Michael J Hands was born in the county town of Shrewsbury but at the age of sixteen he moved with his parents to the small town of Clun, which nestles in the hills in the beautiful Clun Valley close to the border between England and Wales.

After serving in the Royal Air Force he lived in Australia and Essex and during his working life he had many jobs including a farm worker, smallholder, gamekeeper, insurance representative and bank manager before retiring back to Shropshire.

THE BROKEN SHIELD

Best Wishes

This book is dedicated to my wife Sue.
Without her indulgence and understanding I would not have been able to complete.

M. J. HANDS

THE BROKEN SHIELD

AUSTIN & MACAULEY
PUBLISHERS LTD.

A CIP catalogue record for this title is
available from the British Library.

ISBN 978 1 84963 132 7

www.austinmacauley.com

First Published (2012)
Austin & Macauley Publishers Ltd.
25 Canada Square
Canary Wharf
London
E14 5LB

Printed & Bound in Great Britain

Whilst this work is fiction, many of the characters, battles and place names are real. These people lived, loved, fought and died in the 11th century in their attempt (be they Norman, English, Scottish or Welsh) to survive in the turmoil of what was then England.

Other than those long dead warriors and their kinfolk, there is no resemblance to any other person, living or dead.

My thanks go to the skilled men who worked on the farm named LlanEdric with whom I worked for a summer season, who first told me of the legends of 'Wild Edric'.

Many thanks also to my brother Robert and my Grandson Jack whose help and advice have been invaluable.

PROLOGUE

K ing Harold's brother, Earl Tostig and his Viking army have been defeated at the Battle of Stamford Bridge in the north of England.

The Jubilant English army are given no more than a few days to celebrate their victory and tend to their wounded before the news of Duke William of Normandy's landing in the south of England reaches them.

The battered and much reduced English army make a forced march to the south, with many of the wounded falling by the wayside, before they reached the south, surprising the Normans by appearing in formation on the brow of Senlac hill, near the port of Hastings.

The ensuing battle is long and savage with both sides suffering grievous losses, until late in the afternoon King Harold Godwinson is slain by an arrow, causing his battling warriors to falter, thus allowing a lone horseman to shatter the famous English shieldwall.

Harold's housecarls fight to the death and fall around their fallen King.

Norman horsemen pursue the survivors, whilst the rest of the triumphant Norman army celebrate their victory on the gore-covered battlefield.

CHAPTER 1

'Spread out and form a line!' bellowed the man who was obviously the leader of the horsemen. 'Flush 'em out.' he roared, brandishing his spear in the air above his head, and the twenty or so Norman horsemen urged their mounts to either side of him so that within the space of a few minutes they had formed a ragged line in the woodland.

Edric and his two companions watched from the far side of the glade as the horsemen began to ride towards them, riding under a large oak tree that had been browsed by deer, who, during the lean winter months and the springtime, had stood on their hind legs in order to reach the nourishing and succulent young shoots, thus creating something of a canopy just high enough for the horsemen to ride under, with their heads bowed as if in prayer. It was a tactic that cost two of the riders their lives, for they were immediately stabbed and slain by the English fugitives who were hiding in the lower branches.

'Get them,' roared the furious Robert L'estrange who was the Norman leader, causing the rest of his men to urge their mounts over to the tree where the horsemen thrust their weapons upwards into the overhanging branches, bringing down no less than three English warriors, whilst a fourth man dropped down to the ground on his own accord and commenced to run into the woodland, but he was immediately chased by half a dozen horsemen who whooped and bellowed as they speedily caught the man, hacking him to the ground.

Edric and his two companions watched with horror, knowing that should the Norman horsemen continue their ride towards them, then there would be no way that the three fugitives would be able to outrun them, for the two younger men had been struggling to half carry and half drag their wounded lord away, steeling their minds with the knowledge that they would be forced to make a stand and sell their lives as dearly as possible.

However, the God of good fortune was with them, for they were still within earshot of the Normans when they heard the Norman leader bellow to his men. 'The light will be fading soon and I have no wish to be caught in this woodland by more of these English peasants. Rein in your mounts my stout fellows, we return to the Duke,' and the three fugitives breathed a sigh of relief as they watched the Norman horsemen halt their forward movement and turned their steeds away from the exhausted Englishmen.

*****

Yesterday, Senlac Hill had been a serene hillside with the fragrance of sweet grasses and herbs wafting on a soft autumn breeze, alive with the hum of bees and insects as they flitted from flower to flower in their frantic haste to collect the vital nectar that would see most of them through the coming winter.

The air had been melodious with the song of larks as they vied for their unseen patches of territory high above the hillside, before the setting sun would drive them back to their night roosts.

However, this evening the hillside presented a very different scene with the trampled grasses reeking with the blood of men and horses who lay in profusion upon the ravaged hillside, and the sweet song of the larks had been replaced by the harsh squawks of the red kites, ravens, crows and other eaters of carrion who waited impatiently for their feast in ever growing circles, high in the sky above the hill.

Duke William and a cluster of his knights waited on the top of the hill for the arrival of the Kings brother.

He paced backwards and forwards, as was his way, treading carefully along a small area that had been cleared near the site where the final slaughter had taken place.

William's brother, the Bishop Odo had been an dashing warrior in his youth, but his youth and his active lifestyle had been corrupted many years ago by a lifestyle of luxury that had caused his waistline to expand to such an extent that he had attracted the title of 'Odo the Fat', though no man who wished to live would utter such words in his presence, for he was also known as 'Odo the Cruel'.

When the messenger had arrived to summon Odo, the Bishop had immediately left his cot, where he had been resting, emptying the glass of red wine that he had been holding in one hand whilst he continued to gnaw on a roast duck that he held in his other greasy hand.

His servant helped him on with a fresh cloak before he left his tent and made his way through the Norman camp towards the hill, walking through hordes of jubilant warriors who were making their way down the hillside, laden with all the loot they had stripped off the dead.

Odo soon became breathless as he continued to trudge slowly up the slope of Senlac Hill.

However, when he reached the broken spears, shattered shields and the bodies of horses and men that lay in profusion before him, he found that he had great difficulty in hauling his ungainly body through the mayhem of what had been, a few short hours before, one of the most bloody battles in history.

As he trudged higher, the bodies of the dead and wounded were so thickly strewn that he had no option other than to step on and over them, grunting as he heaved himself upwards with the help of his sturdy crook, making the sign of the cross as he did so.

'Help me Father,' moaned a man who lay on the ground before him, holding his one arm up towards to the approaching cleric

Odo looked down with distain towards the man, whose other arm was some three feet away, lying across another slain warrior.

He noticed the dead man's hand was the possessor of a thick gold ring and the severed hand was still clutching a rather expensive and unbloodied sword.

His greedy nature, something that had been with him since he was a child, caused him to stoop in order to pick up the ring, but then he paused before his hand touched it, fearing that some of the celebrating warriors would notice him stooping down. So erring on the side of caution he refrained, muttering to himself, 'I shall have all the gold I want after this day.'

16

He held his perfumed cloth over both his mouth and his nose in order to prevent the nauseating smell of blood, guts and the contents of men's stomachs from upsetting his own delicate stomach, then he quickly made the sign of the cross over the dying man, before hurrying onwards and upwards, treading on the dead as well as the dying in his haste to leave the moaning man behind him, for he could see that the man was in the last moments of his life.

He cursed loudly as he slipped in another large pool of blood as he attempted unsuccessfully to avoid stepping on yet another corpse, hauling his corpulent body laboriously up the slight hill for the second time that day.

To curse was, of course, against God's will, especially for this man who was no ordinary warrior, in fact he was not even an ordinary churchman, but was a bishop, and not merely a bishop, but a bishop who had been ordained by the Holy Father himself in Rome.

He cursed yet again as he gazed down at his brand new, expensive, calfskin boots, noting that the bloodstains were now high up over the ankles and seeping through the eyeholes into his woollen socks, 'Damn, damn, damn and blast,' he said aloud. 'These boots cost me a fortune.'

Odo knew that his brother was somewhere up there on the hill, but he could not see him, in fact he could see nothing before him but the bodies of the dead, lying where they had fallen, twisted in death, bloody and battered, many with arms, legs and even heads missing, lying in pools of their own lifeblood which was seeping into small rivulets of the blood of their former friends and enemies alike as the gore made its glutinous way slowly down the hillside.

The masses of triumphant Norman warriors also blocked his view as they bellowed their roars of victory, forcing him to stretch his tired body upward in the attempt to look either over or around them as they held their arms up towards the heavens. Presumably, he thought, thanking the Lord Jesus Christ for their crushing victory over these English savages.

Bishop Odo had in fact made this tiring journey up Senlac hill once before on this bloody day of October the fourteenth, in the year of our Lord 1066, when he had led one of his brother's elite divisions up towards the waiting English, who had lined the top of the hill, only to follow his men downward in their ignoble confused retreat.

In the short time that he had faced the English shieldwall he had welded his holy cudgel liberally to no avail, for it was against his religious beliefs to brandish a sharpened weapon and to shed the blood of his fellow men.

As he had hastened down the hillside in retreat, he was both disgusted and appalled that some ignorant English peasant had had the audacity to try and kill him.

He quickly glanced around to see if anyone was watching him, noting that all the Norman warriors were attending to their own wounds, drinking themselves silly, or looting the dead.

He savagely kicked the face of a fair-haired Englishman who stared, wide eyed up at him, but the dying man hardly flinched and continued to clutch at the spear that still protruded out of his belly.

'Take that you swine,' he snarled, 'I hope you were the bastard who tried to skewer me earlier,' then he continued his journey upwards towards his brother, smiling quietly to himself as if he had just inherited a kingdom.

For indeed it was a kingdom that he and his brother had just obtained.

*****

Despite the fact that William and his triumphant army held the battlefield, he was a worried man as he watched through the darkening evening's last thin rays as the sun began to drop slowly below the horizon, gazing solemnly as his returning horsemen urged their tired steeds up the slope towards him.

Turning to his half-brother Odo who had just reached him, he mumbled angrily, 'Many of our horsemen who left in this pursuit have not returned. I thought that it was a foolhardy venture to pursue the few miserable survivors, whilst the cream of Saxon England lie dead beneath our feet.'

He gazed across the battlefield and added 'There are still many English warriors who could well be on their way to this battlefield, and our enemies may still outnumber us.'

'Aye, my lord,' replied his brother who was bending with his hands upon his knees as he strove to catch his breath after such an arduous climb, 'for on more than one occasion I feared that it would be our enemies who would be standing victorious upon this very spot, and it would be us who would be hiding in the forest, fearing for our lives.'

William nodded but did not reply, for the same thought had occurred to him during this bloody day on Senlac Hill.

'Have you heard any news from your spies about this second English army that you reported were marching upon us on the yesterday?' said William quietly so that only his half-brother could hear the question.

'No my lord brother,' came the equally hushed answer. 'No news whatsoever. I fear that my spy may well be amongst the slain.'

'Damn and Blast,' swore the Duke. 'They could be upon us at any moment.'

'Aye, they could indeed, that is if they exist at all.'

He added, 'My man was not sure when last I spoke to him.'

'God's blood, does no one know what is going out there?' said the Duke, nodding into the sun that was beginning to sink beneath the wooded horizon, adding, 'My own spies bring no news that is of any use to me. I am as a blind man, unable to see what dangers confront me.'

The two men strode forward to greet a weary knight who was in the act of alighting from his panting, lathered steed.

'Ah my old friend Robert L'estrange! How went it?' said Duke William, forcing himself to smile whilst his weary, aching body told him otherwise.

'Well enough, my lord,' answered L'estrange with a groan, as he placed his hands on his hips and stretched backwards to ease his aching back. 'We chased them until they melted away into the forest. Caught a lot of 'em, but, alas, many more escaped.'

'It was as I had feared,' said the Duke in a more serious voice, 'and should they rally, then we could well have another great bloodletting on the morrow.'

'God help us if it is so,' groaned Bishop Odo.

The Duke was taken aback by the looks of dismay and dread that had appeared on the faces of the men who were with him. 'Nay, nay, my lords, I think not,' smiled Duke William, trying his best to reassure them.

'Today we have broken the back of Harold's England. Oh, I suppose we will have a little unrest here and there, but apart from the odd hiccup now and then, I have no doubt that I shall be crowned at Westminster before Christmastide. Did not the comet foretell of my coming?' he laughed and the noblemen who had gathered around him sniggered and laughed.

Some of the men laughed a little too loudly, showing their nervousness as well as perhaps emphasising their misgivings that this bloody battle at Senlac, may have not have been the one and only battle that would decide if their Duke would, or perhaps would not be, the victor of this island kingdom of England.

Turning, William placed his arm across the shoulders of his corpulent half-brother, then led the way towards the brow of Senlac hill, stepping over and around the bodies of the fallen, shouting to his aides, 'Clear our men off this blood-soaked hill and have them returned to our encampment,' adding in a quieter voice to Odo, 'We shall be safer behind our earthen works for the night, where I shall order the army to kneel and give thanks to God for the victory, as well as the kingdom that he has, this day, bestowed upon me. '

As they neared the encampment, he added almost as an afterthought, 'One of the first things that I shall do when I am King of this land, is to build an abbey upon this mount,' Nodding towards Senlac Hill, 'To thank the good lord for our crushing victory here, this day.'

Some of the men slept the sleep of the exhausted, whilst others slept fitfully, waking in their sleep as if they were yet again experiencing the horrors of yesterday, and some slept not at all.

The Duke of Normandy rose from his warm bed no less than five times during the night, in order to walk the entire perimeter of his encampment, speaking to each individual sentry as he passed them in order to satisfy himself that all was well, asking each man if he had seen or heard anything unusual.

'No my lord,' was the usual reply, except for the odd man here and there who made light of the situation by making remarks like, 'Quiet as a graveyard,' 'Dead quiet,' or 'Silent as the dead.'

As he wearily tried to snatch an hour's sleep, his mind churned with the problems that the morrow would bring. Eventually he fell into a troubled sleep, only to be shaken awake by his brother after what seemed to him to have been no more than a few minutes' sleep. 'Wake brother,' said the rotund Odo. 'Dawn is upon us and the men are restless.'

William rose, stretching his aching joints before crossing to the far side of his spacious tent to the small portable altar where he knelt before the cross, as was his usual habit, praying yet again to thank God for his victory on the yesterday and pleading for the forgiveness of his sins.

He broke his fast with a few bites of freshly baked bread, followed by the breasts of two quail, swilled down with a small goblet of diluted cider, crossed himself yet again before hurrying out of the tent, followed by a boy squire who was still attempting to buckle on the Duke's sword belt.

His eyes were met with what other men may called 'chaos', but it was to him pretty much the same scene that he had witnessed many times before, especially after a successful battle. For whilst some of the men were still in the throes of waking, others were attempting to cook their morning meal, repairing or sharpening their damaged shields and weapons, whilst others were either in the process of making their way up to the scene of yesterday's battle in order to strip the dead of anything of value, whilst others, earlier risers had already done so, and were returning, laden with all manner of things ranging from mail-shirts, weapons, helmets, clothing, whilst some had been lucky enough to have secured silver rings, torques, or coin of silver and of gold.

'Let them have their spoils,' he muttered with a grim smile. 'Lord knows, they earned it on the yesterday.'

Followed by a small group of his knights he strode up the incline towards the top where most of the fighting had taken place, carefully walking around and over the bodies of the fallen until, as he neared the area where the last desperate battle had taken place, he found it more and more difficult to proceed without treading upon the flesh of dead men.

'Which is the body of Harold?' he asked.

'None can tell,' came the reply from an elderly knight who was still out of breath after his ascent up the hill, 'Men have searched for it and still have not found it but they believe that it may be in that pile there' – he indicated to a mound of bodies that were three or four deep – 'but they are all pretty well cut up, so none can be sure which corpse is he.'

William followed by his retinue made his way through the blood and gore towards the pile of bodies where they stopped and gazed silently at the slain.

None dared speak, waiting for a long period as the Duke studied the faces of all of the dead that were visible, before he broke the silence, 'Aye, I can see what you mean, for I knew Harold well enough, indeed I have spent many a happy day hunting with him in my own estates in Normandy. But alas, I cannot see him there,' he nodded towards the slain warriors.

'My lord,' came a voice from the back of the small crowd that had now gathered, 'Some ladies approach,' said the man as he nodded his head towards a small group of four ladies who were making their way as regally as possible through the bodies of fallen men and horses, taking some considerable time before they came to within a few yards of the Duke.

The same man added quietly, 'I do believe that one of them is "Edith Swan-Neck",' nodding towards the tall lady who stood a little ahead of the others.

This lady, who was not only the most beautiful, but was also the youngest of the four ladies who stood facing the Duke.

'God's blood, it is she,' whispered the Duke, for although he had never met, Edith Swanmild, called by some, Edith Swan-Neck, during the time that Harold had been his 'guest' in Normandy. A man who had been his very unwilling guest, and at other times his more than willing hunting companion, Harold Godwinson, had spoken many times of his beautiful wife, especially when he had been in his cups in the great hall of his Norman captor.

Duke William of course knew that the Lady Edith was not the legal wife of Harold, despite the fact that she had been his mistress for the past twenty years and had borne him no less than six children.

He also knew that the English nobles had accepted the union, for it had been the custom of both the English and the Danish peoples to accept a 'handfast marriage', simply because it had been the way of their people for hundreds of years.

The lady approached, made a very small curtsey, before she stood to her full height, which to Williams's surprise, far surpassed his own, and she looked down into William's brown eyes with eyes of blue.

Her pure white eyelashes, and crown of long blonde hair that the morning sun shone through, gave him the impression that it was an angel of God that had suddenly appeared before him.

'I would take the body of my lord and King to give him a good Christian burial,' she said haughtily, speaking the language of Normandy as if it were her native tongue, adding almost sarcastically, 'my Lord Duke.'

'My lady,' answered the Duke, bowing gracefully, ignoring the slight that she had just delivered, 'That I cannot do,' he answered just as haughtily as had been her own short sentence, adding, 'but I will give my old friend Harold and all who fell on this bloody field a good Christian burial, but alas, none can identify him after such a fierce and bloody battle. Yet even if I could identify his body, it would not be prudent for me to allow you to take it.'

'I will know him,' answered Edith, then without further ado or permission, and with the grace of a gazelle, she stepped past the Duke, daintily climbing the mound of bodies, boldly moving from one body to the one underneath and then to the one underneath that, watched with awe by Duke William plus a growing number of Normans who had gathered to catch a glimpse of this renowned English beauty.

A cold shiver suddenly wracked his body.

He turned to his brother who had just joined him saying quietly 'After our trials on this field of battle, and now the bravery of this English lady, I do fear that our holding of this land may not be the easy thing that I had planned.'

His brother nodded and whispered, 'Aye my good brother. These people seem to be like no other race that we have conquered in our many wars and battles.'

'This is he,' came the voice from the lady.

'Bring the body to me,' ordered the Duke, and men rushed to do his bidding.

Edith accompanied the body, which was placed tenderly at the Duke's feet.

'Are you certain lady?' questioned the Duke.

'Aye, I am my lord, Duke, for it is a body that I knew well,' she said stifling a sob as she uttered the words, followed by a small trickle of tears that dripped down her clear, unblemished cheeks, to dampen her white bodice.

A second figure approached from the small retinue. A figure that was stooped by age, wearing the expensive attire of a noble-lady.

'May I present King Harold's mother to you, the Lady Gytha?' said Edith, but the lady who stepped forward did not curtsey or bow to the Duke, merely nodded and looked into Duke William's face with her own, cold, piercing blue eyes.

'Duke William,' said Harold's mother, 'you have your victory, and it is now your Christian duty to allow my son's body to be taken to his home for Christian burial.'

William stared coldly at this woman who had the audacity to tell him what he must or must not do, noting that despite the fact that she was now aged and stooped, her clear almost unlined skin, full mouth and small, perfectly shaped nose pointed to the fact that she must have been a very beautiful woman during her 'beauty years'.

'That I cannot do my lady,' he replied, adding sarcastically, 'for your son was a gallant warrior and a worthy opponent.' He paused for a moment before he continued, 'and I do assure you that I shall bury him with dignity and have a priest read over him.'

Before he continued he stared down at the body of Harold saying. 'Alas I cannot give you his body, for I am certain that there will be Englishmen who may doubt that Harold died on this battlefield, and even if they do believe that he died here, his bones could well be used by those who would gainsay my rule.'

Grimly he added, 'Nay lady, I must bury his body here on this hillside that he defended so gallantly.'

Without further ado he turned, walking quickly away from the mound of dead, leaving the two English ladies and their two serving maidens, thus preventing any further discussion on the matter.

The stern voice of the Lady Gytha stopped him before he had taken more than half a dozen strides.

'Duke William,' she said loudly, 'his body weight in gold will I give to you, if only you will allow me to take my son's remains.'

'Again I must refuse my lady,' answered the Duke as he turned again to face her. 'For with this victory comes England, and with England comes all of its gold,' adding sarcastically, 'including yours.'

'That's what you think,' she hissed quietly so that only her three lady companions could hear her.

'I will bury my gold and all the treasures from our estates before I will allow you to get your murdering hands on it,' was what she said aloud.

William turned again from her, 'Bury him here,' he ordered, pointing to the very spot where Harold's body lay. 'And see to the bodies of the fallen English. Send word to me when the burnings and the burials are done.' Then he turned again, walking slowly down the hill towards his noisy, assembling army at the bottom of the hill.

The Lady Gytha and Edith Swan-Neck returned in the darkness of that night and, accompanied by three servants, they dug up the remains of their beloved Harold, replacing his body with that of a common man, one of the many who still lay unburied on Senlac Hill, reverently taking Harold's battered body to the Great Abbey at Waltham, where they lay it deep in a grave in front of the altar, commanding this loyal mass-priest to bless his body and convey his spirit to Heaven.

*****

Before midday the entire Norman army was on the move, making its way with speed towards the nearest town of Dover, leaving a small contingent behind with orders to burn the slain, then bury their ashes, with further orders to construct a fortress on the top of Senlac Hill.

The army reached the small town before nightfall, where the Duke ordered that Dover to be surrounded but not to be attacked or entered until he gave the order.

By first light on the following morning, his men could see that the Duke had ordered his ships to make their way to the port of Dover. For there, standing in

22

the straits, waiting for the tide to turn, was a large portion of the armada that had carried them to this strange, green, forbidding land a few short, bloody days before.

To say that the town was taken without bloodshed would be a mistruth, for despite the Duke's orders that the town must be taken peacefully, some of the elements of his army, who were perhaps drunk with the sense of their own invincibility, raped, then slew a maiden, slaying the maiden's father who attempted to intervene, thus causing a crowd of onlookers to become enraged. They killed several of the Dukes men, who naturally retaliated, causing the slaughter of more than a third of the population of that town.

William was furious. 'I ordered that we take the town peacefully, and yet these idiots have slain half of the town's population,' he raved, 'I cannot collect taxes from dead people!' he bellowed.

'Bring me the dolts who started this slaughter,' he snapped.

'It cannot be done, my lord Duke,' came the answer, 'I have already made enquiries and the men who caused this mayhem were themselves slain by the citizens.'

'Damn them,' growled the angry Duke, 'I had a mind to make an example of them, to show the rest of this gathering that my orders must be obeyed.'

He stormed off in one of his black moods, a mood that to all who were close to their lord knew that to utter a single word could well bring his terrible wrath down upon their own heads.

Within the hour he had taken control of his mood and returned to the hall, where his captains and lords had assembled. 'We will camp here for one day only,' he ordered.

'I want you, Baskerville–' nodding towards the tall, grey-haired man nearest to him – 'to remain here with half of the men that you brought with you, garrison the town and see that a motte is built for your own protection, should things go ill.' He added, 'See to it that my ships are sent back across the Channel to furnish me with provisions, especially fresh warhorses and fresh warriors, for, as we are all aware, we lost too many good men at Senlac Hill. Should these cursed Englishmen rally, then we will be hard pressed to hold what we have gained.'

Baskerville had already turned to leave the room when the Duke called to him. 'Send riders out to all of my domains on the continent, and to every one of our friendly neighbours, promise land and estates to every warrior who joins me here in England.'

Returning to his assembled captains, he turned to Talbot saying. 'You, my loyal Talbot, you will assemble the army. We march on the morrow.'

'March where my Lord Duke?' asked Talbot, his mind already busy with the things that must be done before the army moved, especially the order of march which he needed to arrange. For both the Bretons and the Normans claimed the right to lead the army on their march into the interior of this new forbidding land.

'Towards the English capital of London,' replied the Duke in a calm, thoughtful voice.

'As you will, my lord.'

William then added, as if talking to himself, and not to the assembled company of lords and captains who had crowded into the room, 'If we can take London, then the rest of the country will fall into my hands like a ripe plum.'

Later on in his life these very words would come back to haunt him.

'Brabazon!' he bellowed, 'Where is that lumbering oaf Brabazon? He should be here with us.

'You,' he pointed at one of the younger men whose name he had momentarily forgotten, 'Fetch Brabazon to me, he is probably in his tent, or in his cups if I know the man. Go,' he roared. 'Be quick about it,' he snarled.

The youngster fled from the tent as if his tunic was on fire, nimbly sidestepping out of the way to prevent himself from colliding into an elderly knight who was in the process of entering the tent.

'You,' said the Duke to another gnarled veteran, 'See to it that sentries are posted and wide awake, and whilst you are at it, assemble all the horsemen who have unwounded mounts, and bid them ride out in a screen for at least two leagues ahead of us. I want them out within the hour.'

Turning to the main throng of men, he muttered, 'I don't want to bump into any more nasty surprises. There may well be ten thousand English warriors out there baying for our blood on the morrow.'

The meeting continued for a further three hours discussing route, provisions and order of march. Destinations, and all the other foreseen and possible unforeseen problems that they may encounter on their march to London.

Hence forcing the assembled lords to remain in his tent, well into the early hours of the morning, before they were allowed out of his presence in order to seek the solitude of their own beds, which in most cases, meant a sheepskin rug thrown upon the damp ground.

It was long after the last man had left when Duke William called for a goblet of mulled wine diluted with water, which he sipped sparingly, for he rarely drank strong wine and abhorred drunkenness amongst his men.

As was his habit, a habit that had been with him since infancy, he knelt before the simple wooden cross to pray, begging forgiveness for his sins and the ills that he had caused others, but being a practical man he also prayed for a speedy and successful end to his campaign.

Only then did he settle his bruised and still aching body upon the travelling bed, which his manservant had prepared for him.

Sleep eluded him as his mind raced from one thing to another.

Should he wait at Dover until his fleet returned with additional men?

Would it be wiser to march his army through the countryside in order to cut off supplies to the city of London before he attacked the city? Or would the boldness of attacking and taking London put an end to all English resistance?

Each of the many problems that raced through his mind had a number of possible outcomes, none of which appeared to present him with a clear-cut conclusion.

It seemed that he had only just closed eyes when his servant was gently touching his shoulder. 'Good morrow sire,' said the valet in an apologetic voice, ''Tis almost dawn and the camp is astir.'

The camp was awake with captains and sergeants-at-arms bellowing at the top of their voices as they assembled their charges into some sort of order, so that they would not incur the wrath of their leader.

The Duke of Normandy and their men would be ready to march at dawn, as ordered.

CHAPTER 2

At the end of a slow, miserable and exhausting journey, the three wet and bedraggled men urged their weary, starving horses to a halt in front of the silent fortress.

'Guards, guards!' yelled Hywell.

A head immediately appeared from the walkway above the gate, and a suspicious face peered down at them through the blackness.

'Who's there?' demanded a gruff voice.

'Lord Edric,' shouted an angry Hywell. 'Open the damned gate.'

They could hear shouts, curses and the clatter and clumping of men making their way down the stairways towards the inside of the stockade where, after another spate of grunting from the sentries as they heaved the heavy oak locking beams out of their positions, the gates eventually swung open just wide enough to allow the weary men to urge their tired horses forward into the courtyard.

Roald and Hywell helped Edric off his horse and literally carried his limp body up to the darkened house where they were forced to halt before the locked and bolted door.

Hywell hammered on the door of the longhall several times, but was forced to wait impatiently for the door to be opened.

Eventually a candle flickered in an upstairs room. Then they saw the light, which disappeared then reappeared again as its bearer descended the stairs as the light flickered along the hallway towards the heavy door.

The bolts were retracted with the clatter of metal upon metal and the door swung open to reveal the sleepy white face of a startled Rowena.

'Oh my God!' she screamed. 'What happened? Where is he hurt?' She rushed forward to cradle Edric's swollen face in her arms.

'We were beaten,' sighed Hywell.

'I can see that you idiot,' snapped Rowena as she attempted to guide her husband through the door. 'Where is my Lord Edric hurt?' she snarled in a way that she had not spoken to man or beast at any time during her lifetime.

''Tis his head, my lady,' said Roald in a quiet voice. 'He was struck on his head by an iron mace, and we haven't been able to get the helmet off his head. He seemed to be recovering until yesterday evening, then he lost consciousness several times during the night, and twice again during the day.'

'Winnifred!' she screamed in a most unladylike voice. 'Where is that damned wench?' she said, then screamed again, 'Godwin, Winnifred, Betilda, Egbert?' causing doors to be opened as the three half-dressed house servants hurried towards their distraught mistress.

The large figure of their son Godwin burst through the far door.

'What's all the shouting?' he grumbled.

'Your father has just returned, and he's wounded,' sobbed the distraught Rowena.

Godwin strode over to the couch and stared silently at the prone figure of his father.

Rowena turned snapping angrily at the girls, 'Get me hot water and a clean handcloth.'

'Egbert, I want you' – she said, pointing at Egbert – 'to make haste to Waldo the blacksmith, and bid him to attend to his lord. Make sure that he brings his tools.'

She then continued to shout at the disappearing figure of Egbert, 'And tell him that the damned helmet that he made for his lordship is bent and will not come off his head.

'Godwin,' said Rowena in as calm a voice that she could muster, 'help me get your father into the bedroom, and we can try to tend to his wound.'

Godwin literally carried Edric into the bedroom, placing him as gently as he was able onto the bed, where Edric flopped onto the feather mattress.

Edric's eyes flickered as he regained consciousness, whispering in a faint voice, 'Godwin? As soon as Waldo gets here, you must help him to get this blasted helmet off, it is very painful.'

Then he closed his eyes and flopped back, uttering another loud sigh, appearing to be a little more contented.

After what was supposed to be a polite knock on the door, but was, in reality an enormous single thump that resounded throughout the interior of the house, the large figure of Waldo burst into the hallway stopping suddenly as he entered the inner-hall, not knowing where Edric had been taken, causing the much smaller figure of Egbert to bump into him, forcing the giant to turn and give the small man a withering look.

'Where is he?' demanded the blacksmith.

'Follow me,' said the little man as he led Waldo into the bedroom.

'Ah, thank God,' said Rowena as the large figure of the blacksmith paused in the doorway.

'Did you bring your tools?' asked Rowena. 'Oh, I can see that you did. Good, now what I want you to do is to get that damned iron helmet off his head, and don't hurt him in the process.' Then she continued, 'You can do that, can you not?' trying hard to smile up into the face of the gigantic blacksmith.

'I can try my lady, but it was the sturdiest helmet that I have ever made, and to be sure it must have been a mighty clout that bent it so, for a lesser helmet would have cracked like an egg.'

Normally a man who, at his most verbal, uttered a grunt and half a dozen words, that was probably the longest sentence that he had spoken during his adult lifetime, as he looked down at the prone figure of his liege lord, where he stood for such a long time that Rowena became annoyed, thinking that the oaf had gone into some sort of a trance.

'Well. Waldo? Well?' she snapped.

'Aye, yer ladyship,' he mumbled, then after yet another long look at Edric, he slowly turned and fumbled in the large wooden chest that he had carried into the house, which he had unceremoniously thumped down onto the rush-strewn oak floorboards, where he knelt down and rummaged amongst his tools before selecting a hammer, chisel, plus a pair of large, two-handled iron tongs.

'Godwin,' he grunted, as he prised one of the points of the tongs under the side of the iron helmet, 'grab hold of this and when I say lift, then lift outwards and upwards, gently mind.'

He then walked to the other side of the bed, prised the ends of his stubby fingers under the far side of the warped helmet, placed his other hand on the shoulder of Edric, nodded towards Godwin and grunted, 'Lift.'

Both of the men were powerful men, in their prime, but their combined effort achieved nothing other than to raise Edric from his bed, causing him to pass out again.

With a disgusted grunt, Waldo stomped over to his tool chest before he returned to Edric's bedside holding a tool, the like of which no one in the room had ever seen before.

'Expensive,' grunted Waldo, 'only one I got,' he said looking at the strange metal saw which had teeth all along its length.

'Just get that blessed helmet off,' hissed Rowena. 'I'll pay you enough silver to buy a dozen of the things if you can just get that damned helmet off him.'

'My lady,' grunted Waldo. Then turning to Godwin, he said, 'Hold the helmet firm,' and when Godwin had leant over in order to grip the helmet Waldo, carefully and using as little pressure as he could, began to draw the metal saw backwards and forwards across one side of the helmet.

At first it appeared as if the saw was making no impression what-so-ever on the helmet, but after ten minutes or so, there appeared to be a faint mark on the shining helmet, and after a further half an hour of work there was a definite ridge, showing where the saw had done its work.

Moving the saw slowly and carefully, Waldo eventually made a deep ridge in the helmet running down from the crown to the rim on the left-hand side.

He stood back, wiping the sweat off his chin with a grubby rag, throwing the now blunt saw back into his toolbox.

'We'll try,' he said, nodding towards Godwin, who stood at the left hand side of the still unconscious Edric.

'Hold him firm,' he said, as he grasped the left-hand side of the helmet with both hands, one each side of the saw marks, and his huge muscles bulged as he strained to pull at the stubborn metal.

Nothing appeared to be happening until, with a sudden crack, the seam opened up like a boiled eggshell and the helmet lifted off with a soft sucking sound, something like the sound that a man makes when he is trying to pull his feet out of soggy marshland.

'Thank God,' sighed Rowena, but then sobbed, as she saw that Edric's head was a mass of tangled, blood-soaked hair, with a large bump the size of a goose egg protruding from where the dent had been.

She grabbed the bowl of hot water from the shaking hands of Betilda and knelt beside Edric whereupon she commenced to gently wipe his bloody forehead and his matted hair.

'There there,' she clucked like a broody hen, 'you'll be all right now my darling, just rest and you will be fine.'

There was no response from the still unconscious Edric, but she continued to talk to him, wiping his head and his brow with a clean cloth, which she had soaked in warm, honey and lavender scented water.

Quietly, Waldo, Betilda and the other servants left the room leaving Godwin standing shocked, as he looked at his distraught mother as she tended his father.

'Will he recover?' he asked his mother in a quiet voice, almost a whisper which was very unusual for a man whose normal voice was usually loud enough to wake the sleepiest man from his dreams. Yet she did not answer him, merely looked up at him with tears streaming down her cheeks, shrugging her shoulders as if in despair. Then after a little while she turned again, saying quietly, 'I shall pray to our Lord Jesus Christ for his deliverance.'

Godwin's four sisters arrived to see their father, taking turns at relieving Rowena whilst she snatched a few brief hours of sleep, staring numbly at the prone figure of their father as he lay still as death on his feather mattress.

Ella, being the eldest of the four sisters felt obliged to take charge, ordering her sisters hither and thither in a vain attempt to ease her father's discomfort.

Liann, the second eldest, obeyed her sister's orders, running down to the cookhouse and then on to the well, in order to bring her father fresh glasses of cool, clear water which she tried to coax his unconscious form into swallowing.

Unfortunately most of the water was lost down his chin soaking his bedclothes, whilst Rene, the third daughter, who had always possessed the gift of healing, usually spending a lot of her spare time helping the sick and infirm of the village and the surrounding countryside, merely changed the bandage which she had placed on her father's forehead at regular intervals, thus keeping the fever from him, for she had seen many such cases of men and women who had slept in this type of a coma, some who had slept for weeks and in some cases for months before they had awakened, as if they had merely been asleep for a single night, awakening with no ill effects whatsoever.

She had also seen some wake up with their minds elf-addled, and most of those people had never regained their minds, lingering on for a few months or perhaps a year or so before passing to the next world.

Then there had been other people who had simply passed from this world during the night without giving any sign of their going.

The youngest daughter had been named Eve after the difficult time that Rowena had carrying her during her pregnancy, had, in her wisdom, taken the name from the first woman who, according to the priests, God had created to accompany Adam in the Garden of Eden.

Eve, like her three other sisters was a hard-working, well-adjusted individual, practical and thrifty. Yet she, like her other sisters could do naught but merely stand and watch, hoping and praying that her father would regain consciousness and return to them, to be the father that they had known and loved before he had left for the disastrous battle at Hastings.

Edric was unconscious for a further two full days, eventually opening his eyes, blinking rapidly as he tried to focus on the first thing he could see, which was the slouched, sleeping form of Rowena who had hardly left his side since the removal of the warped helmet.

It was almost by instinct that Rowena suddenly shook herself awake, staring unbelievingly into the bleary, red-rimmed eyes of her husband.

'You look like my wife,' he said sleepily.

'Oh thank God,' she blurted out with a sob as she moved to hold his hand, stroking his cheek with her other hand, kissing him tenderly on his cheek, whispering into his ear.

'I thought that we had lost you,' she said. Then added, 'Thanks be to God that you have returned to us.'

He said nothing, merely smiled weakly up towards his wife.

The five children stormed into the room like an invading army.

'Quiet,' hissed Rowena. 'Your father has only just wakened. Hush,' she whispered again, 'come quietly to see your sire. One by one,' she insisted, 'not all together.' And the five fully grown children obeyed their mother, dutifully approaching their father, white-faced and trembling with excitement as well as with relief. Each of the siblings stooped to kiss him on his cheeks and on his forehead before retreating in order to allow the next sibling to approach him.

Within a few hours Edric was sitting up and allowing himself to be fed steaming hot beef broth by his adoring wife, whilst his big burly son, their four daughters, Betilda, Winnie and the other household servants looked on, with faces gleaming with joy.

Just as Rowena was wiping out the clay bowl with the last crust of freshly baked bread, Edric's brother, Hal arrived, slightly out of breath, for he had been many miles away when he had received the news of his brother's recovery. He had ridden hard, casually leaving his lathered pony in the courtyard before he burst into the room.

'Ah big brother,' he bellowed in his usual loud voice, 'I see that even those dreaded Normal cudgels are not stout enough to crack your thick skull.'

He did not bother to tell Edric that he had been at his side for much of the time that he had been unconscious, and had only left his side the previous night as he had been more or less forced to leave his brother's side when a messenger had arrived from his own holding, some seven miles away, informing him of a fire that had destroyed the largest of his barns.

He strode over to take his brother's hand in his, slapping Edric on the shoulder, causing an angry Rowena to snap, 'Careful you oaf. He has been to Hell's Halls and back, and is not yet recovered.'

Then, realising what she had said, being a devout Christian, she put her hand to her mouth, saying quietly 'I mean to Heaven and back,' causing all the occupants of the room, even the pallid looking Edric, to smile.

He was stumbling about as if drunk for the following week but on the second week he was much steadier and began to venture outside in the courtyard attempting to mount his Norman warhorse, when a furious Rowena screamed at him through the window.

'Don't you dare!' she bellowed, 'Or I will not be responsible for my actions, Come back inside before you collapse on us again.'

One of the many things that he liked about his wife was the fact that she certainly had a will of her own, and, as many of the servants had found out to their cost, she was not one to be disobeyed. So much to the astonishment to the small crowd of servants and friends, Edric allowed himself to be ushered into the house and sat down in front of the roaring log fire, where Rowena immediately threw a sheepskin rug over his knees and thrust a drinking horn of warm mead into his hands, 'Stay there and drink this,' she said with a pout. 'I will bring you a warm bowl of apple and blackberry pie as soon as it is out of the oven.'

It was a full seven days before he did ride, not for long and not far, but he consoled himself, 'At least I did ride.'

People marvelled at his recovery, for within the month it was almost as if Lord Edric was his old self again. Indeed it appeared that he had never been wounded at all.

However, despite his visits to most of his holdings and speaking jovially to his people, he was utterly shocked that when he totalled up the number of survivors who had returned from the battlefields of Stamford Bridge and Hastings. Realising that, perhaps, only two out of every ten men who had left with him had returned.

The loss of Garth hit him the hardest, for he had known Garth all of his life and Garth had been one of his closest and most loyal of his friends. Yet despite all the enquiries that Edric had made, no one had seen the huge figure of Garth fall, so there remained that small glimmer of hope that, one day, he would look through the window and see the mighty frame of Garth striding towards him.

News from the countryside seemed to alternate between good news and bad news, with some travellers and bards, reporting that Duke William and his army had suffered such heavy losses at Hastings that the few Normans who had survived the battle had returned to Normandy in ignominy.

Whilst other rumours said that the Normans had been reinforced by vast numbers of fresh warriors, not only from the dukedom of Normandy but also from the many dukedoms and kingdoms who were allied to the Duke of Normandy, and with this new influx of men, the Normans were in the process of conquering the southern parts of England, leaving death and destruction in their wake.

Edric, always a practical man, discounted most of these rumours, and, despite the loss of so many able-bodied men from his holdings, he tried as best as he was able to help and reassure his people that all would be well.

One of the rumours that did concern him more than most was the one heard time and time again, and from many different sources, saying that Duke William had sworn to confiscate the holdings, manors and lands of any English nobleman who had fought against him at Hastings, and would give these lands to his own men as a reward for their services.

'Rumours are rumours,' said his wife, 'and it is no good to worry about something that may never happen,' as she turned back to her duties as if she hadn't a care in the world.

*****

Ever since childhood Edric had enjoyed hunting, and now took it up with a vengeance, ranging far up the hillsides and into uninhabited valleys in search of the ever-secretive deer, and wild boar.

The Norman stallion that had brought him home from Hastings now carried the new name of Chieftain, on account that the savage warhorse attempted to bite, kick and dominate everyone and everything that came within reach, including others of his tribe, in order to show his lordship over them. A task that was soon accomplished as the two other stallions in the village speedily acknowledging his leadership over them after the briefest of fights. Yet whilst he was still the savage warhorse that he had been trained to be, he was now Edric's constant companion, quickly learning the ways of his new master, picking up the ways of handling both deer and wild boar with the intelligence that both astounded and delighted his new master.

On numerous occasions Edric would venture so far into the mountains that it would be difficult to return before nightfall, causing him to select a suitable camping site, in readiness to spend the night under the stars, not always in the most pleasant of conditions, especially during the depths of winter.

Rowena seldom worried when Edric spent the night abroad, but on one occasion, when her husband failed to return for four consecutive nights, she began to grow concerned.

She knew of many of Edric's favourite haunts, of valleys and hills that he had spoken of over the past few years, and she began to fear that he had fallen foul of some particularly large and vicious wild boar, or had perhaps taken a tumble off his steed, a stallion which she hated with every bone in her body, and a horse which even the stable boys feared, for the devil horse would only obey orders from Edric who the beast appeared to love with the adoration of a love-struck maiden.

CHAPTER 3

The man had been thrown a good ten feet, landing almost at the bottom of the large oak tree that hid the two men and one woman, causing the woman to gasp aloud at the sight of the bloody and battered figure that now lay a mere six feet in front of her.

She and her two brothers had been in the service of Lord Wilfred of Much Wenlock, staying with him until they had witnessed his death as they stood on a nearby ridge at the end of the battle of Senlac Hill.

The Lord Wilfred had held the manor of Much Wenlock under the patronage of Lord Edric.

The three siblings had hoped that Lord Wilfred's only son would survive, but he too had fallen with others of King Harold's personal bodyguard in the last few, violent moments of the battle.

The Norman horsemen had disappeared into the woodland as suddenly as they had appeared, leaving the three stunned spectators and the twisted, prone figure alone in the silent forest.

Evan of Kenley, his younger brother Vaughan and their sister Myreen, had spent their entire lives in the service of the kindly Lord Wilfred, and they had hidden themselves in a tangle of bushes for many hours before they had ventured out. There they had luckily found a looted cart to which a tired old ox was tethered.

Using the ox-drawn cart they were in the process of making their way home.

They had been deep in the woodland when they had heard, rather than saw the noise of horsemen crashing through the forest, having had just enough time to hide themselves before an English warrior, holding a shield and a huge axe had backed out of the forest.

A few heartbeats later half a dozen horsemen had crashed into the clearing, stabbing and spearing the man before riding into and over him, turning the man into the mangled heap that they now saw before them.

At first sight the two brothers appeared to be identical in every way, both being taller than the average man, big boned with round, ruddy complexions, whilst both men possessed the same happy and jovial nature.

They were the type of men who make friends easily but seldom make enemies. Yet their jovial nature had suddenly been turned into a mood of fear and anguish by the events that had just taken place before them.

Their sister was different in stature and looks, but sported the same happy nature. This had blossomed even more after she had been persuaded by Lord Wilfred of Wenlock to accompany her brothers on Lord Wilfred's 'adventure of a lifetime', begging her to come with him, for she was, he had said, the finest healer in the district, adding, 'Should ill fall upon me, then I would want thee and only thee to be there to attend me.'

Ill had indeed fallen upon him, for the shocked siblings had actually witnessed his demise when he had been hacked to pieces during the final moments of King Harold's last stand.

*****

Myreen was the first to react. Dashing the few short paces to the prone warrior, she placed her finger on the side of his neck to see if there was any life in the body.

'Is he dead?' asked Vaughan in a low voice.

'No,' came the reply. 'He is alive. Quick, give me a hand to move him out of this clearing,' she said, adding, as the two brothers half dragged and half carried him, 'Lay him on the cart, I'll see if I can help him.'

The brothers heaved him, none too gently, onto the cart, causing their sister to chide them, 'Careful you clots, or else you will stub out what little life is left in him.'

'He's no bloody lightweight,' grunted Evan, as he pushed the man into a better position on the cart.

Evan then returned to the clearing, picking up the man's axe and his broken shield, and then he slowly walked backwards towards the edge of the small clearing, removing every scrap of evidence that could show that there had ever been people there.

Once he was within the bushes, he stopped and peered into the open area, searching for the slightest scrap of evidence that could betray their presence. Then with a slight grunt, he heaved the man's heavy war-axe onto his shoulder and returned to the cart.

Myreen was bending over the bloody, mangled body. After what seemed to be an eternity to her brothers, she said, 'Well, his left arm is broken and has been wrenched out of its socket, but the head wound seems to be the most serious so I'd better see what I can do there.'

She turned her head towards her brother and said, 'Vaughan, hand me that flagon of wine,' a chore which Vaughan did rather reluctantly as it was the last half bottle of wine that he had managed to salvage from Lord Wilfred's copious store, before it had been looted by the victorious Normans.

She wiped most of the blood off the man's face and forehead before gently holding the large flap of scalp which she carefully cleaned to ensure that not a single hair or a particle of debris remained on it, before she poured nearly half of the contents of the flagon of the late Lord of Much Wenlock's wine over the flap, as well as onto the man's exposed skull.

She carefully and gently replaced the scalp, then, tearing off a long thin slip of cleanish cloth from her own undershift, she wrapped the cloth as tightly as she could around the unconscious man's head.

She then turned her attention to the man's shoulder. 'Evan?' she said to her elder brother, 'Will you put him into a sitting position and hold him firm, whilst I try to push his shoulder back into its socket?'

It was a manoeuvre that was only accomplished after two failed attempts, with all three breathing a sigh of relief as they heard the shoulder clunk back into its proper position.

'Thank God he's unconscious,' said Vaughan, with a big grin spreading all

33

over his rosy face.

Myreen then commenced prodding and pushing the two pieces of his contorted left arm into a position until she felt that the two pieces of the broken arm bone appeared to have returned to their rightful places before she placed four stout pieces of split hazel around the damaged arm, binding them so that they held the arm in place, then using some of the leather from the warrior's broken shield strap, she made a sling that went around his neck, thus holding the damaged arm firmly in place.

They then packed as much dry fern in and around the still-unconscious man before urging their patient old ox forward along the overgrown path.

The man made no movement or sound whatsoever that day, nor during the night, but as the three siblings prepared to move on the following morning, a distinct and loud groan emitted from the cart.

All three rushed over to the man, who, much to their surprise was, not only awake but was attempting to haul himself up with his one good arm, trying to pull himself upright with the aid of the side of the cart.

'No, no,' hissed the alarmed Myreen. 'Lie still or you'll start the bleeding again.'

The man touched his forehead causing him to grimace as he realised just how sore his head was.

'What happened?' he said. 'Where am I?' Then added, 'Oh yes, I remember, those damned Norman horsemen.'

'You are safe now stranger,' said Evan with a reassuring smile. 'My sister Myreen,' nodding towards his sister, 'she healed you, you will be all right now, just rest a while longer.'

His sister looked at Evan frowning as she did so, as she was far from certain that the man would recover. She had seen men die from far less serious wounds than this.

It was midmorning before they recommenced their journey homeward, for many unwelcome noises came from the forest; sounds of men shouting and of horses moving through the woodland, but, thankfully none came near to the clump of thick undergrowth in which they had concealed themselves.

When they did eventually move, Vaughan followed the cart, doing his best to conceal all evidence of their passing by brushing the grass with a small branch of silver birch, hiding all broken twigs, thus removing all signs of their passing from all but the most experienced of trackers.

The journey was painfully slow, making Evan think that by the time that they had chosen a secluded spot in order to stop for the night, that they had covered no more than three or four miles.

As they sat by a very small, hidden fire, heating a pot of water, which Myreen had insisted that she needed in order to tend to the stranger's wounds, Vaughan remarked to his brother, 'It's going to be a long, dangerous journey, especially with this cart and this wounded man.'

'Aye,' agreed his brother. 'And we don't know anything about him, not even his name or where he comes from.'

Vaughan stood up. 'Well it's time we found out,' and they both strode over to the cart where their sister was busy taking the bandage off the wounded man's head.

'Hail fellow,' said Evan, with a broad smile. 'How are you feeling after today's journey?'

But before the man could answer, Myreen looked up at her elder brother, saying, 'Oh, he seems to be coping quite well, although I'm not too happy about this head wound, it has started to weep here,' pointing towards a small droplet of pus that had started to ooze out from a small gap in the wound.

Evan was just about to ask the man a few questions when Myreen continued. 'I will have to prise it open again and see if I can stop the infection before it gets too bad and causes a real problem.'

She gently opened the wound, causing the man to wince. Yet he made no sound, merely looked straight into Myreen's eyes, as she made a tutting noise at the discovery of a single strand of his hair that had lodged itself under his scalp, nodding to herself, for she felt certain that this single strand of hair was the cause of the small infection that had set in.

The man gritted his teeth, grimacing a little, but made no sound other than a deep grunt that seemed to resonate from somewhere deep inside his chest.

'There,' said Myreen as she delicately removed the offending hair, carefully replacing the inch or so of scalp that she had removed, patting it gently into place, before tying the bandage back into its original place.

'How does the arm feel?' she asked.

'Hurts like hell.' Was the gruff reply, but then he added with something that resembled a sparkle in his eye, 'But I'm sure that with your tender care I will mend soon enough.'

For the third time Evan tried to speak to the man, 'Tell me stranger,' he said smiling his usual smile, 'You have been with us for almost a couple of days now, and we don't even know your name, or where you are from?' He added as an afterthought, 'We are from the town of Much Wenlock, near to the county town of Shrewsbury and we were with our lord Wilfred who was slain in the Battle of Hastings.'

The stranger's eyes widened as he attempted a smile, saying, 'Ah, that is indeed good news for I too have travelled here from the town of Stretton, which is also close to Shrewsbury. But I lost sight of my lord and friend, the lord Edric during the battle, but if my memory serves me correctly, Edric also holds the town of Much Wenlock as one of his many holdings.'

The three siblings nodded and looked at each other in surprise and relief as they realised that the man whose life they had saved was from their own shire, and as such, he should be a friend and mayhap of some help to them in returning to their own homes safe and sound.

Garth grimaced as pain wracked his body, reaching to his head with his undamaged right hand.

'Here,' said Myreen, handing the man a small sliver of willow bark, 'Chew on this for a while, it should help to ease the pain.' She added with a sad smile, 'I haven't had time enough to dry or grind it into a powder, but it should do the same job.'

The man looked up into the girl's eyes with a look that caused her cheeks to redden, a look which did not go unnoticed by the two brothers, who looked at each other in a knowing way, unsure as to whether they should smile, or to attack this strange man who dared to take such a liberty with their sister.

The man chewed on the bark and the pain seemed to ease a little.

'I am called Garth,' said the man in a quiet voice, addressing the remark to the maiden as if they were alone and meeting formally. 'I am a good friend to my lord and master, the lord Edric. Who, alas, I know not whether he still lives, or was killed on Senlac Hill.'

The three siblings were dumbstruck, for they did, of course know of 'Wild Edric', as everyone called him, for he was the liege lord of their own master, the late Lord Wilfred, thus making Edric their own overall liege lord. Yet the thing that had struck them like a thunderbolt was the fact that this man, the man whose life they had saved, was none other than Wild Edric's famous and constant companion, the fabled warrior 'Garth,' nicknamed 'Garth Bloodaxe,' and that very same bloody battleaxe still lay uncleaned beside the man.

The two brothers gazed open mouthed at the man on the cart, but Myreen quickly recovered her wits. 'Well Garth we are pleased to know your name,' she stated sharply, 'But you are still a very sick man, and if you don't lie still and let me tend to your wounds, then you will soon be a very sick dead man, so keep still.'

Garth looked up into her honest brown eyes and smiled, knowing that the temper that she had just tried to show; was her way of showing her concern for him.

He instantly knew, and he knew that she also knew, that it was more than mere concern between healer and patient that had sprung up between them.

Evan reached for the axe, noting the look of concern that instantly crossed the face of the sick man, so he said rather nervously, 'I will clean all the gore off your axe before the rust sets in.'

Garth visibly relaxed, 'Don't worry,' said the younger brother. 'He is no warrior.' Adding, 'Well neither am I really, but he was Lord Wilfred's armourer, so he will make a good job of your axe, and will return it to you as good as new.'

The next day they covered a good six miles, spending the night in a deserted cottage that had obviously been looted either by Normans or Englishmen, for every scrap of food and all of the livestock had disappeared, except for two scrawny cockerels which the two brothers whooped and yelled at as they managed to catch them after a lot of undignified scuffling.

Scrawny or not, the cockerels tasted delicious, and the four travellers went to sleep with the taste of roast chicken still on their lips.

The following day the three siblings propped Garth up against the side of the cart where he would be much more comfortable and would be able see the countryside through which they were travelling, as well as help his three rescuers to keep watch for any dangers.

They did meet the occasional farm folk and villagers, all of who told stories of raiders, rape and pillage, either from bands of Normans or English fugitives from the great battle that had taken place near to the town of Hastings.

As their journey continued, Garth's health improved, with the ever attentive Myreen helping him with his first few steps, steadying his huge frame when dizziness overcame him, and threatened to send him crashing to the floor. But little by little he began to recover some of his former confidence until, after four laborious weeks of very slow progress; he began to walk with the long, confident strides that his former self would have been proud of.

The friendship between Garth and Myreen had blossomed into something more than mere friendship, for they were usually seen lagging behind the two brothers who had taken to the habit of sitting upon their now empty cart, watching their sister and her former patient deep in conversation, or perhaps laughing and giggling like two striplings.

Garth and Myreen's first kiss was something of an embarrassment, occurring as they sat in a meadow underneath a spreading ancient oak that shielded the four travellers from prying eyes.

A moment before, they had been giggling softly at some silly joke that he had cracked, but as they leaned forward towards each other, she leaned over and kissed him quickly on his lips.

He pulled back with the shock of her unexpected kiss.

'Oh, sorry, I shouldn't have,' she flustered.

'No, no,' said the gruff warrior. 'It's fine,' adding, 'I'm,' but didn't finish the sentence. He quickly leaned forward and grabbed her shoulders, pulling her towards him so that he crushed her face into his rough war-shirt, causing her to gasp as the rough shirt scratched her cheeks.

He realised by the sound of her gasp that he had hurt her and eased her away from him, holding her at arm's length as he looked at her beautiful but now scratched face.

'Sorry,' he said, shamefaced, 'didn't think.'

'You big brute,' she said with a smile, 'you don't know your own strength.'

Then stepping forward she stretched up onto her tiptoes, just reaching his chin which she kissed gently, sighing loudly with complete happiness as he placed his one good arm around her and drew her gently to his lips.

The two brothers knew nothing of what had taken place at the other side of the wide trunk of the oak tree, for they were both snoozing happily in the late autumn sun that streamed down through the oak's leafy canopy.

The romance blossomed as the four travellers moved steadily towards the west, through empty fields, deserted villages and silent woodlands. The brothers rode in silence whilst the two lovebirds whispered and giggled like two small children, treating the late autumn days as if God had created that very day for them, and for them alone, and nothing, nor any person had the right to intrude upon their own beautiful, happy, private little world.

For it was indeed a new life for both of them, as Myreen had never looked with love, or even liking upon a man, considering them to be loud, grubby and lazy, fit only for drunkenness and the chasing of women. Whereas Garth, despite his age and his many adventures, had spent his entire life amongst men, as well as his simple love and his devotion to his liege lord, Edric and the Lady Rowena, causing him to lead a life that seemed to give him little or no time for women, whilst the isolation that he had experienced whilst still a boy, in a cave, in the company of other boys, had made him shy, causing him to be uneasy in the company of women. Hence he had always made it his nature to avoid them, finding excuses and other things to occupy his mind.

On the odd occasion the travellers met people, who told stories of bands of Norman invaders riding through the countryside leaving death and devastation in their wake.

Whilst the news of raiders in the district forced the two brothers to glance at each other with worried frowns, jumping in alarm at each unexplained noise that emitted from the woodland.

These supposed dangers did little to dampen the happy mood of Myreen and Garth. They continued their merry way as if they didn't have a care in the world, yet despite his happiness Garth had, for the first time since his recovery, hoisted his famous battle-axe onto his left shoulder, leaving his right, undamaged hand free to hold the hand of his newfound love.

Their entry into the small town of Much Wenlock was not the homecoming that the three siblings had hoped for, as they found the single street deserted with the cottage doors closed and bolted, and it was only upon reaching their now deceased lord's hall that they were able to speak to a human being, catching sight of a man as they walked around the side of a cottage, just as he was in the process of running for cover.

'Wait!' shouted Evan at the top of his voice. 'Alf, Alfred!' He shouted even louder, 'It's me, Evan and Vaughan, don't run, it's only us. We won't hurt you.'

The man slowed down, then stopped and turned cautiously, staring intently at the small party that had just startled him.

'Good lord,' he said. 'It really is you Evan? I thought that you had been killed along with his lordship and most of the men.'

'No, no, Alf,' replied Evan as they approached the still nervous man. 'We are still alive, as you can see,' laughing in his now familiar way, ' and this is Garth,' he said, turning towards Garth who was doing his best to smile and not to frighten the little man who was still staring at the huge warrior who carried a fearsome battle-axe over his left and obviously damaged shoulder.

The man relaxed a little, saying, 'A few of the men returned and told us of how Lord Wilfred was killed, but as the last of the survivors turned up over three weeks ago we had thought that you three had also died in the battle,' then clapping Evan on the shoulder he added, 'And it is right glad I am to see you safe and well.'

He turned and beckoned the travellers to follow him, 'Come with me to my cottage,' he said. 'I will get my wife Ashwen to heat up a pot of lamb stew for you.' He adding with pride, 'Named after the Lady Ashwen of Corby she was, her mother had aims above her station,' he whispered, winking to Evan as he uttered the words.

The cottage was small and warm, and the warmth was more than welcome to the four fugitives after spending so many cold nights shivering under the stars.

The lamb stew was even more welcome, and the pot was quickly emptied leaving the astounded wife gazing at the gargantuan appetite of the huge man who seemed too big to fit into her small cottage.

'By Freya's tits that was good,' belched Garth as he plonked his wooden spoon onto the now empty wooden bowl. 'Don't suppose there is any more?'

'Nay mē hlāford,' came the indignant reply, 'that was the last of it. Not sure where our next meal is coming from.'

Garth looked up at the woman as if he was seeing her for the first time since entering her cottage, noting the distress in her face as this greedy giant who had gobbled down the very last morsel of food that the couple had in their cottage. 'Here good lady,' said the smiling warrior, fishing into the folds of his jerkin, then threw down two silver coins, 'this should pay for the meal and buy you a few more to tide you over until things get back to normal.'

Ashwen's face filled with joy as she gazed almost lovingly at two glistening coins for they were far more than her husband had ever earned from Lord Wilfred for a whole year's work as a farm ploughman. Then she looked at the huge man, seeing him in a very different light, not as a huge brute to be feared, nor as a greedy, selfish glutton as she had previously thought him to be, but as a large, generous man, but still a man with the obvious power of a bull and not a man to anger.

'God bless you mē hlāford,' blurted out the astonished woman as she bent to scoop up the two precious coins, which disappeared magically into a small pocket that lay in the folds of her apron.

Before they settled down for the night Myreen insisted on inspecting Garth's broken arm, and after unwinding the bandage, probing the still painful arm, grunted with satisfaction, 'seems to be mending.' Then asking him for the hundredth time (or so it seemed to Garth) to waggle your fingers, a small exercise which he willingly did as he looked into her eyes, saying with a silly smirk on his face, 'They worked yesterday, and the day before, and the day before that, and they are still working.'

'Good,' she said with a smile, giving him a light kiss on his cheek before she began to re-bandage the arm with a stiff piece of leather and a thong which she had scrounged from their hosts.

After spending a warm, dry and blissful night in the cottage, they woke early, and were on their way as dawn broke over the distant plain.

Evan and Myreen had opted to accompany Garth to his home whilst their younger brother Vaughan decided to return to his homestead in the hamlet of Kenley in order to help the remaining elder brother run the twenty or so acres that the family owned as freemen.

Garth purchased three scraggy ponies from a farmer who seemed to be so worried about the encroaching Norman army that he didn't even bother to haggle over the price, a trend rarely found in farmers, thought Garth as he happily paid way under the usual market price for the ponies.

The trio rode steadily westwards down the beautiful 'Ape dale,' then along the 'Corve dale,' through serene meadows and wooded valleys until, after two days, they finally reached their destination.

*****

Rowena was busy in the barn, helping one of the men tend a sick calf, when a breathless farm boy rushed in, 'My lady! My lady, come quickly, there are strangers approaching.'

She rushed out as the clatter of horses sounded on the cobbles, dreading that she would see a troop of Norman invaders galloping in to burn and pillage her beloved village.

She came to an abrupt halt as she saw that they were not raiders, but Englishmen.

However it took her a little time as she looked from one face to another before she recognized the haggard and changed face of her husband's lifelong friend and companion, Garth.

'Garth!' she screamed, almost in tears as she surged forward towards the huge frame of Garth, now alighting from his pony. 'We thought that you were dead,' she sobbed as she threw herself against the chest of the embarrassed man, who, despite knowing Rowena for many years, had always thought of her as a titled lady and had invariably treated her as such.

'My lady,' muttered the embarrassed man, as he stepped back away from his mistress. 'Dead would I be if it were not for this lady,' turning towards an open mouthed Myreen, he added, 'May I present Myreen to you?' Adding after a short pause, 'My betrothed,' then adding as an afterthought, 'oh and this is her brother.'

He thrust his good arm out towards Rowena. 'May I present the Lady Rowena,' he said, 'the wife of my Lord Edric.'

Myreen made a slight curtsey, whilst her brother bowed his head, saying, in unison, 'Right pleased we are meet you my lady.'

Rowena gave the two brothers a radiant smile, 'Come, come in, you must be exhausted after your long journey,' then turning to the beaming farm boy she said, 'take care of the ponies, see to it that they are fed, watered and bedded down.'

She led the way towards the hall, 'Lord Edric is away hunting,' she explained. 'But you must tell me and Edric of your adventures. Edric was wounded too, struck on the head by an iron mace.' After a thought she went on, 'If it wasn't for Waldo's sturdy workmanship, the blow would surely have split Edric's helmet in two and crushed his head like an egg. But he seems to be well recovered now, although in truth I see so little of him nowadays, he is always away either hunting, or visiting one of the outlying farms.'

Garth was overjoyed that his friend was alive and well, for he had been driven away from Edric during the battle by a solid wedge of Norman horsemen and had long believed that Edric had been killed.

The weary travellers were seated at Rowena's best longboard where they were given a sumptuous meal of roast pork, washed down with the finest beer that any of them could remember.

It was long after darkness had fallen when the door flew open, ushering the arrival of Edric, who strode through the hallway, then into the main room where Rowena, Garth, Evan and Myreen were sitting around the longhearth, for the night had grown chill with the first frost of the winter.

He was stunned when he realised that the large man sitting with his back to him was none other than his old friend Garth.

'God's blood,' he roared, 'tis you! I had grieved for you as being dead these long weeks past.'

Edric strode across the floor to grasp the now standing Garth around his shoulders, only noticing at the last moment, when Garth winched a little, that his left arm was strapped up uselessly at his side.

'What happened to the arm?' he asked.

'Oh I had a slight disagreement with some Norman horsemen,' said Garth with a wry smile. 'But it is mending, thanks to this good lady and her brothers, without whose timely attention I would surely be dead.'

'Nay my lord,' intervened the embarrassed Myreen, 'all I did was to repair a little damage.'

Turning to Myreen, Edric looked into the beautiful and honest face of the lady that had saved the life of his friend saying, 'You have my undying gratitude my lady, for it does my heart good to see that my old friend is alive and recovering from such grievous wounds,' then after a moment he added 'name what I can do to repay you for your service and if it is within my power it will be yours.'

'Nay Edric,' said Rowena. 'You have not yet heard the full story, for our friend Garth and his saviour are to be wed, and from what I have heard, it will be sooner rather than later.'

Rowena thrust a stirrup-cup of mead into her shocked husband's hands saying. 'What think you now my lord?

Edric took a deep, large drink for he was more than a little stunned by the news of his friend's impending marriage.

'Welsh chieftains I can deal with, Norman warriors I have fought, but a thing has come to pass that I believed would never happen, and that is to see you take a wife,' he said as he raised his tankard to his friend and his intended bride.

Then as he emptied his tankard he added, 'As a wedding gift I shall give you one of my best holdings. Choose, and it shall be yours.'

'My lord, I could not,' Garth started to say, but was interrupted by Edric.

'Enough, good friend, it is done. It is strange that the roads that we have travelled are so alike,' said Edric sipping his mead. 'We survived the destruction of our village, then lived in that blasted cave with old Vorta. Together we have fought many battles against Welshmen, Danes and Normans.'

They were both silent for a moment until Edric continued, saying, 'Even stranger still, both of us have been clouted on the head by horsemen, and yet here we are, both reasonably hale and hearty, enjoying a tankard of good English ale in the company of our loved ones.' He then took another small thoughtful sip and said in a more sinister manner, 'You know my old friend, Vorta was wrong about horsemen. He told us time and time again that horsemen were of no value in this wooded country of ours, and yet it was horsemen who shattered our shieldwall at Hastings, and it was bloody horsemen who nearly killed both of us. I think that in the future horsemen could well be the key to any battle.'

They did not seek their beds until the midnight hour was long gone, drinking and recalling not only their latest disastrous adventure, but the many other adventures that they had experienced together. Spending, or so it seemed to the others, far too long laughing over the boyhood pranks that they had played upon one another during the early days when they had spent their youth living in a dank and cold cave on some far hillside, deep in the borderlands.

CHAPTER 4

The men of Canterbury put up a brave but futile resistance against the invaders, whose archers decimated their small army before the Duke unleashed his precious horsemen who rode right over and through the English battle line, sending the few who were not slaughtered into headlong flight.

William snapped out an order to his herald, 'Recall the horsemen, we have few enough left and I don't wish to lose any more pursuing those ragged men.'

The horn sounded, recalling the well-trained horsemen, who immediately reigned in their steeds and reluctantly returned to their position on the right flank of the Norman army.

An hour later, Duke William rode into the township to accept homage from the alderman, who waited with his personal bodyguard numbering a paltry dozen men.

That evening he summoned Vernon and L'estrange to him, both strong and reliable men who had been with him for many years, for each of the two had impoverished their own estates in Normandy in order that both of them could provide a fully manned ship for the Duke's invasion of England.

'When you joined me on this venture,' he said to them as they sipped a silver beaker of his finest wine, 'I promised you rich lands and estates.' Then he added with a rather sinister smile which did not reflect in his cold blue eyes:

'Well, within a few days you shall have your lands, and after we were so kind to allow the survivors from this city of Canterbury to escape and spread the word of our invincible army, you should have no trouble in taking your prizes.

'You,' he said in as friendly a voice as he could muster, staring at L'estrange, 'will take your own men, who if my memory is not at fault, number some one hundred and ten, take them, along with our good friend Vernon, as well as his own stout fellows.

'March to the towns of Margate and Ramsgate, both are good ports with useful harbours, choose between you who has what, evict the local lords and establish yourselves there.

'On the morrow I shall take the rest of our army to the town of London, and once I have taken that city, then the remaining towns in this godforsaken land will all be ours.'

One of the noblemen who was standing just out of the immediate circle that surrounded the Duke muttered to his companion. 'Godforsaken land, if it is such a godforsaken land then why is he going to such pains to conquer the bloody place?

'Gold,' whispered his companion, and then added quietly so that his companion only could hear him. 'Isn't that what you came for?'

Vernon and L'estrange glanced at one another, smiling as they bowed their heads and said almost in unison, 'My thanks, my lord Duke.' Then turning, they left the room, but the Duke added in a less than friendly voice, 'Remember my ruling, my good friends, The silver, coin, manors and land you can have, but the gold comes to me,' adding with a cold smile, 'and if I find that a single gold coin has entered your coffers then your heads shall be forfeit.'

The following morning, the Duke marched at the head of his army, heading northwards, through the lands of the Kentish men, taking whatever livestock, loot and provisions they needed in order to sustain the army.

They evicted English lords from their manors and estates, but otherwise left the peasantry untouched, causing many of the more savage men in the army to curse the Duke, who had already hung no less than six of their comrades for disobeying his paramount order, which had been 'No unnecessary killing'.

A few days later he assembled his men before the walls of the city of London, where he and his lords, knights, as well as his massed warriors had watched helplessly as the massive, iron-studded oaken gates had been slammed shut in their faces.

They sat glumly on their steeds as they watched the citizens of the city peer down at them from their high walls and towers, throwing all manner of offal and insults at the angry Duke and his equally furious men.

The Duke sent his scouts around the walls to search for any weak spots that may offer him a speedy victory and entry into this big, dirty, smelly but vital city. Scouts who, upon their return, made great play that they had found a number of places where they thought that his army may be able gain entry into the stubborn city.

The following morning, accompanied by his brother Odo, plus a number of his lords, the Duke rode out and inspected each one of the suggested sites, but after a long and heated debate, especially with his hot-headed brother, he decided that, although he may be able to breach the wall and enter the city, the cost in men would be too high and would leave his depleted numbers vulnerable to the English of the north and the midlands. For if they were to rally and attack him in an even weaker state than he was in at the present time, then he knew that the odds would be severely stacked against him and he would almost certainly be defeated.

'No!' he bellowed as he stared into the fat, red face of his brother. 'I will not risk losing my army for the sake of an early victory, which could just as easily turn to be an early defeat.

'We will starve them out and then we shall see how many rotten cabbages they will throw at us from their high walls.

'You Fitz-Robert,' he said grimly, pointing to the gnarled figure of Fitz-Robert who stood near the front of the assembled knights in his battered and rusting armour.

'You will be in charge of the siege I don't want any provisions to get into the city, not a thing in, and not a thing out, do you understand?' Looking intently at the grubby, grey-bearded figure, knowing the man well, fully aware that despite the man's appearance and his dour manner, he was one of the most meticulous and efficient knights in the entire army.

'I want you to make doubly sure that no food gets in by using the river,' he emphasised. 'Is that clear?

The man nodded, answering glumly, 'Aye my lord,' adding, 'do I have my lord's permission to blockade the river with some of your ships?' Knowing full well that he had been given a nearly impossible task, as the wide river had literally hundreds of minor streams, marshes, large and small pools, that seeped and oozed out of and into the main course of the river.

The Duke suddenly ceased his pacing backwards and forwards, as was his way when he was trying to solve a particularly difficult problem, saying, 'In fact I will send a messenger to the fleet commander, ordering him to sail half of my entire fleet up the Thames, to be anchored within sight of the city walls. That will put the wind up these stubborn Londoners and help them to decide to open their gates to me and to accept me as their legitimate king.'

The following morning the watchers on their high walls saw that about a third of the Norman army still surrounded their city whilst some two thirds marched off in several directions into the surrounding countryside.

Yet again Duke William instructed his commanders that wherever possible they were to spare the peasants, insisting that the purpose of their enterprise was to 'collect taxes from live peasants, not dead ones.' Yet he still allowed his nobles to confiscate or impound all the livestock and grain that they could find in order to prevent it from being smuggled into the city.

'Evict the English noblemen,' he ordered, 'and I will allocate their holdings to you once the fighting is over, but remember this,' he hissed as he stared into their eyes, 'if a single golden piece finds its way into your coffers then your severed heads will be forfeit. Is that clear?'

The men shifted their feet nervously, answering with a curt nod and the words. 'Aye my lord,' and went their way.

It was a slow, leisurely march through the cold, yet still green countryside, the climate, still far more severe than most of the Normans had ever experienced, although the land was still enjoying what the English Christians called a 'Saint Luke's little summer' which sometimes happened in late autumn, giving the inhabitants a much needed period of warmish sunshine before the onset of winter.

However, this siege of the English capital was slightly different from any they had attempted before, being so far from their homelands, especially so, as it was across a wild and often impassable sea, and against a people who spoke not a word of the god given languages of either France or Normandy

Many of the towns of Kent now threw open their gates to his army and whilst the burgers welcome was far from friendly, with town-reeves and heads of guilds sullenly swearing their oaths to him.

Two weeks later he received word that London had agreed to surrender, and the Lords of London would meet with him to formally hand the city over to him three days hence at the town of Little Berkhamstead.

'Little Berkhamstead,' fumed the Duke. 'Where the Devil is Little Berkhamstead?'

None present had heard of the place.

'Bring in some of the Kentish men who now attend me,' ordered the Duke, 'They should know where it is.'

Within minutes three very nervous English noblemen were ushered into the Duke's presence, 'Ah, good,' said the Duke, 'now what I want from you is for you to tell me where in the name of the saints is the town of Little Berkhamstead?'

The three Englishmen looked at each other shaking their heads but then the elder of the three spoke, 'I have heard of the place, my Lord Duke,' he said in English, 'I am quite sure that it is in the land of the East Saxons, some few miles to the north of London.'

'What say's the man?' fumed the Duke. 'I cannot understand a word that he says.'

The interpreter translated quickly for the Duke, 'My lord Duke, the man says that it is a tiny place, just few miles north of London, in the shire of Essex.'

'Essex, Essex, that wasteland?' raged the Duke. 'Why Essex? Why up there? Miles from where we are now, damn these proud English!'

Then he commenced his pacing up and down, up and down, stopping occasionally to issue orders to the waiting retinue.

'I suspect a trap,' he fumed. 'Send out riders to scour the countryside, find their army, if they have one.' He bellowed, 'I want you, de Lacy,' pointing to a gnarled veteran, 'to assemble all our horsemen, every one, call them in from the outlying districts. Have them attend me at first light on the morrow, then we can arrive at this place Berkhamstead before our hosts, and see whether or not this is a trap set to catch this Norman bear.'

Over fifteen hundred horsemen accompanied their commander, riding through silent fields, deserted villages and hamlets, finding no one to resist them until they reached the small town of Southwark, where a stubborn army of no more than sixty or seventy men lay in wait, hidden in the marsh and reed beds, attacking the massed riders, howling like banshees as they rushed out from the high reeds, throwing the startled mounts into confusion and disarray no less than three times, before they were ridden over and wiped out by the enraged men of Normandy.

The Duke ordered the town to be razed to the ground, sparing no man, woman or child, urging his exhausted men out of the blazing ruins, he led his army across the Thames, leading their horses through marsh and swampland, into and through silent town of Islington then upwards into the southern lands of the East Saxons.

They arrived almost two days before the appointed time, where the Duke found that the people of Little Berkhamstead knew of their coming, and had been ordered to prepare a great feast of welcome for him. A feast and welcome that the astounded people had only just begun to think about, let alone prepare, for the housewives were only in the process of lighting their fires to begin their cooking, whilst the townsmen were still in the process of selecting the cattle, sheep and pigs that were to be slaughtered for the feast.

The aldermen of the town were still in the process of sitting alongside a large trestle table on the village green, drinking their ale, where they were solemnly discussing the details of how their small township would be able to feed the horde of foreign noblemen and warriors who were about to descend upon them.

Duke William ordered his men out of the town, making his fortified encampment near to the River Rib, which was a pleasant, bubbling clear river, meandering through lush meadows, dotted with huge oak trees, now devoid of their leaves, their branches standing out, stark and black, after the last two nights of heavy frost.

He was pleasantly surprised when he had witnessed the people's activities, but was determined not been lulled into a false sense of security.

'Could all be a ruse,' he stated. 'Put on just to fool us.' He sent his scouts out far and wide into the surrounding countryside, looking for the army that, he was still convinced, was out there somewhere.

The appointed day came and dragged on until midday, with no sign whatsoever of the London noblemen, until some time later when a lathered horseman galloped into the village centre, careering his steed to a halt before the Duke.

'They come my Lord,' gasped the sweating man, as he knelt before the Duke.

The Duke, who, all around him could see, was furious, not only with being kept waiting, a thing that would have wrought severe punishment in his own dukedom of Normandy, but he was equally furious with the report which he had just received from one of his own men who should have known better.

'Who comes you idiot?' he bellowed. 'Jesus Christ. An army? A cowherd?'

'Nay lord, sorry my lord,' stuttered the man. 'Nay my lord, they come, my lord. The London lords,' blurted out the flustered man. 'They are here.'

A short while later the small cavalcade of horsemen appeared on the brow of a small rise that led into Little Berkhamstead, slowly making their way down into the town, stopping a little way before they reached the Duke. There the horsemen alighted from their horses, collected a few bundles of possessions from their attendants, formed a ragged procession which appeared to be led by the elder of the three senior lords, then made their way as proudly as they could under the circumstances towards the Duke and his lords.

The small party of English noblemen stopped some six or eight feet from the Duke, where they knelt in unison before him.

The leader holding out before him in his two outstretched hands a small yellow cushion; upon which contained a large iron key.

'My Lord Duke,' said the man.

'This is the key to London, which I humbly offer to you and to your arms.'

The Duke was obviously pleased that, despite his fears of treachery and ambush, things appeared to be going well, however despite the apparent ease that was being shown by these aldermen who were now surrendering the keys to the largest city in the kingdom, he was still suspicious.

Nonetheless, he nodded his head in acknowledgement then walked the two paces forward, taking the key from the cushion which he then held aloft for all to see.

Whilst his nobles and horsemen yelled their approval, his agile mind was thinking, 'Is this really happening? Could this simple iron key be the Key to the city of London?

'Why is it not gold? Or at least silver. The key to any of my own towns in Normandy would be of gold. Am I to inherit a pauper kingdom? Am I still being duped? I have heard just how devious these London burghers can be.'

Yet he still held the large iron key aloft and grinned towards the loud jubilant throng of his men.

The assembled men joined the Duke at the tables that now groaned with food of all descriptions. Ravenous Normans attempted to devour everything within reach, whilst the Duke himself and the London Burghers nibbled at the food and drank sparingly of the wine and local beer, each suspicious of the other. Yet all seemed to go well enough, allowing the evening to end without mishap, much to Duke William's relief.

Late on the following afternoon he led his army through the open gates into the city of London, past the scowling guards, through the crowds of silent Londoners who greeted his army with silence and contempt.

*****

Westminster Abbey was full, packed with a standing throng of noblemen and soldiers, all stern-faced Normans except for a few odd English noblemen who were attending in the hope that by being at the crowning they would be allowed to keep their lands and titles.

A short time before the ceremony a bitter argument had taken place between William and his brother, the good Bishop Odo, who had claimed that he, Odo should have the honour of crowning his brother.

Duke William had bellowed, 'It must be an Englishman who crowns me, or the people will not accept me!' An argument that fell onto the deaf ears of his brother, and an argument that would, in the coming years, fester into a feud that would nearly cause the downfall of William, and would indeed cause his brother to pay an awful price for his pride, spending many of his later years imprisoned, accused of instigating a rebellion against his brother, the King of England.

Duke William did, as usual, have his way, and was crowned by the English Bishop Aldred, Archbishop of York, who loudly proclaimed him 'King of England' at Westminster Abbey on December 25th, in the year of our Lord 1066.

William was the third king crowned King of the English in that fateful year of the comet.

The jubilant throng of Normans roared their approval, counting the wealth that would soon be theirs, whilst the English lords grinned glibly, praying to the Lord that they would be allowed to hold on to their own titles and estates.

King William appeared through the ornate doors of Westminster Abbey, standing on the top step where he raised his hands triumphantly skyward awaiting the acclaim that did not come from the silent, scowling crowd of London folk.

True to his word, during the next few months, William allocated lands and titles to many of the noblemen in his army. Yet much to the dismay and anger of a large number of them, many of the lands and titles were in remote and outlandish parts of the country, some being in towns and villages that no one had ever heard of.

Whilst many of their holdings were in parts of the land that still lay unconquered.

47

CHAPTER 5

The wedding was a happy occasion, as well as being a much-needed diversion from the news that continued to reach the community from the southern regions of the country.

Myreen was radiant in her white knitted woollen dress, tied with a blue girdle around the waist and a matching blue ribbon around her cuffs and neckline. Her hair was bound into two long plaits that reached her waistline.

Garth also cut a fine figure, wearing his best tunic, sporting a wide belt with a huge silver buckle that only a man with his height and stature could wear.

Attached to his belt was a long knife with a bone handle that had thick silver thread wrapped around it in the shape of a stag.

His beard had been trimmed and his hair washed and cut with two short braids, which hung down past his ears tied with silver threads.

The celebrations went on long into the early hours of the following morning, and it was long after the happy couple had retired to their bridal chamber that the final guests either left the hall or sank into drunken oblivion onto the benches or onto the soggy reeds that covered the paved floor.

By midday Garth, Myreen and three servants left for their new home which Edric had bequeathed to them, a home that would seem very familiar to Myreen, for it was none other than the manor and village of Much Wenlock, the former home to the now deceased Lord Wilfred.

Edric and many of the village folk waved a fond farewell to a delighted Garth and his new bride who had, overnight become the Lord and Lady of the small town of Much Wenlock, and of its surrounding lands.

Edric was, once again left without the company of his lifelong friend, but although he sorely missed him, he had plenty of things to occupy his mind.

There was always some disgruntled tenant or minor landlord approaching him with one claim or another, the sort of petty squabbles that always seem to be part of country life, usually concerning either land boundaries, livestock or women.

These minor problems were overshadowed by the news from the south of England, where, it seemed that Duke William, who was now claiming to be 'King William of England', was industriously consolidating his claim, by slowly marching his army northwards, taking towns and villages in his name.

Towns and villages in which he would install a new lord, build a temporary fortress, before moving northwards again and according to the latest reports that Edric had received from the ever increasing flow of refugees, the Norman's had at the present time already begun to infringe into the counties of Gloucestershire and Herefordshire, erecting a castle or motte before moving on to the next town or village.

Then good news arrived telling that the Normans had withdrawn from Herefordshire, in order to return to the valleys of Somerset, where a major rising had taken place, throwing William's carefully laid plans into disarray.

Edric and Rowena celebrated by roasting an ox on the village green, inviting all the villagers and people from the outlying farms and holdings to attend, where they enjoyed roast beef and all the good ale they could drink.

The following morning, despite having a slight hangover, Edric saddled his black stallion and rode into the distant hills seeking his favourite prey, the wily and dangerous wild boar.

That day turned out to be one of the most disastrous days in Edric's life.

The morning started well enough with the weather clement and the countryside green and peaceful, and by midday his two boarhounds had located a small herd of wild pigs, which he tracked and chased until his stallion was beginning to tire. Then, just as Edric was forced to dismount in order to rest his horse, the largest boar that he had ever seen burst out of a clump of bushes and charged towards him.

He had a mere moment in which to grasp his boar-spear, enabling him to level it towards the snorting, furious boar – which, in its frantic attempt to gore Edric hurtled itself straight onto the spear, penetrating the boar's right eye and into its brain, instantly killing the enraged beast. Yet not stopping its wild charge, a charge which sent the already dead animal into the crouching figure of Edric, sending the hunter and the hunted backwards into a tangled heap amongst a mass of nettles.

Covered in blood, with his face and exposed arms stinging from the nettles, he heaved the heavy animal off his chest and lay for a moment on his back before he rose to his feet, wading out of the waist-high nettles, cursing and looking around for a dock leaf which was supposed to be the antidote for nettle stings.

After he relieved the animal of its entrails he had a slight struggle to heave the huge carcass of the boar onto the rear of his Norman saddle, before starting the long journey homeward, looking forward to being greeted by his beautiful Rowena, plus the rest of his household, who he felt sure, would soon have the beast sizzling on a spit, allowing himself and the household to enjoy an evening feast of delicious roast pork.

Late in the afternoon he rode into the strangely quiet village, where the puzzled Edric guided his mount down the muddy track, past silent cottage after silent cottage until he reached his own longhall.

Despite seeing no one, he dismounted, untied the boar and heaved it onto his shoulders, then strode through the open door of his home, halting immediately when he saw the body of the maiden Elfrieda sprawled in the hallway, with her right hand actually lying in the fire, burning furiously but totally unfelt by the staring cold eyes of his wife's once faithful maidservant.

A man suddenly appeared in the door which led into the great hall, and gaped at the static figure of this man with a wild boar on his shoulders, causing the silly smile that the man wore to suddenly leave his dirty, grease-smeared face.

A moment later the man's face altered again as the Edric's hunting spear entered his belly sending the man staggering backwards, crashing to the floor with a loud groan as he clutched at the offending weapon in the dying seconds of his life.

Edric heaved the boar off his shoulders, then stepped over the dead man, walking into the great hall, snatching the man's sword out of its scabbard as he did so, and was shocked to see a large number of men sitting at his own table, eating and drinking.

However, the thing that totally shocked him was the body of his beloved Rowena which lay on the floor, in a large pool of her own precious blood, with her beautiful blue eyes staring unseeingly up at the rafters.

A cold rage filled his brain, which speedily built up to become the red berserker rage that he had sometimes experienced in the heat of battle.

The same red rage that had probably earned him the name of 'Wild Edric'.

However, this rage was coupled with a cold, chilling hatred that he immediately felt for every last one of these men who stood before him.

The nearest man stepped forward and swung his battle-axe towards Edric's head.

Edric easily evaded the clumsy swing, thrusting his sword into the man's throat, taking the axe from the dying man's hand as he fell to the floor.

He now held a battle-axe in his right hand and a short sword in his left as he approached the main bunch of the men who stood dumfounded before him, however they quickly recovered their wits and with loud cries (in a language that he did not recognize) moved en masse towards him.

Much to their surprise, the man did not retreat from them, even though they outnumbered him by eighteen to one. For they were (were they not?) veteran warriors, well-schooled in the arts of war, with the experience of many battles and skirmishes behind them? Yet this stupid man literally launched himself into their midst, thrusting, head butting, elbowing and hacking about him until, within a few short, bloody moments, at least half of their number were either dead or wounded.

One of the men ran for the door, but the floor was now littered with dead or wounded men as well as discarded weapons, and Edric threw his own sword into the man's back like a spear. Then scooped up another similar sword, hurling himself towards the remaining men, catching the now startled and cowering men unawares, slaying a further three before they could move, then pursuing the remaining men with well-rehearsed, deliberate killing blows, that his old mentor Vorta had knocked into his head whilst he was still a boy, until not one of his wife's killers remained standing.

A red mist clouded his eyes and he was indeed an English berserker of old.

His rage was still not sated and he moved from one wounded man to the next, dispatching them with his axe, covering not only the floor with their gore but also splashing their blood over himself as well as half way up the walls.

He heard a whimper and strode over to the longboard expecting to find another wounded Norman cowering under it, but was shocked back into reality when he stooped and saw a small figure of a blood-soaked boy, cowering under the table.

The boy was obviously an English child according to his clothes and his hairstyle.

The sight of the boy stopped him in his frenzied search for a live man to kill, and the only sounds in the bloody, steamy room was the hoarse panting of his own gasps, and the slight whimpering that emitted from the boy.

Recovering a little of his composure, he stared down at the boy, and seeing that he was covered in blood, asked:

'Are you wounded?'

The boy shook his head but said nothing.

'Come,' said Edric, but the boy shrank away from this madman who had just slain every living person in the room except himself.

Edric stooped under the table grabbing the boy's arm, pulling him to his feet, where the child, who appeared to be around the age of perhaps eleven or twelve years old, stood unsteadily amongst the carnage of his former associates.

He dragged the boy outside and into the fresh air saying, 'Sit here for a while and you will feel better.'

The boy flopped down onto the grass until his sobbing slowly abated, then after a while it ceased altogether.

Edric learned that the boy's name was Aldred, who turned out to be a very intelligent young man, wise beyond his years, who told Edric that the men he had slain had all been Normans who had been part of the Norman army that quelled the small rebellion that had taken place in the south. This task that had taken them a few short days, and after the rebellion they had been part of a larger Norman army which had continued to advance up and into the heartland of the country.

The Normans had, according to the boy, already taken control of the towns of Hereford, Ludlow and Shrewsbury, news that shook Edric's body to the core.

'Just another shock to come to terms with in a day of shocks,' he mumbled to himself.

He left the boy, returning to the house, where his old habit of counting automatically took over as he placed the heads of twenty-one Normans outside his front door. He returned to cradle the head of his beloved Rowena in his lap, sobbing his heart out as he kissed her blood-soaked face and hair.

Hal found his brother when he entered the bloodied house an hour after daybreak.

Edric was asleep amongst the headless bodies of his victims, leaning against the wall with the head of his dead wife still cradled on his lap, her hair still damp from his tears.

*****

'Ah brother,' said Hal, as he carefully stepped over the bodies, trying to avoid the pools of dried blood, but stopped abruptly when he realized that Edric was still cradling Rowena's lifeless form in his lap. He approached further until he reached his brother, placing his hand on Edric's shoulder, kneeling quietly beside him.

There was no reaction whatsoever from Edric who appeared to be staring down aimlessly into the face of his dead wife.

Hal placed his hand upon Edric's right hand which held Rowena's head, and attempted to pull it away saying, 'Come brother, there is naught that we can do for her now except give her a decent Christian burial.' But the hand refused to move as if clenched by an iron claw.

He tried again, but neither the hand or the head of Edric moved an inch.

He stood and made his way to the door, returning a few minutes later carrying a tankard of cold beer. He knelt again alongside his brother, raising the tankard to Edric's lips, 'Take a sip of this,' he said, tilting the tankard so that the beer touched his brother's dry lips and dribbled down his beard and off his chin.

'Come with me,' Hal insisted as he tried again to haul Edric off the floor. 'It looks as if you have a few cuts and bruises that need looking at.'

Edric's eyes flickered as he looked up, as if he were wakening from a dream. He licked his lips then looked up into his brother's sad eyes.

Then grasping the tankard, he placed it to his mouth and drank long and deep.

'Hal,' he whispered through his cracked, lips, 'they killed her.'

'I know brother, I know,' said Hal, still shocked by the carnage that surrounded them. 'Think you not they have paid for their sin?

'Not enough, brother,' answered Edric. 'Not enough.'

'Let us carry her to the St Chad's where we can lay her body to rest, then we can speak about what we should do about these Norman swine.'

Edric rose, his limbs protesting at the movement, for he had been sitting on the cold floor for the whole of the night, and was forced to lean against the wall for support until the cramp had left his stiff limbs.

He then stooped and lifted Rowena's body up, protesting when Hal stepped in to assist him.

'Nay, Brother. 'Tis my task, touch her not,' giving him a look that told Hal, as well as any other person who knew him, that to gainsay him, especially at a time such as this, could, and would bring savage retribution upon the perpetrator.

Hal followed his brother, who solemnly carried his dead wife through the small crowd that had gathered outside the house, across the village green and into the churchyard, stopping at the edge which dropped sharply into the valley.

'This will be a fitting place for my lady,' said Edric. 'She loved to look down into the valley to watch her people at their work and at their play.'

'Aye,' answered his brother. 'She did so.'

He carried her limp body into the Church, placing her white, blood-soaked body before the altar saying:

'Into your hands dear Lord, I give the soul of my beloved wife Rowena, welcome her into your kingdom of heaven,' kissing her full upon her lips, he placed her hands together across her body and, after a long, silent prayer, he stood shakily, turned, and left the church.

The brothers dug her grave and, despite many offers, allowed no man to help.

The priest took the funeral service that was attended by every person in the area for she was sorely loved. No person, be it man, woman, or child, could speak ill of her.

The boy Aldred stood apart, speaking to no one, but nonetheless, he made the sign of the cross at the correct moment, allowing the tears to cascade down his dirty, blood-smeared face.

After the short service Edric called for quiet and addressed the throng:

'Friends,' he began, 'my thanks to you for honouring me with your presence on this sad day, but I say to you here and now, that from this moment on, it may not be safe for you to remain here. For when the Normans learn about the slaughter of their men, and they surely will hear of it, if not today, then another day hence, then they will return in greater numbers to seek revenge.'

He then paused for a while, in order to allow what he had said to sink in. He could see his people look at each other in amazement and mutter amongst themselves.

'Aye my friends they will come, and I shall not be here to greet them, for I too will have left this place.

'I think it wise if you all leave this place, for a while at least. Perhaps you could return in a few months' time.'

Again he paused and a voice from the crowd shouted, 'Aye my lord, but where shall we go?'

'Then another voice said, 'My lord, we have nowhere to go.'

'I have thought long and hard about that question,' answered Edric, 'and I think that I can find places for most of you. And I shall answer you Edward, my friend, since you are the one who had courage enough to raise the question.

'I have an empty cottage at Middleton Scriven which has some land for your milking cow. That is yours, rent-free for the foreseeable future.' Then he turned to another of his tenants, a small, grubby man who answered to the name of Lyulf the Lame, due to one of his legs being shorter than the other. 'I would like you Lyulf my old friend to take your wife and children, how many is it now, eleven or twelve?'

'Nay lord, only ten,' was the answer.

'Ah well Lyulf, you take your wife and ten children to the village of Culmington where the Sytch Farm has been empty these ten months past, since poor old Edward died of the flux.'

To another he allocated the Coats Farm at Rattlinghope, a derelict farmhouse, which stood high on the north-western side of the long mountain, 'But it does need a new thatched roof,' he added.

To Wilfred the ploughman he gave Long Meadow Farm, near the village of Wattlesborough.

He sent Ernest the Woodman to the hamlet of Bickton, where he knew of a smallholding whose tenant, old Ned, had recently died

The other empty properties that he knew about were given to families who he thought had needs greater than the others, but after racking his brains could think of no more empty properties or barns.

'The rest of you will have to stay with friends or your kith and kin,' answered Edric. 'Make sure that you take your stock with you,' he added with some venom, 'don't leave these Norman reavers a single chicken. The crops will continue to grow and you can harvest them when you return.'

There was more muttering, some applauding their lord for his consideration, whilst others muttered angrily as the crowd began to leave in groups of muttering, worried people.

The large form of his son Godwin and the even larger form of Garth stood alongside him, deterring any further discontent.

His brother Hal also stood tall beside him, seeing the wisdom of his brother's decisions for he was, as usual, totally committed to do his bidding; but then Edric said to him:

'Brother, I would like you to take your wife and that tall son of yours, and of course your lovely new born daughter, to the hamlet of Bicton.'

Hal was just about to protest when Edric continued, 'No, not the Bicton near Clunn, but the other Bicton near the city of Shrewsbury, where you will be safe. For none will know that you are my kin, and from there you will be able to glean all the news from Shrewsbury and warn me if you hear of aught that should be of concern to me.'

Hal spluttered and protested, but he could see that his elder brother was adamant and could also see the wisdom in his decision, so he reluctantly agreed to go.

He dispersed his four daughters and their families likewise, sending them to the remote parts of the shire where, he hoped, they would remain safe from the Norman invaders.

However, he decided that his son Godwin who was now a strapping ox-like fellow with the shoulders of an archer should remain with him, saying, 'My son, I would like you to stay with me, for you are as yet unmarried and have no children to worry about, and I still may have need of your strong right arm to guard my back.'

Waldo the blacksmith did not turn to leave, nor did Evan, who had become a good friend of Waldo, having much in common with the smithy, with his experience in the making and repairing of armour, swords and maces. 'Waldo and myself will ride with you my lord,' said the ever-cheerful Evan. 'We will both be of use to you.'

They turned to return to Waldo's forge, 'Come Waldo,' he said cheerfully, 'we must see what we can take with us,' and they both walked towards the still burning furnace, which was outside Waldo's single-roomed cottage.

Edric returned to his own house in order to collect a few essentials he thought necessary to take with him.

He knelt by the longhearth in the hallway and dug up the left-hand corner of the still warm hearth which was situated inside the still blood-soaked room where, eventually, he located and heaved out two large leather sacks of gold and silver coins, plus the final two of the great gems which his old mentor Vorta had given him.

He picked up his trusty longbow, plus two quivers of arrows (one hunting arrows and the other heavy war arrows) his axe, and two heavy spears. These he loaded onto the Norman saddle of his stallion, then led the stallion over the village green to Waldo's smithy.

He called Waldo and Evan over to him, 'I have not mentioned this to the others as I think it is in their best interests not to know, but I have decided to move to my manor at Wentnor. It is a pleasant enough village, perched high on a hill and perhaps remote enough to hide us from these Norman dogs for a while.

'Besides,' he added, 'if and when they do find us, I will have made the defences strong enough to make even them to think twice before attacking us. It is a place which we should be able to defend, especially if we can gather as many good men as we can find. From there we may even be able take the fight to these Norman dogs, and help win back our lands.'

At the precise moment that Edric put his foot into the stirrup, his stallion snorted and started forward in such a manner that Edric was forced to hop for a few awkward moments before he eventually heaved himself into the now familiar Norman saddle. Then as he steadied his mount, he saw the reason for the stallion's actions, for riding through the gate was the young dapper figure of Hywell riding his own captured Norman stallion.

Hywell's stallion had also seen Edric's mount and was prancing about, either in happiness or perhaps with anger at seeing another stallion that it might have known from the past.

The stallions slowly calmed down, and then approached each other, nuzzling each other in obvious delight at seeing each other again, which in itself was very unusual, for stallions usually tend to fight rather than make love.

'What brings you back here my young friend?' said the delighted Edric, 'I thought that we had seen the last of you, and you would be long lost in the mists of those dark Welsh mountains of yours.'

'Nay, my good Lord Edric,' came the reply. 'You forget that I am only half Welsh and the other half is as English as your good self. Besides,' he added, 'after the thrilling time that I had with you at Stamford Bridge and Hastings, the rain and fogs of the mountains soon become more than a little boring, and I long for another adventure if you have one to offer.'

'Indeed I do,' answered the delighted Edric, 'for I remember you in the shieldwall at Hastings, and how you saved my life from those damned Norman horsemen,' shaking his head slightly as he recalled the pain and worry that his crushed helmet had caused him (the selfsame helmet that he still wore, but now strongly reinforced by the adept skills of Waldo.)

Recovering from his thoughts, he continued, 'I am still in need of your strong right arm, in fact I would welcome a hundred like you, for I intend to take the fight to these Normans and I will need all the good warriors that I can muster.'

Some of the villagers had already left, whilst others were busy packing their belongings onto carts, gathering and hobbling their livestock, shouting children caught geese and hens, as well as nimble, bleating goats, causing such chaos that despite the fact that Edric was sad as well as angry, it caused bouts of despair that seemed to sweep over him like a cold north wind.

It was eventually with a slight sigh of relief that Edric led his little party through the village and out of the gates, waving and bidding farewell to people, many of whom he had known for most of his adult life.

'Who's the urchin?' asked Hywell, turning in his saddle to stare behind the riders.

Edric then turned in his saddle to look in the direction that Hywell had indicated, and saw the small, grubby figure of the boy Aldred who was skulking behind a bush some fifty feet behind them.

'Come boy,' he shouted, and the boy reluctantly appeared, holding his head down, as he approached the four grim men.

However, despite his black mood, Edric found it hard not to smile at the boy and held his hand out saying, 'Take hold boy, and ride behind me,' heaving the boy up and onto the rear of his mount.

The four travellers and the boy reached Wentnor by midday on the following day, and soon settled into the deserted longhall, employing three of the village maidens who offered their services to cook, clean and to look after the four wet and weary men.

Edric assigned Aldred the duty to tend his own stallion, under the tuition of an experienced groom who was in overall charge of the four horses.

During the next few days Edric sent no fewer than eleven men and youngsters out into the countryside, under the disguise of homeless, landless men, with orders to contact all of the towns and villages in the area, in order to spread the word that Edric was, yet again, raising his standard, with the intention of taking the fight to these Norman invaders in order to drive them from England.

Wild Edric was determined to restore the kingdom to English ownership, hopefully under the leadership of one of King Harold's sons who were, it was rumoured, even as they spoke, raising an army of their own in order to avenge the death of their father.

In the meantime, he spent a large part of his time in training the few men who had already answered his call, but still found a little time to pursue his favourite pastime, that of hunting in the vast Forest of Clun, which literally began within a few hundred yards of his new home.

Whilst his days were busy in the extreme with these new duties he had set himself, the nights were long and mostly sleepless, finding that during the few brief hours of sleep, when his tired and troubled mind allowed him to sleep, he dreamt.

Nor was the dream about his lovely Rowena.

He had the dreams, nay; he had the nightmares that had troubled him for so long whilst he was a child, as well as through his years of youth, even into adulthood.

These nightmares came flooding back almost, it seemed to him, as soon as his head hit the pillow, when he found himself time and time again in the battle line where he had stood proud and confident, only to experience his own death as an enemy spear entered his chest, forcing him to leave this world of men in a haze of a serene, painless cloud, only to find himself standing again in the graveyard, looking down upon his own graveslab, which read.' Here lies Edric, October 10th, (but no year), and he again turned to the spirit that stood beside him and asked the question:

'I know of course that it is the Eve of St Ethelberga and I see that according to my gravestone that I died on October the 10th, but there is no year. What year do I die?'

And the spirit who stood alongside him answered, the same as he answered each night:

'This year.'

*****

He tried to console himself time and time again that 'this year' was 'every year'. Yet with every year that passed he was always pleased to see the tenth day of October pass.

Whilst he had sworn to himself, time and time again, that after the loss of his beloved Rowena, there would never be a woman who could compare with her.

Women were the last thing on his mind, but it was the first day of the Christian month of May, he watched glumly as the village children, bedecked in garlands of flowers danced around the thorn tree that had been planted in the centre of the village green.

He felt that his long face would dampen down the villagers' spring celebration of May Day, so after spending some considerable time petting and talking to his black stallion Chieftain, he eventually left the stallion in his stall and saddled a two-year-old dun gelding which Rowena had named Foxy, due to the fact that its colouring resembled that of a fox, enabling the gelding to mingle into the foliage so well that on many occasions the gelding had taken Edric quietly, almost unseen, to within striking distance of deer, wild boar, as well as the occasional wolf. However, on this occasion he quietly urged Foxy through the gates and out of the village.

He rode through freshly greened woodlands, through dappled glades trampling the young curled ferns beneath the delicate hooves of Foxy, as they made their way quietly, somewhat soothed by the birdsong and the peace of the woods.

By mid-afternoon he had seen spoor of wild boar, deer and wolf, but all had been stale and he caught sight of no living thing, except a few cheeky red squirrels that peered down at him from their lofty perches, high in the oak trees.

He guided Foxy down a steep incline, through the tangle of hazel and beech saplings where he paused at the bottom of the slope, allowing his horse to slake its thirst in the clear, babbling brook that made its way through the narrow valley. As he alighted from his saddle to join the horse and drink from brook, he fancied that he heard the sound of music, but then as he knelt to drink, cursed himself as a fool, putting the supposed sound down to the gurgling and babbling of the brook as it made its way over the many rocks that made up the stream bed.

Eventually he remounted and began to guide Foxy upstream, around boulders, through boggy areas where small springs added their contributions to the brook.

Yet again he imagined that he heard the sound of music. Whilst trying to convince himself that he was imagining it, as he was riding in an area that was completely devoid of human habitation, so there could be no possibility of music coming from such an outlandish area. Yet as he rode on he again heard the strains of music.

This time he was certain that he could distinguish the individual sound of a lyre, then the plucking of a harp, plus the definite, shrill melodious sound of a flute. Then a sound reached his ears which literally made his hair stand on end, for it was the beautiful chorus of a number of girls singing in unison with the music.

The horse's ears shot forward and he came to abrupt halt, forcing Edric to dismount. He had to lead the reluctant horse forward until they reached a large glade, in which he could see a small, round, thatched cottage, with a door and a single window through which Edric could plainly see the shadows of figures passing as people moved about inside the cottage.

Edric tethered his horse to an elder, then walked slowly towards the open door. As he reached the door he could see that the room was ablaze with the light from a large number of candles that festooned the walls, creating a bright, yet hazy light through which he could make out a group of beautiful women in the far corner, one playing a lyre, another a flute, whilst another plucked at a small harp.

Other women sat in various parts of the room or stood in silence as they watched, as if in awe, as another maiden danced slowly by herself in the centre of the room, turning gently with her eyes closed and her hands held high above her head, as she moved sensuously in a small circle in the centre of the room.

All of the maidens were extraordinary beautiful, and, as was his way, he had unconsciously counted seven.

Each of the maidens had long hair of various colours, ranging from deep brown to blond, plaited and adorned with flowers, and were dressed in expensive linen garments of a design that was unknown to him.

He slowly entered the room as if in a dream, failing to notice when the music came to a slow stop with the eldritch fall of a final chord from the lyre.

The maiden in the centre of the room had ceased her hypnotic dance and stood in a ring of light with her eyes now wide open, staring unblinkingly at Edric, her lips curved in a knowing, pleasant and welcoming smile.

Although she had ceased her dancing, white petals of the may blossom appeared to drift slowly onto her head and shoulders, giving her the appearance of what he imagined an angel would look like.

He stopped as though he had walked into an invisible barrier, standing for many moments. Yet it seemed to him like hours, staring, open mouthed at this beautiful woman.

As far as Edric was concerned, she was the only other person in the room, for despite their beauty the other maidens had ceased to exist, whilst the maiden who had entranced him seemed, to him, to be the most beautiful woman that he had ever seen.

The apparition walked slowly the few steps towards him, and it was then that he realised that, for a woman, she was exceedingly tall. Her wide, laughing blue eyes peered at him on exactly the same level as his own eyes, which were in turn dazzled and captivated by the eyes that had stopped a few inches from him.

An aromatic perfume, the like of which he had never smelt before, emanated from her being. Overwhelming his senses. Infecting his brain as if he had been immersed into a cauldron of steamy, perfumed smoke, intoxicating his mind and bewitching him.

'I am named Godda,' she said in a soft, low voice, 'and I am Queen of the Light Elves.'

She spoke with a husky deep velvet voice and automatically assumed that her short statement explained the strange events that had happened to this man over the last few, short minutes.

As if to answer his unasked questions, she continued, 'My sisters and I have awaited your arrival these long years past, for we can only appear in human form upon the first day of spring, before we must return to our own kingdom of Elvengard.'

'My own destiny has been foretold long ago, that I should meet you here, bring joy and happiness to you, and become yours for as long as you wish.'

Then she paused for a moment before she continued to speak, adding, 'Unless you reproach me on account of my sisters, or about this sacred place where we have met. Should you do so then I shall return to my own kingdom and you will never see me again.'

Her abrupt statement, which had been uttered softly and pleasantly, appeared rather strange to Edric. He had seen this beautiful woman only a few moments before, and yet, here she was uttering ultimatums to him, as if he was beholden to her.

Yet even as she spoke he knew himself to be captivated. For her extravagant dress, her stature, plus her utter beauty had sent his head spinning and his heart pounding so much so that he feared it would break free from his chest and present itself on a platter to this so-called 'Queen of the Light Elves'.

As she had been speaking, Godda's sisters had approached the couple and now surrounded them, hissing and scowling that their sister, their beloved sister and Queen was about to be taken from them. Only with great reluctance that, after a sharp, short sentence from Godda, who said loudly: 'You are all aware that this would happen. It is my destiny,' causing them to stand aside, unwillingly, still hissing and scowling. Yet they did allow Edric to take Godda's hand, and lead her through them, out of the doorway and into the coolness of the glade in which the cottage stood.

That evening Edric and Godda lay together under the stars on a bed of dry fern, each pledging their love, promising to be faithful to the other. Vowing to marry at their earliest convenience, eventually falling into a blissful sleep nestled in each other's arms.

As soon as she had wakened in the morning Godda kissed Edric lightly on his cheek then stooped down, taking his hand in her own, in order to study the palm of Edric's right hand, whispering in his ear, 'So it is true that the line of destiny is there. What about this legendary spearmark in your chest? Is that just a myth or have you really been speared through your heart?'

'No,' he muttered, 'I have never been speared.' Then added thoughtfully, 'Until the moment that I saw you on the yesterday, whence my heart was penetrated by your loveliness.'

But even as he uttered the words she was untying the cord of his shirt and lifting the shirt up, over his chest, running her hand over his chest, 'Mm,' she cooed, 'I see where the spear went.'

'Nay, sweet lady, as I said, I have never been speared,' he repeated.

'Not in this life,' she whispered as she kissed his cheek.

CHAPTER 6

'**D**amn these bloody Englishmen,' fumed the normally cool and calculating William, 'Who the devil is it this time?' he asked his already flushed brother Odo, Bishop of Bayeux.

'A man named Edric,' answered Odo. 'Him and some Welsh Kings. Don't know their names,' he added, 'but I understand that they have raised a considerable force.'

'Well they will have to wait until I have dealt with Harold's sons in the North. What is the latest news that you have on them?'

'And what other disasters have occurred whilst I have been in Normandy?'

'No other risings, my lord,' answered Odo, 'but I have sent Earl Brian of Penthievre to deal with Harold's sons.'

'Fine choice, he's a good man. He is an able man who can handle himself well. Fought well at Hastings,' answered Duke William. 'In the meantime, send the garrisons from Winchester and Gloucester, plus any other odds and sods that you can muster to deal with those yokels from the Welsh border.'

Two weeks later Earl Brian's small army met the late King Harold's sons on a bleak moor in the north of England, where they caught the rebellious army on the march, soundly defeating them, sending the few survivors scurrying back to their ships where they returned to Ireland and sank into oblivion.

No sooner had Earl Brian returned in triumph to his own lands than he was disturbed from his bed in the early hours of the morning by a dirty, sweaty rider, who had been sent by William, King of all England, with the disturbing news that the north was, yet again in revolt.

''Tis King Swein Esthrithson, King of Denmark, my lord,' gasped the exhausted rider. 'He has joined Earl Morcar, the Earl of Northumberland, and Edgar Aetheling, plus a small army led by his brother, the Earl of Mercia.

'My lord the King also believes that the earls Waltheof' and Gospatrick may also join them, and if that happens the King will need every man he can muster, and he bids you join him on his march to the north.'

Cursing silently to himself, Earl Brian stumbled from his warm bed, hurriedly dressed, grabbed his chain-linked war-shirt from a chair where he had flung it a few short hours ago and led the tired messenger into his main room, where a servant was already in the process of re-kindling the log fire that still smouldered in the longhearth.

'Summon my warriors!' he yelled to his one and only personal bodyguard, a man named Haiden whom he had chosen for his trustworthiness. That and the man's cantankerous nature, for he had known the man for many years and had served the Earl faithfully.

'Send out riders and assemble my men,' he ordered, 'have them assemble here by noon on the morrow,'

Without a word, Haiden nodded his gnarled head in sullen acknowledgement, and slunk out of the room.

'No need to stir myself yet,' he grumbled to his servant who stood near the door holding a candle. 'Time enough to get a little shut-eye,' he muttered as he snatched the candle out of the man's hands and returned to his still warm bed.

'Let the morrow's problems await the morrow,' he said sleepily and still fully dressed he sank his head into his goose down pillow and fell asleep.

By noon Earl Brian led seventy-nine warriors through the gates of his small but sturdy stockade, knowing that his small army would swell as he marched through his own lands towards the Great North Road, where he was to join King William's army.

Whilst he was fully confident in the fighting ability of his own men, his sour mood was made even worse by the glum faces and the loud grumbles that emitted from his warriors.

He was fully aware that they were none too happy at being called out to fight so soon after their victory against the former King Harold Godwinson's sons. Both the warriors and their leader knew that this coming battle against the King of Denmark, who was one of the most famous warrior-kings in Europe, plus the northern earls who had joined him, would make this enemy a far more difficult enemy to defeat.

It was more than two weeks before he and his men joined King William south of York, where he found William in one of the blackest of his black moods. On that very morning the King had received news that the city of York had been taken, the garrison slaughtered, and, if the reports were to be believed, no less than nine hundred of his men, plus his good friend, Robert de Comines had been slaughtered by a single English warrior.

This particular English warrior, who had slain so many of his men when the Norman survivors from the battle had attempted to escape through the one and only available gate, had been named as the dreaded Earl Waltheof.

'There is also trouble in the Fens,' muttered the Duke. 'Some troublemaker named Hereward. Apparently he is causing such havoc that some of our men are already calling him 'Hereward the Wake'.

'When I meet these rebels I will teach them who is their master or, by the sacred bones of my father, I shall die in the attempt,' hissed the King ominously.

'Still, let us deal with the present situation here in the north,' he said. 'Come, join us Earl Brian,' motioning for Earl Brian to join the other lords who had already been studying a map that lay on a small table near to the fire.

'Here,' pointed the King, 'is where we are, just on the outskirts of York. We march first thing in the morning, and I want you Earl Brian to take this route across these hills here' – pointing to a range of hills west of York – 'whilst I take the bulk of our army up the Great North Road to attack the city from the south.'

Earl Brian merely grunted and nodded his gnarled head.

The King continued. 'Now I do of course realise that you have already had a long march and have only just arrived here, so I shall provide horses for you and your men, whilst we will march on foot, that way we should both arrive at our destinations by sunrise two days from now.'

Earl Brian nodded again in acknowledgement as King William continued. 'Lay waste to every farmstead and holding that you come across and when you have reached York, block the northern side of the city. Slay any fugitives that come your way.'

He stared coldly at Earl Brian, who quickly muttered 'Aye my lord King' and lowered his eyes in order to study the map in detail.

'Good,' said William, 'and as soon as you are in position north of York, see to it that you send a rider to me with news of your position.'

Much to the Duke's surprise, the enemy had left the city of York, allowing him to enter unopposed, greeted glumly by the few citizens who had remained in their homes, not sure whether these new warriors who now strode confidently into their partially destroyed city would continue the slaughter and debauchery that they had experienced over the past few years, or whether they would be allowed to live in peace

The King remained in York, joined by the Earl Brian where they strengthened the partially ruined defences, whilst a large part of the Norman army foraged far and wide, devastating the land, destroying towns, villages, livestock and crops, extinguishing all signs of life between the Humber and the Wash.

Despite the slaughter and devastation, the King and his entourage celebrated Christmas in grand style, eating off silver platters brought especially from Winchester for the occasion, happy and contented that whilst the rest of the shire starved, he and his warriors ate their fill, eating of the finest food that had been brought in from the surrounding countryside.

With spring came the news that his enemies had wintered in the Cheviot Hills and were, once again on the march, so it was with relief and joy that he assembled his men and marched to meet them.

His joy was heightened when on a chilly, damp spring morning heralds arrived at his camp with news that his enemies wished to parley.

Ever the practical and calculating man that he had always been, he readily agreed to parley; and when he met with the rebels his eyes beheld the worried faces of the earls Waltheof and Gospatrick. Whereas his own heart was near bursting with joy with the thought that he may be able to bring this rebellion to an end, by making peace with these two earls, thus avoiding the slaughter of a large number of his own men, or even a possible defeat and with the latter a distinct possibility of the loss of his newly won kingdom.

How he dealt with them later could wait until he was in a stronger position to make that particular decision.

Earl Gospatrick was obviously a man of good breeding, well dressed and well groomed, but to William, Earl Waltheof appeared to be more like a bear than a man, for his huge frame was hidden by a black cloak. Greasy, grey-streaked hair fell without a break down into a beard that merged to cover his rusty war-shirt almost to his waist. Out of this mass of hair protruded two enormous arms that were thicker than most men's thighs.

As the Duke tried to take stock of the two men he mused to himself how this beast of a man and his companion had been able to slay his friend Robert de Comines and nine hundred of his men. Though of course, he doubted the true figure was probably less than half than number.

But whatever the true number turned out to be, this bear-man would certainly send tremors of fear into any foe who faced such a brute in the battle line.

Against his better judgment, William held his hand out to Waltheof. A hand that immediately disappeared inside the man's huge paw and felt that his hand had been inserted into a vice, causing William much pain, but he flickered not an eyelid.

'Good it is to meet such a renowned warrior,' said the King as his hand was finally released and the blood began to regain its path towards his crushed fingers.

The man grunted, and continued to stare at William through piggy grey eyes that peered through his hair-covered face.

Gospatrick on the other hand grasped William's right hand with both of his hands in a sign of genuine friendship. 'Well met,' said Gospatrick with a genuine smile.

Three hours and nine jugs of bitter English ale later (which was consumed by the two earls, whilst the King merely sipped at his one and only glass of cider) they parted, having sealed a truce wherein the two earls as well as each one of their warriors had been granted the King's royal pardon, retaining their lands and titles, providing they vowed never to take up arms against William and his kin ever again.

The two earls were pleased with the pact, as neither of them intended to comply with the agreed terms, for they had both decided long before meeting William that if things went well for them, and they were given the breathing space that they needed, they and the majority of their warriors would make their way either to the east in order to join with Hereward the Wake, or westward to the Welsh Marches and join Wild Edric in order to continue their war to oust this cocky little Norman from English soil.

As for William, he too would bide his time and allow things to settle. He had already planned that, providing he could eliminate these two troublesome earls from the present situation, his army would now remain intact, and be strong enough to deal with the two remaining and growing rebellions, that of Hereward the Wake, plus the English upstart, Wild Edric and his Welsh allies.

'God's bones brother,' whispered Odo into his William's ear, 'you must be going simple in your old age,' he said with a smirk. 'You had those two heathens in the palm of your hand and yet you let them walk free, the rains of this cursed country seem to have addled your brains.'

'You forget yourself brother,' snarled William. 'Those two ruffians still command an army, and if on this day they had failed to rejoin their warriors, their men would soon find themselves another leader, perhaps Hereward or even Edric the Savage, and then we could well lose all of England.

'Nay brother,' he added with a grin, 'by granting those two simpletons amnesty, I have taken one army out of the field, and can deal with them and their disbanded warriors as and when I see fit. We can now concentrate all of our strength on defeating the rebels in the east and along the Welsh border.'

'Just so brother, just so,' said Bishop Odo shamefacedly, as if the decision had been his all along. As they turned and walked back into their sumptuous tent he added, 'send that Saxon turncoat to me, I have need of him this day.'

Odo relayed his brother's command to a guard and the man ran to do his bidding.

A short time later the traitor, Earl Hunwald entered the room still in the act of adjusting his tunic, which was of the finest Norman linen. It was a gift from the King himself.

'My lord King,' said Earl Hunwald as he knelt in front of William.

'I have need of your admirable talents, Earl Hunwald,' said the King, holding out his left hand that Hunwald kissed, leaving a damp patch on the King's knuckles.

William hid his distain, not only of the spittle that this man had left upon his hand, but also from the natural distain that he held for all traitors, for he had said on more than one occasion, *once a traitor always a traitor*. A comment with which his brother Odo wholeheartedly agreed.

'I want you to send two of your best men to join Hereward and his gang of cut-throats in the Fens, and have them report back to me at least once a month. I want to know how many men he has with him, where his lair is and what defences he has in that water wonderland of his.'

Before Earl Hunwald could comment, the King continued. 'And I want you personally to join with that rebel Edric and his wild Welshmen, take someone who you can trust with you. Tell me all you can learn about their stronghold. How many warriors they command and where they intend to strike next, and make sure that you report back to me each and every month. Is that clear?'

The horrified Englishman, not noted for his courage, and who had been appalled with the King's wanton destruction of the northern shires, nodded glumly.

Noting his reluctance, the King continued, 'Do this for me my good Earl Hunwald, and I shall reward you with land and gold beyond your wildest dreams.'

Hunwald smiled sheepishly, obviously heartened by William's mention of land and gold, 'Aye my lord King,' he said, forcing a smile from his sallow continence. 'I shall make arrangements to leave first thing on the morrow.'

True to his word he sent two of his best men to the Fens where they would hopefully join with Hereward and his growing band of rebels. Both were men who had served his family since birth, so he felt, indeed he was confident that they would carry out his wishes and do their duty.

Hunwald took his personal slave with him on his journey to the Welsh borderlands, a man who had been sold to him whilst still a boy of twelve and who had served him with honesty ever since.

Earl Hunwald had named the boy Harold although, in truth, he had never known his real name, nor had he ever asked.

Harold had grown tall and strong in the service of the earl, fluently speaking the language of both Norman and the English, although he had been born to neither of them. Indeed both of the languages were totally alien to him, having spent most of his childhood within the tiny Albian clan of fourteen souls that had been his tribe and sole family until his capture into slavery at the age of ten. Whence he had been sold from master to master until Earl Harold's father, the late earl had bought him for the princely sum of five shillings from an abusive and cruel peddler.

Harold had been taught none of the attributes that a warrior required, but he was skilled in the arts of a valet. He was fully aware of his lord and master's likes and dislikes, as well as the man's strengths – and his weaknesses.

For instance he knew that his lord had a mind like a steel mantrap, as well as being a scheming, cunning and underhand liar, willing to go to almost any lengths in order to improve or even maintain his land and titles. Yet despite all of these things, Harold had developed a certain loyalty to the man. However, now he had reached the age of nineteen he was beginning to question that loyalty, as the memories of his childhood continued to disturb his dreams. He recalled the destruction of his own family and the way in which his own father had fought, slaying no less than four of his attackers before being encircled and cut down by a ring of spearmen.

Nonetheless, at first light on the following morning, he saddled the two horses needed for the journey.

One was of course the stallion of which Earl Hunwald was justly proud of, whilst the second was a scrawny old mare, so heavily laden with the Earl's baggage that Harold had no alternative other than to walk, leading the mare by her bridle.

The journey from the ravaged north was a further shock to both men, and for the first two days they met not a single living being as they travelled through burned farms and villages, past the decaying corpses of men, women, children, cattle and sheep, through clouds of carrion crows and noisy red kites as they were disturbed from their gory meals.

On the third day a few of the farmsteads were undamaged but uninhabited, and it was not until the light was fading that they met their first human being, an ancient, ragged old man who had been too slow or too lame to hide from the foreign killers as they had slaughtered their way through his village.

Earl Hunwald forced the man to sup with them in order to glean news, presenting the near-starving man with a large slice of roast lamb in order to gain his confidence.

'We are good honest Englishmen, like yourself,' he said jovially to the man, 'Pray tell us where are the people who dwelt in these empty towns and farmsteads that we have passed through?'

'Dead,' said the man as he attempted to chew the tough meat with the few teeth that he had left, 'Dead or gone,' he reiterated.

'Gone!' spat the Earl. 'Gone where?' he asked.

After a further pause and a lot more chewing, the man answered, 'North my lord. They said that they would go north, into the kingdom of Malcolm, he who rules in Scotland, or at least the southern part of it. Said they would find succour in the lowlands.'

The Earl was silent, thinking to himself that this may be news that King William should hear, welcome or not. For if thousands of fugitives were to trek northwards into Malcolm's kingdom then, with the obvious hatred that they would now hold for William and his marauding Normans, and being of either English or of Danish descent, they could well provide King Malcolm with a large number of warriors who may well decide to aid him in his lifelong ambition and try, yet again, to conquer the entire north of England.

They continued their journey south, veering off the Great North Road to the westwards through lush, mellow and undamaged country, finding the inhabitants friendly, but very fearful of their new King, for news had already reached them of his devastation of the northern shires.

They travelled across the fertile Cheshire plains, lodging at a grubby inn in the city of Chester for the night in order that the Earl might glean news of the whereabouts of this troublesome countryman of his, this so-called Lord Edric and his Welsh allies. However after spending more silver than he had bargained for in the purchase of warm, bitter beer, he learned nothing other than that the rebels had besieged the town of Shrewsbury, some forty or so miles away.

The following morning they passed out through the town's southern gate making their way southward, along an old disused and neglected Roman road that led to the border fortress of Shrewsbury.

CHAPTER 7

The first few weeks Edric had spent with his new wife, the beautiful Godda, Queen of the Light Elves, or so she claimed to be, he bathed in her radiance. The fact that she claimed to be a light elf did somewhat unsettle him, for tales of the light elf folk who dwelt in the glades of the deep impenetrable forests, were part of the folklore of his own people, and although many claimed to have seen them, so far as he knew no man had ever been approached by them, or indeed had ever spoken to them, for at the first sight of these strange beings, even the bravest man usually turned tail and ran.

All at once the sky was bluer, the birds' song was even more beautiful, and the wildflower meadows more colourful.

Life again seemed worth living.

The wedding had been a quiet affair, despite the fact that every man of noble birth in the area attended, bringing their ladies as well as their unmarried, chattering, and giggling daughters with them.

The church was deathly quiet as the bride and groom repeated their marriage vows, with Edric speaking loudly so that all could hear him pledge his troth. Although the majority of the ceremony was in the teaching of the Christ child, Edric.

Edric still insisted on swearing the oath of his ancestors, saying loudly. 'Our union be unto death when our souls will dwell in the halls of my people, as it always has been, from the beginning.'

People held their breath. Many make the sign of the cross across their chests whilst some of the more pious souls, totally shocked that such pagan words could be uttered in God's church, fully expecting the Lord Jesus Christ to appear and strike down the offender.

The silence continued until it was broken by a voice, not of an angel but of a Queen.

Godda's voice sang through the building like a nightingale, shrill and clear, causing many of the ladies to whisper that this, indeed, was the true voice of a Queen of the Light Elves, crossing themselves in awe as they did so.

Every man, woman and child joined the wedding guests at the wedding feast which was held in both the great hall of the longhall house and upon the village green, where tables laden with food and drink had been laid for the enjoyment of all.

The wedding night itself was very different to that of Edric's previous marriage to his first love, Rowena, for although there was no doubt that his new bride was a virgin, their lovemaking took Edric into new realms that he had not believed to be possible.

Once they had disrobed, they stood some three or four feet apart gazing adoringly at each other. Edric still had the slender waist of a much younger man, and had lost none of the muscles that rippled as he raised his hand to brush a strand of fair hair that had become unbound from the thatch that appeared to be a large part of his charisma.

She, tall and fair with a slender figure, was, he thought without a doubt, equally as beautiful as Rowena (knowing well that he should not compare the two, and yet finding it impossible not to do so) but, although she had similar traits to his first wife, there were a lot of very striking differences.

Although Edric had only been married once before, he had seen the naked bodies of many women, both dead and alive. Yet this maiden now standing before him as his new wife, was indeed very different from any woman he had ever seen. For on her creamy white body the only trace of hair was on her head, and the white arch of her eyebrows, and he gazed in awe at the golden locks that now fell onto her shoulders.

Other than that, there was no trace whatsoever of hair on her body, not on her cheeks, (as there had been with Rowena) or under her arms, or between her legs. Not one single, solitary hair.

And if that was not strange enough… her breasts, well, her breasts were so small and her nipples so wide, so large and so prominent that all he could do was to stare at them, as he slowly brought his hand up to them touching her left nipple. Which he felt grow even larger and harder, until it appeared to push hard into the palm of his hand.

She made a slight mewing sound as she pushed her breast against his hand, causing a burning sensation to commence in the centre of his palm and creep swiftly up his arm and into his entire being.

She smiled at him, her face reddening as her beauty shone out as if from the sun, making her every inch a queen, if not of the light elves, then of his own mortal race.

Godda stepped forward and flung her arms about his neck, kissed his lips with unbridled passion whilst at the same time, she lifted herself up upon him, straddling him with her long legs.

Then, to his delight and much to his surprise, she wiggled her hips and very slowly impaled herself upon him, sighing as she did so, 'How now lord husband?' she murmured but although he heard her, it was as if the voice came from afar.

The only answer that he was able to produce was a low, almost feral groan that rumbled upwards from the depth of his chest.

Throughout their wedding night they made love with wild abandon, time and time again until the first rays of dawn shone through the open window, causing Godda to cry out, as if in alarm, sending her diving for cover, hiding her face under the duck down quilt that served as the only cover Edric ever had on his bed, even during the coldest of the winter months.

'What ails you my love?' said the equally startled Edric, fearing that some attacker or perhaps a wild animal had crept into their room through the open window during their lovemaking.

Then an even greater terror flew through his mind, thinking to himself that perhaps the many weird stories that he had heard about the Light Elves, saying that they were all changelings, and that this beautiful woman who he had just married and spent the night with was, in fact, a changeling, a being that could change her appearance from one form to another.

He saw a strange movement under the quilt, and a moment later the beautiful, fresh face of his bride emerged, smiling radiantly up at him.

'I am with child,' she said almost casually.

The shocked Edric was dumbstruck, unable to grasp the words that his new bride had just uttered. 'Wh – why, how can it be so?' he stammered, 'we have only just...

She held a slim finger up to her lips. 'Ssshh, my dearest Edric,' she whispered as she stretched upwards to place her full lips upon his own. 'Do you forget that I am the Queen of the Light Elves, and I know such things. What is more my sweet, I will bear you a strong son, who we shall name Alfred for it is a name favoured amongst my folk.'

With a smile she returned to her original position with her face protruding from under the quilt and stretched her arms out to him and drew him once again upon her.

Not only was Edric totally captivated by his new bride, he soon realised that he was not alone. All who met her seemed to fall under her spell, and soon the house was awash with callers bringing gifts. Not only from the villagers, but also from all the local nobility, who presented her with gifts in order to meet this exquisite and beautiful woman.

Their bliss however lasted for a few short weeks, as more and more refugees from the ravaged lands that the new King William had wrought upon the land sought refuge in the village.

Many of these newcomers were warriors – scarred, bitter, hard-faced men, with battered shields and dented armour, bearing well-worn weapons, eager to follow a leader of Edric's fame in order continue their fight against the Norman invaders. Others were mere peasants, farmers and tradesmen who had been burned out of their holdings by the marauding Normans.

Edric found that he had less and less time to spend with his new bride and virtually no time at all to continue with his favourite sport of hunting the red deer and wild boar, for many of these newcomers seemed to require his attention, bombarding him with their ills and woes, as well as their pleading for him to lead them against their enemies.

He was beginning to despair that he would be unable to forge this mass of individuals into any kind of disciplined fighting force, ranting and raving at them, pretty well in vain, as they seemed unable to obey any kind of command when it came to remaining in a formation. Each individual appeared to have a different idea of how a battle should be fought and won.

It was with delight and relief that Edric, red in the face from trying to knock this rabble of men into some kind of order, glanced to his rear and saw, a mere fifty paces away, a sight that he felt had been sent to him from God himself.

The elegant figure of Hywell, dressed in white kidskin and riding a fine grey stallion, accompanied by the large, untidy hulk of Garth, were sitting on their horses, just as Edric had always pictured them, with Garth straddling a large mare, with his long legs dangling loosely down and his feet brushing the long grass, as he and his companion made their way across the meadow towards him, whilst the much smaller figure of Hywell sat alongside him. Both wore the silliest and most welcome of grins that he had ever seen.

'Lord Edric,' came the booming voice from the still grinning Garth, 'I thought that you may need a little assistance in clearing these Normans from our land.' Nodding his head towards the smiling figure of Hywell, he went on in a somewhat quieter voice, 'And I met this lad here, wandering aimlessly about in search of a little adventure and persuaded him to join me.'

'Lad he may be,' said Edric as he held his hand out to greet them, 'but he is a lad who proved to be a better man than most, when he fought with me in the shieldwall at Hastings.'

'Glad I am to see you my friends,' said the beaming Edric, 'and it would be no lie if I were to admit that I do indeed need a little help in forging this rabble into something that resembles a disciplined army.'

He dismissed the crowd of men who thronged happily around the famous duo, with grunts and shouts of approval that the famous Garth Bloodaxe and the equally renowned Hywell the Welshman (as he was called) had now joined them.

After Garth's and Hywell's horses had been taken from them and fed, groomed and watered, they sat in the longhall enjoying a tankard of mulled ale.

Edric confessed to them, 'I must admit that there are a lot of good men with me here. Oh, I have weeded out a lot of scroungers and no-hopers, but those who remain here are all good men, brave and skilled fighters. But there appears to be a division between the men of the north and the local Mercians. Both of these groups seem to resent the few Albions who are still with us, whilst all of them seem to object to the Welshmen.

'Although they do not openly oppose me, they seem unwilling to work together as a cohesive group.'

'Fear not Lord Edric,' said Garth as he drained his tankard and held it out to a bench maid for it to be refilled, 'young Hywell and myself will soon have 'em singing the same tune. We'll start on 'em first thing on the morrow. Isn't that right young Hywell?'

'Aye my lord,' answered Hywell with a smile, 'Garth and me will soon knock them into shape.'

'What we will do,' said Garth with a grin, 'is start 'em off with wooden swords, so as we don't have too many casualties, just like old Vorta did with us when we were mere babes. Then we can train 'em in the basics of thrusts and slashes, blocks and parries and teach 'em the necessary footwork to help them in battle, then select the good ones who we will then provide with proper weapons and send the rest into the fields to tend the crops and livestock.' He clapped his huge arm around Howell's shoulders.

'Come lad, we have work to do.'

True to their words, Garth and Hywell joined Edric soon after sunrise the following morning. Mustering the men, they divided them into three more or less equal groups, with each group containing men from the north, Albions, Mercians, plus the Welshmen to begin their training in earnest.

Starting with the tactics that old Vorta had taught Edric and Garth many years ago.

Three short weeks later news reached them that a Norman named Richard Fitzscrob, had installed himself in a nearby valley and had erected (with the help of forced labour from the local populace) a wooden castle which he had named Richard's Castle,

A situation of which Edric had been aware, but the news now reaching him was that Richard Fitzscrob now felt himself strong, or perhaps stupid enough to seize two additional villages that belonged to Edric, the villages of Hopton and Culmington, burning several cottages to the ground and slaying a large number of villagers.

It was an extremely angry Edric who assembled his men, then turned to speak to the small assembled group of Godda, Garth and Hywell. He said, 'I had hoped that King William and his lackeys would leave my holdings alone, especially so with him aware, and I am sure that he is aware, that I have assembled quite a gathering of warriors about me, causing him to realise that I am quite capable of holding my own against anything short of a full blown invasion. Yet this upstart Fitzscrob still dares to take my land and kill my people.'

Then turning to face his assembled men, he said in a loud voice so that all could hear him, 'I had hoped, perhaps foolishly, that these Normans would be content with what they already have, but I have been mistaken. They have now taken more English land and killed even more people who were dear to us.'

He paused for a while, aware of the warrior's anger and that most of them already knew pretty well what he was about to say next.

'Well, enough is enough. Most of you were seasoned warriors when you joined me here, and I am sure that you have your own reasons for continuing your fight against these Norman dogs, but I think the training that you've received here over the last few weeks has made you into some of the fiercest warriors in the country.'

He was prevented from continuing as his men roared their approval and clashed their weapons against the iron rims of their oxhide shields.

When the noise finally abated he continued, holding his own sword and shield high in the air.

'We are now wolves. Lions! Follow me and we will crush these slayers of women and children, drive them back whence they came.'

The noise was even greater than the previous bellows of applause, as the warriors shouted themselves hoarse, clashing their weapons against their shields until Edric thought that many a spearhead would be shaken loose by such abuse, and held his hands high in the air calling for the clamour to cease.

*****

The small army, numbering a mere three hundred and sixty men, left their camp in three divisions, each division led by either Edric, Garth or Hywell, followed by a small band of pack animals. They also bought nearly one hundred sheep, in order to provide them with enough sustenance to enable them to complete their march without plundering their own people and thus preventing the already poor, who some cases had been plundered not only by Normans but also by the few remaining English landholders and noblemen, throwing fresh woes upon the already poor people.

They reached the small, partially completed fortress before midnight. There Edric posted his men, thus preventing anyone from entering or leaving. Yet much to Edric's annoyance, the fortress had been forewarned of their approach, and the gate was firmly closed. The makeshift battlements were ablaze with torches displaying a throng of armed Norman warriors who stood upon them, alert and

71

prepared to defend their keep.

Despite the catcalls and abuse shouted at the besiegers, Edric stationed his men just outside the range of the defenders' archers, who all appeared to be crossbowmen. Then he bade his men to get a good night's sleep, saying, 'On the morrow we shall see if their voices are so bold when we have brought them down from their lofty perches.'

However the following day, as Edric had expected, was taken up with the construction of dozens of ladders plus a number of double hazel hurdles, which his men packed with dry hay obtained from a local farmer's haystack.

That evening he joined his men in a good solid meal of roast lamb, washed down with small beer, before allocating sentries, who were to be relieved every three hours with strict instructions that no living thing, man or beast was to enter or leave the besieged fortress, and should anything – and he stressed the word, anything – odd occur then he was to be wakened immediately.

Fortunately no man disturbed Edric's sleep. Yet dreams and imaginations of possible problems and disasters troubled him for most of the night.

He was roused an hour before first light bleary eyed and irritable by Evan, who had now become his constant companion and friend.

'Time to rise Edric,' said the jovial Evan, who, despite his lower rank in society had never once uttered the word 'lord', as he handed the still half-asleep Edric a jug of mulled ale. In his other hand he held a plate consisting of two large slices of hard bread, a sliced onion and a chunk of cheese.

Edric took both the jug and plate from Evan, thinking silently to himself of the wonderful breakfasts that Rowena used to make him which usually consisted of crushed wheat, dried blackberries and sliced apple covered in warm milk straight from the cow, but on special occasions she would serve him a large plate of grilled bacon, eggs and warm bread, swilled down with warm best beer.

Still, he mused silently to himself, he was on a campaign and the meagre fare that Evan had just handed to him was sufficient for his needs. It was probably more than a lot of his men would be breaking their fast with; so munching on a large chunk of bread and after taking a small bite of the acrid onion, he struggled into his fur-lined leather boots, pulled his mail-shirt over his head, snatched up his shield and war-axe and strode out to rouse his men.

By the time the weak sun showed its hazy face over the hillside he had organised his men into three divisions, then with a whispered command to Garth and Hywell, he led his own division ahead through the misty meadow towards the still silent fortress.

Skylarks and meadow pipits rose before the men as they strode through the wet meadow soaking the men's boots as well as saturating the lower parts of the double, hay-filled hurdles, making the already heavy hurdles so heavy that the four men who carried each hurdle in front of them needed to be helped by a further two men in order to continue their advance towards the fortress.

In truth, their silence had been completely unnecessary. As soon as they had approached within range, the hurdles shuddered as the short, heavy bolts which the crossbowmen used began to thud into the front of them.

No bolts came through these makeshift but effective shields, although Edric and probably a number of the more experienced warriors were well aware that the nearer that they approached to the fortress, the more effective these deadly missiles would become.

They advanced an additional twenty paces before Edric held up his hand and signalled a halt, 'Now!' he bellowed. 'Now you archers,' and his own archers speedily strung their longbows whilst still under the protection of the hurdles, then sent their shafts high in the air towards the fortress and the enemy crossbowmen.

The English archers outnumbered the Norman crossbowmen and sent their yard-long, grey goose shafts high into the air to fall like rain upon the Normans who crowded the palisade of their small fortress, hitting a number and sending the remaining Normans to seek cover behind the wooden walls of their fortress.

Whilst the Norman bowmen made a valiant effort to continue their arrow storm, the fact that the English longbow men could loose the equivalent of three arrows for every one from the crossbowmen. The contest was an unequal one, allowing the attackers to press forward until they were soon below the very stockade itself. Edric gave the order for the scaling ladders to be raised.

'Men must go where arrows went!' he bellowed and raising his shield high above his head. Resting his axe over his shoulder he bounded up the sturdy ladder.

Ten heartbeats later he reached the top, where a burly Norman confronted him, wearing the type of helmet that he now knew belonged to men of that race. The man was stretching and straining with both hands at the top rung of the ladder, striving to push it away from the fortress.

A spear struck Edric's helmet causing his head to ring, yet he still managed to grab his war-axe from his shoulder and strike at the Norman's outstretched arms.

The Norman, who was obviously an experienced warrior, saw the blow coming and released the ladder, which fell back against the stockade with a jarring thud.

Edric clambered up the two remaining rungs and was about to leap onto the walkway when the man who had been trying to dislodge the ladder leapt at him, sword held high as he sheltered behind his steel-rimmed shield.

The Norman's sword clanged against Edric's roundshield, and the blow was delivered with such force that Edric was nearly forced off the ladder.

He thrust his shield hard against the Norman, forcing him back, thus allowing Edric a take a tentative step onto the walkway. There he swung his axe hard against the Norman's own shield, forcing him back a little further.

Other English warriors had followed Edric up the same ladder, whilst still more clambered up the other ladders fighting fiercely to gain admittance onto the walkway.

Whilst Edric was vaguely aware of this, his own adversary was proving to be a hard and valiant warrior, who countered Edric's attacks with his own attacks. It was not until both men were nearing exhaustion that the Norman made the fatal mistake of holding his shield very slightly to one side as he came yet again into the attack. Yet it was enough to allow Edric to swing his axe so that it fell like an eagle just inside the Norman's kite-shaped shield, snapping the leather shield-strap with which he held it, jarring the warrior's arm just enough to allow Edric to continue with a classic figure of eight slash – whereupon he brought the axe upwards, slicing the Norman across the side of his face, neatly removing the man's jaw and the side of his face.

The man dropped his sword and his hand went up to his shattered face.

Edric had not forgotten the long, hard lessons that old Vorta had taught him, one of the first being that a wounded man can still kill you. So whilst he still continued the flight of his axe in the figure of eight, he brought it across with a sinister swish, severing the man's head from his body.

Edric stormed along the walkway, slaying three other men and heaving a fourth to his death on the courtyard below, until the walkway was clear of the enemy and he could stride down the stairway like the avenging warrior that he was.

Furious fights continued all along the walkway on the far side of the fortress, as well as upon the courtyard below, but he could see that his men had already gained the upper hand. The stragglers amongst them, who had not yet been bloodied, were still scaling the ladders before they could tread upon the gory walkway.

The remaining Normans fought doggedly until they were slowly and surely surrounded and cut down one by one by the more numerous English warriors, knowing that they could expect little or no mercy from these avenging men whose farms, homes and villages they had destroyed.

Finally a small knot of eight men – bloody, wounded and exhausted – surrounded by a horde of ferocious English warriors who bayed for their blood, stood in the courtyard ringed by spears and archers with their shafts notched, ready for flight.

'Hold!' bellowed Edric as he approached the throng of his bloodthirsty men. They reluctantly stood aside as he made his way through them, noting that many of them still had the battle fever running through their veins.

'Which of you is Richard Fitzscrob?' he said in a loud voice.

The encircled Normans shook their heads and looked at one another in amazement, and it was then that Edric realised that these men could not understand the good, honest, and easily understood language of the English nation.

'I know their language,' said a refined voice from amongst the Englishmen, and a fresh-faced man of about thirty years of age, still bleeding profusely from a gash along the right side of his face, elbowed his way to the front.

'I am called Edgar of Swanage,' offered the man, 'and I was with Harold Godwinson during his captivity in the land of Normandy. I speak their heathen tongue reasonably well.'

Edric liked the clean cut look of the young man and bade him come forward, 'Glad I am to greet you young Edgar,' he said. 'Pray interpret for me and ask these men which of their number is their leader, the man who is called Richard Fitzscrob.'

Edgar nodded and approached Edric and said in a loud voice, in the tongue of Normandy. 'He who is called Richard Fitzscrob step forward and show yourself.'

No man moved as the Normans shifted their feet unhappily, fully expecting that the next few moments would be their last on God's good earth.

After a long, nervous silence, a voice came from the encircled men, 'He is not here.'

'What says he?' asked an increasingly angry Edric.

'He says he is not here,' answered Edgar.

'Where the devil is he then,' said Edric, 'is he slain?'

Again Edgar addressed the Normans, and after an uneasy pause was told that their leader, Richard Fitzscrob had left for the city of Hereford three days before Edric and his small army had arrived.

Edgar then added, 'The man who had been left in charge was a man named Vernon, and was the very warrior who attacked you when you reached the top of the scaling ladder.'

Edric sighed loudly. 'Damn,' he said, 'I had hoped to bring this business to a speedy end, but it seems that it is not to be so.'

His thoughts were interrupted by the gruff voice of Garth who had shouldered his way through the throng and now stood alongside Edric, his bloody axe still covered in blood and gore.

'Shall we kill them now, my lord.' he said menacingly.

'Not so my friend,' answered Edric, 'I think enough blood has been shed this day. Nay,' he added thoughtfully, 'bid them lay down their weapons and have them guarded, then after we have seen to our own men we shall see to their wounds and have them join us in a thanksgiving feast for our victory.'

'My Lord,' gasped Garth disgustedly, 'they are the enemy, and would not have dealt so kindly with us had they been victorious.'

'True my good Garth, true,' said Edric with a wry smile, 'but dead men are unable to tell us what we want to know, and I think that these men, once their wounds have been tended to, and after they have had a bellyful of good English ale and roast lamb, their tongues may well become looser. Then we could well learn much about their tactics, their numbers and more importantly, learn about their leaders and the way that those leaders act. Perhaps more importantly, the way that they think.'

'Nay, Garth,' he said. 'By sparing the lives of these eight wretches, we may well save the lives of many scores, perhaps hundreds of good honest Englishmen.

'Have it seen to,' he ordered as he walked away towards the huge oak doorway of the fortress, which was now thrown open wide and thronged with his small army.

Twelve English warriors had been killed, plus many more wounded, three seriously with wounds that were likely to be fatal,

Edric did all he could for these men, having them brought into the living quarters of the previous Norman garrison where they were settled onto clean straw mattresses, covered with heavy duck down quilts and made as comfortable as possible.

He then sent out a number of riders to scout the surrounding countryside in order to be forewarned should any further bands of Normans be in the vicinity, and ordered closed the heavy gates of the fortress.

He called his friend Evan over to him, 'Get a couple of men to help you to gather up the stores and provisions that these Normans had, and arrange a feast for this evening out here in the courtyard. Once you have done that, assign two good men to sup with each of the Norman prisoners. Put that youngster Edgar with the one who seems most likely to be friendly towards us.'

'Will do,' said the ever pleasant Evan, adding, 'and I will tell our men to keep an eye on the beggars, especially when they are handling the knives that we keep around the tables.'

'Good man,' said Edric knowing that Evan was meticulous in organizing things of this nature and would leave nothing to chance.

As dusk fell, Evan ordered his men to light the braziers, and organising that the food and ale be laid upon the table in front of the assembly, who were already seated along the makeshift tables that had been set on the cobblestones of the courtyard.

Cheers rose from the English warriors as the roast carcasses of sheep, plus a huge side of beef, was brought out on spits and large serving dishes. Foaming jugs of ale had already been placed on the tables and, although no man, including the separated and escorted Normans, had as yet filled his own personal tankard that lay upon the table in front of them.

Edric who was flanked by Garth on one side and Hywell on the other rose to his feet, holding his right hand high in order to quell the hubbub of noise that came from the assembled warriors.

'Men,' he said in a loud voice, 'we sit here this evening, in a fortress that was built by our enemies on our own land.'

There were loud cheers from the assembled English warriors.

'It is a fortress that we have taken by our blood, and with our courage and by the strength of our arms.

'Fellow warriors,' he said seriously, as he reached down and took his own silver tankard that he held aloft, 'I drink to your courage!' he cried.

Raising the tankard to his lips, he drank deeply, and the silent company looked on as he slowly took the tankard away from his lips. Then he raised it high above his head, nodding to the serving wenches to fill the warrior's empty tankards.

He waited silently until all the tankards were brim full of foaming ale, and then cried 'To England!'

The assembled men stood, raising their foaming tankards aloft, echoing his words.

'To England,' they bellowed, and drank their fill of the dark ale.

Edric had been watching the captured Normans as the toast was taking place, noting that although their tankards had been filled, not one of them had touched the ale which lay in front of them. Yet as the huge plates of roast venison, beef, pork and goose were placed before them, the pangs of hunger were awakened by the aroma that rose from these steaming dishes, causing them to remember that it had been long before dawn since they had eaten.

It was with grudging reluctance that they reached out, greedily snatching the food that had been placed before them, stuffing it ravenously into their mouths.

He hadn't really had time to study his captives, as they had been guarded by the burly Garth and a dozen of his best men, but now he began to study them, noting that some of them were quite dark haired, whilst two of them were very fair. Whilst another was particularly swarthy with a thin, pock marked face.

Edric was fascinated by their expensive and ornate dress, as well as being intrigued by the way that, despite the stubble upon their faces, they were generally clean shaven, with a number of them sporting braids of hair that hung down over their ears, whilst every one of them had back of their heads shaved in the fashion of Normandy, leaving the rest of their hair to form something which

Edric assumed must give them a little added protection for the helmets which they had worn, as the hairline appeared to follow the shape of the Norman helmets.

As he watched them, Edric noticed that one individual who was older than the rest and rather wider in the girth, stretched his right arm out and, glancing sideways as if to see if his fellow countrymen were observing him, snatched up a tankard of ale and drained it in one long, enjoyable swallow, wiping his mouth on his sleeve as he replaced the tankard upon the table nodding to a serving wench, who immediately came to his side to refill the empty vessel.

Edric caught the eye of Edgar and called him over.

'Do you see that man there?' said Edric as he nodded in the direction of the Norman who he had been studying.

Edgar glanced in the direction that Edric had indicated and nodded, 'The fat one?' he asked.

'Aye, that's the one,' answered Edric, 'I will call Edward the younger over to me, and you can take his place beside the Norman, and I want you to befriend him. Encourage him in his liking for our strong ale. Find out all you can about him as well as anything of interest about the rest of our captives. Learn as much as you are able about the rest of the Normans in Mercia and of their intentions and strategy.'

No sooner had Edward the younger been replaced by a jovial Edgar than Edric noticed two strangers who were standing at the open gates being denied entrance by the stern-faced guards.

Edric left his place at the table and hurried over to the small knot of guards who now surrounded the two strangers, standing defensively amidst them and grasping the reins of the strangers' two tired and sweaty horses.

As he approached he noted that the elder of the two appeared to be an expensively dressed Englishman. He wore a good sword with a silver-wired hilt which nestled snugly in a very expensive white deerskin scabbard, a man who was obviously the owner of the fine stallion which he still held onto, despite the sentry holding onto the other side of the stallion's reins.

The younger of the two was equally imposing, but for a number of different reasons. He was quite clearly the Englishman's servant, being dressed in a grubby brown smock with patched breeches, yet his bearing was that of a warrior, having long sturdy legs, narrow waist, broad shoulders and a strong intelligent face topped with a tangled mop of bright red hair.

'An Albian,' thought Edric as he returned his attention to the elder man, however before he could speak the other man puffed his chest out and blustered:

'If you are the master of these fools, bid them release me and take me to Lord Edric, him who I have come to join.' He tried again to shake off one of the guard's strong hands, which was firmly embedded in the man's chubby arm.

Somewhat taken aback by the man's attitude, Edric halted a few feet away from him saying, 'I am Edric, and who pray are you who struts into my camp like a king?'

The man, seemingly startled by this ordinary-looking man standing before him, who claimed to be the famous killer of men, the legendary 'Wild Edric'.

The face of Hunwald turned red, and he said in a much milder manner, 'My lord, pray forgive me, I had been led to believe that you were a man at least seven feet tall and as wide as an English oak.'

Edric smiled wryly, not quite sure whether he had just been flattered or insulted, but also knowing that here was a man with a sharp mind and a ready tongue, as well as being a man who would prove to be either a gallant ally or perhaps a dangerous snake in their midst.

'I am Earl Hunwald of Windermere,' he said releasing his horse to his servant, and holding out his right hand out in greeting, in order to show to the recipient that his hand contained no weapon.

Edric stepped forward and shook the man's hand, noting that it was flaccid and clammy to his touch, causing his mind to scream out and tell him that perhaps his first instinct had been correct. This was not a man to be trusted.

'Glad I am to meet you Earl Hunwald,' said Edric forcing himself to smile as he looked into the cold blue eyes of Hunwald. 'Windermere,' he mused, 'I have not heard of that place. Pray tell, where is that holding?'

'Ah, my lord, it is a wondrous place,' said Hunwald with a smile, 'a land that is far to the north of here, with lakes so deep that they have no bottom, and forest-covered mountains that reach to the sky, 'ah' – he sighed again casting his eyes to the sky as if he was caressing a maiden in the midst of love making – 'and,' he sighed, 'I own the most beautiful manor that you have ever seen, set amongst sweet-smelling meadows fed by crystal clear streams full of fat brown trout.'

'Why leave such a wondrous place?' said the gruff voice of Garth who had joined the group.

'Ah,' sighed the smiling Hunwald, 'if only I could have stayed,' came the glib reply. 'My own lands were taken from me by those bloody Norman dogs, isn't that so, good Harold? Turning to his red-haired servant, but before the young man could answer, he continued, 'Oh I fought. I fought well. Slew six of the ruffians, but they were too many for me and I was forced to flee for my life, isn't that so Harold? We barely escaped with our lives, my servant and I. Isn't that so Harold?' he repeated yet again, and the red-haired youngster seemed forced into agreeing with his master with a hesitant, 'Aye my lord, just so, just so.'

'That is why I have come to offer my strong arm and trusty sword to your good self, Lord Edric,' Then kneeling before Edric, he bowed his head and held his sword, hilt forward to the shocked Edric who had never experienced such melodrama before, and almost burst out laughing. Yet he managed to contain his mirth and touched the man's bowed head, saying, 'Rise good Earl Hunwald. We are glad to welcome you to our band of patriots.'

Hunwald rose to his feet, his face beaming with pleasure as he sheathed his sword, 'My thanks to you my lord,' he said still smiling what looked like a genuine smile of pure joy. 'I shall serve you well and will help you rid our lands of these Norman pigs.'

Edric smiled and bade the newcomer to take his place at the tables whereupon Earl Hunwald gladly sat down and commenced to partake of the food and drink that were placed before him.

The following morning after he had broken his fast, Edric called Edgar to him, 'Now Good Edgar,' he said, 'tell me what, if anything you have learned from that Norman captive who you sat next to at the feast?'

'Well my lord,' he said, 'I really didn't learn much from him despite the fact that we are now good friends and on first name terms. Though I still hate the bastard for the Norman dog that he is.'

'Enough of that,' said Edric, 'what information did you glean from him?'

'Well,' said Edgar, 'I now know that he is called Boland, Boland the good, and was, according to the story that he told me, a man of noble birth, destined for the clergy, but lured into this war by William of Normandy's promises of riches, and the dreams that he could become rich. He said he intended to use those riches to found his own abbey.

'Anyhow,' he continued, 'he joined William's crusade against his own better judgment, and at the insistence of his father, and he was seasick during the voyage over here, and hasn't, according to him, slain any Englishman, acting with goodwill towards our people and treating them as he would treat his own.'

'Well he would say that,' said Edric.

'Just so my lord,' said Edgar, and then continued with a thoughtful frown creasing his forehead.

'He also told me that his people have taken the city of Hereford and the whole of its shire, as well as the city of Shrewsbury, but they have only captured that particular city itself, but have not yet taken that shire, having not yet subdued the surrounding countryside.'

'Good news, and bad news,' said Edric, totally shocked that the invaders had taken the city of Shrewsbury, a town much loved by him.

'But,' added Edgar, 'the shire-reeve of Shrewsbury has bowed his knee to the Normans and has agreed to perform his duties of the law for them.'

'This is news that needs time to digest and not to be acted on in haste,' said Edric stroking his short, bristly beard. A habit he was prone to when tackling a particularly difficult problem.

Later in the morning Edric met with Garth and Hywell, saying, 'I have decided to be lenient with our prisoners and to send them on their way,' continuing as he could see that Garth, who had already said that they should be slain, did not agree with his decision. 'Oh, I know your thoughts on this matter my good friend, but I think that if we show lenience in this matter it could well prove to be a wise move in the long run.'

'Well, as least allow us keep their weapons and armour, 'Tis too good to give away,' Garth said in a disgruntled manner.

'Very well,' answered Edric. 'We will keep the armour, as well as their weapons, then we can let them go to spread the word that we Englishmen can still fight and defeat them, and that we also treat our captives with honour.'

Edric could see that both Garth and Hywell were not happy with his decision as they both grunted assent and nodded grimly as they left him standing some twenty or thirty feet from the group of miserable prisoners.

The Normans were quickly stripped of their war accoutrements, given a small leather satchel containing a chunk of cheese, plus a freshly baked loaf of bread, and then ushered through what remained of the gateway of the fortress that they had so recently owned.

Once his own men had vacated the fortress, three of his men carried out his orders and set the fortress alight, burning the hated place to the ground.

CHAPTER 8

On returning to Wentnor he was shocked to see that the meadows surrounding the village were seething with men.

Men who appeared to be enjoying themselves from the noise that came from the area.

As Hywell rode up to join Edric in the van of his small army, he shaded his eyes against the glare of the sun as he glared at the men, then cupped his hand to his ear and let out a happy yelp. 'Look you now,' he said in a loud, joyous voice. 'Only the Welsh could sing like that. It seems that my Father has joined us.' Only then could Edric make out the melodious songs that had suddenly seemed to separate itself from the rest of the noise that emanated from the camp.

'It cannot be,' uttered the unbelieving Edric.

''Tis so,' answered Hywell. ''Tis Bleddyn himself, king of Gwynedd.' He spurred his horse brutally, galloping ahead to greet his father.

Hywell brought his horse to a skidding halt alongside his father, 'Good it is to see you my lord father,' he said, 'and with such a host. Indeed I did not think it possible for you to gather so many men.'

'Good to see you also, my son,' came the reply, 'and looking so well.' With a grin he added, 'This life of war well suits you. But all of these men are not from our lands, for I persuaded Rhiwallon, king of Powys to join us, as he was a personal friend of Harold Godwinson, and was only too pleased to tread the path of war against these foreigners.'

Hywell found it impossible to hide a smile, thinking to himself that it was merely a few short years ago that both his father and Rhiwallon of Powys would spit at the very mention of the word English, and for them now to join with the English against their enemies would have been unthinkable. Yet here they were in what they had long classed as their enemies' territory, with the pick of their young men, ready to assist the Saxons (as they still called them) in a battle against an enemy who, they all realised, controlled one of the most formidable warrior castes in the continent of Europe.

Rhiwallon rode up to join them, forcing Hywell to recall the one and only time that he had met the famous Prince of Powys. Then, as now, the Prince cut a majestic figure, being a large swarthy man with more jet black hair than a man half his age should wear, which had been tied behind his head with a white sheepskin band, with the colour of the band matching his thick sheepskin jacket that he wore over his very expensive boiled leather war-shirt.

After spending such a long period of time with Edric and his Englishmen, and despite being used to it, the fact that Rhiwallon's face was literally covered with blue tattoos still continued to shock him.

He did, of course, know that the tattoos told strangers of his rank. His tribal markings as well as his standing in his own nation; the large amount of rings that virtually merged into one huge mass also told strangers of the number of men that he had killed in battle.

'Ah, so this is your young whelp,' said Rhiwallon in perfect English with just a mere lilt of a Welsh accent. 'He has grown somewhat since I saw him last.'

Bleddyan gazed towards Hywell, 'Aye Lord Powys he has so, and can wield that sword of his with the best of them. At Hastings he was with the good King Harold, now that was a bad day for all of us, and that's the truth of it.'

Rhiwallon answered with a noncommittal 'mmmm' adding quietly, 'Just so, just so' as he spurred his small rough stallion forward towards Edric who had approached the trio.

'Good to see you Lord Edric,' said Rhiwallon in a jovial way.

'Good to see you too,' came the answer, 'and with such a host behind you, I do hope that you have come to join us and not to fight us,' he said smiling and hoping, but really knowing that the two Welsh Kings had indeed come to join him. Had they come to make war upon him, the village of Wentnor, plus the surrounding farms would already have been ravaged and burned to the ground.

'Aye,' came the reply from Bleddyn, 'We have indeed come to join you in your crusade to clear the land of these invaders,' he touched his ornate sword in a melodramatic way.

Edric was delighted, for with the men that these two Welsh kings had brought with them they had, in a single stroke, pretty well doubled his numbers, chasing away the demons that had been haunting him over the past few months, all too well aware that with the small number of warriors that he had previously assembled, it would only be a matter of time before William of Normandy would turn his attention towards Edric, with the numbers of experienced warriors that the Norman leader controlled, it would have been a foregone conclusion that Edric and his small army would quickly be overwhelmed and destroyed.

However, now that his numbers had doubled, he felt that he had a good chance of at least holding his own against the Normans. Even a remote possibility of beating them, especially if time and circumstances were kind to him, and his battle luck held.

Accompanied by the two Welsh kings, he led his victorious men through the Welsh camps to the sound of shouts of welcome in the Welsh tongue (a thing he never thought that he would hear) and the clamour made by the warriors clashing their swords and spears against the metal rims of their shields, which was sweet music to his ears.

Godda met them at the door, her face beaming with pleasure and holding a tray full of tankards of ale.

'Welcome home husband,' she said happily, 'and to you good kings. Pray alight. Come inside for I have prepared a feast for you to celebrate your victory.'

As Edric, Rhiwallon, Bleddyn, Hywell, Earl Hunwald and Garth dismounted, Edric thought to himself, 'How does she know that we were victorious at Richard's castle?'

Then he shook his head as if to say to himself, 'You idiot, she knows these things. Is she not Queen of the Light Elves?' Cursing himself, only half believing and yet still sceptical about the origins and lineage of his beautiful new wife.

She then astonished him even further when she began to converse with the two Welsh kings in their own language, chattering away and laughing as if it was a language she had been born to. It became quite obvious that they were enjoying themselves as the hall echoed with the bellows of laughter from the two Welsh kings mingling with the more melodious, ladylike chuckles from Edric's wife.

Inside the great hall the tables were laden with all sorts of delicacies, from huge plates of roast beef, venison, half a roast lamb, roast blackbirds, sparrows, pheasant and chicken, alongside steaming plates of pies that Edric knew would be apple and blackberry as he knew well that Godda was aware that apple and blackberry pie, laced with fresh cream, was her husband's favourite meal.

With loud grunts of approval the men sat themselves down on the benches and, just as Edric had plunged his eating knife into a small pheasant, he noticed that his Welsh guests were crossing themselves and had bowed their heads in prayer and had already began to mumble their thanks to God in their own language.

A little shamefaced, he dropped the pheasant which still contained his knife in it onto his wooden plate and joined his guests in their thanks to God.

Much to the amusement of Godda, Edric's head was still bowed when his guests had completed their prayers and were already busy filling their plates, causing him further embarrassment, as he speedily snatched his knife out of the pheasant carcass and brought a large chunk of meat to his mouth, speaking with his mouth half full of meat.

'I hadn't realised how hungry I was until I saw this food,' he said to Rhiwallon, who agreed with him by answering his remark with loud grunt and an even louder belch.

Godda herself refilled their tankards with strong ale and as she approached Edric she pushed her hip hard against his shoulder, then leaning over, she whispered in his ear in her provocative, husky voice, 'How now my lord.'

'Think you that these Welsh kings came here without me summoning them?'

Startled, he looked up to her, and she raised her eyebrows in a knowing way and smiled at him; before she moved on to fill the tankard of her next guest.

After the meal the table was cleared and Godda and her maidens vanished into the bakehouse.

Edric posed the question to the two Welsh kings and Earl Hunwald saying, 'Our combined forces now give us enough strength to fight these invaders, but we have two main cities from whence we need to evict these damned Normans. They have taken the city of Shrewsbury, and also occupy the city of Hereford.'

'The question is which of these cities do we attack first?'

Rhiwallon immediately thumped his fist down on the table, 'Shrewsbury is the most obvious place and when we have taken that city, then Hereford will be more isolated and easier to take.'

Bleddyn said nothing, merely looked towards Edric with a puzzled look on his face, whilst Earl Hunwald merely smiled and nodded.

'Maybe, maybe,' answered Edric. 'But on the other hand I would prefer to take the city of Shrewsbury first. As you all know, most of my own holdings are in that shire and as I am so well known, we would be able recruit a large number of warriors from the city as well as from the shire. It could well double our numbers again, which would make the taking of Hereford and that shire so much easier.'

'That is true,' chipped in Hywell. Garth nodded and grunted assent, but the two Welsh kings stayed silent, apparently unconvinced or perhaps unhappy that they should use their own warriors farther northwards than they had perhaps anticipated.

'No my Lord Edric,' said Rhiwallon. 'I still think that we should take Hereford first and then move on the city of Shrewsbury.' He thrust his bristly grey chin out in defiance.

Bleddyn nodded in agreement, 'Aye Edric, I think that this old rascal is right, we should take Shrewsbury first,' adding with a crafty look towards Rhiwallon, 'and if, God forbid, things should go ill for us, then we are only a stone's throw away from the safety of our Welsh homelands.'

'Shrewsbury it is then my lords,' he said glumly. 'Raise your tankards and let us drink to the taking of Shrewsbury.'

The men raised their tankards to their mouths saying 'To Hereford!' and drained them.

As Harold and the three other servants who shared the stable were about to wrap themselves in their cloaks and find a soft bundle of hay where they could spend the night, they were shocked when the Lady Godda herself entered through the open door carrying so large a platter of food that Harold thought she would drop it. Stepping forward, he said, in the almost forgotten language of the Albions, 'Take care my lady, else the weight be too much for you.'

'Nay my good Harold,' came the pleasant response in his own language, totally shocking him yet again and causing him to stumble and almost crash into her in his haste to assist her. 'I am well used to such burdens,' she continued in the language of the Albions, then turning quickly to the other servants said, in the English tongue, 'Pray allow our guests to help themselves.'

She then turned again towards Harold who, along with the others, was eagerly grabbing handfuls of food and stuffing it greedily into their mouths.

'Come Harold,' she said pleasantly, 'sit with me and tell me how a handsome young man like your good self came to be a servant of one such as Earl Hunwald?'

Harold, despite of himself, opened his heart to the beautiful Lady Godda, who tarried long into the night with him.

*****

Later, when the house was quiet, Earl Hunwald quietly left his room and crept to the stables where his servant, the red-haired Harold slept. he kicked the man awake.

'Come,' he whispered, and Harold followed his master out of the stables away from the three other servants who had been sharing their sleeping accommodation with him.

Earl Hunwald led Harold into a spot that was shaded from the gleam of the full moon saying, 'As soon as I have left I want you to pick a good horse, lead it quietly out and ride as fast as you can to King William with this message, *Edric and his Welsh allies will be attacking the city of Shrewsbury within the next week.* 'Do you understand?' he asked.

His servant nodded and grunted, 'Aye my lord.'

'Good,' said the Earl, 'repeat the message to me.' Harold quietly repeated the message word for word to his master.

'Good,' repeated Earl Hunwald and patted Harold on the shoulder, turned and disappeared into the darkness.

Harold, as ordered, stole silently towards a line of tethered horses. After a few soothing words he stroked a large brown mare along her muzzle, gently untied her, silently saddled and bridled her then led her quietly through the throng of sleeping men and out of the encampment.

He rode at a steady pace through the quiet hamlet of Rattlinghope, following the path which skirted a pleasant babbling brook, leading his horse up the steep hill to the village of Pulverbatch without seeing a single person. He passed through Wrentnal to the larger village of Pontesbury, a village which he carefully by-passed, as he could see that a Norman tower was in the process of being built.

In the failing light he again skirted the city of Shrewsbury, driving his tired mount southwards, which was totally in the wrong direction that he really wanted to go, fording the mighty River Sabrina at the hamlet of Atchem, whence he again turned his horse's head to the north, towards the city of York.

York was where he had been told King William and his army were spending a few months whilst he was assembling his army in order to destroy the many rebellions that seemed to be rising in one or another part of the country. Causing not only Harold, but also his lord, the Earl Hunwald to begin to doubt that King William of England and of Normandy (as he liked to be called) would indeed be able to retain his title of King of this troubled land.

As weary as he was, he continued to ride northwards until his faltering mount staggered, coming to a determined halt, causing Harold to dismount in a small dell alongside a stream. There he hobbled his horse, allowing it to drink, then graze on the lush tussocks of grass that bordered the stream. He gathered a few sticks of dry wood and lit a small, smokeless fire over which he roasted a small, almost rancid chunk of lamb that Earl Hunwald had given him.

As tired as he was, sleep evaded him, his tortured mind flitting as the clouds across the moon on a warm summer's evening. He began to question his loyalty to his master, and yet if he carried this message to King William then he would be betraying the beautiful Godda, as well as her husband Edric, who, he felt were somehow, virtually kin to him.

When dawn finally came with the clamour of the dawn chorus filling the air with the songs of countless birds that dwelt in the woodlands, the birdsong, coupled with the breeze that wafted through the trees, caused his already troubled mind to become totally confused.

He sat on the damp ground, numb and stiff beside the dead fire, unable or perhaps unwilling to walk even the few steps towards his still grazing horse.

The clamour from a pair of mating wood pigeons as they thrashed about in a nearby tree eventually startled him out of his stupor, forcing him to stand and stretch his stiffened legs.

He suddenly realised that he had made a decision, and as he shook his head as if to clear it of a spider's web that had clouded his brain and his eyes, the beautiful face of Godda floated before his eyes, smiling that same bewitching smile with which she had greeted him when she had entered the stables last night.

Was it last night, he asked himself. It could have been, yet the vision seemed to be as old as time itself.

Yes, he answered his own question. It could have been last night. And yet perhaps it happened a lifetime ago.

Or was it another life?

He ambled in a leisurely way over to his horse, still slightly confused about the reason and the possible consequences of his decision, yet adamant that the decision that he had made was in fact the correct one.

He untethered his horse, climbed up and headed back towards the city of Shrewsbury, retracing his steps around the city during the night and finally making camp in a shepherd's hut, out of the persistent drizzle that had drenched both his weary horse and himself since nightfall.

The drizzle persisted throughout the night, pouring through the patchy thatch that served as a cover for the hut, thoroughly soaking both Harold and his tired horse, making the night seem longer than it actually was, leaving Harold wet, tired and irritable.

His low spirits were further dampened when, by midmorning he ran unexpectedly into a group of three horsemen, who by their attire and bearing announced themselves to be Normans.

They had appeared so suddenly around a bend in the overgrown lane he had been riding along it had been impossible to avoid them, so his only option was to continue to urge his tired horse towards them, as if he was fully expecting them and hadn't a care in the world.

Although he was not a warrior, he did by habit keep to the left-hand side of the lane. This being the customary side for men, especially warriors to ride, in order to hold the reins of their steeds with their left hands, leaving their right hands free to use their weapons, should the need arise.

Forcing himself to smile, he urged his horse to one side of the narrow lane in order that the three Normans could pass by, but as they drew alongside him the man who appeared to be the leader of the group reined in his horse, declaring loudly, 'Well now, what do we have here? '

His companions also pulled up their own mounts and hemmed Harold in, against the side of the lane.

The man screwed up his eyes and peered at the red-haired man who merely sat on his horse as he waited, and indeed, willed them to pass by.

But they did not pass, merely urged their own horses closer towards his own horse, hemming him in even further, until his tired mount became restless.

'Does it not seem strange to you my friends that we have met this English serf here astride a good Norman horse? And in broad daylight too.'

The two other Normans grunted their assent to the man's suggestion, pressing ever closer to Harold.

'What say you serf?' growled the leader as his right hand dropped to the hilt of his sword.

His two comrades had already drawn their swords and pointed them menacingly towards Harold's belly.

'Not so my lords,' said Harold in the language of Normandy. 'I am merely a servant of the good Earl Hunwald, who, as you probably know is a loyal subject, indeed a good friend of King William himself.'

Somewhat taken aback that this English serf could speak their language, and in fact he spoke it with an upper-class accent, certainly far better than the majority of the Normans that they knew.

The men lowered their swords and were about to return them to their wool-lined scabbards when the leader said in a rather less menacing voice, 'Hold lads. This rascal may speak our simple Norman tongue but that does not explain what he is doing alone in the middle of the wilderness on a Norman horse. And I don't know about you, but although I've heard about a turncoat named Earl Hunwald, the last I heard about him he was in the city of York with the King.'

'Aye, aye,' growled his companions, as they rested their still unsheathed swords across their laps, not quite sure where this last remark was taking them.

'Not so, My lords,' answered Harold. 'Forsooth, my lord, the good Earl is in the borderlands on a special mission, and it is for him that I do journey with an important message from our King.'

'Let me see the message,' snarled the leader, 'I see no docket about your person.'

'The message is here messires,' said Harold, tapping his forehead with his index finger. 'For it would be foolish indeed if the Earl were to send his written word out into the wilderness with one unarmed servant.'

'This message,' said the now confused leader, 'what manner of word is it?'

'I would not incur the wrath of King William by telling you, and perhaps it would be unwise for you to enquire further.' With a little irony in his voice, Harold added, 'My good lords.'

Then as the confused Normans gazed at one another, seemingly shocked by his answer, Harold urged his horse forward, leaving the three men sitting bemused on their stationary horses, watching him as continue his journey down the lane.

He breathed a loud sigh of relief and wiped the perspiration off his brow with his sleeve as he rode around a bend in the lane, disappearing out of sight of the three horsemen, silently thanking the good Lord for his deliverance, and continued his way through the wet bushes and tree branches that invaded the narrow, pot-holed lane.

When, around midnight, he reached Wentnor he was not too happy as he urged his tired horse through silent fields and deserted campsites. The damp, dead ash from extinguished fires told him that Edric and his army had already left.

He dismounted and left his tired horse before the longhall, banging loudly upon the nail-studded oak door, which was almost immediately opened by the beautiful Lady Godda.

'Come in my good Harold,' said the smiling Godda in the language of the Albions. 'I have been expecting you and I am so pleased that you made the right decision, and did not obey the orders of your traitorous master.'

She turned and beckoned him to follow, 'Come,' she repeated. 'I have prepared a small something for you after your long journey, Come, let me take your cape, you are soaked through to the skin. Sit here,' she cooed, 'by the fire, and wrap yourself in this sheepskin,' handing him a fleece that had been warming by the roaring wood fire.

Godda ushered him over to where a small table had been laid beside a large chair.

She fussed over him like a broody hen, handing him mulled ale and platters of the choicest of meats, chattering away to him as if he was her long-lost brother returning safely from the wars.

'My husband, the Lord Edric and his Welshmen left only this morning. Come now good Harold, eat your fill and you can tell me all about your journey.'

CHAPTER 9

Many of his own men mumbled into their ale about their leader, Hereward. Already some had nicknamed him 'the Wake' due to the savage way in which he treated not only his enemies the Normans, but many of his own people, especially those who had bent their knees to their conquerors. That and the way that he bawled and browbeat his own men; who now sat alongside him at the tables, celebrating their taking of the Isle of Ely.

This island had been named by the local fishermen, due to the vast amount of eels that swarmed in such numbers around the island. So much so that, at times, men found it difficult to propel their light boats through these vast shoals of the long slimy fish.

In truth the taking of Ely could hardly be classed as a victory, for the resistance put up by twenty or so half-trained levies had lasted for no more than a few brief minutes before they had flung open the gates to their attackers.

They were forced to kneel in the mud, where Hereward himself speedily beheaded them.

'Let that be a lesson to all who oppose me,' he had bellowed to the thirty-seven men of his warband, adding, 'and to any other Englishmen who joins these Norman dogs.'

No fewer than seventeen of his men had been with him at the Battle of Hastings, and six had fought at Stamford Bridge. Those six stout men had served under him and his more noble father, Leofric of Bourne, for many years before those two fateful battles.

They were, of course all aware of Hereward's claim to nobility. All knew that he was the Nephew of Earl Ralph the Staller and of his mother, the lady Eagyth, who was the great-great niece of the famous Duke of Oslac.

Being of such nobility, he automatically demanded not only the role of leadership of this small band of warriors, but he also demanded his men's unquestionable obedience and loyalty.

Hereward eventually calmed down and, looking thoughtfully into his half empty tankard muttering half to himself and half to the unwashed old warrior who sat next to him. 'Nine of those bastards were Normans,' adding, after taking a gulp of ale. 'The question is, how did they get here? I thought this place was unknown to them, hidden here amongst these muddy marshlands.'

The gnarled warrior, Aldred of Lincoln, answered angrily, 'There are many amongst these mud hoppers who would sell their own grandmother for a silver penny.'

'I had thought these Fen people to be loyal, but mayhap you are right,' Hereward muttered as he turned his face towards Aldred. He snarled angrily, 'I shall find out who led them here and if he is not already amongst the dead, he will soon wish it were so.'

He thumped his tankard down upon the table, in anger at the thought of good honest Englishmen leading his Norman enemies to this, one of the most secret of places in the Fens, spilling a good half of the contents of his tankard in the process.

'Another thing,' he said. 'What to do about those pious monks at that monastery? Some of them may be Normans. It could well have been one of them who led those Norman scum here.

'What to do,' he repeated over and over again. 'What to do,' speaking as if he was in his cups. 'What to do. What to do?'

He then grabbed his tankard and drained it in one long gulp, 'If I slay them all, then I would suffer the wrath of our own people, and of the Church. Yet if these churchmen favour the Normans, they will always be a thorn in my side, a spy in our midst.'

'Mayhap we could use them.' offered Aldred who, despite his age and his grubby appearance, had more cunning and intelligence than most of Hereward's men, as well as a mind like a steel mantrap.

'How so?' snapped Hereward.

'Well,' came the answer, 'if we could allow them to learn that we intended to attack a particular town or village, they may well send word of our plans to William, who would then set a trap for us and, mayhap, we could trap the trappers.'

'Now that could work,' said Hereward thoughtfully, suddenly as sober as a milkmaid, adding, 'and if we can use them in that way, we will be seen to be friends of the Church as well as being seen by our friends and enemies as a force to be reckoned with. That will draw men to our standard, as well as give us credibility if we ever have the need to treat with that Norman bastard William.

'Drink up my friend,' he said jovially to Aldred. 'Methinks that you could well have earned your ale this day.'

Nearly one month later, after a few brief days of heavy toil when they had laboured to repair and strengthen the half-finished Norman stockade, their forced idleness was beginning to cause Aldred's men to become bored of fishing and lazing about on the small, fly-infested islet set in the middle of miles of mud and reed beds. A grubby Fenman, reeking of fish, shuffled into the men's quarters where Hereward was in the process of instructing one of his newest recruits in one of the finer points of sword play.

'My lord Hereward,' said the warrior who had escorted the man into Hereward's presence, 'this man is an eel fisherman from the western reaches of the Fens. He has insisted on seeing you, says he has news for you and refuses to tell me what it is.'

Hereward gave the sword back to the young warrior, and then walked over to the warrior and the foul-smelling fisherman.

'I am Hereward,' he said to the man who was standing before him with his dirty, grease-smeared hat held before him in both hands, with his head lowered almost onto his chest.

'I seed them milord,' he mumbled.

'Seed?' Hereward corrected himself. 'Saw whom?' he demanded angrily.

'Seed them Normans,' came the mumbled reply from the man whose head was still bowed as if he did not have the right to look a lord in the eyes.

'Well man?' said the easy-to-anger Hereward. 'Where were these Normans?'

'Near to where I lives milord, building a causeway they was, 'undreds of 'em, boats an' all.'

'And where do you live, my good man?' asked Hereward, far more interested in the man's news than he had been a few short moments before.

'Oh oi' lives about four, maybe five miles from 'ere,' came the reply. 'Oi'm an eel fisherman y'see,' as if Hereward hadn't already realised that from the smell of the man.

'They didn't see me though, Oi 'id in the reeds. This 'igh they be,' holding his right arm high above his head.

'Lead me to where you saw them.' ordered Hereward, walking past the man, snatching up his war-axe from where he had left it by the entrance of the hut.

The man led Hereward down to an almost hidden spot at the water's edge, where a flat-bottomed boat lay hidden in the high reeds.

The boat was just about big enough for Hereward and one other warrior to join the man who seemed relieved to have survived the short interview with this fierce warrior, happy to be alive and in his boat, on the marshlands again.

The man's boat had both a paddle and a long pole, enabling the fisherman to cross deep and shallow water as he used both pole and paddle at various stages of the journey. A journey that took them through an ever changing variety of channels, streams, pools and stagnant reed beds, sometimes changing direction so violently that Hereward could swear that they were, at times, heading back towards the camp. He cursed himself for being such a fool to put his life at risk on the word of this smelly peasant who he had only met such a short time before.

He was fingering his war-axe with the intent of embedding it in this smelly peasant's breast, when suddenly the man stopped propelling the boat forward. Placing his pole quietly along the length of the boat, he knelt down as the boat inched slowly towards the edge of the large reed bed through which they had been travelling.

'There they be milord,' said the fisherman pointing to the left, towards the far edge of a small lake.

Hereward leaned forward and saw a virtual hive of activity, where scores of men were working away, cutting reeds that were then in the process of being loaded onto the boats, and carried in the boats towards a ten-foot wide causeway that stretched back as far as the eye could see.

'Damn,' muttered Hereward aloud.

Whereas the fisherman, for a brief moment forgetting himself, put his index finger to his mouth and said 'Ssshh.' Then added, 'Sorry milord, but sound do carry far across these waters.'

''Tis I that should be sorry,' admitted Hereward, 'I should not have doubted your loyalty, Here,' he said with a smile and handing a silver penny to the delighted man.

'Now take us back to Ely,' he said, 'and I want you to gather up as many loyal fishermen that you can muster and have them come to Ely in the evening of the morrow. For I will have work for them, and to each I will give a silver penny, and to your good self I shall give four more.

'Tell me my good man,' said Hereward to the eel fisherman, 'oft-times these waters are teeming with eels, and then they disappear. Where do they go?

'Ha, milord, no one really knows that, do they? But there be a saying amongst us eel folk that goes:

When the willows do come out in bud,
Then the eels do come out of the mud.'

'Ha,' said Hereward with a smile. 'The riddle is solved, for they obviously hide in the mud. See, I have solved the secret that you eel men have sought these many years since.' Smiling at his own genius.

'That may be milord,' came the reply, 'but there be times of the year when a man can dig ten feet down into the mud and find no eels.'

There was a pregnant silence in the boat.

They sailed on in silence until they reached the isle. After unloading his passengers, the eel fisherman calmly paddled off shaking his head, and smiling to himself.

The following evening no less than thirty-one fishermen arrived at Ely to be greeted by Hereward and his assembled warriors, who waited anxiously along the slippery shoreline.

*****

The small flotilla arrived at the scene of the deserted Norman causeway a little before midnight, where Hereward, urging half of his force to disembark onto the causeway whilst he sailed quietly around the sleeping Norman encampment with the remainder of his men.

Three hundred heartbeats later, at the sound of three booms as if from one of the many bitterns that inhabited this watery world, his men came swooping down the causeway and into the Norman camp, literally bowling over the two bleary eyed, startled guards, causing panic as they slaughtered any man who appeared before them.

Seconds later Hereward led his second force into the camp from the opposite direction, crashing into a score or more of half-dressed fugitives, who were running as fast as their legs would allow them away from the mayhem that had been, a few brief moments before a quiet, sleepy haven.

They were dead before they realised what they had run into, as Hereward and his men ran through them as a hot knife goes through butter, then Hereward's men surged onwards until they joined up with the rest of his men who had been guided to the causeway some one hundred yards away catching the fleeing Normans in a pincer movement. Whereupon they continued to slaughter the few Normans who had, thus far, escaped from these reavers of death.

Hereward rested his men and the Fen fishermen until daybreak when, after stripping the dead of their valuable armour and weapons, he sent his warriors to the far end of the causeway with orders to destroy as much of the causeway that they could before any other Norman force may arrive in a vain attempt to the come to the rescue of their already dead countrymen.

It was with much delight, and many loud hoots and catcalls that Hereward and his men watched as over a hundred frustrated Normans were forced to rein in their horses at the place where their once sturdy causeway had been. Where they could do no more than sit on their mounts and glumly watch as Hereward's warriors continued to destroy what was left of the causeway and Norman boats, until there was nothing left except bunches of floating reeds and wooden stakes drifting, aimlessly, in the slow-flowing current.

However just before he left Hereward was slightly peeved as he glanced back over the shoulder of the Fenman, who was busy propelling the flat-bottomed boat away from the destroyed causeway, when he saw the figures of four soggy Normans scrambling out of the water along the banks of a pool. Running wearily to join their frustrated countrymen who were still sitting on their horses watching their enemies slowly float away.

The jubilant but tired men arrived in Ely by noon to be greeted by the few sentries that had been left to guard the camp. Their joyous shouts and triumph was somewhat clouded by the small group of sour-looking monks who stood apart, and were quite obviously not pleased to see Hereward and his men returning to their island in triumph.

News of Hereward's exploits spread far and wide causing many English and Danish warriors to make their way through the Fens to Ely, swelling his already growing army. Amongst the newcomers were two very wet and bedraggled Englishmen who claimed that they had been lost in the Fens for over a week, in their quest to join Hereward and his band, in order to help him in his fight against the Norman invaders.

These were Lynulf and Eldon, men who served the Earl Hunwald, as did their fathers before them, and their fathers before that.

A large number of the newcomers were fugitives or deserters from one army or another, although to be fair, many of the men were from King Harold's own *fyrd*, still totally loyal to the English cause.

He welcomed them all; fugitives, deserters and good men alike, but, the suspicious man that he was, he was very aware that any one of them could be a spy or an assassin, causing him not to allow any of these newcomers to get too close to him, unless he was in the company of his own personal bodyguard. This now consisted of twelve warriors, all of whom were either kin or had proven their loyalty and their worth in battle.

Later that month news reached him that yet another causeway had been started by the Normans some six miles north-east of the Isle of Ely. After speaking to several loyal Fenmen he was pleased to discover that it would be at least another six weeks or so before this causeway would be close enough to Ely to become a real threat to him.

That evening he called his favourite warriors and captains to him in order to explain to them his plans.

'First of all,' he said to them in a loud confident voice, 'it will be at least six weeks before this new causeway can become a real threat to us, and that is allowing that there are no exceptionally high tides or floods to destroy it or to hinder them. Remember that this is not the first time that they have tried to reach us. In fact, it is the third causeway that they have constructed.

'Have no fear,' he said. 'We shall destroy this one just as we destroyed the other two, and we shall send many of these Norman dogs to their deaths in the process.'

The men, heartened by this speech, cheered loudly, clashing their weapons onto the iron rims of their shields in approval.

Hereward held his hand up and waited for the noise to die down, 'We will permit these fools to waste their efforts on this causeway without hampering them too much,' adding, to appease the shocked look that had suddenly fallen upon the faces of his men. 'I will send a half dozen of you just to let them know that we are still here,' he pointed to a small cluster of men who he knew would be more than willing to carry out the task. 'You men can keep them awake at night with a few night attacks, and an arrow or two from the reed beds in the daytime, in order to keep them on their toes.'

The men's sullen faces began to smile again.

'In the meantime,' he continued, 'I want the rest of you to be prepared to move at first light on the morrow.' At that statement loud cheers came from the assembled warriors, whilst others shifted their feet nervously at the thought of more battles and more bloodshed.

'Whilst these fools build their causeway,' he bellowed to drown his boisterous warriors, 'I shall lead you out of the Fens to the west. We shall march around our enemies and take the town of Stamford, which I have been informed has only a small number of Normans who guard the town. We will relieve them of the valuables that these fools who are tiring themselves in our marshlands have left at Stamford, thinking that their gold and silver will be safe inside the town.' He chuckled loudly.

Again the air was filled with cheering and the clamour of his warriors who now saw an easy victory before them, with most of the throng delighted that there would also be a few measly Normans to slay, as well as a rich town to sack.

He again held his hand above his head for silence and waited a while until the noise abated. 'And on our way home we shall take these causeway builders in the rear and send them all to join their ancestors in hell.' then turning his back on his cheering warriors he returned to his quarters, pleased with the tactics that he had devised, and in his own mind, he was totally convinced that his plans were fool proof.

Lynulf and Eldon who had been amongst the assembled warriors slyly looked at each other and smiled.

After a little while they left the assembled warriors, making their way slowly and quietly away from the assembled men until they found a quiet spot where they could talk without being overheard.

'What think you?' asked Lynulf who had always been a follower and not a leader.

'Well,' answered his friend with a sly smile, 'this is what Lord Hunwald sent us here for. So I think that we should gather up our few belongings and get the hell out of this place, then we can get our rewards from Lord Hunwald, or even King William.' He adding with a smile, 'I've always dreamed of having a purse full of gold and a big house, so with a bit of luck we could soon be rich men, come on let's go,' he said as he turned towards the dirty wattle and daub hut that served the two men, plus six others as a home where they began to gather up the few belongings that they had horded over the past few weeks.

The goddess of luck was not with the two men as they crept quietly out of their sleeping quarters and across the island to one of the secret causeways that were known to most of the island's inhabitants.

After stumbling around in the dark for quite some time they eventually found the causeway and were hastening along it, covered by Eostre, the goddess of the dawn who had drawn her cloak over the waters, throwing up her breath in the form of rising mists that drifted in swathes some five or six feet above the marshes.

However the breath of Eostre did not turn out to be the blessing that the two men had thought them to be, for as they hastened along the silent half-hidden causeway, Lynulf stumbled over the sleeping form of one of the many guards who had been stationed at intervals along the causeway, falling heavily over the man who, awakened in such a manner, let out a loud howl as he rose to his feet, heaving himself up with the aid of his spear, which as a result of his many tours of night duty was always attached by a leather thong to his right hand.

Lynulf and Eldon, thinking that the guard was alone, drew their twelve-inch long *seax* from their belts and jumped at the man, stabbing him in his left shoulder. Yet the man was a seasoned warrior, and had suffered wounds of this nature several times in his long career. He knew full well that if he were to allow the wound and the pain to worry him he would be speedily overpowered by these two men, especially so as he was already outnumbered, two against one, and would soon be slain.

So the sentry gritted his teeth, ignored the searing pain in his shoulder and continued to fend off his attackers with his spear. Slowly retreating, he shouted, 'To me! To me!' resulting in three other sentries, who had been sleeping a few yards away from the man, leaping to their feet, attacking his two assailants from their rear, immediately spearing Eldon, who fell onto his face, pierced by two spears, forcing the shocked Lynulf to drop his *seax*, and thrust his hands high in the air.

'I yield, I yield!' he shouted and was knocked to the ground by a heavy blow from one of the spear-wielding guards.

'What shall we do with him?' panted one of the guards.

'Take him to Hereward,' gasped the guard who had been wounded, as he stuffed a grubby rag against the wound and held it hard against his shoulder in order to staunch the flow of blood.

'We two had better stay here just in case there are any more of them whilst you take this carrion to Hereward,' said one of the guards.

Hereward had already assembled his men and was about to order them to march when two of his sentries appeared, bundling a bound prisoner through the warriors, pushing the man onto his knees before their leader.

'We caught two of them trying to flee from the camp,' said one of the warriors. 'They must be spies or deserters otherwise they would not have attacked me. They would have killed me had it not been for my friends.'

'Killed one,' he added, 'This is the other.'

'My thanks to you my friend for your vigilance,' said Hereward, 'however, I cannot delay my mission, Healer?' he called, 'Healer! Where the devil is Healer?'

Healer eventually pushed his way through the crowd and stood in front of Hereward, 'You called my lord,' he said with a cynical smile on his handsome weathered face.

'I did,' answered Hereward as he studied the tall, slim, dark-haired figure of one of the most evil men Hereward had ever encountered, a man who wallowed in torture and the screams of his victims.

'I want you and that nephew of yours, Martin, to question this man,' he nodding towards the still kneeling captive.

'Find out what you can from him and when you have, then I want one of you to urgently find me and tell me what you have learned.' Then turning he bellowed, 'We are done here. March!'

As he made his way to the fore of his warriors, he was slightly concerned by the evil smile that the two 'questioners' gave one another as they led their victim upwards towards Hereward's headquarters. Yet he let the moment pass for he had little or no sympathy for people who betrayed him.

By using the hidden causeways and secret tracks, Hereward and his small army squelched their way for more than three quarters of the day before they were clear of the Fens and the surrounding marshlands, forcing him to call a halt to give his wet, tired men a short rest, as well as to allow the laggards to catch up with the main body of his force.

By midnight they found themselves in the dark reaches of the mighty forest of Rockingham where, for some untold reason, and much to the fury of Hereward, his two guides, people who had professed to know the forest, 'like the back of our hands' presented themselves before him.

'My lord,' said the younger of the two as he bent his knee before Hereward, 'We know not where we are. We must have taken the wrong track back there in the dark.'

Hereward, a man not known for his tact or kind temperament, spun on his heel and as he did so he drew his sword, striking the man's head from his shoulders before the man even knew anything was amiss.

'Now,' he said to the remaining guide who was now trembling with fear with a steam of cold sweat running profusely from his face. 'You had better find the correct route, and be quick about it.'

The man, realising that he was not to share the same fate as his younger companion, breathed a sigh of relief, saying, 'Aye, my lord, that I will.' And turning, he made his way through the silent crowd of men who had just witnessed the anger of their liege lord.

The guide disappeared into the darkness and was never seen again.

Since there was little to be gained by wandering through the wet forest in the dark, he called a halt.

'Get some sleep,' he ordered. 'We will continue our journey on the morrow,' thinking to himself that 'the morrow,' would at least give him daylight, for indeed he considered himself to be an experienced woodsman who would have no problem in heading in the correct direction once the sun rose. Yet as he gazed through the leafy canopy he reckoned that dawn was no more than three or four hours away, and they all needed a rest anyway.

He was awake and on the edge of their camp before the first rays of daylight, staring through the ground mist that rose from the forest floor, studying the four almost hidden paths that led in various directions into the forest.

Not usually a pious man, he suddenly felt the urge to pray, so he knelt on the wet, mossy floor, closed his eyes and held his hands together in prayer, offering his prayers to Saint Peter, imploring him to show the way.

Saint Peter was the one saint that Hereward favoured, for many years ago Hereward had saved the life of the Abbot of Peterborough, and he had, for some unexplained reason, returned a large part of the treasure that had been stolen from the saint's own abbey of Peterborough.

His prayers did not last many moments, for it had been many years since he had prayed, and the schooling in the ways of the clergy that his father, Leofric the good, earl of Mercia had given him, had, for the best part, been long forgotten.

However, as he finished his short prayer he felt the hot, wet breath of the saint upon his cheek. Then cursing himself for being a fool, he realised that if it was in fact Saint Peter breathing his holy breath upon his cheek, it would not smell so foul. So he opened his eyes suddenly and was confronted with the grey face of an old man dressed in the manner of the clergy.

In one flowing motion Hereward leapt to his feet, drawing his sword as he rose. yet the man seemed to be unperturbed, standing, or perhaps hovering, whilst remaining completely still, looking at the tall figure of Hereward who stood a mere six feet away from him.

The apparition slowly turned and floated away from Hereward, who noted that the spirit wafted towards the most little-used path of the four that led out of the clearing. Then it turned his head towards Hereward as if to say, 'Yes, this is the path that you should take, you stupid man.'

Then the apparition simply evaporated like the morning mists, before the eyes of the still static, startled Hereward.

Hereward bellowed at the top of his voice, 'Rouse yourselves my sleeping beauties and follow me, for the guardian angel of Saint Peter has shown me the way.' Then he made his way along the track that the spirit had taken, followed by a long line of still half-asleep, grumbling, half-dressed warriors, still carrying their woollen blankets, weapons and shields.

Stamford was not the easy target that Hereward had thought it to be. The new Norman owners had strengthened the old English palisade, as well as half completed the building of a high stone wall which already encompassed more than three quarters of the town, leaving just one section protected by the old English palisade, which would be the best place for a successful attack. Yet that portion of the town was girdled by the slow-flowing river Welland, and whilst the river did not present Hereward with too much of a problem, it did add another small hurdle for him to overcome.

Relief came from an unexpected quarter the following day. Just as he had assembled his men with hurdles, ladders and ropes and he was on the point of issuing the order to advance, one of his men shouted, 'Look there my lord, the gate is open,' pointing to the gate that was merely a few hundred yards from the assembled Englishmen.

All heads turned towards the gate that had been flung open, and they could see figures of men hacking and thrusting at one another in mortal combat.

'Follow me!' yelled Hereward, as he leapt into the saddle of his horse, a noble black mare called Swallow. Digging his spurs into the hindquarters of the beast, raced towards the open gates yelling at the top of his voice the old Saxon battle cry, 'OUT, OUT, OUT, OUT!'

There were only three others in his assembly who possessed mounts, and they too spurred their own horses after their lord, echoing his cries. They in turn were followed by the mass of his warriors, who made their way as fast as they could towards the open gates of Stamford.

Of the thirty or so citizens of Stamford who had started the rebellion against their new Norman masters, only eight remained standing, and they were surrounded and about to be annihilated by the more heavily armoured, better equipped and more professional Normans. Yet suddenly the Normans were attacked from behind by a banshee from hell in the name of Hereward the Wake, followed by more than a hundred other banshees.

Avenging Englishmen roaring their ancient battle cry of OUT, OUT, OUT!

They hacked and thrust at the Normans, hacking their kite-shaped shields to pieces with their dreaded English battle-axes, giving no quarter nor asking for any.

It was a short, bloody and fierce encounter with more and more half-dressed Norman warriors joining the fray in ones or twos, only to be cut down almost as soon as they had arrived, depriving the Normans of their favourite manoeuvre of forming their nearly impenetrable shieldwall.

No prisoners were taken, as was the way with Hereward, for had he not sworn vengeance upon these invaders? Sworn that none taken in arms against the English would live.

*****

'They are from Ely my lord,' said the Guard.

'Are they armed?' came the curt question.

'Not so, my lord,' snorted the sentry, a pious man who had been destined for the priesthood before his father had been slain at Hastings. 'They are Monks from the Abbey at the Isle of Ely.'

'I have known many monks who carry knives,' said the always-suspicious Duke William. 'Have them enter and bring that other sentry in with you, for whilst I doubt not your word, it is always good to be wary, and Monks can be canny fellows.'

The three churchmen entered, shaven-headed with their arms crossed across their corpulent bellies. 'My lord King,' said the eldest of the three who was obviously a prior, who formally bowed his head.

'What can I do for you my good sires?' asked William acknowledging the bow with a slight nod of his head, rather annoyed to be confronted at this early hour by three men of the Church, who, from his long experience with the clergy, knew that such a meeting usually meant that some boon was about to be asked. He muttered aloud, 'Oh no not another abbey to be built or some land dispute,' as was usually the case.

'Nay, lord King,' came the reply with a smile. 'We seek naught from your good self, but bring you relief from your woes.'

'How so?'

'One named Hereward dwells with us at Ely,' answered the Prior.

Getting more exasperated by the minute William said with a little rancour in his voice, 'Think you that I know it not?'

'Just so, lord King. Just so,' came the smug reply.

'This Hereward is but the latest of a long line of rascals and thieves to come to our retreat, a retreat where we have dwelt in peace and solitude for over two hundred years.'

King Williams's ears pricked up as he thought of the possibilities of where this strange Prior's conversation was leading, nodding and smiling at the man, but saying nothing, he merely waited for the Prior to continue.

'He has irked us somewhat,' continued the Prior. 'He desecrated the church of Saint Peter in Peterborough.'

'Did he not spare the Abbot and return a large part of the treasure to him?' said William quietly.

'That he did,' acknowledged the Prior, 'but he has sorely displeased us on Ely with his blasphemous ways and debauchery, so much so that we would be well pleased if he were elsewhere.'

Now King William saw the reason why these three men had made the tiresome journey through the fen lands to seek him.

His thoughts were interrupted as the Prior continued.

'We have many of the Fen people in our flock, eel fishermen, wildfowlers, reed cutters for thatch, and the like. Men who were born in the marshes and have spent their entire lives there, as did their fathers before them, and there are many secret passages, islands and causeways amongst the reeds, known only to them or perhaps to one or two good friars of my calling.'

'And if one of your people were to lead my warriors along these secret pathways, what would you require in return?' said the King bluntly, knowing that there is nothing for nothing in this world, or, as they say in Normandy, one good turn deserves another.'

'Not a thing lord King,' came the smiling reply. 'But once the hornet's nest has been cleaned out it will be ideal for my people to be allowed to pray to our Lord Jesus Christ in peace once again.'

The King, smiling, was about to answer when the Prior said in a quieter voice so that his two associates, who stood behind him, could not hear:

'Besides, I am weary of dining upon naught but fish and eels, and I have been led to believe that the fair city of Norwich has no Bishop. I do so love the city of Norwich,' he whispered in the King's ear. Smiling to himself as he uttered the quiet words.

The King could not prevent himself from smiling, nor did he try, but grinning from ear to ear (thankful that the boon that had been asked was so small) he placed his arm across the shoulder of the holy man saying, 'and a fine Bishop of Norwich you would make, and that's no lie. But first we have to clean out your hornet's nest, walk a while with me.'

He led the Prior into the inner chamber.

A week later, led by the old Prior himself, who was surprisingly agile, despite his age and the size of his girth, William and six hundred of his warriors followed the man through reed beds so high that at times they could not see the sky, across lakes so shallow that the water only reached up to the Norman's ankles. Through green sludge where they were warned that to take one step to their left or to their right would result in them sinking out of sight within the space of a heartbeat, 'Especially in that heavy armour of yours,' said their smiling guide, as he led them out of the sludge onto a small dry island where he said they could rest for a while.

'Let your men get as much rest as they can,' he said to the King, 'for the island of eels is but a short distance from here, and you told me that you did not want to arrive before nightfall.'

William called his captains to him, 'Keep your men silent,' he said to them, 'and I do mean silent, no fires, no loud talking, nothing. Cheer them up a bit, tell them that things will soon warm up once darkness has fallen.'

As the watery sun fell below the reed beds, the Prior started on his way again, walking along a causeway that was about a foot below the waterline of a slow-flowing stream, totally invisible to any but the trained eyes of the Fen people, who had constructed it many years ago, as well as to perhaps to the one or two holy men who dwelt on the sacred Isle of Ely.

Less than an hour later they approached the Isle of Eels, which was now clearly visible, lit up by large fires around which scores of figures danced and shouted, totally unaware that their revelling was about to be rudely interrupted.

William waited until the last of his men sloshed off the causeway and assembled them in the usual formation with himself and his chosen warriors at the front of a wedged formation, with the three sides covered by the large kite-shaped Norman shields that each man had carried through the Fens, strapped onto his back.

They were amongst and slaughtering the drunken revellers before their foes were aware that anything was amiss, and the unabated slaughter went on until the Normans could find no more enemies to kill.

Leaning on his blood-stained shield amongst the slain, William ordered his captains, 'Find me the body of the man called Hereward the Wake,' he said, adding, 'then have his body identified by that monk who led us here, He knows what he looks like.'

Then smiling to himself, he sat down amongst his personal bodyguard, whereupon he took out a large slice of boiled ham from his pack, which he began to devour, relishing every mouthful, delighted that he had eliminated yet another of his enemies. He devoured the ham until every last morsel had been eaten for he had not realised just how hungry he had been, not having eaten a thing during the march to this isolated island.

His captains returned, with scowling faces, so different from the beaming, happy faces with which they had begun their search for the body of Hereward.

'There is no sign of the rebel Hereward,' said the bravest of the captains, 'but we have found these two,' he added pointing to two bound captives that were being bundled in behind him.

Whilst King William was furious, he was not really too surprised that his arch foe Hereward the Wake had not been slain or captured, muttering aloud, 'I thought it might be so, for I have learned much about this villain, and he is not one to be taken in his bed nor in his cups. Damn the man,' he snarled.

He then turned his attention to the two prisoners who stood before him; both were tall, well-built men.

One was older and the thinner of the two, whilst the second man was younger and heavier, despite his bedraggled appearance. Also he was tied hand and foot, with an additional noose around his neck, had a round rosy face with laughing blue eyes, who, despite his dire circumstances grinned broadly at his captor.

The captain invaded his thoughts, 'They were both sound asleep my King,' he said, 'Drunk as lords, if you will excuse my expression, and they had been torturing this poor wretch,' he added nodding his head towards the doorway where two of his warriors were holding up what remained of a man.

Again the captain spoke. 'We found various parts of this soul scattered around the room, his ears and eyes, and all of his fingers, hands and feet thrown asunder.'

'Hold his head up,' ordered the King, peering at the bloody, eyeless face of the man.

'I know this man,' he gasped, 'He is one of Earl Hunwald's men, probably sent here by Hunwald upon my own orders.' He turned his head in disgust, whereon he spat at the elder of the captives and watched as his spittle dripped slowly down the man's face.'

Martin stared wide-eyed at Healer as the spittle finally reached his chin then slowly dribbled upon his once spotlessly clean and very costly tunic, knowing that they could expect no mercy from this Norman King after torturing one his own.

His assumptions were correct, for the King, trying as hard as he was able to contain his rage said, 'I feel the urge to plunge my own dagger into your black hearts but that would be too speedy a death for such as you.'

He turned to his captains, saying, 'Strip them, and cut off their balls, then tie them to one of those mooring posts,' pointing to the edge of the island where a number of flat-bottomed boats were still moored.

'Tie them to the farthest posts with just their heads and shoulders out of the water and we shall watch while the tide comes in and the eels start to feast on what little remains of their balls before the bastards are sent slowly to hell.'

CHAPTER 10

Four men carrying sacks of turnips mingled with the usual morning crowd of peasants who carried their wares on their backs, or drove their small carts, or ushered a sole milking cow towards the gate. Known as the English Gate, it was one of the two gates that led into the city of Shrewsbury.

The crowd moved slowly over the wooden bridge where they were slowly allowed through the gate by the two burly Norman guards.

Both of the guards, obeying their lord's orders, prodded and searched each and every peasant and his wares before allowing them to proceed through the gateway into the town.

The two guards ordered the four men to place their sacks on the ground at the same time, then wrenched them open and peered down into the open sacks, all at about the same time, and were skewered by four short-bladed *Seaxs*, also at the same time.

The four men urged silence upon the shocked peasants. 'Move to one side,' ordered one of the men, as Edric, the Welsh Kings Bleddyn of Gwynedd, Rhiwallon of Powys and Hywell, followed by a mixture of English and Welsh warriors poured across the bridge and through the English Gate into the city.

On their way up the steep hill towards the castle they bumped into, slew and ran over a small patrol of ten Normans who were on their way down the hill, killed a further four Normans who were merely meandering down the high street, and streamed out from the huddled mass of houses onto and through the open gates of the castle, forcing the shocked cluster of four sentries, whose sole duty had been to guard the gate, to abandon their post, turning on their heels and running into the fortress bellowing at the top of their voices 'To arms, to arms, We are attacked!' Before all four men fell on their faces with several well-placed, yard-long, grey goose shafts in their backs.

Crossbow bolts fired from the castle walls struck a number of the attackers down as they thronged onto the courtyard, 'Hywell,' bellowed Edric, 'Take some of your Welshmen up there and deal with those gadflies.'

'Aye lord,' answered Hywell and gathered a large company of warriors sending them up three of the many stairways that led to the palisade.

Edric noted that a torrent of Normans now gushed out of the entrance that had once been the old Earl of Shrewsbury's quarters, some fully armoured. Others were still in the act of hoisting up their breeches or struggling to fit into the tight chain mail shirts.

Edric had not expected so many warriors to be in the fortress, and could immediately see that his men were sorely outnumbered. 'Form a shieldwall,' he bellowed, then turning to Bleddyn he shouted, 'Have your archers follow Hywell up there,' pointing to the palisade. 'Show these Norman dogs what Welsh bowmen can do.'

Bleddyn smiled evilly, 'Indeed to goodness we shall do just that,' adding as he assembled at least fifty of his men, 'this will be much easier than shooting wild goats off our sacred mountains.' And he trotted lightly in front of his men leading them up the steps and onto the palisade where Hywell and his men, despite the loss of at least a dozen comrades to the deadly bolts from the defenders' crossbows, were in the act of hurling the final Norman bowman over the parapet where he fell screaming loudly, until his screams were cut off with a dull thud.

The Normans, under a huge captain, had also formed a shieldwall and the two lines of shields came together with a mighty crash, followed by the grunts, groans and screams of the two sides as they pushed, heaved, thrust and hacked at their opponents.

Men fell on both sides, but it was soon blatantly obvious to Edric that the Normans, with their larger kite-shaped shields and their well-rehearsed discipline were gaining the advantage against the mixed force of English and Welsh warriors. Who despite their courage, lacked the training and the iron discipline that these professional Norman warriors had attained over the course of their many years of warfare, both on the continent of Europe and here in England.

Relief came from the palisade as Welsh arrows began to rain upon the heads and unprotected backs of the Normans, who now found themselves surrounded by the Welshmen who held the walkways above their heads, and who now showered their them with yard long arrows, sending man after man to the ground, leaving holes in the Norman shieldwall, which allowed the screaming, avenging English and Welsh warriors through, striking left and right with axe, spear and sword.

The shattered Norman shieldwall was soon completely broken, resulting in scores of private duels which took place all across the courtyard, some of these duels were won by the better trained and more heavily protected Normans, but they were now in a minority and were being attacked from both the front and from the rear by their now more numerous enemies.

Some Normans found themselves surrounded by four or five English or Welshmen, causing them to cast down their weapons in disgust, in the hope that their victors would show mercy.

Some were disappointed and were slain on the spot, but more and more were made captives. Their weapons were taken from them as the defeated warriors were bundled into an ever-expanding circle of scowling prisoners who were ushered into one of the corners of the courtyard.

''Tis done,' bellowed Edric, and was cheered by the weary and, in many cases, bleeding victors as they slowly accepted the fact that the fighting was over and began to realise that they were victorious.

Prince Rhiwallon, who was clutching a gaping wound on the right-hand side of his neck that had stained his once white jerkin.

'What shall we do with these?' he asked, nodding his aching head towards the cluster of captives' Many of the captives were wounded, with no less than three lying prone upon the ground. Their fellows were attending two wounded men whilst a third lay unattended.

Edric had, as was his habit, already counted the prisoners who numbered some fifty-three souls, including the three that were on the ground.

'Have your men to usher them into one of those large huts,' he said nodding in the direction of a number of huts that huddled against the walls of the fortress.

The Welsh King issued the order, and a score of his warriors commenced to shepherd the scowling prisoners towards the largest of the huts, urging them on brutally with the hafts of their spears.

'Once they are all safely tucked away in that hut,' said Edric, 'place a few guards on the door and get that young man, what was his name? The one who speaks the language of Normandy.'

'Edgar, my lord,' came the reply from Evan who barely left Edric's side, except in the heat of battle. 'The man's name is Edgar, and he is indeed talented in the way of languages for he knows the sacred language of Wales.'

'Quite so, good Evan,' said Edric. 'Well, get him over here as soon as you can, I have need of such skill.'

Evan disappeared on his errand and returned some time later with the young interpreter at his side.

'You sent for me my lord,' said the youngster who appeared to have prospered somewhat since Edric had last seen him. His tunic was of the finest suede and he sported coloured breeches, knee-high expensive deerskin boots and one of the finest ornate leather belts that Edric had seen in many a day.

'I do indeed,' answered Edric, 'I need your skills in the language of these Normans. Find me one of rank. One who has the gift of self-importance and who will tell you what he knows of the plans of his masters, and tell the guards that you have my permission to speak with them.'

'Aye my lord, I will do my best,' answered the youth as he turned and made his way towards the prisoners' hut, knowing that he had been set a difficult and perhaps a dangerous mission.

He arranged that four of the serving maids and servants prepare and take trays laden with beer, bread and cheese to the Normans and accompanied them, with his sword drawn, on the pretext of protecting the servants.

He listened carefully as the maidens gave out the food and drink, aware that so far as he knew, none of the prisoners knew of his knowledge of their language, as indeed barely one in a thousand Englishmen knew a single word of the Norman tongue of their enemies.

'Beer and cheese,' snarled one man as he snatched a large chunk of cheese off one of the plates, 'don't these ignorant peasants know anything about good food? I'd give my right arm for a glass of good wine and a hock of good Norman ham boiled in garlic wine' he grumbled as he chewed on a mouthful of cheese.

'Different ways in different countries,' mumbled another.

'Aye, that's right,' said the next man sitting beside him as he dabbed at a gaping wound that stretched from his right ear to his chin. 'Better than nothing.'

'That is so,' said his companion. 'At least if they are feeding us, then the chances are that they won't be killing us.'

One or two of the men standing and sitting near him nodded their heads and grunted their approval.

Edgar smiled inwardly to himself thinking that whilst Edric seemed inclined to spare some of his prisoners, he was sure that the Welshmen kings would probably slaughter every mother's son for their clothes alone, plus the right to etch yet another blue tattoo onto their faces in order that they could boast to their friends of the number of foes that they had slain.

'Perhaps on the morrow I might find some ham,' said Edgar in the language of Normandy, startling the astounded Normans who were near enough to hear.

Musing to himself, he was thinking, I am not going to learn much if I can't talk to them, he added loudly, 'And I know the beer is not what you are used to, but it is the main drink here in England, and perhaps in time you may get to like it.'

'I think that highly unlikely,' came a more refined voice from the edge of the crowd. 'Oh it's acceptable if there is nothing else to drink, but what I don't like about it is the dregs that are left in the bottom of the tankard.'

'Ah well,' said Edgar with a smile, 'that's what gives it its body, but if you really don't like the dregs then it is best not to drain the tankard, is it not?'

Not quite a joke, thought Edgar, but perhaps enough to lighten the mood a little, we shall see, as he reached forward and offered the final chunk of cheese to the man who made the comment, smiling again as the man wrinkled up his nose and declined his offer.

The following morning Edgar, with Edric's permission, organised a more substantial meal to break the prisoners' fast, consisting of small beer, freshly baked bread, cheese (again) plus a large platter full of thick slices of fried ham. The Normans crowded noisily around the servants, snatching the food and literally gobbling it down greedily, quickly clearing the trays of the last vestiges of food and drink.

Edgar watched with some amusement, thinking to himself that if the tables had been turned, and the prisoners who were being fed were English, then the English captives would probably have formed a reasonably orderly queue, and waited their turn to be served, rather than fight and push as these ignorant Normans had just done.

Taking the opportunity, he casually walked his way through the crowded hut until he found the Norman who had spoken to him yesterday, and approached the man with a smile saying, 'How now gallant knight. What think you now of the fare?'

The man who had not seen him approach looked up with a start. Then realising who had spoken to him, answered in a more friendly way than he had spoken on their last meeting, 'Aye, Englishman. 'Tis a small improvement on my last meal,' came the answer as the man swallowed a large mouthful of ham. 'But a suckling pig and a roast fowl or two would have been more to my liking.'

Edgar, thinking that the man's answer and his expensive clothing seemed to indicate that he was a man of noble birth and therefore was used to eating richer fare, said 'Oh and I suppose that all of you Normans usually have suckling pig's to break your fast?'

'Not so,' came the reply followed by a snort, 'I am not really with this rabble.' He lifting his chin in a dignified way.

'I am a cousin to my lord, Roger de Montgomerie. He to whom the king has given this shire, and the title of the Earl of Shrewsbury, and my esteemed cousin has appointed me to be his sheriff.

'Alas,' he sighed again, 'a position that I have held for less than one solitary month before you savages attacked us.'

Edgar ignored the man's insult and stayed with him for some time before moving on, chatting as friendly as he could, forcing himself to speak to a number of other prisoners. He tried to select the ones who wore the most expensive clothing and were, perhaps, a little more friendly towards him than some of the others.

After over an hour with the prisoners he left their crowded quarters and sought out Edric. After a number of unhelpful directions, he found him below the watergate leaning against a willow tree, deep in conversation with his erstwhile companion Evan.

'My Lord Edric,' said Edgar. Edric and Evan spun on their heels for they had not seen or heard his approach down the shaded track that led to the deep, placid river named Sabrina.

'Pray forgive me for the interruption, but I think that I have found a man amongst the captives from whom we may be able to glean news.' He explained his thoughts to Edric and his friend who, after carefully listening to the plan that Edgar had devised, agreed saying, 'We shall do as you say, good Edgar, have the man moved to a private room.'

After a thought he added, 'Befriend him, but keep him well guarded, and if you allow him to accompany you outside the fortress, make sure that at least one guard walks with you, I suggest Hugh the bowman. He's a good man, and let the Norman see a demonstration of Hugh's skill so that he is aware that should he be foolish enough to try to escape, then a yard-long shaft with a grey goose feather could easily be placed between his shoulders.'

Hugh the bowman was more than pleased to undertake guard duty. At the present time most of his fellow warriors were labouring with their shirts off, in a hurried attempt to remove scores of rotten timbers from the palisade and replace them with new timbers hauled from the forest of Hughsmond, some four or five miles away to the east.

Edric and Evan continued their conversation.

'The Welsh kings want me to march on to Hereford. But I think that as we are this far north, then, unless we hear that William has his moved his army from the east then we should consider widening our domain in the Midlands by taking and holding the city of Chester.

'The last we heard of him he was bogged down in the eastern Fens, fighting against Hereward and his band of cut-throats.'

'I do agree with you Edric, but we have received no news from Chester, or indeed from the shire of Cheshire these long months past. And the King could have killed or captured Hereward and be marching towards us even as we speak.'

Edric visibly winched at the name 'King'.

'He is not my King,' he spat.

'Sorry my lord. 'Twas but a slip of the tongue.'

'I will send a few horsemen onto the Cheshire plains and see what news they can glean.'

They turned and walked under the watergate and up the slippery, muddy lane, around the castle walls and re-entered the noise and hubbub of the bustling fortress.

*****

The first of the scouts returned nine days later, quickly followed by two others, all reporting to Edric news that he had not wanted to hear.

The enemy has taken the complete shire, they confirmed, and nearly every town and village had been occupied by them, with every town of note now fortified by deep ditches and stockades built of either wood or stone.

But the news that truly horrified Edric and all that heard it, English and Welshmen alike, was that the holy shrine of Saint Werburgh in Chester had been totally destroyed, and the stone from the holy shrine had been dismembered and used to repair the old Roman walls. These were, according to one of the scouts now some thirty feet high and ten feet thick, manned and patrolled by one of King William's most able lieutenants. The town would, if he rumours were to be believed, be impossible to take by storm.

Saint Werburgh was one of the holiest of the Christian saints, for she had been the granddaughter of Ercombert of Kent, and her father, Wulfhere, who was himself the son of Penda, had been one of the fiercest of the kings of Mercia.

She had been a beautiful English princess, who was reputed to be able to perform miraculous deeds, such as bringing dead animals and birds back to life, and when, nine years after her death, her body was exhumed for its removal to a much holier abode, it was found to be totally untouched by the ravages of death, and was still that of a maiden in the first bloom of her life.

The Welsh kings met with Edric in the evening to discuss the situation, and Edric was forced to agree that to attack the city of Chester was out of the question, due to the strength of the fortress.

However all three agreed that they should march into the shire in order to ravage and destroy as many Norman holdings as they were able before they marched southwards towards Hereford.

'That is what we wanted all along,' chorused the two Welsh kings.

'Look you,' said Prince Rhiwallon scowling, for although he had been slightly reluctant to march on Chester, his greed for the rich loot that he had expected to reap from the rich plains of that shire had overruled his good sense, making him the most eager of the three to march to the north.

'There are Normans to kill in the shire of Hereford and rich pickings for our men,' said Prince Rhiwallon. His tattooed face broke out into a wicked grin as his mind thought of the rich pickings that he, as prince of his people would win, for the title of prince gave him the right to one third of all of the rich pickings that his warriors may take from the shire.

King Bleddyn, who disliked being outdone by his friend and rival said, 'After a few weeks of foraging in the Cheshire lowlands I will stay here with a few score of my men and hold the town, just in case these Norman rascals think of returning.' He added with a crafty smile, 'Perhaps some of these idle sods who I have seen lounging about the town can be persuaded to join my warriors,' knowing full well that such a thing was, to say the least, unlikely. As there was still much bitterness between the townspeople of Shrewsbury and the Welsh, probably due to the past five hundred or so years of warfare between the two peoples, a fact that all the men present were aware of, especially the two Welsh kings.

Nonetheless he continued, 'Naturally, as lord of the fortress I shall be entitled to the usual tithes, one tenth of all that enters and leaves the town, is that not so?' he asked.

Edric, fully aware of the law, was forced to nod and grunt his assent, not really happy at the Welsh king's decision, and even less happy that he and a large number of his warriors would not be available to accompany him and his men southwards.

CHAPTER 11

After marauding on a wide scale across the Cheshire plains to within sight of the walled city of Chester, Edric turned his army southwards and commenced his march towards Hereford.

The march was long and dreary, along muddy pot-holed roads, through teeming rain that blew horizontally into the faces of men and beasts as they trudged under dripping woodlands that gave them little or no relief. Edric was forced to call for an early halt and make their camp a mile or so short of his old home of Stretton.

He knew that for the sake of the men and pack animals, he should have spent the night at Stretton. Yet pride and perhaps old memories prevented him from doing so.

During the night the weather became even more savage. The rain turned into sleet, which soaked through the thickest leather, preventing men from sleeping as they huddled together under whatever makeshift cover they could find to shield themselves from the elements.

By daybreak the sleet abated into a fine drizzle which continued until noon, whereupon the skies cleared and a weak sun attempted to peek through the grey clouds that still hung in the heavens.

They marched passed the old fortress of Stretton, from which the people waved and cheered at the small army as it made its way along the old Roman road. No less than ten young, sturdy warriors from the township joined them.

At the hamlet of Stokesay another small band of warriors swelled their numbers, grumbling slightly about the weather, for they had been waiting for Edric for the past three days. Edric greeted these men, especially the leader, a small, thickset man, who wore his grey hair in two braids which hung down the side of his face, onto his calfskin jacket.

'We be from the valley of the Clunn, but this man here' – dragging a reluctant young man forward – 'is from the town of Ludlow, where he says the Normans have occupied the town and erected a fortress on the site where the old ancient British fortress stood.'

'Is that so?' asked Edric.

''Tis so lord Edric,' came the reply in a broad Clunn accent, 'they bin there some weeks now, and 'ave built a large fort. Seen it myself, I have.'

'How big is it?'

'Massive milord, massive,' came the answer.

'As big as the one at Richard's castle?' asked Edric.

'Dunnow,' was the reply. 'Never seed that one.'

Realising that he would get no further with the man, but thanking him for his information, Edric decided that he would need to see the structure for himself before making a decision of whether or not to attack and capture it.

He made camp at the small hamlet of Broomfield, a mere mile away from the town of Ludlow. Ludlow was a prosperous town, noted for its wool trade, spawning many large houses built by wealthy wool merchants. These had, in turn, attracted other tradesmen to the town, making it one of the wealthiest places in the entire county.

Edric told his men that this night they were to make a cold camp. On no occasion were they to light fires or make merry, a point that he stressed to his captains, telling them, 'I know they have had a long march and deserve a tankard of ale for their troubles, but if they drink too much there will be fights, and fights produce noise, and if we want to take yonder fortress then it is best that the Normans are unaware of our presence until we are ready to show ourselves to them.'

Once dusk had fallen he led King Rhiwallon, Hywell, Evan and Garth into the town, up the slippery hill, through deserted wet streets, past rain-sodden thatched houses that led to the mound where they had been told the Normans had built their fortress.

The massive fortress was not as large as they had been led to believe, being about half as large as Shrewsbury castle. Yet while it was mainly constructed of wood, huge piles of stone lay in the deep dry moat ready to be added to the stone wall that was already some four or five feet high.

'I can only see one gate,' whispered Evan.

'Aye,' agreed Rhiwallon, 'and it looks pretty sturdy to me.'

'Strong is a better word,' said Edric in a low voice, as he continued to walk around the perimeter of the fortress, hoping to find an unfinished part of the stockade or a vulnerable point where his men could get in.

Despite slipping and sliding on the embankment on the western side of the fortress, their progress was brought to a halt by a steep precipice. One that ended in a sheer drop to the River Corve which bubbled over huge boulders, some two hundred or so feet below, forcing them to retrace their steps and to return to the one and only gate.

They returned in silence, through the wet streets, down the hill, then back into their camp. Edric led them into the one and only tent that was large enough to accommodate them, evicting several men who had discovered the empty tent and had already commandeered it, and were found to be fast asleep when their leaders entered, forcing the unhappy warriors out into the cold, wet night.

'If we try to take the place by storm,' said Edric, 'we will lose many good men.'

'Only if they see us coming,' chirped Hywell in his high-pitched voice, 'Why not do what my grandfather, Madoc the Lucky did,' he suggested. 'Wait somewhere close to the gates with a few good bowmen, and take the gate that way.'

Edric frowned at the suggestion for it had instantly brought back memories of his childhood, when his own village had been destroyed by Madoc, the only man in those days who owned one of these now more familiar kite-shaped shields. He still remembered Hywell's grandfather as the man who had slain his own Mother and Father.

His dark thoughts were interrupted.

'Might work,' said Garth whose own family had also been slain by Madoc in the same raid, but he was, perhaps a little thicker skinned than Edric, and seemed to have blotted out those bitter childhood memories from his mind.

'I'm for an all-out assault,' growled Rhiwallon, 'got me some of the finest archers in Wales, probably England too,' adding with a satanic grin, 'soon knock those bloody Normans off their precious walls.'

'Sounds a good idea to me,' said the ever-cheerful Earl Hunwald.

The supposedly dim yokel from Clunn, who had been standing in the doorway, stood on his toes so that his face just reached over the shoulder of the man who was directly in front of him, chirped up in his strange accent, ''Scuse me buttin in milords, but me brother Athelbert is a baker in the town, and 'e takes bread into the castle every day, p'haps 'e could open yon gate for 'ee?'

'Where does this brother of yours live?' asked Edric.

'On the 'ill near the castle,' came the reply.

Edric beckoned the man forward. 'Make way for our friend,' he said. 'Tell me young man, how are you called?'

'Oi be Edmund of the black 'ill.'

'I'd like to meet this brother of yours,' said Edric placing his arm around Edmund's shoulder. 'Will you take me to him?'

'Certainly milord,' came the pleasant reply. 'But 'e do start early you know, bein' a baker loike. ''E 'as to be at the fortress by first loight.'

'Well it is nearly midnight now,' said Edric. 'Rhiwallon? Get fifty of those archers of yours and meet me here in an hour.'

Rhiwallon smiled one of his evil smiles forcing the dark blue tattoos to wrinkle up into an even more hideous pattern than it had already was. 'Aye lord Edric,' he said as he left the tent.

Turning to Garth Edric said, 'Have fifty of your best men to follow us up into the town. Keep them hidden in the cottages near the fortress.'

Garth nodded, grunted assent and left on the heels of Rhiwallon.

'Hywell, you and I will accompany Edmund to his brother's house, where we can finalise our plan.'

Giving orders for the bulk of his small army to follow and hold themselves in reserve at the top of the hill, Rhiwallon, Garth and Hywell with their assembled men left the camp soon after Edric had explained his plan to them. Leaving in small groups in order to be as quiet as possible and not raise the suspicion of the townsfolk who, Edric was sure, despite almost all of them being English, there was always the odd man in any group who would sell his grandmother for a silver penny. He did not want some disgruntled soul lumbering up to the gate and raising the alarm.

Thankfully the rain had stopped and Edric noted that the Welsh bowmen were busy holding out each arrow in turn, peering down the shaft which they held in their outstretched arms, looking along the arrow to ensure that it would fly straight and true. Other archers were taking their dry bowstrings out of their greased leather pouches and stringing their bows in readiness for the coming conflict.

'I like the look of your men,' he said to Rhiwallon, who strode alongside him,

'Aye they are good lads,' came the answer, 'many of them have been with me since they were breeched, and every last one of them have the mark of more than one kill tattooed above their eyes.'

Edric said nothing after that last remark for, although he knew that some of the Welsh warrior's tattoos represented men killed in battle, there were so many other tattoos on the men's faces, depicting tribes, families, married men and probably a dozen other reasons. He had never known what each different mark meant, considering it wise never to broach the subject with them.

As they moved up the slippery hill, he strayed into a dream which took him into his last battle, when he had fought with Madoc the Lucky, Hywel's own grandfather. He could still see the man's grinning face floated before him, his yellow teeth, and his reeking breath causing him to remember, or perhaps he imagined that he remembered that on Madoc's face, which had hovered a few inches above his own, as the Welsh chieftain had attempted to drive his famous long knife into Edric's belly, he saw a mass of blue tattoos above the man's eyes, and wondered if some of those hideous tattoos had represented the slaying of his own parents.

The thoughts brought a spasm of shudders throughout his body, causing him to turn his mind towards the matter in hand.

Before they reached the bakery his men had been dispersing, slipping into alleyways and corners, behind carts and into shadowy doorways where, upon the command of their leaders, they would bellow their war-cries and assault the Normans who now held the town.

Edmund halted before one of the doors, looked carefully around him before he knocked twice, then paused and knocked again, paused again, then knocked twice.

''Tis our family signal,' he whispered to Edric. 'No one else knows it.' An instant later a light appeared from inside the house, and a large individual opened the door, a man who was so unlike Edmund as chalk is to cheese.

'Let us in,' he whispered, and the door opened just enough to allow the three individuals through. 'This be me brother Athelbert,' he said. 'He be the foinest baker in Ludler.'

Where Edmund was small, ferrety faced and grubby, Athelbert was tall, enormously fat, with a large round face that gleamed as if it had been scoured with sandstone.

Athelbert nodded towards Edric and Garth without a word, then he was ushered down a short hallway led like a tame bull by his smaller brother into the room where Edmund spoke to him in such a manner that, to Edric, it seemed that it was as if a lord was talking to his serf.

Athelbert turned and disappeared into a room at the rear of the house whilst Edmund returned to Edric, ''E's gotta get back to 'is bakin' milords,' he explained. 'Else this last batch will be burned, follow me and we'll have a tankard of small beer and warm ourselves by 'is fire while we waits.' He led them into yet another room where a small log fire crackled away, taking the chill off the damp, morning air.

'Will he lead us into the castle?' asked Edric

'Oh 'e'll do it milord, but 'e's non too happy though. See it's 'is livelihood innit? Made 'im wealthy loike, but I promised 'im that you will see him roite if 'e 'elps us.'

Edric nodded, still unsure whether or not this plan was going to work but grunted his thanks just as a pretty young girl entered with a foaming jug of small beer and three empty tankards. These she promptly filled and handed to her uncle, Edric and Garth.

CHAPTER 12

Earl Hunwald stood in a darkened alleyway a mere hundred yards from the front gate of the fortress. This was illuminated by two large torches positioned on either side of the gate, plus two additional and larger torches that threw a beam of light from the stone battlements above the gate some twenty or so feet beyond the actual gate itself, allowing Edric to be able to identify the figures of four sentries, two on either side of the gate.

Earl Hunwald was standing behind two warriors who, tired of standing in a damp alley and staring into the darkness, had decided to squat and roll a dice for a silver ring which lay in front of them on the muddy, slimy ground.

'That's three to me and one to you,' said one man happily. 'That puts me two up. Another two and I shall be the owner of your fine ring.'

The second man scowled, taking up the dice, which he placed in the cup of both hands, shaking them rigorously by his right ear before he threw the dice onto the floor.

'Five,' said the man.

The other man nodded and grunted in agreement then took the dice.

'My turn,' he said, then shaking the dice much the same as the other man had done, but with much more vigour. He cast the dice onto the ground and leant forward to see how it had landed.

The razor-sharp dagger, which Hunwald had silently slipped out of its oily fleece-lined sheath, slashed across the man's outstretched neck sending a cascade of blood onto the floor. Slowly the dying man collapsed into the growing pool of his own blood.

His friend, stunned and not quite able to register what had just happened, looked up into the smiling face of Earl Hunwald, allowing Hunwald to grab the man's hair, thrust his head forward and draw his knife across the back of the man's neck, severing the spinal cord and sending the man onto the back of his already dead friend.

Earl Hunwald wiped his knife on the second man's jerkin, replaced it carefully into its sheath, then fumbled about in the blood until he found the ring that the two men had been dicing for.

He wiped the ring clean before placing it carefully into one of the many pockets in his jerkin, 'Shame to let a gem such as this go to waste,' he mumbled to himself, as he carefully looked around to ensure that no one had witnessed his actions.

Not a thing stirred in the street ahead of him. After a second, long look, he crept slowly out, flitting silently from shadow to shadow, making his way towards the gateway.

He had not gone totally unseen, for as he silently glided past an alley that was partially blocked by a small cart, a Welsh bowman caught a fleeting glimpse of a figure as it passed from one shadow to another.

The man nudged his companion who was one of ten archers, huddled together in the darkness, 'Look you there,' he whispered in an excited voice, 'I just saw someone go past, heading for the fort they was.'

'Where?' asked the other fellow who was in fact the first man's cousin, 'There, look you.' he said pointing towards a dark spot where he had seen the shadow disappear into.

'Can't see nothing,' came the reply, but then just as he had finished speaking, the shadow moved from one spot to another, which was a little nearer to the gateway.

'Good God Owen,' he said. 'You're right, I see him too. Hey you lot,' he whispered in a slightly louder voice, 'String your bows, I think we have a spy trying to warn those Norman dogs.'

'Better warn Lord Rhiwallon,' said Owen. 'You Elwyn, you're the youngest, sprint over to that house, yes that's the one two doors away, and tell his lordship that we think there's a spy trying to get to the gate.'

Elwyn leapt to his feet and speedily sprinted to the door which, much to his surprise, was unlatched, allowing him to burst in where he found Lord Rhiwallon, Lord Edric, Garth and Edmund seated by the now dying embers of a fire.

'Lord, come quick,' gasped Elwyn. 'We think we have spotted a traitor trying to reach the gate and raise the alarm.'

Each man snatched up his weapons and shield and rushed to the door. 'Where?' demanded Rhiwallon, peering into the still darkened streets.

'We saw him there,' answered Elwyn, pointing to the deep shadows where the man had been last seen.

'Can't see him now,' said Rhiwallon.

'Neither can I,' confirmed Edric who was also peering into the blackness.

'Where are the archers?' demanded Edric.

'With me, my lord,' answered the youth. 'Two or three doorways down.'

'Lead the way.'

'Aye my lord,' said the youth as he noiselessly led the way back to his friends.

They followed him silently into the alleyway where the bowmen were hidden and although they had expected some reaction to their supposed sighting of a traitor, they had not really expected to be joined by his lordship himself, AND Lord Edric (nicknamed the Wild, also called by some, Edric the Savage.)

'How many bowmen do you have here?' demanded Rhiwallon.

'Ten my lord,' came the answer.

To Edric it had been a futile question, for as he had entered the alleyway, and despite the poor light, he had already counted ten men.

'I still do not see him,' said Edric, 'but if he really is where you say he is, then he is already within shouting distance of the fort and could raise the alarm at any moment.'

Turning to Garth he said, 'Be ready with that hunting horn and upon my order, give the signal to attack, for it seems that our carefully laid plans to use the baker may come to naught.

'Lord Rhiwallon? Get your bowmen out of this damp alleyway. Have three of them to aim their shafts towards the spy, and the rest of them to send their shafts at those four sentries on the walls.' He added grimly, 'Then with the few scaling ladders and ropes that we have and with a little help from Woden we shall wipe out this nest of wasps.'

'Jesus Christ's help,' corrected Rhiwallon grimly.

'Quite so, quite so,' mumbled Edric, realising that at times like these, he had often been unsure whether or not he was a true Christian, preferring Woden, the god of war to the peace-loving Christian god, whose priests were continually droning on about 'turning the other cheek'.

After quite a long time a shadow moved into the open and raced towards the gate. Only to be overtaken by three yard-long shafts that thudded into his back with such force that they sent him onto his face in a puddle on the side of the street.

'What was tha'?' said one of the sentries, but was prevented from finishing the sentence by two arrows, one in his chest and a second in his throat.

The three other sentries fell, studded with arrows, grunting with shock and horror as they tumbled onto the walkway from which they had been peering into the blackness in one vain, last attempt to see what the slight noise that they had heard as Earl Hunwald fell.

Garth blew one deep note and his horn and charged forward towards the gate, followed by a horde of screaming English and Welsh warriors, pleased to be in action after waiting around in damp alleyways and dark doorways for so long.

They reached the gate and walls, milling about in confusion until, after what seemed to be a terminally long wait, three men with ladders arrived, plus half a dozen with knotted ropes with slats of wood tied on the end.

The ladders were immediately placed against the wall whilst the men who held the ropes heaved them over the parapet, hoping that the slats would catch on something in order for them to clamber up.

Suddenly a solitary sentry appeared on the walkway and began shouting at the top of his voice, 'Alarm, alarm, alarm!' whilst hacking at one of the ropes that had lodged itself in a cranny.

The moments that it took the guard to cut through the rope cost him his life. Even as he shouted, Edric was scaling one of the ladders whilst Garth was scrambling up another. A wiry Welsh warrior was nearing the top of the third ladder, all reaching the top at practically the same moment, and leaping onto the walkway.

Garth was the nearest to the guard. Realising that an enemy had actually gained the walkway, he thrust his shield in front of him and, taking up the conventional stance, thrust his short sword in front of him as he advanced towards the crouching figure of the big Englishman. This may have been a good move if he had additional warriors alongside him who had formed a small shieldwall, or even if the man who faced him had been an ordinary English warrior. Yet Garth, with his massive size, his huge strength and his years of combat experience was no ordinary warrior, and immediately charged the guard.

He struck his own shield against his opponent's shield with such force that the man was thrust backwards as if he had been a bag of feathers. He landed on his back with his shield still in front of him, protecting his face and chest, with his sword still pointing upwards towards Garth's groin.

Garth almost casually, but with great force, hooked his great war-axe over the man's shield and wrenched it away from the man, then brought the axe down with a thud into the man's chest.

Whilst this personal combat had taken place, many other vicious fights were taking place on the walkway as well as on the stairs, causing the inside of the castle to echo with the clash of weapons and the shouts and screams of the dying men, rousing the remainder of the sleeping garrison.

Norman warriors began to erupt out of many of the doorways, which were situated on the ground floor in and around the main keep. Soon the courtyard, stairways and walkways were alive with Normans, many in various stages of dress and undress, but all carrying shields and weapons, running towards the attackers who were still in the process of gaining access to the fortress by way of the three ladders and the few precarious ropes now hanging over the walls on both sides of the gate.

'Quick!' bellowed Edric. 'Follow me down there.' He pointed to the gate, 'Help me open the gate and let our men in.'

Not waiting to see if anyone had heard him, or looking to see if any warriors were following him, Edric leapt from the walkway onto the cobbled courtyard, rolling, exactly as old Vorta had taught him many, many years ago. He ended up on his feet with his shield held before him and his sword ready to fend off any attack.

One man bellowed the old Saxon war-cry which was quickly taken up by the rest of the English attackers, including the men who were still outside the wall as they roared, 'OUT, OUT, OUT!'

Edric's waiting was swiftly ended as a huge Norman warrior, whose helmet covered his head and had cheek guards with a steel neck brace, but wore no mail and nothing whatsoever below his waist, charged into him, forcing him back several paces. Yet without breaking through his guard, as Edric returned the Norman's attack with a savage swipe of his sword which, in turn, was parried by the Norman's iron-rimmed shield.

He retreated a further two paces, pleasingly aware of more and more of his own warriors swinging themselves down from the walkway into the courtyard. A few tried to jump, and of the few that tried, one broke his ankle in the attempt and was speedily slain by two furious defenders.

The Norman charged into him again, thrusting his kite-shaped shield into Edric's smaller round-shield with such force that he drove Edric back yet again towards the inner side of the fortress's wall.

Two more Norman warriors joined the first man and Edric found himself facing three screaming and half-dressed, yet fully armed warriors who, forming a small shieldwall, advanced towards him, their kite-shaped shields showing no more than their eyes, out of which protruded two wicked-looking Norman swords, plus one long spear.

The man in the centre of the trio jabbed his spear over the locked shields towards Edric's face, narrowly missing his eyes as the razor-sharp, leaf-shaped spearhead glanced off his helmet, leaving a loud ringing sound in his head as Edric attempted to sidestep the blow, parrying a sword thrust with his shield and meeting the third man's sword thrust with his own sword.

Edric was driven back until he reached the stockade wall and could go no further as he parried and attempted to ward off the attack from the three determined warriors who were vigorously trying to slay him.

Help came from a most unexpected quarter. To his amazement, Edric saw the fat, lumbering figure of Athelbert the Baker, still white with flour, swing himself down off the stockade to one side of the Normans, and, armed with no more than a large, well-worn knife, he hurled himself bodily into the Norman trio, knocking two of them to the floor whilst he sank his knife into the unprotected neck of the third.

Before the two Normans could recover, Edric pounced on them like a lion, slaying them with two deadly strokes of his sword before they could scramble to their feet

Similar combats were taking place all over the courtyard with the still outnumbered English warriors being eliminated one by one as the more heavily armoured and better trained Normans, now under the command of a knight who had suddenly emerged and taken control of the situation, and had begun to organise his men into a solid shieldwall.

Edric realised that all would soon be lost unless he could reach the gate and open it, in order to allow the rest of his men into the fortress. Then, and only then, might he just have enough men to break the Norman shieldwall.

'Follow me,' he bellowed to the few men who were within hearing distance, then followed by half a dozen men, including the large, lumbering figure of Athelbert, as well as the killing machine who bore the name of Garth Bloodaxe, they charged towards the gate. Bowling men over as they charged, reaching the gate that was guarded by no less than ten stern-faced Normans, who – upon seeing these blood-covered savages bearing down upon them, knocking warrior after warrior to the ground as they did so, felt their courage drain away, like a light April shower that used to drain into the soft white sands, on the serene beach in Normandy where this small contingent of Normans had once called home.

One man turned and ran and his friends, seeing the wisdom of his ways, followed him, leaving the gate, that had been their sole duty to guard, totally unguarded.

Garth and Athelbert heaved the heavy blocking beam off its hinges and the single gate swung open. To the delight and cheers of the horde of English and Welsh warriors who had been assembled around the gate, awaiting their turns to scale the ladders and ropes in order to gain access to the fortress.

They surged in en masse, crashing into the Norman shieldwall, roaring OUT! OUT! as they fell upon their opponents.

The Norman shieldwall did not break.

The young, the rash and the inexperienced died within moments, whilst the veterans, Welsh and English stood back, as the Norman shieldwall began to advance, the English were slowly forced backwards towards the open gate through which they had, a few brief minutes before charged through with such gusto.

'Give me your best men,' yelled Edric to the Welsh king, who immediately nominated ten of his largest and most experienced warriors. 'They will smash yon puny wall,' bellowed Rhiwallon, as his men clustered around their lord and Edric, who had in turn beckoned a small number of his own men to him.

'Give me your axe,' he said to one youthful warrior, 'and you can have my own sword until I return your axe to you.' Then, grasping the axe, he said in a sinister voice, 'Garth, I want you and half a dozen axemen to join me in the van of our men. The rest of you follow us. As soon as we have broken through, you can create havoc amongst them.'

'Quickly now, follow me!' he bellowed. He then led his men forward, stopping some five feet from the Norman line, just out of the range of the hedge of spears that protruded out of their shieldwall.

'You know what to do,' he bellowed, 'when I say go, GO!' he shouted and his battle line surged forward.

One of his axemen was instantly skewered by a spear before he reached the shields, but all of the remaining men in the van of the attack managed to hook their battle-axes over the rim of the shields in order to pull them down and allow his own spearmen to attack the parts of the Normans that would be exposed by this very risky manoeuvre.

However, most of the Normans were seasoned warriors and were well aware of these sorts of tactics, having experienced them in continental Europe. They knew that in order to prevent their shields from being wrenched downwards by this manoeuvre, all they had to do was to thrust their one knee forward against their own shields to counterbalance the move, thus preventing their shield from tilting forward.

Almost all of the Norman warriors performed the manoeuvre correctly, thus counteracting the English warriors' ploy and denying their opponents the luxury of exposing their bodies to their attackers weapons. Yet in three cases the shields did come down, and in two of these cases, the shield straps were wrenched so violently that they snapped, yielding the shields useless and allowing their owners to be attacked by spears from their English attackers.

Garth had hooked his axe over the rim of the Norman's shield and had physically heaved the shield, including the man who still held on to his shield, completely off his feet. Whereupon he dispatched him with a savage blow that took the man's head clean off, sending it rolling forward below the feet of the dead warrior's stunned companions.

Garth then stepped forward swinging his axe to the right, then to the left, slaying two Normans in the process, thus making a large hole in the Norman shieldwall.

Edric, who had been fighting alongside Garth, followed by more and more men, charged into the broken shieldwall, dealing death and destruction as they went, and causing panic amongst their enemies – who until this very moment had believed, and had been told, time and time again, that they were invincible, and there was no power on earth that could break a Norman shieldwall.

To Edric, who was aware of most of the fights that were taking place around him, knew full well that 'battle luck' was either with you or perhaps against you, for he had seen many warriors die who did not deserve to die, whilst others who were perhaps either stupid or careless, or both, and as such they should have died, yet they did not, and survived the slaughter.

The English and Welsh warriors offered no quarter, killing any Norman that they could find, clearing the courtyard of their foes, except for a small knot of bloodied Normans who clustered around their battered and broken shields in one corner of the enclosure.

'Archers,' bellowed Rhiwallon, and twenty or thirty Welsh bowmen trotted forward, many holding wads of dry sphagnum moss against wounds that they had received in the fighting, 'Kill that lot,' he ordered and the bowmen casually stretched their bowstrings taut and sent a deadly shower of arrows into the huddle of Normans who attempted to shelter behind their shattered shields.

'No!' shouted Edric, as he suddenly realised what his ally was doing, but it was too late. At least a quarter of the defeated Normans had already fallen to the arrow storm.

He quickly made his way to the angry Rhiwallon, who was furious that his orders had been countermanded. 'I ordered them slain,' said Rhiwallon, glaring into the bloody face of Edric, his own blue tattoos appearing to grow with his fury. 'Who are you to gainsay my orders?' he snarled.

'Not so, good Rhiwallon,' said Edric, forcing himself to smile at the still scowling Welsh king, 'We need information and we cannot get news from dead Normans, also' – he placed his arm across the man's shoulder in order to consolidate the friendship that he had with Rhiwallon, a friendship that he now felt he was in danger of losing – 'a few Norman prisoners can be no bad thing, if not for ransom, then perhaps the slave block in Brittany.' He knew full well that much of Rhiwallon's great wealth did not come from the selling of wool (as he had so often claimed) nor did it come from the specks of gold that could be found in the Welsh mountains, but did indeed come from the buying and the selling of slaves.

A sly smile creased the Welsh king's face, making the tattoos around the corners of his eyes rise as if in pleasure, 'Quite right my friend,' he said. 'I was allowing my hatred of these dogs to over-ride my good sense. That's enough now my beauties,' he shouted to his men, 'disarm the rest and lock 'em up somewhere safe.' Then turning to Edric and placing his own blood-soaked right arm across Edric's shoulders, he said in a jovial way, 'Come my friend, let us seek out a cosy nook and a jug or two of this famous Norman wine that these dogs are always going on about.' And he led Edric through an iron studded-door into what must have been the castle commander's quarters.

'Pah!' he exclaimed in disgust as he overturned several leather bottles which had obviously been emptied the previous night. 'Naught here but empty flagons, come, follow me, I have a nose for good wine,' and he led the way through another doorway, halting abruptly as soon as he had entered the room.

He had halted so suddenly that Edric nearly bumped into him, causing Edric to be on his guard, snatching the sword out of its wool lined sheath in readiness to confront the danger that had caused the Welsh prince to stop so abruptly.

Yet Rhiwallon had not reached for his weapon, and as Edric could not see past the large figure of the king, he surmised that one of three things must have happened, the first was that the Welshman had been pierced with a spear and was already dead but had not yet fallen, the second was that he was threatened by an enemy or, perhaps, a number of his enemies who covered him with either longbows or those deadly little dart-throwing crossbows.

Or perhaps in the third instance he was not menaced by any danger at all, and was, perhaps, standing in amazement at some fine Norman painting or tapestry, or maybe a vast chest of jewels.

CHAPTER 13

Rhiwallon stepped a couple of paces forward allowing Edric to enter the room warily, with his sword held forward in readiness for a fight. Yet his sword-arm slowly drooped downwards as he stared, mouth open at the two expensively dressed, extremely beautiful women who stood in the centre of the room, each holding a glass of red wine, one also holding a bottle in her other hand, both smiling sweetly at the two heathens who had just interrupted their party.

'One each,' said Rhiwallon with a gruff voice.

'Nay friend,' came the reply, 'I am forsworn.'

'Pity, I'll be forced to take the two then,' grinning like a Cheshire cat as he entered the room.

Edric replaced his sword, trying to look casual as he did so.

The two ladies did not attempt to move but stood close together as the two blood-splattered warriors approached them.

'Fear not,' said Edric, 'we mean you no harm,' but the ladies remained silent and did not respond to him.

'They don't understand you,' said Rhiwallon, 'Let me try.' He spoke kind words in the language of Wales, explaining that nobles such as he and his friend Edric were bound by a code of conduct which demanded that they treated ladies of noble birth with kindness and compassion, whilst silently cursing himself for being such a fool, as these two ladies were the kind of women that most men met only in their dreams, or perhaps when they are in their cups.

Again the ladies glanced at each other and shook their heads, saying 'No,' several times, obviously unable to understand what the Welsh king had said.

'Wait here,' said Edric. 'I'll go and find someone who speaks their language and don't let them out of your sight.'

'Hardly likely, my friend, two beautiful ladies and a jug full of wine. Now am I likely to desert them? I ask you.' Stepping forward and reaching for the bottle which the lady promptly gave him, then after a quick glance around the room.

He walked over to a table at the far end of the room where a number of empty glasses awaited him.

Edric speedily left the room and began searching for Edgar, who was the only man that he knew who could speak the language of the Normans.

After an exhaustive search through throngs of jubilant Welsh and English warriors, who were scattered all over the fortress, some looting or squabbling over various pieces of loot, or dicing for an odd item of value, or else binding their own wounds or tending to the wounds of a fellow warrior, he eventually found Edgar who was in the process of consoling Edmund of Clunn who was openly weeping over the large body of his brother, Athelbert.

''E never should 'ave come 'ere,' he sobbed, 'weren't cut out for fightin', was 'e?' He sobbed as he looked up into the sad face of Edgar.

'He was a good man,' said Edric, 'and a fine warrior. I am sad for your loss, does he have any children,' asked Edric.

'Aye lord, 'e do 'ave four little 'uns, well one of 'em is as big as me.' He added, ''Es a pretty good baker an all, perhaps 'im and me can take over where poor Athelbert left orf.' He tried hard to force his lips into something that resembled a smile.

Edric placed his hand on Edgar's shoulder saying, 'Come with me young Edgar, I have need of your services,' leaving the grieving Edmund with his brother's body as he and Edgar made their way to the room where he had left Rhiwallon and the two Norman ladies.

He found the three laughing as if not one of them had a care in the world, due to the strange antics that Rhiwallon was performing with one empty glass balanced on each of his shoulders, whilst the full bottle was balanced on his forehead as he hopped about like a four-year-old child, singing in his deep baritone voice that neither Edric or the Norman ladies could understand.

The appearance of Edric and Edgar caused Rhiwallon to lose concentration and both of the expensive glasses to crash to the floor sending shards of glass in all directions, followed by screeches of laughter from the ladies. Yet it did not cause the Welsh king to drop the full bottle of wine, which remained safely in his strong hands.

'Here is our interpreter,' said Edric to Rhiwallon who was striding over to the far table to obtain more glasses for the ladies, Edric and himself.

'Good, let us hear from these two foreigners what we will,' he said in a voice that had changed from a laughing youngster into a stern king of his realm in the space of two seconds flat.

Edric nodded to Edgar, 'Ask who is the lady here and who is the servant,' he said.

'Oh that's simple my Lord,' answered Edgar. 'The lady in blue is the mistress and the other lady is her companion, for only ladies of nobility can wear such attire.'

'Oh,' said Edric, stunned that such a simple solution had eluded him. 'Well ask them, or rather ask her if her lord is amongst the slain. Or perhaps he is captured, then ask her that if it is so, would she be kind enough to point him out to us so that if he is alive, we may honour him and treat him according to his rank? And if he is amongst the slain then we can bury him with the full honours that a man of his rank deserves.'

After what seemed to Edric and the Welsh king to be a long, heated and garbled tirade of gobbledegook from Edgar, a rather amused Edgar turned to Edric.

'The ladies say that their lord is the Lord Ralph Mortimer, this lady's Husband.' He pointed to the lady. 'She is named Isabella and her husband, luckily for him,' he added with a wry smile, 'is away with William of Normandy, fighting Hereward the wake in some distant marshlands in the east of the country.'

'Not so lucky for her though, is it?' said Rhiwallon with a lecherous smile.

'Maybe not,' answered Edric, 'but in her, we have a valuable asset,' adding, 'worth her weight in gold, like as not.'

'No virgin though,' said the King, 'so no one will know if the mare has been ridden once or twice, will they?'

'That may be so, my friend,' answered Edric with a frown. 'But this mare has a tongue, and seems to be much spirited if I am not mistaken.' Looking towards the scowling Welshman, he added, 'There must be a score of willing fillies in yon township to sate your urges without losing this pretty cartload of gold, and maybe your head for the sake of one broken mare.'

Rhiwallon scowled, drained his glass and stormed out of the room snarling profanities as he went.

Edric assigned two warriors to guard the ladies, then walked out into the courtyard, somewhat confused as just how he should handle these two, strange Norman ladies.

He shouted at a couple of his men, 'Close those damn gates, and post sentries up on the walkways all around the fortress.' Then he called another of his captains over to him, saying, 'Send out half a dozen mounted men and have them position themselves on the roads both to the north and to the south of the town, in order to give us due warning, should any Normans reinforcements approach.'

The man sped off to do Edric's bidding.

He then called the rest of his captains to him and ordered them to allocate sleeping quarters for their men inside the fortress, and then to arrange for food, drink and medical attention to be given out to those who needed it.

Once he was satisfied all was in order, he made his way through the gates towards the small town, stopping to look at the body of the man who the Welsh archers had shot as he had sprinted towards the gate in order to alert the sentries of Edric's pending attack. It was still lying face down on the cobbles with the three arrows protruding out of his back, now resting in congealed pools of blood.

Edric stooped and heaved the body onto its back, breaking one of the arrows in the process. Then stepped back in shock as the still smiling face (or was it a grimace?) as the English Earl Hunwald stared up at him with unseeing eyes.

'So here we have our traitor,' he said aloud, for no man was near, 'And one of our own.' Stepping away in disgust, knowing that an Englishman, and a nobleman at that, had been caught in the act of betraying his own kind to these damned invaders.

He shouted to one of his own men who stood guard at the gates less than fifty yards away, 'Get rid of this traitor's body, throw it into yonder river and let the fishes dine on the traitor's flesh.'

The guard nodded, 'Aye my lord.' None too happy that he had been taken from the simple task of lolling against the gate to be given such an unpleasant task. Yet his mood lightened somewhat when he rifled through the dead man's leather purse and found himself to be the owner of seven silver shillings plus the most beautiful ring that he had ever seen, so after heaving the body across his shoulders, he staggered two hundred yards to the edge of the bank, and with a sigh of contentment, he heaved the corpse over the edge and watched as it tumbled down the embankment into the river. 'My thanks to you my lord,' he said aloud, his face beaming, 'for you have made me a wealthy man.'

Edric moved on into the town, stopping off at the baker's shop, where he found Edmund of Clunn, who was already busy, assisting the eldest son of his dead brother, tossing lumps of fresh dough into the ovens, where they were in the process of baking their second batch of round, mouth-watering loaves.

After expressing his sorrow, yet again at the loss of Athelbert, he persuaded Edmund, to supply the fortress with a large supply of bread and pastries, and to organise two good cooks to attend Edric that evening in order that they may cater for ten people.

'And I want them to be skilled in their craft,' he said sternly, 'for they will be cooking for kings and other people of noble birth.'

The man, who at first he'd thought to be a witless oaf, bargained long and hard before agreeing on the price of ten silver pennies, plus three silver pennies for each of the cooks, which was, in Edric's mind quite an outrageous sum, forcing him to realise that behind the man's bland, rather silly face, there was a brilliant and astute mind.

The people of the town appeared to have recovered from the short and savage bloodletting that had taken place so recently in their midst. The town had reverted to the busy, noisy and crowded place it had always been, with tradesmen standing in the doorways of their premises, or pushing their barrows along the cobbled streets, shouting at the top of their voices in an attempt to attract buyers.

Here and there were farmers' wives or their milkmaids standing by the milking cows that they had driven into the town that morning, in readiness to provide fresh milk to the townspeople. Others stood by pens of fowl, or else prodded their squealing piglets which were tied by a strong leather thong, in order to attract buyers.

He did not tarry too long in the crowded streets and eventually wandered down to the wide river that gurgled its way over boulders beneath the fortress.

He sat on a large branch of a fallen willow tree, gazing melancholy into the bubbling waters, contemplating the events that had taken place in the past few weeks, partially thrilled. Yet in another way he dreaded the revenge that William of Normandy would take, realising that if all that he heard about the man were to be believed, then he was certainly not a man who would sit idly on his hands and allow a complete shire to be taken from him without exacting a savage vengeance.

As he sat there with the noonday sun directly overhead so hot that he was forced to move along the log some five or six feet into a more shaded position, his mind alive with plans, pondering what would be the best counter-move for him to make when William eventually marched into his shire. 'Because,' he said aloud, 'as sure as God made little apples William will march.'

He had not realised just how long he sat there, considering all the possible problems and possible answers to those problems, as well as dreaming of his beautiful wife Godda, who was, when he left her a few short weeks ago, heavily pregnant, causing him yet more pangs of regret for not being at her side.

And yet he rather enjoyed the afternoon.

He was alone, basking in the sun, but was eventually brought back to reality by the voice of Hywell, who was shouting at the top of his voice, as he walked down the hill towards the river.

'Lord Edric, Lord Edric!' he repeated as he approached. ''Tis nigh evening, and the ladies are waiting, King Rhiwallon is already in his cups and threatens to disgrace himself and us before the Norman ladies.'

Edric had no clean clothes of his own to change into but, after a quick splash of cold water from the river, he quickly strode up the hill then back into the castle where he rifled amongst the bodies of the dead Normans. Despite the fact that he was not the first Englishman to do so, he eventually found a more or less presentable shirt with a mere splatter of blood on it. It had obviously once belonged to a man of noble birth, for the style and material were of the finest quality.

Dusk had arrived as he walked into the great hall.

He realised that Edmund of Clunn and his many assistants had been extremely busy, for the hall was bathed in the light of numerous braziers that studded the walls, a crackling log fire blazed away in the huge hearth, and the long trestle table was laid for ten places, exactly as he had ordered. Yet despite this, no food decked the table, and the diners stood around in small groups holding either goblets of wine or tankards of ale.

Edric's eyes immediately fell upon the ladies, who stood together in the company of Rhiwallon, Garth and Hywell. They were all listening so intensely to what the Welsh prince was saying that, at first, no one noticed that he had entered the room. It was not until Garth glanced towards the doorway, catching a glimpse of him as he stood there assessing the situation, that his presence was made known.

'Ha. There you are my lord,' he shouted, obviously pleased to have a reason to leave the presence of the Welsh prince who had been dominating the conversation for the past hour in an order to impress the Lady Isabella, a task in which he was dismally failing, which was quite obvious to every person in the room excepting Prince Rhiwallon himself.

'Good Edric,' said Rhiwallon in his deep voice, 'thank the good Lord you have arrived, we can now eat, I'm bloody ravenous.' Slurring his words he spilt half of his wine onto the floor as he waved his arm into the air.

'My apologies for keeping you waiting,' said Edric as he walked towards the group, 'I was down by the river,' he added in a futile attempt to explain away his absence.

'Shall we eat then?' asked Rhiwallon. 'Where is that Edmund of Clunn? Will someone summon him and tell him to delight us with his culinary skills.'

Hywell made his way through the door that led to the kitchens. Returning a few minutes later he said, 'Edmund says that the food is all prepared and he will be with us in a few minutes.'

'Good,' sighed Rhiwallon as he plonked himself down into the nearest chair, then grabbing his own eating knife, shouted at the top of his voice, 'Come now Edmund, we are waiting,' before suddenly collapsing as he had been struck by a cudgel, falling head first onto the table, nearly impaling himself onto his own eating knife in the process.

Edric was alarmed and rushed forward to help his friend and ally, but Hywell laid his hand on Edric's shoulder, 'Nay, my lord, there is naught wrong with him except an excess of wine. He will be right as rain in a little while, You'll see.'

His remark was followed by a loud, gurgling snore that emanated from the drunken man.

Edric took Edgar the interpreter aside and quietly instructed him to stay as close as possible to the two Norman ladies on the pretext of translating whenever possible, but more importantly in order that he was close enough to overhear their chatter and to learn anything that he thought might be of value to Edric with regard to the numbers and military dispositions of the Duke of Normandy (he still could not bring it onto himself to call him 'King') and to report back to Edric if and when he had any important news.

The rest of the diners took their seats, and it was with a wry smile that he watched the two Norman ladies choose their seats well away from the sleeping Welshman.

The Lady Isabella and her companion, who was named Catherine, sat opposite Edric and Garth, chattered away and giggling in their own language like two young girls as they waited for the food to be served.

Edmund of Clunn entered the room, grinning like an idiot as he carried a large metal pot full of steaming beef broth.

He was followed by an assortment of kitchen maids, cooks and their helpers, each carrying large platters filled with roasted geese, fowl, the complete carcass of a young pig, half a side of roasted venison, a year-old roast lamb, plus a huge side of roast beef, all of which were placed onto the stout table before the delighted and expectant diners.

'There thee be, milord.' exclaimed the still beaming Edmund, 'Oi do 'ope it is to milord's likin'.' stepping back with pride as one of his helpers nudged her way in front of him to offer Edric a bowl of steaming broth.

Edric nodded his thanks and leant backwards to allow the maid to serve him with two large wooden spoonfuls of the delicious-smelling soup.

He thanked the girl and looked around the table to be met with the smiling faces of his guests, and much to his delight the two Norman ladies were also beaming with glee and chattering away like two finches on a sunny spring morning.

The only exception was the still sleeping figure of Rhiwallon, who was now lolling dangerously over the one side of his large chair.

Edric rose from his own seat and walked over to the Welsh king, shaking him by his shoulders as rigorously as he could until the man wakened with a loud grunt, uttering as if nothing untoward had taken place and seemingly as sober as a priest on a Sunday, 'Wonderful! Food at last.'

As he leant forward to wrench a complete hind leg off the roast pig, he added 'I'm starving,' and proceeded to gnaw away at the leg uttering contented grunts in the process.

Despite the feast that was set before him, Edric's appetite failed him, causing him to pick at a slice of roast lamb and a few boiled peas, looking at his fellow diners with interest. He noted that whilst most, and especially the large figure of Garth were tucking into huge piles of meat, the two ladies ate small portions of roast pork which they cut into small, delicate slices with their small, bone handled eating knives, chattering gaily to each other as they did so.

'My lady,' asked Edric as he leaned forward across the table, offering them the small wooden box of salt as he did so. 'Is the food to your liking?' momentarily forgetting that they did not speak the English language until the ladies ceased their birdlike chatter and stared blankly towards him across the table.

Edgar the interpreter immediately realised the situation, came to Edric's rescue saying in the language of Normandy.

'My Lady Isabella, My lord, Edric wishes to enquire if the food is to your liking?'

'Iss good,' came the reply in English, followed by a smile and a giggle from both of the ladies, then the Lady Isabella gave Edric a radiant smile as she spoke the words, followed by a distinct raising of her eyebrows.

Edric returned the smile, realising for the first time that perhaps this Norman lady was not so ignorant of the English language as she had led him to believe.

The meal was finished with some of the finest pastries that Edric had ever tasted, made, he was assured by Edmund of Clunn, 'mesell and me nephew' as he said as he placed the piping-hot dishes onto the table in front of the delighted diners.

The pastries did whet Edric's appetite and he helped himself to a large slice of apple and blackberry pie smothered by fresh cream, which he speedily devoured. Had it not been for the presence of the foreign ladies, he could have been tempted to have a second plateful, but erring on the side of good manners, he declined.

After the pastries, the serving maids filled the diner's goblets up with wine or beer, causing the evening to become merrier and noisier, especially the Welsh king who had matched the two Norman ladies drink for drink. Rhiwallon grew so drunk that he slurred his words so badly it was impossible to distinguish whether he was speaking in English, Welsh, or was perhaps trying to converse with the ladies in their own language. Whatever it was, Edric mused quietly to himself, he was sure that no one could understand much of it, except for an odd word here and there.

By contrast, the two ladies appeared to be totally unaffected by the amount of wine that they had drunk, and continued to speak to each other as well as to Edgar in their usual happy manner, with no apparent side effects whatsoever from the large amount of wine that they had consumed.

As the hour approached midnight, Edric was ready to retire to his sleeping quarters when he noticed that the door, which had been discreetly closed by the servants when they had cleared away the remains of the meal, quietly swung open. To admit a small, ragged person, leaning heavily upon a short bent oaken stick, which had strange carvings reaching from top of the stick to bottom.

Edric jumped up in alarm, 'Guards, guards!' he shouted, startling his guests, causing the men to reach for their weapons and the ladies to emit a muffled scream as their hands flew to their faces in alarm.

Two guards immediately appeared at the door, some ten feet behind the figure, which had ceased its progress into the room and now stood.

'Are you asleep?' shouted Edric angrily. 'Your orders were to let no one in. How come you allowed this creature in?'

'We did not see him – er – her, my lord.'

'No one passed us, my lord,' said the other.

'What do you mean, no one passed you? What is this then?' He pointed to the strange small figure that had not moved, other than to raise its head and look directly towards Edric.

'How did he get inside the fortress in the first place?' said Garth who now stood behind Edric, holding his famous 'Bloodaxe' in his right hand.

The small person held up his (or her) right hand and appeared to be leaning heavily upon the stout stick, then walked a few paces towards the table.

'No need for the axe,' said a squeaky voice that could have belonged to either a man or a woman, or even a child, 'I will not harm you, that is of course, unless you harm me first. And if that were to be the case then neither Odin or the Christ god would be able to help you.'

Garth grunted, relaxing a little, allowing the head of his famous axe to rest on the floor beside him.

'I am named Mono, Mono of the Meadows,' the shrill childlike voice announced, then without another word, the figure shuffled forward and sat on one of the vacant chairs. Reaching forward and it grasped a half-full goblet of wine, which it brought up to its nose, sniffed loudly a couple of times before sipping the wine, then with a smack of its lips, it squeaked, 'Good.' Then tipped the glass up, completely emptying it.

'Well Mono of the Meadows,' growled Edric, rather annoyed that this thing, which he had still been unable to decide whether it was a man or a woman, had the audacity to enter his hall unannounced and uninvited, then plonk itself down at his table and help itself to his wine as if it was its God-given right to do so, 'now that you have decided to join us, perhaps you will be good enough to tell us what it is you want of us?'

'Ha ha ha,' it cackled. 'I want nothing from you Lord of the Saxons. The winds brought me here.'

Then the otherworldly strange beings eyes looked up towards the blackened rafters of the room so that only the whites of its eyes could be seen, and its child-like voice said. 'My destiny is to save you.'

'Save us? We are in no danger here, for we have just conquered this fortress and I am surrounded by some of the finest warriors in the whole of England and Wales.'

Mono of the Meadows continued as if he had not spoken, for now Edric had decided that it was a she and not a he, as well as convincing himself that she was indeed either a witch or perhaps even a changeling:

'Although I must admit that I am acquiring a taste for this fine Norman wine,' holding her goblet towards Edric for it to be refilled.

Swallowing his pride, and deciding that this witch meant him no harm, he silently decided that he would prefer to have a witch as a friend rather than as an enemy. He refilled her goblet to the brim, causing her wrinkled face to break into something that resembled a toothless smile.

'Thank you kindly my lord,' taking a large swallow and smacking her lips again, she chuckled with pleasure as the warm wine careered down her gullet and into her scrawny stomach.

Edric studied her, attempting to disregard the greasy, knotted hair that hung down over her face, trying to imagine her age and how she might look in clean clothes and perhaps after soaking in a hot tub for a few hours. He came to no conclusion except to decide that she was not, perhaps, a hag in her eighties, and adjusting his estimation a little, deciding that she could be aged anywhere between the age of forty up to perhaps fifty, or even sixty.

Her eyes were grey, but one was dark grey whilst the other was perhaps more blue than grey. He was unsure, for it seemed to him that she avoided his direct gaze and always appeared to be either studying the floor or gazing up at the ceiling. And when she looked upwards, all that he could see were the whites of her eyes.

She emptied her goblet, throwing it into the fireplace where it shattered into a thousand pieces. Then she sank further down into the deep chair, shivered as if it was midwinter, and her eyes retreated into themselves showing nothing but iris-less white.

'Can't let my demons infect you. Can I?' she squeaked, as if that explained the expensive glass that she had just destroyed.

After a long silence which allowed the small crowd to relax a little, she began to speak, quietly at first but then in a louder, shrill, childlike sing-song voice, much the same as a man might expect a five-year-old child to recite a rhyme. She said:

Oh I know you savage Edric.
Of your travels and your battles,
With the Vikings and the Welshmen.
Of your fight with Ivor half-face,
And of Vorta, and of Madoc.
Oh I see your past and future.
Lives long gone, yet still to come.
I see a King, high and mighty.
Serving wine in golden goblets.
'Tis not for love he fills your goblet.
Nor because he likes your whiskers.
For that wine will cost you dearly.
Watch him as a hawk looks down
Upon the skylark singing sweetly.
High above the summer hayfield.
Knowing not that death awaits him.
Treat him with both care and caution.
As you would a slimy serpent.
See his lips for they are smiling,
But his eyes show nought but coldness.
Trust him not, for he is evil.
I see Princes, Welsh and Norman
Princes flocking all around you.'
Like the magpies in the May tree.
Like the sparrows in the Rick-yard.
Chatter-chatter, flatter-flatter.
Trust them not, they will desert you.
Fate will send you to the Northlands.
Through the wall that once was Roman.
O'er the moorlands life will take you.
To the mountains and the heather.
Where the north wind shrieks like demons.
Fight your battles, swing your sword arm.
You will win, and set some free.
Fight the heathen o'er the wall.

Fight them with your skill and cunning.
Chase them not when they are running.
Cornered polecats can be lethal.
Beware also of black water.
Blackened by the peat of ages.
Wade not through the blackened water.
For the black will change its colour.
Blood of men will taint the water
Blood from men who died in battle.
Screaming to their God in Heaven.
To the Christ child, and to Woden.
To the Druids, and the Sun God.
But if you wish not to join them.
Go not in the blood-red river.

She shuddered violently and red spittle dribbled out of the side of her slack mouth.

No one spoke, and the room was silent except for the odd crackle from a log that someone had thrown onto the fire in order to give it life.

Another cackle came from the seemingly unconscious Mona, whose white eyes still stared, unseeingly, up towards the smoky rafters.

And I see a King who serves you.
Blood red wine in golden goblets,
Two Queens,' she whispered in her childlike voice.
Two Queens I see. A black and white one.
The white one's gone, the black one stays.
There is much blood.
You too, Wild Edric,
Edric the Savage, you too will go.
You will tread the path of ages.

She shuddered so much that she virtually slid out of the chair, and was only prevented from reaching the floor by the strong arm of Edric. Dashing forward, he caught her before her body reached the floor, heaving her bodily up into the large wooden chair, where he held her for several minutes before her spasms ceased.

'Go,' Edric said with disgust to Rhiwallon who now seemed to be surprisingly sober.

'Go where? Is that good or bad? Doesn't make sense,' said the Welsh king, who was by now stone cold sober.

'Nah,' grunted Rhiwallon. 'Hogwash. She's spouting a load of rubbish.'

However as he had just ended saying the word 'rubbish', Rhiwallon looked down at Mona. Only to find her staring up at him, with a strange, knowing smile on her withered lips.

'We shall see, Welshman, shall we not?' she cackled and reached out towards yet another half-empty goblet of wine, which she emptied in one long, satisfying gulp.

The two Norman ladies, white-faced and frightened at what they had just seen and heard, made their excuses, speeding towards their bedchambers hand in hand as if for protection, whilst the men refilled their glasses with the last of the wine, or filled their tankards with the more plentiful beer, which still remained on the table. Then made their way slowly towards the large fireplace, where they stood and began to discuss the strange omens that had just been predicted by their uninvited guest.

'Kings and queens,' muttered Hywell. 'They could only be our new so-called King, William of Normandy.' He made a point of spitting into the fire as he uttered the man's name.

''Tis so,' said Garth, 'but there's not much chance of William serving Edric with wine, unless it has a good dose of poison in it.' He laughed nervously at his own joke.

'You did not hear correctly,' said Edric, 'The Witch said 'a king and queens.' and the way I interpret that is, one king and more than one queen.'

'Perhaps she meant Godda? She's a queen,' said Rhiwallon.

'Ask her, see if she remembers,' butted in Hywell, and they turned towards the table, which revealed several empty goblets and ten empty chairs.

After scanning the room, they found it completely empty of people except the men who were with him and the two guards on the one and only door of the room.

'Where did she go?' shouted Edric to the guards who still stood near the doorway.

'No one has passed us since the Norman ladies left, my lord,' said the eldest of the guards in a very shaky voice. 'We thought the witch was with you.'

Several of the men shivered whilst others crossed themselves, or reached for the Christian crosses. However, Garth touched the heavy stone copy of Thor's hammer that he wore around his neck suspended by a greasy leather thong.

'The witch has gone,' said Hywell, stating the obvious, and emptied his tankard, nearly choking in the process.

The men continued to talk and drink into the early hours of the wet, dull morning, discussing many things, especially the witch, Mono of the Meadows before they retired to their individual sleeping quarters, as a watery sun tried to penetrate through the low clouds that seemed to envelope both the fortress and the town.

Edric staggered into his sleeping quarters and flung himself down on top of the large oak bed that once belonged to the Norman lord who had so lately been in possession of both the bed and the fortress, and was soon competing with Thor the Thunderer with his loud snoring.

*****

Hugo de la Venn was lowborn, yet he had dined with kings and princes and called every nobleman in Normandy, Burgundy and France by their Christian names.

He smiled to himself in the cold chill of the morning as he landed lightly upon the cobbled stones inside the walls of the fortress, thinking to himself just how easy this task was going to be compared with the last man that he had slain, for Hugo de la Venn was known as the finest assassin on the continent of Europe. He had worked for most of the nobles in almost every country in western Europe, as well as with other nations, as far afield as the city of Constantinople.

His last task had been in Gascony where a particularly troublesome nobleman had earned himself a reputation as a brigand, plundering and killing far beyond the territory of his own small estate. It had been Hugo's mission to eliminate this particular nobleman, who had recently inherited a castle from his father, a solid stone castle that stood on a small but steep crag overlooking his small domain.

The castle had walls of stone, ten feet thick and fifty feet high, built by the finest masons of the time.

The one and only door was constructed from oak beams four feet thick and studded with hand-forged bolts, with a single, small eyehole through which the ever alert guards peered before opening the gate to anyone, be he friend or foe.

Scaling the wall on a moonless night had been more difficult than his usual assignment, but the things that had caused him the most trouble on that particular night had not been the wall, or the three guards whose task it had been to protect their lord. They had been strangled easily enough, one by one.

The four boarhounds that slept in the room with their owner had, however, been an unexpected and difficult problem. A problem that had only been solved after peering through the half-opened door – which he speedily shut. Noting that two of the hounds had already wakened and had peered directly at him, he quietly closed the door, then made his way down to where he thought the kitchens might be. After several wrong turnings he found them, strangling a kitchen maid who had been in the process of lighting the morning fire

He unhooked four large joints of venison that hung above the dead girl's body, took them back to the lord's bedchamber and silently lured the hounds out of the room, giving each of them a joint of venison to keep them occupied, whilst he had silently slipped into the bedchamber, slit the man's throat and made his escape using a rope which he eventually found in the stables.

This puny fortress of Ludlow, built half of stone and half of wooden stakes, had proved to be simple to scale.

He had passed the sleepy men on the palisade as if he had been a shadow, for indeed he did look like a shadow, dressed in black with a black hood over his thin, evil-looking blackened face.

He bumped into one unfortunate maid, who died before she knew what was happening, slumping to the floor with his help as he held her and the night-pot she had been carrying in order to throw its contents out of a nearby window, gently easing both the maid and her pot silently to the floor.

He eventually located Lord Edric's sleeping quarters and eased himself gently through the door into the darkened room, thinking to himself how easy this was going to be, and what a fool this stupid Englishman was not to have guards or dogs, or even a couple of geese, to protect him whilst he slept.

With his razor-sharp knife in his right hand he crept silently towards the sleeping figure who still lolled, fully clothed on his bed. He was about to draw his knife across the sleeping man's exposed throat... when a childlike voice said from a few feet behind him.

'Assassin, 'tis not his time.'

He spun around, blade before him, to be confronted with a tiny, childlike figure who stood not three feet from him.

He could see that the tiny figure possessed no weapon, so he smiled, smugly to himself, stepping forward to deal with her. Yet he was stopped as if he had crashed into an invisible wall.

'Not so,' came a whispering childlike voice, ''Tis not his time, but it is yours.'

He stood, unable to move, helpless in the power of this shadow, and a chill wind suddenly engulfed him, as if he was standing on a hilltop in midwinter in the Bavarian Alps where he had been whelped.

'You do not want to breathe, you can stop breathing,' it hissed. 'You will stop breathing,' she repeated. 'You will stop breathing.'

'Stupid dolt,' he thought to himself as he tried yet again to move in and slash at the figure with his knife, but found that he could not move.

'You do not want to breathe...'

A smirk that had been on his lips slowly vanished as his hand flew to his throat, and he gasped, choked, let out a long sigh and slowly collapsed to the floor, where his body writhed for a few brief moments before it lay still.

The sound of the assassin's knife clattering onto the floor had roused Edric from his drunken slumber, causing him to sit up in bed. He looked around him, until his still sleep-ridden eyes eventually focused upon the body that was sprawled at the feet of the witch who called herself Mono of the Meadows.

'What... What's going on?' he stammered.

'Shhh, Lord Edric,' came the shrill-like reply. 'The slayer is slain.'

Now fully conscious, he leapt out of his bed, grabbing his sword in one swift motion as he rose.

Looking down at the dead man he asked. 'Is he alone?' Then stooping down to examine the body, said, 'There are no marks on him. How did he die?'

'Who is he?' So many questions,' sighed the witch, then started to recite as if she was a children's teller of stories, in her birdlike childish voice she said:

The killer stalked you on his own.
Do not ask me how he died.
For that I cannot tell you.
I am your guardian angel.
And have slain the slayer.

She paused for a brief moment as if she was being strangled and her voice could not emerge out of her open, toothless mouth. Then her face relaxed a little and her childlike voice continued the rhyme:

But there are others have no doubt.
As white as driven snow.
One is good and one is bad.
It is for me to know.

She was about to continue when she was interrupted by a piercing scream that echoed from the kitchens as one of the maids stumbled upon the body of her slain friend, causing Edric to leap to his feet and sprint down the corridor, leaping down the wooden staircase and into the kitchen, where he found the sobbing maid. She had now been joined by other members of the household, who were standing in a small huddle around the dead maid, gazing silently at the twisted form of the unfortunate girl.

Garth, Godwin and Hywell appeared, all in a state of undress.

'Check the fortress,' Edric shouted to Garth. 'Make sure there are no more intruders here, and send those dozy guards to me.'

Garth dashed off to obey his liege lord.

Edric then made his way back to his sleeping quarters which were empty except for the body of the assassin which lay untouched and unattended, for no man had dared to enter Lord Edric's quarters without his permission.

He knelt beside the body in order to examine the man's knife that lay beside the body, noting that it was one of the finest knives that he had ever seen, nodding to himself as he noted that it was definitely not an English blade. It looked as if it had been birthed in one of the finest forges on the continent.

He slid the black sheath from the assassin's belt, then rifled through his sparse black clothing to see if the man carried anything that might point towards the man's identity, or even to his master, in order to give Edric some clue as to who had hired such a professional assassin.

Inside the man's shirt he located a small, soft moleskin purse that contained naught except three golden coins, each bearing the stamp of Normandy. 'Mayhap that answers my question,' he muttered to himself as he rose from the body.

Hywell, Garth and Rhiwallon joined him, entering his room, where they stood and silently looked down at the body.

'Evil-looking sod,' said Rhiwallon.

'He is that,' said Garth, 'but how did he get this far, past the guards?'

'More to the point,' said Rhiwallon shaking his head as he spoke, 'how did the devil die? There's not a mark on the body and his neck don't look broke to me.'

'Good question,' said Edric. 'The very same question that I asked Mona of the Meadows, when she stood over him.'

'She was here?' gasped Garth and shivered at the thought.

'That witch?' grunted Rhiwallon.

Godwin looked about him as if the witch was standing beside him, but there was no sign of her.

'Witch she might be,' said the sombre figure of Garth, 'but it seems that she has saved Lord Edric's life, has she not?'

The three men grunted their approval as they moved out of the doorway and proceeded to make their way downstairs.

'I'll get some of the men to take the two bodies away,' said Evan who had now joined them. 'And we shall give the girl a good Christian burial. But I think we should throw the assassin into the ditch and let the scavengers eat their fill.'

The men nodded and grunted their approval as they made their way to the kitchen to break their fast.

CHAPTER 14

'Lord King,' gasped the messenger who had been ushered before King William, still panting, as he knelt, mud-splattered from the journey that he had made across half of the centre of England.

'Dire news sire,' he said as he lowered his eyes to the ground. 'Edric and his army of Saxons and Welshmen have taken the city of Shrewsbury, as well as several other fortresses including the town of Ludlow, belonging to his lordship, the Lord Ralph Mortimer.

'Reports say that they have ravaged the shire of Cheshire, slaughtering every Norman in their path, and even as we speak, they are threatening to march into the shire of Hereford and take that city, along with the rest of that shire.'

William and the assembled lords were shocked at the news, having spent the past few months pursuing the will o' the wisp, Hereward and his small force of rebels who had escaped from the battle at Ely.

'Damn these English,' spat the King. 'Don't these people know when they are conquered?'

'Would you, lord King?' came the sly reply from Odo, the King's half-brother.

The King stopped his pacing and glared at his brother, but then commenced his pacing.

After a few more minutes of pacing backwards and forwards, he stopped abruptly saying, 'Odo, have the lords of my council attend me here, at noon on the morrow, and order them to cease whatever they are doing, and that includes chasing any of the other rebels, including Hereward, in those damnation marshes of his.'

'As you will my lord King,' said his brother as he made his exit from the room.

The following morning the noblemen of the King's council rode into the courtyard, many soaked through to the skin from the constant downpour that had persisted since it had begun late on the evening of the yesterday.

'Damn this bloody English weather,' grumbled one of the lords, who had been brought up on his father's warm estate in the foothills of the Pyrenees. Doesn't it ever do anything other than rain in this god forsaken country?' then wished that he had kept his mouth closed as he saw none other than William of Normandy standing in the courtyard, not more than six feet away from him.

'Beg pardon my King,' said the man, attempting to smile and make light of his remark, then seeing that the King was smiling, he added, 'But of course, all this beautiful rain,' holding his hands and his wet face up towards the heavens, 'makes this land so beautiful and so very green, does it not my lord King?'

William said nothing but smiled at the man's quick thinking and turned his own face skywards, musing to himself that in truth the man had been correct. Silently he wished himself to be once again in his beloved Normandy with his loving wife Matilda, who had just presented him with his sixth child, albeit, much to his annoyance, she had turned out to be another girl, and not the son that he had wished for.

The lords had all arrived before noon and joined their King in the great hall where they were invited to sit at their allotted places and given a choice between some locally brewed warm ale that the King's manservant had acquired, or a goblet full of good Norman wine.

With the exception of two of the lords, all had chosen the wine, looking upon the English ale as a peasant's drink and not fit for the noblemen of Europe.

William called them to order by banging the hilt of his jewelled dagger hard upon the oak table, saying:

'My good nobles, I have called you here so that there will be no mistakes or excuses when you' – and as he uttered the word, you he looked directly into the cold blue eyes of his own brother, and then slowly to every single man in the room before he continued speaking – 'ALL of you, when you carry out the strategy that I have spent half of the night dwelling upon.'

He again looked slowly at the assembled lords before continuing. 'As many of you know, over the past few months a lot of you have been with me chasing this will o' the wisp Hereward and his cut-throats halfway across the countryside. Yet we have failed to bring him to battle. This wolf's head continues to sting us here and there, before he disappears, only to re-appear in another part of the country to sting us again.'

He paused for a moment, bringing a tankard of apple juice to his lips for he rarely touched the juice of either the grain or the grape.

'We also have a small rebellion in the West Country, as well as more rumours from the north about Malcolm of Scotland, and more seriously still I have just received news that half of the warriors in Wales have joined the man that they call 'Wild Edric'. They have already taken the city of Shrewsbury and the whole of that shire, plus many smaller fortresses including the border town of Ludlow, and even as I speak to you, he is preparing to take his army into the shire of Hereford and take that city along with the complete shire.'

Then he added, 'And if we lose that shire then we lose the whole of the west and this 'Wild Edric' will attract warriors from every shire in England and will threaten our very existence in this country.'

He paused again as he watched the reaction of his council, many of whom he had bestowed with towns and villages in Shropshire and Herefordshire. The King noticed the looks of shock that fell upon their faces as they realised that the manors that the King had given them, manors that were, even now, making them into rich men.

Manors, they realised, that if these rebellions festered on and were allowed to grow, could just as easily to be taken away from them, (despite the fact that fewer than half of them had ever visited their new domains.)

He continued, 'I require the service of you my Lord Vernon,' looking at the young Lord Vernon, who despite his youth, was already almost bald-headed and the few short hairs that remained on his head were cut so short that he did look as if he possessed not a single hair on his head. The few short hairs that he did possess appeared to have migrated to his chin to form a short, sparse fair beard.

'You my Lord Vernon, and your horsemen are to scour the countryside in the

135

search for Hereward, he who is called "The Wake".'

'Leave messages at every town and village, saying that I, King William of Normandy and of England will grant him a pardon and will allow him and his cut-throats – don't call them cut-throats of course – I will offer them a full pardon if they cease their raids and swear allegiance to me.

'Leave word that they can attend me here on the first day of the new month, and I swear by all that is holy that I shall grant them amnesty and restore their holdings to them.'

There were shouts of alarm, much muttering and the thumping of fists and tankards upon the table, as the assembled lords protested against their King's new edict.

'My lord King,' said one bolder than his peers. 'If you grant a pardon to this cut-throat, then it will send a message to every murderer in the land that the King is weak and not fit to govern.'

William held his anger, but all could see that he was furious that his edict had been challenged.

'Do you think to call me weak, my Lord Challinor?' he said almost at a whisper, but loud enough for all to detect the menace in his voice.

'No, no, of course not my lord King,' said the now trembling Challinor, wishing that he had been as wise as his fellow noblemen and kept his mouth shut. 'I was just saying, my lord King, that it may not be the right message to send to the people,' he demurred trying as best he could to squirm out of the dangerous position that he had plunged himself into.

'Let me put it another way, my lords,' said William in a more civil tone, 'We do not have enough men to garrison the towns and the castles we now own, as well as to fight this Hereward, AND hold the north as well as the West Country, PLUS put down this rebellion along the Welsh borderlands.

'What think you that I should do?' he hissed the challenge.

The assembled lords looked at one another whilst others gazed silently at the floor, but not one of them uttered a single word.

King William let this sink in until his noblemen nodded, and began to mutter quietly amongst themselves, and then he held his hand up for silence.

After a short pause silence again prevailed, allowing him to continue. 'What I also want you to do my good Lord Vernon, you too Fitzbowes, and you my Lord Sieward, is to send ten riders out into the very heart of England, and let it be known that I shall re-establish the Saxon *Fyrd*, and have every warrior who belonged to the *Fyrd* join me here at any time during the next two months.'

The room erupted in a roar of disapproval from the assembled lords, with shouts of, NAY, NAY, NAY! and the hollow sound of gnarled, sword-callused hands thumping onto the stout oaken table.

William stood defiant of his council, allowing them to voice their protests for many minutes before, again, holding his hand up for silence. When the noise continued, he nodded silently to the two guards who he had placed at the door in anticipation of this very thing. Who quietly opened the door to allow fifty heavily armed warriors of his own personal bodyguards to enter.

The noise immediately ceased as the shocked noblemen, who had all been disarmed before attending the meeting and carried no more than their eating knives and ornamental swords, realised that they had, yet again, been out-manoeuvred by their King, and that they would now have no option other than to comply with his decisions.

'We need warriors, do we not?' he snarled.

'Aye,' came the reply from the assembly, although all did not utter it.

'These men of the *fyrd* are warriors, are they not?' he asked.

'Aye,' came the reply but from fewer voices.

'Those of you who were at Hastings with me know that only too well, for it was a close run thing, was it not so'?

'Aye,' came the mumbled reply from the assembled men.

'Forsooth, I had three stallions slain under me on that day, never have I been in such peril, and yet you seem loth to accept these men as fellow warriors, do you not?'

'But lord King,' stammered one man. 'They are the enemy. How can we trust them?'

'They are as likely to sink one of those English axes into our heads, rather than into the heads of our enemies.'

'That may be so,' conceded William, 'but did you note that not one of Harold's housecarls deserted him until death swept them away? And why do you think they died rather than to ask for quarter?' he asked.

'Because they hated us,' ventured one.

'Because they loved Harold,' growled another.

However, before any more theories came from the table, William said, 'Not so, my lords, I have made many enquiries regarding their deaths, and have discovered the reason that they died to the last man.' Pausing for a space of ten heartbeats as he looked at his assembled lords before going on.' It was simply due to their oath,' wagging his finger towards them, he emphasised the point.

'Harold's housecarls gave their lives because they had given their word. They had sworn a blood oath to Harold and died rather than dishonour it. How many of you would have died rather than cry quarter, had I been slain at Hastings?' he challenged.

'I would, I would!' every man in the room bellowed, thumping their fists onto the stout oaken table until it trembled.

He looked around at them and knew that some of them indeed would willingly have died to protect his honour, whilst others averted their eyes from his gaze, and he knew that those men would have bowed their knees and begged for their own miserable lives.

He paused for a brief moment before continuing, 'I shall extract a similar oath from every English warrior who would join us, then with them fighting for us and not against us, we shall bring peace to this land and you, my lords, shall have the holdings and the riches that I have promised you.'

At long last there were the nods and grunts of approval that he had been looking for, allowing him to walk around the room, placing his hands on the shoulders of a man here and there, thus ending the meeting.

*****

On the first day of the month the sentries announced the approach of a large body of men riding an assortment of horses ranging from large carthorses to

137

ragged mountain ponies, complimented by the vast range of weapons that they bore.

Some carried the dreaded English longbow, whilst others held the much shorter ash hunting bows.

All the men carried swords and axes of various types, half hidden under the round English war-shields that dangled from their saddle horns.

William watched them clatter into the cobbled courtyard, aware that not only he was watching them, but also fully aware they were also being watched by over one hundred eyes, from the other men who he had been placed in hiding at various strategic places within the fortress, just in case this savage Hereward the Wake intended to dishonour the truce that he had been offered.

King William met Hereward at the door, holding out his right hand in friendship.

His hand was gripped by the right hand of the English outlaw in a vice-like grip that would have sent a lesser man onto his knees in agony, but William had been tutored from an early age on how to deal with such things. He returned the grip, staring into the eyes of this tall, fair-haired Englishman, noting the man's lean, intelligent face that was looking back at him, gazing into his own eyes with eyes that were steady and inquiring.

He also realised that this man reminded him of someone else who he had met, but for the love of Jesus, the man's grip seemed to prevent him from recalling who that person was. For Hereward's eyes were grey with his left eye being far lighter that his right eye.

'Well met,' said William in the tongue of Normandy. 'It is good that you have come.'

Then, much to his surprise, Hereward replied in the language of Normandy without the slightest accent, 'Just so, just so. You and I have jousted from a distance for long enough. 'Tis time we met, man to man.'

William was somewhat taken aback, not only by the man's straight talking, but also by his mastery and knowledge of the Norman language.

He speedily recognised the fact that this man was no ordinary peasant and was a man of noble birth, something that his advisors, men who were supposed to know these things, had omitted to tell him.

'As a matter of prudence, I do not allow weapons into my hallway,' said William in as pleasant a manner as possible, and was slightly alarmed as the right hand of Hereward sped towards the hilt of his dagger that graced his belt.

Hereward controlled himself and, smiling as he did so, unbuckled his belt handing the dagger, belt and all to the King, saying, 'I came to listen to your terms, not to kill you.'

William took the belt, but before handing it to one of the two personal bodyguards who stood at the door, he noted that both the intricately woven belt, the ornate scabbard and the blade were unlike any others he had yet seen. So obviously English, yet of a quality that would put the finest armourers in Normandy to shame.

'Come,' said William. 'It will be more genial if we talk inside,' leading the way through the doorway and into the great hall, which was empty except for a serving girl who had just placed beer, wine, bread, cheese, plus a cold roasted goose onto the table, before she curtseyed and left the room.

William sat at one side of the table, not at the end, as was his right, and offered a seat opposite to him, which Hereward took. Yet only after quickly looking around the room, as if he were looking for assassins or traps,

Both helped themselves to the food, with William pouring himself a goblet of wine (doing this as a gesture in order that he did not offend his guest) while Hereward poured himself a tankard full of ale, tore off a leg from the roast goose, broke off a piece of cheese and a chunk of warm bread, which he began to eat and drink at the same time.

'Here's to your hospitality, and to an amicable agreement,' he said, holding his tankard aloft before bringing it to his mouth.

'I accept your toast Lord Hereward,' answered William, bringing the wine to his lips just enough to allow a drop or two to pass through before returning the virtually untouched wine to the table.

He had called the man *Lord* Hereward on purpose for two separate reasons. One was to give Hereward a taste of what it was like to be called 'Lord', and secondly because he felt that he had been slighted by this arrogant English rebel who had not yet used the word, 'King' or even *Mē Hlāford* in the few short sentences that he had so far uttered.

However, not allowing his personal feelings to stand in the way of an agreement that could, after all, mean the difference between holding onto this kingdom or losing it. He ignored the suspected insult that he felt had been given, not sure if it had been the man's intention or not to insult him, forcing himself to continue to be pleasant to the Englishman saying, 'How now, Lord Hereward, have you come to lay aside your war with me and to live amongst us in peace, on your own domain, swearing loyalty to me? And in return I shall grant yourself and all of those warriors in the courtyard out there a full amnesty, absolving you all from any crimes that you have committed against me.'

'CRIME?' shouted Hereward as he leapt to his feet, walking away from the King, then turning and walked more slowly towards William. 'I have committed no crime, I have blooded my sword against you, and against your Normans in defence of my land, and that is not a crime.'

Not willing to bandy words and get into a heated argument that could well dash all hopes of an agreement being reached between them, William held his hand up in alarm.

'Well good Hereward,' he said with as friendly a smile that he could muster, whilst his inner body seethed with anger at this English cut-throat's arrogance, 'Let us mellow the word and say that you will be forgiven for any deeds that you have carried out in the defence of your country, during the past three years.'

Allowing the man to calm down a little, he calmly sat on his seat, leant back a little and took yet another sip of the wine, inwardly crossing himself as he did so, saying 'Could we not at least agree on that?'

Renowned for being a hothead and a man in possession of a furious and impetuous temper, Hereward nonetheless realised that this man was honour bound to act with generosity towards him whilst he was a guest under his roof, and as such, he also knew that this 'so-called King' had been placed in such a position that now allowed Hereward to extract far more out of him than he had ever dreamed possible.

'What about my father's estate in Leicestershire, can that be kept?'

'Of course,' answered the King, knowing now that he had snared his prey.

'And my own estate in the Fenlands?'

'Naturally, any lands and estates that belonged to you as well as your direct family will be yours again. With a full royal pardon granted to you, your men, and to your kinfolk.

'But,' he added, 'neither your warriors nor yourself must take up arms against my people. If that happens then I shall do all that is within my power to hunt you down, and have you hung, drawn and quartered. Is that understood?'

'Aye,' said Hereward. 'My lord, King.'

'And you will swear a blood oath to be my man, in life and in limb?'

This time his question was not so speedily answered as the man gazed into his half empty tankard for what to William seemed to be an eternity.

'Aye, My lord King,' came the quieter, choked reply.

'Ah,' thought King William. 'I have him, and with him I have the kingdom.'

Then a cloud drifted over his mind that dampened his mood as he thought of Wild Edric and his Welsh rebels who were still wreaking havoc in the Welsh borderlands.

Hereward drained his tankard, then bent to kneel before the King, taking the King's right hand in his own, and somewhat reluctantly raised his face to place his lips upon the ring on the King's middle finger, thus making him a man of the King, free from the crimes of rebellion, murder and treason.

CHAPTER 15

The combined English and Welsh army marched for three days, meeting no opposition other than the atrocious summer weather, with torrents of rainwater drenching them to the skin, filling the streams to overflowing, and turning the rivers into impassable torrents. This forced the tired, soaking men to tramp upstream through the muddy, rain-soaked meadows until an acceptable ford could be found.

During the last of these crossings, three men had been swept to their deaths when an uprooted tree had careered down the swollen river, scattering the terrified string of men in all directions, and it was not until the evening camp that Edric had been told of the three lost warriors.

The city of Hereford opened its gates to Edric, but the town's aldermen pleaded with Edric not to allow his Welshmen through their gates.

'We have had too many Welsh raiders in our shire over the years to welcome them now,' said the senior alderman. 'Only ten months ago a Welsh raiding party descended upon the township of Ross upon the Wye, burning three farmsteads, and murdering a youngster who tried to protect his cattle.

'Nay, Lord Edric, you and your men are most welcome, but it is too much to ask us to accept your Welshmen in our city, allies or not.'

Edric returned to the waiting Welsh king who stood amongst his aggrieved warriors with a scowl on his tattooed face, as he watched the stern-faced Edric approach him.

'So it is nay then?' said Rhiwallon grimly, 'We are good enough to rid them of yon Normans but not good enough to enter their poxy town.'

'Sorry,' answered Edric, 'but it seems that your people tend to keep to their old ways and enter this shire, taking a few cows now and then and that don't please them too much. Pity.'

'They are not my people,' spat the angry Rhiwallon, 'they were from Gwent, nothing to do with us.' he spat and turned away in disgust.

'Come with me my children,' he bellowed at his warriors, as he turned his back on Edric, leading his men back to make their camp in the damp meadows by the muddy river.

Fearing that the snub may cause the angry Rhiwallon to take his men back into their mountain fastness and thus weaken his small army, Edric forced his own, very unhappy men to remain outside the walls, and to make their own camp in the wet watermeadows alongside the river Wye, alongside Rhiwallon and his Welshmen. But not before he had bargained long and hard, in order to purchase a herd of fifty-year-old steers from the leading alderman of the city, ordering his men to drive them into the combined camps of his army.

This cheered up both English and Welshmen, and they soon had sides of beef sizzling over huge fires, thus allowing Edric, Garth and Evan to re-enter the town in order to dine with the city aldermen, whilst his small army feasted on the cattle, serenaded by the beautiful singing of happy, well-fed Welshmen.

Nonetheless, Edric was cheered when he heard the singing and the raucous behaviour from his men beyond the city walls as they feasted long into the late hours of the evening.

The army rested in and around the city for a further three days. Then much to Edric's surprise, on the fourth morning he was interrupted by Evan, who escorted a messenger into Edric's sleeping quarters.

'My lord,' panted Evan who had obviously hurried to see him. 'Dire news, My lord,' he blurted. 'Rhiwallon and his Welshmen have gone.'

'Gone? Gone where?' asked the bemused Edric, thinking to himself that as of yesterday, he had noticed a little uneasiness about the Welsh king and his captains, thus assuming that he had become tired of waiting outside the walls of Hereford and had decided to take his men home to the safety of their lofty mountains.

'I'm not sure,' said Evan. 'But it looks as if they have gone south, towards the shire of Gloucester.'

'God's blood,' swore Edric, 'what possessed the man to do that?' he fumed. 'The fool has split our army in two, and with it he has made us easy meat for William of Normandy, who will now be able to eat us up bit by bit.'

He stormed down the staircase, meeting Garth who was on his way up.

'Have you heard the news?' he shouted at the top of his voice.

'Aye lord, I was on my way up to tell you.'

'What news of William?'

'Still in the east,' came the reply.

'Good,' said Edric with relief, 'at least we don't have to meet him on the morrow.'

'True, my lord,' grunted the gruff voice of Garth, 'but sooner or later we are going to have to meet with him one way or another.'

They both strode to the breakfast table that was laid out with all manner of fare, ranging from cold fowl, a goose, freshly baked bread and cold oatmeal, but they both ignored most of the food, merely snatched a chunk of bread and a handful of cold roast goose which they ate as they walked through the door and out into the courtyard.

Edric issued orders to Garth. 'Send three. No, send four riders after Rhiwallon. His trail should be easy enough to follow, and have one of them to return to me each eventide with news of his progress.'

'Aye lord.'

'Then have our men ready to march by noon on the morrow and by that time we should know what our Welsh allies are up to. In the meantime, now that Rhiwallon has left us, we can allow our men into the town, and see to it that they are quartered in some dry lodgings.' Then almost as an afterthought, he added, 'Oh, purchase as many sheep or cows as is necessary to give them a good meal or two,' then digging into his leather purse that hung on his belt he handed Garth three golden coins. 'This should suffice,' he said, as he walked through the open gates, leaving Garth to do his bidding.

It was a day of bad news. Just as the feeble sun was directly above his head, Edric was confronted with another exhausted, mud-splattered messenger.

Kneeling before Edric the man gasped out the news that he had carried with him for two days and one night, through flooded rivers and rain-soaked meadows to tell his liege lord.

'News my lord,' he spluttered in a voice that showed just how exhausted the man was, 'Hereward, he who is called the Wake, has made his peace, and is now William of Normandy's man.'

That was the entire message that the man had to say.

Not a long complicated message, but devastating news nonetheless, for everyone knew that with the final rebellion now over in the east of England, William was now at liberty to throw the full weight of his army across the country to the one remaining rebellion that must be extinguished, if he was to reconquer the shires lost to Edric and consolidate his rule.

Edric's now diminished army had, in the space of a few short hours, not only been halved in size but was also now in danger of being confronted with the full force of the Norman military machine, who would, no doubt, now be baying for vengeance.

And, Edric mused, this was the very same Norman army that had been let loose on the north of England, and had left those northern shires devastated and devoid of life. So much so, that it would certainly take them many generations to recover.

'My thanks for the news, unwelcome though it is. I suggest that you now go down to the kitchens and get some hot food and drink into you, then have a few hours' sleep,' As the man nodded his head and turned to go, he added, 'Attend me when you have fully rested, for I have a further task for you.'

Edric called his captains to him where he issued further orders.

'Garth,' he said, 'I would like you to send a man to the city of Shrewsbury and inform our friend Bleddyn of Hereward's surrender and of the strong likelihood of William's probable invasion.

'Hwyell, I want you to send a few good horsemen to the surrounding towns and villages, in order to recruit as many good men as you are able. Remember,' he added seriously, 'we do not want farm yokels with pitchforks and sickles. We want warriors, men who have stood in a shieldwall and who know how to handle themselves.'

*****

Rhiwallon and his small army sped south burning and killing as they went, leaving a wide wake of burning farms, charred villages and a ravished population behind them, driving a huge herd of captured cattle and a mass of stolen sheep before them.

Edric's four scouts followed his progress, which was a simple task, for the horizon was festooned by black smoke spiralling up from burnt farmsteads and villages, blackening the cloudless blue sky.

By the time that the first and second scout had reported back to Edric, it appeared that Rhiwallon had reached the River Lugg, where they had been confronted by a band of fifty heavily armoured Normans who stood in a solid phalanx on the one and only bridge that guarded the southern half of that shire.

Rhiwallon bade his archers to clear the bridge, a task that they set to with gusto, sending volley after volley of arrows towards the arrogant Normans – not only high, so that the shafts might fall upon the heads of the Normans, but also from the left and right bank of the Lugg.

To no avail, for the Normans, experienced warriors to a man who had performed this type of a task many times before and from far more numerous, and better armed adversaries. They held their large, kite-shaped shields not only above their heads, but also to the sides of their much rehearsed formation, rendering the deadly arrows harmless, as they stuck into the shields, but failed to penetrate through to the warriors' inside, who were totally protected by their solid snake-like construction.

Rhiwallon then sent fifty of his best warriors forward to the bridge. Yet this was only wide enough to allow four men across at a time, and the Welsh warriors were again met with the Normans impenetrable shieldwall from which protruded a virtual hedge of razor-sharp spears, skewering the few men who were foolish enough to allow themselves to get too close.

After several hours of fighting and the loss of twenty-five of his finest men, good men, men who would be sorely missed and mourned in their villages when he returned to his own kingdom.

He began to fear that his leadership may well be questioned if he were to lose any more men, especially so if he were not achieve a victory. So after considering the situation for a while he roared at the two captains who were nearest to him, in the most confident voice that he could muster:

'Ah well, my lads, why bother with these few stubborn Normans here when there are just as rich pickings to be had on this side of the Lugg? We will return home to our beloved mountains, and will, I doubt not, pick up a few trinkets on our way.'

A hearty cheer from all who heard it, causing the news to speedily pass from man to man, until every man in his small army had heard the welcome news.

His men began to retreat from the banks of the Lugg, leaving the tired but jubilant Normans on the bridge which they had defended so well.

Edric's third scout arrived to report the events of the day, insisting that the Normans had won the day, and that the small Welsh army had now reversed its order of march and was now heading northwest, towards the fastness of the Welsh mountains.

'Serves him right for deserting us,' spat Garth. 'What we should do now is to relieve him of the sheep and cattle that he has stolen from the Englishmen in that shire.'

'The thought had crossed my mind,' said Edric thoughtfully, 'but prior to this act of bad faith, he has been a good man, and I think that we could not have taken Shrewsbury or Ludlow without his bowmen.'

'And we might need him and his bowmen again.' said the less agitated Hywell.

'True, true,' said Edric. 'Perhaps it would be wise to see what William of Normandy has planned for us before we turn our friend Rhiwallon into an enemy.'

Edric and his small army tarried in the city of Hereford for more than a month and still there was no news of King William's invasion, causing the Aldermen to approach him with complaints of drunkenness and debauchery being carried out by his bored warriors who had nothing better to do other than to inhabit the taverns and brothels that huddled along the banks of the Wye.

'There are fights and killings every night,' claimed the spokesman. 'In fact, day by day it is getting worse.' He added. 'Three of our people were stabbed last night, one of them was the son of my good friend, Gerald of Kington, who, thanks be to God' – crossing himself as he uttered the words – 'is not too badly injured, and with a little luck should make a full recovery.'

The alderman who was standing directly behind him then spoke, 'That is not the only problem that we have. You and your men are depleting our food supplies and have just about drunk the last of our best beer.'

Edric looked for the first time at the man and saw a sallow, thin face individual with a wispy grey beard and eyes that appeared to be so narrow that Edric wondered if the man was blind.

'Surely that can be no bad thing,' he said in a pleasant way, 'if you and your people have nearly been drunk out of house and home, then you have all been made rich men from the inflated prices that you have been charging my warriors for your fare.'

'Not so, my lord Edric' answered the leading alderman, snorting down his nose in indignation as he spoke, 'for my good friend here, and myself, are God-fearing men and profit not from the demon drink.'

Edric placated the aldermen as best he could, saying that he would keep a tighter hold on his men and would take them out of the city as soon as he had word of the movements of King William and his army.

He sent his captains into the city each evening for the following two weeks in an attempt to curtail the drunkenness and the fighting. Yet although this had some effect, causing the rowdiness to lessen, it still continued, but perhaps on a somewhat lesser scale.

He called his captains together on the twentieth day of September, a bright, sunny day, with the welcome autumn sun warming the damp meadows and woodlands with its warmth, enhancing the colours of the beech, oak, and other trees of the forest who were in the process of turning into their vivid autumn colours.

'Winter is all but upon us,' he said to them, 'and still William of Normandy tarries in the south and the East Midlands, amassing men and consolidating his holdings there.

'It is, in my opinion, almost too late for him to launch an attack across country before the roads and the rivers become impassable for an army of that size.'

He let this logical explanation sink into the minds of his captains, hoping that one of them might come up with some bright suggestion which his mind had failed to grasp. Yet there was an ominous silence from his men, so he continued, 'If he were to make a winter march, through countryside which we know far better than him and his Normans, then the advantage would remain with us.'

'But my Lord Edric,' said the ever-smiling Evan, 'is it not true that he is recruiting warriors from King Harold's old *Fyrd*?

'That is what we've heard,' conceded Edric.

'Well if that is so,' added Evan, 'then those English traitors will also know the terrain, is that not true?'

'Aye,' came the agreement from around the room. 'Aye.'

Edric, more than a little angry that his good friend Evan, who was also his constant companion, had indeed discovered something that he had not thought of, so he said in a quiet, but sinister voice, 'Of course that is true, he may well have Englishmen with him, indeed I would be surprised if it were not so. But many of our warriors are from the Midland shires and I personally know of several of our men who have hunted these plains and valleys since they were boys. And I know, for a fact, that they would guide us and that would, I am convinced, give us a distinct advantage should if we were forced to meet William in battle.'

There were further murmurs and rumblings from the men and it was clear to Edric that their hearts were not feeling good about the winter campaign that he had hoped to mount. They too were well aware that the fighting season was pretty well over. Edric really had no option other than to bend to their wishes and disband the rest of his small army.

'I think it best,' he conceded, 'that we leave Hereford on the morrow, and allow our men to go their separate ways until such time as we need you again. However,' he added, 'I shall keep fifty of the best men with me at Wentnor.'

*****

The aldermen had mixed feelings, as they and many of their citizens watched from the walls of their city, as Edric and his small army faded from view in the morning mist.

'Who will defend us if the Normans come?' said one.

'You wanted Edric to go,' said another accusingly.

'We are well rid of them,' spat a third vehemently, 'They stabbed my daughter's son.'

'If what I heard was correct, then he had it coming to him,' said the first man, 'he always did have a big mouth.' He added, 'Too cocky for his own good.'

'It still leaves us with a bit of a problem. What exactly do we tell the Normans when they come, and they surely will come? We are too wealthy a city for them to leave vacant.'

'They will come,' the Burgher mumbled unhappily to himself, as he turned to walk down the wooden stairway.

'Leave that to me,' said the Town-Reeve, 'I'll sort out the Normans,' adding, 'All they want is money and power, and dead citizens will give them neither.'

They glanced once again as the last of Edric's banners disappeared in the mist and they made their way solemnly down the stairway and into the city.

*****

William had problems on his mind other than the loss of Shrewsbury and Hereford. The two shires with their sparse population, would produce only a small proportion of the revenue that he needed for his wars on the continent as well as here in his new Kingdom of England.

The more pressing matter that concerned him was the news that in the late summer Prince Aethlething, who was the great-grandson of the late King Ethelred, (He who had been named, 'The unready, or (ill-advised) had invaded

146

the north of England, and with the help of a strong army of Danes, under their warrior King, Sweyn, plus a large number of English Nobles. They had already taken the city of York as well as much of the surrounding countryside, slaying every Norman in the process, except the few whom they considered to be worthy of ransom.

The King had been forced to call out his army yet again, and with the aid of the few warriors who had served under King Harold in his *fyrd*, he made a forced march, first to Stafford in order to quell a minor resurrection that had taken place in that city, before he turning his face to the north, marching along the Great North Road towards the city of York.

He met with Prince Aethlething and his Danish allies in the following August, on the meadows before York, where the King's enemies outnumbered his own battle-hardened army by a ratio of at least two to one.

However, the battle had been short but bloody, lasting for less than an hour, and had been decided by King William's mounted knights who simply rode around the long Danish shieldwall, where they attacked their Norman King's enemies from the rear, coming to within a hair's breadth of slaying or capturing King Sweyn himself, sending his oath-men into such a panic that they crowded around him and virtually bundled him to the rear of his battle line and onto his waiting ships on the river Humber.

Upon seeing their King retreat, the remaining warriors of his army followed their King, losing many of their number in the process.

King William entered the city of York again to the sullen faces of its inhabitants of whom a large number were akin to the Danes.

That winter, far from hibernating from the sleet, snow and biting frosts, the Normans did not sit idle by their firesides. William had ordered most of his noblemen to return to their domains, telling them to construct fortresses, 'To hold the natives down.

'Place your castles in strategic places,' he ordered them. Build a mound with a wooden fortress, and a motte surrounded with earthen works. Later, when you are secure, I will have masons brought from Normandy to convert your fortress into more robust castles of stone.'

Later that autumn, he met with King Sweyn under a flag of truce and was rumoured to have paid the Dane a vast sum of Danegeld providing that the Danish King took his fleet elsewhere, promising to harass England no more.

It was a fact that the Danish King left England's shores and spent the winter somewhere in Ireland.

CHAPTER 16

Life at Wentnor passed pleasantly that winter, with Edric enjoying the company of Godda and their newborn son Alfred.

Whilst Godda accepted the presence of the two lady Norman prisoners, she would not have them sleep in the manor, insisting that they spent their time in a cottage some one hundred yards away on the outskirts of the village.

Edric, against his better judgment, agreed to her wishes. Yet he did insist that two of his most trusted men must live in a separate room in the cottage, with orders to keep an eye on the ladies, 'Trust them not an inch, for I trust them not at all,' he ordered. 'One of you must be with them at all times, morning, noon and night. Have your own women in the cottage with you and tell them also to keep a sharp eye on the ladies, get not too close or too friendly with them, and do not, on any occasion' – he wagged his finger at them – 'let them near any of the horses, for I have noted how well these Norman ladies ride.'

The two men nodded. The elder of the two, a grey-bearded man who had served Edric for more than ten years said, 'Rest assured my lord, we shall watch them as a hawk watches a sparrow before he strikes.' He then followed the younger man who had already left to collect his few personal belongings.

One dark and dismal day, after they had eaten their evening meal, Edric plucked up the courage and broached the subject, whilst Godda was holding up a large patch of linen, smiling to herself at the delicacy of her own needlework.

'Godda,' he said pleasantly, causing Godda to look up from the needlework that she had been stitching in the light of the fire, looking radiant as ever in the light from the fire that enhanced her beautiful features. 'Much as I love the lad, I have found it difficult to take to the name Alfred, and from now on I shall call him Ælnoth after my father's father.'

She stared intently into his eyes for a full minute before she answered in a cool, calm and pleasant voice, 'As you will my dear. Then we shall both call him Ælnoth.' Thoughtfully she added, 'A good enough name, although I am loth to abandon the name of Alfred so the fortunate young man shall have not one, but shall have two names.' She then returned her attention back to her needlework, thus allowing the matter to be settled without another word being said.

In the middle days of 'the month of the wolf' called January by the Christians, one of Edric's spies arrived, having travelled through two feet of standing snow, and snowdrifts some six feet high to bring news. 'My lord,' said the shivering man as he stood near the fire in Edric's great hall, as torrents of water dripped from his sodden clothes onto the newly laid rushes that Godda's maidens had laid not an hour since.

'William of Normandy has again left these shores. The rumours say that there has been a revolt in one of his provinces, close to the border with his neighbour Burgundy, and it is, apparently a very serious rebellion against his rule, for the prince of that state has a large army and threatens the very security of William's holdings in the land of Normandy.'

'Who did he leave in charge of England?' asked Edric as he handed the still shivering messenger a cup of warmed ale.

'I believe he has left his brother Odo in charge, my lord,' answered the man as he brought the cup to his lips and sipped the warm liquid.

'My thanks for the news,' said Edric. 'Drink up and warm yourself, I will get one of my men to show you to your quarters and provide you with dry clothing. Stay a few nights and wait until the weather is more clement before you return to your duties, and attend me again if you have any further news.'

He then opened his moleskin wallet and handed the man three silver pieces, causing the man's cold face to light up, for three silver pieces was more than a freeman could expect to earn in a whole year.

'My thanks to you my lord,' said the man as he turned and left, still holding the warm cup in his hands.

As the man left the room, another form entered a moment before the door closed.

Mono of the Meadows shuffled forward towards the fire where she stood holding her hands so close to the flames that both Edric and Godda thought she must burn them. Yet after what seemed a long, long time, she turned to face them and said in her strange childlike, croaky voice that had now become so familiar, 'Ah, I do so hate this cold weather.'

This evening she appeared dirtier and more pallid than usual, making it difficult for Edric to imagine that she had once been young and pretty.

'Oh! I have not always been so,' she croaked, as if she could read his thoughts. 'Many, many years ago, at the time of your grandfather's grandfather, when I was spawned' – her eyes sped up towards the rafters, showing but yellowy white, as was oft-times her way – 'oh, I was once young and pretty. Hair the colour of the sun, and skin so smooth, so smooth,' she sighed as she ran her dirty, uncut fingernails over her bristly chin. 'As smooth as yours Elf Queen,' she added now looking directly at Godda.

'Then Fenrir the wolf-god came to me during the night, and spoke to me saying that his tribe will go south until the spring arrives, for these hills and valleys will be full of blood and unsafe to dwell in.'

Godda, perhaps believing more deeply than her husband, shivered uncontrollably, leaning onto her husband's arms as if for protection.

'Wolf-god?' sneered Edric. 'What can he know? If he exists at all, which I doubt.'

For whilst he was perhaps not as superstitious as many of his peers and especially his lovely wife Godda, who seemed to read strange prophecies into the smallest of occurrences that happened in and around their home, he had to admit that he had been forced on many occasions to eat his words as her dreams and her prophecies had been proved to be correct.

He held her close and consoled her. 'Come now beloved,' he cooed in his gruff voice. 'Wolves are forest creatures and their life is one of blood, killing and of being killed. There is naught to fear.

'Still it may be wise not to enter the forests until spring is here,' he added, as he looked towards the small witch, who had now turned again towards the fire and was, once again, warming her small, claw-like hands.

A cackle of approval emitted from her throat as she shuffled out of the room.

The blood month of winterfall came and went with the slaughter and salting of the domestic animals that had been fattened up over the summer months. Now their meat would be needed in order to sustain the people though the harsh winter months.

The following few months were tedious in the extreme for Edric as well as the other men who would normally have spent the winter months out in the forests and woodlands, hunting deer, wild boar and other animals in order to supplement their diet of oatmeal, dried fruit, nuts and smoked beef, lamb and pork.

However, the first few months of the new year had been the coldest that the oldest amongst them could remember, and for the whole month no one had heard the usual chorus of the wolves throwing their eerie howls into the chill night air.

Many of the men whiled away the daylight hours repairing their houses, their weapons and their tools. Whilst most evenings were spent in front of a roaring wood fire, gambling, concocting or the telling riddles, or perhaps recanting the tales and sagas of their forefathers, and the folklore of their people.

When the Christian month of April finally arrived with its normal watery sunshine and heavy showers, Edric mounted his favourite hunting horse, slung his small, ash hunting bow across his shoulders, and holding his boar spear in his right hand, he guided his mount along the rutted pathway into the vast forest of Clunn.

He had been riding for less than an hour when he encountered the sparse remains of a red deer that lay in a clearing beneath a gnarled oak tree.

Stepping down from his horse, he examined the gory remains that consisted on little more than a few torn strips of the animal's hide, gnawed apparently, by some other animal whilst the still bloody bones appeared to have been torn off the animal and strewn around the once pleasant glade.

The grass surrounding the carcass had been trampled flat, yet revealed no obvious clue as to who or what had exactly slain and devoured the animal.

In the next valley he came across a similar scene, although this animal had once been a large wild boar that had been killed and eaten some weeks ago.

In the next glade, a mere twenty feet away, were the remains of at least three sows and more piglets than he could distinguish, with legs, and portions of the remains of their bodies strewn about, now lying on the blackened, congealed, gory ground.

His mind flew back to the words that Mona had uttered in one of her many weird warnings. Had she not said something about the forests being stained with blood, or something like that? And had not he and all who heard the prophecy thought that the blood would be that of man? Well, he thought to himself, perhaps this was the blood that she had foreseen, the blood of wild pig and of deer, not that of the human kind.

Smiling to himself, he thought what fools he and his people had been to take her warning to mean: 'the blood of men,' staying at home, afraid to enter the forest for a large part of the winter and the springtide!

Again, he alighted from his horse in order to examine yet another corpse, noting that whilst most of this carcass had been devoured by an animal, he could also see that there were two distinct cuts along the left hip joint. Cuts that could only have been made by a knife, and from these clues he quickly deducted that this particular animal had been attacked, killed and eaten by both a human as well as an animal predator.

Still puzzled by his findings, wondering to himself who, or what manner of man and beast dwelt in the woods, especially during the past winter, he mounted his nervous horse, continuing his ride into the woodland hoping to come across the culprits.

The afternoon passed without any further finds, but as he settled down for the night wrapped in his bearskin cape, he began to feel uneasy, having the distinct feeling that he was being watched. Yet he was assured that there was naught amiss, for when he looked at his horse, she was calmly chewing away at a succulent patch of grass that grew near to the small stream, showing no sign of alarm.

Knowing from long experience that the horse's senses of hearing and smell were far superior to that of mankind, he drew the bearskin cape up over his shoulders and soon fell asleep.

A loud snort from his horse brought him out of his deep sleep, waking to the misty dawning of a new day.

He sat bolt upright with his right hand grasping his boar spear whilst his left hand flew to his ten-inch hunting knife.

Nothing. Yet the hairs that stood up on the back of his neck caused him to disbelieve his own eyes, warnings that screamed out to him that there was something to be alarmed about.

At any second he expected an arrow or a spear to fly out of the undergrowth and send him to meet his maker, yet nothing happened.

Relaxing slightly, with an exhalation of relief, he heaved himself to his feet and began to make his way towards his tethered horse, which was now staring along the small stream with its nostrils flared and its ears lying back along his head with its eyes wide with alarm.

As he laid his hand upon the horse's neck in order to calm the beast, two enormous hunting hounds suddenly appeared out of the bushes and raced along the side of the stream towards him. *Just like those Irish killer dogs I used to have*, he thought as he calmly waited for them to reach him, knowing that if he were to turn and run they would be upon him in an instant, quickly sending him to the afterlife.

They were some fifteen feet from him and in the act of hurling themselves at his throat when he saw, out of the corner of his eye, another of the hounds, accompanied by what appeared to be a huge bear, yet he had no time to assure himself whether it was a bear or not, before the leading hound was in the air and leaping for his throat. He sidestepped the hound's drooling fangs by a hairsbreadth, plunging his spear upwards and into the hound's heart as he did so.

The second hound that had been only a couple of feet behind its mate landed with its feet upon Edric's chest, knocking him to the ground in the process, whilst its carnivorous mouth sought his neck.

Edric tried his best to fend the hound off with his right hand whilst at the same time stretching his head and neck out of the hound's reach, trying, without success to plunge his hunting knife past the hound's long legs and into its heart.

The hound's legs clawed across his chest and abdomen leaving red, bleeding welts which Edric did not even feel as he, at last, managed to plunge his knife upward and into the hound's belly a couple of times before a third thrust plunged into its heart instantly killing the beast.

He heaved the enormous weight of the hound off him, and as he struggled to his feet, he found himself confronted by a third hound which was being held in check by a huge, ragged giant, the being that he had first thought to be a large black bear.

'You've killed my two hounds,' snarled the figure menacingly as he pointed a spear at him, a spear that Edric quickly assessed as being 'home made' for it was no more than a sturdy pole topped by a crudely shaped lump of flint.

'Crude but deadly,' thought Edric, for he had seen many a good man slain by flint spears, arrows and axes.

''Twas either them or me,' said Edric, still somewhat out of breath from his recent fight with the two huge hounds, adding. 'If you did not want them slain then you should not have set them upon me.' As he stooped down to grasp his own spear which he wrenched out of the body of the first hound that he had slain, for despite the risk of angering the man by retrieving his boar spear, he felt very exposed facing this huge bearskined giant, plus the man's remaining hound with nothing more than a hunting knife.

'UGGGR!' snarled the man, unsure whether or not to avenge the killing of his two hounds by slaying this arrogant man who stood before him, but for some reason unknown to him, the man hesitated, for he had seen how easily the man had killed his pets and was unsure as to whether or not he and his remaining hound could prevail over a man such as this.

Whilst the man hesitated, Edric had his first opportunity to study the man, noting that what he saw did make a huge impression on him. The man must have stood nearly seven feet in height, and he appeared to be almost as wide as he was tall. However, Edric thought. The huge black bearskin coat that the man wore probably added to his girth; but even so, he must be pretty damned big, with or without the coat.

The man's hair and beard were greasy and filthy, adding to the overall picture that made him appear more like a beast than a man.

The man suddenly took up an aggressive stance and, in accordance to the laws of the day, he slapped his left palm twice with the haft of his spear, and then stared towards Edric, waiting for his reply.

Edric, of course, had no option other than to accept the man's challenge. Yet he did so with some reluctance, for although he thought that he was an experienced enough warrior to beat this huge man, the outcome of such a fight was not, in his mind, a foregone conclusion. The giant stood at least ten inches taller than Edric.

The man was also probably half as heavy again, and the spear that he brandished in his right hand, although roughly made, was nearly twice as thick as Edric's own sturdy boar spear, and sported a hand-cut flint that was at least ten inches long.

He reluctantly slapped his left palm with his boar spear and took up his fighting stance, waiting for the man to attack him. He thought he would probably come in one lumbering rush.

How wrong could he be? The man approached him slowly and prodded his spear towards Edric's head with such speed that he felt the flint nip the side of his ear.

He moved sideways prodding his own spear forward as he went, seeking a flaw in the man's defence. Yet the giant was so light on his feet and so experienced with his lumbering spear that Edric could detect no weakness.

The two men circled each other, probing forward with their weapons to no avail, each man swinging, thrusting and parrying each advance, with the crashing sound of wood upon wood echoing in the stillness of the clearing.

Edric scored the first hit, which was a wide swipe at the man's head but landed on his left shoulder with a thump, drawing no blood, and seemed to have no effect whatsoever upon the man.

His second success slashed the giant's left arm, leaving a neat tear in his leather sleeve with a few spots of blood dripping from the cut.

Edric attacked with renewed vigour, lunging and striking with his smaller boar spear against the more robust spear of his opponent, driving him back until the giant's back reached the base of a broad oak tree, prevented him from retreating any farther. Yet the base of the tree also hampered Edric who could still thrust forward with his spear point but could not now lunge from either the left or the right.

His opponent stepped away from the oak, raining blows onto Edric's shaft causing the lighter spear to fray and creak. Fearing that the shaft would snap in two if the giant continued, Edric retreated, dodging and sidestepping most of the blows, hoping that he would be presented with the opportunity of making one final thrust, and wound his adversary, thus bringing the contest to a close.

The giant began to give the impression of tiring, gasping and puffing as he parried blow by blow against his more nimble opponent, but the feigned tiredness turned out to be naught but a ruse, for as he backed away from Edric's attack, he suddenly reversed his stance, switching his spear from his right hand to his left and swung blow after blow with such power and ferocity that Edric was forced backwards yet again. Then, as he reversed even further back, his heel struck the body of one of the dead hounds and he toppled backwards, for a brief moment leaving himself open to attack; an attack which came so suddenly that his opponent struck out, catching Edric on the side of his head, and sent him unconscious to the ground.

His head spun with bolts of lightning that shot before his eyes as he struggled to kneel, to rise to his feet. Yet once he reached his knees he felt the coldness of the flint spearhead touch his neck, forcing him to stay where he was. Lifting his eyes, he tried to focus on the huge man who now stood over him.

He was unable to shake his head in order to clear the mist that swam before him. He could do no other than to stare up at the man, thinking that his time had come.

He had heard old wives' tales about the moment when men die, rumours that their lives flash before them, and true enough, the beautiful face of his first wife, the lovely Rowena smiled the smile that he had long thought forgotten, Then the hairy face of his old mentor, Vorta appeared before him, grim as ever, and Edric's memory told him that he could not even once remember Vorta produce anything that resembled a smile.

Vorta's face disappeared to be replaced by a blindingly bright light that dazzled his eyes, and out of this light appeared the wrinkled face of Mono of the Meadows. Who looked down at him, then turned her face upwards towards the giant who held Edric's life in his hands.

As plainly as he had ever heard a voice speak, man, woman or child, Her voice said, loudly, pleasantly, firmly and clearly, 'Nay, strike not, this man must live.'

Then she was gone.

The giant withdrew his spear, with a look of awe and amazement on his face, he mumbled, as if to himself, 'Nay I must not.' He retreated a couple of paces from Edric, leaned heavily upon his spear, panting as if he had just run a mile.

Edric's muddled thoughts were interrupted by the man who turned away, and walked towards his hound which he then untied, pulled savagely on the stout rope that held the hound in check, and said gruffly, 'Come,' and turned to leave.

Somewhat surprised, Edric staggered to his feet, saying quietly, 'Hold. There is no need to go, Come. I will help you bury your hounds.'

The man hesitated, but then carried on walking away. 'Oh well,' said Edric a little louder. 'I will have to bury the poor creatures myself.'

As if he had suddenly wakened out of a trance, the giant said, 'Don't touch 'em,' and turned to glare at Edric, who thought that the man looked as if he might attack him yet again.

'I'll bury them,' growled the man.

'As you will,' said Edric in a pleasant manner. 'Then I shall light a fire and you can share the spoils of my hunting, little though it is,' knowing that he had but one small chunk of venison, which he would now have to divide between himself, this gigantic man and his huge hound.

They both went about their tasks and when they had done, they waited while the venison roasted on a spit over the fire.

'What are you called?' asked Edric.

'I am Ordgar.'

Edric knew that the name Ordgar meant 'spear point' so he said with a chuckle, 'So you are named Spearpoint, you must have been a pretty little baby to have been named so.'

The man had probably heard the pun before and half smiled. 'Aye,' he said in a more pleasant way, 'Perhaps my mother should have named me after a cudgel rather than a slender spear point.' He ending his sentence with a half grunt.

'I am called Edric.'

The name meant nothing to the man who merely nodded in his direction and grunted, 'Edric.'

'Tell me Ordgar,' said Edric, 'why did you not slay me when you had me at your mercy?'

'Don't know,' came the sullen reply, 'mayhap I should have,' he grunted as he looked rather savagely into Edric's eyes.

Edric heaved the small chunk of venison off the fire, cut it in half and handed half to Ordgar, who immediately cut his half in two and handed the smaller of the pieces to his hound, who snatched it from his hand and slunk off, quickly and noisily devouring the meat. Then it returned to Ordgar's side and looked up at his master with eyes that quite plainly said. 'Give me more.'

As he chewed his half-cooked chunk of venison, Edric looked at Ordgar and said, 'I think that I shall call you Ordgar the Bear.'

The man looked up from his meat, made a grunted assent, and then returned his attention to the rapidly vanishing piece of venison.

*****

When he wakened in the morning, both Ordgar and the hound lay nearby. The man still slept, whilst the hound's eyes watched Edric as he stretched himself, took up his hunting bow and the sheath that contained his arrows, and quietly crept out of the clearing.

It was almost as if the god of the hunt was with him, for no sooner had he left the glade than he was presented with a year-old stag busy slaking its thirst from the stream.

The buck had not heard or seen Edric's approach and fell an instant later to a heavy ash arrow that pierced its heart. Within a few minutes of leaving the glade he returned carrying enough venison to sate his own hunger, plus that of the enormous man that he had just met, and the enormous man's equally enormous hound.

Edric did not break his fast until his chunk of venison was properly roasted on the newly awakened fire, and watched with interest, plus perhaps a little revulsion as both the hound and its master chewed their chunks of raw venison with relish and grunts of satisfaction, dribbling blood down both of their whiskers, as they both devoured vast quantities of bloody meat.

He called across the glade farewell to 'Ordgar the Bear' as he threw less than half of the remains of the stag over his horse, and began to walk away from the glade, and was rather surprised when he looked behind him to find Ordgar the Bear was no more than six feet behind him, leading the hound which had now been released from its rope and was following its master like a lady's lap-dog.

'I go with you,' he said almost apologetically, as he strode to catch up with Edric and walked alongside him. 'Nowhere else to go,' he added.

'That's fine,' answered Edric, 'I will find you somewhere to live when we reach my place.'

The two men led their respective animals along woodland paths, through dappled glades, up wooded hillsides and across the hilltops of bracken, brambles and heather. They talked as they made their way over fallen trees, around patches of marshland and thickets too dense for them to penetrate, scattering birds, mice and other kinds of wildlife before them.

Edric learned that Ordgar was not the old man that he had surmised him to be, but was a mere youngster of some twenty-five years of age. When Edric attempted to imagine what manner of man lay beneath his matted beard, greasy hair and dirt smattered face, he found it difficult to imagine the face of a much younger man lurking beneath all that hair and the grime.

Slowly, with words that the man found some difficulty in remembering, he told Edric as much about his life in the forest that he could recall. Edric was appalled to learn that Ordgar the Bear had been abandoned some twenty years previously by his father, who had lost his wife to the plague. Then, finding that he could not cope with his young son, he had simply disappeared one dark winter's night deserting his five-year-old son as he slept, leaving him completely alone in a deserted, flea-ridden hovel in the middle of the forest.

Since that time Ordgar and his hounds had ranged far and wide, living on anything from nuts, wild fruits and berries and of course, any game that they came across. Only staying in one place long enough to kill or scare away all of the wildlife in that particular part of the forest, before moving on to fresh territory.

When Ordgar first began to speak to Edric, his vocabulary and speech were garbled and hesitant. Edric presumed that this was because Ordgar had had little or no contact with humans during the last twenty years, and had spoken to naught but hounds during those long, lonely years. Yet as the hours passed, the language and the words came back to him, until Edric's head began to ache with the tirade of words that came, virtually non-stop out of Ordgar's mouth, telling of his life and the incidents and adventures that had befallen him during his life without people, spending as much time speaking about the hounds which meant so much to him, likening them to the family that he had never really had.

The hounds had originated from one near-dead puppy that he had found abandoned in a burned-out cottage some years before, and that particular bitch had eventually mated with a wolf, giving birth to the three hounds that had attacked Edric a couple of days ago, now.

'Alas,' he sighed, 'all I have left now is my beauty here, and I'm pretty sure that she is with pup, 'cause she was on heat a couple of weeks ago and disappeared for three days before she returned to me, and a big white male wolf followed us for many days after that, so we shall see, shall we not?'

'Should be interesting if she is in pup,' conceded Edric, 'for if she is, the pups will be more wolf than hound.'

Ordgar grunted and nodded.

They led their respective animals over the wet moorland, past the newly built mill and the many new duck ponds that had been created in the wet ground, where a gander hissed and chased them as they invaded his territory.

They wearily made their way up the hill and into the small village of Wentnor, through the gate of the small palisade that surrounded the newly constructed fortress, and across the small green to where the longhall stood.

Godda opened the door at the precise moment that Edric's hand touched the wooden latch, 'Welcome back my Lord Edric,' she said, smiling at him for a brief moment before she threw her arms around him, embracing him in a tight hug, then she looked over his shoulder towards the towering figure of his companion, speedily switching her gaze from him to his hound. A sight of which immediately caused her happy face to alter to a more serious contenance.

'Wolves are not friendly with my elf folk,' she said quietly into his ear.

'Nay, my love,' he answered, ''tis not a wolf, only half so, and I am sure that she will not harm you whilst in the company of this man, Ordgar the Bear.'

'Ordgar the Bear,' she said politely. 'I foresaw your coming, but not that of your dog.'

'My lady,' said the giant in the most polite and civil voice that Edric had yet heard him utter, for he seemed to have been instantly captivated by her beauty and stared at her in complete awe, almost, but not quite servile. 'My hound will not harm a hair of your head, nor any of your kin. For she is, like myself, a devoted servant of your good self and of your husband, Lord Edric.

Edric was rather surprised by the man's statement. He had given Ordgar no hint of his standing in the community, yet the man had accepted the fact that Godda and Edric were of the nobility as if he had always known it to be so.

After a welcome drink of mulled ale, plus a quick snack of newly baked bread, a chunk of cheese and half a partridge, he said as casually as he could to his wife, 'That witch, Mono of the Meadow, have her sent to me.'

'I have not seen her for several days, she left about the same time that you went on your hunting trip,' came the reply. Yet not asking why Edric seemed keen to speak with the witch, but giving him a glance that seemed to tell Edric that she knew only too well the whereabouts of Mono of the Meadows.

As if by magic, the door slowly opened, and in shuffled the wizened figure of Mono of the Meadows, who approached them, looking first towards Edric with a knowing smile, then turning to gaze upwards towards the gigantic figure of Ordgar the Bear who had ceased his idle chatter, and was staring down, white-faced, at the small, grubby figure as if he had seen a ghost. And indeed he was seeing a ghost, for the face that looked up at him was a face that he knew he had seen before, but the face was hidden in the grey mists that floated inside his brain, refusing to reveal its knowledge to him, despite the fact that he tried and tried in vain to recall when and where he had seen this grey, wizened old hag before.

'We have met before,' said the crone in her shrill, childlike voice.

Ordgar found it impossible to speak, shaking in fear for the first time in his life. He managed a single nod of his huge matted head.

'It was in the forest,' she said as if she had read his thoughts.

He nodded again and this time managed to utter a grunt.

Without further ado she turned and left the pale, shivering giant, shuffling over towards the corner of the room where the mother hound who had just given birth, and was allowing her seven wet, newborn pups to nuzzle their mother for her milk.

Of the seven pups, two had the appearance of purebred wolves, four were pure white and one, and the largest, was dark brown, like the mother.

The bitch wagged her tail and muzzled the rear ends of a couple of her pups, making no attempt to stop Mono as she picked up the brown pup.

'When it is weaned, bring this pup to me,' she said in her childish, birdlike voice then replacing the pup to continue its suckling.

No one answered.

She looked at them as if in disgust as she shuffled towards the table, poured herself a tankard of mulled ale from the jug, sipped the ale, making a grimace with her pock marked face, said, 'Ug, this stuff will rot your guts, I long for warm mead,' then drained the tankard, plonking the empty tankard upon the heavy oaken table before she shuffled her way out of the room.

Ordgar was given a bed with a dozen other men who were crowded into one of the small cottages that had been built alongside the inside of the palisade. Yet whilst he appeared to have been accepted by the men, Edric eventually learned that he never actually slept inside the cottage, but left his allotted place each evening to sleep with his hound, wrapped in his bearskin, under the thatched, open-sided woodshed.

It was not many days before Ordgar the Bear found a new friend in Waldo the blacksmith, who appeared to one of the few people in the village who was unafraid of Ordgar's hound. For the hound simply lay on her back, belly up, at any opportunity for the huge blacksmith to tickle her belly.

All of the seven pups lived, and soon became a pack of their own, creating havoc in the small village, controlled only by Ordgar the Bear, Godda and Edric.

This small pack however was soon reduced when, one evening, Mono of the Meadows returned. She walked over to the pups that should have been weaned some days ago, but were still in the habit of pestering their indulgent mother to produce yet more milk for them.

She knelt down, said something that the people who were watching were unable to hear. Then, as the astounded onlookers watched, the brown puppy disengaged itself from its siblings and, wagging its tail, simply followed Mono as she made her way towards the longhall's cookhouse which always seemed to be the first place that Mono always visited.

CHAPTER 17

William of Normandy, or King William of England as he preferred to be called, remained in the Dukedom of Normandy, raising troops and assembling stonemasons who were to accompany him on his next journey across the sea to England. At the same time he was forced to quell a number of minor rebellions, that seemed to erupt like pimples on a teenaged boy, first in one place, and no sooner had that particular pimple been squeezed out of existence, than another appeared somewhere else, requiring his attention.

He and his small army ranged across Normandy, Maine, Aquitaine, Basse and Brittany, bringing lords to heel, lords who had wrongly considered that now that their liege lord, William of Normandy had taken England, where most of his army was embroiled in either holding, or re-conquering various parts of that country, he would have neither the men or the inclination to miss their annual rents, nor would he notice if they invaded their neighbours lands, taking an extra valley here or an additional village there.

How wrong could they have been? For he fell upon them with vengeance, as a gyrfalcon swoops upon an unsuspecting skylark that hovers in the warm summer air, razing their fortresses and either slaying them or taking them and their men into his service to help him quell the few remaining lords who dared to deny him.

He took them with his own troops to the ports along the Normandy coast, or in the less extreme cases he may take one or all of their children to reside with him or with one of his loyal knights in far off castles in order to ensure the loyalty of their knightly fathers.

Dire news reached him via his spies, informing him that despite leaving England in the firm hands of his half-brother, Bishop Odo, the earls Waltheof and Ralph who was Earl of Northfolk, were conspiring against him, raising men and drawing warriors from their shires.

Whilst the news from the Welsh border shires were better, the city of Hereford having been restored to his arms. The Welsh king who had occupied it for more than a year had abandoned the city of Shrewsbury, and the main rebel of those shires, the man who was named Wild Edric or Edric the Savage had apparently disappeared into the vastness of the never-ending forests that covered those two shires.

The disappearance of Edric was a double-edged sword to King William, for he knew not whether the man had been slain, had died by some other means, or had simply withdrawn his forces and was now, gathering an even bigger army; an army that could swoop out of the forests at any time and sweep his own forces out of those shires, thus putting his complete English kingdom in jeopardy yet again.

His two loves, other than warfare, were his wife and his children, plus of course, his lifelong love for hunting,

If the pressures and problems weighed too heavily upon his shoulders, he would suddenly stop his pacing backwards and forwards, hurl the parchments onto the floor, and without a word stride out of the room, make his way to the stables where he would choose one of the many horses that he kept there.

He would hurl himself into the saddle, snatch up a short ash hunting bow and leather bag of hunting arrows, or perhaps a boar spear, call a couple of his favourite huntsmen and hounds to him, and spur his horse through the castle gates, into the woodlands, not returning until well after dusk, sweaty, bedraggled and exhausted, but ready to face his many problems on the morrow.

Williams's favourite son Robert, a strong young man of nineteen summers now felt himself old and mature enough to suggest to his father that he should be left in charge of Normandy, whilst his father returned to England in order to quell the English rebellions.

'My lord King,' he said one evening as he sat with his father and one of his younger brothers before a roaring log fire, sipping his mulled wine as delicately as he was able, knowing full well that his father approved of neither the juice of the grape or of the grain.

'It makes sense, does it not? My brothers and myself will look after your interests here in Normandy and Aquitaine, and we will keep our borders secure, whilst you take the bulk of our men to England and scour the land of those grubby Saxons.'

'Uncivilised savages,' spat the younger brother.

William looked with interest at the younger son, then turned his gaze towards Robert, who, from the day that he had been born had always been his favourite, seeing him now, as if for the first time, he noticed that the boy had grown and was, almost a man.

'Certainly,' he mused to himself. 'The boy has grown. He is bigger and has more muscle than I had at his age, and yes, he looks promising on the practice field and can joust with one or two of my better knights, but he has never yet seen blood shed on the battlefield. Never once has he been forced to defend himself against a man who really wanted to kill him. Yes, my knights have fought him, many with some gusto, but he knew that they had stayed their hands, for some of the better ones could have slain him on more than one occasion.'

Then, as he gazed back at his fresh-faced son, his eyes swam, as if in a mist, and he found himself back at Hastings, facing the English shieldwall, and those bloody axes. Oh, those axes.

He shuddered.

He felt himself falling off his stallion as he again heard the stallion squeal in agony, and heard the butcher's clump as an English war-axe bite into the animal's neck.

A second bout of shivers racked his body and he shook his head, trying to shake the image out of his mind's eye.

He put his hand out to prevent himself from falling.

'Father, Father!' cried Robert, jumping up from his seat as he rushed towards his father.

William shook himself awake.

The decision had already been made for him.

Robert was far too young.

He was far too inexperienced, too tender to be subjected to the gory work of battle.

'I'm all right,' he said, shaking his head again to try to destroy the vision of the bloodshed that he had seen at Hastings. Yet he could not, and the lonely figure of his friend, his fool, the lovable Tailifer, swam across his vision, tossing his sword high in the air, then catching it on its downward journey as he advance up the slight hill, smiling like a child who had been given a new toy.

Advancing, then dying from a single stroke from one of those deadly English war-axes.

Robert thrust his own goblet of mulled wine towards his father's lips, but the goblet was pushed aside.

'No, my son,' said the now recovering William. ''Twas but a bad dream.'

'A nightmare by the looks of it,' said the younger brother with a snigger, causing his father to glower at him, cursing him for being a fool.

'No, my dear Robert,' he said as he ruffled the boy's raven-black hair, 'In truth, the boy may be right, and the English may be uncivilised savages, but in warfare I have yet to meet their match, and I think that you are far too young to test your skills against an English war-axe.'

'But Father,' he was cut short by William, who, losing his patience, gave his son a mighty cuff across his ear, sending him sprawling across the room.

'Enough,' he bellowed, 'enough I say,' and strode out of the room, leaving the two boys alone, one grinning broadly at the discomfort of his elder brother whilst the other seething with anger and indignation at being treated with such distain.

'He'll bloody well regret that one day,' said Robert rubbing the side of his head. He'll bloody well regret it, you'll see,' he repeated.

William slept little that night, tossing and turning, much to the annoyance of his wife Matilda. She was often kept from her sleep because of her husband's restlessness, so much so that this night she left marital bed, spending the night on the floor on an old feather mattress that she lifted out of one of the several chests that stood against the walls in their sleeping quarters.

He was up, had broken his fast and was hunting in the forests before dawn, followed by two sleepy huntsmen and two equally sleepy deerhounds, having a fruitless day, seeing neither deer nor boar, returning to his castle in a more foul mood than he had left.

During the hunt his mind had not been on hunting. He had driven his steed furiously through marshlands and bramble bushes, up hillsides and through wooded dales, unable to scour from his mind the words that his eldest son had said, as well as the things that had been left unsaid, the previous evening.

He had, of course, always been aware of Robert's drive and of his ambition, but in his mind, what he had heard yesterday had been little more than a hooded threat saying that unless he gave his son more power, or even a province of his own, then he would grasp the first opportunity open to him, and would take the power.

Power which he considered to be his by right of birth, for he was, he had often argued, a son of the King of England, lord of Normandy, Aquitaine, Brittany, Maine, plus a dozen other smaller states that now made up his father's vast empire.

'He is too much like me,' said William to himself. 'I'd better watch this young son of mine, or I could wake up with a knife in my ribs, and then he'll inherit the lot.' Muttering aloud, causing one of his grooms to glance up at his Lord, eyes wide open in amazement that his lordship should start talking to himself.

The groom looked towards a stable boy who was forking out last night's manure, and raised his eyebrows in a knowing way, then brought his head down speedily lest his lordship should see the look.

William stalked into the hall in order to finalise his plans to return to England, but not without first dictating many letters to his scribes, sending riders hither and thither with orders and demands in order to satisfy himself that his domains here on the mainland were secure.

CHAPTER 18

The weather had been very wet, holding the spring ploughing back by more than two weeks, causing the ploughmen to curse and lash their animals with the long whips that they carried as they, and their lumbering oxen, trudged their way up and down the heavy, rain-soaked fields.

The month of May was also wet, causing the weeds to grow at double their normal rate, or so it seemed to the people who attempted to keep them in check.

For Edric and his fifty warriors it had been a time not only for repairing their weapons and equipment, as well as practicing their skills on the one meadow that Edric had kept aside for that particular purpose, but also for repairing and strengthening their small fortress.

They had deepened the dry moat, in readiness for the attack from the Normans that, he felt, must come, especially now that the winter had passed. They too must realise that the expected improvement in the weather would allow the campaigning season to begin once again.

Whilst Godda spent a lot of her time with the two Norman ladies, the Lady Isabella and her companion Catherine, conversing with them freely in both English and the language of Normandy. These ladies caused Edric some concern, as no emissaries had arrived from Isabella's husband, the Lord Mortimer, forcing Edric to consider sending one of his own men to find Lord Mortimer in order to negotiate the return of his wife.

Edgar the interpreter was the obvious choice but whilst Edgar was a likeable and intelligent young man, he was no warrior, which would mean that Edric would be forced to send perhaps half a dozen warriors with Edgar, in order to protect him from the many bands of lawless men who now inhabited the land, mainly due to the Norman habit of burning farms and villages.

Would Edgar and his small retinue of warriors be too large or too small?

If there were too few, then they would be left open to attack, which could result in Edric losing both Edgar and his companions.

Yet if he sent too many men with Edgar, they would be seen as an aggressive force, thus provoke an attack by any Norman force that they might meet.

Another unknown factor was the whereabouts of Lord Mortimer. Was he alive or dead?

Was he even in the country?

No one seemed to know.

Or, had he returned to Normandy?

No news whatsoever had been heard of the man for over a year.

That evening he broached the subject with Godda. 'What do you think I should do about Isabella and Catherine?' he asked. 'Do you think it wise to try and find Lord Ralph Mortimer, and let him know that we are holding his wife and her companion here? Or should we just release them? Send them off with an escort and let them find Mortimer?

'I always thought that Mortimer knew that we were holding his wife,' he said, scowling slightly as he did so, 'and that he probably did not want her back. Perhaps he is glad to see the back of her.'

Godda interrupted him, as if Edric had not spoken, as was her way. 'If you should send her back to her husband then you can kiss goodbye to any ransom that you thought that you had hoped to receive,' she said sweetly, 'and you may lose five or six good men into the bargain, because the two women can't travel alone in these uncertain times, and Mortimer seems to be a man who you should be wary of.'

'What you say may well be true,' said Edric as he stood up, and holding his jug of ale in his right hand, walked over to the fireplace. 'What I will do,' he said thoughtfully, 'is send a couple of men to the cities of Hereford and Shrewsbury, and have them spread the word amongst the Norman garrisons that Mortimer's wife is being held captive by me, and that I want a ransom of fifty. No. I want a ransom of one hundred pounds' weight of silver for her return.

'That should do the trick. News will soon reach Mortimer and his pride and his good name will force him to pay up for the safe return of his wife. She is, after all, quite a beauty. Is she not?'

Godda snorted at his remark. 'I wouldn't call her a raving beauty,' she said and stormed out of the room.

The following morning, Evan and Edgar the interpreter left Wentnor. Evan headed south towards Hereford while Edgar headed for the city of Shrewsbury, both were mounted on shaggy Welsh hill ponies, sturdy, tireless mounts but grubby enough not to cause any interest, should meet any inquisitive Normans.

The message that they carried was verbal, saying that, 'If Lord Ralph Mortimer wanted his wife the Lady Isabella and her handmaiden returned to him, then he was to meet Edric, with no more than two menservants, at the forum in the ruined Roman city below the mountain called the Wrekin at midday, on midsummer's day' – this was the summer solstice, some five weeks hence – 'with one hundred pounds' weight of silver.'

Both men were back within three weeks, having accomplished their mission of broadcasting the news of the two Norman ladies' capture, assuring Edric that all he could do now was to wait for the news to reach Isabella's husband, and hope that his reaction would produce the results that he wanted.

Edric spent those weeks in the usual way, hunting, overseeing the work on the small fortress, settling petty disputes between farmers and cottagers which were usually arguments over borders or who owned this cow or ram, as well as helping with the numerous tasks that needed to be done with his own livestock.

Sheep shearing was the one task that he disliked more than any other, and had nothing but admiration for the shepherds, as they and their young helpers, caught the heavy sheep, clipped them with handheld metal shears, then rolled the wool into bundles in readiness for either transporting the heavily laden wagons to the nearest wool merchant, or stored a smaller portion of the fleeces in one of the barns where the fleeces would be spun, and knitted into garments, rugs and blankets during the long, dark winter months.

The month of June, called Ærra Līda by English people, came in with long sunny days, followed by weeks of clear blue skies, drying the ground that had once been saturated during the winter and spring months.

The hot weather now turned the earth into rock-hard soil, drying the ground so severely that fissures gaped so deep that a grown man could stretch his arm down some of the cracks and still not touch the bottom. Yet the people ignored such trivialities, whistling and singing as they went about their tasks, enjoying the long hot days, and the warm evenings that allowed them to sit outside their cottages in order to enjoy long days that remained light until nearly midnight.

Edric and Godda spent many happy evenings with the two Norman ladies, Garth and his lovely wife Myreen, sitting outside the longhall, sipping ale, and elderflower wine, enjoying one another's company and the sweet smell of the freshly lugged hay that was now stacked up to the rafters in the nearby barns.

Both Godda and the Lady Isabella had laboured long and hard in teaching Edric the language of Normandy, and although he had grasped a large portion of it, he still found it extremely difficult to get his tongue around some of the more difficult words, much to the amusement of the ladies.

'Why can't they speak plain simple English?' he said laughingly to Godda one evening whilst she was struggling to get him to pronounce a particularly difficult phrase. 'Even English children of two and three years of age have no trouble with our language,' he said, but she scowled, then gave a wry smile, for she had heard that one before.

He left a full week before the summer solstice, sadly recalling vividly the time when he had left his first wife alone, only to return to find the beautiful Rowena's body, battered and mutilated. So on this occasion he left the bulk of his warriors in the fortress in order to take care of Godda and the rest of the people who were under his protection, taking only ten men with him, plus of course the two Norman noblewomen.

The small band of men escorted the two ladies along the western side of the Long mountain passing through the tiny hamlet of Ratlinghope, then across the hilltop, and down the steep side of a hillside named Cathercott where there lived a local family who dwelt in a single, neat, whitewashed cottage that lay half hidden in a small dell. They were a jovial, happy family of nine or ten children, who cheered and waved at the men as they made their way past the cottage, carefully riding down the slope into a narrow valley, through a marshy patch of land and then up the steep incline into the small, fortified longhall of Pulverbatch.

A mile or so further on they trudged through another small village, named Longden and Edric could see why it was so named, for it stretched for a couple of miles along the side of a babbling brook.

He purposely avoided the city of Shrewsbury, crossing the wide River Sabrina at a shallow ford near the hamlet of Atchem, where the remains of a once proud Roman bridge still stood on one side of the river. Then they continued southwards until they reached the outskirts of the deserted Roman city, a mere mile or so further on.

They made a cold camp in a small wood, near to the river, where they ate a meal of cold Lamb, cheese, bread and honey, swilled down with beer for the men, and homemade elderflower wine for the ladies.

Edric allowed no fires to be lit and had two warriors stand guard, with orders that the warriors were to be replaced by fresh men every three hours during the night.

He was awake, and walking in the eerie silent, ruined city an hour before dawn, accompanied by two of Ordgar the Bear's pups who were now full grown, each now the size of a well-grown calf.

His eyes peered into every gaping window and doorway, sniffing the air in order to detect the slightest hint of wood smoke, or the smell of damp leather or any other stench that indicates the presence of humankind.

After an hour of wandering through the weed-choked, deserted streets, he was about to start his journey back to his camp when the two hounds abruptly halted as if they were joined at the hip. Their bristles went up and they stared towards a large derelict building, uttering low growls.

'Down boys,' he said in a whisper, and the two well-trained hounds immediately dropped onto their bellies and looked up to their master.

He patted both of the hounds on their heads. 'What is it?' he said. 'What do you see?' straining his eyes through the hazy light of a new day, but could see nothing but more ruined buildings that stretched away into the distance, with the large mound of the Wrekin looming high in the far background.

'Stay,' he said quietly to the hounds, causing them to relax and sit on the dusty ground as he crept forward as quietly as he was able, through the dry grass and scattered rubble that lay on the once perfect Roman street.

He reached the wall of the building that the hounds had stared at, peered through a window, but could see nothing but darkness, no sign of a fire, no smell of horses or of human presence, and he was in the process of standing up straight in order to move to the next building when the muffled sound of a man snoring reached his ears.

The sound, slight though it was, came from deep within the building that he had already been peering into.

He thought it unwise to enter into a darkened room where men may be sleeping, especially as he had no idea how many men may be in there. So he remained where he was for the space of a hundred heartbeats, but heard no further sounds from the room, causing him to consider the possibilities of whether or not he had imagined the first sound.

He felt sure that it was the sound of a man sleeping, but began to think to himself that if the room had been full of sleeping men then the noises would normally have been greater than a single snore from a single man.

It could, perhaps, be a family of English people in there, mayhap a shepherd or a drover sheltering for the night. On the other hand, from what he knew of the superstitions of his own people, then it was perhaps unlikely to be one of his own people for they tended to shun places like this, considering them to be unlucky and inhabited by ghosts and demons.

Far more likely to be Normans, he thought. The question is, how many? It might be just one or two, but of course it may be many, many more.

Possibly waiting for him and his two Norman ladies to appear and walk into their carefully prepared trap.

He silently returned to his two hounds. 'Heel,' he said to them, and they followed him out of the street to another building some one hundred yards away, where the three of them, silently and carefully entered the ruined house, took up a position near a window that was half covered with ivy and an elder tree, then peeping carefully through the window that overlooked the street and the building where he had heard the snoring coming from, he crouched down and waited.

He did not have to wait for long. For a few short minutes after he had positioned himself where he could peer out of the window without being seen, a figure suddenly emerged out of the doorway of the far building, stretched his arms skywards, stretched again and yawned loudly, obviously unaware that he was being watched. He then scratched himself under his left armpit and bellowed, 'Come on you lazy sods, shift yer asses!' then turned to re-enter the room.

Edric began to hear more noises, consisting of grunts, groans, moans and shouts, coming from within the building. However he was unable to make out what was actually being said, but was convinced that the noise that emanated from the building could only be made by a considerably large number of men.

Eventually no less than thirty-one men gathered outside the building, where the man who was obviously their leader assembled them into a formation that was alien to Edric.

Edric could now see that the assembled men were, without a doubt, Normans, for although they wore many different types of attire, nearly all of them had their hair cut in the Norman way, with the back of their necks shaven, showing the now familiar 'pudding bowl' style that the Normans habitually wore.

Edric mused for a moment about their strange hairstyle, and came to the conclusion that they favoured this style in order to allow their cone-shaped helmets to fit more comfortably onto their heads, as well as to offer the wearer a little additional protection.

He watched as they assembled, then moved off, passing the house in which he was hiding, chattering and laughing like 'a killing of crows'.

Keeping his two hounds quiet by whispering soothing words to them, he allowed the Normans to pass. Then he silently followed them down one street into another for more than half an hour, always allowing them to pass out of sight before exposing himself and his two hounds, just in case a man at the rear of the company felt the urge to look behind him.

It was not really a surprise to Edric when the marching men reached the centre of the ruined city and disappeared through the archway that led into the round building that was quite obviously the 'Forum'.

This now presented Edric with a fresh problem. He could not follow the men through the ruined archway in case he was seen, forcing him to follow the wall around the outside of the Forum in order to find another way in, and, if possible, learn a little more about the Normans trap that they were quite obviously planning for him.

He eventually came to a small entrance where the old wooden doors had rotted away. Carefully pushing his way through a tangle of nettles that were nearly as high as his face, he emerged into what appeared to be a tunnel that must have originally reached up into the inside the forum, with a flight of wooden stairs that probably led to the top of the walls, but was now nothing other than sagging walls and rotten timbers, which were hanging treacherously in all directions, as well as hampering his own (and his hounds') progress.

'Sit,' he said to the hounds, and they both sat. 'Stay,' he said and stroked both of them in turn on their heads and fondled their ears.

The hounds looked up lovingly at their master, and then lay down as they had been told.

He made his way carefully over and under the rotting timbers, through brambles and around young trees of all descriptions that had taken root in what must have been, many years ago, a bustling, thriving community, until he eventually reached a position where he could see a large portion of the circle.

This would be the arena where men had, according to the stories that he had heard, fought, not only each other, but had pitted their wits and their strong right arms against beasts the like of which he had never seen, but had heard many bloodthirsty stories about them since his childhood: of lions that were eight feet long with fangs as long as a man's hunting knife, hyenas and striped cats called tigers, and of elephants as big as a house. Beasts that he knew the names of, but had no real idea of what they looked like.

Edric's eyes followed the leader as he walked casually around the arena, stopping now and again to allocate a man here, and another there, then watching as the man went to his allocated position, either nodding that all was in order or perhaps bellowing to the man until that particular man had been moved to another, more suitable position, before moving on to find a hiding place for the next man.

*****

Edric watched until all the Normans had been allocated a position and the leader bellowed, 'Right, now that you all know your positions, I want you make sure that you know exactly where your position is. Get some dry hay or bracken and make yourselves a comfortable nest, and when you have done that, meet me at the entrance, and we will have an evening meal together, because it'll be the last meal that you will have until this job is over.'

As the leader turned to leave, his men slowly emerged from their hiding places, and he shouted, 'I want you all in position by midnight, so make certain that you have all got a water bottle, and a hunk of dried bread or a slice of meat to get you through the day, and make sure that you have all had a piss and a shit, and then not a word out of any of you, do you hear? Not a word until you hear my command.'

Edric waited for some time before making his way back to the hounds then he led them back to where he had left his men and the two Norman ladies some three or more hours ago.

'Thank God,' said Garth as he greeted Edric. 'We were beginning to think that you had been slain or had lost your way.'

'Well as you can see I neither lost my way or have been slain,' he answered with a wry smile as he passed the large figure of Garth, and made his way towards the two Norman ladies who were huddled together in a shady spot under a large oak tree, where they could gaze upon the tranquil river that flowed lazily past them not twenty yards away.

'My lady,' said Edric as he approached them, 'have you and your companion eaten?'

'We have Lord Edric,' answered the Lady Isabella. 'Your men have been most courteous,' she added with a dazzling smile that completely captivated

Edric, making his knees tremble and an excited shiver throb through him, sending his mind into something of a turmoil of longing and desire. Yet the desire lasted for one brief moment, as he reminded himself that he already had a life-mate in the form of the beautiful Godda.

'Is my husband, Lord Mortimer waiting for me up there?' asked Lady Isabella nodding in the direction whence Edric had returned.

'Nay my lady, he is not,' answered Edric with a wry smile. 'But a large number of his men are.'

Garth who had been with Edric as he approached the ladies, gave a grunt, saying, 'I thought it might be a trap. Damn bloody Normans, there's not one of 'em that you can trust.' Forgetting as he uttered the words that the two ladies were standing a mere three or four feet from him, were indeed Norman ladies.

The two women carried on as if Garth had not spoken, giving no indication that they had just been insulted.

'I am sure that my Lord Edric will know what to do, and will deliver me safely to my husband, the good Lord Mortimer,' said Isabella, still radiating her much rehearsed smile. A smile that had from the time of her childhood, captivated all who met her, both male and female, young and old, serf and nobleman, belying the beautiful ladies true nature and her brilliant brain.

A brilliant brain, coupled with her beauty had catapulted her from being the bastard daughter of a minor baron, to the wife of one of King William's wealthiest and most trusted lords.

'Just so, just so,' said Edric in a non-committed way, as he placed his arm across the shoulder of Garth and led him away from the two Norman ladies.

'I hope she is right,' said the ever-blunt Garth.

'She certainly is,' answered Edric. 'And if it works, then we shall be rid of these two troublesome ladies, and have a hundred pounds' weight of silver jingling in our saddlebags by noon on the morrow.'

Early the following morning Edric, followed by his ten warriors, plus Garth, Ordgar the Bear, Waldo the Blacksmith, plus the two Norman ladies, made their way carefully through the silent, weed-covered, ruined streets of the Roman city. They halted when Edric considered them to be within perhaps a quarter of a mile from the main gate of the Forum, at a spot where he knew the Norman warriors were waiting for him to walk into their carefully laid trap.

As a result of the previous day's reconnoitring, he knew that there were only three streets that led directly to the one large gate through which the Norman ambushers had passed, and which, if his assumptions were correct, the gate through which Ralph Mortimer would pass. If indeed, the good Lord Mortimer came at all, and had not sent one of his lackeys in his stead.

He stationed his party in a couple of deserted houses near the centre street, some two hundred yards from the forum, then sent two of his warriors down each of the three streets, with instructions that, 'If and when you see a body of Normans approaching, make your way back to me as quickly as you can, and make sure that they don't see you. Is that clear?'

Each of the six men nodded and grunted. 'Aye, my lord,' and went their separate ways.

Shortly before noon the two warriors who had been watching the central street came rushing in. 'They come, my lord,' panted one of the men.

'How many?'

'About twenty I think,' answered the warrior.

'How far behind you are they?'

'Not far, my lord, they ride quickly.'

'You go up that street and bring in the other warriors back here,' he said pointing to the left-hand street. 'And you run up the other street and bring back the other two.' he said, and the two warriors ran off like hares being chased by hounds.

'Half of you men hide yourself in those buildings over there.' He pointed to the other side of the street. 'The rest of you stay here, and don't make a sound or do anything unless I order it.'

The men also touched their foreheads with their knuckles in acknowledgement and ran to do their liege lord's bidding.

'You ladies come with me,' said Edric harshly, 'and you Garth, Ordgar and Waldo, follow me.' He strode out into the street and proceeded to walk towards the forum, stopping when he had covered approximately twenty yards.

*****

The twenty-five horsemen trotted gaily around the bend of the street which was littered with broken rubble from the several buildings that had collapsed, urging their mounts through clusters of brambles, nettles and saplings that had taken root in the once spotlessly kept Roman road. Now the rubble preventing them from galloping as was their leaders' original intention.

As soon as they saw the three figures and what they took to be two half-grown foals standing in the middle of the street, some thirty or so yards in front of him, Ralph Mortimer who was leading the small cavalcade, on his much prized and extremely expensive Arab stallion, hauled savagely on the reins, causing his steed to slide to a halt in a cloud of dust.

'What in God's teeth is this?' he cursed, as his fellow riders reined in behind him.

'Don't know, my lord,' said the knight nearest to him, 'but I will soon find out,' spurring his horse forward towards the three men. Lord Ralph and the rest of his men followed the bold knight Sir Bondevile, a man who was known for his bravery, and indeed sometimes for the rash deeds that he oftimes performed.

'There are, after all, only three of them!' he shouted over his shoulder as he approached the three waiting Englishmen.

'Plus two foals,' shouted one of the men in his retinue, and laughed at his remark, then added. 'Probably some farm yokels who want a hand-out.' This brought more chuckles from his fellow riders.

Lord Ralph Mortimer snarled 'Shut yer face you idiot!' Spurring his mount a little closer to the three waiting men, he exclaimed in awe. 'They're not bloody foals, they are bloody dogs.'

'Buggering dogs,' mumbled one of the men. 'I hate the buggering things.'

'Hounds,' corrected Bondevile, Damn great things. I've heard about their war hounds. Bloody Saxons used to use them in war,' adding a few seconds later, 'but I haven't seen any on this trip.'

'Nor any that bloody big.' added someone at the rear of the company.

Mortimer reined his nervous horse some ten feet in front of the three men.

'By the Christ God,' he whispered to Bondevile, 'forget the bloody dogs, just look at the size of those men, they are bloody enormous.'

'I'm not looking at the dogs or the bloody men,' came the whispered reply, 'I'm looking at those fucking great axes.'

Mortimer shifted his gaze momentarily from the men to the huge axes that each of the three men carried, resting the heavy axe heads on the ground in front of them, alongside their kite-shaped shields.

He visible shivered as he remembered the havoc that axe-men such as these had caused at the battle at Hastings, shivering again as he recalled King William's horse screaming as its guts gushed out to become entangled in the stallion's legs as it thrashed about in agony, nearly kicking the King as he had attempted to scramble to his feet.

He shifted his gaze back to the three men, and this time he studied the shields, thinking to himself, 'They have Norman shields. Now, how in hell's name did they get them? Probably from slain Normans!'

Then he looked again at the man in the centre, the smallest of the three, the one who had one of those huge hounds on either side of him. He was probably the leader, perhaps even the man they called 'Wild Edric', whilst the two giants on either side of him were probably his personal bodyguards.

He was about to order his men to encircle the three and cut them down when, out of the corner of his eye he almost felt, rather than saw a movement, and as he glanced sideways towards the derelict building, he saw a hand, holding what could only be one of the famous English longbows, for the tip or an arrow gleamed as the sunlight caught it through the open window.

Not just three of them, he mused to himself, crafty sods, but just how many?

Could be a dozen or more, but there was no way of telling.

Mortimer's calculating mind assessed the possible odds.

His numbers here were a mere twenty-five, but there were another thirty of his finest warriors in the Forum. But of course it would take time for them to reach him, and in those few vital minutes, there was no doubt in his mind that many of the men here, and very possibly himself, would have fallen, either to arrows, or to the hounds, who would no doubt panic the horses, or to those damned axes which glistened a few feet in front of him.

No, the risk was too great.

The odds were against him coming out alive from any conflict with these English giants.

'Would any of you gentlemen happen to be the Lord Edric?' asked Lord Mortimer, forcing himself to smile.

The man in the centre answered, as he knew he would.

'I am he,' said the man in slightly imperfect Norman.

He let out an audible sigh of relief, thinking to himself that the man was at least civilised enough to speak the Norman tongue, and the feeling that a steel-tipped arrow was going to thud into his back at any second, almost went away.

Mortimer continued to smile as he dismounted, handing the reins to the nearest warrior.

'Dismount you oafs,' he snapped to his men, and they rather unwillingly dismounted from their restless mounts, looking about them. For in fact many of them had also seen the gleam of arrowheads and movements in the buildings that skirted the street.

He approached the trio, taking off his steel mitten as he did so, holding out his right hand in the universal greeting of friendship, and of course in order to reassure this Saxon wolf's head that he held no weapon in his right hand.

Edric, who, when he had been standing in between his two body-guards had looked to be smaller than most men, but as he shook the hand of Edric, he was surprised to see that Edric was at least two inches taller than himself, and he was nearly six feet in his hose. Taller than most of the men in his entourage, causing him again to shift his gaze from Edric towards the two giant bodyguards, causing him to gaze up at them, his mouth gaping open in amazement as he realised that whilst from the back of his stallion they had looked tall, but now, from ground height, both men were absolutely enormous.

Edric, seeing Mortimer's shocked countenance, remarked, 'Garth Bloodaxe and Ordgar the Bear do tend to have that effect upon men.'

Feeling at a distinct disadvantage, despite having twenty-five men behind him, Mortimer blustered a little.

'My, my wife, the Lady Isabella, is she here? Is she well?'

'She is here my lord and she is safe and well,' answered Edric, eager to get this distasteful business over and done with. Especially before the additional thirty or so warriors who were at this very moment waiting for his arrival in the Forum realised that something was amiss, and left their hiding places to join Ralph Mortimer and his men here, a manoeuvre that would speedily tip the odds against him.

'Waldo bring out the ladies,' he shouted, and the huge figure of Waldo the blacksmith appeared in the open door, ushering out the Lady Isabella and her companion, Catherine with his bulk towering over them making them look like little girls of perhaps ten or twelve years of age.

'God's blood,' gasped Ralph Mortimer under his breath. 'Don't these bloody Englishmen come in normal sizes?'

Edric heard the remark and smiled to himself, for this was the only reason that he had brought Waldo with him on this trip.

He had paid Waldo four silver pieces to make himself an outsized mail-shirt, plus a helmet to fit his large head, as well as a shield and a war-axe, and he had to admit to himself that the blacksmith did look the part, as he ushered the two Norman ladies across the street towards the waiting men. Yet Edric knew full well that, whilst Waldo was probably one of the finest blacksmiths and strongest men in the shire, he was literally a hopeless warrior, with little or no sense of timing or co-ordination whatsoever, making him more of a liability to his own men than a danger to any enemy.

As the ladies approached, Edric turned to the Lord Ralph Mortimer. 'Well here is your lady wife and her companion, perhaps now would be a good time to see the ransom money.'

Lord Mortimer, who was used to being treated with far more finesse and courtesy by men of lower rank, and that meant most men, was taken aback at such rudeness, cursing to himself at the thought that this Saxon lowlife did not trust a man of his rank, and he was about to order his men to take the dog down a peg or two, when his mind was forced to reconsider such a hasty decision. Not only because of the three enormous men and their huge hounds who now stood before him, but also the gleam of those damned arrowheads and spear points that constantly glistened from the derelict buildings on both sides of the street.

'Bondevile,' he snarled to his aide, 'have the two pack animals brought up,' and his aide turned and beckoned to the two men who held the two pack animals in the centre of Lord Mortimer's warriors. 'Bring the pack animals up,' he ordered to the man who had been called Bondevile, and two servants urged the two pack animals up to the front of Mortimer's men.

'Check the silver,' said Edric quietly to Garth, and Garth heaved his axe onto his shoulder, allowing his shield to fall to the floor with a loud thud, as he walked the few paces forward to the waiting animals.

He checked each of the four leather saddlebags in turn, digging his hands deep into them to ensure that the silver coins did indeed go to the bottom of the bags and had not been substituted by copper or perhaps stones or the like, before returning to Edric, 'All seems to be in order my lord,' he said, 'although it would take an age to count it to make sure,'

'No need for that,' answered Edric, 'for I am sure that a man of Lord Mortimer's reputation would not stoop so low as to short-change us.' He smiled as he uttered the words and looked directly into Mortimer's eyes, where for the first time since they had met, he saw a flicker of fear.

'It seems that we have a deal, my Lord Mortimer,' he said.

Mortimer nodded, 'It would seem so.' Then for the first time since his wife had appeared, he stepped towards her, placed his right hand on her hip and gave her a light kiss on her cheek, 'Come my dear,' he said quietly, 'I shall take you home,' and, taking her hand in his, he made his way back to the comparative safety in the centre of his horsemen.

'Come,' said Edric, grinning from ear to ear, 'We are done here, so let us make haste before those idiots who are waiting for us in the Forum realise that we are not going to walk into their trap, and come howling after us like a pack of hungry hounds.'

As soon as Mortimer and his Normans had disappeared around the bend, Edric's men emerged from their hiding places, and he led his men down an alleyway, which entered into the western road that led to and from the Forum, into the small overgrown courtyard where their horses were tied.

They speedily mounted and hastened down the wide, weed-choked street towards the edge of the ruined city.

As they finally left the last of the silent city behind them, Edric thought that he heard a sigh of relief from his men as they entered the scattered woodlands, where, it seemed to him, the birds began to sing again. The breeze stirred the leaves and the land smelled of greenery and of blossom, being fresh and untainted by the decaying, weed-choked aura of the deserted Roman city.

Despite his fears of an ambush Edric urged his mount forward through the shallow ford to the far bank of the fast flowing Sabrina, pausing only once as his horse became nervous when it stepped into one of the many hidden holes that pitted the river bed of the badly maintained ford, causing the following horses to neigh and whinny in panic, giving their riders some concern until they eventually re-gained control of their mounts.

He smiled to himself with a little satisfaction when he found that there were no waiting Normans hidden in the bushes on the far side of the river and he urged his mount up the steep bank, where he dismounted and tethered his horse to a nearby sapling. His men did likewise as he beckoned them to join him.

'We are a mere fourteen men,' he said, stroking his short beard as he looked around at his men, 'and if we are to be followed, which is a distinct possibility, then we are likely to be followed by anything up to fifty Normans, all intent on regaining the fortune that their liege lord has just paid us for the ladies.

'What I want you to do Waldo,' he said, turning to the huge blacksmith, 'is to take the two packhorses and make your way home as quickly as you are able, and deliver the silver safely to Godda.

'You, Edward and your brother Aella, you will accompany him and make sure that nothing happens to him or to the money,' he said grimly. 'I want that silver delivered safely to Godda and then I shall give you all your share when I join you at Wentnor.'

Waldo, and the two men nodded and turned to remount their horses, untied the ropes that tethered the pack animals, then led them northward along the bush-covered road.

Edric then turned his attention to the rest of his men.

'We shall remain here for a couple of hours and hope that the Normans haven't taken it into their thick heads to follow us. But if they do, then this is the ideal place to stop them, in fact it's probably the only place that we can stop them. So string your longbows, hide yourselves along the riverbank overlooking the ford, and do not do anything until you hear my order to shoot.'

Just as his men were turning, he said, 'Oh, I think it would be wise to use bodkins as most of the Normans with Lord Mortimer were armoured.'

His men nodded, and grunted consent, knowing full well that arrows with steel-tipped bodkins were the only arrows that would penetrate Norman chain mail.

They then returned to their horses, where they untied their bows from the saddle horns, took the bows out of their leather casements, brought out the bow-strings from a separate bag that was wool lined in order to keep the strings dry, strung their bows. Then, taking a bundle of arrows, they made their way towards the riverbank, where they hid themselves and settled down to await developments.

They did not have long to wait, for within ten minutes they heard the thunder of horses' hooves, followed a few minutes later by a flurry of activity as a horde of horsemen crashed out of the bushes on the far side of the river, and splashed, fearlessly onto the ford.

'Hold,' bellowed Edric, knowing full well that although his voice was loud enough to carry to his warriors, it was unlikely that the Normans could hear him as they cursed and drove their steeds across the wide ford.

'Hold, Hold,' he said again. 'Loose!' and his own arrow preceded those of his men by a split second, taking the leader in his chest, piercing his chain mail and flinging him backwards off his saddle, into the face of the horseman directly behind him.

Three more mén were hit, plus two horses, sending the remaining horses into a panic, and driving no less than five horsemen off the narrow ford into deeper water where they floundered and wallowed, their riders reluctant to dismount from their horses, knowing that their heavy chain mail would immediately send them to the bottom of the deep River Sabrina.

A second volley, then a third emptied more saddles as dead and wounded men either lay in the shallows of the ford or sank in the deeper water.

Several wounded horsemen and a number of wounded mounts retreated to the far bank, but two brave men spurred their mounts forward and sped up the bank towards the Englishmen.

The leader was met by Garth. Who had discarded his bow and rose to meet the horseman, shield in one hand and his dreaded axe in the other.

The horseman lunged down with his sword, which clanged against the rim of Garth's shield, as Garth swung the axe slicing the man's leg off at the top of his thigh as the axe carried on and lodged itself in the ribs of the man's steed, sending both horse and man to the ground in a welter of flaying hooves and spraying blood.

The second horseman appeared to ride through the Englishmen with impunity. It was not until much later, when the battle was over, that Edric found the man lying on the ground by his placid, grazing mount, dying from a grey goose shaft that had gone clean through the man, chain mail, leather and torso, with a mere foot of the shaft protruding from both his back and his front.

Meanwhile the remaining Norman horsemen milled about on the far side of the river bank, appearing to be involved in a heated argument as some of the braver ones, or perhaps more foolhardy ones, argued that they should attack again. Whilst the wiser, or perhaps the less brave of the men said that they had done enough, and saw little point in dying for a few bags of silver, of which, even if they survived, they would see little or none.

'Cowherds!' bellowed Lord Bondevile, who had been placed in charge of the pursuing Normans with orders to retrieve the silver that these English savages had stolen from his liege lord. Savagely he spurred his stallion down the riverbank onto the ford, followed by three reluctant lackeys.

The first bodkin pierced Bondevile as he reached the centre of the river, the second a few yards further as his horse struggled out of a small pot-hole in the river bed, the third shaft sent him plunging onto a shallow part of the ford where he lay, arms splayed out and staring at the sky with unseeing eyes.

Two of the following horsemen fell to arrows whilst the third man made his retreat with a bodkin through his left shoulder.

The remaining eighteen or twenty horsemen (for one of the rare times in his life, Edric had omitted to count them) turned their mounts about and, leaving their slain comrades, spurred their horses back down the road from which they had erupted a few short minutes beforehand.

Several of Edric's warriors stood and began to make their way back to their tethered horses. Six others made their way towards the river, intent on relieving the dead Normans of any valuables that they may have been carrying.

'Hold your positions,' he called to them. 'Stay where you are, it might be a trick,' bringing the men back to their positions where they sat or squatted down, gazing across the body-strewn ford.

He forced the men to remain in their positions for a further hour before he bade them to loosen the strings of their longbows. Only then did he allow his men to relieve the Norman corpses of their mail, their weapons and any valuables that they contained, before ordering them to mount their horses and continue their journey homewards.

Despite the fact that it was midsummer, the skies were full of black thunder clouds, sending Thor's fire-arrows across the dark skies, before the dark clouds released their contents onto the sodden travellers, as they made their way through the small village of Cressage, along the bottom of a crest of hills named White-rock Edge eventually following a meandering stream through waterlogged meadows and reed-beds, from which they sent flurries of water fowl rising from beneath the horses' hooves, unnerving the tired but still skittish beasts.

Edric urged them on, through the hamlets of Longville, Shepton and Rushbury, finally stopping for the night at the small village of Plowden, totally exhausted and soaked through to the skin.

'Only a few miles more and we would be home,' grumbled a Garth as he took off his wet coat and attempted to wring out some of the rainwater, before he threw an equally wet sheepskin blanket over his head and settled beneath a small oak tree in order to try and get some sleep before resuming their journey on the morrow.

Similar scenes were taking place all over the campsite as the men tried to tend to their horses and settle the beasts, and themselves, down for the night.

Dawn broke early, as the darkness at this time of year lasted for a mere four or five hours, waking the still sodden men and beasts after their wet and uncomfortable few hours' sleep.

Fires were reluctantly kindled into life, and half a dozen legs of lamb were soon sizzling over them, dripping their juices into the fires and sending mouth-watering aromas towards the hungry men, who were forced to wait until the raw meat was at least half cooked before slices were cut and handed around, to be devoured, scalding many a man's gullet.

They saddled up and were on their way within the hour, arriving home before noon, to be welcomed a crowd of solemn villagers, who were standing in silent groups, avoiding eye contact with Edric and his warriors as the horsemen rode slowly through them.

Godda met him at the door, red-eyed from weeping, looking like a woman who had not slept at all that night.

'Thank God you are back,' she screamed almost hysterically. 'Where the devil have you been? You should have been back yesterday. If only you had been back yesterday,' she repeated, then flung herself at him, sobbing on his chest and beating her fists against his shoulder.

'What on earth is wrong?' said Edric, looking around to see what was amiss.

The small fortress was intact.

There was no sign of a fire, or of raiders.

No signs of battle and no wounded men.

No widows were wailing.

All seemed to be in order. Yet obviously some disaster had taken place, but what?

'It's Ælnoth,' she screamed into his ear, almost deafening him. 'He's gone missing, he's gone,' she repeated between sobs. 'One moment he was there and the next he had disappeared. No one has seen him since midday yesterday.

'We have searched the house, searched the fortress, the village, the stream and the woods beyond, every man woman and child in the village has searched high, low and level, and still there is no sign of him,' she said falling into another fit of sobbing, soaking his shirt with her tears. Her body shook so fearfully he feared she was in the throes of a seizure, and would collapse to the floor at any moment.

'Godwin is still out looking, and I fear too for his safety.'

'Oh, Godwin is big enough to take care of himself,' answered Edric with the confidence that he did not really feel.

'Oh, I know that Godwin is safe but it is little Ælnoth that I fear for,' she wept.

'He's dead,' she sobbed, 'I know it. He's dead, either drowned in the river, or taken by wolves.'

'I thought he was always attended by those two Valkyries of yours, Betilda and Winnie,' he said accusingly.

'They were with him and they've gone too.'

'Where were they seen last?'

'Down by the river.'

'The river is too shallow. Three people can't have drowned in that.'

'It's almost dry,' said Godda.

'Right,' said Edric. 'You two men go downstream and you two go upstream. Take one side of the river each, and go as far as you can until nightfall.'

'Garth? You join me and we will ride in a circle around the village and see if we can pick up their trail.'

Edric and Garth rode out of the village until they reached the limit of the ploughed and cultivated area, before turning their horses southwards in order to make a broad ride around the boundaries of the village, riding slowly about twenty feet apart, with their eyes scanning the ground for the slightest sign of the missing trio.

CHAPTER 19

The four ponies were tethered to a half-grown elm tree, whilst Ulric, his sister Freya and Walter sat around a small fire waiting for the water in the blackened cauldron to come to a boil before Freya added the dried oats and berries which would make their meagre evening meal.

Freya was the eldest of the trio, a mere ten months the elder of her brother who had just reached the age of eighteen.

Her demure looks belied her true nature, for she was indeed a beauty, tall with a slim waist, a large high bosom and long, fair hair. She carried herself with the poise that a queen would be proud of, having a noble face that was round, perhaps a little too round, interposed with a pert nose, startling blue eyes and a mouth that held the promise that every man dreamed of.

Her brother and his friend Walter were only too aware of her beauty, but both were cowed by her domineering nature and the sexual demands that she forced upon both of them.

This was the first time they had stopped since seizing the child, a full day and a night ago. Both the riders and their ponies were now totally exhausted.

The thrill and excitement had worn off long ago, leaving the two male abductors with a fear that brought them out in a cold sweat.

Freya, however, appeared to be untouched by any form of fear. Indeed, despite the fatigue that had just begun to affect her, she was enjoying the whole adventure, laughing and making jokes with the two young men as they rode southwards.

'What if they find us?' said Walter as he stared into the fire.

'Then your worries will be over,' snarled Freya, for despite being the only female in the group, she was undoubtedly the leader and had always dominated her younger brother as well as his friend Walter.

'They won't find us now,' added Walter, hoping that he was correct. 'We have come too far.'

He always appeared to be the dimmest of the three, but was in fact far more intelligent than the other two put together.

Freya, on the other hand, despite her beauty and her pretty name, had a sadistic and cruel nature. It was she who, despite the protests from her brother and Walter, had taken great delight in torturing the captured boys' two companions, cutting the throat of the skinny one and laughing as she choked to death on her own blood. Then she'd tied the fat one to a tree, stripped her naked, slowly sliced off her breasts one by one, drooling as she did so, then literally peeled long wide strips of skin off her startling white, fat body until the woman had fainted. Yet an unconscious woman was no sport for Freya, who splashed cold water onto the woman's face time and time again in order revive her, and once the woman had regained consciousness she had continued to torture the woman until she had uttered a long groan and died.

She had then moved over to Walter, her eyes glazed over with lust, literally pushing him to the floor, yanked his breeches down, hoisted her own skirt up and straddled him, riding him for a long time before she had screamed loudly in her passion and rolling off him; she then lay alongside him chuckling happily to herself as if someone had just told her a raucous joke.

A few minutes later it was her brother's turn, who had turned his back on the copulating couple, pretending to be asleep. Yet he was roughly wakened when his sister hauled him over onto his back, ravishing him in much the same way that she had used Walter until she screamed abuse as a second climax surged through her young, insatiable body.

The boy sat apart from his abductors with his hands still tied behind his back, totally shocked by the events that he had just witnessed. Despite his resolve not to cry out and to bear any indignities that may befall him with the type of bravery that his parents would have expected of him, the spectacles that he had just been forced to witness caused tears to stream down his face. His body was racked by throbbing, silent, sobs.

A dirty rag that had been stuffed into his mouth had only been removed three times in order to force a few drops of brackish water into the boy's mouth, just enough to keep him alive.

'How old did the hag say he was?' asked Freya.

'About five I think.'

'Big for five,' she remarked with a sadistic smile.

'Don't get any ideas,' said her younger brother. 'He's no good to us dead.'

'Pity,' she said, still grinning as she looked towards the boy. 'I could really have some fun with him.'

'Better get some food and water into him, or we can kiss our reward goodbye,' said Walter thoughtfully. 'Is that porridge ready yet?'

'Nearly.'

'Well hurry it up. I'm just about dead on my feet.'

Walter shuffled over to the boy and removed the gag from his mouth.

The boy licked his dry lips with his swollen tongue, but uttered no sound, just continued to stare up at Walter and his two companions through his tear-stained red eyes.

'Is he dumb?' snarled Freya, then shouted, 'Are you dumb boy?'

Ælnoth didn't answer, just stared.

Walter returned to the fire, scooped four big spoonfuls of porridge out of the still simmering pot and returned to the boy.

He first held his own water bottle to the boy's lips, tipped it up and allowed the boy to take three or four swallows of the warm, brackish water, before taking the bottle away. He then began to shove spoonfuls of piping-hot porridge into the boy's mouth, burning the child's mouth and his throat in the process.

'There, that's done,' he mumbled. 'Now I can eat my own supper in peace.' He walked over to his two companions who were already in the process of devouring the porridge that they had scooped into their own, rather dirty wooden bowls.

'Sod,' swore Walter. 'You two haven't left me much,' he grumbled.

'Shouldn't have given the brat so much, should you?' snapped Freya, as she rolled another spoonful of hot porridge around the inside of her mouth in a vain attempt to prevent the porridge from scalding her own mouth.

They quickly finished their meal, fed and watered the ponies with the last of the small bundles of hay that each pony had carried in a small sack attached to the saddles, then returned to the fire.

'Better get some shut-eye,' ordered Freya. 'We will be on our way at the crack of dawn.'

'It's still daylight,' grumbled Ulric.

'Of course it is, you stupid idiot,' snarled Freya. 'It's bloody midsummer isn't it?'

Walter walked over to the boy, untied his hands then yanked them to the front of the boy, and retied them in the front, pulled the young captive over to the fire where he lay down, pulling the boy down beside him, then tied the loose piece of the thong from the boy's rope to his own wrist, saying, 'Now boy, you get some sleep, and don't try nothing, 'cos I'm a light sleeper, and I have been known to knife people in my sleep.' He hadn't really, but he just said that to frighten Ælnoth, in order make sure that he didn't try to escape during the night.

Ælnoth did indeed intend to try to escape during the night, but was so exhausted by his ordeal and so traumatised by the torture and death of Betilda and Winnie that the moment his head hit the unyielding earth, he fell into a deep sleep. Only to be wakened at the crack of dawn by the towering figure of an angry Freya who viciously kicked him awake.

'Wake up you little swine!' she spat, and was in the process of delivering another blow with her right foot as he sat upright, wiping the sleep out of his red-rimmed eyes.

The fact that he was awake did not deter her and she struck him another savage blow with her foot, pushing him onto the body of the still-sleeping figure of Walter.

'What the hell,' grumbled the groggy Walter as he shoved the boy's body off him. Yet looking up he saw the menacing figure of Freya, and thought better of continuing the tirade that he had been on the point of uttering.

'Had a bad night?' he asked.

A grunt was the only answer he got.

'I slept like a log,' he said happily, knowing that his statement would needle the already irritable Freya.

Another grunt, followed by an order, 'Fetch some dry sticks and get the fire going.'

Half an hour later, after a few spoonfuls of hot porridge, washed down by fresh water from a nearby stream, they were on their way, urging their ponies down the overgrown track that had once been a well-kept Roman road.

'I hope the bugger is in Canterbury when we get there,' grumbled Ulric.

'How far do you think Canterbury is?' he asked his sister.

'Don't know,' came the muttered reply. 'But I reckon it will take us at least a couple of weeks, that's if we aren't caught first.'

'Do you know where Canterbury is?' asked the brother.

'No, not really, but I know its south. I've got a tongue in my head, so we can make enquiries along the way.'

'The problem is,' cut in Walter, 'if and when we get to Canterbury, and IF King William or his fat brother Odo is there, then how are we going to get to see

180

him?'

'I'll send him one of the boy's ears,' interrupted Freya.

Walter continued in his slow, deliberate manner, 'An ear is an ear, could be anyone's ear. William probably doesn't even know that Edric has a son, and even if he does, it is unlikely that he is aware that the boy has been taken.'

'You should have thought of that before you urged us to go along with your hare-brained scheme,' snapped Freya. 'Perhaps I should kill the boy, then we could head south and no one would be any the wiser.'

'And we will be none the richer,' intervened Walter.

Then he added, 'I think we should keep the boy alive a little while longer while I' – then he changed the 'I' for a 'we' – 'we can think of a way to tell King William that Wild Edric's son has been taken prisoner by us and that we want a fat reward for the boy. Perhaps you should go,' he said turning towards Freya.

'Not bloody likely,' came the snorted reply.

'No matter, I'll think of a way,' said the ever thoughtful, wily Walter.

They rode on in silence, each keeping their thoughts hidden, seemingly unaware that the boy, Ælnoth was listening, with interest, with apprehension and with dread to their morbid, callous and devious conversation.

After a silence that lasted for more than an hour as they made their way towards the south, Walter suddenly blurted out, 'I know what we will do. At the next town and in every town and village that we pass through, we will mingle with people who have dealings with the Normans, you know, butchers, bakers, candlestick makers, masons, carpenters and the like, spread the word amongst them, you know, those sort of people like to gossip. Tell them that we have heard that Wild Edric's son is being held and taken to Canterbury, to be given to King William, or to the King's brother, Bishop Odo. Word will soon reach the King, or his fat brother, and when we do arrive he will be more than ready to see us.'

'Given, given,' snorted the indignant Freya. 'We are not giving him to anybody. We want a bloody reward for our services.'

'I know that,' said Walter, looking angrily at Freya. 'But we are only saying, 'giving', so that the news reaches the King that we have the boy.'

'Ah, I see,' said Freya, smiling now, and approving of Walter's plan, 'and then, when we reach the fat bishop, we can demand our reward.'

'Ask,' Walter, repeated. 'Ask for a reward might be a better way of putting it.'

'As you will,' said the scowling Freya, as she spurred her pony ahead to edge it around a particularly large clump of blackberry briars that had nearly choked up the narrow pathway.

*****

'There is no sign of them in the woods,' said a furious Edric. 'They must have taken the road south, that's the only logical way to go. No one but a fool would go north or westwards into the mountains.'

'A fool, Or a Welshman,' added Garth.

'Or a Welshman,' agreed Edric, 'but I think they have gone south, don't ask me why, but I feel it in my bones that we need to go south if we are to find them.'

'So be it,' agreed Garth.

'We will call in at the village first, there may be news there, and we can stock up with a few provisions to see us through the next few days.'

Godda greeted them at the door, and it was obvious from her face that Ælnoth had not been found.

She was, however, calmer, almost happy, 'He is alive,' she said. 'Both Mono and myself have seen him,'

Edric startled by her statement, said, 'Seen him? Seen him where?'

'No, not seen him, really seen him, felt him. Oh it is impossible to explain to you, but we know, we have both seen him alive,' she repeated, wringing her hands together on the front of her tear-stained dress.

'Heavens, woman,' he shouted. 'Where have you seen him?'

'South,' came the squeaky, childlike reply, not from Godda, but from Mono of the Meadows who had almost magically appeared from behind. Or was it from the side of Godda? Edric was unsure, as well as being totally shocked by the sudden appearance of the strange little witch.

'They went south,' she repeated with a childlike cackle.

'There,' exclaimed Edric, 'I said south, quickly now, grab some food and drink so that Garth and myself can be on our way.' He alighted from his horse to embrace the lovely Godda, whilst the serving wenches scuttled away to obey his orders.

Ten minutes later they were galloping out of the village on fresh horses. Edric astride his Norman stallion, Chieftain, whilst Garth's large figure rode a heavier captured Norman stallion that was better suited to carry such a large man.

They guided their horses as fast as was prudent along the weed-tangled road, avoiding the potholes, fallen trees and tangles of nettles and blackberries, until, late in the evening a white object caught Edric's eye, some twenty or thirty feet off the road, set back in a cluster of young birch trees.

Edric reined Chieftain to a halt, nearly causing a collision between his own mount and Garth's horse that was following close behind.

'What the…! What the devil's wrong?' shouted the annoyed giant who had never really felt at home on the back of a horse, and needed no excuse to dismount and walk.

'Something up there,' said Edric, pointing to the birch trees.

'What?'

'Don't know, let's find out,' he said as he spurred his steed off the road towards the small copse of birch trees.

Edric's face was pale with anger as he dismounted, for he had seen death before, too many times to be shocked by death alone. But this was different.

The two naked bodies had been people he knew, people he had loved.

Winnie, or what was left of her, had been tied to a tree, mutilated, skinned and disembowelled, then left to die a slow, lingering death, whilst the head of Betilda lay some four feet away from her torso, grinning up at him in a macabre way, as if it was saying to Edric, almost pleading with him, to re-unite her head with the rest of her body.

'Christ's blood,' swore Garth as he joined Edric. 'Who in the name of Odin did this foul deed?'

'By all that is holy, we shall find out,' growled Edric. 'Scout around,' he said. 'See if there is any sign of my son, we can bury the girls later.'

They both walked in ever widening circles around the area to no avail. So they buried the two murdered women in a shallow grave and, after saying a few words commending their souls to either Heaven or Valhalla, they walked slowly and sadly to their horses.

'Well there was no sign of Ælnoth, thank God,' said Edric, 'but from the signs that they have left we now know that there are three of them, and that one of them is a woman.'

'A woman,' answered Garth, 'Who would think that a woman could be party to this?'

'Oh, I don't know,' said Edric grimly, stroking his short blond beard as if in thought. 'I've known some cruel bitches in my time.'

'Aye, you're right there, worse than men some of 'em.'

'I'm going to make damn sure that I don't get captured by this one.'

'She will receive no quarter from me,' grunted his companion.

'Bloody right.'

They rode on, watering their horses in the streams that cross-crossed the flat landscape, snatching a few hours' sleep when the darkness made it unsafe to follow on the disused and overgrown road.

Each person they stopped and asked, shook their heads, 'Nay,' was the answer they heard from each and every one of them, until late in the evening they met a shepherd driving his flock into their pens for the night.

'Aye, lord,' he said. 'Three of 'em there were, and a child, ridin' Welsh 'ill ponies. Young folk; two boys and a girl, the girl was a looker, seen 'er close up. A beauty, she was. That's a fact.'

'When was that? Which way were they heading?' said the excited Edric, delighted to know that they were on the right track and that his son was still alive.

''Bout this time, nearly two days ago, it was, 'eadin' south. Lonnon probably,' and he leapt to his left in order to prevent a large black faced ram from dashing past him.

'Damn 'im,' he swore as he brutally shoved the ram back towards the rest of his flock that were now pouring through the hurdle into their night pens.

Edric fished out a silver coin and flipped it to the shepherd who caught it, dropping his crook in the process, 'Thank 'ee koindley sur,' beamed the delighted man, touching his woollen cap with the index finger of his right hand before turning to close the wicket.

'That's good news,' said Garth.

'It is indeed, but we are still a long way behind them. Now that we know where they are heading, we can make up some of the time,' answered Edric. 'We will get a little sleep tonight.'

'None at all, if I know you,' answered Garth with a wry smile.

The trail became stale at the small town of Bromyard, but they carried on, eventually hearing news that their quarry had preceded them by a day when they reached the outskirts of the large town of Worcester, where, despite asking many people, the trail again went cold.

In the beautiful vale of Evesham they hailed a peasant who was cleaning out a ditch alongside the road. 'Good day my man,' shouted Edric to the man who was bent in two and nearly hidden in the deep, muck-filled ditch.

'Have you seen four young people pass this way, mounted on shaggy brown

183

ponies?'

'Indeed I have good sire,' came the reply from the mud-splattered, bone-thin man as he stretched himself upright, uttering a groan as he did so. 'They passed me not more than two hours since. Ridin' hard, they were. Nearly sent me flyin' into yon ditch they did,' he said sadly, wiping his brow with a dirty rag that he had fished out of his pocket.

Again a delighted Edric flipped a coin to the man, 'My thanks to you my friend,' he shouted as he dug his heels into his mount. 'You have just made my day.' and, followed by an equally delighted Garth, they disappeared in a cloud of pebbles and dust.

'An' you 'ave made mine,' said the man to himself, as he put the coin between his teeth to make sure that the silver coin which he had just earned so easily was in fact a real silver and not one of those fake things that people had told him to be wary of.

'That be worth a year's wages, that be,' he muttered to himself as he carefully folded the dirty rag around the coin and deposited it into the one and only good pocket that he had in his grubby breeches.

The two men rode their tired mounts as hard as they could until the dusk prevented them from continuing, without seeing a single soul.

'We had better stop and rest the horses,' said Garth, 'for I fear that if we continue they will drop dead beneath us, then we will never catch up with young Ælnoth.'

The sound of his son's name seemed to bring Edric back to reality and for the first time in many hours and he realised that both his own mount and that of his friend Garth's were wringing wet with sweat, foaming at the mouth and pretty well on the point of exhaustion.

He dismounted, furious that he had not caught up with his son and his abductors, furious that his mount did not have the stamina to continue.

He was angry at Garth for calling a halt.

He was also furious at himself, and with the world, that he, Edric the Wild, Edric the Savage, warrior, victor, lord of numerous estates could not catch up with and deal with three puny children. Who had so far, not only outwitted him, but had outridden him, as well.

They unsaddled the horses, wiped them down with doeskin cloths, allowed them to drink at a nearby stream, tethered them and left them to graze, before gnawing ravenously on chunks of dried beef and stale bread.

'We must have missed them,' said Edric angrily.

'Or they have turned off,' suggested Garth.

'Aye, but where?'

'Don't know, we will have to backtrack as soon as it is light, they can't have got far.'

'Could have seen us coming and hidden.'

'Aye,' was the answer. 'You could be right.'

Edric and Garth had no way of knowing how right they had been in their assumptions; for indeed they had been seen as they spurred their steeds furiously down a long stretch of the dusty road.

*****

184

Freya had called a halt on a small hillock and as she was in the act of dismounting from her pony she gazed at the boy, who she could see was looking along the road over which they had just travelled, and there was a gleam in his eye and a look of awe on his face that told her all that she needed to know.

Ælnoth had indeed recognised his father's black stallion, Chieftain, and the huge figure of Garth, as Garth continued to savagely spur his mount in order to keep up with Edric. As the two pursuers urged their mounts along one of the few stretches of clear road that they had travelled upon, the youngster had been unable to hide his joy at seeing his father riding to his rescue.

It was that joy upon his face that told Freya that the two riders who were spurring their mounts furiously along the road a mere quarter of a mile behind them were the pursuers that she had feared all along, might be following them.

'Quick!' squealed Freya with panic in her voice.

'Follow me into those trees,' and they spurred their ponies towards a thick clump of trees that were some one hundred yards or so away from the road.

They had only just hidden themselves in the woodland when the two riders spurred their horses onto the crest of the hill, then thundered past them along the road. Neither of the men glanced towards the small wood that concealed the four young riders.

'Thank Christ for that,' whispered a shocked Walter.

'What are you whispering for, you fool?' snarled Freya,

'They can't bloody well hear us.'

Then she turned her horse's head into the wood and urged it along a faint deer track, 'Follow me,' she said, leading the way and pulling the loose reins of Ælnoth's pony behind her. They'll go galloping along for hours before they realise that they've lost us, and but that time it'll be dark, so we had better get a move on. Jump to it!' she ordered. The two youngsters urged their ponies after Freya's and Ælnoth's who were in the process of disappearing along the path and into the deep woodland.

*****

'Damn and blast!' shouted Edric as he hauled on Chieftain's reins, bringing the sweating beast to a halt in the half-light of a glade, where the encroaching trees had met above the overgrown road, preventing most of the remaining evening light from reaching the ground. You are right. We have lost them. They must have turned off the road.'

'Damn and blast,' he said again, furious with himself.

Garth, whose horse had been unable to keep up with Edric's stallion, brought the tired beast to a more gentle halt beside Edric, said nothing. He had known for the last half hour that they should have overtaken their prey some miles back, but had followed his friend in the forlorn hope that he had been wrong.

'What now, my lord?' he asked.

'We will rest the horses here and get a little sleep,' answered Edric, 'then we will have to retrace our steps in the morning, and see if we can find out where they left the road.'

Garth grunted in agreement and groaned loudly as he eased his stiff limbs out of the uncomfortable saddle, for the riding of horses was one of the pet hates of his life.

They lit a small fire, tended their mounts and lay down on their saddle blankets watching the dark clouds flit a cross the watery moon.

Both men were silent.

Each man alone, lost in his own thoughts.

Edric, bone tired, yet furious at himself with the thought that these children could have outwitted him yet again, and dreading what harm his infant son was having to endure at the hands of these young killers. He cursed himself again and again for not bringing two or three of his hounds with him.

Garth's thoughts were of his own love, the beautiful Myreen, who he could almost feel resting upon his huge hairy chest, purring as she often did whilst he stroked her hair and caressed her naked figure, a figure that was still the envy of many women half her age.

'Ahh,' he sighed aloud, startling his companion who immediately jumped to his feet, war-axe in hand.

'What's amiss,' hissed Edric

''Tis nought, I was but dreaming,'

'Well dream quieter, I was near asleep,' growled the still furious Edric, as he lay down and covered himself with the blanket in another attempt to snatch a few hours' sleep.

Despite being tired after such a gruelling day, Edric's troubled mind prevented him from sleeping.

The moon disappeared behind black clouds and a roll of thunder rumbled in the distance.

'Don't like that,' grumbled Garth as he tossed and turned on the hard ground that was still damp, despite the fact that Garth had chosen to clear the prickly leaves from beneath a holly tree in order to sleep beneath its protective leaves.

'Thunder never killed anyone,' muttered Edric.

Lightning flashed through the blackness, and Edric automatically counted the seconds, as he always had done since he was a child, before the following clap of thunder boomed in the heavens. 'Still a long way off,' he said. 'With luck we will probably miss the worst of it.'

Then he turned his face away from the lightning in an attempt to get some sleep.

Sleep still eluded him, or so it seemed, for he felt himself flying. Soaring over dull forests, over cloudy mountains and valleys, over wastelands and deserts, until, after what seemed to be an eternity, he was suddenly plunged downwards into a black hole.

It was not a large hole. Perhaps the same size as a peasant's house, and he flew down the sides of this pit, where the upper bodies of men and women protruded, waving their arms and screaming in despair.

His body dived downwards, through the searing heat and the noise, as these half-people clawed and grabbed at him, raking his face and his clothes with their nails, until he finally reached the bottom. Yet his journey did not end there, for he was catapulted along, through miles and miles of screaming, sweaty, half-people who protruded from the top, the bottom and the sides of the tunnel until he finally came to a halt, hovering over a vast, blood-red, bubbling fire.

He, accompanied by hundreds of other souls, fell, and as he fell he found himself standing once again in front of his own gravestone that read, as usual. Edric; Died October 10th.

He woke with a shout of terror, soaked in sweat.

'What is it?' Garth roared as he sat upright, plunging his head into the prickly holly tree that he had been sleeping under, cursing loudly as he withdrew his head out of the savage leaves.

Edric was still shaking his head in order to clear the dreadful images that were still running riot inside his brain. At last they slowly dimmed and vanished, causing him to sigh loudly in relief that it was only a dream.

He realised that his nightmare had in fact been naught but a dream, and he wiped his forehead with his blanket, still seeing the images that he had experienced in his dream.

Then he answered Garth's question.

'I have just seen hell.'

The gravity of Edric's statement shocked Garth, who could do naught but stare at his lord, the man who had been his friend since childhood.

A man whom he had always thought of as being afraid of nothing or no one.

And he could only repeat the word that Edric had uttered.

'Hell?'

'Hell,' said Edric again, shaking his head as he tried, in vain to dislodge the searing hot images that still burned inside his head.

His mind was in turmoil, 'What caused that nightmare?' he mused, 'does it have anything to do with Ælnoth?'

Was his son dead or alive? Had something happened to him? Had he suffered the same fate as poor Winnie and Betilda?

Had little Ælnoth gone to hell? Surely not, for the boy was a mere child, only five years of age and had committed no sin.

No, he tried to reason with himself.

He was the one who had seen hell.

He was certainly the one who had sinned, not little Ælnoth.

God alone knows how many men I have killed.

The faces of many of his victims flew before his eyes and had often kept him awake at night.

The vision of hell had been for him.

He had been warned.

But warned of what? he asked himself. Yes, he had slain men, but in every case they had been men who had deserved to die or had been fully intent on taking his own life, had they not?

But then there were those Normans who had slain his beloved Rowena. They had signed their own death warrants.

Those men had deserved to die, and hell or no hell, he had no regrets whatsoever when he thought of their dying.

His mind spun until he could bear no more and he rose, flung his heavy coat over his head and walked alone in the darkness and the rain, in order to clear this vision of hell from his head.

Flashes of lightning lit up the sky above them, then Thor clashed his sword against his war-shield time and time again, before drenching the two mere

187

mortals below him with his spittle.

Edric, usually fearless and sensible, shook like a leaf in the north wind, as the deluge descended upon him, causing him to snatch up his sodden blanket and retreat from the God of Thunder's displeasure, joining Garth under the prickly, protective holly tree.

CHAPTER 20

Freya, Ulric and Walter suffered from no such nightmares, having spent the night in a warm cottage, fussed over by the wife of a mole trapper, enjoying the old lady's hospitality and sleeping before a roaring log fire wrapped up in wolf skins, which was, apparently just a sideline for the trapper, who was not at home on this rare occasion.

The previous evening they had dined on roast venison, and had broken their fast this morning with a bowl of oats, swimming in warm milk laced with wild honey.

'He don't usually stay out at night,' said Alice. 'Must be the rain, probably flooded the river so he can't get through. He'll be back by midday, never you mind.'

Freya sent a sly glance across the room to Ulric, and winked, 'Oh that will be nice,' she said, beaming her well-rehearsed radiant smile, a smile that automatically made people, especially men, warm to her, often sending the male gender into a love-haze that such a beautiful young girl should give them such a smile.

The same smile usually told women that here was a girl just like their own daughters, a delicate and vulnerable maiden in this wicked world, ruled by brutal men.

'I do hope that he arrives before we go, I really would like to meet him,' said Freya, again turning her head away from Alice and pulling a face at Ulric, who in turn was forced to turn away, lest the woman saw the mirth that was on his own face?

Alice turned to the fire and bent over to push a log further into the flames, allowing Freya ample time to withdraw her knife from the sheath hidden beneath her tunic and plunge it into Alice's back.

Alice gave a loud sigh and collapsed into the fireplace, with her head lying a few inches away from the flames, which ignited her hair into a brilliant blaze that lasted for only a few seconds before sizzling out.

Alice of Attwood did not feel the flames.

'What the hell did you do that for?' gasped a shocked Walter. 'She was a harmless old dear.'

'Aye,' answered Freya gleaming with pleasure and dribbling saliva out of the corner of her mouth, 'she was a harmless old dear who could tell anyone that we three and the brat passed this way. No witnesses,' she hissed menacingly.

'Come on. Grab as much food as you can carry and let's get out of here,' she snarled, snatching up the half-eaten loaf of bread, plus three apples that were the remains of their breakfast, then shoving the captive Ælnoth before her she pushed her way out through the door.

The two youths knew better than to argue with her when she was in one of her moods, and set about gathering up all the food that they could find, before following her out of the door towards the lean-to stables where they had left their ponies.

They quickly loaded their spoils onto the ponies, mounted and urged their mounts down the muddy pathway southwards.

*****

Aldred of Attwood was slightly bothered when soon after midday he led his pony into the yard and tethered it in the lean-to stable that had been its home since he had acquired the piebald over four years ago. For it was rare for the Attwoods to receive visitors, and by the look of the hoofmarks in the mud, at least three or four ponies had left their prints on the muddy ground.

'Alice? Alice!' he called, fully expecting his wife to appear at the doorway, as she always had done over the thirty-two years that they had spent together, especially on the odd occasions that he had spent the night away from their cottage. Usually she greeted him with a hug and a kiss upon his now grey bearded cheek.

'Alice?' he called again as he walked up to the cottage door, which was half open, 'Strange,' he thought and called again, 'Alice, my love, sorry but I couldn't make it home last night. The river was in spate and I couldn't get through. Spent the night with the Oaks...' He failed to finish the sentence as he saw the body of his wife sprawled across the hearth.

'Oh no!' he cried and rushed across to her, kneeling beside her, then lifting her head onto his lap, he cradled her singed head in his arms. 'Alice, Alice, my darling!' he sobbed. 'Who could do such a thing? There there my lover, you will be all right,' he wailed, knowing full well that she would not be all right, but hoping, beyond hope that he might be wrong.

Her eyes fluttered then opened, and she looked up into the adoring, damp eyes of the man that she had loved since the age of fourteen, so long, long ago.

'Who did this my love?' he sobbed as the tears dribbled out of the corner of his eyes and down onto the face of his wife.

'A girl,' she whispered almost inaudibly. 'A beautiful girl, and two boys,' then her eyes closed and he thought that he had lost her, but after a while they fluttered open again and she whispered, 'She did this... a captive boy,' then she became delirious and whispered 'Canterbury, Canterbury,' before she fell asleep forever.

*****

Edric and Garth were mounted before dawn, cursing as they waited for the light to grow strong enough for them to retrace the tracks that they had made the previous.

'God damn it,' swore Edric. 'Where's the light? Any other morning it would have been daylight half an hour since.'

''Tis the cloud,' muttered Garth raising his eyes skyward. 'Stops the sun getting through.'

'What sun? We haven't seen the sun these two days past.'

Garth tried to make light of it, knowing that Edric was furious that he had not yet rescued his son from these murderous youngsters, realising that he was worried sick that young Ælnoth had, or still could, suffer the same fate as his two nurses.

'It will soon be light enough for us to start, and I am sure that we will soon find their tracks and find the boy.'

Eventually dawn arrived and Edric viciously spurred Chieftain into action, immediately regretting his brutality for he dearly loved his savage Norman stallion.

'You take this side of the track and I will take the other!' he shouted back to Garth who was already some twenty feet behind him.

'Aye my lord.'

'Look for any disturbance that will show us where they left the road,' he ordered.

'Aye my lord,' came the answer from Garth, who grumbled under his breath so that his lord and friend could not hear him. 'Why else would I be sitting astride this old nag at this time of the morning, soaked through to the skin, without a bite to break my fast?'

After the first spurt of speed they both slowed their horses down to a walking pace scanning each deer track and trail for sign of the fugitives.

By midmorning they had followed the road right back to the spot where, the previous day, they had seen the peasant cleaning out a ditch. Yet this morning there was no peasant and, more importantly, no sign of their prey.

There were recent tracks aplenty, of deer, wild boar, foxes and badgers, plus an assortment of wildfowl, but no sign whatsoever of the four ponies that they were seeking.

'The damned thunderstorm has washed away their tracks,' shouted Garth, stating the obvious.

'We have no other choice than to go back up the road and look again,' said Edric, 'but this time we will ride at least a hundred yards out from the road.'

They urged their horses out from the road, through sparse woodland and heather, as they began to ride back yet again, searching the damp undergrowth and moorland for the spore that they were seeking.

About half way back, Edric's eye passed over a small copse of trees, and he was in the act of turning away when something made him look again at a dark patch within the trees. As he focused his eyes on the spot, a very slight movement caught his eye.

He called his mount to a halt. 'Whoa boy,' he said quietly to Chieftain, and the stallion immediately obeyed, standing still while Edric stared at the spot where he thought he had seen movement.

'Yes,' he said to himself, 'there it is again. Garth, Garth!' he called, halting Garth in his tracks.

'My Lord?' came the gruff reply, as he spurred his mount across the two hundred or so yards that separated them. He reined his horse alongside Edric. 'What is it?' he asked. 'What do you see?'

'Over there,' nodding his head in the direction of the movement, without taking his eyes off the spot. 'I saw some movement in that dark spot in that small copse.'

Garth's eyes followed his directions. 'I see nothing,' he said.

Even as he spoke, a face moved forward out of the darkness.

Not a boy's face, as he had hoped. Not even a human face, but the face of an old gnarled grey wolf.

'It's bloody wolf,' snarled Edric.

'Just so, my lord,' said his companion, 'funny though.'

'Funny, what's funny about it? We're not hunting for bloody wolves. Our quarry is far more dangerous than a mangy wolf.'

'Odd though. Is it not my lord? He's coming right at us.'

'Mmmm, so he is. Now that is strange.'

''Tis' Fenrir, the wolf-god,' whispered the pagan Garth.

Edric turned his face towards Garth for a brief moment, noting the look of awe that was on the face of his friend.

The wolf padded slowly towards the men, stopping a mere ten feet away. Then, looking up towards Edric, it turned his head not once, but twice towards the spot from where he had emerged, at the edge of the copse, then turned, and very slowly padded back the way that he had come.

The hairs stood up on the back of Edric's neck.

'He is showing us the way,' he said quietly.

'Aye, he certainly is,' said the still shivering Garth, urging his horse behind Edric's stallion, as they both followed the old wolf-god up the half-hidden deer-path.

The wolf did not hurry, even though Chieftain nearly stepped on his tail, but continued very slowly into the darkness of the copse. Where, much to Edric's surprise, the half-hidden deer-path broadened out into a well-defined track where, partially protected by the overhanging trees, most of the previous night's storm had not penetrated. The distinct prints of pony hooves showed bright and clear along the muddy track.

'Well, would you believe that?' said an astonished Edric. 'Woden has sent his wolf-god to guide us,' he blurted out, forgetting in the heat of the moment that he had long since been converted to Christianity.

Garth merely smiled and nodded.

They followed the wolf for more than a mile until, as they turned a sharp bend in the track they realised that he was no longer with them.

'He has carried out his duties,' said Edric. 'My thanks to you god of the wolf-folk, we will now, hopefully find my son, for why else would Woden have sent you to show us the way?'

Garth was more mixed up than ever, for try as he might over the last ten or was it fifteen years, he had attempted, time and time again, to understand the religion that Rowena had forced Edric to convert to. Yet here was absolute proof of the power of the old religion, otherwise why had it not been the Christ-child who had shown himself and pointed the way to rescue little Ælnoth?

The track twisted this way and that, through streams, around marshes and over fallen trees, until all of a sudden they found themselves out of the woodland, standing in a clearing leading to two small meadows, in which a small, thatched cottage stood where a single milch cow stood calmly chewing the cud.

They approached the cottage, glancing at a newly dug grave that was to one side of the cottage, dismounted, and walked to the door.

The door was wide open.

'Come in,' said a voice, 'and take what you will, for I have naught left but my life, and you can gladly have that.'

Edric entered the cottage, followed by the large figure of Garth who had to bend nearly double to ease his frame through the low portal.

'We want naught from you good sire,' said Edric looking at the old man sitting on a stool before the unlit fireplace. 'Except, mayhap, a little information, if it pleases you.'

'Please me?' said the man, looking up for the first time. 'Nothing in this world pleases me anymore, except perhaps that I could follow my Alice into the afterworld.'

'And take the swine who slew my good Alice with me,' he added.

'I am truly sorry for your loss,' said Edric, as he sat on a bench opposite the old man, 'do you know who it was that slew your wife?' he asked.

The man looked up for the first time since Edric and Garth had entered the cottage. It was obvious to the two men that the cottager had been weeping, for his unwashed face and his beard were still damp from the tears that he had shed.

'No, not really,' said the man. 'But my Alice mumbled a few words before she left me,' and further tears cascaded down his dirty cheeks.

'What did she say?' asked Edric as sympathetically as he could.

'She was rambling and said only a few words that I could make out, something about children, a girl, now what else was it she said?' he stopped and scratched his head and held his hand over his brow as he attempted to recall what his dying wife had said a few brief moments before she had died.

'No,' he said shaking his head. 'There was something else she said but I cannot bring it to mind, probably some nonsense for she was sore in pain.' He shook his head again as if to clear his mind of the agony that he had seen as his loving wife suffered in her last moments of life.

Trying not to show his frustration and anger that the man could not remember anything more specific or useful to his search for his abducted son, Edric tried to question the man again, handing him a tankard of ale that Garth had somehow found in the small, ransacked cottage.

'Here.' he said thrusting the tankard into the man's still shaking hand. 'Drink this, it will help.'

The man took the tankard, and nodding his thanks took a deep gulp. Then as if a holy vision had come to him, he said, 'Canterbury! That's what it was. She muttered something about Canterbury.'

'That must be where they are heading,' gasped Garth, who since childhood had always been rather naïve, having an annoying habit of stating the obvious.

Edric thanked the man and hurried out of the door followed by his dutiful friend and liegeman, Garth.

Within the space of ten heartbeats they had mounted their horses and were half way across the one and only field that separated the cottage from the never-ending forest, spurring their horses towards the distant town of Canterbury.

CHAPTER 21

After a long and difficult winter campaign William had completed his conquest of the county of Maine.

It had been a campaign that had cost him nearly a third of his small army, with most of those losses taking place in the final battle, when he had defeated his enemy with a classic pincer movement. In this he had held his cavalry back whilst his foes had thrust forward into the centre of his army, then at a critical moment he had thrown in his heavy cavalry, using a classical encircling movement which had led to a great slaughter of his enemies, leaving a mere four hundred and sixty-two men able to kneel and swear allegiance to him.

Only seventeen men had refused to kneel, and of those, twelve were related in kinship to the earl of the county of Maine who had fallen in the battle.

Those men had been slain by King William's executioner, the huge, ugly, ungainly Hugh de la Hormavile, who had grinned and made lewd jokes as he had beheaded the men in front of the victors and the conquered warriors.

That evening, shortly after he and his lords had supped, a bedraggled and mud-splattered courier hammered on the door with the pommel of his dagger, begging permission to enter and have an audience with the King.

'Let him in,' bade William, knowing that a messenger such as this seldom brought good news, beckoning the man forward.

'Well, what is it?' he snapped at the man, feeling totally exhausted after the strains of battle and especially after witnessing the necessary killing of the late earl's kin and followers.

The man knelt, 'Dire news, my lord King,' said the man handing a wet leather pouch up to the King.

The King snatched the pouch out of the man's hands, and then handed it to his scribe, a white-haired, hunched backed Jew.

'Open this and read it aloud,' he snapped, then turning to the still kneeling man, he said, 'Well, man you must know the news, for I see the pouch bears the crest of my brother Odo, so let me have the bad news before this oaf cuts his fingers off trying to slice through the wet leather?'

'Dire news my King,' the man repeated, his voice wavering as he uttered the words. 'The lords Waltheof and Ralph, the Earl of Norfolk have risen against you.'

'Geoffrey of Coutances is raising an army to protect your realm, but your lord brother Odo fears he will not meet with success, for the rebels are many and well supplied with arms. The English rebels have also been reinforced with men from many of the English shires and from the Northmen.'

'Christ on the Rood,' said King William quietly, fully aware that the news that he'd just received was probably more than two weeks old and, if any battle was going to be fought back in England, then the battle would already have taken place and the result had already been decided.

Therefore, he thought to himself, there was little or nothing that he could do at this precise moment of time, and he needed a level head plus a little time in order to collect his thoughts, in order to decide what to do, for only after careful thought, and after considering all the possibilities, would he be able use his limited resources in the best possible way to preserves his vast empire which now covered a large part of what had once belonged to the King of France, plus his new realm of England.

He knelt to pray, asking the Lord Jesus Christ for help, praying aloud. Praying, 'that after all the battles that I have fought and all the good men I had lost, had not been in vain and that by this one throw of the dice. A throw that had already been cast could now have lost me the kingdom of England.

'God forbid that I need to fight another Hastings in order to regain England,' he said under his breath, 'mayhap I would not be so fortunate a second time.'

William's son Robert Curthose, who had been standing alongside his father, seized the opportunity that he had long been waiting for and stepped forward saying quietly into his father's ear.

'Father, perhaps now is the time for you to let me serve you by ruling Normandy and Mainè, whilst you take your warriors and secure your Kingdom of England.'

His suggestion caused his father to have one of his nervous coughing fits that only abated when a glass of water was speedily brought up from the kitchens, and thrust into the still coughing King's outstretched hand.

He quickly sipped the cool liquid, and the coughing slowly subsided.

The furious King turned to his son and with an uncharacteristic snarl and said. 'You must be mad, you are still a boy and would lose my kingdom within a month.'

Not many of his lords were close enough to hear the exchange between the king and his son. Yet all present were well aware that something untoward had taken place between the two, for both Father and son turned away from each other, with the latter stomping out of the room followed by four of his close henchmen and their retinue of advisers and servants.

Robert left the castle within the hour with upwards of two hundred knights plus their men at arms, riding furiously towards his fathers' estates where he knew he would be able to raise more men, fully determined now to take what his father had so savagely denied him.

King William was wakened by his squire an hour before dawn with the news of his eldest son's departure, and of his intentions. Yet the king had already placed one of his most trustworthy spies in Robert's retinue and had, on many occasions received information about Robert's intentions before his son had been able to put his aims into action. However, on this occasion his spy had been forced by circumstances to accompany Lord Robert on his exodus from the castle.

Thus the spy had no opportunity to reach King William in person, relying upon a trusted friend to carry the news to William.

A polite knock on the door and his closest confidant, Vernon the younger entered, buckling his belt as he did so, his shirt still unbuttoned showing his frail chest.

Vernon the younger had entered Williams service some ten years ago at the age of fourteen, and was now the closest thing that William had as a real friend, a man on whom he could totally rely, and a man who would tell him the truth, the real facts and details of most situations, and not the flowery flattery that most of his minions uttered.

For many of King William's retinue were the court followers who usually spouted words that they thought that their king would like to hear, or perhaps some other words of flattery that would give them some advantage. Perhaps granting a particular favour that they were seeking they shied away from bad news like a fawn hiding in the high fern, watching the hunter pass by.

Vernon the younger was, despite his youth, already balding but was still a man of boundless energy, clever and agile, and a man astute enough to assess a situation correctly in a heartbeat. He was also a man who would keep his steel nerve in the most dangerous of situations.

'I have heard the news, my lord King,' he said as he entered.

'Aye, so have I,' answered William. 'Why could the puppy not wait until I gave him a kingdom, or at least until I had reached my dotage,' he added, as he struggled to hoist up his tight hose. 'The good Lord knows that I love the boy. Have I not indulged his whims? Have I not allowed him to mate with half of the serving wenches on my estates, filling the villages with his bastards? Have I not given him a full quarter of my men-at-arms and crossbowmen to use, as he will? God knows I have spoilt the boy. How could he betray me so?'

'He is a boy no longer my lord King,' answered Vernon. 'He is a full nineteen years now, a man full grown,' he added with a wry smile as he walked over to a chest, where he picked up a jewel-studded sword belt and handed it to the King.

'And if the stories are true, did you not lead your own father's knights in a charge in Aquitaine at the age of fourteen, winning the day, thus rescuing your father from an ignoble defeat?'

The King grunted, slightly annoyed that Vernon should bring up such a thing at a time like this, as well as making excuses for his son's ill behaviour.

As if to press the point even further, Vernon added. 'And, my lord King, at the age of nineteen were you not wed to your beautiful Matilda, and already lord over a full third share of Normandy?'

The King grunted again, knowing full well that Vernon was, yet again, quite correct in his statement, but he was still angry over the actions of his wayward son.

'What you say my dear Vernon, is, as usual quite so, but had my father been in a situation such as this, and in danger of losing half his kingdom, I would have done the thing that a dutiful son is supposed to do, and that would be to support my father, NOT run off in a tantrum with half of his knights and half of his men.'

Vernon did not answer, merely nodded his head, knowing that whatever he said, the King was not in a listening mood, and he would take whatever action necessary to ensure that he still had complete control of both of his realms of Normandy and England.

It took the King most of the day and the following evening to arrange the administration and policing of Maine, but he and his knights and men-at-arms were on the march one hour after dawn on the following day, marching along the same road that his son Robert had taken two days beforehand.

He had intended to increase his numbers so that he could achieve his two goals.

The first and most important course of action was to stop and restrain the rebellion that his son seemed intent on causing, and the second, which was of equal in importance, and that was to muster as many men as he could, in the shortest time possible, and sail for England in order to assure himself that England was still safely under his control.

However by midday on the third day after leaving Maine, a messenger from England reached him with the most welcome news. The rebellion of Waltheof and Ralph, the Earl of Norfolk had been quashed, and that his loyal kinsman, Geoffrey of Countaces had routed the rebels, who had the right foot cut off from all of the major conspirators, forcing the surviving Norman, English and Northmen to kneel and swear allegiance to King William, upon pain of death.

'Wonderful news,' beamed the delighted William. 'Although I would have slain the lot of 'em; once a traitor always a traitor.' he spat. 'Now I can use my full force and bring my wayward son to heel. Vernon? Where the devil is Vernon?'

'He is in the stables, my lord King,' answered a servant. 'One of the brood mares has gone lame,' he explained.

'Fetch him,' ordered William, muttering to himself as he grabbed a chicken leg off the table, saying with a mouthful of chicken, 'what the devil is he bothering with a damned horse for? What does he think I employ those lazy grooms and stable boys for?'

Vernon arrived reeking of horse manure and sweat.

'Where the dickens have you been?' stormed William, knowing of course where Vernon had been, but still felt it necessary to make the point that Vernon was growing rich attending him and not looking after sick horses.

Vernon, as he had expected, was delighted with the news from England, quickly turning his agile mind towards the current and only major problem that still beset the King.

'If I may be so bold, my lord King,' he said gently. 'What we need to do is to cage your son somewhere convenient, convenient to us and not to him of course, thus preventing him from recruiting more men, as well as to prevent him from creating a major problem for you.' He was fully aware, of course that his son was already causing his father a major headache, but attempting (unsuccessfully it seemed) to put the King's mind at ease, by trying to tell the King that the problem was a mere hiccup, and not something that he should be unduly concerned about.

Later the same day a messenger from one of his spies arrived with news that Robert had taken the castle and town of Rouen, and was busy recruiting warriors from the surrounding countryside.

'Great news,' exclaimed the jubilant King, clapping his hands in joy. 'Now we have the puppy boxed up in a kennel of his own making. Well, so be it, let him stew there for a day or two whilst I arrange for the nails to be hammered in a little firmer. Vernon!' he shouted, and Vernon, who had only been in the next room, appeared in the doorway, 'Send a rider to my fleet and have them shift their position to the straits outside Rouen, with orders that no sails whatsoever are to move in or out of the estuary.'

He paced up and down in the room like a caged bear, as was his habit when he tussled with a particular problem.

Within ten days William and his vastly increased army were camped outside the walls of Rouen, sealing the city off completely from the surrounding countryside. There they watched the King's son and the defenders stride along the castle walls where they, in turn, could view the King's vast array camped in the meadows that surrounded the small town, plus the royal fleet which now lay in the estuary, thus preventing any food, reinforcements or assistance from reaching the castle from the seaward side.

'Now we have the silly young fool bottled up, what shall we do with him?' said the King to his assembled lords, not really asking for their advice but merely probing to see if any of them would be brainy enough, or perhaps foolish enough, to come forward with any bright ideas.

'We could send the fleet in against their sea wall,' spouted a beardless youth, a youngster who had recently been disinherited, as a younger son from his father's fiefdom, and was eager to please, and to show his worth to his new master.

The rest of the assembled lords snorted and snickered like a small herd of horses, with one of the older men intervening by saying, 'And run the risk of losing the King's fleet as well as slaying the King's son, I think not,' he snorted with distain.

The youth's face reddened and he turned his eyes downwards, towards the floor but made no retort, now only too aware that his suggestion had been slightly foolhardy, to say the least.

The King who was now in a much happier frame of mind, strode over towards the young man and placed his arm across the youngster's shoulder saying, 'Well your suggestion was at least an opinion, and you were the only one amongst these many lords who was bold enough to voice one, and for that alone you are to be commended. I shall have you attend me in my hall when I return to England.'

The young man's head came up and he gazed adoringly into the hazel eyes of the King of England.

William's army camped outside Rouen for a full week without making any attempt to storm the town. Yet on the ninth day of the siege, Vernon, escorted by two or three other noblemen asked him what his plans were, the only answer that they received from him were the words.

'Let him stew.'

The stalemate was broken on the sixteenth day by the arrival of Matilda of Flanders, wife to the King and mother to his nine children.

William greeted his wife with joy, for being a religious and pious man, he had fallen in love and wed the young Matilda when she was a mere child of twelve, the daughter of a tanner, a dealer in skins and hides, a man who spent half of his life in other men's piss, as he cleaned and dyed his leatherware.

The match had been much opposed by his father Duke Robert of Normandy, who had ranted and raved at his son, threatening to disown the boy if he went ahead with the marriage.

However the stubborn William did go ahead and the wedding had taken place without his father.

The Duke Robert did not attend the ceremony, but Robert loved his bastard son so, and relented, taking the boy into his own keep, schooling him in the arts of a gentleman, and teaching him the ways of war and the life of a warrior.

Matilda was still a comely woman at the age of thirty-two, and threw her arms about William, kissing him on both cheeks, a show of affection that was generally frowned upon in noble society.

'Welcome my love,' whispered the King, slightly embarrassed by his wife's unladylike show of affection. 'It is wonderful to see you, but what brings you to these wild lands, far from the comforts of your own keep?'

'Silly man,' she chided him, patting him lovingly upon his stubbly cheek. 'What think you has brought me here, though I do admit that the journey was tiresome. What else am I to do when I find the love of my life fighting with his own son?'

'It cannot be so.'

'It must not be so,' she cooed.

'I have come to make peace between my two boys.'

This outburst, so unusual for a woman of her nature, was even more so for a woman to say such a thing to her lord and master, especially if that master happened to be the Duke of Normandy and the King of England.

Especially if that was the warrior King who had conquered Normandy, Aquitaine, Flanders and Maine, not to mention the island kingdom of England.

Her statement had somewhat shocked William who had never heard her speak so forcefully, and he felt more than a little abashed knowing that his wife was quite correct, knowing full well that, indeed, he should not be making war against his own son.

However, William felt that as he had not started the feud, and had in fact preventing it so far from getting out of hand, for he had not yet actually attacked his son, thus, things were not really as black as his darling wife seemed to think.

And it was the son and not the father who had slain his opposite's envoy and sent his head back to the father in a leather sack, with a note which said the words, 'Who now is the silly boy?'

His thoughts were interrupted by Matilda who said in a sweet voice as she refreshed herself with a glass of red wine, 'I shall change my clothing and swill my face before I visit my son. Giselle, Giselle, where is that silly girl? Ah there you are,' she said with a little relief, as the maid appeared in the doorway, curtseying as she did so, 'My Lady Queen?' she said sweetly.

'Yes,' answered the Queen, 'Have my clothes unpacked and lay out my blue dress. No, on second thoughts I will wear the yellow one, more colourful,' she explained. 'And have my banner brought out and mount it on a shaft. I want my son to see what manner of person approaches his keep.'

*****

Later that afternoon, Matilda rode out towards the fortress, dressed in her bright yellow dress and accompanied by two of her ladies, plus one mounted knight who held her banner high, showing her coloured pendant off proudly, so that her son would recognise her heraldry, thus prevent his bowmen from showering her and her small retinue with arrows or bolts.

Nonetheless they were closely scrutinised by the sentries who stood high on the two towers on either side of the sturdy, bolt-ridden gates.

''Tis her ladyship the Queen,' she heard one of the sentries shout to men below. 'Open the gates.'

The gates swung open, allowing the Queen and her company through, clanging noisily behind her.

The noise startled her two ladies, but the Queen appeared not to have heard them. She rode casually up to the mounting steps and gracefully stepped off her mare, scornfully rejecting the helping hand that was held out by a knight.

Robert came striding across the courtyard towards her, his face beaming with delight.

'How like his father he is,' she mused. 'That walk; the way he struts and moves his shoulders, and the face. Indeed it could be my beloved William twenty years ago, striding towards me.

'How now Robert,' she said sternly as he strode up to her, holding her shoulders as he kissed his mother on both cheeks. 'What is all this nonsense,' she said, looking up at her son; for he was now a good twelve inches taller than she, 'twas not always so, she thought as her face softened, gazing up into the soft brown eyes of her favourite son.

'What is this nonsense between you and your father?' she repeated.

'He treats me like a child, scorns my suggestions and belittles me in front of my peers,' he spat venomously. 'He must hate me to treat me so,' he said, his voice breaking with emotion.

'Tush, boy,' she said quietly. 'He does not hate you. 'He loves you dearly, and denies you these things that you so sorely crave, in order to protect you from harm.'

'Protect me? Protect Me!' he raved, almost jumping up and down with frustration. 'Protect me from what? I am a man full grown, am I not? It is I who should be protecting him.'

'I know. I know my sweet,' she cooed, 'I know, but forsooth, he does sorely love you, as do I, and it breaks my heart in two to see you quarrel with your father.

'Oh I know he can be a difficult man,' she continued in a soothing, motherly voice. 'He has had to be. And still must continue to be so in order to hold on to what he has taken from the world. And it is not for himself that he has become what he is. It is for you boys that he has carved out such a kingdom.'

She paused for a while as his anger abated.

'It is you boys who will inherit his kingdom, but you must give him time. Yes, he is growing old, but he is still a strong and vibrant man, not yet past his prime. Give him time,' she cooed, 'and all of his realm will go to you boys.

'It would be foolish, would it not,' she continued, 'to wage war against your own father and lose all that will be yours by right of inheritance in a few short years' time. If you were to win and slay him, God forbid,' she said, wiping a fake tear from her eye, 'then civil war would probably follow, for many of his noblemen would not follow you. Indeed some may have designs upon his Kingdom themselves. And if you were to lose against him, and lose you probably will, then mayhap he would disinherit you and settle on one of your younger brothers, sending you into exile, penniless and landless.'

'All you say is true Mother. But I will not walk unarmed and shamed into his camp, like a beggar asking for his charity.'

'And I would not expect you to, proud young man that you are,' she said softly. 'I will return to your father and have him meet you halfway between his camp and your fortress, with banners flying, fanfares blaring and drums a-beating, with all the pomp and ceremony that should be shown when a king meets a prince, especially so, if that king and that prince are father and son.'

The meeting was agreed with father and son meeting exactly halfway between their two armies, as drawn up in front of Rouen.

Both men were reluctant to make the first move and it was the redoubtable Vernon who broke the deadlock as father and son halted some ten feet apart, staring at each other, with neither a smile nor a frown bedecking the face of either one of them.

'Come now, my lord King,' said the smiling Vernon, moving alongside King William, 'is it not bliss to see your favourite son again, and in such good health?'

The King, nudged out of his mood, stepped forward towards Robert and embraced him, kissing him rather coldly on his cheek, 'Aye,' he said as he stepped back. 'It is good to see you again my son. We should not fall out, you and I, for we are so alike, hot tempered, impetuous and prone to take hasty actions. Come now. Let us be friends, for all that I have, will one day belong to my heirs.'

Robert then stepped forward and embraced his father, then knelt before him, saying, 'Forgive me lord King. I acted too hastily; I always did allow my head to rule my heart.'

'Come my boy,' said the king, 'Let us sup together and put this unpleasant episode behind us. We will join your mother, who, if I know her well enough, will have a spread fit for a king waiting for us in her tent.' He smiled slightly at his own joke, whilst his son, happy now that the difficult moment that he had dreaded had now passed, walked alongside his father as they made their way through the cheering warriors towards Matilda's large tent that had been erected next to the king's own quarters.

The evening was spent in celebration with the knights and nobles consuming vast amounts of food and wine, delighted to be eating and drinking with men who only a few short hours ago they may well have been killing.

During one of the quieter moments of the evening, William, sipping sparingly on the only glass of red wine that he had held during the entire evening, sought the company of Vernon, ''Twas well done my lord King,' said Vernon quietly.

'Thank the good Lord Jesus,' answered King William, adding, 'and now to England.

*****

Freya led her brother Ulric and Walter on, pulling the silent figure of Ælnoth behind them as they followed the woodland path up a slight incline then around a bend that had been caused by the falling of a huge oak tree. There she suddenly hauled savagely on the reins of her pony in alarm, for not ten paces in front of her were a party of at least a dozen Normans who stood and sat in a group around a fire upon which a huge piece of venison was sizzling.

Three other Normans were sitting quietly on their horses some ten feet away, staring longingly at the roasting venison that would, they hoped, soon be ready to eat, for they had not touched a morsel of food since leaving the fortress of their lord, some eight hours ago.

Her agile mind quickly assessed the situation, forcing her to realise that to turn tail and run would avail her naught, for their weary ponies would be speedily overhauled by the much larger and more powerful horses of the Normans. So, beaming the most radiant smile that she could muster under the circumstances, she urged her pony forward smiling merrily at the men who were all staring at the four young people who had interrupted their pending meal.

The Norman warrior's thoughts had immediately flown from the sizzling venison to the approaching woman as they stared, boggle-eyed at the beautiful blonde vision who rode to within a few feet of them, admiring her as she daintily dismounted and stood before them with her hands on her hips and a dazzling smile upon her generous lips.

'It is well that I have met up with you good men at long last, but in truth I had thought that you should have met me two days since at the river crossing at Chipping Norton,' she said loudly in the most haughty manner that she could muster.

No man replied, and all looked in awe that this young girl. Nay, this beautiful young woman who stood before them and had the affront to address them so, for no man there knew what the lady was talking about.

A burly man, who sported the shoulders of a swordsman and a face that showed the result of too many battles, pushed his way through the throng and stood in front of his men. He had the almost mandatory hairstyle of the Norman warrior, with his hair cut and shaved high up upon the back of his neck, with a thick fringe of black hair, mottled with white reaching to his eyebrows.

'What say you missy?' he said in a gruff, heavily accented voice. 'We know nothing of meeting with you or any other wench for that matter, but are out here patrolling our lordship's new domain, seeking cut-throats and wolf-heads who have been raiding his lordship's holdings.'

He turned his head slightly towards another man, younger and seemingly better bred, for he wore an expensive hose and held an elaborate embossed war-shield.

'What say you Waldorf?' he growled. 'Do you know what this wench is prattling on about?'

But before the man called Waldorf could answer, Freya intervened saying angrily, in a very loud and refined voice. 'Wench! Wench, do you dare to call me Wench. Let not these ragged clothes cloud your vision, for I would be ill advised to wear silk when travelling the woodlands, would I not? And we shall see who the wench is when Bishop Odo's men get here with their orders to escort me to his holding in Canterbury.'

The mention of Bishop Odo had the desired effect upon the men, causing most of the Norman heads to suddenly look at her with perhaps more on their minds than rape and plunder, whilst one or two of the more timid souls took a pace backwards, with one man gasping aloud at the name of the churchman who was universally known to be a harsh and cruel man.

'No offence was intended lady,' muttered the leader in a much more civil manner. 'We were not to know that you were on an errand for the good Bishop.

We are, after all, merely honest warriors carrying out the orders of our liege lord.'

'That is quite all right my good man,' she answered haughtily in the finest voice that she could muster, a voice that she had rehearsed in many a woodland clearing over the past four years, a voice and mannerisms that she had originally learned at the tender age of fourteen when she had spent a few short months as a mistress of a sadistic Norman lord, and a voice that she now spoke with such perfection that even the most snooty of the landed gentry would swear that she was a Norman lady born and bred.

'You are forgiven my good man,' then added with one of her famous smiles. 'But only on the condition that you and these fine fellows of yours will escort us through these treacherous woodlands, until we chance upon our true escort, and if we do not meet them then you must accompany us to the outskirts of Canterbury.'

The man was in the process of coughing and about to deny such a preposterous demand, when he was interrupted by the refined voice of Freya, 'I will, of course, inform the Bishop of your kindness.'

'Your servant my lady,' said the man reluctantly, not really knowing how he had been cajoled by this woman into taking his men miles off their original course. More importantly, he knew that his lord would be furious when he came to learn what had happened, for by escorting this lady and her companions would mean that they would be gone for many days, important days in which his lordship would, he knew, certainly withhold their daily pay.

'May I offer you and your companions a little venison?' he said beckoning her towards the fire where the hindquarters of a deer sizzled on a spit.

'You may indeed,' she answered with a smile. 'Come Ulric, you too Walter and bring the brat.'

After they had eaten, the leader approached Freya. 'He doesn't talk much, does he?' Nodding towards Ælnoth.

'No he does not,' came the answer. 'He has not spoken a single word since we took him. In fact we are not sure whether or not he can speak. Oh, he understands us well enough, but he either nods or shakes his head when we ask him questions, but says not a word. Really strange,' she said smiling towards the man, shaking her golden locks as if in awe of the boy.

'Please excuse my rudeness,' said the man as he sat alongside Freya, 'but we have not been properly introduced. My name is Hugo,' he said, placing a gnarled hand on his chest. 'Some call me Hugo the Slayer,' he added proudly with a wry smile that crossed his scarred face.

'Just so, Hugo.' answered Freya, 'it is good to make your acquaintance, Hugo,' adding in her sweet, refined voice, 'and what part of Normandy do you come from?'

'Nay, lady I am not of Normandy, I am a true Breton, through and through.'

That was what Freya had hoped, for her Norman lover had told her many things about his homeland of Normandy as well of the Duke's dependency of Brittany.

She also knew that Hugo, being a Breton, would probably know little about Normandy. Knowledge that she hoped would give her an advantage in her dealings with this lout of a sergeant.

'And I am called Freya. Although my real title is the Lady Freya of Louviers,' she added with a radiant smile.

'Louviers,' he mused, 'I have heard of it my lady, but know little of it.'

'Oh it is a beautiful place, deep in the countryside of our beloved Normandy,' she sighed. 'My father has a chateau there,' she lied, 'high on a small hillock, overlooking his domain which is green and pleasant.

'Sunny and warm,' she said with a sad smile, 'unlike this cold, wet country. Oh, how I do long to return to my beautiful Louviers, as soon as the good Bishop Odo will allow it.'

She sighed again and gazed longingly into the dying embers of the fire.

After a long silence, she said, 'My two companions over there are called Ulric and Walter' – she nodded towards the two young men who were sprawled on the damp floor on the other side of the fire – 'and it is their sole purpose in life to care for my every need, although to be quite honest with you, my dear Hugo, they both fall dismally short of their duties.

'They are not the type of companions that I would have chosen,' she said sadly, 'Heaven alone knows why Bishop Odo chose them,' adding quietly, 'I suspect he sent them to keep an eye on me, for the boy that we hold is a prize much valued by the Bishop.'

'Why is that'?

'Can't really say,' came the quiet answer as she wrapped herself in the dry sheepskin to ward off the night chill, and then turned her back on him in order to avoid any more difficult questions and, of course, to attempt to get some sleep.

CHAPTER 22

'We have seen no sign since noon,' grumbled an angry Edric.

'Aye,' answered his companion, who was in the act of dismounting in order to stretch his limbs which were so stiff after the last few days of unaccustomed riding, he felt that his legs were so numb that they would not be able to support his large frame unless he could get off this bony beast and walk for a pace or two. 'Not since Fenrir the wolf-god left us.'

Edric had always known that his friend Garth had never taken to the new religion of the Christ child, despite a few half-hearted attempts that he had taken towards Christianity, he still doggedly followed the old gods.

Edric chose to ignore Garth's remark, saying, 'The light is going so I think that here is as good a place as any to spend the night.'

'I don't know why we don't go on a little further,' Garth grumbled, 'you never know, we might find someone who has seen them, or even find a cosy cottage where we can spend the night.' He felt unhappy that he was about to spend yet another uncomfortable night under the stars on the damp ground, which was beginning to cause him so much pain, especially on his left shoulder where he had taken a spear thrust some eight or ten years ago.

Edric grunted approval, saying, 'Right then, we will get to the top of that rise yonder and see what we shall see.' Spurring his mount forward, leaving Garth standing beside his own tired horse as he watched his friend disappear from sight.

Garth wearily mounted his horse and urged the animal forward in Edric's wake, finally catching up with him on the rise of a small hill.

Edric had already dismounted and was squatting on the ground staring into a lush, wooded valley.

'I see smoke there,' he said pointing downwards.

'Where?' said Garth, straining his eyes in the direction of Edric's pointed finger. 'Oh, Yes, I see it too,' he answered after a slight pause. 'Let's make for it then. It might even be them.' Without waiting for Edric's approval he spurred his horse over the crest of the hill and down the slope into the valley.

Slightly annoyed at his companions' unusual show of haste, Edric quickly remounted Chieftain, following Garth down the overgrown track into the growing darkness of the early evening.

As they neared the area where they estimated they had seen the smoke, Edric lightly touched Garth's arm, brought his finger to his lips to indicate silence, and dismounted.

Garth followed suit and they both tied the reins of their mounts to a sturdy sapling, before proceeding through the undergrowth along the side of the track towards what appeared to be a large clearing in the forest.

Long before they saw the light from the fire, both men could smell the delicious aroma of roasting venison, for venison has a smell of such richness that distinguishes it from any other meat.

At the far end of the clearing they could see a number of men seated and standing around a fire, plus a line of tethered horses that were in the process of being given a few handfuls of hay before they were to be settled down for the night.

'Bloody Normans,' hissed Edric.

'Aye,' snarled Garth quietly.

'Gods blood,' swore Edric. 'The smell of that roast venison is making my belly think that my throat has been cut.'

'Me too,' answered Garth as he wiped the saliva that had dribbled out of his mouth, 'I'm so bloody hungry I could eat a scabby oxen, horns an' all.'

'How many of them do you think there are?' asked Garth.

'I can count fourteen or even fifteen,' whispered Edric, 'although there could be more the other side of the horses that I can't see.'

'We can take sixteen motley Normans, no bother,' growled Garth.

'Probably,' answered Edric, 'but I think it would be wise to wait a while and let them settle down for the night.'

'As you wish my Lord Edric,' whispered Garth in his gruff voice, adding with a smirk. 'Let the dogs enjoy their last evening on earth, but, to be sure, I do begrudge them that venison that they are scoffing.'

Edric ignored the remark despite the fact that he could also smell the roast venison and those same aromas were informing his belly that it was, yet again, desperately in need of being filled.

'Can't see little Ælnoth,' he said quietly.

'Neither can I; can't see those three young killers either.'

'We will circle their camp and see if they are on the other side of the fire,' said Edric as he slowly backed away, disappearing silently into the undergrowth.

Darkness had taken hold by the time they had slowly and silently circled the Normans camp. 'Still can't see 'em,' whispered Garth.

'They must be there somewhere,' said Edric quietly.

'I think it's time to cut a few throats,' said the ever-bloodthirsty Garth switching his great war-axe into his left hand as he withdrew his *seax* from its sheath, and began to slither forward on his belly towards the nearest sentry, whose outline was silhouetted against the glow of the fire.

Ten minutes later the dying sentry was laid gently, almost reverently to the ground by Garth, cooing into the man's ear, as if he was trying to cajole a baby to sleep.

The second sentry was dispatched by Edric equally as efficiently but the man was taller and much heavier than Edric, causing Edric a little concern as the man struggled in his death throes, uttering a loud guttural growl as he hit the floor.

A man, who was either not asleep or had been wakened by the sentries growl, shouted, 'Who's there?' But when he received no reply, he appeared to be satisfied by the silence and speedily huddled back under his sheepskin blanket, against the chill of the night.

They waited a long time before they crawled silently towards the remainder of the sleeping Normans, slaying the men one by one, until Garth placed his hand, as usual, over the mouth of his next intended victim. Only to find, much to his surprise that the man was still wide awake and had, before he could react plunged his dagger into Garth's side.

With an agonised grunt Garth grabbed the man's hand and wrenched the hand, still clutching the dagger, out of his side, slashing his own razor-sharp *seax* across the man's throat, sending him to his maker. Yet not before the man had roared and gurgled his last, loud cry in his final moments of life.

Shouts and bellows echoed around them as the remaining Normans stumbled out of their wraps, realising that they were under attack.

During the following few brief moments of confusion, Edric quickly realising that the time of knives had passed and switched his knife to his left hand. At the same time he drew his sword, dispatching two foes before they could react to their enemy within.

Garth, clutching his left side in order to stem the flow of blood that he could feel saturating his shirt, dropped his knife and, wielding his axe in his right hand, let out his savage war-cry, charging into a cluster of three Normans, instantly slaying one with a downward swing, taking half the face off another as he brought his blood-stained axe upwards.

Edric, his bloodlust up, furious that these Normans could be in league with the three young killers who had taken his son, struck right and left, stabbing and hacking at any man foolhardy, or perhaps brave enough to come near him, until no man stood in front of him, whence he strode across the clearing seeking out his next victim until the only people alive in the clearing were himself and Garth. He was now leaning heavily on the haft of his axe, his head bowed onto his massive chest.

Edric, leaning on his own sword now that the slaying was over, stared towards Garth. Staring, almost unbelieving as he watched his lifelong friend slowly topple over and fall, face-first onto the churned up, bloody ground.

He rushed over to Garth, kneeling at his side as he tried to roll the huge figure of his friend onto his back so that he could see the wound. With a gigantic heave he managed to turn him onto his back and, by merely looking into the eyes of Garth, he knew the wound to be serious.

'Take your hand away,' he ordered. 'Let me see.'

With a muted groan Garth removed his hand and Edric could see the blood oozing out from a deep cut in his side, some eight or ten inches above his hip bone.

'Is it bad?'

'No, you will be fine,' Edric lied.

'Press your hand against the wound for a moment while I look around and get something to stop the bleeding.'

Edric searched the dead Norman bodies until he found a suitable piece of linen. This he cut into strips with his blood-stained knife, then returned to Garth and commenced to press a wad of the material against the wound, wrapping the cloth around Garth's waist until he felt it was tight enough to quell the bleeding.

He helped Garth up to a sitting position. Then with a lot of heaving, pushing and shoving, he managed to get Garth up onto his feet, and helped him over to the fire where he propped him up against two Norman saddles, and wrapped half a dozen sheepskin blankets around his now grey-faced friend.

He walked over to the still forms of the dead Normans, moving from one Norman body to the next in hope that one of them may still be alive, hoping beyond hope that he just may find someone alive, someone who would be able to give him information about his son and the three young killers who had abducted him.

The last man he visited was indeed alive, although, Edric could see, his last moments were nigh. He gave the man a sip of wine from one of the many bottles that were lying in the clearing.

'Here my good man,' he said, in the language of Normandy, 'drink some of this fine French wine. It will make you feel better,' he raised the bottle to the man's lips.

After the man had gulped down a mouthful of wine, Edric said as pleasantly as he was able, 'Did you see anything of a captive boy and three young people who were holding him?'

The man looked up to him and nodded.

'You did!' exclaimed the elated Edric, scarcely able to conceal his joy. 'And where are they now? Do you know?' Trying desperately to hold himself back from shaking the answers out of the dying man.

'Don't know,' gasped the man, coughing blood as he spoke. 'They didn't turn up.'

'Turn up? Turn up?' exclaimed Edric and shook the man. 'What do you mean, turn up?'

The man's head lolled to one side, and he said no more.

*****

Edric stripped the dead of their weapons and valuables, though for the life of him, he did not know why. Maybe it was habit, or mayhap it was the anger that was still in him, for he was now alone, burdened with a wounded comrade and could do naught with the weapons and accruements of twenty-two dead men.

He then dragged the bodies out of the clearing and inspected the horses, still hoping to find some sort of evidence that his son had been here, returning dejected and exhausted to the still figure of Garth.

'Is there any sign of him?' asked Garth.

'No, afraid not,' came the sad answer, then changing the subject he said, 'Come Garth, let me get you lying down and we shall see how you are on the morrow, and then we can decide what to do next.'

It took some time to arrange a bed of three sheepskins for Garth to sleep upon. When that was done, he covered his friend with a further two sheepskins, gave him a drink of good Norman wine, then attempted to settle down beside his friend in order to await the coming of the dawn.

Despite the fact that he was exhausted, Edric slept little with his mind racing from one thing to another with each question being followed by yet another.

They had trailed his son directly to this band of Normans, yet he had not been found here.

Where, therefore was he?

What connection did the three young killers have with these Normans?'

Why had Ælnoth been taken in the first place?

If it was a ransom that they were after, then why did they run from this particular band of Normans?

Had these Normans paid the ransom or not?

Are they still in hiding? Nearby?

He stood up and walked to the edge of the clearing, then made his way into the sparse woodland, walking around the perimeter of the clearing no less than three times without seeing a single sign of his son or his abductors. There was only one distinct path leading out of the clearing which did bear the signs of the comings and goings of a number of horses, but no distinct signs of the ponies that he and Garth had been following for the last few days.

Had Ælnoth and his abductors been taken further south by another group of Normans? And if so where and why?

Canterbury?

Why Canterbury?

Questions, questions, questions...

He must have finally dozed off, for when the rain running down the back of his neck woke him, it was full daylight.

Glancing across the now dead fire he could see that Garth was still asleep with just the top portion of his face protruding from beneath the sheepskin rugs that Edric had swathed him in the previous evening. He sliced off three or four portions off the now cold and wet venison that still remained on a spit over the dead fire, thrusting a slice into his own mouth as he walked over to Garth, gently shaking him awake.

'Wake up old friend,' he said. 'How do you feel this morning?'

'Fine,' came the reply. 'I feel fine.' Yet as he attempted to rise from beneath the sheepskins, Edric could see the pain in the face of his friend as he struggled to raise himself into a sitting position, but even this task was too much for the big man, and he fell back onto his bed.

'At least you do seem to be a bit better than you were last night,' said Edric, 'here, have a mouthful of this venison and a swig of this fine French wine, that should help,' as held up a thin slice of venison and a half-filled bottle of red wine.

He raised the bottle to Garth's lips, tipping it slightly in order to pour the liquid into his mouth and did, indeed manage to get some into his mouth, but much more dribbled down his short beard and onto his shirt.

'Try the venison,' he said holding a slice forward, but Garth shook his head, mumbling, 'I cannot.'

Frustrated and in a quandary as to what to do next, he walked away towards the tethered horses, tending to Chieftain first, whispering quietly into the savage stallion's ears whilst he stroked his neck, with the stallion responded by nuzzling Edric's neck and ear.

He then moved to Garth's mount, then on to the twenty-two horses plus the two pack animals who had up until the previous evening, belonged to the now deceased Normans. He spoke quietly to them as he gave each one a small bagful of oats, plus a leather bucket of water which he had to fetch from a nearby stream.

'Though what I shall do with you my beauties, I really know not,' he said aloud.

For the horses were, like most of the Norman mounts that he had encountered, truly top class horses, oat-fed and groomed to perfection.

He eventually returned to Garth, still pondering over what he should do, not only with Garth but also concerned as to what he could do with these fine and expensive Norman horses.

By midday the drizzle had ceased, allowing a thin sun to peer through the light clouds that covered the forest.

Edric had decided to remain with his wounded friend for perhaps another day or so, fully aware that the longer he tarried here, the further away Ælnoth and his captors would be.

Gazing into the newly kindled fire, as he waited for a chunk of venison to cook, he became aware that the horses had started to snicker and had suddenly become restless, as if they had sensed danger.

He rose to his feet, stooping to pick up Garth's famous axe, and as he rose clutching the axe, a man emerged out of the forest and stepped into the clearing.

He was a big man, sporting a unkempt black beard and dressed in what had once been an expensive tunic. That was now so ragged and mud-encrusted that he looked like one of the many beggars and wolf-heads who now roamed the countryside.

Before Edric reached the man, the man said in a quiet, somewhat cultured voice,

'What have we here?'

Then another much rougher voice from behind Edric answered, 'Not much, I think. Just another accursed Norman, I would wager.'

Then yet another voice came from third man who emerged from the woodland:

'Just kill the sod and let's be on our way.'

CHAPTER 23

Edric turned towards the voice only to see at least a dozen men enter the clearing, noting that they were all youngish men, armed with a varied assortment of weapons, including four longbows, all of which were drawn and ready for use.

These men had the look of hard men, battle-hardened and merciless, well used to the shieldwall and to the killing.

He immediately knew that if he were to make a wrong move then he would be quickly slain, allowing these men to rob him, then move on without giving him a second thought, pretty well delighted with themselves to have slain the man that they had mistaken for a Norman, taking the pile of Norman loot which he had assembled plus a small herd of expensive Norman horses.

Quickly realising that his life hung by a thread, and that the first aggressive move that he made would result in a yard-long, grey goose feather shaft sending him to the afterlife, he said in the calmest and strongest voice that he could muster. 'I am no Norman, but an honest Englishman, tending my friend yonder,' he pointed to the prone figure of Garth whose head still protruded from out of his sheepskin bed, 'and it was bloody Normans that nearly killed my friend.'

'A likely tale,' said the man who appeared to be the leader.

'Yeah,' said another of the band, 'he probably wounded him himself and is about to rob the poor sod and make off with them their horses,'

'Aye,' said another individual who was even dirtier than the rest of the band, but held a spotlessly clean sword in his right hand. 'Them's valuable 'osses them are.'

'They are indeed,' intervened Edric, adding with a flourish of Garth's huge battle-axe. 'But before you sell the horses you must own them.'

'Brave words stranger,' snarled the leader as he advanced towards Edric, 'but it seems to me that there are eleven of us and just one of you, which does give us a slight advantage, wouldn't you agree?'

'Perhaps you should put that question to the twenty-two dead Normans over yonder,' answered Edric, nodding towards the clump of undergrowth where he had dumped the dead Normans.

A flicker of doubt fled across the face of the leader, who suddenly halted in his tracks, a mere six feet away from Edric, a whisker out of the range of the huge axe that this stranger held, almost casually in his right hand.

'Take a look over there,' he ordered, and two men turned, walking a few paces into the bushes, returning a few minutes later. ''Tis right Oscar,' said one, ''tis like a bloody slaughterhouse in there,' spitting as he uttered the words as if to expel the smell and the sight of the Norman corpses from his body.

The leader, slightly unnerved, and unsure of what to do next as a result of this quickly changing situation, stepped back a couple of paces to within the straggling line of a small knot of his companions, lowered his sword and conferred quietly with his men, muttering amongst themselves just out of Edric's earshot, then the leader detached himself from his companions and, followed by them, they all walked over to see the bodies.

After a short while, he and his men returned to Edric, who had not moved and was, waiting, seemingly casually, still leaning on the axe-shaft.

'Well?' he said.

''Twould seem so,' answered the leader, 'and I expect you want us to believe that you and your friend yonder slew that lot?'

Edric merely nodded.

Then, after a long silence he said, 'I am called Edric, some folk have called me Edric the Wild, whilst others have named me Edric the Savage, and my friend there is Garth Bloodaxe.'

He paused a few moments to allow that statement to register, then added. 'We are both Englishmen, born and bred. We are here, pursuing three young killers who have slain my servants and have abducted my son, and we believe that another band of Normans have taken him further south into captivity.'

'He can't be Edric,' came a voice from the crowd, 'I heard that Edric was seven feet tall and had a scar across his right hand caused when Woden himself gave him his first sword.'

'Aye,' snarled another large grubby man, 'and he is supposed to have had a spear thrust through his heart and lived to tell the tale.'

'Left a mark and a hole as big as yer fist,' added the first man.

'I am Edric,' roared Edric loud enough to be heard above the mutterings, 'although I must admit that some of the stories about me may have been exaggerated a little.'

Then holding up his right hand, for all to see the straight line that went in a deep straight line across the palm of his right hand.

The men suddenly went silent, craning their necks in order to see the line across his palm.

Then, as if partly convinced, they retreated back to their original places, where the muted muttering continued until the large grubby man took a pace forward and said, 'What about the spear wound then? Show us that.'

Somewhat reluctantly, Edric unbuckled his belt, allowing the belt, *seax* and small knife to fall to the floor, pulling his leather shirt up to his neck.

Again the men shuffled forward to stare at his chest, where they could see for themselves the large indentation that had been with Edric since the day of his birth. It was this very dent in his chest that had caused the legends and stories about him, making him a legend in his lifetime for he had been speared through his heart, had he not? Yet he lived to tell the tale.

Gasps and grunts followed their inspection.

Eventually they shuffled back, looking at one another in awe and amazement that they should actually meet with a man who had been, and still was a living legend amongst their people. A man about whom they had heard many stories from the storytellers and minstrels who wandered from village to village, earning their bread by telling, and no doubt embellishing the legends and stories of the English people.

The mutterings ceased. Yet before any of them could speak, Edric said, 'We thought that those Normans there,' nodding in the direction of the slain Normans, 'held my son, but he was not amongst them. He has, apparently been taken further south by another band of their countrymen.'

There was now a nodding of heads, plus a few grunts of approval as the men began to believe him. Many of them had heard of the exploits of both Edric and of Garth, but as the leader was about to speak he was forestalled yet again by Edric who added, 'Now by the right of conquest, those horses and all these Norman weapons and accruements belong to me. But if you will join me in my quest, in helping me to hunt down these people who are holding my son, and help me rescue him, I will not only give each one of you a fine Norman steed, plus a spare mount, and a share of the spoils that lie under those sheepskins there, as well as a purse of silver, plus of course a fair share of any further booty that we may take.'

At the mention of silver and loot, the men's faces altered from the serious, bloody-minded faces of men bent on killing this stranger only a few short minutes ago, to the smiles of men thinking of riches, and the power that riches would give them, land, farms, power and women.

He silenced their grunts of approval by holding up his hand saying. 'Of course, I only want men willing to fight for me, men who will swear a blood-oath to me, no faint hearts, no old men or weaklings.'

The leader, the man called Oscar, who had obviously once been a man of learning and a man of worth, a trait that had made him the leader of this pack of wolf-heads, turned to face Edric.

'What manner of blood oath?' he asked, and as he spoke, Edric noted that the man's sword lifted a little and he held his large round shield just a smidgen higher.

'I am a man well respected in the borderlands,' said Edric, 'some might say, perhaps rightly so, that I am also feared a little, and I have survived many a battle including our fight against these invaders at Senlac Hill, near to the town of Hastings.'

Before anyone else spoke, Edric continued, saying, 'And the oath that I expect each and every one of you to swear is this.'

He paused for a moment, glancing from one worried face to the next, before he continued, 'Men who have fought with me have oft-times been men who I have grown up with and have known for many years. Men I knew that I could trust, whilst your good selves and myself have met a few short heartbeats ago, and I know naught of you.

'I will demand that those men who join me must swear their loyalty not only to myself but to each other, and will state after me, thus:

'I Earl Edric of the borderlands – you will of course state your own name – do swear, that I shall fight unto death, to defend my fellow warriors in this band, and should any of my fellow warriors fall in battle, I will recover his body to give my fellow warrior either a good Christian burial or send him into the afterlife in the way of the old gods. I will protect all women and children, and do my utmost to regain the sovereign land of my country England from these Norman invaders.

'This I swear.'

He waved his *seax* in front of him then drew the blade across his left hand and turned his hand over to allow the blood to dribble into a wooden tankard that was half filled with stale Norman wine.

Oscar stepped forward, nodding his approval as he moved, and was about to take the oath. Yet before he spoke, Edric again held his hand upwards, saying, 'You are about to take a solemn oath before our men and myself. You seem to be a man of honour so I will accept your oath Oscar, for I can see by the gashes in your sword and the white scars on your arms that you are a man well used to standing in the shieldwall, but let not yourself, or any man who stands here, in this place swears this oath, who had not proved himself in battle, or has any intention of deserting us, or breaking his sacred oath, for as sure as God made little apples, that man will be hunted down and slain by either myself or one of you, for he will have broken this sacred blood-oath.'

'I too fought at Hastings,' said Oscar, 'together with at least half of my men here. Many of the others are good men who I would trust with my life.'

'I am pleased to hear it, for you will be doing just that,' said Edric smiling as he placed his right hand reassuringly on Oscar's shoulder, then turning to the assembled men he said:

'No one will think any the less of you and name you a nithing if you do not join us. I will give you my blessing, plus a good Norman horse if you would rather return to your farms and loved ones.'

To his surprise, after a short pause, five men stepped forward.

One man, a thin middle aged man dressed in what could only be described as rags, touched his forehead muttering, 'I have a wife and three little 'uns at 'ome and they needs me.'

'Go with my blessing,' said Edric, and the man moved away.

Another, younger man, hardly more than a boy, nursing a hand that had three fingers missing, said, 'I would be of no use to you my lord, as I was once a good bowman. But I now need to recapture some of my old skill before I tackle those bloody Norman dogs again.'

The other three merely touched their foreheads with their right hands, lowered their eyes and moved away towards the tethered horses.

Oscar grumbled in his now familiar deep, refined voice. 'Do you not think it unfair, my Lord Edric, that those five men who are leaving us should have the pick of the finest horses?'

'Hold,' called Edric at the departing men, who immediately stopped and turned towards him. 'Wait there until these men have sworn their blood-oath.'

The men stood still and waited while, first Oscar, then Aldred, followed by the rest of the men swore the oath, cut their hands and allowed their blood to be mingled with the wine and the blood of Edric.

Edric then took the tankard, brought it up to his lips, took a mouthful of the stale wine mixed with his own blood and the blood of his men, swallowed the liquid and said, 'This sacred oath I do so swear,' passing the tankard to the next man, then on to the next man until the near emptied cup returned to him.

'We are all men of the same blood,' he said in a loud, serious voice, 'and we are now sworn by this blood-oath to defend each other to the death.' He flung the cup and its meagre contents into the fire.

'Aye,' cheered the men, 'to the death.'

Edric then turned to Aldred saying, 'Chose five steeds for those men.'

Aldred trotted off to do his bidding.

'Just so, just so,' said Oscar in an approving voice. 'He knows his horses, does Aldred. He's a good man with horses.'

Edric nodded his head in agreement as the man named Aldred loped off in order to catch up with the five men who were leaving, then Edric suddenly remembered the savage nature of his own stallion Chieftain and called, 'Aldred, stay well clear of my own black stallion if you would like to see this eventide, for if ever there was a killer horse then it is he.'

Aldred waved his hand in acknowledgement and turned to catch up with the five men who had already reached the horses and were standing glumly and somewhat ashamed, waiting for him.

Edric made his way to the prone figure of Garth, followed by Oscar and the remaining five men.

'How are you feeling old friend?' asked the concerned Edric.

'Oh, I'm fine,' said Garth in a quiet voice, looking up into the eyes of his liege lord.

'I can see that you are little improved, but you still need to see a healer, but where to find one in this county' he said thoughtfully.

'Perhaps I can help my lord,' came a high-pitched voice.

Turning, Edric noted that the voice had come from a rather unlikely source, for the man who had uttered the words was a large fellow, well over six feet in height, a man with a healthy, ruddy complexion and a mop of fair hair that was tied at the nape of his neck by a rag that had once, perhaps in better times, been bright yellow. Yet now, like most of the clothing of these men who had just sworn the blood-oath to him and to themselves, was nought but a dirty rag.

'This is Hugh of Worcester,' said Oscar, 'he is a good man, though a little strange at times, isn't that so Hugh?' he said with a smile as he reached into the crowd and gently pulled the big man forward. 'Come on Hugh. Tell us how you can help Lord Edric's friend. That's a good fellow.'

The big man stepped gingerly forward, looking first at Oscar and then Edric, casting his eyes to the ground as he mumbled in his strange high-pitched, almost girlish voice that all of his previous friends were used to hearing. Yet it was a voice that seemed to Edric and Garth to be out of place amongst this company of hard-bitten warriors

'I was born and bred not five miles from here, my lord, and my mother and my sister are still there.'

'That's good Hugh,' said Oscar in a kindly, almost fatherly way. 'But how is that going to help this poor man here?' nodding towards the prone figure of Garth.

Hugh seemed confused by the question and gazed down at Oscar with an expression that almost said to Oscar, 'How can you be so stupid as to not understand what I am saying.'

'She's good with sickness and wounds, she is! Everybody knows that. They comes from miles around to be cured by her they does, always giving her things like geese and chickens, and one man gave her a fine cow for curing his wife of the flux.' Then as an afterthought, he added, 'Good milker too.'

'Will you take us to your mother?' asked Edric, trying to hide his excitement that this man was, seemingly, holding out a sliver of hope that may help Garth to recover from his stab wound.

'Of course he will,' answered Oscar, 'won't you Hugh?'

He, still looking somewhat vacant, nodded his head.

'Aye, so long as you don't hurt her.'

'We won't hurt her Hugh,' said Edric in as soft voice as he could muster. 'In fact if she can heal my friend I will give her a full purse of silver, and make her a rich woman.'

The man's eyes seemed to focus upon Edric's face and something between a smirk and a smile appeared, 'Come on then, this way,' in his high-pitched, girlish voice, then he turned to his left, walked over to the horses where he grabbed two of the nearest and started to stride out of the clearing.

'Wait for us Hugh,' shouted Oscar as he and his men scrambled for their meagre belongings, running towards the waiting horses in order to choose a steed.

Edric scooped up the Norman loot, weapons and belongings which he wrapped in a heavy horse blanket, throwing the blanket over the back of his own stallion, saying, 'I will share this loot out later, once we have reached the house of the healer.'

Edric could see that Hugh was having a little difficulty with one of the horses that he had chosen, calling to him. 'Do you know how to ride Hugh?'

'Aye I do my lord,' came the reply in a rough, harsh voice that was totally different from the girlish voice that the man had been using before. 'Born and bred with horses I was, before them damned Normans killed my father and stole our two brood mares.' He climbed up into the unfamiliar Norman saddle with a silly grin on his face.

Edric, somewhat startled in the change that had taken place in the man, glanced around towards Oscar who had already mounted a large roan stallion and was sitting astride it with a wide grin on his face.

'Hastings,' he said, as if that explained everything.

'Hastings,' mused Edric to himself. That might explain the loss of the man's horses but did not, it seemed to him, explain the change in the man's voice, as well as his demeanour, still that was of little consequence providing that this strange man could take them to a healer and stem the blood that was still seeping out of Garth's side.

*****

As gently as possible Edric helped three other men lift Garth onto a makeshift litter made of a leather cloak stretched over two stout hazel rods, covered him with two sheepskins, tying the stretcher between two of the quieter horses. Then, led by Hugh, they followed him down the overgrown pathway through the damp woodland.

Following the sturdy figure of Hugh who was riding a large dun stallion with the ease of an accomplished rider, they reached the cottage of his mother a little before noon.

The cottage was not what Edric had expected. It was no wattle and daub hut stuck in the middle of a forest, but he saw before him a substantial property built of sturdy oak logs, sporting a new thatch, surrounded by a neat vegetable garden and well-tended farmland.

Edric dismounted and with the help of two of the other men, carried Garth, as gently as possible through the doorway into a large room. This consisted of a large oak table with two benches, one either side of the table, plus a number of benches and cots along each of the two side walls.

As his eyes adjusted to the darkness of the room, a room that had a single source of light which shone out from a large stone-lined fireplace, he could see that most of the cots in the room were occupied, and on most of the benches sat people, silent, yet perhaps inquisitive at this crowd of strange men who had just invaded their silent room.

A small figure rose from a high-backed chair that was facing the fire, revealing to Edric a woman who looked like a bent hag, or perhaps a witch, for she leaned heavily on a stout ash stick.

Her white hair stood out from her head against the firelight giving the impression that she had just been struck by a bolt of lightning.

'Damn and blast,' muttered Edric under his breath, 'She's just a bloody old Witch.'

'She is no such thing,' said a loud indignant feminine voice that came from behind his left shoulder.

He turned towards the sound of the voice, and was shocked to see a woman standing a mere three feet from him. 'She is merely an old woman and probably the most gentle and most kind old lady that you will ever meet.' said the woman in a low, sultry voice.

Edric was shocked at the devastatingly beautiful face that stared back at him. Her blue eyes, highlighted by the firelight gleamed from a young, clean, perfectly shaped face, surrounded by shock of raven-black hair which fell in pleats both to her left and to her right, meeting at the back of her head, tied with a white ribbon.

'I am the one you seek,' she said, then without waiting for a reply from the still dumfounded Edric, she speedily knelt beside the prone figure of Garth, placing the palm of her hand upon his forehead. 'Mmm...' she muttered, 'he has a raging fever,' then turning to her mother she said, 'Mother, be a darling and bring me the jar of crushed willow leaves, some comfrey, a little feverfew, some crushed foxglove leaves and we shall see if we can break his fever.'

She then lifted Garth's shirt and dabbed at the wound with a piece of white, sweet-smelling cloth, and turning her head, called in her sultry deep voice, 'Mother, dear, bring the honey and the woundwort'.

She then attended Garth's wound, giving him a small wooden cup of her own medicine, which she forced him to drink, spilling a small amount down his tangled beard, smiling gently as he coughed and spluttered as he attempted to swallow the foul-smelling concoction.

As she stood, she said to the still silent Edric, 'Carry your friend over there and put him in that cot,' then, as if for the first time she noticed her brother, she said pleasantly, 'Ah, brother Hugh,' ''tis good to see you again, especially so soon after that dreadful battle at Senlac Hill. But of course I knew that you would come home unscathed.'

'Of course you did sister,' answered Hugh in a high-pitched womanly voice, a voice that Edric had learned to expect from him when he was excited or perhaps a little unsure of himself.

Hugh cleared his throat and said in a voice that was one moment the voice of a woman, but had now altered into the deep voice of a man. 'This is my sister Winnifred the Healer. She is the one I told you about,'

Then turning to his sister he reverted again to his manly voice, saying, 'That is so is it not sister? You can heal him, can't you?'

'Time will tell,' answered Winnifred in a noncommittal, deep sultry voice, which seemed to Edric to be even deeper than the voice of her brother.

'You and your men will have to sleep in the barn,' she said to Edric. 'As you can see, we do not have room for you in here. Besides, your noisy roistering would do little to help my patients heal.' then she turned and disappeared into a small passageway that led into another room.

'Thank you for your kindness,' answered Edric, 'but alas we cannot stay, for we have urgent business in the south.'

Edric knelt by the bedside of his friend, saying, 'We shall leave you in this maiden's capable hands whilst we continue our chase.' Then touching Garth's shoulder, he added, 'I shall pick you up on the way back, when I've got Ælnoth.' he turned and ushered his men out through the doorway towards their tethered horses.

'Mount up,' he ordered. 'We have a lot of catching up to do.'

CHAPTER 24

'Why doesn't the boy speak?' asked Hugo, nodding his head towards the figure of Ælnoth who was nodding, half asleep on his pony.

'I don't really know,' answered Freya. 'He has not uttered one single, solitary word since we took him.'

'Perhaps he is dumb.'

'Perhaps so,' she said nodding her head, wishing that this long, tiresome journey would end and she could stop trying to be pleasant to this stupid Norman sergeant.

A little while later, as if he had read her mind, he said, 'Another three or four hours and we should be in Canterbury. And I must say that I shall not be sorry to see that blessed place, although I dread to think what my lord will have to say when we return home. I wager he thinks us dead by now.' Then, almost as if he was talking to himself, he added, 'We were only supposed to be away for three nights.'

They reached the outskirts of the town before dusk, passing through the gates with little more than a casual glance from the two tired sentries who had been on duty since daybreak, considering this small contingent of Norman horsemen to be just one of many who had passed through the gate during the day.

Freya insisted that her escort (as she thought of them) accompany her to the very gates of the residence of Bishop Odo, holding her left hand out limply to allow Hugo to bow his head and place his lips on the back of her outstretched hand.

'My thanks for your company Hugo,' she said haughtily.

'I shall inform my Lord Odo of your diligence and of your good behaviour, and he will no doubt relay his own thanks on to your own lord.'

He was about to commence his long rehearsed speech but was prevented to do so by Freya who said hastily:

'My thanks to you again,' as she turned her back on him, striding forcefully past the solitary sentry, and through the gates, followed by Ulric, Walter and the fettered boy Ælnoth.

Much to her annoyance, she was kept waiting for what seemed to be an eternity before she was ushered through room after room until, at long last, she passed through yet another door to halt, slightly out of breath, before the corpulent figure of Bishop Odo.

'Ah yes!' he boomed, 'I do remember you, but had long since thought that you had either died, or had mayhap altered your mission just a little, and had decided to go straight to my brother, the King.

She curtseyed, bowing her head for a brief moment before she raised her eyes again to gaze into the face of the fat bishop, convinced that he, bishop or no, like a hundred men before him, would be totally captivated by her beauty.

She rose, giving him the most radiant smile that she could muster, a smile that she had rehearsed time and time again in front of the cracked mirror that her brother had once carried for her.

'Ah!' she thought as she saw him melt before her, 'I have him.'

'Your obedient servant my Lord Bishop,' she said in a quiet, refined voice, adding. 'I have captured the son of the rebel Edric of the borderlands and have brought him to you as ordered.'

'Well well,' he said stroking his sparse beard thoughtfully. 'Have you so?'

'I have indeed, my lord, he is in the entrance hall, guarded by my two servants.'

He turned to the servant, who had escorted her to the Bishop and barked, 'Well man, don't just stand there looking stupid, bring the young captive in to me.'

The man turned and nearly tripped over his own feet in his haste to do the Bishop's bidding.

The Bishop only had time to walk the few paces to a table and pour himself a silver goblet of sparkling red wine before the servant barged through the door, totally out of breath, dragging the bedraggled and tired-looking Ælnoth behind him.

'Ah, so this is the boy is it?'

'It is my lord,' said the delighted Freya.

'The son of Wild Edric. The man who has caused such havoc in our borderlands?'

'It is my lord,' she repeated.

'How do I know it is he?' he asked with more than a little sarcasm in his voice.

'My lord,' spluttered the shocked Freya, for this meeting appeared to be running down a lane that she had not explored.

'Well, this boy could be anyone,' snarled Odo as he sipped from the silver goblet, gazing at Freya over the rim. 'Could be any urchin off the streets, well boy, what have you to say for yourself? Are you the son of Edric the savage?'

'He is so,' intervened Freya, 'I swear he is. We took him from Edric's own household, right from under the very nose of the monster himself.'

'And I am expected to believe the word of an adulteress like yourself?' adding, 'Oh I know all about you, I have ears in every shire. I know only too well how you treated that poor husband of yours, drove him to suicide, so I heard.' He adding with a cynical sneer, 'Some say it was poison. I want to hear from the boy. Speak up young man. Who is your sire?'

'My lord,' said Freya. 'I am afraid he is mute. He has not uttered a single word since we captured him.'

'A likely tale,' he snarled, 'and so very convenient.' He emptied the goblet, which he flung onto the floor, as if in a rage.

'You bring me a mute and expect me to honour you with good honest Norman silver?'

A child's voice piped up, 'Lord Edric is my sire, and the Lady Godda my mother.'

Freya took a step back, staring down at Ælnoth in amazement.

'I thought you said he was mute,' snarled Bishop Odo.

'I... I... I thought he was, my lord,' she spluttered, still stunned that this infant who had been roped and mistreated by her for nearly two weeks. A child who was supposedly weak and afraid, who had not uttered a single word, had now chosen this moment to break his silence.

Then she added in a demure and timid voice. 'He has spoken not a single word since we took him.'

A shiver went through her body, as if a ghost had walked over her grave.

'If that is so,' said Odo haughtily, 'why have you not spoken to this lady whilst you were in her care?'

'She... she killed Betilda and Winnie,' he said shakily, feeling his eyes watering as he grappled to regain control of his emotions. 'Cut them up she did.'

Ælnoth then fished inside his soiled shirt and withdrew a small kidskin pouch, from which, after fiddling around for a brief moment, he brought forth a small ring that he placed on his right index finger, holding it aloft for the Bishop to see.

'My father gave me this ring for my fifth birthday,' he said proudly.

The Bishop bent down to examine the ring and brought the boy's hand up to his face, 'What says it?' he demanded. ''Tis too small for me to read.'

His servant bent down to scrutinise the ring, 'It says, *Ælnoth from Edric.*'

'Pah, and I am supposed to believe that, perhaps searching for yet another way in which he could avoid paying this bitch the silver that he had promised her?' Then turning to a second servant who was in the process of retreating to the doorway, he called, 'You there, you can read, can you not?'

The man nodded, 'I can my lord Bishop.'

'Well. Come here and read this. Your eyes are younger than mine. Quickly now for I have more pressing matters to attend to,' he said, thinking of the roast duckling and suckling pig that he knew must now be waiting for him in his newly furnished dining hall.

The man rushed forward and bent to examine the ring until his face was almost touching the ring, reading aloud, he said in a shaky voice, '*To my dear son Ælnoth from Edric* my Lord Bishop.'

'Just so,' said Odo, trying to consider whether or not this ring was proof enough to convince him that this child was indeed the son of the English barbarian Edric. Deciding that it was, he reluctantly crossed over to a small chest that rested on the corner of a large polished oak table, inserted one of the keys that hung on his belt, and pulled forth a small leather purse.

He jangled the purse up and down a couple of times, felt the weight in his hand in order to assure himself that he was not paying too much, then tossed it towards Freya who deftly caught it, smiling broadly as she did so.

'Now go!' he growled, unhappy that had just been forced to part with a goodly portion of his precious silver.

Freya curtseyed, smiled, and was ushered out through the door whilst Bishop Odo waddled as quickly as he was able through a second door towards his dining hall and the feast that awaited him there.

*****

Edric was more than pleased with the first day's progress of their renewed hunt, for Hugh and Oscar proved their worth by riding some way ahead of the main band, leading them unerringly through woodland, along stream beds, past towns and village, avoiding all of the larger populations, returning from time to time in order to explain the reason that he was taking this route and not that as well as to point out the newly constructed fortresses that proved to Edric that beyond doubt those particular places had already been over ran by their Norman enemies.

His new pathfinders followed the scent of the fugitives like bloodhounds, gleaning information from farmer and peasant alike, their persistence paying off by occasional sightings of their prey.

Canterbury appeared before them on the second day, a large cluster of buildings ranging from wattle and daub hovels to large substantial buildings encircled by a newly built town wall, with no fewer than ten towers situated fifty or sixty yards apart all along the palisade.

'Didn't used to be like that,' said Oscar.

'So you know the town?' asked Edric.

'Like the back of my own hand,' came the reply. 'Used to go there with my father when I was a boy.'

'You will know where the Bishop lives?' queried Edric.

'He's likely to have taken him to the old bishops' of Canterbury's palace,' said Oscar thoughtfully.

'Tonight you will show me,' said Edric grimly.

They camped deep in the centre of a small wood, tended to their weary horses, then snatched a little sleep after gnawing on cold mutton and dried stockfish.

Edric chose Cledwyn the Welshman, a small, wiry, middle-aged warrior to accompany Oscar and himself and, after leaving the rest of his men and the horses some quarter of a mile from the town, the three men proceeded on foot towards the northern edge of the palisade.

The three men crept silently up to the newly built stonewall, exactly half way between two of the towers.

Edric untied the rope that he had prepared earlier, swung it in a wide circle over his head and flung it, with the iron cloth-covered hook uppermost, up and over the wall.

It landed somewhere inside with a dull thump.

He waited the space of fifty heartbeats before he began to pull on the rope, which, much to his relief, eventually lodged itself upon some unseen object and refused to budge any further.

He tested the rope a couple of times before he scrambled silently upwards, followed by Oscar and then by Cledwyn, who tumbled into a heap alongside him on the walkway.

Edric hauled the rope upwards then dropped it over the inside of the palisade, and one by one they landed on the ground ready to confront any enemy who may have been foolish enough to approach them.

After pausing for a short while, Oscar led the way, and they followed him through the winding streets and alleyways towards the Bishop's residence.

The palace was a large substantial building simply awash with light from the many candles that lit up each and every one of the many rooms that faced them.

They crept as silently as possible through the bushes that surrounded the building peering into the candle-lit rooms one by one, being eventually rewarded by the sight of Ælnoth who was sitting at a table tucking into what could only be called a feast, especially to the hidden watchers who had not eaten a meal like that since the last Christmastide.

Hiding in the dark, safe from being seen, Edric could see two other young men at the table. One was a dark-haired youth of perhaps ten or eleven years of age whilst the other was maybe a year older, much taller, but pitifully thin.

Both of these boys had their hair cut after the Norman fashion, whilst his own son stood out as a Saxon with his long fair hair held in place at the back of his neck by a leather strap.

'What shall we do with them?' whispered a voice from beside him.

'Bash 'em on the head and leave 'em,' whispered Cledwyn.

'No,' hissed Edric quietly. 'We take them with us. Two can play this game of hostages. Follow me,' and he ran, leaving his two comrades standing with their mouths open for a moment before they too, chased after him towards the door that was a few short yards away.

Edric burst through the door like a whirlwind, crashing into a servant who had just entered carrying a bowl of fruits, sending the startled man and his tray of fruits to the floor in a loud crash.

Almost casually he swiped the startled man across the side of his head with the hilt of his *seax*, sending the unconscious servant back to the floor that he was in the process of rising from. Then Edric strode manfully across to his equally startled son who he lifted high and hugged him tightly against his dirty, sweat-stained coat, almost unable to believe that, after all of the trials and tribulations of the past few weeks, he had, at long last, not only found his son hale and hearty but actually had him safe and well in his arms.

'Father!' sobbed the boy, overwhelmed by the entry of his famous father, a father who he had thought to be hundreds of miles away. 'I knew you would come for me. I knew you would come,' he repeated tearfully.

'Take them,' Edric ordered nodding to the two other boys, and Cledwyn grabbed the fair haired boy whilst Oscar chased the dark-haired boy a few paces before catching him by the scruff of his neck, hauling the struggling boy after him as he made his way to the door.

'Let's go,' Edric said, as he carried his son out of the door and into the blackness of the night.

He and his comrades tied and gagged the two Norman boys, and after a single scare when, just as they had clambered up upon the walkway, they thought that a sentry had seen them – but the man was, fortunately much too interested in the leather bottle of wine that he was in the process of emptying than in carrying out his duties of being an alert sentry – and they passed silently and unseen.

The three men silently scaled down the rope, each man carrying a boy across his shoulders.

They rejoined their comrades before midnight and by dawn were more than twenty miles north of Canterbury, homeward bound.

*****

The journey to the house near Worcester where they had left Garth in the care

223

of Winnifred the healer took them a day and a half of unpleasant travelling along muddy lanes, through rain-soaked woodlands, wading through swollen steams and muddy rivers due to the torrential downpour that did not show any sign of letting up.

However, towards the middle of the afternoon, as Hugh led them the last half-mile towards his mother's house the clouds appeared to drift slowly to the east, revealing a clear blue sky, leaving the cool breeze which began to dry out the bedraggled travellers' clothing.

As they came within sight of the house they could see Winnifred and her mother who were standing at the door, as if they knew that Edric and his party would be arriving at that precise moment.

As Edric approached nearer he could see that both Winnifred and her Mother carried trays laden with wooden jugs full of ale, plus a large wooden plate full of all manner of sliced meats.

The men dismounted, hauled the three boys off their mounts, and after a few words of welcome, began to stuff their empty bellies with strong ale and good food.

As Edric was taking a long swig of ale, he nearly choked as the large figure of Garth staggered unsteadily into the doorway and stood, leaning against the doorpost, with a wide, boyish grin across his usually grim face.

'Well, well,' spluttered Edric, 'indeed, it is good to see you up and about.'

But before Garth could answer, the gentle, deep voice from Winnifred who was standing alongside Edric said, 'Yes but it against my wishes, for I have bade him time and time again to stay in bed, for he is not yet well enough to be out of his cot.' Then moving towards the still unsteady figure of the big man, she added 'Come now Garth, you will never get better if you continue to gainsay my orders,' and placing her hand on his elbow ushered him back inside the house towards his unmade bed.

Edric could not fail to notice the way he obeyed her and looked at her, feeling certain that the long gaze that Winnifred returned was not the glance that a nurse would normally give to a patient. Yet Edric knew beyond any shadow of a doubt how much in love his friend Garth was with his wife Myreen, and felt certain that, knowing Garth as he did, there would be no way that Garth would betray that love.

Yet what he had seen pass between the two was a concern that bothered him for many days and nights to come.

Winnifred returned to the small gathering of newcomers and the few residents of that holding who had arrived to greet Edric, shouting their praise for this famous man who had successfully rescued his son from the dreaded Normans.

'My congratulations to you my Lord Edric,' she said. 'Your son looks hale and well, despite his ordeal.'

'Aye, he does so,' answered Edric trying to speak and be polite, and not spit out the large chunk of pork that he was chewing. 'He is a stout little fellow, but I fear that he will never forget or forgive the slaying of poor Betilda and Winnie. He was close to both of them and the way that those three young savages tortured and slew them is bound to have made an impression on the mind of one so young.'

'I will speak with him.' she said, and then returned to her house to tend a young shepherd boy who had been savaged by a wild boar.

That evening, after they had eaten, Winnifred awaited the opportunity to join Ælnoth who was standing in the doorway, looking wistfully into the distance.

She placed her hand on his shoulder saying. 'It is such a lovely evening that I thought that I might walk down to the river and watch the otters. Come on, I wager that you have never seen the otters splashing about in the shallows.'

'I have so,' he answered. 'We have lots of them in the stream at Wentnor.' Yet he still tagged along behind her as she walked ahead through the meadow and down towards the river.

Ælnoth eventually trotted a few paces to catch up with Winnifred and, as Edric watched them walk slowly through the meadow, he noticed that Ælnoth reached up and held Winnifred's hand, and then as they walked hand in hand he gave a little skip as he walked alongside her.

They returned long after dark and although Edric never knew what was said or what happened on that balmy summer evening, Ælnoth returned bubbling with joy and excitement, having almost reverted back to the Ælnoth that Edric had previously known.

Edric, his son and his newly found band of warriors remained with Winnifred the Healer for a further three weeks before Garth was pronounced fit enough to travel, and it was with some reluctance, plus a few tears (from Ælnoth) and mayhap more than a little reluctance from the usually gruff Garth, whose peck on the cheek from the beautiful healer seemed to last a second or two longer than it should have, convincing Edric that his friend and the beautiful healer had fallen in love with each other.

Before their final departure, Edric placed his hand on Winnifred's elbow and led her a few paces from the gathering. Speaking low so that no one else could hear, he whispered, 'Lady, I thank you from the bottom of my heart for what you have done for my friend, but set not your heart upon him for he is spoken for and dearly loves his wife.'

'My Lord Edric,' she answered. 'I know that he had a wife and loved her well enough, for he has spoken much of her. But alas, she is no more.'

'What do you mean by that,' said the shocked Edric in a loud voice, causing the small gathering of warriors and village folk to cease their chatter and to stare at him, realising that something was amiss.

He glared back at them, causing them to avert their eyes from him, but when he turned to confront Winnifred, she merely smiled one of those unassuming, enigmatic smiles that it seemed to him that she alone could produce, casually turning her back on him and walked slowly back towards her house.

Winnifred's words troubled Edric on the long slow ride to Wentnor, casting a black shadow over the joy of seeing his lovely Godda and his beloved homeland again.

CHAPTER 25

Everything at Wentnor was the same and yet not the same, for all that Godda sobbed with happiness and emotion at the safe return of her son, kissing his face, and his head, touching him all over as if to assure herself that it was really him, and that had he really been returned to her all in one piece.

Something seemed to be wrong, and for a long time Edric could not think what it was. Yet something was not quite right as he watched Godda, still clutching her son, gracefully meeting with the men who had accompanied him to Wentnor. He sensed that she was acting rather aloof and strange, smiling gracefully as she met each of the men, yet behind the smile, something was being withheld.

Something, Edric thought, that was perhaps too great a burden for her to reveal to him at this particular moment, a moment of joy, euphoria and happiness.

He arranged quarters for the men and had two burly men assist the exhausted Garth into his sleeping quarters before following Godda and Ælnoth into the longhall. There he found that his wife had already instructed her maids to tend to the table that had already been laid out with all the favourite foods that Edric and Ælnoth liked: hot crispy pork, a large side of well-done beef, roast duck, roast turnips swimming in thick brown gravy, plus his favourite pudding being a freshly baked apple and blackberry pie, as well as several bowls of fresh cream.

Edric sat in his usual chair at the head of the table and he tucked into the feast that his wife had set before him.

He lovingly watched her as she sat opposite, hauling her stocky son onto her lap before she picked at the food on the table, eating a little herself but feeding Ælnoth with titbit after titbit of his favourite food as if he was a babe still in his swaddling clothes.

'Let the boy down,' he said in a gentle voice. 'He has more than proved himself over the past few weeks and I am sure that he would rather feed himself.'

Almost reluctantly she helped Ælnoth to the floor and he skipped joyfully towards the middle of the large table, hauling himself up onto his own chair where he happily grabbed a small freshly baked loaf and a handful of pork which he began stuffing into his mouth as if he had not had a good meal for months.

Edric ordered his serving man to bring the two captive boys to them. When they arrived a short time later, he bade them join him at the table.

'Sit here alongside Ælnoth,' he said to the fair-haired boy, who willingly sat and immediately began helping himself to the feast on the table, whilst the dark-haired boy was far more reluctant and sat, straight-backed on his seat, folded his arms and stared straight ahead refusing to speak or partake of the food.

'Come boy,' said Godda, 'help yourself, you must be starving after your long journey.'

The boy stared at her with open hatred in his face, then looked away. 'I would rather die,' he snapped in a high voice, heavy with the accent of

Normandy.

Godda looked towards Edric who grimaced, raised his eyebrows as if to say, 'So what, let the ungrateful wretch starve.' Yet Godda smiled sweetly, rose and crossed over to the boy, stooping beside him, she placed her arm across his shoulder and put her warm, rosy face against his and whispered in his ear, 'Just try a little piece of this delicious roast lamb for me, it will melt in your mouth, and you must eat a little food in order to give you strength to survive your time with us.'

'I am the son of the Lord of Brittany,' he said haughtily, 'and my father will come with a thousand knights to rescue me, so you had better let me go now or else he will have you hung, drawn and quartered.'

'Tush, such talk, when all we want is to treat you well and let you experience some of our good English food and hospitality.'

'Pah!' he spat. 'This is not fit for swine. At home I would now be dining on larks eggs and roast quail. You English are savages.'

She could see that perhaps Edric had been right, and perhaps the correct thing to do would be to leave him alone to starve. Yet she was, after all, Queen of the Light Elves, and as such not used to being disobeyed, so she smiled sweetly, kissed his cheek, selected a small piece of succulent lamb which she stabbed with his eating knife and brought it up to his mouth.

Perhaps it was the scent of this beautiful woman who reminded him of his own mother who had wept so when he had been forced to accompany Duke William on his trip to England (*and* held by the Duke in order to obtain total obedience from the boy's father) or perhaps it was merely hunger taking control of him, but involuntary, his mouth opened and he allowed the meat to enter, causing his juices to flow. Whereupon they literally took over, finding the meat which had been spiced with mint and wild garlic, to be unbelievably delicious.

'My thanks, my lady,' he mumbled, somewhat reluctantly. 'But I am no longer a child and can feed myself.' He then reached up, holding Godda's hand with one hand whilst his other gently took the knife from her, he proceeded to slice a larger piece of meat off the joint, and ravenously devoured it.

Edric smiled, then he turned his attention to his own son who had continued to gnaw on a leg of lamb. Speaking as casually as he could without trying to alarm his wife, he asked her.

'Is all well with our holdings?' and before Godda could reply, he added, 'all seems to be in order but I do sense that there is a problem that you seem reluctant to discuss with me.'

'Things are the same here, but we are being flooded with refugees who are being driven out of their homes. None close to us as yet, but I do fear that these invaders will soon be here amongst us.'

She took a sip from her wine goblet saying. 'They have a big garrison in Chester which is controlling most of that shire, and Shrewsbury has been given to someone called Roger de Montgomery, who now calls himself the Earl of Shrewsbury. And from what little news we have here, it is rumoured that the old Earl was thrown into his own dungeon where he was left unattended to starved to death.'

Edric could only gaze down the table at his beautiful wife, who was quite obviously upset, but she carried on speaking as if the floodgates of her mind had opened, as if it was vital for her to relay all of this disturbing news to her newly arrived husband at this precise moment. A moment which should have been full of happiness and joy at the homecoming of their son, nonetheless she continued to speak.

'The town of Oswestry is under the control of a Norman knight named Alan Fitzflaad, and the new King William has put him in charge of overseeing the complete borderlands between Mercia and the Welsh mountains, which, if I am not mistaken, encompass your own lands, my Lord Edric, causing us to fall under his sway.'

Edric, realising the gravity of the situation that his wife was trying to explain to him, asked, 'What about Ludlow, Hereford and Streeton over the hill?'

'All are Norman now, and they are building huge stone castles everywhere.'

'God's blood,' swore Edric, thumping his own glass goblet down onto the oak table, spilling a large quantity of its contents onto the table's surface.

'And they are forcing our people to work for them as slaves,' she added.

'But surely there are not enough skilled men who can fashion stone in the Norman way, are there?'

'Oh they have brought their own stonemasons over from France and Normandy. Promising them riches in land, gold and silver that they have stolen from us, as well as promising them titles; our lands and our titles.'

'Have you seen aught of them whilst I was away?' he asked.

'Not yet, but it is only a matter of time before they come here,' she answered.

'The strange thing is,' he mused almost to himself, 'is that when we were at Canterbury, they still had the old English wooden palisade inside their new stone walls.' After a moment's thought he added, 'Why did they not knock them down? It would have been the most logical thing to do. I would have knocked 'em down and used the wood for something else.'

'I think, husband, that may well be their next job, and the wooden palisade will only be destroyed when the stonemasons thought that their stonework strong enough to be walked upon.'

Edric could only nod, glumly as he raised his tankard to his mouth.

'Then we have a lot to consider, do we not? But I shall not dwell too much on what might or what might not happen. The morrow will suffice for us to dwell on those particular problems. Tonight I shall finish this good wine and eat my fill of this feast that you have set before me, then hopefully enjoy a good night's sleep in a soft feather bed, and face the morrow with a full belly and a lighter heart.'

For the rest of the evening the 'Norman problem' was not mentioned by Edric or by Godda who, despite their happiness of being together, and the joy of having their son back home, plus the two captured boys, thrust the Norman incursions and the enslavement of their people to the back of their minds. Nonetheless it still cast a shadow over what should have been a very happy occasion.

It was in the morning as they were breaking their fast that Edric mentioned Garth.

'Is all well with Garth's own manor at Much Wenlock?'

The spoonful of warm bran that Godda was about to place into her mouth hovered an inch from her lips as both her arm and her mouth froze, as if a sudden frost had engulfed her.

She slowly replaced the uneaten spoonful of bran onto her earthenware plate, saying, 'Alas my lord, I have delayed the news of Wenlock. For it pains me to tell you, even now, some weeks after it had happened...' she seemed unable to continue and reached for a tankard of warm milk which she brought to her lips, sipping at its contents.

'Tell me? Tell me what? For goodness' sake wife, tell me what has happened at Much Wenlock?'

''Tis bad news Edric,' she answered. 'Garth's longhall was burned to the ground,' she sobbed, 'Burned to the ground, with everyone in it.'

'Myreen?' he growled.

'Aye, my lord, Myreen, the children, everyone.'

'Normans?'

'Aye my lord.'

'By God, they shall pay for this devil's work,' he swore at the top of his voice and stormed out of the room.

As he walked across the village green towards Garth's house, the words of Winnifred the Healer suddenly hit him as if someone had clouted him with a club, causing him to cease his walking. He tried to recall the exact words that the healer had said.

It was, 'his wife is dead.' No, he corrected himself. She had said, 'She is no more.'

But thinking as hard as he was able he could not recall the exact words that Winnifred had uttered. Yet what he was sure about was the fact that she had known, those many days since, that the wife of Garth was dead.

How could that be? he asked himself, but could come up with no logical answer. He had no other option but to continue to make his way towards his friend's house, dreading the moment when he would find Garth and break the dreadful news to him.

He found Garth eating bacon, cheese and wild garlic with freshly baked bread.

'Edric,' he said in a startled voice as Edric burst through the door and walked across the flagstones towards his friend.

'Prepare yourself my old friend,' said Edric in as gentle a voice that he could muster under the emotion that was welling up within him. 'I have bad news for you, and I'm afraid that there is no easy way for me to say it, so I will give it you straight from the chest, no ribbons or frills, but it is dire.'

Garth stood, still somewhat unsteadily after his recent injury. 'Well?' he said in a more normal voice, 'Well, what is it?'

''Tis your wife, Myreen,' he whispered. 'Your house at Wenlock has been burned to the ground with Myreen and the children in it.'

Garth staggered over to a settle that was alongside the fire and sat on it with a thump. 'Not the girls?' he asked.

'Aye, I'm afraid so.'

'Normans?' he asked.

'Aye, Normans.'

'By Woden's balls!' he bellowed, hurling the chunk of cheese that he was in the process of eating, across the room. 'Someone will pay for this!' He then held his head in his hands and sobbed his heart out.

Garth's grief knew no bounds, making him totally unapproachable as he wandered about the small village, through the surrounding fields and woodlands, avoiding human contact, snarling savagely at anyone who was foolish enough to approach him.

He even avoided Edric, who on the two occasions that he attempted to speak to his friend, received nought but a nod or a mumbled reply before Garth turned on his heel and made off.

Other than the sorrow that he felt for his friend's loss, Edric was, yet again, totally amazed when he recalled that Winnifred the Healer had intimated about the demise of Garth's wife some days before they had reached home.

Perhaps she was a witch, he thought to himself.

Yes. That was it. The healer was indeed a witch.

Later on that very evening, after they had eaten their final mean of the day, Edric spoke about his feelings, telling Godda how Winnifred the Healer had known about the death of Myreen long before news of the massacre had been made know, venting his anger whilst he spoke to Godda.

'How could she have known?' he spat. 'Out there in the forest, miles from anywhere.'

'How could she have known?' he repeated. 'She must be a witch.'

'Well, she might be a witch,' said Godda with a kind smile crossing her face as she witnessed the turmoil that was causing her husband so much anger. 'But then again, she may not be,' she added. 'For there are many folk who have the gift of seeing events that have taken place in some far-off land, and in some cases they have the gift to see things have not yet taken place. Things still to come.

'It happens to me more often than I would like, for it is not always pleasant things that these premonitions foretell.' She reached across, placing her hand on the arm of her husband, saying:

'There is one thing that I can say of the lady Winnifred. If she is a witch, she certainly is what my folk would call a white witch, and not a witch who spins the web of evil, for I have heard many things about Winnifred and know these things.'

She removed her arm, then took his hand leading him up the stairs towards their bedroom where, after a short period of time she lay upon him, making love to him in a way that only a Queen of the Light Elves could, after which they fell asleep in each other's embrace.

CHAPTER 26

Bishop Odo raged and swore when he was told the news that he had not only lost the son of the English renegade Edric, a boy who had so recently cost him a large bag of English silver, but he had also lost the two other hostages that he had been holding for his brother the King.

He smashed a very expensive chalice against the wall and had two of his servants executed for their lack of diligence. Then he sent every man woman and child who had been in the house at the time of the abduction into serfdom in the fields, replacing them with eager recruits who had recently arrived from Normandy.

'That's not going to matter much when my brother finds out that he has lost those boys,' he muttered to one of his knights. 'The King was holding them to assure him that their fathers remained loyal to him back home in Normandy and in his province of Brittany.

'He will have my head for this.' he fumed.

'Not so my lord Bishop,' one of the knights dared to say. 'He will be angry, no doubt about that, but he is a God-fearing man and his vows will stay his hand from harming his own brother, especially so as you are a man of the Church.'

'Christ's teeth, I hope so.' Then Odo snarled, 'That bitch Freya. I feel she had a hand in this deed, who else knew that I held Edric's boy here? Go Blondell,' he screamed. 'Find that bitch! Bring her to me.'

Blondell, a young knight from Brittany, who had been wounded at Hastings and was still limping about upon his barely healed leg that had been sliced to the bone by some English peasant, was now a man who had been speedily converted from a pleasant, placid individual into an adamant hater of anything English. A man who had, since the battle, tortured and killed more than a dozen Englishmen for the mere crime of bearing a weapon, be it sword, spear, axe or hunting knife, the latter which was essential for the existence of every peasant, a tool which he or she needed for the simple tasks of everyday existence.

Blondell smiled, nodded as he slowly limped out of the room followed by his two, equally sadistic retainers, Bugger and Renault.

'My lord Bishop,' spoke Sir Ralph Trevelle, 'perhaps the King will not hear of this mishap,' he said with a wry smile as he placed his hand upon the Bishop's shoulder, gently ushering him out of earshot of the small gathering of followers who seemed to accompany the Bishop for most of the time.

'How so?' asked the Bishop, looking and hoping that the man could come up with a way out of this unexpected problem.

'If we were to recapture the boys,' he whispered into the Bishop's ear, 'before the news reaches your brother's ears, then all would be well, would it not?'

'Oh, and how would I do that? I haven't a clue as to who took them, or where they are likely to be now.'

Running his hand over his bald head, he added. 'They could be anywhere by now, even back with their own sires in Brittany, or even Normandy.'

'Nay, my good lord Bishop,' answered the crafty Trevelle. 'The Norman and the Breton have been with you for more than a year, and their own sires seem content enough to serve your brother on the continent, as well as sharing the spoils of war with your brother.'

He went on with a sly smile, 'Your first thoughts were correct. I am sure the culprit is the woman Freya. She took the Englishman's son, and I am certain that it was this renegade Englishman Edric has reclaimed his own son, and at the same time taken the other boys just because they were there.'

'You could be correct my dear Trevelle,' sighed the Bishop, somewhat relieved that this man who had been a close companion of his for some fifteen or more years, still retained the logical, practical mind that had assisted Odo on many occasion over those years. This was one of the main reasons that he kept the man close to him.

'But, even if you are correct, we still have no idea where those boys are now.'

'Just so my lord, Just so, but when Blondell returns with the woman, we will know where she took the boy from and thus, where he has been returned to.'

'God's blood, Trevelle,' exclaimed Odo, 'what would I do without that devious mind of yours? Come,' he placed his arm around Trevelle's shoulder, guiding him over to a huge, oaken cupboard that contained some of his large collection of French and Burgundian wines, 'let us drown our sorrows and await Blondell's return. God willing let it be soon.'

Blondell returned before noon on the second day dragging a bedraggled Freya behind him.

'Here is the woman you seek my lord Bishop,' said the smiling man as he stooped down to rub the wound in his right leg that had been causing him so much pain during the last few days.

'Well done my good Lord Blondell,' said the smiling Bishop as he gazed casually at Freya, who looked very unlike the refined lady who had walked so gracefully into this very same room less than a week ago.

'I see your leg is still troubling you,' he said to Blondell, trying very unsuccessfully to look concerned.

'Just so, my lord Bishop,' answered Blondell, ''Tis this damned English rain, always seems to play up when it's cold and wet.'

'And that is most of the time,' said the Bishop with a wry smile, delighted that the woman who held the key to his future, in fact to all of their futures, stood before him. The fact that she was dirty, unwashed and bedraggled concerned him little. What did concern him that a steady drip of muddy water that dripped from her tunic. It was creating a large puddle on his newly polished, very expensive, oak floor.

He strode regally over to her.

'Hold her head up.' he ordered, deigning to touch her dirty hair with his own spotlessly clean hands.

Blondell grabbed a handful of hair, which draped over her bowed head and yanked her head up so that the Bishop could look into her face.

The Bishop was, yet again, struck by the girl's beauty, noting that, despite the mud that had been washed down her cheeks by the riverlets of her apparent tears, her radiant beauty shone like a light in the darkness.

Then remembering just how sadistic and devious this beautiful girl was, he said to Blondell. 'Take her to the ladies' chambers and have the maids clean her up, give her some garb more fitting for riding, then take fifty of your finest men and have her lead you to the place where she found Wild Edric's son, and bring those two brats back to me within the week.'

'My lord Bishop, wh – wh – what shall I do about Edric and his son? What are your orders if I should be forced to negotiate for the two boys?' he asked nervously.

'Negotiate?' screamed the Bishop. 'Negotiate! You should not have to negotiate with fifty men behind you,'

Then rubbing his bald head with his sweaty palm, he remembered that this Wild Edric was no ordinary wolf's head, recalling that he had been a major player in the recent rebellion that had devastated a number of shires along the Western midlands, plus a large tract of the borderlands, as well as into the multiple kingdoms of Wales. After a long pause he added, 'Oh well, yes. Negotiate it you must, but only as a last resort.'

'My, my lord Bishop,' said the still nervous Blondell. 'What am I allowed to offer for the boys?'

'Offer? Offer?' huffed the Bishop, then with a gesture of annoyance, throwing his hands in the air as a gesture of finality, he turned and walked away, saying over his shoulder, 'Oh, offer anything you please, we will soon have his village, then whatever you have promised him will be naught but forgotten words.'

Blondell, a man who had been brought up to be a loyal man and was also a man whose word had always been his bond, was about to gainsay the Bishop, but his memory suddenly prevented him from doing so. For in the few short years that he had been in the close company of King William and his half-brother, Bishop Odo, he had seen the Bishop torture and snuff out the lives of men who had not only been loyal to him, but had been far closer to the Bishop than Blondell could ever be. In his agile mind he quickly realised that their loyalty had been worth no more than the buzzing of a fly to their master, therefore his own life would be worth even less.

He nodded curtly to the Bishop, muttered. 'It will be done my lord,' turned and ushered out Freya through the door, in order to escort her down to the ladies' chambers.

However as they reached the door Freya stopped, saying, 'I will be taking him nowhere,' in the best, most refined and controlled voice that she could produce, adding, 'I brought the brat to you and that was the end of our agreement. I'll not go into the wilderness again, not for you, not for the King himself.'

'You will go where you are told,' stormed the furious Bishop, 'or I will have your hair shaved and give you to my warriors,' he laughed at the thought of it.

'Do as you will,' she replied with a defiant shake of her head, then stuck her chin out and added, 'anyhow I might fancy a week-long session with your puny men. I'd probably have them all shagged out by then.'

Bishop Odo was about to order her to be taken out but speedily realised that whatever treatment he dealt out to her at this particular moment might well give him the satisfaction of knowing that he had won this petty battle, but it would certainly not get the hostages back. This would in no way placate his brother's anger if and when the King should learn of the missing hostages.

He needed those two boys back and he needed them back fast.

Before his brother the King heard of their abduction.

And that was what he hoped might well be the case, but he did have serious doubts, for he knew well that his brother had many spies in the town, and feared that the news of the boys' abduction was already winging its way across the English Channel to the King.

Still, he mused thoughtfully, if he recaptured the boys and had them safely back in his care before his brother returned to England, then the damage would be reduced, and the King's wrath would be no more than a bellow or two.

'Right my lady,' he said scornfully, bowing his head slightly. 'Take my friend Blondell to where that Saxon brigand has taken them, then bring the two youngsters back to me, and I will bestow a manor plus a large village to you. I will also give you the choice of half a dozen of my finest knights to make an honest woman of you. How does that suit you?

She ceased her struggles from the two men-at-arms who had taken hold of her, tossing her head so that her hair cascaded over her face, thus hiding her eyes from him. Then she brushed her hair from her face and looked directly into his eyes.

'You swear it?'

'I do so swear,' he said as he placed his right hand upon the thick silver cross that dangled from an equally thick silver chain across his chest.

'And the manor and wealth will be in my name and not some knight who is your second cousin twice removed?'

'Nay dear lady, all will be yours, forever.'

'When do we leave?' she asked, beaming with joy from ear to ear.

'At first light,' was the answer.

Bishop Odo abruptly turned his back on he and strode through a doorway towards his bedchamber, followed by the small crowd of his personal servants.

Blondell strode some way behind the Bishop and his retinue but speedily caught up with the group as soon as they had entered the bishop's bedchamber

'I could have made her take me, without you being so generous, my lord Bishop,' said Blondell as he helped Odo to unclip a golden brooch that held his tunic.

'Generous, generous,' said the smiling Bishop. 'I have not been at all generous. I shall merely kick some measly Saxon out of his manor and give it to her, and have her choose a husband from one of five loyal men that I, myself shall select.'

*****

An hour after dawn Blondell led his fifty men, plus Freya and a sturdy maidservant on horseback through the gates, past the tired sentries who had been on duty for most of the night, clattering across the newly constructed drawbridge and along the muddy lane that served as a main highway from the town towards the north and the western borderlands.

CHAPTER 27

Edric was in the process of mustering his men in the courtyard, choosing the youngest and the fittest from amongst the large crowd of warriors who were eager to accompany him on this particular venture.

He selected Ordgar the Bear, who held two of his huge wolfhounds on strong leather leashes, but left Waldo the blacksmith whose skills as a smithy far exceeded the inexperience and clumsiness that he had shown as a warrior.

Then from out of the smithy door came two figures, one of which was very familiar to him, being his old friend Garth, but although the other man looked familiar, he failed to recognise him.

'Welcome friend Garth,' he said clapping his friend on the shoulder. 'I was beginning to wonder if you were going to join us.'

'Mighty Thor himself could not stop me from avenging the murder of my lovely Myreen,' he said grimly, causing Edric to realise that the two days that had passed since they had received the news of the burning of Garth's longhall and the death of his wife, the only woman that he had ever had true feelings for, had done naught to quell his anger. He could still see the rage bubbling out from his friend's eyes.

'Who is your friend?' asked Edric, nodding towards the stranger who stood alongside Garth?

'Come now my Lord Edric you must know my friend,' said Garth with a grim smile, then turning around he said. 'Take that helmet off and show your face,' and the man placed his shield and spear on the ground, then raising both of his hands he struggled to wrench the tight-fitting helmet off his head.

It was, Edric noted, a brand new helmet, which had metal cheek guards, plus a wide nose guard that protruded downwards from the gleaming helmet.

As the helmet came clear he raised his head to face Edric, revealing the round, rosy face of his friend Evan.

'Evan!' exclaimed Edric in wonder. 'What on earth are you doing geared up for war?

''Tis my right my lord,' came the reply from a grim-faced Evan, 'for as Myreen was Garth's wife, was she not also my sister?'

'Aye, of course she was,' answered Edric. 'But we will avenge her death for you. You are not a man of war. You are a man of peace and I have never heard of anyone who does not like you or, indeed, of anyone who you do not like.'

'Perhaps so, my lord, but it is my right to help slay the swine who killed my sister and her two daughters, and if I can just taste the blood of one of them, my lovely Myreen can sleep peacefully in heaven knowing that she has been avenged.'

'Don't concern yourself over him,' grunted Garth. 'I'll look after him, I have sworn to keep him safe. The two of us will avenge Myreen.'

'So be it,' muttered Edric, still unhappy that Evan, the man who was every man's friend, a man who was one of the most gentle men that he had ever known, was now geared up for war and ready to accompany the war band against such well-armed and seasoned men who now held the township of Much Wenlock.

From the men of the blood-oath he chose Cledwyn the Welshman, Oscar, Hugh the brother of Winnifred the Healer, and Aldred, bidding the remaining men to remain with Waldo in order to protect Godda and Ælnoth.

'Guard them with your lives,' he said, 'for if aught befalls them it will be with your lives that you will pay.'

The three men brought their right fists up to their foreheads in acknowledgement of Edric's grim order, each answering in a grim manner, 'Aye my lord.'

Edric and his war band of thirty-five men rode their mounts through the hamlets of Eyton and Plowden, following the valley a mile or so before turning south to the Dale of Corve where they rode along a well-trodden pathway through the beautiful village of Diddlebury. Through Munslow where the longhall now lay empty and forlorn, then they turned eastwards through Longville in the Dale and Easthope, both now deserted, having been burned to the ground some weeks ago.

They saw no living soul until a little before midnight they saw lights which told them that they had reached the township of Much Wenlock.

Edric led his men into a small spinney where he bade them dismount. 'We will camp here for a while, so see to your horses and try to snatch a couple of hours sleep, for I intend to attack them before dawn.'

A few grunts and groans followed his announcement as the aching men dismounted, stretching their stiff limbs.

Edric beckoned to Cledwyn the Welshman. 'Bring your longbow and we will have a look around.'

After tending to their horses, Edric and Cledwyn made their way quietly down the steep incline that led to the town, keeping out of the bright moonlight as much as possible. They drifted like shadows from the shade of one tree or bush to another, until they were in the muddy track that served as a roadway that made its way straight through the town.

They flitted from the shadow of one darkened thatched cottage to the next until they were confronted to what could only be the encampment. This appeared to house some of the Norman invaders, for it consisted of a dry ditch, topped by pointed stakes that protruded out of the top of the dry moat, which was, in turn, topped by the beginnings of a castle wall. Yet the half constructed wall had, so far, only reached the height of some ten or twelve feet in height.

Beyond the ditch and the incomplete wall stood a round tower or keep, itself unfinished but reaching perhaps fifteen feet high.

'The buggers have been busy,' whispered Cledwyn.

Edric nodded in reply saying a quiet. 'Aye, they have that.'

'Let's take a closer look,' he said as he crept quietly down into the dry moat, then levered himself up through the stakes until he reached the top. He felt rather than heard Cledwyn join him as they surveyed the open space that lay between them and the stone castle.

'Can't see a sentry,' whispered Edric. And was about to stand up in order to sprint across the open space towards the tower, when he felt Cledwyn tug on the sleeve of his tunic.

'There's one there, look you,' whispered Cledwyn nodding towards the shadows cast by a large stack of wood that had been piled up near the doorway.

Edric strained his eyes, concentrating on the shadows by the wood stack, and saw one dark shape move slowly in the shadows towards a second similar figure.

'Thanks be to Woden for your eyesight,' he whispered, and heard the hardly audible reply:

'You mean to the Christ god,' adding with a smile that Edric could not see. 'My lord Edric.'

They made their way back to the spinney without mishap, where the rest of the war band were huddled under their blankets or sheepskin saddlecloth, most, Edric suspected, would be wide awake with the anticipation of the coming battle. Yet here and there he could detect the contented snoring of one or two of his men.

'Some folk can sleep on a clothes line,' he muttered to himself as he walked over to the tethered horses where he fondled the head and mane of his beloved stallion, Chieftain.

'There, there my beauty,' he cooed to him, 'I suppose you are raring to go and will charge into battle like a banshee on the morrow?' He then placed a kiss on the stallion's head, whispering again to the stallion, 'But tomorrow will be man's work and not fit for you my fierce beauty,' before he returned to his men in order to try and get at least an hour or two of sleep.

Two hours later he was up and shaking his warriors awake, but in truth, most of the men either sat up or stood before he reached them.

He gathered them in a cluster around him, quietly explaining his strategy, before leading them silently down the hill, through the still sleeping village, down into the dry moat, then up through the stakes. They stopped at the very spot where he and Cledwyn had lain just a few hours before.

'Cledwyn, I want you to take three other bowmen and make your way along this ditch until you are roughly behind the tower. Then two of you make your way to the left, whilst the other two make your way to the right until you should meet at the same distance away from that doorway.'

The four men nodded, anticipating their roles before Edric actually told them,

He continued, 'At a given signal from me, I shall be here, I want you to loose your arrows and take out those two sentries, SILENTLY,' he hissed and wagged his finger at them as if they were infants.

'The signal will be four hoots of an owl, got it?

They nodded or grunted that they had understood his orders.

'Then the rest of us will join you and we will take the tower. Off you go.'

Darkness had just begun to give way to the dawn as the four men disappeared in the gloom.

Cledwyn and one of the bowman crept silently to the left whilst the other two warriors disappeared along the dry moat to the right.

To Edric, it seemed to be a long, long time before the four men appeared.

The first to come into view was Cledwyn the Welshman, sidling along the wall with his bow strung and an arrow at the ready.

Two or three paces behind him came the second man.

He motioned to Cledwyn to remain where he was, just out of sight of the sentries until, at long last, or so it seemed to Edric, the other two bowmen came creeping around the other side of the wall.

*****

An owl hooted four times.

The four men moved forward. Edric watched with bated breath as they stood, drew their bowstrings back to their ears and loosed their shafts.

Three shafts struck home. Yet the fourth arrow glanced off the shoulder of one of the guards. The startled man's hand flew to his wounded shoulder as he staggered a couple of paces to where he had dropped his spear, before the experienced Cledwyn sent a second arrow into the man's heart sending him to the ground with little more than a sad groan.

'Follow me!' whispered Edric, and followed by the rest of his men they sprinted as fast as they could over the uneven ground to join the four bowmen at the gate.

'Well done men.' he said quietly, hoping that the Normans who were still inside the tower had heard nothing.

'Now I want you to pile all this wood against the door,' he said, 'and grab as much straw as you can from that pile there,' indicating a large stack of straw that had been brought in for thatching.

Within minutes all the available wood the Normans had intended to use for the beams, rafters and flooring of their new castle had been piled up against the doorway together with the dry straw.

'Right, now set fire to it. We will burn the bastards out.' And four or five men knelt around the enormous pile of inflammables, striking their flints, igniting the straw and kindling sticks that the men had gathered.

Edric and his men drew back from the flames.

'What will they do now?' asked the infuriated Garth, who was itching to get to grips with the men who had murdered his wife.

'Job to say really,' answered Edric, 'they may burn or choke to death or they may wait for the fire to burn itself out and then come storming out behind their shields. Or they may come bubbling over that half-finished wall at any moment,' looking up at the wall. 'In any case, we must be ready for them. Bows at the ready,' shouted Edric. 'You men who don't have a bow, help me sling some of these burning logs over the wall and let's see what sort of a hornet's nest we can stir up.'

Bellows, curses and shouting echoed from the inside of the tower, then for a brief moment, all went quiet, followed by the loud voice of one man shouting orders.

The sound of metal upon metal came to the ears of Edric and his men who were still throwing blazing straw and burning logs over the wall.

As Edric had predicted.

The hornet's nest had been well and truly stirred up, for the Normans, prevented from emerging through the blazing gateway by the fire and, unable to face their attackers from the partly finished wall, came surging over the wall like a flood, dropping from the wall like fledgling sparrows, or perhaps more like hawks, amongst their antagonists.

Most of the men landed on their feet but many others sprawled as they landed on and amongst the piles of broken stone and other building material that the workmen had left strewn about on the site when they had ceased their work after their labour had ended yesterday evening.

Edric's archers had not been idle. Three Normans lay where they had landed, dead or wounded pierced with deadly arrows.

Yet the fifteen or so Normans, fierce warriors, savage men who had either been trained from boyhood into the ways of warfare, or had learned their trade on the battlefields of Normandy, Brittany, France and probably Hastings quickly regained their feet, and stood with their large, kite-shaped shields held forward forming an instant, formidable shieldwall.

'Such discipline,' muttered Edric, almost in admiration as he launched his battle-axe at the nearest shield. Only to find that his axe merely stuck in the rim of the shield, only managing to release it with an enormous heave, cursing as his opponent's spear almost grazed his left ear, causing him to step back a pace, to join his own men who appeared, just for a moment, to be standing, unsure of themselves as to whether they should attack or retreat before this formidable and disciplined enemy formation.

A roar of triumph came from the Normans.

Yet the roar quickly subsided as they were attacked from an unexpected quarter, and much to the amazement Edric and his men.

Evan. Yes, Evan the friendly. Evan the man who was every man's friend, raced the few paces forward then using his spear as an athlete would use a vaulting pole.

He launched himself over the Norman shieldwall, landing nimbly on his feet behind the astonished men, quickly spun round, and thrust his spear upwards and under the helmet of the nearest Norman – who barely had time to turn around before the spear took his life.

He then withdrew his spear and, shouting in a voice that none recognised, bellowed, 'That was for Myreen, you bastards!' withdrawing his spear from the fallen man, thrusting it into the next man's neck, scraping the astonished man there but causing the warrior to take a step backwards, leaving a hole in the Norman shieldwall large enough to allow Garth Bloodaxe to shoulder his way through, swinging his huge battleaxe with deadly accuracy, sending man after man to meet their maker.

Ordgar released his two huge hounds and they covered the ground between the two factions in a few seconds, leaping into the space that Evan and Garth had made, causing fear and then panic amongst his enemies as the Normans tried in vain to tackle this new and unexpected menace that had just appeared before them.

Far too late for two of their men as the huge hounds pounced on the two unlucky defenders sending them to the ground, screaming and unable to use their heavy shields and long swords.

The elder of these two men tried to hide under his kite-shaped shield but the hound still managed to attack his exposed arms and face, until Ordgar stepped forward to slay both men.

Edric and the remaining warriors joined the melee, eliminating the few remaining Normans with clinical ease as they surrounded their prey, attacking from the front and the rear until the last Norman fell, savage and unbowed, but very dead.

The triumphant Englishmen were left standing amongst the carnage that they had caused, somewhat amazed as to how they had so suddenly managed to overcome what had initially been a solid and determined body of warriors, gazing at each other as they gasped for breath after the exertion of the past few minutes.

Then, as was their custom, Edric's triumphant warriors began to attend to their wounds (and there were many, but thankfully, none serious) before they moved amongst the dead Normans in order to relieve them of their weapons, chainmail shirts and anything else of value.

The fire in the gateway had burned low and, with a little effort, Edric was able to lead his men into the still smoke-filled tower, where he found a large knot of people huddled in a corner.

Most were men but with a sprinkling of women and children.

'Labourers,' came a mutter from a blood-splattered Evan who had returned to his usual place, a few paces behind Edric, 'workmen and slaves who have been working on the tower,' he added as if Edric was a youngster and needed a further explanation as what the word 'labourer' meant.

'Slave labourers,' he added.

'Mmm,' muttered Edric loudly, 'I wonder if any of them are these famous stonemasons that the Normans are bringing over from Normandy. Let's see,' he mumbled as if to answer his own question, as he walked slowly over to the crowd of people who had risen from their crouched positions and were now facing him, many with open fear on their faces, whilst some of the women clutched their children close to them in abject fear, sobbing quietly to themselves.

'Are there any Norman stonemasons here?' he demanded.

After a prolonged silence and many stares in the direction of a small knot of men, one man stood forward said, in heavily accented English, 'Aye my lord, me and my friends here are masons.'

'Bring them forward,' he ordered his men, and half a dozen of his bloodied warriors stepped forward towards the masons.

'We were forced to come!' gasped the man who was now being held by two grim-faced English warriors, fully expecting to be executed on the spot by these savage men, who he had been told were savages, men who delighted in feasting on Norman children.

Struggling against his captors, he gasped, 'They took me from my wife and children, said they would kill them if I did not come.'

The three other masons grunted and nodded, with one of them speaking in words that, if Edric had not learned the tongue of Normandy from the captive Norman lady Isabella, he would never have been able to understand.

'That's correct my lord,' he spluttered. 'They forced us all to come here, I would much rather have stayed in sunny Normandy than come here to this cold, rainy, wet land.'

Edric held his right hand high, as if to stay off their execution, although in fact it had never occurred to him to slay them. They would be much more use to him alive.

'I will spare your lives,' he said quietly in the language of Normandy, 'even though you have built this alien tower in my Country. I will take you with me to my own beloved borderlands where you can build one of your towers for me and mayhap you will pass on your skills to some of my own people, then if you build a tower for me fast and stout, then mayhap I shall allow you to return to your homelands across the water.

'Bring them with us!' he ordered, as he turned towards another small knot of ladies, who, he noted, were dressed in fine clothing, not the usual drab rags that the rest of this particular knot of people were wearing.

'What have we here?' he said.

'Norman ladies,' answered Evan who gazed in wonder and obvious hatred at the clean, well-dressed and apparently noble women.

The tallest of the women stepped towards Edric, saying haughtily, in a slow, heavily accented English, 'Messier, you have slain our menfolk. Surely you will spare their grieving widows?'

'Like you spared my own sister,' snarled the still enraged Evan.

'Hold, good friend,' said Edric. 'There is no need for us to stoop as low as our enemies. I think that there has been enough slaughter this day. Don't you agree?'

'Sorry my lord,' said Evan, calming down a little, looking with unashamed malice at the Norman ladies.

A second lady approached him.

She was at least a head shorter than the other, and whilst her clothes were of a foreign design, they too had been made of good quality material. Yet still not as fine as the clothes of the tall lady, for on closer inspection Edric could see that the cuffs were frayed and the dress had more than one patch around the waistband.

'I am English, like your good self, my lord,' she said in the refined voice of an English noblewoman. 'And these Norman dogs' – nodding towards the bodies of the dead Normans that she could see through the open gateway – 'slaughtered my mother, my father and my two brothers before they took me off into captivity.

'I thank the good Lord God that you killed 'em,' she added as she held her two hands aloft as if she was praying to a god in the sky.

'Come, dear lady,' said Edric and held his hand out to her, drawing her towards him in friendship. Yet as she reached out and held his hand she turned her head beckoning towards two of the other ladies, saying, 'They are English too, captured, like I was by these damned Normans.'

Edric smiled and bade them come forward.

The two other English ladies made their way towards Edric, smiling happily as they did so, leaving the tall Norman lady and two others standing to one side of the now free English captives.

'I will spare your lives,' he said to the tall Norman lady and her two companions, 'even though you may not deserve such lenience. But a number my warriors are in dire need of a woman so I shall let them choose you, and I care not whether they choose you for a wife or for a bondswoman.'

Eight or ten English warriors crowded forward, jostling and joking with one another as they vied against each other for the three Norman ladies. However in the midst of the turmoil the tall Norman lady shouted at the top of her voice.

'My husband escaped and he will exact terrible revenge on you for this insult.'

'Hold,' roared Edric to his men. 'Bring her to me,' and two scowling men brought the tall lady over to him, unhappy to have been deprived of the pleasure that they had, a moment ago, expected to enjoy.

'What do you mean escaped?'

'He escaped over the far wall,' she replied with a sneer, 'with two of his best warriors.'

'Damn,' swore Edric, 'I had thought that we had got them all, yet it appears that the man most responsible for the death of Myreen and her children has escaped.

Evan, who had been, as usual, no more than three feet away from Edric was totally shocked to hear the news, for the revenge that he had sought and surmised that he had already exacted upon the killers of his sister, had suddenly been turned sour, by the knowledge that the leader of the Normans, the very man who had been the main perpetrator of the crime, had escaped from their clutches.

Garth, who had been in another part of the courtyard, noting the worried faces of Evan and Lord Edric, hurried over to them. 'What's amiss?' he asked as he reached them.

'The Norman lord and a couple of his men have escaped,' said Edric, then turning to one of the freed English women he asked. 'What is this man called?'

'He is named Chaumont, my lord,' answered the girl. 'Chaumont the Cruel, we called him.'

'Then he is the swine that I must hunt down,' said Garth grimly.

'And I,' said an equally grim Evan.

'Nay, Evan,' said Garth. 'I can do this deed alone.'

'I too need to do this,' he snarled, 'and if you will not allow me to go with you then I shall go alone and avenge my sister and the girls.'

Seeing the determination on his friend's face, Garth nodded saying, 'So be it my little friend, but you stay well behind me, and I really do mean *behind me*, for my friend Bloodaxe needs a lot of space to do his job properly,' fondly he stroked the still bloody blade of his huge war-axe.

Edric watched his two friends walk over to their horses. 'Take care now,' he shouted after them. 'Men like this Chaumont do not die easily.'

But the only reply he received was a casual wave from the huge frame of Garth.

Still angry at losing three of his enemies, and worried about his two friends who had left to chase them, Edric turned to the waiting men who still held the tall Norman lady by her arms. 'Take her,' he said, 'willingly or no, she was party to this thing. She is yours,' and the grinning men pulled the woman away, through the gate and out of his sight.

Later, he called his men together saying, 'We are done here. It's time we returned to Wentnor.' Turning to the large group of people who the Normans had used as slave labour to work on their tower, he said, 'I think it wise if you also left, go to stay with your friends or relatives, and if that is not possible, then hide in the forests until this thing is forgotten.'

Most of the men and women turned and made their way towards the gateway, leaving three men and one woman standing by him.

'We've have nowhere to go my lord,' said the eldest in a rather cultured voice, indicating that he had been a man of some standing before the Norman invasion. His clothing was of expensive leather but was now muddied and ripped in several places.

'Could we not go with you and serve you in some way, my lord?' he asked.

'Aye you could come with me, but I have all the servants that a man could want, and I certainly do not need any more. What I do need are good fighting men, men good with a sword, spear or bow.'

'My father was a man of standing,' said the man. 'Before these damned Norman dogs killed him, he trained me from an early age in the arts of war, and, though I say it, though mayhap I should not, I am as good as any a man with a sword, and do have some skill with a longbow.'

'I too have been a hunter,' chipped in the youngest of the trio. 'Used to keep my father's house well supplied with wild boar and venison.'

'What about you?' Edric asked the third man.

'Nay, my lord, I am naught but a farm labourer. Good with sheep though. I was a shepherd for Lord Garth and Lady Myreen, though his lordship didn't know me when he was here. I was always out on the hillside with my sheep, see,' he said in a quiet voice that was barely audible.

A woman, who was dressed in rags with a black cowl over her head that obscured most of her face, removed the cowl to reveal the face of a young girl of perhaps thirteen or fourteen years of age, Under the dirt and grime that was smeared on her face, plus the greasy fair hair that hung down hiding her face even further from prying eyes, there was a pretty, or even a beautiful face of an attractive young woman.

Somewhat shocking her, he asked, 'And you, what do you do?'

'I do a little sewing and embroidery my lord,' came the answer accompanied with a little curtsey. 'My father would not allow me to work on the farm,' as if that statement explained everything that Edric required to know about her.

'Her father owned a large farm at Cressage,' explained the younger man, 'owned most of the rich bottomland along the river. Wealthy, he was.'

'Oh, I see,' said Edric, 'then you had better come with us as well. I think that my wife Godda will welcome you into our house.'

He then turned from the four new recruits to his household, shouting to his men, 'Mount up, we leave for home, come on now,' he called to a small group of men who appeared to be squabbling over a large piece of Norman tapestry.

*****

Edric and his small army rode leisurely along the ridge from which they could admire the panoramic views to the left and to the right, then guided their mounts slowly down the slippery pathway towards Easthope and past the hamlet of Longville in the Dale.

They were a mile or so before reaching the hamlet of Diddlebury when Hugh appeared in front of them, spurring his horse in his haste to reach them.

He skidded his mount to a halt before Edric in a shower of grass, sticks and mud. 'My lord, my lord!' he gasped in his high girl-like voice, the voice that he always seemed to turn to when he was excited. 'Up ahead,' he said. 'Up ahead, tracks, my lord. Normans by the look of it, they shoe their horses different from us,' then as he delivered his message and calmed down a little, he added in a totally different gruff voice. 'No more than an hour ahead, my lord.'

Edric spurred Chieftain forward, causing his savage stallion to respond by immediately leaping ahead like a salmon jumping a weir.

By dusk Edric and Hugh were waiting for the rest of his party by the side of a lane half a mile before Newton.

He held up his hand in greeting as Garth urged his horse alongside Chieftain.

'They are camped at Newton,' he said in a quiet voice, 'about half a mile ahead.'

'Don't seem to be in any hurry,' whispered Hugh, with a grim smile.

CHAPTER 28

Freya had, once again, urged Blondell to halt when there had been at least two hours of daylight left.

She was in no hurry to reach Wentnor for she feared, with some justification, that when they reached the village, someone may recognise her or put two and two together. Or perhaps, she mused, that if this Norman Blondell and his men were to be outwitted or even defeated in battle by Wild Edric, then her life would certainly be forfeit.

Her devious mind had studied all the angles, telling herself that she had, perhaps, a fifty-fifty chance of returning safe and sound from this mission. Yet her greedy nature overrode her caution as she had studied Blondell and his men, noting that each of the men had been handpicked, and on the whole she had been pleased with the efficiency and the caution in which Blondell handled his duties. She felt reasonably confident that he could bring this expedition to a satisfactory conclusion, without mishap, or perhaps more importantly, without the loss of her own very precious life.

She had, nonetheless, hedged her bets by exchanging the quiet mare that had originally carried her out of Canterbury for a large, spirited gelding that she felt could outrun most horses. That exchange had merely cost her a few kind words, a smile and a stroke of a besotted and lonely Norman warrior's cheek

Not that she was relying totally on a fast horse if things went awry, for on the first night of their quest she had quietly joined Blondell under his blanket.

This was the fourth night that she had crawled under his blanket.

A blanket which Blondell had placed some way from the prying eyes of his men, where he waited, as usual, in a state of high anticipation for the union that he now knew from the experience of the last few nights was about to take place.

Tonight was slightly different for they had spent the three previous night's sleeping under the stars, but tonight Blondell had evicted a family of peasant farmers out of their cottage and was now lying on the largest of the two beds that had been placed along two of the walls of the one-roomed farmhouse.

Freya, as usual took the top position, sinuously crawling on top of him, muffling his deep groans with a long, savage kiss before she straddled him, whereupon she commenced without further ado to ride him like an unbroken horse.

She pinioned his hands with her own, throwing her head back in ecstasy as her hips and buttocks shivered in the first of the many climaxes that she hoped would take place during the coming night, or before the man tired and his manhood shrivelled to nothing.

Of course she did not love the man. In fact she did not love, and never had loved any man, but had learned from an early age that her beauty lured men to her like moths to a candle. Old men who could only dream of possessing her, young men with the energy and inexperience of young wolves, married men who came fresh from their wives, returning to them when they had finished with her, peasants smelling of cow manure and with hands calloused from their toil in the fields, and lords wearing silk, smelling of lavender, who worshiped her beauty, second only to the gold and silver that they held in their money belts, which many of them did not remove even in the throes of their lovemaking.

Lying on her back alongside the exhausted Blondell she mused to herself, thinking that if only one of those rich lords could possess not only the energy of youth, plus the roughness and callous ways of a peasant, yet still retain their riches, then that would be the man that she may, just may, be able to live with for the rest of her life.

She could, she smiled to herself as her devious, agile mind ran riot within her head, ride him all day and half the night, enjoying his rough ways and his rough hands, and still live the life of luxury each and every day until the day she died.

She smiled into the darkness, then shook her head in frustration, for she would never find such a man. Even if she did, he would probably be an overpowering bully or a skinflint, and that certainly wouldn't suit her, for although sex was her overriding passion, money and the spending of money came a very close second.

Blondell stirred besides her, turning onto his side and threw his right arm across her, crushing her breasts as he did so.

She felt a stirring and then a definite throb between her legs, so she moved onto her side then heaved him over onto his back, fondling his manhood until it had grown hard enough for her liking, then climbing on top of the still sleeping man, she rode him until she had satisfied herself for the fifth time during the night.

Before dawn she had left the cottage and returned to her own blanket, thinking, but not really caring, whether or not any of Blondell's warriors knew what had taken place during the night.

Blondell emerged through the cottage doorway, stretching his arms aloft and yawning as he did so, surveying the well-rehearsed scene of his men who had already kindled their morning fires, and were in the process of roasting a few chunks of beef over the fires or boiling up oatmeal mixed with dried blackberries, plus the few precious drops of milk that they had horded for occasions such as this.

He snatched a chunk of hard bread off his servant, eating it greedily as he walked around the small encampment to ensure that all was well, issuing orders here and there, not because the orders were really necessary as each one of his men had been hand-picked, and had all been together for the last three years.

Campaigning in Normandy, France and England, working together as the well-trained team that they were, laughing and joking as they did so, so that the odd order that Blondell issued was merely to reiterate his authority. Yet in some way, he thought, it took his men's thoughts away from the beautiful young woman that he was now totally in love with and who occupied his bed-place every night on this otherwise tedious expedition.

'De Bracy,' he shouted, calling the dark De Bracy over to him. 'You and your two men scout ahead as usual. Are you ready?'

'Aye, my Lord Blondell, we are, or at least we will be as soon as Boloftee brings up the mounts. Boloftee?' he bellowed as loud as he dared, for his long experience on these sort of raids had taught him just how far a voice can carry on the clear morning air. 'Ah! Here he is,' he exclaimed with satisfaction, as the Boloftee appeared leading three horses from the far side of the camp where they had been tethered for the night.

The three men mounted then without a word, rode westwards out of the camp.

*****

'Hugh, I want you to scout ahead with Cledwyn,' said Edric quietly to the young man. 'Keep well out of sight and send Cledwyn back to me when, and if they change their route of march. I'm pretty certain that they are heading for Wentnor, but they may go further along the Clunn valley, and if they do, I want you to send Cledwyn ahead of them to warn the townsfolk of Clunn, then I want you to ride back here to me and let me know so that I can make my own plans.'

He watched as the two men mounted their horses and rode off before calling Aeldred over to him. 'Aeldred,' he said, 'you know the way over the long mountain to Wentnor, do you not?'

'Aye. my lord Edric.'

'Well, I want you to take the track over the hill to Stretton. Then go up and over the Burway, then over the long mountain to the track that leads down through Prolley Moor to Wentnor, warn my Lady Godda that the Normans are probably heading her way, and urge her to call in all our people, close the gates and keep them shut until we arrive. Is that clear?'

'Clear as a bell my lord.'

'Good man, off you go.'

He then returned to the rest of his men. Squatting down amongst them for a moment or two as he chewed on a chunk of hard, dried bread and a wedge of cheese, he said:

'We can relax for an hour or two and see what news Hugh and Cledwyn bring us before we need stir ourselves. But I would ask you all to look to your mounts and be ready to ride at a moment's notice. Remember,' he added as he looked around the small circle of his men, 'as I have said, we can relax for a while. But keep your voices down as you all know how sound can carry along these hills and valleys.'

Then he lay on his back, closing his eyes in order to give his men the impression that he was going to have a nap and that he hadn't a care in the world, hiding the fact that there were always angles and factors that could go awry with the most careful of plans.

He knew full well that both Hugh and Cledwyn were excellent hunters, well used to the ways of the forest. Yet even they could make mistakes, perhaps taken unawares, killed or captured.

Then there was Aeldred, who was a good enough horseman, and a man who knew this part of the countryside reasonably well, but there were scree slides, were there not? And deep pit-bogs that had taken the lives of many a weary horse and its rider.

Then there was the odd wolf's head lurking in the shadows ready to send an arrow or a well-aimed spear into a weary traveller just for the price of a groat or a crust of dry bread.

Nonetheless, he closed his eyes to give his men the impression that he had fallen off into a pleasant, dreamless sleep, whilst in fact his mind jumped from one subject to another, giving him something of a headache.

Much to his own surprise, he did sleep for some time and was only awakened by the approach of Hugh, who had returned in a flurry of dust, reining in his mount within a few yards of him.

Edric stood, stretching his arms aloft and yawned before he strode the few paces towards the waiting man who stood holding the reins of his horse.

'What news?' he asked. 'Have they turned off down the Clunn road?'

'Not so, my lord,' came the answer. 'I fear that they are heading towards your own holding of Wentnor, but they do not seem to be in much of a hurry.'

'Good. That will give Aeldred time enough to reach Godda and warn her of their approach.'

Then he clapped Hugh on the shoulder, guiding him over towards the fire where a half side of lamb sizzled on a spit.

He scooped up a half empty flagon of small beer and handed it to Hugh. 'Here, have a mouthful of this. Help yourself to the roast lamb, then get some rest, you must be tired after your long ride. One of you men look after his horse,' he shouted, and a man walked slowly over towards Hugh's still sweating horse in order to feed, water and groom it.

An hour later he ordered the men to mount and they rode off down the muddy track that served as a main highway down the centre of the valley, towards Walford, which was a small hamlet consisting of a mill, a large fishpond plus two large farmsteads and a scatter of tiny cottages.

Walford was deserted with the exception of one old lady who sat outside a dilapidated cottage, rocking backwards and forwards on a rickety old chair.

'Good day to you lady,' called Edric to her as he rode up to her, not sure if the woman was sick in the head.

When the woman slowly looked up towards him and gave him a smile that revealed two remaining long brown teeth. Edric thought that she had indeed lost her mind, but then the stupid smile that she could produce at will to people, whether they were her friends, family or perhaps strangers, suddenly disappeared and her face became the face of a sane person.

'And a good day to you *frēa*,' she said with a chuckle. 'You be the second group of horsemen who passed this way on this warm summer day' – then she spat into the dust before her feet before she went on – 'but the first lot were foreigners, bloody Norman dogs if I be not mistook. Though to be honest with you I never did see a Norman before this day, and hope never to see another one before I meets me maker.'

'Is that so dear lady,' said Edric as he dismounted, motioning the rest of his retinue to follow.

''Tis so *frēa*,' she replied, 'but it was a strange thing with that lot.'

'Strange, how so?'

'Well, *frēa*, I bin sittin' here this day, trying to think to meself what it was that was odd about 'em, and then it struck me.' She stopped speaking, chuckling to herself before she resumed her rocking backwards and forwards on her rickety old chair.

Edric, trying to maintain the pleasantness of his conversation with the old woman whilst at the same time attempting to restrain his own eagerness in order to learn what was strange about the party of Normans that he was following. He was eager to resume his pursuit, which in his mind was now becoming very urgent now that they were getting closer to his wife and the village of Wentnor.

'And what was it that was so strange about them?' he asked pleasantly.

The woman ceased her chuckling, which in truth was beginning to annoy him, and said. 'Well, young *frēa*, they was all fine, strong young men. Except the one, and at first I couldn't see why that one was different, then it 'it me. You see. It was a woman, oh, dressed up in man's gear she was, but she was a woman. I swear it.'

'A woman, are you sure?' he exclaimed.

'Aye *frēa*, sure as I stand 'ere. Or sit 'ere. Definite, it was a woman.'

'Now that is strange,' said Edric as he turned towards his men.

'Why would a party of Norman warriors on this kind of an expedition hinder themselves with a woman?' he asked himself out loud.

'Perhaps she is a captive,' said one of his men.

'Or maybe she's the wife or mistress of one of 'em,' said another.

'Yes,' he answered thoughtfully. 'You are probably right, she's likely to be one of their women or a captive belonging to one of them. Naught there to worry about.' he added as if to clear his own head of the misgivings that were still spinning about in his head.

After a short rest, he sent Hugh out ahead on a fresh horse, then followed him at an easy trot, passing along the valley, bypassing the three cottages that made up the tiny village of Marshbrook, then turning up the narrow valley towards Plowden, eventually heading northwards along the side of the long mountain towards Wentnor.

They veered to the west again, crossing the thickly wooded valley, before they began to urge their horses up the incline that led to the village. Yet some half a mile before reaching the village they were stopped by Hugh who guided his horse from a thick stand of birch tress onto the track, holding his hand aloft as a signal for Edric and his men to halt.

'They are a couple of hundred yards up ahead,' he said quietly as he urged his horse alongside Edric's stallion, Chieftain. Who as usual was unhappy to have other members of his tribe near to him, trying his best to bite Hugh's gelding, but was prevented from doing so by a savage yank of the reins that wrenched the savage stallion away from his intended victim.

'Steady boy,' snarled Edric, fully aware that if Chieftain had succeeded in biting the gelding, then the squeals of fighting and injured horses could easily have reached the ears of the men who they were following, which would have placed Edric and his men in a difficult position. The Normans were on the higher ground and they were certainly more numerous and probably more experienced in battle than many of the men in Edric's party.

When the stallion calmed down Edric said quietly, 'What are they up to then?'

'They have tethered their horses and left two men to guard them,' Hugh answered, adding. 'the rest of them are on their way up towards the stockade.'

'Time to act then,' he said. 'Dismount men, and tie your horses to those birch trees, then follow me, quietly now.'

He dismounted, drew his sword and began to climb the incline towards the point where the Normans had left their horses.

'Let me go ahead my lord,' said Hugh. 'I'll take care of the men who are guarding their horses.'

'Take a couple of men with you just to make sure.'

'By your leave Lord Edric, I'd rather be alone, not used to hunting with other men,' Hugh explained.

'So be it,' whispered Edric, 'but we will be just a few short paces behind you and at the first sign of trouble, we will come running.'

Hugh nodded and padded effortlessly and silently up the hill.

CHAPTER 29

Edric waited a hundred heartbeats before he motioned his men forward, leading them as quietly as possible upwards towards Wentnor.

When they reached the Norman horses they found Hugh standing over the body of one man whilst a second man knelt at his feet with his head bowed and his hands tied behind his back.

'Well done,' said Edric quietly as he approached. 'Why did you spare this man?

''Tis not a man my lord,' answered Hugh, as he reached forward to pull the kneeling man's head upwards to reveal the pretty – nay – the beautiful face of a young woman. He grabbed the top of her brown leather hat and snatched it off her head, revealing a mass of dark auburn hair which fell down over her shoulders like a cascade of beach leaves caught in the gust of an autumn wind. 'And I could not kill one such as she.'

'Stand up woman,' he ordered.

The woman obeyed and stood facing him with a haughty look; a look that told him that this was no peasant woman, but was a person well used to ordering people about and having servants to obey her.

She smiled up into Edric's face, noting the astounded look on his face, a look that she had seen on many a man's face since as long as she could remember, a look that she knew from long experience that she could use to her advantage.

'My thanks to you my lord,' she said in a very refined voice that had, he thought, an accent that was of English nobility, as well as a mere hint of Norman French. ''Tis just as well this oaf of yours did not kill me along with my poor guardian Robert,' she nodded to the prone body of the Norman whose throat Hugh had cut a few short heartbeats ago.

'For had this oaf slain me, then my poor husband the noble Lord Blondell would never have forgiven you and he would have hunted you down until he had wreaked his revenge upon you and all of your kin.'

Before Edric could answer, she continued with a shake of her head that sent her mass of hair from one side of her face to the other:

'As you have spared me, I think that he will do naught more than to continue his mission to regain the two children who were abducted from the palace of Bishop Odo, which is the only intent that he has on this mission of his, for he does not wish more bloodshed.

'He merely wished to make peace with the brigand named Edric the Englishman, and to pay him a fair price for the boys.' She knew full well that this man who stood before her was, in fact, the brigand named Edric the Englishman, or as his friends and enemies alike called him (usually behind his back) Wild Edric.

He knew that she knew that he was Edric, and he knew that she knew that he knew who he was, and he also knew that he had just been insulted, but for some strange reason, he ignored the insult.

'God's blood,' he thought to himself. 'This woman is unbelievably beautiful, so young, yet so confident and self-assured, but whilst her lips and her face smile up at me, her eyes tell me another tale, perhaps they are too steady, too icy-blue, what is it?' he asked himself, and in truth he could not allow himself to believe that this extremely young and beautiful woman could really be anything other than what she appeared to be.

He shook his head, as if to clear the muddled thoughts that clouded his head.

'And where is your husband now?' he asked

'He has gone up ahead towards the fortress to meet with this man Edric,' was the firm reply.

'Then perhaps we should go up and find him,' he said. Without further ado he waved his arm aloft and bade his men to follow him as he strode past the woman making his way upwards towards the small township of Wentnor and towards his Norman enemies.

Nearly two hundred yards were covered before he could see the Normans who were standing in a cluster some way ahead.

As was his old habit, he counted their numbers automatically, reckoning that there were at least forty-nine of them grouped around the man who was probably their leader, as well as the husband of the woman who was in the act of being escorted up the steep incline by two of his men.

He halted motioning to his men to form a semicircle around him, saying. 'You men remain here. I will take the woman up with me and speak with their leader. But be ready for treachery. Be on your guard.'

As the woman joined him, he realised that he had been so astounded by her beauty that he had not even asked her name. 'Your name lady?' he demanded gruffly.

'I am called the Lady Freya of Overneul,' she stated with a haughty shake of her head.

'Come, we shall have a word with your husband, what was his name again?'

'He is the Lord Blondell, and he a trusted friend of King William as well as a loyal man to the King's brother, Bishop Odo of Canterbury.'

He stooped to grab her hand then stalked upwards, dragging the still gasping Lady Freya behind him.

He was brought to an abrupt halt a mere eight or ten feet from the cluster of warriors who were still crowding around their leader, by three men who had been standing to one side of the group and had seen him approaching.

'What have we here?' said one of the men, as he pointed his sword at Edric's chest, then his eyes fell upon Freya who was still two paces behind Edric, standing with her head bowed, gasping for breath after the short but strenuous climb.

'Oh, I do crave your pardon my lady,' said the man. 'I did not realise that it was you.'

All eyes turned towards Edric and Freya, then the warriors moved aside as Blondell made his way to the front.

'Ah, my love,' exclaimed Freya, who wrenched her hand free, running quickly up to Blondell, throwing her arms around him. As she stood on her toes pretending to kiss his cheek, whispering quietly into his ear, 'This is the traitor called Edric, and I am your lady wife.'

Blondell's eyes lit up with surprise, a look that did not go unnoticed by Edric.

However, Blondell quickly recovered his composure, saying, 'My lady wife tells me that you are the famous English warrior, Edric, and if that is the case, then I am right proud to meet you, for it is to you that I have travelled these many long miles to see.'

'With so many warriors?' came Edric's quick retort.

'Alas so,' said Blondell with a wry smile. 'These men are my personal bodyguard. Men who always accompany me on such a sensitive missions as this,' then he replaced his sword into its scabbard and held out his right hand in greeting.

Edric shook his hand, despite the feeling that he'd better not trust the man although, as soon as he shook hands with him, he almost immediately warmed to the him, due to his friendly smile and the man's firm handshake.

'And what is this sensitive mission?' he asked, remembering what the Lady Freya had told him, but anxious to hear confirmation from her husband.

'I have been asked by my Lord Bishop Odo, who has the full consent of King William to ask you for the return of the two young noblemen who were taken from their lodgings in Canterbury.'

Edric remained silent for a moment, both annoyed yet somewhat amused by this Norman's apparent honesty, as well as by his bluntness.

'Why should I return the boys to you?' he asked. 'My own son Ælnoth was taken from me and I did not go cap in hand, begging for his return.'

'I am aware of that,' answered Blondell. 'And if it is any consolation to you, I offer you my sincere apologies. But what has been done cannot be undone.'

'And if I refuse?'

'Then I shall be left with no other alternative other than to take them,' answered Blondell. 'Over the bodies of your men if necessary,' nodding his head towards the remainder of Edric's men who had followed him up the incline, and who now stood some thirty or forty feet down the hill from him.

Before Edric could answer, Blondell continued, 'And I might point out to you that all of my fifty warriors are men proven in battle. We also hold the higher ground and outnumber you at least two to one.'

'Is that so?' replied Edric, casually pointing uphill, towards the half-finished stone and wooden stockade. This was, in some places half covered by wooden scaffold, and encompassed by a stone wall that reached half way up the upright poles of the old wooden stockade.

The gate now stood open, and before the gate stood a figure that he recognized as his wife, the Lady Godda. Despite the fact that she wore a shirt of chain mail, a helmet, and held a round English shield in front of her, standing proudly before her assembled men carrying a sturdy spear in her right hand.

Arrayed to her left and to her right stood every able-bodied man that she had been able to muster, forming a battle line three men deep and some fifty yards long stretching almost to the curvature of the mound.

'My men are also proven warriors,' answered the now smiling Edric, 'and as for "the high ground" and who outnumbers who, that is, I think, now something of a moot point.'

The Norman was totally shocked into silence, realizing that he had been out-manoeuvred.

'It appears that you have me at a disadvantage,' muttered Blondell, adding in a barely audible voice, so that he would not lose face in front of his men. 'But of course I did not come all this way to fight a battle I came with my Lord Bishop's approval in order to negotiate terms for the release of our two young men.'

'That being the case,' answered Edric as he steeled himself and began to make his way through the crush of scowling Normans, 'perhaps you and your lady wife would like to continue our conversation, not out here in the wind, but in the warmth of my longhall.'

'Do I have your word that we will not be harmed?' demanded Blondell at the top of his voice.

Edric stopped, turned and with a face as red as sunset, answered the Normans insult in a low sinister voice, 'Do you question my word as an English nobleman?' but before the stunned Blondell could answer, Edric said:

'Bring half a dozen of your men with you, if you have a mind to, but leave the rest here. All of you will be safe in my lands,' then he strode out manfully, furious that this Norman stripling should question his hospitality.

Blondell speedily chose six of his best men, taking Freya by her right arm. They followed Edric up the steep incline towards Godda and through the open gates of Wentnor.

Edric embraced his wife saying quietly to her, 'Disperse the men so that these Norman dogs do not see them and realize that most of them are farm labourers and household servants.'

She turned to the towering figure of the blacksmith, saying, 'Have the men return to their duties. Quickly now,' she hissed, allowing the smithy to turn and usher the men through the gate, ordering them to vanish from sight as quickly as they possibly could.

Blondell followed Edric and Godda through the gateway, grimacing silently to himself as he compared the crude wooden structure of his small fortress with the great stone towers that Blondell and the other Norman lords were building across the length and breadth of England.

As they proceeded through the courtyard Edric halted the Normans saying, 'Your men can bed down in the stables, they are clean and dry, and I will have food and drink sent to them in a little while.'

Blondell's face darted here and there in order to make a mental note of the construction and the manpower of this small fortress, but his head stopped abruptly as he noticed three men who stood out from the local English people like a sore thumb. For the men wore the dusty garb of stonemasons, and who, from the look of their demeanour and their stature, were quite obviously men of either Normandy or of Brittany.

Edric noted Blondell's startled face but chose to ignore it. Instead he turned to Blondell, saying with the most pleasant smile that he could muster, 'You and your Lady will be my honoured guests in my house, where my Lady Godda and her maidens will see to your every comfort.'

Blondell could not help smile, for the most comfortable Saxon home that he had ever seen in this miserable country had been naught but damp, straw-strewn hovels.

He felt that there was no way any of these English houses could compare with his own home in sunny Brittany, for he literally hated these dark, dank, wattle and daub, flea-ridden hovels that passed for homes in this dull, wet and miserable country.

As he stepped through the door he cursed himself for being a fool, for the hallway was a light and airy room, warmed by roaring log fire.

His astonishment was heightened as he followed Edric through a second door into what he surmised must be the Great Hall, for it was spotlessly clean, with the sun streaming through two large windows onto an enormous table that was literally groaning with a vast array of food. Roast joints of beef, venison. lamb and pork, surrounded with roast fowl which included three or four carcasses of rare pheasants, doves, partridge and common farmyard fowl, all still covered in their plumage, surrounded by vegetables of all sorts, amid glasses of sparkling red wine.

As Blondell entered the room he stopped and stared, open mouthed at the feast, several young maidens brought in yet more trays of steaming hot bread, fresh from the oven, ushered in by one of the most beautiful women he had ever seen.

'Ah,' said Edric, 'this is my wife, the Lady Godda,' and he stepped forward to take Godda's hand as he presented her to Blondell.

Blondell's eyes met the blue-grey eyes of Godda, causing him to blush as he realized that he was staring, open mouthed at her.

'My lady,' he stammered in Norman French, 'it is my honour to meet with you.'

He bowed from his waist, as he gazed up longingly into the blue-grey eyes of this tall, beautiful Englishwoman.

'The honour is mine messier,' came the reply in the same language. 'You and your lady wife are most welcome in my home.'

'My lady,' he answered. 'May I present my lady wife, Freya,' he lied, as he grasped the hand of Freya in order to present her to Godda.

'It is a great honour to meet you my lady,' said Freya as she curtseyed before the tall woman.

Godda took her hand for a brief moment and with a rather haughty look she replied, 'Just so, just so.'

Then she turned towards Edric and said, 'Edric, I'm sure that our guests would like to be shown to their bowers to change out of their travelling clothes and may freshen up a little before they eat.'

Edric, slightly shocked by his wife's sudden request, as he had expected to sit down to the table immediately and tackle the mouth-watering feast that had been laid out for them; he realised that all was not well with Godda, who was obviously feeling ill at ease for some reason or other. Something that had, seemingly totally escaped him, as he had been feeling quite pleased with the way that things had turned out, at least up until that moment, so he turned to his guests saying in a gruff voice:

'How remiss of me my dear, I'm sure they would like to spend a few moments alone before they join us for dinner. Edna?' he beckoned one of the young maidens over to him. 'Pray take our guests to their room and see to their needs.'

The girl made a slight courtesy then led Blondell, Freya and their two servants out of the room, to their sleep-quarters.

As the door closed behind them, Edric turned to his wife and said, 'I thought that we were all going to eat now. My belly thinks that my throat has been cut. God's blood woman, I'm so hungry I could eat a scabby donkey, hooves and all. Now, tell me what this is all about. What's wrong?'

'Husband, have you no eyes?'

'Of course I have eyes, why, what's amiss?'

'The girl.'

'Aye. The girl, the Lady Freya.'

'The Lady Freya indeed,' said Godda with a snort and a shake of her head. 'Well didn't you see?'

'Oh for the good Lord's sake, see what?'

'The girl is evil.'

'Evil. Why? What did she say?'

'Oh, for goodness' sake, you are like all the rest of you men. All you see is a pretty face, but you don't see the real person.'

'So what's wrong with a pretty face? She is naught but a girl wed to Blondell the Norman.'

'Oh for goodness' sake,' snorted his wife, who was now becoming annoyed with Edric, but then she remembered that he was only a mere mortal and not of the Light Elves that were her real kin.

'She exudes evil,' she snorted. It covers her like a cloud,' and as she spoke she visibly shivered, clasping her arms about her body as if a freezing wind had just chilled her. 'I want her out of my house.'

'Our house,' he corrected her.

'My house, our house, I don't care whose house it is. I want her out. Get her out,' she hissed menacingly.

'I can't ask them to leave now,' he answered. 'They are our honoured guests, and I would be dishonoured to withdraw the hospitality which I have already given to them. Besides,' he added stroking his chin as if in meditation, 'I have given my word to negotiate the return of the two Norman boys, and with luck I may be able to wring a lasting peace out of this man Blondell.'

She stamped her foot in a fit of temper. 'What about our own boy? What about Ælnoth? What if he is murdered in his sleep by this evil bitch? Or abducted in the middle of the night and taken off to, to the Lord knows where?'

'I'll have a man guard him tonight if that will put your mind at rest. And if I can reach an agreement with Blondell tonight, I will get rid of them first thing in the morning.'

CHAPTER 30

He was about to explain to Godda how important an agreement would be, and the many advantages that he thought that they all might gain, when Blondell and Freya walked back into the room.

They had both changed out of the clothes that they had worn on their journey. Blondell now wore his favourite lamb's wool jacket, with a pair of comfortable breeches that were tied about his waist with a wide leather, silver-buckled belt, being the self-same belt that his father had presented to him before he had left his parents on this, the adventure of his lifetime.

Freya also wore her favourite clothes. In fact they were the only additional clothing that she had hastily thrown into her travelling bag before she had been forced to leave Canterbury in such a hurry.

It was also the most glamorous and revealing attire that she had purchased with the money that Bishop Odo had given her for her part in the abduction of Eric's son Ælnoth, consisting of a tight lambs wool skirt with a white, figure-hugging, knitted woollen blouse, with a very deep, plunging neckline which displayed more of her bosom than was proper, and was so outrageous that it caused Edric to cease speaking in mid-sentence and stare open mouthed at this beautiful woman who had suddenly lit up his dining hall as if the room had been invaded by the daughter of the sun.

Godda, on the other hand, was outraged that this woman who was, in her opinion, a very unwelcome guest in her house, flaunting her body in front of her husband and her servants, as if she was a madame in a French brothel.

She was about to vent her indignation when her husband, who had almost recovered his composure, said 'Ah, my Lord Blondell, here you are, and most welcome too.' He gestured towards the table which was still groaning with the rapidly cooling food, 'Please, take a seat and join my good wife and myself in our supper.'

The four people sat at the table, with Blondell on one side facing Edric and Freya alongside Blondell, facing Godda, and Edric, as was his way stabbed a roast partridge with his eating knife and was about to place it onto his plate when Blondell, placing his hands together in front of him and closing his eyes, said in a loud voice.

'Good fare. Good meat. Good Lord let's eat.'

Both Edric and Godda were somewhat shocked, as well as a little amused and bewildered. Godda more so, due to the fact that she was, after all, Queen of the Light Elves and, as such, was not of the Christian faith.

But as far as Edric was concerned he, of course, now professed to be a Christian, although in his deep conscious he still respected the old gods, Woden, Thunor and the other ancient Saxon gods, silently cursed himself for not having foreseen that his guest, being a Norman, was quite obviously a Christian, and as such would have expected grace to be said before eating.

However, he was not sure whether the grace that Blondell had spoken had been a serious and a proper grace or had been something of a joke, despite the fact that Blondell's face had remained grave as he had uttered the words. So Edric made no remark and, as soon as Blondell had finished, plopped the roast partridge down onto his plate.

The evening went reasonably well. Blondell and Edric spoke in friendly terms, finding that they had much in common, especially warfare and hunting, the usual pursuits of both English and Norman Noblemen.

However, the two ladies obviously did not share their men's jovial evening, barely conversing, despite several attempts that Freya made towards Godda, only to receive a polite smile, which was as far that Godda would go to make 'that woman' (as she later called her) feel at ease.

When they had eaten their fill, Edric rose from the table and with a half-filled glass of red wine said, 'Praise raise your glasses and join me in a toast,'

The two guests and his wife stood and he said, 'To peace and prosperity between our two peoples.' The other three echoed his words before they, too, drained their glasses.

'Come my lord,' said Edric, beckoning Blondell to sit on an oak settle at one side of the fire, whilst Edric sat, heavily on another settle beside the longhearth. 'We have things to discuss.'

'That we do,' replied Blondell, his voice slurring very slightly from the amount of red wine that he had drank during the evening.

'You want these two boys back,' Said Edric bluntly.

'I do indeed.'

'Well, to tell you the truth,' said Edric, 'I must admit that I do like the boys, for they are great company for my son Ælnoth, and he will sorely miss them should I send them away.'

Blondell was about to speak, but was interrupted by Edric who said. 'His French has been much improved since they came here, and a tutor would cost me many silver coins to replace them,' he lied.

Blondell also knew that he lied (or that he was perhaps toying with him) for he knew full well that both Edric and Godda spoke excellent Norman French, so it would cost them naught for their son to be educated in that tongue. Nonetheless, even in his half-inebriated state he realised that Edric had just raised the subject of money.

'If silver coinage is a problem, then the good Bishop Odo has provided me with enough coinage to pay for a tutor to teach the boy our language.'

Edric ignored the remark saying. 'If I did let you take the boys, where would the gain be? I am a rich man. I have more silver than I can spend, and I have a small army of proven warriors here with me who would willingly take up arms for me,' adding carefully, 'should I ever need them.' Then staring into the wide, brown eyes of the Norman, he emphasised the point:

'What would I gain?'

'Nay, I shall tell you.'

'I see naught much to gain, but there is much that I would lose. I would lose two valuable hostages would I not? Hostages that could well keep your Norman wolves from my front door.'

He was about to go on about his land, his farmers and their farms, his fishing rights from the mills and ponds that were a vital part of the food needed by his tenants to sustain them through the winters. Yet he was rather rudely interrupted by Blondell, who appeared to be in his cups, although Edric had his doubts about the man's capacity to drink. Had he not boasted of the vineyards and of the fine wine that his father's servants made on the vast estate that his father owned on the continent?

'Of course, my good Edric, you are quite correct that the two boys may well keep my people from your front door,' he slurred, 'but by holding them here, they could just as easily provoke my Lord Bishop into sending an army into your lands to rescue them, which surely must be the greater of the two evils.'

He lifted his glass and drained it, slamming it down upon the oaken table, then shouted drunkenly for more, as if he was the lord of this hall, and not merely a guest of his host, the Lord Edric.

Edric had known all along that what Blondell had just said had always been a distinct possibility but he tried not to show his displeasure, allowing his mind to accept the fact that this man may or may not be in his cups, trying his best to smile as a servant filled Blondell's empty glass yet again.

'You are quite correct that the hostages may well invoke an invasion by your people. But as you can see for yourself, we do have sufficient warriors here who are not only ready, but more than willing to meet your men on the field of war. In fact they are becoming quite bored with all this inactivity, making it something of a trial to prevent them from invading your territory.'

He took a small sip of wine in order to allow what he had said to sink into the supposedly drink-fuddled mind of the Norman before he continued, saying, 'And I might add, that if I were to raise my standard against you, other shires would certainly join me.

'Then you could well have a full-scale rising on your hands, and that, I think would not please your Bishop Odo, or his brother the King, who does, so I hear, have his own battles to fight in far-off France.'

'True, True,' answered Blondell, who was slightly shocked to learn that this Englishman, who dwelt in this remote, hill-skirted valley should know of King William's problems in France, answered hesitatingly 'Oh I do agree with you my Lord Edric, that certainly is something that should be avoided at all costs, which is surely all the more reason why you should take my offer of the one hundred pounds weight of silver for the boys, plus my word. And if I give you my word, then I am giving you the sacred word of the King of England himself, that so long as you shall live, no Norman nor any allies of my people shall invade or take any land or estates that belong to you or your kin.'

Edric realized that the hours of eating, drinking, and assessing each other had come to an end and that the time of hard bargaining was now reaching its climax. Finding, much to his own surprise that he had come to actually like and admire this man, who now had, he thought, finally put all his cards on the table, he nodded and thoughtfully stroked his chin as if he was considering Blondell's offer.

'There would of course be the usual conditions,' added Blondell with a grimace crossing his handsome face.

'What kind of conditions?' scowled Edric.

'Well as a freeman, and a lord of your own domain, you will be expected, along with every other nobleman in England, be he an Englishman or Norman, you would be required supply men and arms for King William, should the need arise.'

He added after a slight pause, 'Of course, 'tis an unlikely possibility, for as you know, the King already has a large standing army. In fact he already has many Saxons – I mean English – warriors already fighting for him. Many who followed the late King Harold and fought with him at Hastings.'

Edric nodded, for he already knew of the many English warriors who had joined William's ranks, either from boredom, or perhaps because they had been evicted from their farms and manors, or mayhap they had no other option other than to use their strong right arms and their fighting skills for the very tyrant who had evicted them.

He gazed into his wine, considering Blondell's words.

'You would provide proven warriors only,' he said.

'Agreed.'

'No farm boys with pitchforks and sickles?'

'No.'

'Nor the old or the young?'

'Of course.'

Neither man spoke for a long, long time and, as if by the stroke of a wand from the Light Elf Queen herself, Blondell appeared to instantly sober up.

'What think you my good Edric,' he asked.

'Aye, Blondell,' said Edric with a wry smile, reaching across the table to clasp the right hand of the Norman.

'We have an agreement?'

A little later the two men retired to join their respective 'wives', with Blondell falling into the deep feather bed alongside Freya.

'How went it?' she purred.

'Aye, it went well.'

'We have the boys?'

'Aye we have them, or at least we will have them on the morrow, although I have seen neither hide nor hair of them since we arrived.'

'Oh, we will get them first thing in the morning. Then we can get out of this grubby hellhole,' she snarled, hoping beyond hope that the boy Ælnoth did not see her.

Silently praying that if he did see her he would not recognize her, and spoil what seemed to be a fitting ending to this expedition with this boring Norman.

Despite his love for her, or perhaps it was the wine, when she demanded her wicked way with him that evening, straddling him in her usual rough way, even the vision of such a beautiful woman gazing down at him, with her full breasts almost obscuring her face, and her hips gyrating along his manhood, he found it difficult to return her passion. Much to her disgust, he let out a large groan of relief when it was all over, turning away from her and falling asleep almost as his head hit the duck-down pillow.

Two rooms away a similar conversation was taking place between Edric and Godda, but there was a subtle and important difference. As Edric explained the agreement he had reached with Blondell, he lay on his side facing his wife, caressing her beautiful, smooth face, lovingly running his fingers down her shoulders, now and then stroking her breasts, then tenderly allowing his index finger to run gently over her large nipples, whilst she, in turn, ran her fingers through his hair and twisted ringlets in the long locks that dangled down the side of his face as she listened intently to the hopes and to the fears of her husband, as he struggled to explain the advantages, as well as the possible the pitfalls that he could possibly be led into, by dealing with these Normans.

She listened intently but was quick to point out that, 'thus far these Norman invaders have shown no honour whatsoever in their dealings with their English subjects. Nonetheless,' she pointed out as she nuzzled into his neck, planting kisses on his neck and his shoulders as she spoke, 'with the boys gone, and the agreement that we have with Blondell, life should be a little safer and far less complicated without us having to watch the boys every move in case they steal a couple of ponies and spurred their way out of here.'

'True,' he said as he turned his head to meet her lips, planting a long loving kiss upon them. 'We will certainly be no worse off, and several bags of silver to the good which we could use to bribe some of those wild Welsh kings to bring their men to join our cause, should the need arise.

'And I do think,' he added, 'that our little Ælnoth is getting a mite too close to those two Norman whelps, and I am not too sure that I like that.'

They talked long into the night before they fell into a deep sleep in each other's arms.

CHAPTER 31

Blondell and Freya were wakened by the noise of people working and the clatter of the kitchens that must have been directly below their room.

'What in God's name is all that noise?' grumbled Freya as she shook her head in a vain attempt to clear her fuddled mind from the after effects of the last evening's drink, of which she had over-indulged.

'Oh my head,' she groaned, 'what sort of bloody poison were those peasants giving us last night?'

'Shhh, keep your voice down,' he hissed, 'or they will hear you.'

'I don't really care if they do,' came the indignant reply, but of course she did care, and he knew that she cared, but totally understood the anxiety that she was feeling. He too was extremely concerned about two very important points regarding the agreement that he had reached with his host on the yesterday evening.

The first point that concerned him was whether or not his host, the Lord Edric, could remember the deal that they had struck after both of them had consumed such a vast amount of wine. Secondly, he, like Freya, was extremely fearful that the moment that they entered the room the boy, Ælnoth, who would almost certainly be there, would immediately recognise Freya as the woman who had abducted him and murdered and mutilated his two nursemaids, causing the wrath of their host, Wild Edric to fall upon their heads, which at best would result in their agreement being annulled whilst, at the worst, they would be immediately put to death.

They both dressed, neither speaking to the other.

Freya was literally shaking with fear and apprehension as they descended the stairs, while Blondell, trying his best to hide his own fear, slipped a thin Norman dagger into one of his riding boots and another, longer blade into his belt, under the back of his leather riding jacket.

They entered the room together, relieved to see that the sole occupants of the room were Edric and his wife Godda, who were sitting at the table, sipping from earthenware beakers what looked like warm milk.

'Ah there you are,' said Edric loudly. 'We were wondering if you had both overslept, and had decided to spend the rest of the day in bed,' he said, with a smile on his face.

'Aye, we nearly did,' answered Blondell with a pleasant chuckle. 'It is sometimes very difficult to leave such a good feather bed on a cold morning such as this.'

Edric was slightly dumbfounded by Blondell's statement, for it was mid-summer, was it not, and the sun had been up for more than two hours?

Servants brought in steaming hot plates of crispy bacon, fried eggs, beef sausages, hot freshly baked chunks of bread and jugs of foaming small beer.

'Our agreement of last night still stands?' asked the anxious Blondell.

'Of course, why should it not?' answered Edric with a mouth full of sausage.

Blondell was about to continue the conversation when the clatter of small feet came from along the corridor and the door burst open revealing the three boys.

The moment they entered the room, all three stood still with their mouths open, for no one had mentioned to them that the house was entertaining Norman guests. The sight of the two expensively dressed strangers sitting at their dining table came as a shock to all three of the youngsters.

'Ah, here are the boys,' exclaimed Blondell, who clapped his hands, as if in glee, beckoning the boys over to him. 'Come over to me young men,' he said jovially. 'My wife and my good self have come to take you home.'

'Home,' exclaimed the youngest of the three. 'Home to Normandy,' he said joyfully, jumping happily and clapping his hands as he said the words.

'Well, yes of course, But first we must stop at Canterbury, to pay our respects to the Bishop,' said Blondell with as cheerful a voice as he could muster.

'Oh,' said the boy, obviously disappointed.

'Him,' said the elder of the two, his hopes raised and then dashed in the space of a few moments.

Nonetheless, the two young Normans were still pleased to see someone who could at least take them a step or two nearer to their loved ones in Normandy, and slowly approached the man as if seeing Freya for the first time. Like moths to a candle they both walked silently up to her, touching her dress and her arms, as if they could not really believe that such a beautiful creature not only existed, but had made the long and difficult journey with the sole intention of rescuing them, in order to take them home.

Ælnoth had not moved, but stood still as if rooted to the spot.

'Come here son,' said Edric curtly. 'Pay your respects to our guests, then you can break your fast before saying farewell to your two friends here.'

But Ælnoth slowly shook his head, remaining exactly where he was, just inside the room.

'Come now Ælnoth! It is not like you to be rude to our guests,' said Godda as pleasantly as she was able in the presence of Freya, to whom, incidentally, she had not yet spoken.

'Come now,' she hissed with just a little venom in her voice.

'He is probably sad to see his playmates go,' said Blondell,

'Aye, that's it,' said Freya, beaming from ear to ear with one of her famous, well-rehearsed smiles.

Ælnoth felt himself wetting himself, then suddenly turned and raced from the room as fast as his legs would carry him.

Godda jumped to her feet, sending one of her precious, very expensive glasses to the floor with a crash, and ran after her son. Yet he had dashed through the open door and, by the time she had reached the door, he was already halfway across the courtyard, making for the open gate and the fields and woods beyond.

'Ælnoth, Ælnoth!' she screamed, most unladylike, 'come back here at once and say farewell to your friends.'

But her son sped onwards, past the two bewildered guards and through the small encampment of Normans. Within a few moments he had disappeared into the woodland.

Swearing under her breath, Godda returned, red-faced, to Edric and her two guests.

The four adults and the two boys made small talk in order to cover their embarrassment whilst they hastily finished their breakfast, allowing Blondell and Freya to rise from the table rather earlier than would have normally been polite to do so, rising from the breakfast table in something of a haste. Then grasping their travelling bags, they made their way towards the doorway and to the four waiting horses that Blondell and Freya had brought with them, plus two ponies that had been made ready for the two Norman boys.

'My apologies for the rudeness that my son has shown,' Godda forced herself to say to this Norman and to the woman, who she now realised that she actually detested.

'We should have brought our son up to show better manners with guests, but here we are in the middle of the wilderness, and we see so few strangers.' She shrugged her shoulders as if that explained Ælnoth's flight.

'He should, at least have said his goodbyes to his friends,' she added as she patted the youngest boy on the head, then stooped to place a light kiss on his forehead. As she stooped to kiss the elder boy, she said, 'Have a safe journey, and I do hope that you will soon be home, safe and sound with your families in Normandy.'

The younger of the boy's eyes watered again at the thought of leaving this little haven where he and his friend had been so happy, thinking also of the image that he always carried in his mind of the meeting that he envisaged would take place when he reached home, and the time when he would be cuddling into the warm breasts of his loving, corpulent mother whom he adored, as well as shaking the hand of his stern-faced warrior father, and plunging into the warm, deep river that encircled their stone fortress, shouting and laughing with the sons of his father's knights.

After a few words of thanks and words of farewell, Blondell and Freya mounted their waiting horses, then followed by the two boys who were each astride a small well-trained Welsh mountain pony, the four 'guests' again thanked their hosts for their kindness before they rode slowly across the green and out of the gate.

'Well, that's that,' said Edric as he watched the Norman warriors mount their horses and follow Blondell and Freya as the entire band of Normans urged their horses down the slope that led to the one and only pathway that crossed the wet and boggy plain known locally as Prolley Moor.

'Yes,' agreed Godda, 'that's that. 'But I still have that feeling that our guests were not quite genuine. Oh, I liked him well enough, for a Norman anyway, but the woman – argg! If I were not a queen I would have spat in her face. The woman was evil. Pure evil! I'm glad to see the back of her.'

'I could see no harm in her,' offered Edric, 'in fact I thought that she was very beddable,' he teased.

'Oh you men,' came the reply followed with a playful slap on his cheek, for she knew that he was merely jesting with her. I think you should go and look for Ælnoth,' she said seriously. 'It is not like him to just run off like that, and in front of guests.'

'No, I agree, it was a bit strange,' answered Edric, 'but he has been through a bit of a traumatic time of late, and then losing his two playmates, who he did genuinely seem to like.'

'It's all been a bit too much for him,' agreed Godda.

'I'll saddle Chieftain and go and look for him. The stallion needs to stretch his legs a bit. It seems ages since he's had a good run.'

As he walked over the courtyard towards the stables she called after him.

'When you find him, be gentle! Remember he is still only a child.'

He waved his hand above his head in acknowledgement as he walked through the stable door towards the stallion, which seemed to know that his master had entered his domain in order to take him for a gallop through the countryside.

'Well, well, Chieftain you dirty great heathen,' he said as he gently stroked his nuzzle, causing the stallion to respond by pushing his shiny nose into Edric's chest with the joy of seeing the only human being in the world that he enjoyed being near.

Edric cantered through the gates. As soon as they had left the standing wheat behind he allowed Chieftain to have his head, and the savage stallion whinnied with delight as he surged forward for more than half a mile before the thickness of the woodland forced him to slow to a trot and then to a slow walk.

Edric began calling into the silent greenwood, 'Ælnoth! Ælnoth! Come on out Ælnoth, we are not angry with you. Ælnoth, where are you?'

After an hour or so he stopped to rest his mount as well as to ease his aching back. He made his camp in midday at a favourite spot where he and Ælnoth had camped a number of times when he had taken his son hunting, hoping that perhaps the boy had made his way to that particular spot and may be resting under the lone beech tree. There they had made their camp site and had spent many a happy night out under the stars, but alas there was no sign of him and the empty woods that had given both of them so much joy in the past, seemed silent, eerie and sinister.

'Still,' he said out loud, 'he is well used to the forest and will come to no harm.' As if to reassure himself, and chase away the fears that were, only now, beginning to form in his mind.

Dangers, real and imaginary began to flood his mind.

Wolves, peat bogs, as well as perhaps the most dangerous of all: bears.

'Bloody bears,' he cursed to himself, knowing that bears were probably one of the worst dangers that a small child like Ælnoth had to fear.

And then he cursed again as he thought of the packs of wolves that roamed these parts. He realised that wolves were probably just as much a threat as the bears, perhaps more so, for once they had the scent of a small, vulnerable child in the forest, they could and would mercilessly hunt him down, and would not leave so much as a scrap of his leather shoes to show that here, on this patch of woodland, had once lived his precious son.

He stuffed a large chunk of cold pork into his mouth before he walked the few paces to where Chieftain had found a small patch of grass in a small forest glade.

'Come on old friend,' he said softly to the stallion as he hauled himself up into the saddle and rode down the small valley to resume his search.

*****

Less than ten miles away Blondell turned in his saddle to speak to Freya. 'Well, my love, that went well, did it not?'

'Thanks be to the lord,' said Freya, beaming with glee. 'The boy didn't recognise me and we came away with our two boys, safe and sound. That miserable turd of a Bishop will be so pleased that we have saved his neck from his brother's wrath that the old sod should pay us in gold not bloody silver.'

'Aye,' he answered. 'We seem to be clear, although I tend to think that the boy did recognise you, and that was what made him turn on his heels and run from us. But I must admit to you that I have been half expecting Edric and his men to appear behind us, since the moment that we left Wentnor. But thanks be to the good lord, he hasn't yet appeared.'

Then he turned in his saddle for the hundredth time since they had left Wentnor. Gazing behind him, he added, 'But it's not too late for him to wrench the truth out of that stupid son of his and come haring after us, so I think it best that we walk the horses for half an hour, then ride throughout the night to put as much distance as possible between him and us.'

He shouted to his men, 'Dismount and walk your mounts!'

His men immediately obeyed him, dismounting and leading their sweaty mounts as they followed their leader along the muddy, overgrown lane that appeared to be the main highway in these parts.

'What was that all about?' he asked. 'You calling yourself my wife, the Lady Freya of where, did you say?'

'Overneul,' she answered with a chuckle.

'Overneul, where the devil is Overneul?' he asked.

'No idea,' she laughed out loud, her chuckle echoing over the flower-strewn meadows that they were leading their horses through. 'Just a place that I heard of once, many moons ago.'

'God's blood,' he said laughing with her, realizing that he was more in love than ever with this beautiful, clever, and devious woman. 'What am I going to do with you?'

She gave him one of her most loving smiles and gently touched his arm.

'Ah, you stupid man,' she thought, 'if you only knew,' and chuckled again enjoying the joke of being his wife, with the title of 'Lady Freya of Overneul', all over again.

'And what was it about being my wife?' he said in a much more serious tone.

'Well, that's what you want. Isn't it?'

'Oh, it is. It is,' he answered in a croaky emotional voice.

'Do you really mean it? Will you really marry me?'

'Only if you are a good boy,' she said playfully, with a toss of her head that sent her mass of hair from one side of her face to the other, but thinking to herself. 'I don't really want to be wed to this penniless oaf. How in God's name do I get out of this one?'

'Oh, I will be a good boy, you can count on that,' he said beaming from ear to ear. 'I'll be the best husband that you could wish for. And I shall treat you like a real queen.'

'But I will probably give you a double dose of hemlock,' she said under her breath, 'before I shall tie myself to a pauper such as you.'

Still smiling, he turned his head to the rear of the column, thankful that there was still no sign of any pursuit, called to his men 'Mount up!' and his troop mounted and followed him at a canter. He tried to put as much distance between himself and any possible pursuit that Edric might attempt.

They had a speedy and peaceful journey for the next fifteen miles and it was not until they were riding single file along a narrow tree-covered valley when the first arrow struck.

They were tired and saddle-sore, causing many of the men to grumble and groan aloud, beseeching their lord to call a halt when the leading rider grunted... then silently slid off his horse with a grey goose-fletched arrow protruding from his chest.

Cries of alarm brought the weary men alert and, being the proven warriors that they were, they immediately twisted in their saddles in order to wrench their shields forward so that the shields covered the bulk of their bodies, then automatically moved into a bunch in order to provide as much protection as was possible from the hidden bowmen.

'Protect the boys!' called Blondell, and his men immediately spurred their mounts around the two boys, Blondell and Freya. Yet as speedily as they had acted, two more men fell, skewered by yard-long arrows that appeared to fly out of the greenery that surrounded them, causing some of the battle-hardened warriors to shiver in fear as they realised that even in their knot of shields, horses and warriors, they were still not safe from these deadly arrows. Although they scanned the hillsides on both sides of the valley, no one seemed to know where the hidden bowmen were.

'You six men stay here and shield the boys and Freya,' called Blondell, 'and upon my command, the rest of you scatter up the hillside on both sides of this valley and flush these rogues out.'

'Sod the boys, what about me?' yelled the furious Freya as she attempted to hide behind one of the shields.

Blondell was forced to ignore her as he brought his own horse around in order to face one side of the valley, before he called, 'Go!' causing he and the rest of his men to spur their already skittish mounts out of the cluster of horses and riders up the hillside like a covey of partridge that had been frightened into flight, spurring their horses through bracken, bushes and small trees in their eagerness to get to grips with the hidden archers.

Yelling at the top of their voices, the riders slashed at the bushes and stunted trees that hindered them, urging their mounts upwards, as they attempted to find the hidden archers.

Another man fell clutching at his chest. Yet his comrades paid him no attention for they knew that within a few seconds another deadly arrow would claim another of them unless they could locate the hidden bowmen.

'He's up here!' shouted a gnarled warrior as he urged his horse upwards, 'and there's only one of 'em. Follow me,' he yelled to the rest of the men on his side of the hill who speedily rallied to his call, whilst the men who were half way up the other hillside turned their horses, urging them down that side of the hill in order to join in the hunt for the man who had already slain four of their number.

The number of horsemen hunting the archer was now so great that it was not long before the man was forced to reveal his hiding place. Yet not before the archer had loosed one last shaft, which took the leading Norman full in the face, did he turn and run up the steepening hillside. Yet as fleet of foot as he was, he could not outrun the horsemen who were now vying with one another to reach the man.

Two riders reached him at more or less the same moment, with each man bringing his sword downwards in unison.

One man missed the runner completely as the running man swerved to avoid the stroke. Yet his sharp swerving threw him into the other man's path, whose sword cut down into the man's bobbing head, cutting through the back of his neck, sending the man down onto the sloping hillside.

They crowded their mounts around the fallen man, where one Norman dismounted and heaved the man over onto his back.

'Sweet Jesus,' he exclaimed, 'he naught but a boy,' as he stared down at the face of a youth who could not have seen no more than, perhaps, sixteen or seventeen summers.

'Aye, maybe he is a boy, but the filthy peasant slew five of our number, including my own cousin Robert,' snarled another and spat at the boy who was obviously in the final moments of his life.

'Bastard,' snarled another. 'Just look at the bugger's shoulders.'

'Aye,' said another, 'and he is naught but a boy.'

'They train with them bows from childhood,' said another.

'I will wager you ten pieces of silver that you can't bend that bow back to your ear like this young bugger could.' (He was a man who so liked the word 'Bugger' that his comrades actually called him, 'Bugger').

The man refused as he had heard just how hard it was to master the dreaded English longbow. Yet another, much younger warrior, fresh from the continent, leapt from his horse.

'No problem,' he said scornfully and picked up the boy's fallen bow. I've been using the Norman crossbow since I was a child,' he boasted.

Quickly and what looked to the rest of the men who crowded around with interest, the youngster expertly notched an arrow.

'Stand clear!' he shouted. 'Move to one side so that I can loose the bloody thing.'

Then he stretched the string, bending the bow until the string reached his chest, then with a grunt and an extra effort, he pulled until it reached his chin, whereupon his fingers suddenly weakened and the arrow flew, not straight, as it was intended, but to one side, skimming along the flanks of one of the horses, causing the mount to rear and throw its rider to the ground with a crash.

Guffaws and roars of laughter came from the assembled crowd.

'Thought you said you could ride a horse,' said one with a chuckle.

Whilst Bugger offered his advice, saying, 'The whole idea of riding is to stay in the buggering saddle.' As he bent over, holding onto his knees, loud with laughter.

The man scrambled to his feet, with nothing damaged except his pride. He stepped quickly forward clouting Bugger across the side of his face, sending the older man back against one of the surrounding horses.

'Swine!' rasped Bugger, reaching for the long knife that hung in his belt.

But before he could draw the weapon, Blondell, who had finally reached the crowd, cried, 'Stop! Put the knife away you old fool, I've lost enough good men already today, and I will not lose another over a silly, boyhood prank.

'Mount up!' he shouted. 'Darkness is near and I want to get out of this bloody valley and find a safer place to spend the night.'

As Freya rode alongside Blondell, noting that he had not spoken for quite some time, she leant towards him and said in an unusually quiet voice. 'What ails you my Lord? You have not said a single word this long hour past.'

After a long pause he answered her.

''Tis that boy back there, that archer, he was but a boy, and yet he attacked fifty of us, and slew five of my fierce Normans. I was merely thinking to myself that if these people found themselves a leader, and that leader organized an army of boys and men such as that boy, then they could kick us out of this island of England as easily as a knife goes through warm butter.'

She was about to come up with some smart answer and poo-poo his idea, when he continued, saying, 'I was also thinking that we have just met such a man, for if the Lord Edric were to raise his standard against us, and raise an army of bowmen such as that boy, then by making this peace treaty with Edric, I could well have prevented such a rebellion that could have reconquered this land of England for the English.'

She looked towards him, seeing him in a somewhat different light, for she had always seen him as an impoverished, brutal and untried young warrior, but nodded silently to herself as she had begun to realise that perhaps there was a deeper and more noble side to this young man whose love she had played with so frivolously.

A little while later he added, 'I have him sworn to live in peace with us, so long as our people leave his lands alone.'

'You could well be right, my lord,' said Freya, with one of her radiant smiles. 'And I shall make it my duty to ensure that the good Bishop Odo is made aware of your achievements.' To herself she thought, 'Perhaps it is well that I have not yet used hemlock on this one, for he may well rise in rank as well as in wealth. And if he rises then I too would rise with him. Then I would already know what sort of a man that I was getting, and I would know that if I were to wed this one, he would be one that I would be able to control.'

She leant across, stretching in her saddle to touch his hand with fondness.

Night had fallen before he called a halt in a good-sized farm that lay alongside the track that served as a road in an area that was known as the Chilcotts, after instructing his men to appoint watchmen on either side of the road.

He ordered the rest of the men to make themselves as comfortable as possible in the farm buildings, while he had his men evict the aged farmer and his wife from their bedroom saying. 'You can spend the night here in this room whilst my wife and myself will have your bedroom, But fear not, for it will only be for one night and providing you do not misbehave, you will come to no harm and we will be on our way on the morrow.'

The unhappy couple shuffled off into the main room where the woman opened an ancient oaken chest that lay alongside one of the walls, and brought out a number of woollen blankets, which she then placed on top of the sheepskin rugs that lay in front of the large hearth. Within a few minutes she had constructed a very comfortable sleeping place for the two of them.

They were wakened before dawn with noises coming from the adjacent room and after a hurried kiss and a scramble to find their discarded clothing that had been strewn about the room, Blondell and Freya dressed and entered the main room of the farmhouse to find that the farmer's wife in the process of baking bread, as well as frying eggs and bacon for their breaking of their fast.

'*Mon-Dieu*,' said Blondell to himself, drooling at the smell of the delicious breakfast that was being prepared for them. 'Now that is one of the things that I do like about this country. It is the sort of fare that gives a man a good boost to start his day.' And he sat down upon the wooden bench that lay alongside the scrubbed oak table in readiness to break his fast.

Freya emerged out of the bedroom a little while later, just in time for the farmer's wife to bring out the wooden trenchers brimming with bacon, eggs, sausages and freshly baked bread for both of them before she returned to the fireplace to collect two additional plates for her husband and herself.

The couple joined Freya and Blondell at the far side of the table made from rough wood where they immediately commenced to devour their breakfasts.

Frey snorted and looked down her nose at the couple, whispering to Blondell, 'Are you going to allow them to eat with us? I am not used to sharing my table with peasants.'

'Be silent woman,' he snarled with an unusual air of authority, ''Tis their table and their food that we are eating. Besides I think they are not peasants, but freeborn.'

She snorted indignantly but held her peace, for she was enjoying the delicious food after the cold fare that she had been forced to eat on the journey.

*****

They reached the outskirts of Canterbury by the following evening and walked into the Bishops hallway with the two boys just as the candles were being lit.

'By the good Lords grace,' beamed the Bishop as he strode to greet them, patting the two Norman boys on the head, saying. 'Well now young sires. There's glad I am to see you home.'

But the elder boy scowled. 'We are not yet home my Lord Bishop.' This caused the fat Bishop's mood to change from jovial to dour, and he growled, 'Well it will be home for a while yet.'

He bellowed at the top of his voice 'Squire!' and the door opened to reveal a pimply youth of perhaps sixteen summers who entered the room and bowed his head formally to the Bishop.

'Take these two boys to the rooms that we have prepared for them,' he ordered, and added as the boys were ushered out of the room. 'And make sure that they have at least one servant with them at all times.'

After a thought he added in an even louder voice. 'And I do mean AT ALL TIMES. IS THAT UNDERSTOOD?'

'Yes my Lord Bishop,' came the subdued reply at the squire left the room.

'And now I suppose you will want your reward for what I am forced to admit, and with some reluctance, was a job well done?'

He was about to continue but was rather rudely interrupted by Freya. 'My

Lord Bishop, might I be so bold as to mention to you that not only have we returned these two hostages to you but also that my good friend Blondell has made a treaty with the rebel, Edric? – Who, I must say is a great lord in the borderlands, and a man that could well have raised an army against us.'

She paused for a moment to allow the Bishop a little time for her words to sink into his rather large, fat head, before she continued, 'And by this treaty he has thus secured the peace of several shires of England as well as some of the Welsh territories for us, which, I think it is safe to say, will please your brother the King.'

'Err – um,' the Bishop cleared his throat, as was often his way when he needed a moment to think, and this was such a moment. He had not realized that this young Blondell and the whore, to whom he had given the task of rescuing the two captive boys before his brother the King had found out that they had been abducted, had not only carried out his order (itself quite a coup, and something that he had not really believed that they would be able to do) now he was being told by this beautiful whore, that they had also eliminated the only remaining serious threat to his brother's rule since Hereward the Wake had been pacified.

Again, in order to give himself just a little more time to assess the situation in his mind, he asked, 'And exactly what was the treaty that you agreed with Edric?'

'Only that he will keep the peace with us and will rein in his warriors, for he already has a small army with him, and could easily be capable of bringing half of Wales to his banner if what we have heard is true. And, my Lord Bishop, I personally do think it to be true.

'The truce will hold, providing that we do not attack him or encroach on his lands. He will keep the peace with us.'

'Hmm,' sighed the Bishop. 'Well that is something I must admit.'

'Not only that, my Lord Bishop,' said the eager Blondell, 'but he has also agreed to provide us with veteran warriors should the need arise.'

'Hmm,' said the Bishop again, warming to Blondell and to his achievement.

'Also,' added Blondell, 'if Edric and his wild men are fighting for us, then they will have little time to fight against us.'

'And they will be under our control,' added the Bishop with a sly smile crossing his face.

'Just so my Lord, Just so.'

Odo began to smile.

Then his devious mind began to work, thinking to himself, 'This enterprise has already cost me a king's ransom in silver and now these two are each expecting an even larger reward for their work. He is expecting a village and a manor, whilst she is expecting silver and the choice of one out of three, or was it five noblemen to make an honest woman out of her?'

He had already noticed the doe-eyed looks that Blondell had been giving Freya and his devious mind already knew from those looks that the man was head over heels in love with the girl. So, he thought to himself, why go through the tiresome bother of bringing noblemen from the far ends of the land, when he already had a willing subject here that would not only save me the trouble, but also a sack-full of silver, as well as being a solution that would satisfy all three of them?

'Blondell,' he said haughtily, 'I shall bestow upon you' the township of

Yeoton and all the lands thereof, which even if I say it myself, is a wealthy town in the West Country, made rich by wheat and wool, but I shall give you this prize on one condition and on one condition only.'

'My good Lord Bishop,' exclaimed the delighted Blondell, for he had heard of the town and knew what the Bishop said to be true, and his agile mind was already calculating that if he were to be made the Lord of Yeoton.

Thus he, the youngest of four sons of a minor nobleman, would immediately be many times more wealthy than ever his father had been. Thus this adventure that he had embarked on a mere two years since, would have paid off in a way far beyond his wildest dreams.

The Bishop could see by the starry look in Blondell's eyes that the young Norman would agree to almost anything if he were to be made Lord of Yeoton so he added in what was, despite a vague attempt to disguise it, a very crafty and evil voice, the condition is that you take this lovely lady, Freya here–' and he turned towards Freya who had been following the conversation intently, wandering to herself just what this hateful, devious old Bishop was up to, '–to be your wedded wife, for I have promised her that she would wed a nobleman, and I am, as everyone knows,' he lied, 'a man of my word, so that will be my reward to both of you, for the services that you have rendered unto me.'

Blondell was flabbergasted, being totally dumbstruck by the thought of not only becoming the Lord of Yeoton but was to be given the hand of the love of his life by the will of the great Bishop Odo himself.

'My Lord Bishop, what can I say?' He knelt before the Bishop, bowing his head as he did so.

The Bishop held out his hand regally allowing Blondell to kiss the huge ring that was on the Bishop's right hand; a ring that Blondell willing kissed with all the reverence that he could muster.

'I agree and thank you from the bottom of my heart,' said Blondell, with the emotion of the moment bringing unmanly tears to his eyes. 'Henceforth I shall be your man in life and limb. Ask of me what you will and it shall be done.'

Freya was dumbstruck that her fate had been agreed whilst she had stood stock-still and she had allowed herself to be traded like a hen on a market stall. 'But, but my Lord Bishop,' she began to protest.

'There, there my child, no further thanks are necessary,' soothed the Bishop as he held out his heavily ringed hand to her, which she dumbly stooped and kissed, saying, 'Serve myself and my brother the King in your new holding.' And before she could utter another word, with a sweeping gesture, he turned and exited the room, leaving the two, now properly betrothed people, standing alone in the large draughty room.

Neither of them realized how long they had stood in the room as they tried to come to terms with the events that had taken place in the last few minutes, when the door suddenly burst open and the Bishop's personal servant bustled through, stopping before the still shocked couple where he made a slight bow to Blondell, saying haughtily. 'May I show you out, my lord.'

The servant's voice was refined and respectful, and he turned beckoning them to follow him out of the room.

Blondell and his new betrothed meekly followed him.

Blondell's face glowed with pride for although his warriors' had oftimes called him 'lord', this had been the first time that he felt that he had the right to be called 'lord'.

Once outside the Bishop's palace he grasped her hand and crooked her hand onto the inside of his elbow as they strutted across the courtyard as if they were the king and queen of the realm.

CHAPTER 32

The evening had turned wet and the fine drizzle had soaked both Edric and Chieftain as they made their way through the wet, leafy world of the forest searching for Ælnoth.

He rode until it was too dark to venture further, halting in order to feed the last of the oats to Chieftain. After tethering the stallion he huddled down under his cloak on the hard ground, chewing on a chunk of dried meat that he had brought with him, finally falling into a fitful, wet and uncomfortable sleep.

Chieftain, who, with the first glimpse of daylight showing in the east, had hobbled over to Edric, wakened him by playfully pushing his nose into his master's sleeping face.

Grumbling under his breath, Edric rose, stiff from his night's sleep and stretched his cramped limbs before he strode stiffly over to a small stream where he knelt and splashed a few handfuls of cold water over his still sleep-ridden face.

He ate the few remaining chunks of dried meat before he resumed his search, urging his mount deep into the forest to the more remote parts where he thought his son may have wandered. He called out for the boy at regular intervals, hoping that sooner or later he would find his son hale and well.

To no avail, and by the time dusk was falling he had made his way back to the village of Wentnor where he found his wife, haggard and drawn with her face wet from tears.

'You have not found him!' she almost screamed as she threw herself into his arms, weeping openly on his shoulder.

'Nay,' was the sad reply as he stroked her hair, 'not a sign of the boy.'

He led her over to the blazing fireplace where he stooped to warm his cold hands, and to dry out his still wet clothing, when the door opened, and through it came the small, wizened figure of Mono of the Meadows accompanied by the brown puppy who was now over a year old and had already reached the same height as its owner, but looked as if it weighed twice as much as her.

She shuffled over to the roaring fire, accompanied by the huge hound, and then sat down so close to it that Edric feared that she would soon become part of it.

'I heard that the boy is missing,' she hissed in her squeaky shrill voice. 'I am here now,' she stated the obvious, 'And I have not yet been offered the courtesy of a drink to quench an old woman's thirst.' She made a sound that resembled tut-tut and slowly shook her head from side to side.

Godda was so shocked by the sudden appearance of the wizened old woman that she suddenly jumped up, as if a hornet had stung her. 'Oh my good Lord!' she exclaimed as she looked at the ragged apparition that had sat almost in the fire itself.

Then she rushed from the room as if in a panic, shouting to the servants to bring wine, beer and food for her husband as well as for the ever hungry and ever thirsty Mono of the Meadows.

Serving maids soon appeared carrying an assortment of food, beer and wine, plus two wooden plates, jugs and wine goblets.

Edric offered a wine goblet to Mono, who shook her scraggy head, and said in her singsong childlike voice, 'What would I want with that tiny thing?' She reached over to snatch a large leather tankard from one of the maids. 'This is more like it,' she cackled as she held it aloft to be filled. 'Wine,' she ordered, and the girl filled the large tankard to the brim, thinking to herself, 'Here, you old Witch, take the lot, and I will wager that it is too much for you. And I hope it chokes you.'

Mono grunted something unintelligible, gazing at the girl with venom before she suddenly shook her head and scuttled over to a large wooden settle where she sat, sipping at the wine. Then to everyone's surprise, she suddenly spat into the tankard and watched her spittle move slowly in the red wine.

'What is it, my dear Mono?' asked Edric who was concerned that his guest may have been served wine that the vinegar fly had tainted and had been turned into vinegar.

She made no reaction to having heard him speak, but continued to stare into the tankard, watching her spittle mix with the clear wine.

Edric looked towards Godda who had also taken a glass of the red wine and had, in fact already sipped it and found it to be as good as ever. She raised her eyebrows, smiling at her husband as if to assure him that the wine was good.

He placed his own tankard of beer on the table and poured himself half a glass of the red wine. This he sipped and, although it did taste a little odd, he surmised that his palate had already been tainted by the beer, so he took another, larger mouthful of wine which he sloshed loudly around his mouth and slowly swallowed it.

'The wine is good,' he said almost indignantly.

He looked at the wizened old lady, concerned, partly because he had originally thought that he might have poisoned her, but just as much bothered because, most people (including himself) were a little afraid of her. Almost everyone acknowledged that she was indeed the most ancient of women, as well as being a very famous soothsayer, or perhaps a very famous witch, who had been about long before most of the people's grandfather's grandfather.

No one in the room spoke, but the silence was suddenly broken by a strange, shrill noise that appeared to emanate from somewhere inside the chest of the old soothsayer.

A shiver convulsed Edric's body and he could feel his hair stand on end, causing him to visibly shiver.

He glanced over to his wife and could see that she too was afraid, for she stood completely still, as if frozen stiff, with a face that was as white as the driven snow.

The silence, which had lasted for perhaps half a hundred heartbeats, was suddenly broken by a low snarl from the hound followed by the shrill, childish voice of Mono, who was still gazing into her wine, as if in a trance:

Ah, I see the child a-running.
Through the pasture. O'er the meadow.

Trampling down the growing barley.
Through the marshland. O'er the hilltop.
Splashing through the stream I see him.
Falling on the bank with tiredness.
Rising now, then running further.
O'er the hill that has the sharpstones.
Down the valley of the sedges,
Frightened curlews rise before him.
Startled crows soar from the carcass,
Of the stag, that fell last winter.
Lying now as if a dormouse.
Curled up, snug inside his cavern.
Sleeps the dormant sleep of winter.
By the stream, that flows to Moorston.

She stopped abruptly, and her head fell upon her scrawny chest as she dropped her wine and slowly slid towards the floor.

Edric, who was closest to her, dashed forward, just managing to catch the old woman just before she reached the flagstones, whereupon he lifted her light body up as if she was a child he carried her towards the door.

Godda was but a pace behind him, stunned by what she had just heard and trying, unsuccessfully to make sense of it, but, at the same time she was concerned for the old lady who lay in her husband's arms as if she was dead.

'Place her on the spare sleeping bower,' she said quietly to her husband. 'I will get her a calming potion from the kitchen.'

Almost as soon as had Edric laid her on the bed, Godda joined him with a warm infusion of a concoction that consisted of ingredients that only she knew.

She stooped down to the prone figure of Mono, lifting her head, and then gently allowed the warm liquid to seep slowly between the unconscious woman's slack lips.

'There,' said Godda, 'that should give her a restful sleep. She should be as good as new in a few hours.'

Edric nodded his head without saying anything, hoping that his wife's potion would work, and that the old witch would recover from the deep sleep that she had so suddenly fallen into.

As they left the room, Edric scratched his chin, which had always been a habit of his when he had a particularly difficult problem, saying 'What did you make of when she said?'

'I'm not sure,' came the answer. 'But I think that she was following Ælnoth when he ran away, and was, somehow trying to tell us where he went.'

'That's what I thought,' said Edric. 'But the good thing was, she said that he was alive.'

'Well,' answered Godda, 'that was not really what she said, was it? What she really said was that he was curled up in a cavern, like a dormouse. She didn't say that he was alive, He could be dead and in his grave.'

'Nor did she say he was dead,' said Edric angrily.

Godda thought for a moment before she answered, saying, 'No, she did not, but what she did say was that he was somewhere by a brook that flows to, or through Moorston.'

Well, I've never heard of Moorston. What the devil is Moorston?

'Or, where the devil is Moorston,' he interceded. 'It sounds more like a place name to me, don't you think?'

'Aye, you are probably right, but I haven't heard of a place called Moorston.'

As they walked back into the main room, Edric said, 'What I will do is to write everything that she said down whilst it's still fresh in my mind, then first thing in the morning I will ride out through the gate and try to follow the directions that I think she was trying to give us.'

'I will come with you.' said Godda with conviction.

'And me,' boomed the loud voice of his son Godwin, who was Edric's son by his first wife Rowena.

'No,' Edric replied. 'I would rather you stayed here and keep your eye on things whilst we are gone.'

To which Godwin nodded and said. 'As you wish Father,' and left the room.

*****

The two worried searchers passed through the gate just as a watery sun peeped over the eastern hillside, bringing the two sentries into a bout of reawakened energy as Edric and Godda rode silently past them, for they had been somewhat startled by the sudden appearance of their lord and his lady.

They rode through the wet, dew-laden grass, over the meadow that had not yet been grazed, for it was being kept aside, in order to be made into hay for the winter, frightening numerous skylarks off their nests as they trampled, uncaringly over the young barley, into the marshland beyond, where their mounts struggled knee deep through the clinging mud as they threaded their way from one piece of less wet ground to the next. After what seemed like a titanic struggle that had no end, they eventually found themselves on dryer ground which led them to higher and higher ground, until they eventually reached the heather covered hillside.

'Well, I can remember Mono's ranting thus far,' said Godda, who had found the last hour or so of riding quite a strain. 'Where did she say to go next? What did you write down?'

Edric fumbled into the leather pouch which carried not only the piece of vellum on which he had written the words that he and his wife had remembered Mono saying, but also a small leather flask of wine, a larger flask of water, plus a hand-sized lump of cheese and several chunks of cooked meat.

'Ah, here we are,' he said as he gingerly brought the small piece of vellum out of the pouch. Holding it up, he carefully read it aloud, saying, 'Through the stream, she said, then past the sharpstones, whatever the sharpstones are.'

'Well if we ride over the top of this hill and head downwards,' said Godda, 'then we should reach a stream, let's just hope that it is the correct stream, for there seems to be a stream in every valley that we come to. What then?' she asked.

'Something about sharpstones, probably a patch of flint or something like that,' came the answer.

But as they rode on he noticed that to his right was the hill that he seemed to recall one of the locals call the stiperstones some years ago.'

An eerie place, a place avoided by sensible folk, as it was rumoured that the Devil himself resided there, and was often seen sitting on his chair.

A chair that consisted of a cluster of huge, ragged rocks, which from a certain angle formed the shape of a large chair

'There's the sharpstones' he shouted excitedly. 'Damn me,' he swore, 'I'd completely forgotten about that.

'Thank goodness for that,' said Godda. 'We are still following Mono's dream then.'

'Aye,' came the happy reply. 'Now we are supposed to go down some valley full of sedges,' he said.

'God's blood,' she swore, which was the first time that he had ever heard her swear, 'every blessed valley around here is full of sedges. How are we expected to know which valley to take?'

She grunted in disgust and goaded her horse forward towards the brow of the hill.

When they reached the brow they could see a small deer track leading downwards where a small, sparkling stream meandered through the soggy valley bottom. Beyond the stream was another small hill and to either side of that hill there were two valleys, both leading off to the west.

'Well there's the stream and that is where Ælnoth wearied and fell on the bank. But which of those two valleys did he take?'

'The one with the curlews,' answered Godda.

'Let's hope that there are not curlews in both of the valleys.'

'Oh, stop being so doleful,' snapped Godda. 'We will find him.'

'I'm sure you are right and we will find him, but the thought of him curled up in some cavern makes me wonder whether he will be dead or alive when we do find him,' answered Edric as a feeling of doom and gloom descended, yet again, upon him.

'You take the left-hand valley' said Godda, as they began their descent. 'And I will take the other one, then we can meet on the far side where the hill seems to end.'

'Very well,' answered Edric in a miserable voice, 'and let's hope that one of us finds the remains of a stag, so that we know that we are following the way that our son took.'

'All we've got to do then is find this thing or this place called Moorston, which we have never heard of,' answered his now weary and saddle-sore wife, as they urged their horses down the trail towards the stream.

At the head of the valley they both went their separate ways with naught more than a wave, disappearing from each other's sight within the space of a few minutes as they headed for their respective valleys.

A few hundred yards into the soggy valley, Edric disturbed a pair of curlews who soared into the air with a whirring of wings and the curly, curly, curly song of their clan.

Halfway down the valley a second pair rose before him filling the valley with their eerie song.

Godda met him as arranged, stepping wearily down from her horse, stretching her aching back and rubbing the inside of her thighs which were now so painful that she swore to herself that, once this trip was over, she would never mount another horse as long as she lived.

'Ælnoth came up my valley!' shouted the much happier Edric whilst still sitting comfortably on Chieftain, for this ride was quite routine for him, even a little tedious, for he had spent more hours in the saddle than he cared to remember. 'I saw two pairs of curlews, so we are still on the right trail.'

'There were also two pairs in my valley,' came the weary reply from his wife.

'Damn!' he swore and looked up ahead to where the ground began to rise again. 'Let's hope that we can find the carcass of the stag.' He strained his eyes against the brilliant light of the morning, 'Look for the crows and red kites. They should lead us to the carcass. Mount up!' he said.

'Don't order me about, I'm not one of your serfs,' said the indignant Godda, but she grasped the reins and hauled herself up again, groaning slightly as she did so.

They saw no crows or red kites in the air. Yet after a long climb up the next hill and the equally difficult downhill ride, they followed the valley around a bend startling an enormous flock of crows that were busily feeding on the stinking remains of a stag.

The equally startled horses sent most of the birds into the air with a loud chorus of noise from the black cloud of birds that had been frightened by the approaching horses and riders.

A few of the crows were so fat that they could only manage to hop a few short yards before they flopped to the ground, too gorged to launch themselves into the air.

As the majority of the birds rose high in the air the noise grew less, allowing the two riders to calm their mounts who had become skittish due to the birds.

'Well well, here we have our stag,' said Edric as he sat on his now calmed down stallion.

'Thank the good Lord,' came the reply.

'Now we need to find this Moorston.'

About a mile further down the valley they dismounted in order to give their horses a rest, and in order to stave off the pangs of hunger, for they had been riding since dawn and now the sun was at its zenith, high over their heads.

Edric brought the food and drinks out of his satchel, handing some of it to his wife while he uncorked the water bottle, taking a long drink from it before handing it to Godda.

She shook her head and said with a weary smile. 'I think I deserve something a little stronger,' nodding towards the smaller bottle of wine that lay alongside Edric. Taking the hint, he passed the leather wine bottle over to her saying, 'Not too much now, we may well have a long ride ahead of us and I don't want you falling off yonder nag.' He tried to smile a little as he said it, attempting to mellow his warning a little.

They ate and drank in silence as they rested from their ride, with Edric reading the parchment for the tenth time as he attempted to decipher the words that he had remembered, and had written down, in a vain attempt to find out exactly who or what Moorston was.

After what was, to the weary Godda, an all too short break, they mounted their respective horses and proceeded down the valley, which so far had been a wild and uncultivated and completely free from human habitation. Yet as luck would have it, they eventually happened upon a sole shepherd who with his black and white sheepdog, were keeping vigilance over a flock of forty or fifty black-faced sheep.

At their approach the startled shepherd began to usher his sheep out of their way as he and his flock headed for a small patch of woodland, some two hundred yards away.

'Good morrow to you my good man,' yelled Edric at the top of his voice, and walked Chieftain slowly towards the man. 'We mean you no harm,' adding with a smile as he neared the man. 'We are just travelling through. A fine bright morning,' Edric went on cheerfully, as he looked upwards towards the high morning cloud, knowing how these English yeomen liked few things better than to talk about the weather.

'Aye,' replied the man. 'Won't stay foin long though,' he added.

'Oh?' answered Edric. 'Looks fine enough to me.'

'Aye, but it be a mackerel sky, bain't it?

'Mackerel sky?' said Edric looking up to see what the man meant, for the sky had white and blue wisps, similar to the belly of a mackerel, although the question immediately arose in Edric's mind as to how a simple herder of sheep, who dwelt here in the middle of England, knew what the belly of a mackerel looked like.

'See what Oi means *frēa*,' said the man, as he touched his woollen cap with his forefinger, for it seemed that he had, at last realized that he was in the company of a nobleman and his lady.

Then he recited a little rhyme his strange accent:

Mackerel sky,
Mackerel sky.
Not long wet.
Not long dry

He then whistled and his dog immediately lay down a few yards away from the round huddle that the sheep had formed, then the man turned towards Edric, standing with his legs akimbo and his shepherds crook held in front of him, as if it was some sort of protective weapon.

'What is the nearest village from here called?' asked Edric in a pleasant manner.

'Well Chirbury be over there,' he said, as he removed his cap and pointed to his left, 'and Rorrington be over yonder.' He pointed to his right.

'Oh,' said Edric, rather disappointed, 'we are looking for Moorston.'

'No place like that *frēa*,' came the answer.

They had just nudged their mounts into movement when the shepherd added. 'There be a place called Marton, over yonder to the west, though I have never been there myself,' he said as he nodded his head, as if to agree with his own statement.

'Good lord!' exclaimed the excited Godda, 'that could well be it, for, to be sure, she was rambling a lot towards the end. Where is this place?' she said to the man, smiling down into the shepherd's still bemused face.

'Don't really know my lady,' he said. 'Somewhere in that direction, I think.' pointing towards a range of hills that rose through the haze in the distance.

Edric plunged his hand into his leather bag and, fishing out a silver coin, tossed the coin to the startled shepherd, who nimbly caught the coin and with a delighted look on his face said. 'My thanks to ee my lord. May you and your lady find what you be seeking.'

They held their hands high to the man as they goaded their horses into a trot across the woodland meadow towards the distant hills.

The track soon disappeared, forcing them to make their way through several miles of what could be called nothing but wilderness, before finding meadows that had once been grazed by sheep, cattle or perhaps deer.

Eventually finding a meandering stream that they followed as it led them westwards, sometimes along its bank, and oft-times along the shallow bed of the stream itself.

Tired and slightly disillusioned at wandering through this desolate area, and not seeing any further sign of human habitation except for an area where a village or a farmstead had once stood, they began to ride on the side of the stream when Edric noticed the remains of what had once been a small fire down on a flat area of grass that had been washed down by last winter's floods.

'What's that down there?' he said pointing towards the ashes.

'What? Where?' came the reply, for Godda had been riding on the far side of her husband and did not have a clear view of the streambed.

'There, look,' he said. 'Someone's had a fire down there,' so he pulled on the reins causing Chieftain to stop, whereupon he dismounted, walked the few paces towards the edge of the bank, and looked down.

'Come quick!' he exclaimed as he jumped down the three feet onto the small patch of grass where the now extinguished fire was, noticing that there were a few fish bones strewn about the sides of the ashes.

He was about to touch the ashes to try to discover just how long the fire had been out, when he noticed something black, a little to his left, and perhaps a foot or so above the grass ledge on which he was standing.

'God's blood,' he shouted aloud, as he could see that the patch of darkness was in fact a round hole in the side of the river bank, and a mere two feet inside the hole was the tussled head of fair hair that he instantly recognised as the head of his son.

'Godda,' he said loudly. 'Come down quickly. Ælnoth is here, but I fear that we are too late.'

Godda literally fell onto the grassy bank beside him, landing on her hands and knees, uttering a very unladylike grunt.

'Where?' she gasped, and then turned her head to follow Edric's gaze at the small hole a few feet away from the pair.

Even as she spoke, the head moved a little and there was a slight groan that emitted from the small cavern.

'Oh my God,' she sobbed, 'he's alive,' and she rushed forward to grasp the boy who appeared to be awakening from a deep sleep.

'I can't get him out,' she said as she grasped the boy's shoulders and tried to heave him out of his nest.

Edric eased his wife out of the way as gently as he could, then stretched his arms into the nest of dried ferns, grasping his son under his armpits and gently eased his son out of the tiny cavern in which the boy had obviously spent a number of days and nights.

Ælnoth flopped out and landed onto the grassy knoll, as if he was a trout being landed by a fisherman, turning onto his back to stare vacantly up into the faces of his mother and father.

'Oh, he's alive,' wept Godda again, as she reached down and lifted his limp body up onto her heaving breast, sobbing and crying with joy as she held him so tightly that Edric thought that she might suffocate the boy.

'For God's sake let the boy breathe, or you will smother him before we can see if he is in good health, or is suffering from something after his ordeal.'

Upon hearing what Edric had said, she suddenly realized that her husband may well be correct, and that her son could, indeed, be suffering from the effects of spending three days and two nights fending for himself in the wilderness.

She held him at arm's length, gazing lovingly into his still sleepy eyes, thinking to herself that he seemed to have lost some weight in the few days that he had been missing.

'Are you well my love?' she asked, but received no response. 'Are you hungry?' but again she received no reply. Yet when she and Edric helped him up the riverbank to the higher ground and brought out a leg of roast chicken, the youngster snatched it out of her hand and sank his teeth into it as if he had not eaten for a week.

During the journey home he clung to his mother just as tightly as she clung to him, nestling himself into her lap as they rode wearily towards Wentnor.

They made their overnight camp under the stars, sitting around a small fire before sleeping together, with Ælnoth wedged in between his mother and his father, warm and snug under their horse blankets.

Edric spent a restless night and felt sure that his wife was awake for long periods of the night. He felt her rise on more than one occasion, listening as she walked to the fire to throw on a few sticks in order to keep it alight.

Edric was up at dawn, stretching his arms aloft in the dim light, gazing around him into the damp mist that hung on the hillside. He then stooped over the still glowing fire, throwing dried grass onto it before he blew it back into life, throwing a few more dry sticks onto it before he walked over to the horses where he rifled into one of the saddle bags and fished out a small sack of flour. This he put into a small earthenware bowl, poured in a small amount of water, then stirred it into a paste before placing the bowl in the embers of the fire.

'Oh, there you are,' came Godda's sleepy voice. 'What are you doing?'

'Making an oat mixture for the boy there,' answered Edric. 'I think that you and I will have to chew on a bit of dried meat for the morning.' He grimaced. 'We should make Wentnor by midday.'

'Thank goodness,' replied Godda. 'I do want to get Ælnoth home as soon as possible and get some real food inside him, and settle him in his own duck-down bed.'

'Aye,' agreed Edric, looking over at his sleeping son.

They reached Wentnor a little after noon, greeted by the villagers with much cheering and joyous revelry. They urged their horses through the crowd of happy people, then after they had dismounted they handed the reins to one of the young grooms.

The three travellers walked across the village green and into the warm longhall, where, much to their surprise, a warm beef stew was simmering in a large pot, and warm ale was waiting them on a small table near the hearth.

A delighted Godwin greeted them at the door, taking his young brother out of Edric's arms, whereupon he carried him up to his bed where Godda cooed and clucked like a broody hen over her still exhausted son.

As soon as Edric had descended the stairs he was confronted with a very pleasant surprise, for no other than his old friend Garth, followed by Evan of Wenlock, barged their way through the door and greeted Edric.

'Hail, Lord Edric,' gushed the huge, grubby travel-stained Garth. 'I've just heard the good news. How is the boy? Is he well?'

'He seems to be in fair health,' answered Edric.

'Has he said the reason for his running off like that?'

'Nay, he has not get uttered a word.'

'Oh, probably shock.'

'Maybe, but exactly what shocked him speechless?' said Edric glumly.

'Give him a hot meal and a good night's sleep and he will tell you all about it in the morning,' said the still jovial Garth.

'Now I see you were expecting me,' he added with a grin as he walked over to the warm ale and the pot of stew, helping himself to both, filling both his wooden bowl and tankard so full that he spilt some of the precious steaming hot soup all over his breeches.

Evan followed his mentor, filling his own bowl and tankard, but with less generous quantities.

Godda stayed with Ælnoth in his bower leaving the three men to enjoy their stew and ale as they sat around the blazing log fire.

'Well, did you get those Norman swine?' asked Edric.

'Nay, they escaped,' snarled Garth as he spat a small chunk of gristle into the fire.

'They heard that we were after them, so they took a ship to God knows where,' said Evan quietly.

'Probably Normandy,' said Garth angrily, 'to join William the Bastard in his war for the French king.'

Evan nodded as he scooped another spoonful of stew into his mouth. 'We will never find them now,' he said with a shake of his head, then added, 'and we don't even know what they look like.'

They ate in silence for most of the afternoon enjoying a few tankards of mulled ale while they exchanged details of some of the events that had taken place since they parted months ago at Much Wenlock.

Later that evening their conversation was interrupted when Godda walked into the room, ushering her son before her.

Ælnoth stopped abruptly, causing his mother to bump into him, nearly knocking him over.

'What on earth?' she said, leaning down to her son whose face was one of total shock and agony.

'She, she's not here is she?' he sobbed, uttering the first words that he had spoken since they had found him huddled in his small cavern.

'Who?' said his mother. 'Who is not here?'

'She,' stammered the shaking boy, 'the one who killed Betilda and Winnie.'

'Who?' said his shocked mother. 'Surely you don't mean the Lady Freya?'

The boy nodded.

'I can't believe it,' uttered Edric.

'I can,' answered Godda. 'I always knew that there was something evil about the woman,' she added angrily. 'She had a cloud of evil that hung over her like a dark cloud on a mountain, but I knew how important the peace treaty was to you, so I held my tongue and allowed her to stay in my house.'

Then she knelt down and held her son close to her, whispering softly into his ear.

'Yes my dearest, she has gone. You are quite safe now. She has gone for good.'

The youngster ceased his sobbing, then wiped the tears from his cheek with the back of his hand, flinging his arms around his mother's neck to kiss her on the cheek, then, after a big hug he released her and walked slowly over to his father.

'It's all right now son,' he said. 'You'll never see that woman again. Now come to the table with me to break your fast.'

He reached down to take his son's hand and led him to the table where they all sat down to eat, thoroughly enjoying the first good meal that they had shared together for quite some time.

CHAPTER 33

After a wet and tiresome journey which had taken them through marshes and woodlands, over hills and through sparsely populated valleys, Blondell, Freya and her two serving maidens, with their escort of ten hand-picked men, were approaching their domain of Yeoton, making their way westwards through the hamlet of Marston Magna, fording the river at the aptly named hamlet of Muddiford. There several of the men were forced to jump into the river to wrench two of the pack animals out of the clinging mud that had given the place its name over a hundred years ago.

They trudged up Muddiford Hill then eventually down the long winding slope, into the small, straggling township of Yeoton.

Yeoton was a big disappointment to both its new lord and his lady. It consisted of no more than perhaps twenty or so cottages clustered around a small, run-down longhall, set amidst a few fields that had been ploughed and planted, plus perhaps twenty or so fields that held a few scrawny cows and sheep grazing amongst the clumps of nettles, thistles and blackberry briars.

'Christ's bone,' swore Blondell. 'What a God-forsaken place.'

Freya was too disappointed with her new home to make any remark at all, then, as was her way, she said, trying to be optimistic, 'Oh, it's not too bad. We will soon get these peasants to knock the place into some sort of order.'

'Mmmm,' grunted Blondell, not really convinced.

She could see that her new husband was downhearted, and tried to cheer him up a little, saying, 'See over yonder,' pointing to the south. 'There's a fair-sized farm over there, and I'll wager there will be others dotted about. We'll be fine here. We will soon knock the place into shape.'

But he was still not convinced as he gazed about with a look on his face that was enough to turn milk sour.

They reined their horses to a halt in front of the longhall which, now that they were closer, they could see that it was completely empty, with the door half open and a few rags flapping in the slight breeze through the open windows.

'God. What a dump,' he swore again.

Freya nudged her horse towards a small group of villagers who had gathered some twenty or so feet away, gazing curiously and very nervously towards this large group of foreigners who had suddenly appeared in their small community.

'Who lived there?' demanded Freya, pointing to the empty longhall.

'It belonged to Lord Edward of Yeoton,' answered a large, scruffy man who looked like he may have been the village blacksmith. 'But he was slain at Hastings,' the man said sullenly.

'His only son, too,' said another.

Freya virtually ignored the two men who had spoken and said in a loud, refined voice. 'Well, we are the new owners.'

Then in an even louder voice she added. 'I am the Lady Freya, and my husband over yonder is Lord Blondell, and you all belong to us now, even those amongst you who were freeborn.

'We are your new lord and lady, and you, your holdings your crops and livestock now belong to us.'

Then she turned to her husband who was in the process of urging his weary horse towards her, saying, 'And the first thing that we will change is the name of this dismal place. What sort of a stupid name is Yeoton? Henceforth we shall call our new holding, Yeovil.'

Her husband just nodded without the slightest expression on his face, mumbling to himself, that perhaps they should call the place, Hellton, or perhaps Hades after the Greek name for Hell.

Then he gazed over towards the farm that his wife had pointed to, trying to force himself to think that it was not too unlike some of the half prosperous farms in his homeland, but daydreaming of his home only made him even more miserable. So he stood high in the saddle in order to look at the surrounding land, and with the eye of a warrior he eventually spotted a small hillock a little way out of the village. Turning his horse in that direction, he violently dug his spurs into the side of his tired mount and trotted off towards the hill.

He was already off his horse and clambering up the brush-covered hill, heaving himself upwards by grabbing the branches and trunks of the small bushes and trees that covered the uncultivated hill, noting the profusion of bluebell, primrose, hyacinths and other wild flowers, before any of his equally tired men caught up with him, thinking to himself, 'What a pity it will be when these beautiful wildflowers are destroyed in the construction of my new tower.'

To his surprise he found that the top of the small hillock was more or less flat. Indicating to him that, at some time in the distant past, it had probably been a hill-fort or settlement long before the English came to this land.

His sergeant at arms joined him, followed by six others as they had left three men to guard the horses and baggage animals.

He beckoned the sergeant to him. 'Giffard,' he said, 'Make a secure camp at the bottom of the hill for tonight, then, first thing in the morning I want you and two men to accompany me on a quick tour of our new home,' then almost as an afterthought, he added, 'Oh and before we go, muster all the villagers at the longhall and we can learn how far our new domain stretches, how many farms there are, and how close we are to our nearest Norman neighbours.' As he walked over to the far edge of the hill, he added thoughtfully, 'Let's hope there are some more good honest Norman folk about, and not more of these scraggy English peasants.'

Giffard nodded and touched his forehead with his knuckle to acknowledge his lordship's orders, but made no comment, thinking to himself, 'It was a scraggy English peasant boy who slew five of our chosen men on our way home to Canterbury not two weeks since, and yet this silly young man who is now my liege lord, still thinks that these people are harmless bloody peasants.'

Nonetheless, he swallowed his fiery Breton pride and went about his duty.

*****

After a hasty breakfast Blondell led Gifford and two other men to the disused longhall where he found a cluster of thirty or so villagers of varying ages ranging from mothers with babes in their arms, to grey-bearded grandsires stooped with age.

Reining in his horse before them he looked down upon the throng of his villagers, and said in a loud voice, 'I am sure that by now you all know who I am, but just in case there are those amongst you who do not. I will reiterate it for you.'

He cleared his throat, saying loudly. 'I am the Lord Blondell, appointed by your King, King William of Normandy, Brittany, and of England, who has made me the rightful owner of your township.

'A township that will, from now onwards, be known as Yeovil.'

He waited for a moment to allow what he had said to sink into their thick peasant skulls, nodding with satisfaction as he saw his comments register with them before he continued.

'I see that the planting has been done, and the spring hay harvest is in, so it will be no hardship for you to attend to my needs each day from dawn to dusk, with the exception of the Lord's day and those of you who have *boeuf* to milk,' then seeing the looks of confusion that crossed the faces of many of the audience, he added the English word, 'Cows' and smiled to himself as he saw looks of recognition and an occasional smile on one or two of the more intelligent amongst them.

'After milking,' he continued, 'you *boeuf* men will join every other able-bodied man and woman to help us to construct my new residence on yonder hill.' He pointed to the hillock a few hundred yards away.

'And you mutton herders will hand your flocks over to boys under the age of ten,' he looked at the assembled crowd, adding, 'any boy aged ten years or over will work on the hill with the rest of you.'

Then he realized that more blank looks had yet again crossed their faces.

He hurriedly added, 'Mutton, sheep, sheep herders.'

They appeared to understand him and apart from the odd mutter and grumble that emerged from the throng, no person raised a verbal objection and the crowd stayed silent with their heads bowed.

'One other thing,' he said breaking the silence. 'Is there one among you who can ride a horse and who knows the extent of your former lord's holdings?'

After a long silence, one elderly man with a cropped white beard and a shock of white hair stepped forward.

'I can ride a horse, and know where Lord Edwards land ends,' he said touching his forehead as he spoke.

Blondell glared down at the man, then speaking loudly so that all could hear, he bellowed. 'When you address me, you call me MY LORD or LORD BLONDELL, is that clear?' he shouted.

'Yes my lord,' muttered the man.

'I am sorry, I did not hear you?' demanded Blondell. 'Louder, so that all your friends can hear.'

'Yes my lord, I beg your forgiveness my lord,' said the man loudly, fearing for his life from this young Norman upstart.

'That's better,' huffed Blondell, 'Now mount up on that nag,' he pointed to one of the pack horses that his men had saddled, 'and show me my land.'

As the man mounted his horse, Blondell said haughtily to him, 'What name are you known by?'

'I am called Edward of the Ashes.'

'Herrum,' Blondell cleared his throat, as was his way sometimes when he needed a little time in order to digest bits of information or perhaps, to answer a tricky question before he asked in a very rough manner.

'Were you related to the late Lord Edward?'

'His father and my own sire were brothers,' came the half expected reply. 'And I am freeborn.'

'Well Edward,' he said, as he looked into the round blue eyes that stared back at him from under pure white eyebrows. 'I shall allow you to remain a free-man so long as you serve me well, but do not cross me, for although I consider myself to be a kind man, my kindness should not be mistook for weakness, and should you betray me then you and your kin will feel the full weight of my wrath.'

'Is that clear?'

'Aye, my lord, crystal clear.'

'Good, now show me my land.'

CHAPTER 34

On the last day of the month of July – called *Se Æterra Līda* by the old English – just as Edric and Godda had finished their breakfast, they heard shouting and cheering coming from the outside of their house.

Hurrying to the door, still chewing the final morsels of a pork sausage, Edric opened the door and was surprised to see a cluster of villagers and warriors standing around a man who was obviously a messenger. He was still attempting to lead his foam-mouthed, still sweating gelding through the crowd.

Edric made his way towards the crowd and could see from their faces that the man had brought happy news. He approached the man, saying, 'Well man, what news have you for me?'

'I am seeking Lord Edric Sylvaticus, Are you he?'

'I am,' answered Edric. 'What is the news?' he demanded rather anxiously.

'Great news, My lord Edric,' answered the man. 'Well, great news indeed, if you are an Englishman that is, and not such good news if you are one of the French and Norman invaders.'

'Good Lord man, spit it out, what is this great news?'

'King William, he who is called the Bastard: he is dead my lord, Killed in France, fighting for the French King at a place called Vexin.'

'When did he die?' asked Edric.

'A good month since,' came the reply.

'Then it is indeed great news,' answered Edric with a smile. 'Who rules England now that William is gone?'

'From what I hear,' said the messenger, 'I am led to believe that his son, William is already on the throne in London.'

'Blast,' swore Edric, 'another William.' He stroked his chin thoughtfully as he spoke. 'I have heard of this son. It is he who they call William Rufus,' he said, 'and from what I have heard about the boy he is no better than his father, and now that he has the throne, he could turn out to be a more savage king than ever his father was.'

He turned away from the messenger and the still jubilant crowd deep in thought before turning back to the man to say, 'Was there no English rising? Did no man come forward to challenge the pup?'

'Not as far as I know my lord. All the English lords with a few exceptions have been replaced by foreigners, and alas there seems to be no man of royal blood left in the land who will stand for us.'

'What about King Harold's sons?' questioned Edric.

'Still in Ireland I suppose,' came the mumbled reply.

Edric turned away to return to the house and to Godda in order to discuss this latest turn of events, with Godda pressing Edric to lead a rising against this new King. In vain, for Edric was only too well aware that he did not have enough men needed to attack and hold the numerous stone towers and battlements that he knew the Normans had already erected.

The May fayre seemed a long way off now, just a happy memory of that first day in the month of May, when lords, ladies, freemen and peasants enjoyed a day off from the general toil of life, relaxing on the village green where they had all enjoyed the spectacle of the village maidens dancing around the holly thorn, accompanied by the merry music from a piper, flautist, drummer and the happy songs from a small group of singers.

Edric and Godda had provided the food and drink which had been laid onto stout trestle tables which groaned under the weight of a spit-roasted yearling bullock, two new lambs, six suckling pigs plus numerous fowl of many varieties, surrounded by freshly baked bread and pies made from the last of the winter stored fruit.

The atmosphere had been one of loud gaiety, growing ever louder as the day progressed, finally ending at midnight when most of the food and ale had been either consumed or carried off by villagers, thanking their benefactor and his beautiful wife Godda, who they still believed really was 'Queen of the Light Elves.'

Ælnoth seemed to have recovered from his ordeal, apart from the odd bout of silence that occurred from time to time.

'It is his way of dealing with things,' explained Godda, as she watched her son ride his pony. A pony that Edric had presented him on his fifth birthday some seven months ago, and a gift which the boy had positively ignored until a week ago, when Ælnoth had been persuaded by Aeldred, the young groom to inspect the pony. Aeldred had lied saying that the pony had not eaten for days and was pining away for lack of attention.

He had eventually been coaxed to feed the pony a handful of hay, then to stroke his silken nuzzle, and finally tempted to sit in the child's saddle, before being led around the stackyard. After a few minutes he was surprised to find that he was enjoying himself so much that he could not prevent himself from laughing and chuckling at this newly found source of pleasure, so much so that the groom had trouble in persuading the happy youngster to dismount.

'That's long enough for your first time,' said the Aeldred.

'Just a little while longer,' pleaded the boy.

'Nay young sire,' answered Aeldred. 'Your father will kill me if you fall and hurt yourself,' said the nervous young man who had, at long last, realized that by luring his lordship's son onto the pony had not been, perhaps, such a good idea after all.

Reluctantly the boy scrambled off the pony, joining Aeldred on the ground, chatting happily to the groom, delighted with himself that he had, in his mind, mastered the art of riding in one easy lesson.

He left Aeldred who led the pony off to the stables, dancing happily across the yard and into the house, shouting, 'Father! Father, I have been riding the pony you gave me.' Then he stopped suddenly for a moment before he bounded into the room looking for his father, shouting. 'I shall name him Badger, that's a good name, 'cos he is pretty well the same colour as a Badger. Don't you think so Father?'

'Your Father's out,' said his mother quietly. 'But we can tell him the good news when he returns from the hunt.'

'Oh!' exclaimed her son, then with a shrug of his shoulders he sat at the table and helped himself to one of his mother's fresh-baked buns, and echoed his mother's words with a mouthful of bun. 'That's all right, we will tell him when he comes in from the hunt.'

Unfortunately, by the time that Edric came in, weary, wet and empty handed, Ælnoth had been abed for two hours.

Godda thrust a tankard of mulled ale into his hand asking. 'No luck today husband?'

'No, the day has been too hot and the deer have taken to the shade, didn't see hide nor hair of a single deer,' he grumbled. 'Had a miserable day, dreadful, even Chieftain played me up, wouldn't settle.' He tried to explain with a shrug.

'Oh dear,' replied Godda, aware that her husband was not in the best of moods, so she said as pleasantly as she could, 'Still, I don't suppose we will starve.'

Then she handed her husband a platter consisting of cold roast beef, a chunk of bread and a wedge of cheese, saying, 'Ælnoth has had a good day today. Young Aeldred had him up on that pony that you gave him some months since.'

'Mmm,' said Edric. 'Good, coming out of his shell at last.'

'Oh, he'll be fine,' she said trying to smile. 'Just give him a little time.'

Edric sat down heavily on the oak settle, grunting as he struggled out of his wet leather riding boots, sighing with relief as he did so. 'Must be getting old,' he remarked as he attempted to dry his wet feet by the fire. 'I never used to ache like this when I was young.'

Godda frowned to herself, thinking, 'Something is amiss. He has never complained about the cold, the wet or of his aches and pains before. Is he bored with me, or perhaps it is the mundane life that he has been leading of late? Mayhap this life of country gentlemen does not sit well on the shoulders of a man who has spent more than half of his life in war.'

She stood at the table and looked at him as he thrust his feet closer to the fire.

'What is it?' Her mind flitted from one possibility to another as she sought to put her finger on whatever was bothering him, adding as she pecked him on his cheek, ' The love of my life.'

He struggled out of his wet shirt and breeches which he flung in a heap on the floor, saying grumpily, 'Fetch me a blanket or a clean shirt.'

She turned and left the room hurriedly to fetch him a clean set of clothing, grumbling to herself. 'He has never spoken to me like that before,' she mused. 'No "please". No "dear" or "dearest", as had always been his way'

She returned with a dry shirt and breeches, which he put on, grumbling and complaining as he did so.

He sat down again and stretched his cold hands towards the fire, saying, 'I suppose I might as well tell you. You would have found out sooner or later anyway.'

'Oh dear God,' she thought to herself as she walked slowly to the seat on the other side of the hearth. 'He has found another woman. What will become of me now? 'What about young Ælnoth? Could I take him back with me to my own folk? My sisters would surely kill him, for they like not people who are not of their own kin.'

These thoughts flooded her mind as she sat and looked through the light of the fire towards her husband, who she could see was clearly disturbed about the news which he was about to hurl at her. 'This could be the sort of news that will shatter my happiness, the joy that we have shared for a much too short a period of time.'

'On the way home this evening,' he began, staring intently across the fire to her. 'I came across a party of Normans, men who had been calling on all of the landowners in Mercia and were seeking me out.'

She looked up, startled, yet somewhat relieved that it was Normans who had upset their idyllic life, and had not been some woman, younger and prettier than her.

'Oh, they were not just looking for me,' he continued. 'They were messengers sent by this new King William to every nobleman, be he Norman, Saxon, Dane or Celt in the country, with the news that the King is to assemble a great army on the first day of July, and we must all meet him at York with our men, and accompany him on his quest to evict King Malcolm of the lowland Scots from northern England.'

She took a long breath as she digested the news before she said as cheerfully as she could. 'Oh, that's not so bad is it?' Although the words that she had uttered were not really her true feelings.

'You will be in your element with a shield in one hand and a battle-axe in the other.'

'I had thought that I had seen the last of other men's blood and guts,' he answered thoughtfully, 'and sought naught more than to dwell here in this beautiful part of my country and watch my children grow and flourish.'

He sighed heavily and drained the ale, which had now gone cold in its tankard.

'It seems it is not to be so. I must also take one hundred warriors,' he added, 'and that is a lot of men and will leave only a few men to guard you from English and Welsh wolf-heads, should they take it into their stupid heads that there is gold and silver waiting for them here at Wentnor. Easy pickings for them.'

'Must you go?' she asked as a tear welled up in her eye and cascaded down her cheek. 'You are no longer a young man. War is a young man's game. Can you not send the men, and let one of your younger captains lead them?'

'Not so,' he said sadly. 'For I have given my word to young Blondell and his murderous wife, is that not so?'

She nodded sadly, knowing full well what a proud man he was.

A man who would risk his life rather than break an oath.

She kissed him tenderly on his cheek and said in her sultry voice, 'I know my dearest. I know that you must go. It is your path in life. Your destiny.'

She moved over to sit beside him, placing her arm around his shoulders, kissing him tenderly on his cheek, then brushing his long hair to one side, kissed his neck, tasting the sweat of the days hunt, and the cold dampness from the rain that still lingered on his body.

In fact Edric himself had difficulty in understanding his own feelings. On one side of the blade, he was sad to be leaving his beautiful and adoring wife, worried for Ælnoth who was only just getting over the difficulties that he had experienced at the hands of that vile woman Freya, as well as concerned for his lands and his people. He would be leaving them without the protection of their Lord, leaving them vulnerable to thieves, wolf-heads and raiders.

On the other side of the blade, his blood boiled within him at the thought that once again he would be leading men into battle. The thrill and anticipation that always preceded a war trail surged through his body, eager once again of stepping into the unknown.

The clash of metal against metal.

The noise,

The elation.

The shouts and the joy of victory.

His mood lightened a little, and he returned Godda's kisses.

*****

The turmoil that invaded his head evaporated within a few minutes of his head hitting the duck-down pillow, but the dreams that followed were not of joy and elation, for they took him back to his youth, where he again experienced the long series of skirmishes and battles that he had fought with his arch-enemy Madoc the Lucky.

His dreams forcing him to toss and turn in his sleep as he battled again with the Welsh giants, Ivor half-face and his equally ugly and equally gigantic brother, Elwyn, twisting and turning in his sleep as he evaded the giants' mighty sweeps with the huge battle-axe that could cut a man in half with a single blow.

He parried a blow with his shield, thrusting the shield suddenly forward in order to catch the axe in mid-flight, before the full force of the blow could reach him. Yet as he did so, the shield (in fact it was his fist) struck his wife so violently on her chest that she thought that the house had collapsed, and sat up in the bed, clutching her bruised chest and gasping for breath.

'God's blood,' she croaked. 'What... what in heaven's name was that?' She stretched out her arm towards the oak chest where the candles lay. She struck a flint and lit the candle, throwing a sparse light into the darkened room.

'Edric? Edric!' she repeated, shaking her sleeping husband by the shoulder violently, until he finally opened his eyes and gazed sleepily up to her.

'What? What is it?' he grumbled.

'Something struck me on the chest. There is someone in the room. Get up and find him'

Still half asleep, he stumbled up and out of the bed, holding the candle aloft in one hand, grasping his sharp *seax* in his other hand as he peered into the corners and recesses of the room.

'Nothing here,' he growled, angry that he had been wakened from what he thought had been a deep sleep. Then he somehow remembered the dream, and the battle that he had just had with the Welsh giant, Ivor half-face. He returned to the bed and held his still shaking wife close to him.

'It was a dream,' he said. 'I was in a fight with Madoc and the giant twins, and I must have flung my arms about and hit you.'

'Well, you nearly damned well killed me,' she gasped, still finding it difficult to breath. 'Any more dreams like that and you will be sleeping alone.'

Then with a huff, still holding her sore chest, she turned her back on him and nestled down in the bed in an attempt to return to sleep for what remained of the night.

Sleep evaded her, for the pain in her chest was so great. So she suffered in silence, as she listened to the grunts and the snoring of her husband as he returned to his dreams of the past, or, perhaps the dreams of the coming conflict, or even of the arrangements that had to be made as he took this new path towards the conquests of the future.

He rose at first light and looked down at his wife whose eyes were still closed, a ruse that she had used before in order to convince Edric that she was asleep, although she had not slept a single wink (or so it seemed) since being so rudely awakened by what, in her mind, had been the sky falling in.

In the dim light of the dawn he quickly dressed, dashed out of the room into the scullery, startling a bleary eyed kitchen maid as he stormed through the door, snatched a chunk of warm bread and a small wedge of cheese off the table, and was out of the door before the maiden had time to bend her leg or bow her head, in the usual curtsey with which she usually greeted Lord Edric and the Lady Godda each morning.

Apart from a few laggards, most of his men were up and enjoying their breakfast when he burst into their dining hall. Stuffing the last crumbs of cheese into his mouth, he began organizing his men for the coming war-trail.

He called Garth and his other captains over to him, telling them the news, then discussed with them which of the warriors would go with them, and which of the men who were either too old, or were perhaps suffering from some injury or battle wound, or mayhap were too young and inexperienced for the coming battle.

All agreed that every man of the blood-oath should go with the exception of Edgar of Worcester, who had recently suffered a broken leg when he foolishly tried to take a newborn bull calf from its dam, thus enraging the mother who had charged and hurled him into a fence, breaking his left leg in the process.

Of the remaining warriors in his service, he decided to leave fifteen young men and eight of the greybeards at home in order to protect the village.

'That means that we can muster twenty-seven men from Wentnor and Prolley Moor so we need to find another sixty-three from the rest of the shire.'

'That's quite a number,' remarked Garth, scratching his greying beard.

'Yes it is,' answered Edric. 'But if we put our minds to it, I'm sure we can make up the number.' He added thoughtfully, 'I can think of quite a few good warriors, bowmen and spearmen who might be weary of life on the farm, and would enjoy a good hike up to the north of England.'

'Aye,' agreed Garth. 'Now that you mention it, I too can think of a few who would be only too pleased to join us.'

'We can but try,' said Edric, 'although I will order no man to join us. Any man who comes with us must do so willingly. We want hawks not sparrows. Hawks fly alone and one such hawk is Ordgar, Ordgar the Bear and his hounds might join us.'

'Yes, he would be an asset and I have heard that he lives in a hut under the long mountain, somewhere by the fish pools.'

'Good, I will send a man to tell him of his good fortune,' said Edric grinning, knowing full well that Ordgar had oft times grumbled about the tedium of living the quiet life, longing for a little action again, and a chance to raise that formidable spear of his.

'I would like you to make a journey into the Welsh mountains,' said Edric to his friend, 'in order to recruit a few Welshmen for me.'

Garth looked up with a frown crossing his already furrowed brow. 'Wales,' he echoed. Why Wales? This is not a Welshmen's war! Let them squabble amongst themselves, leastways that keeps them happy and well away from us.'

'Aye, maybe that is so, but a few good Welsh bowmen will not be amiss amongst those Heathens north of the Roman wall,' Edric replied. 'And, as you know I am right fond of young Hywell the son of Gwynneth and my friend Bleddyn, and he has a strong right arm and can send an arrow two hundred paces into the heart of a man. And' – he emphasised the point with the point of his finger – 'he may well bring a dozen or so strong Welshmen with him, now that would be no bad thing, don't you think?'

Garth reluctantly nodded, grunting in agreement, saying, 'As you wish. I will journey into the mountains and see if I can find Hywell. But as you know I am not the best of men to find my way through those rain-sodden mountains, and could well get myself well and truly lost, so you may never see me again.' He smiled wryly as he said it, but it was in fact a true statement, for whilst Garth was a good and faithful friend and a famous warrior of note, he did not have the best sense of direction.

Very often finding himself completely lost when travelling through unfamiliar countryside.

'Oh, I have already thought of that,' answered Edric. 'I will have young Emrys show you the way, he hails from the same tribe as Hywell so he will be able to lead you straight to Bleddyn.'

Before Garth could raise any further objections, Edric continued, 'And whilst you are enjoying yourself in those beautiful Welsh valleys, I will tour the shire and select a few more strong fellows to accompany us on our grand venture, in order to assist our new King to rid himself of his troublesome northern neighbour.'

He left Garth to make his own arrangements for his trip into the Welsh mountains before he walked across the village green to speak with Waldo the blacksmith, whom he found, as usual, clanging away with his hammer.

On this occasion he was straightening a bent spear point.

He waited quietly to one side of Waldo who was too intent on his work to have noticed that his lord and master had entered his dark, hot, noisy domain.

Edric watched as Waldo's muscular arms rose and fell as he brought the heavy hammer down with precision onto the exact part of the glowing spear point that was by now almost straight, wishing to himself that Waldo's strength could have been used in another way. He would have made a powerful warrior but, try as he might, Waldo had shown time and time again that whilst he was probably the finest blacksmith and weapon smith in the shire, his skills as a warrior were literally non-existent. The co-ordination which he had in the smithy left him the moment the huge man met an opponent who was intent on harming him.

Edric shook his head, thinking to himself. 'Is the man a coward? Or is there some other, more deep-rooted reason why this man, who is built like a prize bull, is unable to harm his fellow man?'

At that moment his thoughts were interrupted when Waldo took the still red-hot metal and plunged it into a leather bucket of cold water before he placed the cooling spear point on a blackened bench. Looking up for the first time, he noticed Edric standing in the shadows.

'Oh, Lord Edric!' said the man, nodding his head in respect.

'Good morrow to you smith,' greeted Edric. 'I have news that will bring a lot of extra work for you,' he said as he walked towards the door, eager to gain a breath or two of fresh air after the hot humidity of the blacksmith's forge.

Waldo joined Edric and stood in the doorway as if he was reluctant to vacate his beloved smithy and venture into the clear morning air.

'I have been bidden by the King to take one hundred men in order to join him in his war with Malcolm of Scotland. So I will be sending each one of those hundred men to you within the next six weeks, and I want you to provide each man with an iron helmet, that is if he does not already have one, an iron-rimmed shield, plus of course either a spear, sword or axe.'

The Blacksmith looked startled at the amount of work that was suddenly being thrust upon him.

'I cannot do it my lord,' he said in his deep voice. ''Tis too much. Too many, for I am but one man.'

'Oh, I shall provide you with three young men to help you, and I do know for a fact that one of them is well schooled in your craft, for he is the son of a smithy in the town of Shrewsbury.'

Before Waldo could agree or disagree with what his master was saying, Edric continued, 'You could use the other two lads for repairing damaged shields, weapons and armour. Get them to fetch and carry for you and to do any other odd jobs that need doing.

'And if you need more help, then you only have to send one of the boys to me and I will provide you with whatever you ask for.'

He then plunged his hand into his leather purse, taking out ten silver coins, which he handed to the smith saying, 'This should be enough for you to purchase ample material for your needs, but if it is not, then come to me.'

Edric left the stunned blacksmith standing in the doorway of his smithy gazing at the handful of silver coins that had been thrust into his hand.

Edric turned to walk away, saying, 'Good Waldo, this is a thing that must be done. No ifs or buts, for I want every one of the men who will be marching north with me to be fully equipped for the fight ahead. Is that clear?'

Waldo's mouth opened but no words emerged from it, but he did nod his head in acknowledgement to the already receding figure of Lord Edric.

Within two weeks Waldo had his additional 'smiths' to help him, in his own and a newly constructed forge, and the two forges blazed with noise and activity non-stop, day and night, with a constant flow of warriors clustered around the buildings, with some of them trying to assist the sweating smiths, but in the most part getting in the way and impeding the blacksmith's work, or standing in noisy groups, waiting for their particular piece of metalwork to be finished.

This idleness began to annoy Edric, who eventually approached the waiting men with six longbows draped across his shoulder, plus several bundles of arrows, which he dumped in front of them.

'Here,' he said grumpily. 'Set up a target on the far side of the green and hone your skills with the bow, for they may well be needed in the fray to come.'

Speedily turning his back on the dumbfounded men as he stalked back towards the armoury, which was slowly being filled with the accoutrements of war.

*****

The journey, thus far, had been far more pleasant than Garth had anticipated, for the weather was dry and warm.

He had never truly been at home on a horse, but this mare was an old nag, wide, slow and sure footed, which made the journey an easy enough ride as the old grey mare made her way up the valleys and along the stream beds which seemed to be alive with fish as well as fish-eating birds.

The skies were alive with the song of larks, the screeches of buzzards, plus a hundred other varieties of birds, some of which he was unfamiliar with, for he had never before ventured this far into the mountains.

Emrys was a pleasant enough young man, who, despite his unkempt appearance, was good company, jovial and happy, as well as being one of the few youngsters who seemed to enjoy helping the old man (for that was what he thought of his companion,) despite knowing the fearsome reputation that hung around Garth like an ominous mist.

He was also quite nervous of the evil-looking battle-axe that was never more than a few inches from the old man's right hand. He tried his best to limit his constant chatter to happy and pleasant things, taking every opportunity to make a point of saying friendly things about England and the English.

He would dismount from his own shaggy hill pony in order to lead Garth's aged mare over the more dangerous stretches of boulder-strewn hillsides and streambeds, guiding them gently across the loose scree that littered the steep slopes.

Deeper and deeper into the mountainous wilderness they rode, seeing no sign of human habitation other than the odd ring of stones, or the odd patch of blackened earth where some traveller or hunter had rested to make a fire.

Towards evening Emrys pointed ahead saying, 'We will spend the night in the next valley.'

'Why what's there?' said Garth with a smirk. 'More bloody hills and valleys I would wager.'

'Not so my old friend,' said the young man with a smile, 'yonder valley holds a lake that has the biggest trout that you have ever seen, and at the foot of that hill over there' – he pointed to his left, towards a huge cloud topped mountain – 'lives an old shepherd who is my own father's cousin, or at least he was, the last time I saw him, for that was at least six or seven years ago, when I first made my way out of the mountains into England.'

He urged his pony forward as if in anticipation of seeing his old kinsman again, but said over his shoulder, 'But he was an old man even then, and I cannot shake the thought out of my mind that he had, even then, seen too many of our harsh Welsh winters.'

They rode their mounts over the rise, past what Garth thought looked like the source of the stream they had been following. Then, much to the delight of Emrys and to the relief of Garth, they could see in the distance, perhaps some half a mile away, the distinct outline of a tiny lime-washed cottage.

Small, scraggy looking white-faced sheep grazed peacefully on the short-cropped grass that grew along the shoreline of the lake's peat-darkened waters, but they merely lifted their heads and moved lazily out of the way as the two horsemen rode through them towards the cottage.

A thin wisp of smoke rose from the stone chimney into the clear mountain air.

'Ah!' exclaimed Emrys happily. 'It looks like someone is home,' as he dismounted in front of the cottage, leaving his pony to graze, leaping up the two steps with one large bound, whereupon he thumped his fist on the faded oak door, before he lifted the latch and strode into the darkened room, shouting. 'Wake up uncle Dyffid, you have visitors!'

Garth, who had remained on his tired mount, watched with amusement as his young companion disappeared through the door. Yet as no further sounds emitted from the cottage, his amusement turned to concern, causing him to dismount, grasping his trusty battle-axe in his right hand, and a shield in his left as he walked towards the half-opened front door.

He nudged the front door until it was fully open and looked cautiously into the darkened room.

As his eyes became accustomed to the darkness he stepped further into the room, ready at the first sight or sound of danger to launch himself at any one or anything that should emerge out of the darkness.

No attacker appeared, and after a long, ominous silence he heard the sound of a slight groan that came from one corner of the room.

He moved closer and eventually managed to make out a prone figure lying on a roughly hewn, sheepskin-covered bed, and the figure of Emrys, who was kneeling at the bedside, holding the hand of the man in the bed.

'Oh, come on in,' mumbled Emrys. 'For a moment I had forgotten all about you,' then turning his head towards the man, who seemed to Garth to be deathly white, he said. 'This is my companion, Uncle. He is an Englishman called Garth.' As if that was a valid explanation for Garth's presence here in the high fortress of the Welsh mountains he returned his attention towards the man in the bed.

The man's eyes stared towards Garth, and he made a slight nod with his head, before his eyes closed for a moment, eventually re-opening as they focused again on the face of his kinsman.

'He has been savaged by a bear,' said Emrys. 'Look.' And he drew back the sheepskin covers to reveal the shoulder of his uncle, where a mass of still bleeding raw flesh, from his neck to his elbow showed evidence of the teeth marks of a mountain bear.

The man said something in a thin weak voice, in a language that Garth knew to be the Welsh tongue.

'What did he say?' asked Garth.

'Oh, he said that the bear killed his dog.'

'Oh!'

The man spoke again, and Emrys turned his head towards Garth, and said, 'He says that if it hadn't been for his dog, the bear would certainly have killed him.' He looked up at Garth and said in a quiet voice, 'He is dying. Isn't there something we can do?'

'Stop the bleeding for a start,' grumbled Garth.

'But how? The nearest healer is at least a day's ride away.'

'Oh, I know a little about bleeding,' said Garth. 'I've had my hide patched up more than once.' He moved over to the window and opened the shutters, then set his axe down close to the bed.

Turning to Emrys, he said. 'You know these parts, do you not?' but before Emrys could answer, he continued, 'Go out and collect a handful of young willow leaves, and a bunch of comfrey, a single root of wolfsbane. Oh and a handful of clean sphagnum moss. I will stoke up the fire whilst you are gone in order to give the old fellow a bit of warmth.'

A little while later Emrys burst through the door and threw down the things that he had been bidden to find, saying, 'I had to go halfway up the damned mountain to find that blessed wolfsbane, 'tis not an easy thing to find this time of the year.'

Garth merely nodded, choosing some half a dozen willow leaves, a sprig of comfrey, and a mere sliver of the root of the wolfsbane which he chopped as finely as he could and placed the minced concoction into a small bowl of water which was boiling on the embers on the edge of the fire.

'There,' he said with a sad smile. 'I will leave it to simmer for a while, then cool it in the stream, but we must drain off the liquid before giving it to him, and it should, with a little help from Woden, fight his fever, clean the blood and prevent gangrene from setting in.'

At the mention of the heathen god, Woden, Emrys crossed himself and muttered a quick prayer, for although he had grown to like his huge companion, he completely scorned the old Saxon gods, for he and his people had been devout Christians for more than two hundred years.

Garth had not seen Emrys cross himself and seemed completely oblivious to the feelings of his young companion. He continued to kneel beside the bed, cleaning away much of the gore and mangled flesh from the man's arm as well as from the shoulder wounds, before applying a thick wad of moss over the entire wound, saying, 'There, that should do it. Hand me that tankard, and help me hold his head up, while I try to coax as much of this mixture as I can down his gullet.'

Despite being as gentle as they could, it appeared to Emrys that only half of the liquid actually entered the mouth of his uncle, and perhaps half of that was actually swallowed by the sick man, the rest ending up in his grizzled grey beard, or staining his already filthy shirt.

'There, there,' said Emrys. 'Well done, good Uncle Dyffid. You will be fine now.'

'He should sleep soon,' said Garth, as he stood up and stretched his aching back, then he walked stiffly towards the door, carrying his huge battle-axe in his right hand, for he rarely went anywhere without his razor-sharp friend.

Emrys joined him as he stood in the doorway, gazing over the still waters of the lake. 'Beautiful is it not?' said the youngster.

'Aye, it is that.'

Then Garth walked down the steps, crossed the tiny stream that ran alongside the cottage, walking slowly along the pebbled shoreline, his head turning from the dark waters of the lake towards the hillside that rose sharply to his left.

He heard the footsteps of Emrys as the boy followed a couple of paces behind him.

'I thought that I ought to accompany you,' he exclaimed in a jovial voice, 'just in case you meet the bear that savaged my uncle.'

'If we did meet him, I'd warrant that you would soon take to your heels and leave me to face him,' said Garth with a chuckle in his deep voice.

Emrys made a snort in the back of his throat but said nothing

'Well this is where he attacked him, look-you, there is his sheepdog,' pointing to the stiff remains of the mangled dog that lay beside a boulder. 'And there is the remains of his meal,' he added, as they approached a mass of wool scattered amongst the few bloodied bones, which were the sole remains of one of Dyffid's finest ewes.

'Mmm,' muttered Garth as he peered up the hillside and into the tangled undergrowth.

A few brief moments later, as he cursed himself for stubbing his toe on a hidden rock, an enormous roar emitted from behind him, and the huge brown figure of a mountain bear came bounding down the hillside towards them as fast as a warhorse at full gallop.

Just as Garth had predicted a few moments ago, Emrys turned on his heels and ran back towards the cottage as fast as his legs could carry him, hoping to reach the cottage before the bear would reach him. Yet Garth was under no such illusions, knowing full well that even if he did turn and run, there was absolutely no way that, considering his bulky figure as well as his age, he would be able to outrun the charging bear.

So he did the only thing left for him to do, and that was to stand his ground and face the charging animal. He held his axe in both hands, high above his head, and waiting for the slavering animal to reach him.

It took the animal a few brief moments to reach Garth. Yet in those few brief moments, Garth's mind flew back towards the time when he was a mere stripling of perhaps sixteen summers, living with his friend Edric in that cold cave on that bleak hillside, with old Vorta and the rest of his friends, when, on one of his hunting expeditions he had been attacked by a bear that had ripped his clothes to shreds and gave him the fright of his young life.

He shivered at the memory, but was instantly brought back to awful reality as the enormous bear reached him and reared up onto its hind legs with its four-inch claws shining out from its outstretched arms.

The animal's slavering mouth opened wide, showing its huge fangs ready to rip him apart.

Garth faced the bear with his legs akimbo and swung his enormous axe around in an arc, taking the bear high in its neck, severing the beast's spinal cord, instantly killing it but causing the beast to fall forward onto its slayer, pinning the shocked man down with its bulk, drenching him with its lifeblood.

Garth's arms and his axe were wedged between him and the bear, making it impossible for him to move, and try as he might, even his great strength found it impossible to move the animal's heavy carcass off him.

With just the top of his shoulders and his head protruding from under the beast, he felt anything but elated.

In fact a wave of fear passed through him for probably the first time in his life, for he knew that at that moment he was as harmless as a babe in arms, and should the bear's mate, a wolf, fox, or mayhap a crow be attracted by the smell of blood, then he would certainly lose his eyes or even his life.

As the wave of nausea passed, he gazed up towards the weak sun that shone through the misty clouds and saw the shape of a figure, as if one of Woden's handmaidens had appeared from the heavens to save him.

The figure stooped down towards his face and the maiden's beautiful face changed into the pimply, dirty face of Emrys.

'Well that was the bravest thing that I ever did see,' he said, as he shook his head sadly and added, 'but how the devil I can get this monster off you is altogether another thing?'

He stood up and walked around the dead bear, stooping a couple of times, grunting with exertion as he attempted to heave one of the beast's legs and arms in a vain attempt to move it off his old friend.

'It's no good,' he sighed. 'I can't shift the thing.' He walked around it again looking for a solution.

'Get the bloody horse,' gasped Garth, who was now having trouble breathing due to the great weight that lay on his chest. 'Tie a rope to an arm and a leg and pull this damn thing off me.'

'I was just about to say the same thing,' lied Emrys, grinning broadly before he raced back towards the cottage where the horses had been hobbled, and were happily munching on the lush grass that covered a small hillock.

He returned a few minutes later, but what seemed to be an age to the trapped man whose face had now turned to a greenish colour through lack of oxygen.

Emrys speedily tied a rope to one arm and one leg of the dead beast then looped the rope around the saddle horn, turned the horse away and with a cluck or two urged it forward.

The carcass seemed to have a mind of its own and refused to budge. Yet as if it realized that it was fighting a losing battle, making a noise that sounded like a man wrenching his boot out of a bog, the clinging blood loosened its hold and the body rolled lazily off Garth, flopping onto its back, lying alongside Garth as he gasped, filling his lungs with fresh mountain air.

He sat up, still gasping. 'My God,' he croaked. 'I thought that I was on my way to Valhalla. Killed by a bloody dead bear,'

'No my friend,' said Emrys with a very serious and very unusual look on his young face. 'Your time is not now.'

CHAPTER 35

Edric rode Chieftain hard around the parts of the shire that he still held, avoiding the two main towns of Ludlow and Shrewsbury, which were now held by Norman lords in the Kings name.

However, he did spend the night with Walter de Lacy, who, despite being a Norman, was a man who dwelt in relative peace at the hamlet of Stokesay. Walter was a man with whom Edric had spent many a happy day either dining in his great hall, or hunting in the great forest of Clunn, for Walter was a man who excelled at hunting wild boar and the red deer whose numbers teemed in the uninhabited depths of the forest.

Walter was a man of such energy who, despite reaching the age of sixty summers, was only too pleased to promise to join Edric with ten men from his lands when Edric marched to the north in June.

In many of the hamlets there were no men suitable for Edric's purpose. Yet he recruited eight warriors in Streeton, two in Walford, and nine proven men in the tiny hamlet of Golding, six from one family alone. All good men, armed and seasoned warriors.

When he reached the limit of his own territory, he had a mere seventeen men, which painted a true picture of the county, a picture that was slowly proving to him that far more warriors had been slain at Stamford Bridge and at Hastings, than he had first thought. Of the men who had returned from those battles, some had left the county, whilst others had already found employment for their arms in the service of either King William, or some other Norman lord. As for the remainder of those who had returned, many had arms missing as well as other serious wounds and the few who were still whole, seemed to prefer farming to fighting.

However, as word of his errand became known, more and more warriors did eventually make their way to him, or else he found them waiting along the route that they knew he would be taking. Most of them were experienced warriors, proudly bearing the usual scars along their arms and faces, showing that they had once (or perhaps more than once) stood in a shieldwall, in order to face their country's enemies. Yet Edric was forced to reject many of the younger men who wanted to join him, for he had seen far too many young and inexperienced lads who had plenty of courage, but had lacked the experience and discipline that a man needed in battle, noting time and time again that they were always the first to fall, leaving gaps in the shieldwall. Gaps which the enemy would surge through, wreaking havoc amongst the fallen youngsters fellow warriors.

Of course there were always exceptions, such as one young man who had no more than eighteen winters behind him, who simply refused to take 'NO' for an answer, actually challenging Edric to a duel, saying, 'Come on then! Fight me, for I am as skilled as any man here,' waving his *seax* at the small crowd of warriors who stood in a loose semicircle in order to watch Edric select his men, either nodding their approval or muttering amongst themselves as one man after another was either accepted or turned away.

'Nay boy,' said Edric, 'I cannot fight you. Go back to your farm and come to me at Wentnor in a couple of years' time.'

He then turned his back to speak to another man who had just been chosen, only to experience the touch of cold steel at the back of his neck.

'Fight me, or die,' came a snarl from the youngster.

Edric stood completely still for he could feel a trickle of blood running down his neck, then whirled around with all the speed that he could muster, knocking the short blade away with his left hand, whilst in the same movement, in the flick of an eye, he had his own *seax* in his right hand and stood facing his attacker.

'Perhaps that was not the wisest thing that you have ever done,' said Edric quietly, with a grim smile as he wiped the blood from the back of his neck with his left hand, then studied his bloodied hand whilst he still kept one eye on the impetuous youngster.

The young man lunged forward.

Edric merely moved his head and twisted his shoulder a little to watch the sharp *seax* fly past him. Yet then he was forced to jump savagely aside as the boy brought his weapon back, hoping to slash his opponent with a return cut.

'Damn,' swore Edric, thinking to himself, 'perhaps the boy is reasonably good with a weapon. He certainly is fast.'

The youngster slashed again but this time it was a good ten or twelve inches from his opponent's throat and Edric did not even bother to move. The boy stepped closer and sent his *seax* in a wide arc towards Edric's chest, allowing Edric a brief second in which he stepped forward, blocking the cut with his left arm, and at the same time bringing the hilt of his own *seax* upwards and under the boy's chin. There it struck the boy with such force that his head shot backwards and he tumbled backwards, landing on the ground with a loud thump.

There were a few grunts of approval from the spectators and the odd man here and there clapped his hands a few times; but they were, after all, mostly gnarled warriors who had seen, and had been in frays much more violent and dangerous that the one that they had just witnessed. In their minds, there had never been any doubt who would be the victor in this small tussle that they had just witnessed.

Edric bent over the prone figure of the boy, slapping his face a couple of times until the boy's eyes opened.

He sat up and rubbed his aching chin then probed into his mouth with his index finger examining his teeth, which he imagined had been either broken or loosened by the sudden blow that to him had seemed to come out of nowhere to send him to the floor.

The youngster rose and staggered a pace before his head cleared, standing shakily as he faced Edric with a wry smile on his young rosy, unshaven face.

'No hard feelings, my Lord Edric,' he said with a smile as he held his right hand out in friendship.

'Of course not,' answered Edric, but immediately turned away to continue his selection from the small knot of six or seven men who had been waiting their turn.

'Do I go with you then?' came the voice from behind him as the young man dogged his footsteps.

Edric stopped and turned again to face the impudent youngster. 'My word,' he said. 'You are keen.'

'That I am, my lord.'

'By what name are you known?'

'I am called Thurston of Wem.'

'Wem? That is a town north of Shrewsbury is it not?'

'It is, but it now belongs to Lord Surley who is one of Lord Talbot's lackeys.'

'Well, I will say this for you, Thurston of Wem, you really are eager. I can see that you are well provided for in the weapons of war, but do you have a horse?'

'I do, My lord, and can ride as well as any man.'

'In that case it will cost me none of my hard-earned silver to allow you to ride with me. But should that hot temper of yours, or your long tongue cause me any grief, then you will soon be riding that nag of yours back to Wem.'

He bowed his head, and then with a grin that spread from ear to ear across his young face, he said, 'My thanks to you my lord, I will perform great deeds for you in the North.'

'Just fight well and stay alive,' answered Edric as he turned and beckoned the next man forward.

It turned out to be a long day in a month of long days with Edric rejecting four out of every five men who came before him. By the middle of the month of May his small army numbered a mere sixty-eight men, yet each of those sixty-eight men had been tried and tested either on the battlefield, or had faced Edric in a mock battle, which had been performed on the one small piece of level land in the centre of Wentnor. Edric received several cuts and slashes, but most of his opponents had come out of the fray with savage cuts and bruises, apart from one man who had fallen badly, breaking his right wrist, thus eliminating himself from the enterprise.

The trickle of men seemed to dry up in the last few days of May, giving Edric more and more time to train his men, a thing which he fell to with gusto, shouting and bullying them into what he hoped would be the finest and most disciplined unit to join King William's army. Yet to date that hope was far from being fulfilled for, whilst most of his men were seasoned warriors, most of them had little or no idea of coordinated attack or retreat, causing Edric to shake his head in despair at the shambles that seemed to erupt whenever he attempted something that even resembling a difficult movement.

Also, much to his disappointment, he had recruited a mere eleven archers.

These were men who bore white scars on their left arms from the lash of their bowstrings, and possessed bodies that appeared to be misshapen due to the muscles that they had developed on their arms, chests and shoulders.

He was rather disappointed with this small number of men, but on the other side of the blade, he was happy with the quality of the men that he had chosen.

Remembering one of the lessons that old Vorta had drilled into his young head when he was a boy, reiterating it time and time again by saying, 'Ten trained warriors could easily defeat fifty farmers.'

He expected that an odd man would join him over the next couple of weeks but feared that he would not have the expected number of men ready, unless

Garth re-appeared out of the Welsh mountains with a good number of Welsh bowmen.

*****

Garth, however, was just as frustrated as was his lord and friend Edric. He had been forced to linger for a further two days whilst he and Emrys nursed the wounded Dyffid who seemed to alternate from appearing to be well on the way towards a speedy recovery, only to fall back into a virtual coma a few hours later.

Garth had tried all the remedies he knew including using up the large supply of honey that he had found in a large earthenware jar on a shelf in the cottage.

He had soaked the man's wounds in the herb that the old people called all-heal forcing the old man to drink a concoction of one large spoonful of honey, juice from willow leaves and (even though he was not sure of the correct amount, which he knew could be a remedy that could kill just as easy as it could cure) he even used the juice from the leaves of mistletoe.

Yet the man still hovered between life and death.

On the third morning Garth opened the door and was about to gaze across the misty lake. Yet was totally shocked when he saw some twenty feet away, on the edge of the tree line, veiled by the morning mist, the outlines of more than a dozen horsemen sitting silently on their mounts, gazing at him.

He gripped his great war-axe tighter, bringing it up across his chest. Yet at that moment he felt a nudge behind him, and the small figure of Emrys joined him in the doorway.

'By Thor's blood,' swore Garth. 'Who the devil are they?'

He started to walk towards the waiting horsemen, but stopped just as suddenly as he started for the moment he began to approach them, at least half of them brought up their small hunting bows and stretching their bowstrings fully taunt, aimed their stocky hunting arrows at his chest.

Courageous he may be, but his long experience in the ways of war instantly told him that one man, no matter how brave he may be, or even how speedy he may run, would have little or no chance against half a dozen bowmen, especially so, if they happened to be mounted bowmen.

'Wait!' yelled Emrys as he strode past Garth. Holding his right hand aloft he walked boldly up towards the still silent riders, who still pointed their short hunting bows at the now stationary figure of Garth.

Garth watched as Emrys walked up to the riders, where he began to speak to them. Although he could not hear what they were saying, even if he could have heard, he would have been unable to understand the language, but the bows were slowly lowered.

Then the bowmen removed the arrows and replaced them in the quivers the riders had attached to their saddles, indicating to him that the danger had passed.

Their voices grew louder, followed by nods and smiles, then a laugh from one of the men, who dismounted and, followed by the rest of the band who remained in their saddles, they led their small, shaggy hill ponies forward towards Garth.

'So you are the famous Garth Bloodaxe, are you not?' said the man who appeared to be the leader of this small band of riders. Yet whilst Garth did understand what the man had said, he found it difficult to follow the man's speech. It had a lilt to it that, in Garth's mind almost making the man sound as if he was drunk.

'I am,' said Garth, forcing his lips into a difficult and unaccustomed smile, very surprised that his name was known in these far off, distant mountains.

'There's glad I am to meet you,' said the leader as he dismounted and strode forward with his right hand stretched out in friendship.

Garth took his hand and was pleased to feel the strength and the genuine warmth that the man's hand conveyed to him.

'And you have slain the very bear that we have been hunting for these last six days,' he said with a wide grin emitting from out of his grey mottled beard.

However, before Garth could do aught but nod, the man continued, 'And the bear nearly took you to heaven with him, so I hear from my young nephew here.'

This was rather a lot for Garth to take in all in one go. He now realized what Emrys had been telling them that had caused the riders to chuckle, but he had also just learned that this man, the leader of this band of hunters, was none other than another uncle of his companion Emrys, so he spoke without thinking, saying, 'Nephew? So you are another uncle of young Emrys. How many uncles does the boy have?'

'Oh, bloody dozens,' cried the man, laughing as the words left his lips, and the rest of the group joined in the laughter. The man explained, 'I am Evan the Bwylch, leader of this small band of rogues and he' – he pointed towards a man of a similar age – 'is my brother, Evan the Betwys; and that man there' – he pointed to a small thin man on a mangy pony – 'is Evan the Bryn, and, him, him, and him,' he said, 'are also my brothers, and there are four others at home, and between us we have fifty-seven children, and we are all related to everyone who lives in and around Llanyfydd, and Trefnant, so the good Lord alone knows how many uncles and nephews and nieces the boy has.'

After another bout of laughing, with one of the younger men rolling about on the floor in fits of laughter, they eventually calmed down, until Evan the Bwylch said, as he wiped the tears from under his eyes, 'Young Emrys also tells me that you not only slew the bear, but have tarried here longer than you wished to do so, in order to tend to the wounds of Dyffid of Pen-y-felin.'

Again, Garth nodded, for he had not realised that young Emrys had told this man so much in so short a time.

Evan continued, 'And that you are in our mountains looking for men to join your new King William in his war against Malcolm of Scotland.'

Garth nodded in agreement, realising what a difficult task Lord Edric had given him. For in truth, he could see no real reason why these men should travel to the far ends of the country to serve a man they had been at war with from the first few weeks that William and his Norman warriors had first set their booted feet on the shores of this land. Yet he knew how these men from their warrior based society prided themselves as fearless warriors; men who loved to fight. He also knew that promise of loot and wealth would also add to their eagerness to join him.

Evan the Bwylch interrupted his thoughts by saying, in a voice that had such a strong Welsh accent making it very difficult to understand what the man was saying, 'We will take you and Uncle Dyffid with us to Rhuddlan with us, where

Blodwyn the Healer will look after Dyffid, and you can plead your cause with our Prince, Bleddyn the Blessed.'

A litter was speedily made from the willow trees that grew alongside the lake and Dyffid was placed on it.

The men speedily covered the litter with two fleeces that were selected from the many fleeces that lined the walls of Dyffid's cottage. He was then strapped tightly to the litter that had been slung between two of the older and quieter ponies, and they slowly made their way westwards towards their tribal homelands at Rhuddlan.

The journey to Rhuddlan was slow and tiresome, due to the litter that held Dyffid, taking the riders over a day and a half before they reached the town that stood on a small rise alongside a crystal-clear river that appeared to be teeming with fish.

As soon as the leading horsemen appeared in the valley the sound of horns seemed to echo from one hillside to the next, causing Garth to smile with inner knowledge and perhaps with a little pleasure as he saw people and animals being driven through the gates of the small fortress, long before the riders were within half a mile of the town.

What seemed like moments later, the gates were thrown wide open allowing scores of people to seethe through the open gates shouting and waving their arms high in the air with joy at seeing the party of hunters that had left their own township many days ago, loudly cheering at their menfolk's safe return.

'Ah,' exclaimed Evan the Bwylch. 'I see that they have finally recognised us, about time too.' He made a grunting noise in throat.

Their cheers grew louder when they saw the bearskin draped over the saddle of the proud Evan the Bwylch. Yet when they saw Garth who was lagging at the rear of the horsemen, their shouts of joy fell silent. They sullenly watched his huge frame that seemed to swamp his mount, as he rode silently through the crowd.

They passed through the gates, and were forced to push their way through the crowds of people who had ceased their chores and had come to watch the return of the hunting party, groaning loudly as they noticed the sick man on the litter, and the strange Englishman whose name was now being whispered from one man to another. 'It's Garth Bloodaxe. Sweet heaven; just look at the size of that battleaxe!' For they had all heard stories of Wild Edric and his close companion, Garth bloodaxe.

Dyffid was taken out of the small cavalcade towards the hut of Blodwyn the Healer. This hut was unlike the rest of the dwellings, standing apart from the other houses which seemed to crowd one upon another in such a fashion that, on several occasions, the riders found it difficult to move through the township towards the King's dwelling.

When the riders reached a small clear spot that in some ways resembled an English village green, they reined in their ponies before a large thatched building that was obviously the residence of the King.

The crowd's mutterings seemed to Garth to resemble a windy day in the forest when the treetops are blown about, sometimes in noisy gusts, whilst at other times in hushed, almost reverent whispers.

The noise slowly abated as the large oak, nail-studded door was thrown open, to allow the wizened figure of a white-bearded, bald-headed man to hobble through. A man who seemed so ancient he could only walk slowly with the support of a sturdy youth who held him firmly on his right side, whilst in his other hand he leant heavily upon a stout ornately carved stick.

'Ah, it is my old friend Garth Bloodaxe,' said the man in a weak, croaky voice.

Garth looked closer at the man but failed to recognize him despite the fact that the man's voice did seem familiar.

'Oh, I see that you do not know your old friend,' he croaked.

Garth shook his head and said with a half-smile. 'No, I'm sorry to say, although your face does look familiar.'

'I admit that I have aged a little since we last met, but I did not think I'd changed that much.' He shook his head as he spoke, as his face tried its best to muster a sad smile.

Garth could not think what to say, certain that the man was mistaken and that he had never met him before and he was perhaps in his dotage, going the way that he had seen many old people go.

'We last fought together at Hereford,' said the other, 'and I would have thought that you would at least know your old friend Bleddyn.'

Garth was shocked, as well as being slightly shamefaced for not recognizing Bleddyn. For the man had once been a good friend of his, and yet in the few short years that had passed, he had changed from being a strong, robust and virile man into an old man, a man who looked far older than his years.

'Of course, how remiss of me not to recognize you,' said Garth, as he approached Bleddyn, placing his huge arms around the wizened man's shoulders. He kissed him on his cheek, saying, 'I too must be getting old, for it seems that a lot of water has passed under the bridge since we last met.'

'You are being too kind old friend,' said the Welsh King. 'I know full well how ill the years have treated me, and that my days on this earth are numbered.'

Garth gazed with fondness at the man, remembering some of the happier times that they had shared, but unable (as was his way) to put his feelings into words.

Bleddyn, seeing Garth's dilemma said, 'Nay my friend, the bards already sing of my death. It is certain. Both the priests and the druids tell me so.'

'All death is certain,' answered Garth with a wry smile.

Bleddyn gave a happier smile, nodding his head weakly in agreement, then his thin face broke into a sad smile when a commotion broke out in the crowd, and a younger man pushed his way through the throng.

'I'll wager that you will recognize this youngster,' he wheezed.

Garth turned to face the crowd and looked for the reason that had broken the crowd's silence, and was surprised to see the sturdy figure of Hywell ap-Bleddyn.

'Hywell, son of Bleddyn,' cried Garth as he strode to meet the young man, whose arms were already wide open as he, in turn, strode forward in order to greet his old friend Garth.

'There's good it is to see you,' beamed Hywell, as the two met and reached up and placed his hands on Garth's enormous shoulders, adding, 'and it really is you, just as big and as ugly as ever.'

Garth chuckled with the joy at seeing his friend again and thumped the younger man on the back with one of his huge hands, knocking the breath out of the younger man's lungs.

'Come Father,' said Hywell. 'Let us sit and provide our honoured guest with food and wine for he must be weary after his long journey. And I am sure that we all have a lot of tales to tell, for many a long year has passed since we last met.'

Garth was ushered through a large oak door into a larger room where servants were in the process of bringing in food and drink which they were placing unceremoniously onto a large table before literally running back towards the scullery, which Garth assumed to be to the rear of the house, in order to bring in more food and drink.

Suddenly the hall went quiet, causing Garth to pause whilst in the motion of bringing his drinking tankard up to his mouth. He looked over the motionless tankard to see that three women had entered the room and were standing silently near the door, watching the men.

'Ah, I think that you may remember my lady wife, the fair Davina,' said Bleddyn, as he nodded towards his wife, who upon his acknowledgement of her presence, slowly walked, followed by her two maidservants, across the room, striding haughtily past the now silent men with her head held high and her ample chest thrust forward. Whereupon, on reaching Bleddyn she gave a slight curtsey, kissing her aging husband on his pallid cheek,

She then moved to Hywell who she also kissed on his cheek and uttered a single word, 'Son,' before turning her face towards their guest.

She made a deep curtsey towards Garth and said, 'I remember you Garth of the Bloodaxe, even if you do not remember me.'

'Oh, I remember you well my lady,' answered Garth, adding, 'but for your courage at Winnington, my Lord Edric would not be alive this day.'

''Twas not courage but was anger that slew my father,' she replied haughtily, abruptly turning again towards her husband saying, 'Come Bleddyn, you look tired and it is time for the healer who awaits you in your chamber.

Bleddyn merely nodded, rose from his chair and was helped out of the room by his wife.

Garth watched with interest as Bleddyn and his wife left the room, remembering the last time that he had seen Hywell's mother, which was at the battle of Winnington, when she had slain her own father, Madoc the Lucky.

At that time she had been one of the few Welsh battle-maidens in her father's army, and had fought against Edric and his English warriors with savage fury, but had, for a reason known only to herself, slain her own father in order to prevent further bloodshed.

'Yes,' he thought to himself as he watched them leave, 'She is still the wild Welsh battle-maiden that she has always been. A true daughter of her father Madoc the Lucky, perhaps a little heavier, but still a beauty. Aye, he mused, still quite a beauty. She has found her kingdom here. Good for her.'

'Idris!' called Hywell to a servant, forcing Garth out of his melancholy mood. 'Go and fetch Evan the Bwylch and,' turning to Garth, he asked him, 'What was the name of the youngster who brought you here?'

'Emrys,' answered Garth.

'Aye, that was the name.' And he bellowed at the top of his voice. 'And bring young Emrys and a couple of Evan the Bwylch's brothers. There's plenty here for all.' As he grabbed a roast partridge which he began to devour.

The man nodded and hastened through the door to carry out Hywell's bidding.

During the meal, as Hywell continued to stuff prodigious amounts of roast pork into his mouth, he quizzed Garth about his mission.

'How many men will Edric be taking?' he asked.

'Around a hundred.'

'How long will the war last?' he asked peering into his friend's eyes as he spoke.

'Who can say?' was the answer. 'Till it ends,'

'What about the loot?' he asked casually as if it was of little importance, knowing full well, as did Garth, that loot and booty was one of the main reasons that warriors, and especially the chieftains and the kings of Wales joined this sort of an enterprise.

'All gold goes to William.'

'Hum,' he rubbed his short brown beard. 'What about the silver?'

'Yours for the taking.'

'Cattle? Sheep? Women?'

'Aye, as many as you can carry,' answered Garth with a laugh as he emptied his wooden flagon of its dark brown beer.

'Well, to be honest with you,' confided Hywell, 'life here is sweet, but tedious, and in truth I could certainly use a little excitement. And I must admit that I have always had a yen to see the Roman wall, which is, I believe something to behold.'

'Wouldn't know,' answered Garth. 'Never seen it myself, probably a bit like Offa's Dyke, I suppose.'

'I have a lot of young men here who are bored with sheep and cattle and would readily join me if there is loot and women to be had.'

Garth nodded and held his flagon out to the serving wench for a re-fill.

'I'll not take anyone mind you,' said Garth. 'Only the best; good bowmen and they must be steady.'

'Oh I'll help Edric fill his ranks,' said Hywell as he took a sip at his own silver tankard, and carried on as if he was speaking to himself. 'Aye, they must be steady. Proven warriors, I know of many a good man who will be only too willing to stretch their legs for a bit of excitement and a slave woman or two.' He smiled evilly as he spoke. 'There's Pryce ap-Owen, and Howell of Ruthin, now he's a good man with a bow, can take a squirrel out of a tree at a hundred paces, can't go back to Ruthin though, killed his brother-in-law there. Hang him they would, if he dare to set foot in the place.'

And so he went on, naming men of the village and the surrounding valleys, selecting some whilst he rejected others, for one reason or another.

Some were too old.

Some had injuries, old and new, or ailed in one way or another.

Some he rejected because of their temperaments, being too foolhardy or too timid, making remarks like. 'Scared of his own shadow that one.' Or, 'Never goes out at night, frightened like.' Or, 'Many a maiden in the village is braver than him.'

As the evening progressed more and more men joined them, filling the hall with men drinking, chatting and singing until Garth and Hywell could hardly hear themselves speak until a young woman strode into this world of men. Closing the door gently behind her, she strode into the middle of the room where she stood and nodded towards a youth by the doorway holding a large harp. The young man smiled and, heaving the harp upright, he strained as he carried the heavy instrument up to the woman, where he deposited it alongside her, placing a three-legged stool that he had carried strapped to his back, alongside the harp.

The noisy room fell into a hush as the woman sat on the stool and plucked a single note on the harp.

''Tis Myfanwye the harpist,' whispered Hwyell, causing Garth to study the woman more closely, discovering to his surprise that she was in fact a very young girl, hardly more than a child with a startling white face that was partially covered by a tangle of dark hair that fell almost to her breast.

She plucked at the harp, slowly at first. A lilt that seemed to send every man into a trance, before taking them into the valleys and hills of their country as her fingers raced over the strings with such speed that the melodies that she played seemed to be plucked out of the very air the men breathed, or perhaps out of the clouds that covered the mountains and not of earthly making.

Myfanwye the harpist played late into the night and not a single warrior, drunk or sober so much as coughed to interrupt her beautiful music.

When she eventually left the men continued their drinking late into the night and eventually went slightly tipsy but happily to their beds.

Hywell with the thoughts of the thrill of battles to come and of the loot that he would bring home, whilst Garth drifted off to sleep dreaming of how pleased Edric would be when he arrived back in Wentnor with a large contingent of armed Welshmen.

CHAPTER 36

'I'm not riding to the far ends of the country to fight the damned Scots,' stormed Blondell. 'Why should I risk everything I have here when I can send Bugger and a few of the men in my place?'

'Oh I just thought that it would be a good gesture, and would show your gratitude and your loyalty to our new King,' answered Freya, 'and who knows, you may perform some daring deeds, and he would then bestow more manors and lands upon us.'

But in truth her head was really spinning, for she had already planned that her husband would indeed ride to the north with some of the men, especially one or two of the older men to whom she had taken a dislike. Plus the fact that she thought, indeed she hoped that he would be stupid enough to go and get himself killed. That would leave her a rich young widow, free to pursue her affair with Edward, who was the son of the shire-reeve with whom she had already met on a number of occasions. He was a lusty young man, some eleven years younger than her, and was completely besotted with the beautiful Lady Freya from Yeovil.

'No,' reiterated her Husband. 'I am not for this war, 'I will send Bugger and five of my fine Normans plus a few no-good English layabouts and ne'er-do-wells. Kit 'em up with a spear and a shield and send them up to swell King William's army. That should be enough to satisfy my quota.'

'They'll not miss me,' he added as he stormed out of the room, then out of the front door of the newly built manor house and across the courtyard towards the men's quarters.

'Damn and blast,' swore Freya, muttering quietly to herself. 'So it looks like I have to go back to the hemlock, or perhaps put a few toadstools into the next mushroom stew.' Slowly she followed her husband out of the room, smiling to herself as she envisaged her next meeting with the young and lusty Edward.

CHAPTER 37

Horns sounded from the small tower, sending men towards their weapons and the women and children to the safety of the fortress.

All eyes peered through the morning mist towards the plain where a large knot of marching men loomed. Their heads and shoulders were above the morning mist, appearing to the watchers as if they were being attacked by armed men who had no legs.

The attacking army were gliding silently across the plain towards them, their weapons shining in the morning sun.

Herd boys drove their cattle through the gates before the gates were slammed shut with a loud thud, and shepherds whistled and yelled at their dogs as they drove their small flocks of sheep around the lower slopes below the small town, hoping to reach the dense forest of Clunn before the attackers could reach them.

Godda joined Edric on the parapet where they both shielded their eyes against the glare of the sun that had appeared over the long mountain a mere hour ago.

'Who are they?' asked Godda.

'Can't make them out,' answered her husband. Then he shouted to a young man who had joined them and said in a loud voice, 'Your eyes are younger than mine, Edwin, can you see who they are?'

'Nay, Lord Edric,' came the answer. 'They show no banners.'

'How are they dressed?' asked Edric.

'Can't really see my lord, But I think that they be not Englishmen.'

The marching men vanished under the brow of the hill, giving Edric time to leave his wife on the walkway, then dash down the steps and across the green towards his longhall, where he quickly snatched up his mail-shirt and after struggling as quickly as he could into it, grabbed his sword and shield before he raced back across the green and up the steps to re-join Godda and the other man on the walkway.

'Where are they now?' he asked.

'Still under the hill.'

'They will be up with us soon,' answered the sentry.

'Archers. Are you ready?' Edric shouted.

'Ready!' came the reply as the bowmen tested their strings.

'Don't loose until I give the word,' snapped Edric as he looked along the line of archers who stood on the walkway, gazing nervously down the slope that led up to the small fortress of Wentnor.

The tops of the spears, then helmets appeared over the brow, followed by faces that slowly became clearer, led by the figure of a giant of a man who strode some ten paces before the main band of men.

Edric whooped for joy, dropping his shield as he held his hands high in the air.

'Hold your shafts!' he yelled. 'They are friends, and are led by none other than that big oaf, Garth.' He turned and ran down the wooden steps taking them two at a time as he made for the gate.

'Open the gates,' he yelled to the startled guards, who had been unable to see the approaching band of warriors from their position on the inside of the gates. They looked quite alarmed when they saw their lord and master hurtling towards them, waving his arms as if he was a madman.

He was through the gates and half-way down the hill before Garth and his Welshmen saw him, causing a couple of them to grasp for their weapons, thinking themselves attacked by one of those legendary Saxon and Norse berserkers.

Garth met him halfway, slapping and hugging his friend and leader in a very un-English way.

At last they calmed down a little; Garth, from the euphoria of fulfilling his mission and returning home, without mishap, and with a large contingent of Welsh warriors. Edric delighted, not only to see his old friend again but more than pleased to see the large band of grim Welsh warriors aligned behind him.

'How many?' asked Edric.

'Sixty-one.'

'Wonderful, now we really are a force to be reckoned with. With the seventy-three men who I have gathered, your sixty-one gives us a total of one hundred and thirty-four. Are they all good men?' he asked.

'Aye, my lord they are. All chosen men by Hywell and Bleddyn themselves.'

'Are they both here? I cannot see them.'

'Nay, Lord Edric,' came the answer with a shake of his massive head. 'King Bleddyn is on his deathbed and his son Hywell could not leave him. It is important that he is with his father in his last moments, or he cannot inherit the Kingdom. It is their custom. But, he has promised to join us as soon as his inheritance is secure.'

'And Rhiwallon?'

'Nay, my Lord, he too is past his days of war.'

'Oh, I see. That is sad news, I have fond memories of both of them.'

'They did desert you at Hereford,' Garth reminded him.

'Maybe so, but they had enjoyed their little war and had amassed the loot that they joined us for so in their minds it was time for them to go home. It is their way.'

'Aye,' grunted Garth, for although he too held both of the men in high esteem, he still found their ways alien to the way that he and his people thought, In his own mind he considered that once a man had betrayed him (as he thought their actions had) then nothing but death could wipe out the dishonour.

He shook his head as if to clear his mind of such thoughts, then turned towards Edric saying with more than a little pride in his gruff voice. 'Enough of old wounds, let me introduce you to my small army,' and beckoned a rough-looking man forward.

'This is Evan the Bwylch who is a chieftain amongst his people, and a man, who I have been told can shoot a swallow out of the air with that longbow of his.'

Evan the Bwylch placed his bow into his left hand as he gripped Edric's hand with his own right hand in a grip that would have crippled the hand of a lesser man. 'Right proud I am to meet you, Edric Sylvaticus, although from what I have heard of you, I had expected you to be a giant of a man, at least twice the size of our good friend here,' he nodded towards Garth and, smiling at his own joke, or at least what Edric hoped had been a joke, and not a slight, for although he had given Edric his full name, he had not called him 'my lord,' nor had he nodded his head in acknowledgement of Edric's status.

Edric looked into the man's warm grey eyes but could see no malice there, merely friendliness and strength, so he smiled back, warmly thanking the man for joining his venture. He said it with a slight Welsh accent, a habit that he always found himself falling into whenever he was in the company of Welshmen.

'Pleased I am that you and your men have come to join us, and I must say that your warriors do have the look of men who will stand in a shieldwall and will give a good account of themselves in battle.'

'They will that, have no fear,' came the reply.

Then he added, as if as an afterthought. 'Handpicked they are, every last one of them. The best bowmen in the whole of Wales they are.' With an impish grin that would have done a fourteen-year-old girl credit, he added, 'And England too.'

'Mayhap, we shall see,' retorted Edric, trying to match the man's boast and his smile.

'Come,' said Edric as he turned and accompanied Evan the Bwylch up towards the small fortress, 'I will show you where your men can make their encampment, but you, of course will share my own house as my honoured guest.'

'My brother too,' said the Welsh leader.

'I beg your pardon,' said Edric, shocked by the Welsh chieftain's bluntness.

'My brother too,' repeated Evan the Bwylch, 'or he will be offended, for he is my own brother is he not?'

Edric was in half a mind to refuse the demand, fearing that if he agreed to invite this brother into his home, then there may be other brothers in the band who might also be offended. Then perhaps he would offend the whole warband, causing the lot of them to turn tail and he would lose sixty-one Welshmen in one fell swoop.

'How many other brothers do you have here?' asked Edric, trying his best to smile and be friendly as he uttered the words.

'Ha-ha,' laughed Evan the Bwylch, saying with a grin. 'He is the only one here with us today, all the others decided to stay home and protect the sheep, and of course to support Prince Hywell's claim to his kingdom.'

'In that case,' said Edric with a slight smile and a lot of relief, 'he is more than welcome to join us.'

Evan the Bwylch turned and beckoned his brother forward, and a man, slightly younger and much the same height as his brother stepped out of the knot of Welshmen who had clustered around the two leaders.

'This is my brother, Evan the Betwys.' He indicated to a man who was practically an identical twin to his brother except for a row of white hairs that marred his otherwise perfectly black, trimmed beard that adorned the lower half of his face. The white hairs were a scar from some distant battle some years since.

The man nodded respectfully to Edric and said with a smile, 'Good it is to meet you Lord Edric, for your deeds are much talked about in the mountains of

Wales.'

Edric shook the man's hand and beckoned him to follow him into the longhall, saying, 'You are both very welcome in my house.' As he entered the second room, he added, 'My wife Godda will have a serving girl show you to your room as soon as you have eaten.'

As the men warily entered the front door, they both took off their leather war-caps and said almost in unison, 'God bless this house,' which was a normal thing to do for a man of Wales as he entered any house, other than his own.

They sat respectfully at the table, eating with the manners of men used to having servants (or perhaps slaves) to wait upon them.

After they had both drank three tankards of Godda's best ale and consumed most of the contents of the table, including two helpings of Godda's famous apple and blackberry pie, covered with fresh cream. They sat back and, rubbing their bloated stomachs, complimenting her on the meal, saying, again almost in unison, 'Best apple and blackberry pie I have ever eaten.'

No mention was made upon the rest of the meal, just the pie.

After they had been shown to their sleeping quarters, Godda said to Edric, with a very distinct huff in her voice, 'So they liked my apple and blackberry pie, but what about the rest of the meal? Was that not good enough for them? I'll warrant they don't get a spread as good as that very often up in their Welsh mountains.' She then haughtily stormed out of the room.

Edric smiled to himself, shaking his head, for he knew full well that, bleak as the Welsh mountains were, there was indeed an abundance of good food to be had there, not only from the wild game that teemed in the mountains and valleys, but also from the lowlands and valley bottoms which produced beef, lamb, oats, barley and root crops second to none.

When they eventually went to bed, Edric mellowed her mood a little by saying, with a chuckle, 'Well I agree with them. Your apple and blackberry pie is the best I've ever tasted too.'

After a hearty breakfast the two Welsh chieftains accompanied Edric down the slope to the lower ground where both his own men and the newly arrived Welshmen were camped. Then with the help of his newly found friends the three of them, plus the towering figure of Garth, began organizing their men into some sort of order.

'First we must arrange the men into three spear groups. The first should be the bowmen, both Welsh and English, who, I suggest should be under your leadership,' he turned to the younger brother.

'The second should be the bulk of our forces who we will need to train to hold a shieldwall, and that, I think should be my own duty, if you agree,' he said as he turned to the elder brother Evan the Bwylch.

The elder brother nodded, slightly bemused, still not knowing what part Edric wanted him to play in the proceedings.

'And again, if you agree,' said Edric, 'I would like you to train your third of our men as a reserve force who will be able to fill any gap and plug any hole that may appear anywhere in our line.'

Evan the Bwylch still looked a little bemused and very disappointed for he was a man of action, and a man who much preferred to be in the forefront of any battle and not loitering around behind the fighting men waiting to be called, or mayhap never to be called into the fight.

Edric could see the concern on his face, so he tried to console the man by saying to him.

'If, God forbid, I should fall, or mayhap your own brother is slain – and we all pray that will not happen – then you and Garth must take command of our men and try to save the day as well as the rest of our men.'

The man's face mellowed a little, and then broke out into a smile as Edric added, 'Your men must be able to protect our archers, AND fill in any gaps that should appear in the shieldwall.'

Stressing the point, he added, 'They must always be in a position to dash through our wall to slay and pursue our enemies if and when they turn tail and run.'

He was nodding now, as he began to agree with Edric, saying, 'Aye Edric, that seems fair enough, but don't even dream of excluding me or my men from the fighting, cause, look you, that is not going to happen.'

The organizing of the three arms of their small army proved to be even more difficult than he had anticipated. All of the Welshmen without exception wanted to be in the shieldwall and thus, in the fore of any fighting that might take place. It was only by a lot of persuasion, plus a lot of bullying that the two Welsh chieftains finally managed to persuade about a third of their warriors to join Evan the Bwylch in his third division.

Edric was more than delighted with the Welsh archers. They were as good, if not better than his own English bowmen, but the Welsh warriors who were to form part of Edric's shieldwall simply refused to obey orders, declining to remain in the shieldwall when they rehearsed attacks on the shieldwall. Charging out to pursue their own private battles with the attacking warriors, they literally seethed out of the shieldwall, leaving huge holes through which any average enemy commander would use to his advantage and that, as Edric knew full well, would almost certainly lead to defeat.

Three days of strenuous training.

Three days of shouting and bellowing orders until their throats were sore improved the situation a little but Edric realized that, in the heat of a real battle, the Welsh warriors would almost certainly return to their old ways, leaving the shieldwall open, thus exposing their comrades to fend for themselves.

The only man who did not take part in the training was the large ragged figure of Ordgar the Bear, who sat impassively on a grassy bank alongside his wolfhound as the two of them passively watched the sweating warriors perform the same manoeuvre, over and over again, until such time as their mentors deemed it to be satisfactory.

Edric knew well that Ordgar would not fit into any formal formation and that the only way that this huge man and his equally huge dog could be used in war would be to use them as a battering ram when trying to break through a stubborn shieldwall. Or perhaps scatter a particularly difficult knot of determined warriors, besides, none of the other men could tolerate the man or his dog, perhaps, he thought it was because that together they made a ferocious team, or maybe it was that they both smelled as foul as one another.

Edric's Norman friend Walter de Lacy appeared at noon on the day before Edric had named as 'the day of departure' bringing with him the ten men, as he had promised.

De Lacy rode a white stallion which was bedecked with chain mail, whilst he wore a gaudy, expensive chain mail suit plus the most ornate helmet that Edric had ever seen. For around the edge of his mail and around the rim of the helmet, a master craftsman – for none other than a master craftsman – had installed the alternating gold and silver links that had been individually cut and welded around the entire shirt as well as the rim of the helmet.

His saddle, sword and scabbard were equally ornate, having inlaid gold around the hilt and the pommel.

Whilst Edric admired the workmanship, he had grave misgivings about the use of such soft metals as gold and silver in battle. They would surely break when struck by sword, axe or mace, and this sort of ornate display would certainly make its wearer stand out in a shieldwall, thus making its owner a prime target for every opponent seeking loot from the battlefield.

He greeted his friend genially saying, 'Welcome good Walter, you and your fine fellows are most welcome,' then invited the Norman lord into his home, as was the custom when one lord greeted another.

Nonetheless the day for leaving arrived much too early for Edric's liking. With much shouting, loud lowing from the cattle, plus the ceaseless bleating from the sheep that were to accompany the warriors for food on the hoof Edric and his small army left the safety of their small fortress and streamed down the hillside and into the valley on their journey northwards

Travelling only as fast as the sheep and cattle would allow they journeyed along the valley towards the hamlet of Hope trudging down the winding, heavily wooded Hope Valley, making their first camp alongside a pleasant, crystal-clear stream at Pontesford.

The Welshmen had commenced to sing almost as soon as they had left Westbury and it seemed to Edric and, he felt sure, to most of his fellow Englishmen that as much as they enjoyed the singing, and despite the fact that hardly any of them could understand a single word, they enjoyed the pleasant melodies. For their Welsh allies seemed to sing when they were happy, sing when they were miserable, sing when their feet ached, sing when they were wet through to the skin.

Eventually the singing did annoy one or two of Edric's warriors causing a few to grumble, as one grim-faced English warrior commented with a wry smile. 'Don't the buggers ever stop bloody singing?'

They sang marching songs as they walked

Merry songs, when they crossed bogs and marshes.

Sad, lyrical songs as they waded through streams and rivers, soaked to the skin but still they sang as they held their weapons high above their heads in order to keep them dry.

Some of the songs were sad laments as they stoically trudged on through the pouring rain.

On the first night four of the sheep were slaughtered, and most of the men enjoyed a meal of roast lamb, plus a bite or two of dried stockfish, which was the usual stable diet of warriors on the war-trail.

On the second day they crossed the wide river Sabrina at Montford where there had once been a Roman bridge. Yet that had long since been washed away when the Sabrina had been in spate, an occurrence that usually happened several times each winter and oft-times in the spring and summer seasons.

Pressing on until they reached the old fortress of Oswestry, where the unfortunate King Oswald had lost his life and his township to Hywell's grandsire, the Welsh chieftain Madoc the lucky, many years ago.

The following day they had a long march along the flatlands to the fortress of Chester where they camped outside the town and partook of the many meats and pies that the citizens brought out to them. Yet despite the fact that they were on the King's errand, the Norman caretaker, perhaps fearing treachery, did not open his gates to them.

After Chester, the dilapidated Roman road went westwards to Flint and Holywell and then eastwards towards the Midland shires, leading them away from the sweet-smelling estuary and into the heartlands of the country.

In ten days they were near their destination, making their way up the Roman road that had been called the Great North Road for over a hundred years, but in Edric's mind had been sorely misnamed, for it was now little more than a muddy track, meandering around bogs and marshes that had once been drained, wading through streams and rivers that had once been crossed by Roman bridges. It also forced the weary men to march around forest giants that had fallen across the road, where past travellers and local inhabitants had simply made their way around the fallen trees rather than hack their way through, or even haul them off the once proud road, hence the road had many hairpin bends where once it had been straight.

After a cold breakfast of dry meat, a handful of oatmeal and a bite of dried stockfish, Edric and his men left the peasants with whom they had spent the night and proceeded at a steady pace through the empty countryside until they reached the main highway. They fell in with a large throng of warriors who were all hurrying along the muddy, rutted road towards the gathering point that the King had set up some ten miles to the north.

That evening the new Prince Hywell, with two of his father's personal bodyguards appeared as fresh as a spring day, looking as if they had all been out for a pleasant day's ride.

'Well now,' said the smiling Welsh Prince, 'I was worried that it would all be over long before we caught up with you. And here you are, only halfway up and nary a Scottish warrior in sight, idling here and enjoying yourself on the banks of yon river.'

Edric was delighted to see his old friend again, and in truth had discounted the fact that Hywell would join them, surmising that Hywell's father could have lingered for many days or perhaps weeks, which would have meant that Hywell would be forced to stay with him.

He had also thought that there might have been a problem with some of his rival kinfolk, which could well have forced Hywell to remain in the Welsh mountains until his small realm had been made more secure.

The warriors were accompanied by the usual horde of camp followers who ranged from wives or girlfriends of the warriors, helpers and servants, cooks, and shield carriers, farriers driving their two-wheeled carts, that carried the tools of their trade, butchers driving small herds of cattle, shepherds and goat men ushering their animals along with the help of well-trained dogs, as well as numerous other people. Many of these were, or so it appeared to Edric, little or no use whatsoever to the army, and were likely to be naught but an hindrance when the army met with the enemy.

After a tense couple of hours, which seemed to consist of constantly trying to steer Chieftain away from any man or animal who shuffled too close to him and was, therefore in dire danger of being bitten or trampled to death by the savage stallion, Edric was pleased when, at long last, the mass of men who made up this huge army eventually halted for the night.

*****

Edric and his small army eventually reached the outskirts of the King's encampment.

Leaving his men in an area where they could spend the night, he was eventually directed to the area where he was told that the King would be. After making his way through the huge encampment where, after many mis-directions, he eventually approached the heavily guarded palisade of sharpened logs that surrounded a large white tent that served as the King's temporary quarters.

He and de Lacy approached the two savage-looking sentries who stood outside the entrance of the very elaborate tent saying, 'I am Edric of the borderlands, and have been summoned by the King to attend him.'

The elder and most senior of the two sentries looked down his nose at the mud-splattered, weary traveller, and with a look of sheer contempt said to the other man, 'Watch him while I see if he is allowed in.' He turned to Edric and said, 'What was your name again?'

'Lord Edric of the sylvatieus borderlands,' answered Edric, rather annoyed by the guards' attitude, so he added with more than a little contempt of his own. 'Wild Edric, some call me, and if you don't shift your carcass and tell the King that I am here with over a hundred and thirty seasoned warriors, you will find out just how wild I can be.'

The man, unaffected by the threat, casually turned and disappeared into the depths of the tent.

Edric heard shouting within and, although he could not make out what was being said, he guessed that it had been the King, for the guard literally ran out of the tent (minus the spear that had accompanied him into the tent) with his iron helmet askew and a very red blotch on his right cheek.

'The King bids you to attend him,' he stammered.

An amused Edric and de Lacy strode past him, Edric brushing his shoulder as he did so, savagely nudging the man out of his way.

He found the young King William, called by many William Rufus due to his ruddy complexion, surrounded by a knot of his noblemen who were all bent over a table discussing details of a map that was laid out before them.

All heads turned to Edric as he entered, then one man left the group and with his right hand stretched out in greeting and with a smile on his clean-shaven face moved towards Edric.

'Welcome, welcome, Lord Edric.' And he shook Edric's hand with vigour that quietly shocked Edric, that a man of such slight stature should have the grip of a blacksmith.

Directly behind the King stood a man so large that he immediately reminded Edric of Ivor Half-face for he was indeed a giant of a man, dark of skin and dark of hair. Like many men in this new King's army, he also sported no beard, merely a thick moustache which drooped downward at the sides of his mouth, after the English fashion, but Edric was sure that the man was not of his people.

Yet it was neither the man's stature nor his demeanour that caught the attention of Edric, for it was the enormous gold-painted iron mace that he held across his chest. A mace that looked as if it weighed as much as a normal man, yet the man held it there as if it was a willow twig.

Edric's mind was brought back to reality as the King said, 'And I am led to believe that you have brought me over a hundred men. That is good news.' The King said with a smile, 'Do you have any longbow men with you?'

But before Edric could answer, the King went on, 'and any of your famous axe-men?'

Edric was again about to answer, when the King continued speaking, 'God's blood, they caused us much pain at Hastings. Did they not Mourchermon?' He turned to the man whom he had addressed as 'Mourchermon' who was a large man, older than most of the group, bearing a gaping hole where his left ear should have been, which emphasised an enormous scar that ran down the left hand side of his face where his cheek should have been, a wound that could only have been caused by the blow from an axe.

'Aye, my lord King,' answered the man with a scowl.

Edric ignored the man's scowling face and looked back towards the King, saying, 'I have brought forty-seven archers and thirty-three axe-men, the rest are spear and swordsmen, my lord,' answered Edric.

'Good, good,' beamed the King. 'Nay, nay that is more than good, 'magnificque.' That is the word for it, 'Magnificque.'

'My good friend Walter de Lacy also accompanied me with ten of his own men,' added Edric.

'De Lacy? de Lacy?' he repeated, then turned to one of his captains and said to him, 'de Lacy? Do I know the man?'

'I think he was here before Hastings my lord King.'

'Ah,' said the King, totally ignoring de Lacy, as he speedily turned his attention to the rough drawing on a sheet of vellum that lay across the low travelling chest. 'Come, come with me,' he said jovially, 'let us see what you make of my plans, come, look at this map and tell me what you think.' Touching Edric on his shoulder as he accompanied him to the table where he excitedly explained his strategy and of his hope to bring King Malcolm to battle on a field of his choosing.

The meeting lasted well into the night with most of the noblemen having their say which was, Edric noted, pretty well a total agreement with every suggestion that the King came up, plus a few flowery, flattering words thrown in here and there.

Later the mood changed from one of seriousness to a mood of gay abandon, and although most of the noblemen drank copious amounts of wine, the King sipped sparingly at his glass. Edric noted this was the one and only glass that William had all evening.

The King half-filled his glass out of the decanter, and then filled a silver tankard and handed it brimming to Edric with a smile, 'Drink up Lord Edric,' he said, 'and let us put our differences to rest and work together for the good of England.'

Edric reluctantly took the ornately embossed silver tankard from William and held it out as the King filled it up with the sparkling red liquid, and as he had watched the tankard being filled he mused to himself that here, at least, was a part of the prediction that Mona of the Meadows had foretold some years ago.

What was it she said?

You shall break your fast with peasants and sup with Kings?

She also said, 'A king shall fill your goblet.'

It was so long ago that he really had forgotten her words.

Or was it? 'A King shall serve you,' that she had said, and sure enough, the most powerful King that had ever ruled England, and possibly the most powerful King from the continent of Europe, had done just that.

He smiled to himself as King William finished filling the tankard, who then took up his own golden cup. This was slightly smaller than Edric's, but was jewel encrusted with precious stones that glistened in the candlelight as the King struck it against Edric's tankard, spilling some of the contents from both of the tankards, splashing the red droplets onto both of their tunics.

He held the cup aloft for all to see, 'Let there be peace in my kingdom between Norman and Englishmen, so that all may prosper.'

Many of the noblemen cheered and held up their drinking horns, tankards and in some cases, expensive glasses, echoing the words of their leader. Once William brought the tankard to his lips and sipped the sparkling liquid, they followed suit, many of them hurling the empty vessels into the fireplace, where the glasses shattered into a hundred pieces, the drinking horns hissed and sizzled in the fire, and the wooden tankards merely burned until naught was left of them but a blackened shell.

'You see, Lord Edric,' said William still smiling, whilst Edric could see that the King's mouth formed into a smile, he could see no sign of a smile in his cold blue eyes. 'We Normans are not so different from you Englishmen. Was not my own great grandsire a Northman, a Viking? And we still follow many of the old ways, for we still clash our drinking vessels together before drinking, in order to chase away the demons that may be lurking in our wine and beer, and often destroy the vessels so that the devils will not survive to harm us in the future.'

Edric smiled and nodded saying. 'Just so, lord King, just so,' but King William gave a wry smile as he noted that Edric still had his own drinking vessel in his right hand, almost full and intact, thinking to himself that there were indeed many similarities that existed between the Normans and their newly conquered subjects. Yet on the other side of the sword there were also just as many differences, and Edric wondered to himself whether or not this King was the man who could, perhaps, heal some of those differences.

The remainder of the evening that he spent in the company of this new King passed pleasantly enough with perhaps one or two of these Norman lords distaining to speak to him or when they did they did so in a haughty manner, much as a conqueror would speak to the conquered. This caused Edric some concern but then he thought back to the Battle of Hastings when he had met men such as these, smiling inwardly as he did so, thinking that they were not quite so haughty when they had met up with an English war-axe and an English shieldwall.

As the evening was drawing to a close, Edric found himself standing alongside the King as they watched some of the younger warriors stagger and reel from the effects of the wine, many raising their voices, not in anger but in loud, boisterous songs, emptying their tankards in one long gulp then holding them aloft as they called for them to be refilled.

The King made a remark to Edric.

A remark which Edric thought to be a wise and sober remark to be made by one so young. For the King said in a low voice as he looked down into his own golden goblet that still contained most of its contents after such a long night: 'Youth and good wine are wasted on the young.'

Edric smiled at the remark, nodding in agreement with the King. For although he was not drunk, he did admit that he did have a pleasant warm feeling in his gut, as he bade the King goodnight and left the Kings pavilion. He made his way through the huge camp towards his own men, where he found that almost all of his them were fast asleep after their long journey, apart from a tight ring of sentries who had been posted around the perimeter.

He also noted with some satisfaction that, inside the ring of sentries, the men had arranged their sleeping arrangements so that they slept around the tight knot of the remaining sheep and cattle that they had brought with them, thus preventing them from being stolen by any of their so called allies.

Despite the fact that his men were footsore and very tired, some of his Welshmen were singing yet again. Only this time it was not one of their marching songs but was a song of the distant past, for Edric occasionally understood a word or two of the Welsh tongue and distinctly heard the words *Romans* and *Saxons* mentioned, but decided that it would be prudent of him not to read too much into the song.

CHAPTER 38

When he had married Ingibiorg, he naturally expected that Cumbria and Northumberland would automatically become his.

She was – was she not? – the daughter of Thorfinn?

Certainly he had titles enough of his own in the north, and the people were Norse, were they not?

Oh there were a few smatterings of Saxons here and there, but in the main they were her people, and now that she was his, then they must also be his.

Or so he had argued.

And his own mother had been Sybilla of Northumberland, so that alone should have given him that shire. Would it not?

But he had lost Northumberland to the first William in the year 1070, and the lovely Ingibiorg had only given him one son, who they had named Duncan after his own father. Yet now William the Bastard's own son, the second William was proving to be just as troublesome as his damn father.

'Och, man, I'll show him who is lord of the Northlands,' he swore. 'Was I not crowned King at Scone twenty-five years ago? I have waited long enough? Too long some say. My second wife Margaret has not only given me six strapping sons, but by her birth right of being the sister of Edgar the Aetheling, son of Edmund the Exile of England, has given me the right to the whole of England, not to this Norman popinjay, William, son of William the Bastard.

'Am I not Malcolm Canmore, son of Duncan, King of Scotland? Lord of the house of Canmore?

'Did I not rid Scotland of that monster Macbeth and kill his evil son Lulach?'

And so Malcolm, King of Scotland, chuntered and talked more to himself than to the three onlookers as he walked up and down in his huge great hall, admiring his new shirt of chain mail in the full-length mirror as he strutted backwards and forwards in front of a long mirror before his admiring wife and two of their younger sons.

Then he turned to his wife saying, 'Margaret has that idiot Ian got back yet?'

'I have not seen him beloved,' came the sweet reply from Margaret who was still attempting to teach her husband some of the more refined English customs that she had brought with her north of the Roman wall.

He scowled at his wife's reply.

'Damn and blast the man,' he stormed, 'where the devil can he have got to? He should have been back here weeks ago.'

'I will send one of the boys to look for him,' she answered sweetly as she rose from the couch that she had been reclining on, walking slowly to the door where she called in her ladylike voice.

'Alexander, Alexander my dear, are you there?'

A few moments later a tussled-haired youth of some ten winters rushed into the room.

'Yes, my lady,' gasped her second eldest son, panting not only from dashing into the house when he had heard his mother call him, but also from the boisterous game of kickball that he had been engaged in with two of his other brothers, plus half a dozen of the grooms and servants.

'Take your pony up the north road and see if there is any sign of Ian. Your father is getting anxious.'

'Yes Mother,' said the boy, only too pleased to leap onto the back of his black pony and race up the north road as fast as the pony's legs would carry him, enjoying the thrill of racing his pony through the heather (for of course he would distain from riding along the track that served as a main road to their fortress) and spur him onto the topmost peak. There he would be able to see at least a mile of the north road until it disappeared behind the black mountain in the distance.

Both of his parents watched him leave the room. She with eyes that shone with pride, and his father, perhaps with a little pride, but also with the envy that every old man sees in a youngster of that age, who seem to abound with the energy of the young and never seem to walk anywhere, but run, run, run.

'Ahh,' he sighed, 'if only I had that boy's energy we would be dining on venison in London today, not on this windy hilltop in these wild northlands.'

'Or perhaps the beautiful city of Winchester, my dear,' added his wife sweetly.

'Och, Winchester, London, anywhere you fancy, just as soon as I can gather the clans and thrash young William's hide.'

Then he added vehemently, 'Och man, I hope those bloody Picts come this time. They let me down last time I called for a gathering, you know?'

'Yes dear, I do know,' she said quietly.

He paced in front of the mirror again, admiring his fine figure, then added in a loud frustrated voice, 'God blind me, where the devil has Ian got to?'

In the meantime his son Alexander had reached the top of the hill and was sitting on his pony gazing down the glen trying to make out whether his eyes were playing tricks with him. –He imagined he saw figures of men appearing and disappearing again through the mists that always followed the rain in that part of the country.

No, there it was again! Spearheads gleaming in the sun, and then a couple of horsemen appeared, followed by scores. No! It was Hundreds of men appearing out of the mist, as if they were ghosts emerging from the underworld.

Then he heard the faint, eerie sound of the pipes, which sent the hackles on his neck rising.

His pony's ears went back in alarm and he became skittish, causing Alexander to pull hard on the bridle but that only caused his mount to become even more restless despite the savage bit which Alexander always kept in the pony's mouth. The pony backed away, then turned away from the noise and galloped away from the eerie noise that had unsettled him so.

Alexander let the pony have his head as it made for the path that served as a main road to his father's fortress, allowing the animal to take him thundering down the path and through the gates past startled sentries who made no attempt to stop their prince from driving his pony into and through the crowded streets up to his father's palace.

He left the exhausted pony in the courtyard, before racing at breakneck speed to his father's quarters, bursting into the room where he had last seen his parents only to find the room empty.

'Father, father!' he shouted as he raced through one room into another until he eventually found his father in the kitchen munching his way through a half-eaten roast grouse.

'I've seen them Father,' he shouted breathlessly, 'I've seen them.'

'Seen who, you young fool. Seen who?'

'Ian and the men.'

'God blind me,' which were his favourite words of blasphemy. 'You mean he has actually come at long last.' He strode over to the window and gazed out over the town walls and into the distance.

'Canna see them. Are you sure? Where were they? How many men did he have?'

'On the north road Father,' said his son who had now ceased panting and spoke in a more controlled, yet still excited voice. 'Coming down the Barra Glen and he had hundreds of men behind him.'

'So ye didna see Ian hiself?' said the canny Malcolm, suddenly suspicious that what this excited son of his had seen may not have been his herald Ian of McLain, and the men that he had been sent to gather. It could be, just could be, an army of his enemy William the second of England, who had stolen the march on him and had somehow eluded all of Malcolm's agents, spies and informants, and was now about to appear before his fortress with an army that would surely rip down his tiny fortress stone by stone.

He leant out of the window so far that his wife feared that he would fall onto the battlements, for he was well into his middle age, and good living and fine food had given him the girth that many a girl in her eighth month would be proud of.

'Ware husband,' she shouted as she rushed to grab him around his corpulent waist to prevent him from falling out of the window.

He paid her little attention for he was in the process of bellowing to his guards who were a good one hundred yards away, lolling against the still open gates of his fortress.

'Close the gates,' he roared.

Fortunately the wind was blowing in their direction so they actually heard the savage words of their King and began to usher a few people out of the way before they heaved the heavy gates forward, slamming them together with a loud crash.

Then they casually strode over to one side of the gateway where they bent over to heave the large oak beam that was used to wedge the gates firmly shut.

Malcolm was about to bellow to his captain who was now standing below his window, and order him to assemble his small army when he felt a timid tug on his tunic. Glancing behind him he saw his son Alexander who took a step backwards, standing white-faced with his mouth wide open before his large, frightening father.

'What is it now boy,' snarled Malcolm, 'can't you see I'm busy? The English could be upon us in a few minutes. What is it boy? Spit it out.'

'The pipes, my lord,' stammered Alexander, fearful of his father's wrath.

'The pipes?' echoed his father, 'what about 'em?'

'I heard the pipes Father, so it couldna be the English.'

'Och, shut yer face boy, do ye think that the English have no pipers? Could be a ruse,' he added, half convinced now that it could well be Ian and not William of England who was nearing his keep.

Nonetheless, he still shouted down to his captain, 'Call out the men, and make sure that they are properly armed. Snap to it, mon.'

He then turned, nearly knocking his son off his feet, as he stormed out of the room surprisingly quickly for such a large man.

Within seconds he was in the courtyard, bellowing to the grooms for a horse, which appeared as if by magic. For the grooms as usual, had finished their chores by this time of day, and had been munching on hard cheese, enjoying freshly baked bread out of the King's own kitchen, when they had heard their King bellowing out of his window so they had anticipated the King's need for a mount and had thus, saddled and bridled at least six horses in readiness for their King's command.

His captain joined him as well as two of his bodyguard who followed by more of the King's personal bodyguard of twelve chosen warriors, where they were forced to wait for many minutes whilst the guards hauled the blocking beam off the gates and opened them, thus allowing the King and his party to gallop through the gates and along the winding path towards the brow of the hill where his son had sat for over an hour, some little time ago.

They reached the brow without incident, seeing naught but buzzards and a few skylarks, where the King sat on his favourite dun mare gazing down the Barra Glen. Then he gasped aloud with pure delight as he saw a dark horde of men led by half a dozen horsemen, noticing that ahead of the main body of men rode three other horsemen, and the middle rider held aloft a pennant, clearly showing the arms of Canmore.

Still cautious, as was his nature, or perhaps he had learned caution from the many alliances, acts of treachery and treason that had assailed him over the years since he had been King, he was still reluctant to spur his horse down the hill towards the approaching body of men.

'We will wait awhile,' he said to his Captain. 'All may not be what it seems.'

He glanced behind him in order to calculate, yet again, just how far it was to the safety of his gates as well as just how long it would take him to reach them, should the need arise.

Grunting contentedly to himself, he knew that he was in no immediate danger so he twisted a little in the saddle in order to ease his aching back, as he and his escort calmly watched the vast horde of men make their way slowly up the hill towards them. It was not until the approaching men were some one hundred yards from them that Ian, knowing only too well just how cautious and suspicious his King could be, deemed it prudent to remove his helmet and waved it aloft.

Only then did Malcolm relax, smile and lift his hand in acknowledgement, whispering aloud, 'Thank the Christ for that.'

As expected he did not spur his horse forward to meet them, but allowed them to ride up to him before he spoke.

'Right welcome ye are Ian,' he said aloud for all to hear. 'How many men do you bring? Who are these good men who have joined us?'

'My lord King,' answered Ian, 'I have over two thousand and four hundred men here and have been promised more by the chieftains of the great glen. I will introduce them to you properly when they have settled into their prospective camps, and when you are in your throne room ready to receive them.'

'Good, good,' said Malcolm, with a wide smile on his face. 'I will lead my army to the town, where the men can camp in the meadows to the west, and I will see their chieftains after the noonday meal.'

It took the remainder of the morning and most of the afternoon for the men to arrange themselves in some sort of order, with each faction setting up their own separate encampments slightly apart from their neighbours.

Late in the afternoon the chieftains were eventually assembled in the outer chamber of the King's abode, allowing Ian McLain to usher them into his presence one by one.

Ian escorted each man into the King's presence, past the rows of lords, ladies and their children to where King Malcolm sat on his carved oak throne that had been placed on a raised dais so that no man could be above him.

'This is Ranald, second son of Clan Ranald.' said Ian as he bowed his head slightly to his king, 'and he has brought twenty-seven of his warriors to fight for you my lord King.'

Ranald nodded his head in respect.

'Welcome Ranald, I am pleased that you have answered my call and brought your brawny warriors with you.'

The man smiled, made a slight bow and retreated out of the King's presence.

The next man was Macdonald of Glen Kingie, and the same procedure occurred, with the exception of the number of men that Macdonald had brought to the gathering.

Then came Stewart of Appin, a sixth son of the chief by his third wife. This did not go unnoticed by the canny King Malcolm, for Stewart of Appin was a mere boy who brought with him a measly eleven men.

An insult that Malcolm vowed he would not forget.

Macgregor of Glengyle brought ninety men and was clapped on the shoulder with the words. 'I will remember your loyalty Macgregor.'

Three hundred men from Argyll came under the second son of their chief, for few chieftains risked sending their first born and heir.

Forty-one came from Luce bay, all hard men by the look of the white scars that they bore.

Wigtown and Kirkcudbright sent six hundred and twenty-two, a good enough number of men. Yet they were men who Malcolm doubted, for they appeared to be fishermen and crofters who would be new to the ways of war.

'Probably bloody fishermen,' he muttered loudly enough for those who were close to him to hear. 'They'll be na' damn good in a battle line,' he added.

The chiefs and leaders of the assembled horde continued to be presented to him for what seemed like hours to him before the last contingent of leaders were presented. 'Thank the good Lord for that,' he muttered to himself as he was beginning to weary with the faces that continually presented themselves before him.

Near the end of the knot of chieftains came the men from Northumberland, who were led by their leader, a huge bull of a man who answered to the name of Lyulf of Hexham and a man who greeted Malcolm with a salute that reminded Malcolm of the kind of salute that the Roman legions were rumoured to have used, that of a right arm outstretched and held aloft towards their leaders.

Lynulf had assembled a mass of warriors, nearing twelve hundred in number, as well as seven longships of Vikings who had joined him merely for the plunder, plus a large number renegade English fugitives who were either wolf-heads, or had been chased from their farms and villages by the ravaging of the north that had been carried out by William the Bastard, all of whom were seeking either revenge or booty as well as baying for Norman blood. Nonetheless, they were most welcome in this new army of King Malcolm.

There were also men from Cumbria. Men who had settled there over a hundred years ago and still spoke the language of the Norsemen. Good men. Hard men.

Men who had also been burned out of their homes, by Williams's ravages of the North.

These men were fewer in number, merely one hundred and seventy-three, but they looked capable of taking on three times that number of enemies and proving to be victorious.

The last chieftain to be brought into Malcolm's great hall was a gnarled Viking, wearing the usual sheepskin over his rusty mail-shirt.

Malcolm noted that the man's bearing was that of a chieftain and a warrior despite the fact that his chain mail shirt did show signs of rust. The rust appeared to have taken root in places where the mail had been battered and broken, however, the rest of the man's appearance was that of a true Viking.

He was thinking to himself, 'I would wager that this man could well be one of their famous berserkers and he could have even more berserkers in his warband. They are famous for breeding such madmen are they not?' he mused to himself.

Ian whispered in his ear, interrupting Malcolm's thoughts, 'This is the chieftain of one hundred and twenty Vikings, Chief Rolf of Scania. He is a famous warrior and leader amongst the peoples of the north.'

'Welcome Rolf of Scania, I have heard of your deeds,' Malcolm lied, 'and make you welcome in my home. I shall appoint you and your brave men to a place of honour in my battle line.'

Rolf nodded, and said, 'My thanks King Malcolm. It is an honour to serve you' – he too lied, for he knew, and he knew that King Malcolm knew, that the only reason that Rolf had persuaded his men it had been a good idea to join with Malcolm, was simply a matter of gold and silver.

Rolf turned to follow the rest of the leaders and chieftains out of the great hall to join their own men on the fields outside the township, only to find that a number of his own men waiting for him outside the gates, where he was showered with the usual tirade of questions; questions that he surmised that all the other leaders and chieftains were also being asked at this precise moment.

When do we eat?

When are we leaving?

Where are we going?

How many men are in this host?

How strong are the English?

The usual questions usually asked by the usual men.

He eventually settled the men down after they had all had a flagon or two of warm ale and a chunk of pork plus a couple of dried codfish that had for centuries past been the staple diet for men of the longships. Rolf hated to admit it, a food which, although some men seemed to thrive on, he personally hated the bloody stuff, and avoided it like the plague, eating dried codfish only as long as there was another option other than starving to death.

CHAPTER 39

Word flew through the ranks that King William himself had left the army in order to quell yet another rebellion in the county of Cornwall, and had transferred leadership to his second in command, a well-known and proven leader, by the name of Robert de Mowbray.

Mowbray had immediately called together his leaders, most of whom seemed to know and respect this new leader, with the exception of a few newcomers like Edric. He had only seen the man on two occasions, and had never actually spoken to him.

Nonetheless, when he was called to Mowbray's tent he had no other alternative other than to accept Robert de Mowbray as the overall commander of William's army of the north, and quickly warmed to the man who showed naught but friendliness towards him, showering him with compliments about deeds done long ago and all but forgotten by Edric himself.

The army of the north left York, marching slowly through Norton and Pickering towards the coast where they followed the Great North Road, halting for two days at Gateshead before marching towards the new Norman town, which was to be called Newcastle upon the Tyne. There the new castle itself was in the process of being completed, situated on a mound near a wide river crossing, thus dominating the river and preventing Viking or any other marauders from entering the estuary, as well as protecting the town itself.

It was here that small groups of weary warriors left their encampment to trudge the few miles farther north in order to gaze upon the Roman wall, where many of the men, who after a few brief minutes of staring up at the crumbling structure, shrugged their shoulders in disgust before they returned dejectedly to their camp.

Many other men, who were perhaps a little more perceptive or intelligent, stood and gazed in awe at the massive structure.

A structure that after several hundreds of years still stood some twenty or so feet high and eight feet thick, with a walkway that was wide enough for a small cart to traverse, causing many a man to stare in awe at the sheer size of the wall as it stretched away into the distance.

'Bloody wonderful,' remarked one gnarled warrior.

'Wouldn't like to attack that place with my puny spear,' said another.

'Oh, I don't know,' spat another, perhaps more brave or boastful than his fellows, 'I could knock a few bloody Romans off that with this.' He spat again as he patted the yew longbow that he held in his left hand.

A week later, and after a long march, Mowbray made a defensive dry moat as he camped his army on Gloster Hill, for his scouts had warned him that the army of King Malcolm was near, having gleaned information from the local inhabitants who had told him that the Scots had laid siege to the fortress of Alnwick (pronounced Annick, by the locals in a dialect that few could understand).

Mowbray ordered a cold camp, with no cooking fires and no lights of any kind, fearing that the enemy would learn of their position and would either retreat northwards or, possibly make an attack on their flimsy fortifications.

'I don't want them to know that we are here. Let the men eat whatever cold provisions they have with them. There must be no fires of any kind. No drunkenness and no noise whatsoever. See to it that they get as much sleep as possible as I want every man dressed and ready to march before first light. I want to bring this war to a speedy conclusion, and remember' – he wagged his mailed finger to his commanders – 'they will outnumber us by two to one so do not show the enemy any mercy, for as sure as God made little apples, they will show you none.'

The leaders were dismissed and left to join their men.

Edric knew exactly where his own men were in this large camp, for his Welshmen were singing a soft song of love, a certain indication that they were missing their loved ones who were some hundreds of miles to the south.

He called Garth and Evan the Bwylch to him and gave them his orders saying, 'Rouse the men half an hour before dawn, and make sure that every man has had something to eat and drink for it may be a long day. God alone knows when we might eat again.

'Robert de Mowbray, the Earl of Northumbria,' Edric said gruffly to his captains, giving Robert his full title to stress the gravity of the coming day, 'has given orders that the army is to march before dawn with the hope of watching Malcolm unawares, for he believes that Malcolm is besieging the fortress of Alnwick and thinks that if we can approach the Scots from their rear...'

He added as cheerfully as he could, 'And he has little doubt that we will win the day.' *Perhaps a little white lie at this stage may do more good than harm*, he mused.

Garth and Evan nodded dutifully then left to see to their men.

*****

The drizzle had ceased soon after midnight and by the time that the following dawn had arrived Mowbray's army had broken their fast with cold meat, or perhaps a chunk of hard cheese, washed down with water from the nearby stream, or in some cases with the remains of wine or stale beer that had been saved by some of the more serious-minded men.

Edric rode Chieftain, and was accompanied by Garth, Evan the Bwylch and his brother who were also mounted. This allowed the three men to proudly lead their mixed contingent of English and Welshmen somewhere in the centre of the mass of men that made up Mowbray's army.

A few wisps of smoke rose from the blackened remains of the town of Alnwick, that had been set alight some three days ago. Grey wisps of smoke still rose into the clear morning air some half a mile away to the west.

Mowbray halted his army just below the crest of a small hill where he called his captains to him, beckoning them to follow him up to the crest of the hill. At one time this had been cleared of its trees but the secondary growth of oak, ash and hazel had now reached the height of a man on a horse, allowing the riders to stand in their stirrups in order to gaze at the scene below.

'I have approached the town from this direction,' he said in a voice just loud enough for the four captains to hear, 'for two reasons.

'The first reason is that we are now north of our enemy, which means that we have cut off his retreat towards his homelands, and the second reason is, I am sure, clear to you all. For my spies have told me that this very hill on which we survey the Scots is clear enough for our army to pass through, but is also just dense enough to hide us whilst we are doing so.'

The four men nodded in agreement.

'Thus,' continued Mowbray, 'although Malcolm's army outnumber us, we still have the element of surprise giving us the advantage'

Again the four men nodded, although Edric felt, and was sure that he was not alone in feeling that the whilst the slight element of surprise did give them an advantage, he was not quite convinced that the small advantage of surprise was going to be enough for them to overcome an enemy that was nearly twice their number.

'You, Lord Edric and your men will hold the right flank.

'You Brunt and your men will ride with Edric.

'And you, Walter de Lacy, merge yourself and your men with Edric and his Welshmen.

'Mallony, I want you and our good friend here, Front de Beof, with your men to hold the left and I shall lead the main body of our men in the centre.

'Come,' said Mowbray as he turned his mount and urged his mount downhill to where his army waited.

It took more than an hour to re-arrange the army into the three separate bodies with each tense minute seeming more like an hour, as it allowed the enemy to discover their presence.

Finally Robert de Mowbray gave the order and his army moved, painfully slowly, or so it seemed to Edric, up and over the crest of the hill. Then down through the scrubland towards the valley, where the pleasant River Alne meandered through the meadows as it made its way eastwards towards the sea.

As the first men emerged from the scrublands into the open, shouts of alarm came from the besiegers, followed by the sound of horns and the weird screeching of the Scottish pipes.

Men streamed out of their campsites whilst many others abandoned their attack upon the castle, hurling themselves down the hill, into and across the river Alne, wading and swimming in their eagerness to get to grips with this new enemy that had so suddenly appeared on their flank.

About half of Mowbray's army were out of the scrubland when the first Scots loped up the slanting hillside and threw themselves at the thin shieldwall that had been formed some one hundred yards on the downhill slope, striking the wall with such violence and ferocity that the thin wall, that was a mere two or three men deep, was forced backwards up the slight slope.

But it was that very slope that gave the English a slight advantage and allowed them the vital time that they needed for more men, who were still emerging out of the scrublands, to rush downhill in order to reinforce their battered shieldwall.

Men had already fallen by the time that Edric and his men emerged, so he quickly ushered his warriors into a line and they trotted down the slope in formation, bolstering the sagging line as well as extending the English front further to the right, overlapping some of the attackers who were quickly struck down.

Evan the Bwylch forced himself into the wall beside Edric bellowing loudly, with a wide grin across his unshaven face. 'This is more like it Bach. Let's get at 'em and see what gold the buggers have on 'em.'

Edric smiled to himself, delighted to have a man like Evan beside him in the shieldwall, as he blocked a spear thrust with his shield, then swung his sword down onto his attacker's own shield, causing the man to reel back as Edric's sword cut through the outer rim of the man's shield severing its arm-strap and rendered it useless.

'That was a hefty cut,' bellowed Evan merrily as he took a blow from an axe easily on his own shield, and then he thrust at the man with his own spear, catching the man high in his shoulder, sending him tumbling backwards down the hillside clutching his badly wounded shoulder.

Edric nodded. Then, grunting in approval, he stepped forward, bellowing to his men, 'Forward! Show no mercy,' and the men stepped forward catching many of their attackers off balance, either slaying them or forcing them into a slow retreat down the hillside towards the River Alne.

Arrows zipped overhead into several of the tightly packed bunches of Scots as they laboured up the incline

The English shieldwall moved slowly forward, hacking and thrusting as it moved slowly down the slope. English warriors bellowed their ancient war cry of OUT! OUT! OUT! OUT! at the top of their voices.

Edric glanced to his left in order to see that there were no gaps in the line of warriors as they strode solidly down the slope, grimly noticing that there was, in fact, one gap. Yet he immediately saw the reason for it. In the middle of the small gap strode a giant of a man accompanied by a huge hound.

A large warrior whose face was painted blue, and whose hair had been plastered with lime that penetrated through the blue dye, suddenly confronted Edric, and in the brief moments before the two men clashed, Edric was reminded of the Welsh chieftain, Madoc the Lucky, and the time when the painted and tattooed face of Madoc was inches away from his own face and staring down at him, full of hatred, as Madoc lay on top of him and was forcing his razor sharp knife down in an attempt to kill him.

The memory disappeared as the man – who Edric had now realised was a Pict – leapt forward, savagely thrusting his small shield into Edric's own shield with a loud crash scowling as he did so, showing his yellow teeth as he tried to force Edric's shield to one side in order to slice at him with his own heavy sword.

Edric was a little surprised at the man's strength, as well as the man's savageness, fully aware of the fact that the man's own shield possessed a sharp steel point which protruded out at least a foot from the centre of his shield, and that point was now firmly locked into Edric's own kite-shaped shield and was slowly forcing his shield to the side.

The man snarled again, revealing a row of sharpened yellow teeth, and as he strained to wrench Edric's shield, Edric caught a glimpse of the man's left hand which was encased in the straps of his shield, making a mental picture in his own mind that the hand of his adversary contained a knife that was at least a foot long.

The Pict's heavy sword slashed downwards. Yet Edric had anticipated the move and caught the cut in mid-air with his own sword, quickly bringing his own blade downwards towards the man's right shoulder, but the Pict was as agile as a five-year-old and danced easily away from the cut, whilst still maintaining his pressure on Edric's shield.

Edric could feel his own left arm giving way, and had by now realized that his opponent was no ordinary warrior but was, quite obviously, a renowned man of some standing within his tribe, as well as a man well versed in warfare, and by the looks of things, well used to being the victor and not the victim.

The very nature, stance, and actions of this savage Pictish warrior, plus the fact that the man had three weapons, each one quite capable of killing his opponent, caused Edric to reassess the situation in his mind. He suddenly remembered a long-forgotten tactic that his old mentor Vorta had knocked into his head when he had been a boy, so he suddenly stepped to his left, dragging both of the locked shields with him as he did so, until he was standing in approximately the same position that his opponent had been a few brief seconds ago. Realizing, of course that he had his back to the rest of the Scottish line, and was still vulnerable from this opponent's allies, but he considered that in this case the ruse was worth the risk.

The manoeuvre caught his opponent off guard for a brief moment, but that moment was all that Edric had hoped for, as he swung his sword upwards and then downwards slashing through the unprotected neck of the Pict and sending him dying to the ground.

Edric speedily placed his foot on the man's shield and wrenched his own shield free, just in time to raise it aloft in order to take an axe blow aimed at his head by yet another screaming Pict.

This man was, however, a youth, probably an untried boy, who immediately left his own body open to attack as he faced Edric, allowing Edric time enough to thrust his sword into the boy's side sending him to the ground to lie alongside his fellow Pict.

The two blue-painted men lay side by side in death.

As in most battles a lull had occurred, allowing both sides to catch their breath, and as Edric panted with exhaustion, he gazed along the line of English, Welsh and Norman shieldwall. He then looked down towards the Scottish line which, in fact, was not so much a line but was more of a number of knots of battle groups, with each of the individual group forming its own small shieldwall.

The ground between the two armies was already littered with the dead and wounded.

He noticed that each of the opposing battle groups differed from each other in a number of ways, for one group wore short kilts, a bit like a maiden who had not yet reached womanhood. Yet there was of course no mistaking these men for maidens, for they wore full beards and were in the most part, stout-looking fellows with the bearing and wide shoulders of warriors.

The Picts were another group that differed from their fellows for they were painted blue from head to foot, whilst some had painted their hair blue over the spiky limed hair. Others had left the white lime showing, making them look all the more bizarre to men like Edric's who were unused to witnessing such scenes.

The third battle group and the most numerous were men who appeared to

Edric to be Englishmen, for they looked very much like his own men. Apart from a few exceptions, they wore clothes and held weapons, *seax*, axes, swords and spears that were identical to his own warriors.

He shook his head in disbelief, hoping that he and his men would not find themselves lined up against his own people, but then he remembered speaking to some of the Norman warriors who had mentioned that a large part of Malcolm's army was made up of Saxons and Danes who had fled from Cumbria and Northumberland when William the Bastard had laid waste to the North of England.

He looked both to his right and to his left to see how his own warriors had fared in the fighting, noting that there were several bundles of bodies littered along the line, plus a number of men sitting and either tending to their own wounds or else being attended by their kinfolk and fellow warriors.

However, despite searching the lines on both sides of him no less than three times he was unable to identify the tall figure of his friend Walter de Lacy and his small band of warriors that he had brought with him from Stokesay.

*****

De Lacy and his ten men had, for some unexplained reason become separated from Edric's main body of men, and de Lacy, no longer being a young man, felt a wave of panic overcome him as a large number of blue men (de Lacy had never seen or even heard of the race which men called 'Picts') appeared to his front and savagely attacked the thin shieldwall of Norman warriors who were in front of de Lacy's own men, breaking like a wave upon the Normans who bravely stood their ground, which was soon littered with bodies of both Normans and Picts.

He could see gaps appearing in the thin shieldwall that the Normans had held, and, with a gulp and a lump in his throat, he roared at the top of his voice, in order that his voice would be heard over the clash of weapons, and the savage war cries of the opposing forces, plus the groans mingled with the screams of the wounded and dying warriors, 'Forward, Follow me!' and he ran forward towards his struggling Norman allies, followed by his men.

They split up into small groups in order to fill the gaps in the shieldwall, hacking and thrusting valiantly with their weapons, bringing down and wounding many enemy warriors. Despite the fact that most of them were not really warriors and had been, up to a few short weeks ago, mere shepherds, and farm workers of one kind or another, they were perhaps not the top quality warriors that they appeared to be, despite being dressed up in the new mail-shirts and wielding their new swords, spears and axes.

However, their very presence and the fact that they had appeared at such an opportune moment, just as it had seemed that this section of the Norman shieldwall was on the verge of being overwhelmed by the 'blue men', these fresh men turned the tide of the fight, causing the Picts to waver as these new warriors stepped into the breeches, causing the Picts to pause for a brief moment, forcing them to step backwards a few paces, as if to evaluate their own tactics.

The Normans held no such reservations, being battle-hardened and well used to the to-ing and fro-ing of the battle lines, and although their arms ached from hacking away for the past half-hour with their heavy weapons, they surged forward and clashed into the hesitating Pictish men, cutting more and more men down until one huge man whose limed hair stood some six or eight inches up from the top of his head, bellowed an order in his own language and his men immediately turned on their heels, and retreated in some semblance of good order. They disappeared over the brow of the hill, leaving the exhausted Norman warriors standing in bewilderment, looking at one another in something of a daze.

Most of the Normans appeared to be totally amazed. The fight that they had been in sore danger of losing a few short minutes ago had suddenly turned into a victory so speedy and so thorough, that their enemies either slain or melting away before them so speedily, they were left totally dumbfounded.

The Norman leader put his weight onto his kite-shaped shield as his heavy sword dropped onto the trampled turf out of his weary hand, and he reached up to remove his helmet, revealing his sweat-soaked face and hair.

De Lacy stared at the man in awe, for it was none other than Robert de Mowbray. De Mowbray took off his mailed gauntlet and wiped his sweaty forehead with the kid-skin glove that had helped to protect his hand, then looked towards de Lacy and said with a wry smile 'Walter, my good fellow.' (This was the first time that Mowbray had spoken to de Lacy, in fact it was the first time that he had acknowledged the existence of the minor lord of Stokesay). So it was a very shocked Walter de Lacy that held out his right hand to have it shaken in a very friendly way by the high and mighty Lord Robert de Mowbray, Lord of Alnwick and of the mighty fortress of Bamborough.

'You and your good fellows from Mercia saved my neck this day,' he said, 'and it is a favour that I shall be loath to forget.'

He was still grasping de Lacy's right hand and shaking it rigorously, as he added, grinning from ear to ear, 'Come to me after the battle and we shall share a flagon of burgundy together.'

Mowbray then turned away, leaving the dumbstruck de Lacy standing in awe amongst his smiling men, as Mowbray bellowed to his squire, 'Fetch my steed, and be quick about it.'

Despite the fact that the teenage squire ran as fast as he could to the rear of the line, where the horses were tethered, leaping over the bodies of men, both friend and foe, who had been slain in the battle, and evading the grasping hands of the wounded who pleaded with him to stop and help them, it was quite some time before he returned to the fuming Mowbray with his charger, panting as he handed the reins to his lordship, who cuffed the boy around the ears for his trouble, and cursed him for taking so long.

'Where the devil have you been boy?' he swore. 'I did not give you leave to go to York for the bloody nag.'

Then he dug his spurs savagely into the stallion's flanks causing the horse to leap ahead, sending the squire tumbling onto the bloody turf.

*****

Suddenly as if a dark cloud had descended on him, Edric felt his mood alter, causing him to wish he were not here. He cursed himself for giving his word to that oaf Blondell.

'I would wager that he is not here today,' he mused to himself.

His thoughts were interrupted by none other than Robert de Mowbray who rode his stallion out in front of the English line, waving his sword above his head as he bellowed at the top of his voice, 'Charge! No quarter! No quarter!' and spurred his mount into action followed by the rest of his mounted warriors who had been waiting impatiently behind the ridge, where they had been riding their warhorses in a wide circle in order to prevent their highly strung, kicking, biting, highly trained warhorses from savaging one another.

The savage Norman stallions had been held out of each other's way in some semblance of control by their sweating, cursing riders, and well out of sight of King Malcolm's eagle-eyed scouts. Yet now they were given their heads they galloped over the crest of the hill and down the slope, where they crashed into the enemy ranks like an avalanche.

More arrows flew over the heads of the English warriors and over the mounted Normans who were already causing confusion and dismay amongst the Scottish army. The horses surged over the banks of the River Alne, splashing through the bloody river, forcing the Scots to panic as the advancing horsemen surged towards them, running as fast as they were able through the river, leaving their backs vulnerable to the English and Welsh archers.

Edric did notice that some of the enemy did sling their round shields over their backs in order to afford some protection from the storm of arrows as well as a futile attempt to protect them from the Norman horsemen, who were now decimating their ranks.

The riders crashed into the retreating Scots, slashing and spearing at will as they urged their savage stallions into the knots of warriors who had bunched together as they turned to face the horsemen.

But the battle was a sword with two blades for Edric saw many of the horses go down, either speared or disembowelled by the nimble Scots, who pounced upon the fallen horsemen, thrusting and slashing as the riders tried, in vain, to disentangle themselves from their fallen horses.

Edric and his men who were still on the right of the main body of the English army, neared the river, fighting their way through groups of the enemy who chose to fight rather than cross to the far side of the river, dispatching them with sword, axe, spear and arrow.

Edric had, for a few brief moments been engaged in a fight with a man of perhaps thirty summers, but the man had realized that he was outclassed, and had quickly turned, leaping into the river to escape.

But the river offered no hiding place from the deadly spears and arrows that sent man after man to a watery grave, and this unfortunate man was no exception. As he reached the centre of the river he was pierced by no less than three arrows, and his body was soon floating downstream amongst many of his fellow warriors.

Edric's next opponent was a sturdy young fellow, hardly old enough to have a beard, but despite the boy's young age, he was well dressed in expensive chain mail and sported an ornately carved shield and an expensive sword with an engraved gold and silver hilt.

The youngster made a lightening slash with his sword that clanged against the rim of Edric's shield, numbing Edric's arm a little from the force of the blow. Edric parried the next cut and the next, thrusting his shield up into the boy's face but the young man simply danced away.

Edric stepped solidly forward showering blow after blow at the bobbing figure of the young man who simply parried his blows with his shield or sword, or danced nimbly out of harm's way like a maiden dancing around a holy thorn on Mayday.

A blow, as fast as a gyrfalcon, shot over Edric's shield, glancing off his shoulder.

'God's blood,' swore Edric as he gasped for breath, thinking to himself. 'The boy is fast. I must be getting old. A few years back I would not have been caught like that,' as he cast a brief glance where the youngster's blade had ripped through the shoulder of his jerkin, noting that the cut had been prevented from reaching his skin by the expensive mail-shirt he was wearing.

He parried another lightning blow with his shield, quickly retaliating, narrowly missing the young warrior's neck.

'I am flesh and blood like other men,' he thought as he parried yet another jab. 'I bleed. I feel pain. One day there will be a slip. Or a stray arrow, perhaps a thrown spear or a misjudgement of some kind, and then Edric the Wild will be no more. Not that I fear death,' he mused as he circled the man seeking an opening, 'for it is a warrior's way to die in battle, and to sit in the hall of the afterworld with his father and his father before him, to drink ale and sing the songs of his people. For it is a lucky man to die a hero's death, with a sword in his hand, whilst those unlucky enough not to die in battle will wither away slowly, their limbs weakened by age, and their bodies slowly decaying until they die a slow death in agony.

'So hack away young man. Do your worst!'

He paused, stepping back for a brief moment, slightly out of breath and more than a little frustrated that he, Edric the fearless warrior; Edric the slayer of Madoc the Welshman. Edric the famous warrior and chieftain had not been able to conquer this boy, this stripling who was dancing around him like a maiden, slashing and prodding, full of confidence that he would soon be stripping this old man of his expensive sword and armour.

The young warrior appeared to sense that this old man who stalked before him was tiring, and with the cock-sure confidence of youth, he raised his razor-sharp sword high to deliver a death blow. Yet with horror he suddenly realized, too late, that he had delayed that split second too long as his opponent's sword sped upwards with the speed of a gyrfalcon, and sliced through his neck.

Edric stepped back a pace in order to regain his breath, glancing along the line of his men, noting with surprise and more than a little satisfaction that all of his bowmen were still obeying his orders and were standing six or eight feet behind the shieldwall, sending their arrows unerringly up and over his own men and into the still packed ranks of their foes.

'Damn and blast!' swore one of the archers as his bowstring snapped just as he was about to loose an arrow, 'and I haven't got a spare string for my bow,' he fumed, flinging the bow to the ground in disgust. He turned to the long line of his fellow archers and bellowed, 'Have any of you lot got an extra bowstring?'

Several men shook their heads for, although they always carried a spare string to their bows in the small leather waterproof satchels that hung on their belts, they were loath to give their own spare strings away, just in case their own bowstring snapped and they would be left helpless, like their stupid comrade, who was now standing in the middle of a battle with a weapon that was no good to man or beast.

'Stupid sod,' snarled one man.

'Aye,' nodded another as he notched another arrow to his bow. 'A man should always carry at least one extra string to his bow.'

A man further along the line who was, perhaps, a little more sympathetic to a fellow archer, as well as being fully aware that the loss of a single archer meant that their power would be diminished, and a single bowman had, in some cases meant the difference between victory and defeat, thus he bellowed to the archer who had, by now started to panic. 'I have an extra string, come and get it,' and the man picked up his fallen longbow, hurrying towards the man who threw the string to him.

The distraught bowman caught the string and speedily strung his bow, before returning to the bloody business of sending his own deadly shafts into the enemy.

'Always carry an extra string to your bow,' the man snarled and turned his face towards the enemy.

Yet another enemy warrior appeared before Edric, soaked to the skin and dripping with blood mixed with water, as if he had emerged from the water like an otter that had just caught a fish. This warrior, who was much older than the young warrior that Edric had just slain, but similar in colouring and stature, standing out from the darker lime smeared Scots and Picts.

The man's lighter skin and fair hair were typical of the English people, or perhaps he could be a Dane, having the wide of shoulders of an archer, or mayhap the shoulders of a man used to rowing a longship across the seas.

The man sported a neatly trimmed beard that was mottled with grey.

The warrior swung a huge war-axe that crashed into Edric's shield with such force that it shattered the aspen, bullskin-covered shield, lodging itself around the iron boss, in the centre of the shield.

But as the sweating warrior strained to wrench the shield out of Edric's grasp he left himself open to Edric's sword, an error which, to a veteran warrior of Edric's experience, presented Edric with an opening that was a gift from the gods. It allowed Edric to jab his razor-sharp sword forward into the man's unprotected side.

Almost as if in a dream, Edric saw the man's face, as if for the first time, and in that face he saw the face of his own long dead father, gazing into his own eyes, smiling, pleading, as the man fell slowly backwards and disappeared beneath the water of the blood-red river.

Edric stooped to retrieve his broken shield, heaving it out of the bloody water, staring at it in awe for it still had his opponent's axe embedded in the boss, but the blow had completely shattered it, rendering the shield completely useless, so he flung it back into the river in disgust.

The fighting continued on both sides of the river with the crash of shields. The riverbank echoed with clash of weapons and the grunts and screams of the wounded and dying. Arrows and spears flew from both sides, striking shields and men, killing many men, whilst sending more and more wounded men to the rear, limping with the aid of their spears or else being carried by their comrades to a place of relative safety.

Ordgar the Bear was in his element, swinging his huge iron mace with gay abandon, totally fearless as he waded into a shieldwall of thirty or so enemy warriors who stood defiantly in his path, vying with two of his huge hunting dogs which loped along each side of him as the three of them crashed bodily into the shieldwall sending men in all directions as if they were made of chaff. He swung his mace around with dazzling wide circles as it crashed into shield, helmet and body whilst at the same time he parried his enemies incoming weapons with the elegance and grace of a dancer, amazing the Scots and 'blue men' that such a large, cumbersome man could move so quickly, bellowing like a madman as he sent man after man to the floor where they were pounced upon by his huge canine associates, who ripped savagely at the fallen men's necks.

*****

The huge figure of Garth leaned onto the weapon that was known throughout the kingdom as Garth's Bloodaxe, yet during the battle that had just ceased whilst the two sides enjoyed a brief respite before the battle re-commenced, his famous axe was still unbloodied, despite the fact that it had shattered at least three of his enemies' shields and rendered another two completely useless. The owners of those shields had simply withdrawn unhurt from the fray to disappear into the mass of enemy faces that had closed their ranks as soon as the fugitives had entered them.

Edric could see Robert de Mowbray sitting quietly on his horse some way to his left whilst de Mowbray studied the progress of his army.

Mowbray held his sword aloft and urged the army forward.

All along the line the commanders of each body of warriors followed the command of their leader and either rode or walked out in front of their men and bellowed their orders.

'Advance!'

In front of the adjoining contingent stood a man who would not have caused Garth more than a second look, for although this particular warrior wore expensive armour and a shining battle-axe. He was smaller man than most, and did not, in Garth's opinion have the look of 'a leader of men' about him.

But then the man bellowed out in a very loud and deep voice. 'Men of Chaumont! Follow me and kill the bastards!'

At first, the voice and order meant nothing to Garth, but then from the depths of his mind something seemed to stir.

'Why?' he thought to himself.

Then a moment later he realized that the word 'Chaumont' had triggered a memory in his mind, but what was it?

When and where had he heard that name before?

He had led his men halfway down the slope and was nearing the front ranks of the Scottish army when he suddenly ceased his determined striding down the slope, causing his own men to falter and stop, as he suddenly remembered where he had heard that name before.

'Chaumont the Cruel! One of those prisoners had called the killer of his beloved wife so very long ago.

'By the very balls of Odin!' he bellowed out aloud, causing some of his men to gape at him with open mouths, wondering what on earth had stopped their leader in mid stride.

'My lord Garth, are you wounded?' asked one of the men nearest to him.

'Ha, what?' said Garth, still remembering with a growing hatred where he had met the man before. 'Eh – oh no,' spluttered Garth. 'You take charge of the men. Go now, keep at the devils whilst they are on the run. I have other more pressing duties.' With that he veered off to his left and left the gaping, newly promoted warrior standing in front of the dozen or so men who had remained with Garth.

He made his way through a bunch of Norman warriors, one of whom mistaking him for an enemy warrior and slashed at him with his sword. A slash which Garth parried easily on his round shield, and just as easily, head butted the ignorant Norman in the face, then spat at him in disgust as the man reeled back, dazed by the blow.

'I'm one of you. You bloody idiot. Got it, friend?' he rasped into the stricken man's face.

The man nodded dumbly, backing away from this gigantic warrior who, he now realised, could so easily have killed him, rather than merely breaking his nose, a nose which he was now tenderly feeling, as the blood streamed down his sparse beard and off his chin.

The injured man's companions, having seen and heard the small fracas that had just taken place, stepped aside to allow Garth to make his way through them towards the place where he had last seen the man that he now realized was Chaumont the Cruel.

Men like Chaumont are not the kind of men who are caught asleep in their cots. Chaumont had just witnessed the small scuffle that had taken place amongst his warriors, so he watched cautiously as this giant of a man, who was quite obviously an English warrior, made his way through his men towards him.

He was not unduly worried. He had never seen the man before, and was well aware that the King had recruited many English warriors into his army, indeed, the King had a number of trustworthy English warriors in his personal bodyguard.

But he was a wary man.

His caution and his suspicion had caused him to be promoted from the rank of sergeant at arms into a nobleman, knighted by none other than the King himself. His agile, devious mind had kept him alive on a number of potentially dangerous occasions such as this.

But now Sir Chaumont, late lord of the township of Much Wenlock, who was now a commander in charge of one hundred men, admittedly they were mere Bretons and not top quality Norman troops, nonetheless he began to become alarmed as this huge warrior, whose evil eyes were staring unerringly at him as the man stalked through his own men as if they were stalks of cut barley.

His belly contracted as he looked in alarm at the huge battle-axe that the man carried, for he knew that these English war-axes were the most fearsome weapons on earth, and had not only caused havoc at Hastings, but had also wrought death and destruction wherever he and his Norman colleagues had encountered them.

He gripped his heavy sword. At the same time brought his kite-shaped shield up so that its upper rim touched his mouth.

'What can I do?' he thought. 'I cannot turn tail and run, for my own men would probably run with me, and that could lose the battle. And,' he mused, 'if the battle is lost here, because of me, then the King would lose the whole of the north, and then I would surely face the executioner's axe.'

The thoughts flew through his mind, like a swallow catching midges in the summer sky. And then the man was upon him.

But the huge man did not attack him, merely halted some six or eight feet in front of him and glared at the much smaller man.

'Are you Chaumont of Much Wenlock?' accused the man.

'What of it?'

'I am Garth, also of Much Wenlock.'

'The man's face, which had been ruddy up to that point, suddenly paled as if he had just felt the raven of death pass over him; for he had heard stories of and about the former lord of the manor that King William had given to him.

'My wife and daughters were in the town when you burned it,' snarled Garth.

'I knew them not.' Chaumont blurted out, for he knew that his day had come, but was determined not to leave this world as a coward.

'You killed them,' snarled Garth, 'and now I shall avenge them!' raising his huge war-axe high to strike the death blow through the man's shield. But before he could bring the axe down, a shower of arrows from the Scottish army fell as though a hailstorm falling out of a clear summer sky, striking down three or four of the nearest warriors to them and peppering many of the Norman shields that had been held aloft as protection from the deadly storm. They fell all around Garth and Chaumont, standing in the ground like corn, but left Garth and the slayer of his family untouched with the exception of one single arrow.

And that arrow stood out like a signpost from between the Norman's eyes, causing the man to topple to the ground, like a tree in the forest that is felled by a woodman's axe.

'ARRRGH!' bellowed Garth as he held his shield and axe high above his head, stretching his body to its full height as he held his face towards the sky. 'WODEN!' hollered Garth at the top of his voice, 'His life was mine to take.' he bellowed again and again. 'His life was mine!' he screamed again at the top of his voice like a berserker of old, and then he brought his weapon down and took the head off the already dead man, then gazed around at the Normans who stood about, completely dazed at the loss of their leader, unsure whether or not they should attempt to avenge him.

However, they hesitated too long and realised that if they were to attack this huge English avenger then they too were likely to end up headless, so they turned their heads towards the Scots and walked rather slowly down the slope towards them.

More arrows fell striking shields, helmets and men, but not one touched the English avenger as he strode through the Normans to rejoin his men who were, at this precise moment in time, battling half-heartedly with a large cluster of opposing warriors

Yet as he made his way out of the Norman lines he thought he was being attacked by a large, grey-bearded Norman and raised his shield in order to protect himself... before he realised that the man was not actually attacking him, but was merely falling towards him, for he had been pierced in the shoulder by a thick, blue-fletched arrow.

The man fell at Garth's feet clutching at the arrow that protruded from his left shoulder, and as Garth gazed down at the man, the man kept uttering one single word over and over again as the red-faced man strained to wrench the arrow from his shoulder.

'Bugger!' screamed the man. 'Bugger!'

Garth rejoined his men, cleaving his way through the few remaining enemy warriors with the fury that he had hoped to wreak upon Chaumont, bellowing at the top of his voice, OUT! OUT! OUT! OUT! as he slew man after man seeing the face of Chaumont on each of the blue men as they fell to his axe.

CHAPTER 40

'What am I doing here?' panted Edric, cursing loudly to himself, as he leaned heavily on his sword. 'Yes, I have given my word, pledged my sword to these butchers of men.

'So what?

'Is my honour so powerful?

'Is it worth so much death?

'Worth so much, that I am killing my own countrymen for the sake of my enemies?

'These Normans, who have ravaged my country.

'These enemies.

'These murderers of my King.

'Yet here I am, a slayer of sheep, whilst the wolves look on with glee, and praise me for the dastardly deeds that I am doing in their name. What price is my word worth?'

Mowbray's army followed their leaders as they waded and splashed across the Alne, driving the remnants of Malcolm's army before them, leaving Edric still many yards behind the main battle line, still battling with a stubborn group of twenty or so Picts. These had formed a small shieldwall, and were fighting savagely to prevent themselves from being forced down the side of the river bank and into the water.

He, almost unwillingly, walked to the aid of his men in their fight with the lime covered blue men.

Hywell barged his way through a small knot of English warriors and squeezed into the shieldwall beside Edric. He looked up into Edric's face, saying, 'How goes the battle my lord? Are we winning?' Grinning up at him with wicked smile on his face.

Edric looked down on his Welsh friend, for he was at least four inches taller than the Welshman, then he waved his own bloody sword in the air for the adrenalin was still cascading through his veins, he answered, 'Aye my little Welsh King, I do think that we have them on the run.'

Then they both turned to look at Robert de Mowbray who had moved out ahead of his main battle line that was some one hundred yards apart from the Scottish main line.

Hywell suddenly bellowed his war cry and hurled himself forward into the small knot of blue men who were still resisting, literally throwing himself into the Picts, hacking to his right and to his left until the stubborn Pictish men were decimated and reduced to four men who finally yielded, thus allowing themselves to be taken as prisoners, for all of the four men were badly wounded, and incapable of resisting any further.

Hywell strode back up the slope towards Edric grinning like a cat that had just had the cream, triumphantly waving his bloodied sword high above his head.

'Now these Pictish men from behind the wall will know to fear the next Welshman that they meet,' he said whooping loudly.

Edric and his men were still on the right flank of the English army but a small gap had appeared between the two bodies of warriors. Edric noticed that a tight band of the enemy were heading for the gap, so he speedily began to muster his men in order to confront them. He was about to order his men to close in to the left when he noticed something familiar about the advancing warriors.

This group was neither Scots or English, nor were they blue-painted Picts, or men of Northumbria, for they were dressed in the manner of men of Norsemen, and were advancing in their customary wedge formation led by a large man who sported a shield that, as the man neared him, Edric instantly recognized.

'Rolf!' he bellowed, 'Rolf! Can it really be you?'

The leader came to an abrupt halt causing several of his men to crash into the back of him, causing a roar of cursing and grunts of disapproval about their leader's sudden halt, for they were just about to get clear of the slaughter.

'By Odin's balls,' came the gruff reply as he recognised Edric. 'Edric the bloody Saxon, I don't believe it!' he gasped as he removed his helmet to reveal a near bald head, (for when Edric had last seen him he had been in the possession of a thick head of greying hair).

'What the hell are you doing on this bloody field?' bellowed the Viking leader.

'Same as you, I'll wager.'

'I think not,' said Rolf with a wide grin cracking his lined sweaty face. He added, 'We are here for gold, but I prefer to spend my gold in this world not in Valhalla.'

If I remember correctly you turned down your share in the plunder when we last met, and we had to twist your arm to get you to take a little of our silver with you.

Edric noticed how Rolf had emphasized the word OUR, smiling to himself as he recalled the love that these wolves of the seas had for their gods, gold and silver.

'Quickly Rolf,' bellowed Edric. 'Get your men through this gap and away to safety before you are noticed. Mayhap we will meet again sometime,' he shouted again as Rolf urged his men through the gap, up and into the scrubland beyond.

'My thanks to you Edric the Saxon,' bellowed Rolf, adding with a sad smirk that crossed his face. 'Yet again you have saved my skin, for we have already lost too many good Vikings here today. I will repay the debt someday,' he bellowed as the last of his men passed him.

'Come to Wentnor on the Welsh Borderlands,' shouted Edric. 'You will be made welcome there.'

Then with one backward wave of his hand, Rolf and his men vanished into the bushes.

Edric led his men to the riverbank, fighting small pockets of the enemy who stood on the bank, forcing them on the shingle that stretched out into a bend in the river

In the meantime Malcolm had ordered his captains call the survivors back.

The drums banged out the signal for retreat and the tired, beaten survivors who heard the summons, and those few timid souls who had not yet crossed the river, retreated, some reluctantly and some thanking God that they did not again have to face those ferocious Norman and English warriors who still stood before them, waist deep in the blood-red river.

Edric suddenly realised that his opponents had suddenly vanished, as he stood isolated and alone in the river.

As he stood in the slow flowing water memories suddenly flooded his mind.

Memories of Mono of the Meadows and of her predictions.

'Wade not the red river,' she had said, and yet here he was, knee deep in a river that had turned red by the blood of men.

He stepped quickly backwards, shivering like a leaf in an autumn gale, wondering to himself if he had fallen foul to the curse.

'Damn Freya's tits,' he swore aloud, as he realised that he was covered in perspiration.

'Has my wringing-wet body been caused by his exertions in the battle, or was it from the river itself,' he wondered, 'or from the fear of the curse that Mono of the meadows foretold so many years ago?'

Garth brought him back to reality, placing his hand on Edric's shoulder, saying, 'My lord, my lord Edric, are you wounded?'

He shook his head, as a duck does, nearly dislodging his helmet. 'I am unharmed, thank you, but I have just seen the ghost of Mono of the Meadows I remember that she warned me not to wade the red river, and just look at that.'

He nodded his head towards the water, which was still flowing past his feet. For it was, for the most part, a pinky red in colour with larger patches of deep red here and there.

Garth shivered, for he was one of the most superstitious men that Edric had ever known.

Edric stepped backwards a few paces to join Garth on the shingle beach.

Almost as soon as he had reached Garth, a loud cheer could be heard from the castle. The gates swung open and the men of the besieged garrison flooded out to attack the rear of Malcolm's diminishing army, which was at that time facing in the opposite direction, as the beleaguered Scots tried to defend its line against Mowbray's English, Norman and Welshmen.

He and Garth watched in awe as the Scots army was engulfed by the now more numerous English army, who seethed forward, slaughtering and maiming as they went, until they met in the centre over the bodies of King Malcolm, his son Edward and the rest of the Scottish army.

'God's blood,' swore Garth aloud. 'They will take no prisoners.' Shaking his head in disbelief as he watched the last few Scots fall to the merciless English army.

'No, they will not,' answered Edric, 'for they will not want a repeat performance of this in a couple of years' time.'

'No,' he repeated. 'This day will end the rebellion, and from now onwards both Northumberland and Cumbria will remain English.'

*****

Some hours later; for Edric would not cross the Alne until the waters had cleared, he led his men across the river and up the mound to the castle, where he left his men camped on the body-strewn mound, noting with wry humour that Evan and his Welshmen, joined by an equal number of Englishmen, were soon busy moving from one slain warrior to the next, relieving the bodies of anything of value.

He and Garth walked through the unguarded gates to join Robert de Mowbray in the great hall, where he and his captains, plus many men of middle rank, were busy celebrating their victory.

Mowbray spotted Edric and walked casually over to him, saying. 'A great day, hey lord Edric? A fine victory. Think you not?'

'Aye my lord Mowbray,' answered Edric with a nod and a forced smile. 'Your victory here today has secured the north for the King.'

'Indeed, indeed,' said Mowbray as he placed his arm around the shoulder of Edric. 'Your men fought well, especially your bowmen, and I fear that without them, mayhap we could have lost the day.

'And yet,' he continued as he turned his head and looked into Edric's eyes as he spoke. 'Did I not see some of our enemies pass through your shieldwall?'

Edric held his gaze and answered with a forced smile. 'Your eyes did not deceive you my Lord. A few men did pass through a gap but they were of no significance. Merely a few beaten men of no worth.'

Edric never knew whether Mowbray accepted his explanation or not, but the man's brown eyes did flicker a little as Edric had spoken the words, and Mowbray answered him with a non-committal, 'Hrrrm.'

'Nonetheless,' said Mowbray, after a few moments of silence, 'Saint Brice has been kind to us this day.' Then he stroked his grey-mottled beard, before he added, 'I shall build a shrine to him when I next go home to Bamburgh.'

Whilst Edric had heard of Saint Brice, he really knew nothing about him, or even her, for he knew not whether Saint Brice was a male or female saint, and he was also totally unaware that this day, the thirteenth day of November was in fact. Saint Brice's Day. So he shrugged his shoulders, agreeing with Mowbray, nodding and grunting in assent.

Sipping at his silver goblet of red wine, he said, 'Lord Mowbray, as soon as my men are rested and the wounded fit to travel, I shall, with your permission, commence the journey home, for my Welshmen grow uneasy when they are so far from their own lands.'

'Of course Edric,' said Mowbray with a smile. 'There is so little reason to stay here any longer. Our job has been done, and done well, though I say it myself.'

Edric thanked him, realizing that whilst Mowbray, was now virtually 'Lord of the North,' he would not want an army of this size camping on his doorstep, eating every bushel of oats and wheat, and devouring every last domestic beast as well as the beasts of the hunt from the shires of Northumberland and Cumbria.

True to his word Robert de Mowbray, Lord of Alnwick, Lord of Bamburgh, Victor of the Battle of Alnwick and now, lord of the North, did not forget his vow to the lowly Walter de Lacy, for he sought him out that very evening, bestowing him with two additional manors, saying, 'My good friend Walter, without your timely intervention, I do fear that we could well have come second in today's tournament, and I shall whisper words of your bravery and of your valour into the King's ear.'

He left the delighted Walter beaming with delight at his leader's generous words.

CHAPTER 41

When Edric returned to his own men he found that Garth had been busy counting their losses in dead and wounded, reporting to him that out of the one hundred and thirty-six men who had marched north with him, seventeen had been killed, plus some forty-one wounded, eight seriously, with at least five who were not expected to last through the coming night.

A delighted de Lacy had now rejoined Edric's men, glowing with pride and delight of all that he had accomplished, and particularly pleased that despite three of his men being wounded, one seriously, he had in fact not lost a single man in the battle.

Edric accompanied Garth to the wounded where they found that most of the men had wounds varying from small cuts and gashes to the more serious cases where one man had lost an arm, another a leg, whilst many more had been wounded by a spear or sword thrust.

Edric was sad to hear that Evan the Bwylch's brother, Evan the Betwys had been slain, and he was equally sad to see that one of the more seriously wounded was none other than the boy, Thurston of Wem, the youngster who had fought him whilst they were still at Wentnor, the very boy who had pleaded with Edric to be allowed to accompany him on this venture.

The boy stared up at Edric through the bloody bandage that had been wrapped tightly around his head, and reached up with his right hand towards Edric in a vain attempt to shake the hand of his leader, but the effort was too much and the arm flopped back down.

Edric knelt beside Thurston, and took his hand, yet when he looked for the other arm he could see naught but a bloody stump where the young man's left hand should have been.

'You fought well Thurston,' he lied, for he had not seen the boy on one single occasion in the knot of men, who had fought with and around him,

The boy smiled and he tried to speak, but words would not come through his shattered mouth that looked like either a Scottish or perhaps a Pictish battle-axe had battered it.

Edric stooped further down placing his ear by the youngster's mouth but could hear naught but a gurgle that abruptly ceased, followed by a loud sigh as the boy's spirit left him.

Edric closed the youngster's eyes and blessed the boy with the sign of the cross, but as he regained his feet he could feel the tears cascading down his unwashed cheeks and into his blood-soaked beard.

Evan the Bwylch shared Edric's sorrow at the death of one so young and they stood together in silence for many minutes before they moved on to comfort and help the other wounded men.

It was a further nine days before Edric thought it suitable to resume their long march back to Mercia, despite the fact that three of the wounded still needed to be carried on litters that were slung between two of the more docile horses.

The journey was slow and miserable for the weather had turned cold and very wet, with the rain pouring down, making it nearly impossible to prevent their weapons and armour from becoming rusty.

The consistent downpour soaked their leather jerkins so much they began to fall apart as if they were made out of rose petals and not of the hide of mature bulls from which they had been made.

Nonetheless the journey did eventually end with the loss of one of the three wounded men. He gasped his last breath virtually within sight of home, despite the urging and the tender care from one man (a Welshman named Gwylliam of Gwent) and they did, at last, wearily begin their climb the hill that led to the small fortress of Wentnor.

The sentries on the fortress walls had seen the returning warriors, they ordered that the horns be sounded in order to alert the township, causing the people to rush up the wooden steps and onto the palisade in order to watch the returning men as they made their way across the soggy marshlands of Prolley Moor.

They chattered excitedly amongst themselves as they watched the marchers disappear from sight below the brow of the hill, only to reappear a little while later as they made their way up the hill towards the crowds of people that had now assembled in front of the fortress gates in order to welcome their returning heroes.

It seemed to Edric and his warriors that every man, woman and child in the township and the district had turned out to greet them as the people crowded around them as they approached the gates, where Edric's reluctant warriors and Evan and his Welshmen remained outside the gates in order to make their temporary encampment.

Both the English and Welsh warriors were soon rolling the dice and squabbling over the loot that they had taken from the fallen men of Malcolm's defeated army, whilst still munching happily on the freshly baked bread and warm cakes that Godda and her maidens had provided for them.

Nonetheless they watched with drooling mouths as the sheep and pigs that Edric had provided for them sizzled over blazing fires.

Edric rode Chieftain through the cheering crowds, then across the village green towards the longhall, where he could see Godda standing amongst half a dozen of her friends and servants as they waited for him.

He dismounted and handed the reins to a groom, 'Welcome home my lord,' said the boy as he led the stallion towards the stables.

Edric nodded and smiled at the boy in acknowledgement.

He turned around to find Godda standing in front of him with her arms akimbo, as if he had been out on one of his many hunting trips (and not the dangerous war trail that he had actually been on) as if she was saying to him. 'Where in the good Lord's name have you been? Your dinner is cold.'

He smiled to himself, and then his face broke out into a wide grin as he stepped towards her, crushing her in his arms against his sweaty, damp leather jerkin. He kissed her lips, tenderly at first, but then with a passion which he had thought to be long dormant.

She unashamedly threw her arms around his neck, returning his kisses,

351

kissing his cheeks, lips, nose and neck as she whispered into his ear, 'Thank God you are home safe and sound, although of course,' she whispered as she kissed his ear again, 'I always knew that you would return to me unscathed.'

'Witch,' he chided as he drew away from her a little, admiring her beauty before he gently pulled her towards him again to kiss her on her full red lips, and they walked hand in hand into the longhall with a happy Ælnoth holding the other hand of his warrior father.

He stripped off his damp clothes and his rusting mail-shirt, leaving them in a heap on the floor in front of the fire. Godda handed him clean and dry clothes saying, 'Put these on and make yourself comfortable in your favourite chair,' nodding towards the old carved oak armchair that he always sat in, whilst I go to the kitchen and organise a feast for you and your men.' She added with a smile, 'for I would be a poor lady if I could not put on a feast to be remembered for the Victors of the Scots.'

She disappeared through the door into the kitchen.

Almost immediately one of the serving girls appeared with his favourite tankard brimming with warm ale and a tray of cold meats and fresh bread.

'My Lord Edric,' said the girl as she curtseyed, placing the tray and ale on a small table beside him.

He took a deep drink from the tankard, and then placed a chunk of roast venison in his mouth. However, the next thing he could remember was being shaken awake by his wife, as she chided him, 'Come now sleepy head, there will be time enough to sleep, when we have feasted with your men.'

*****

Edric wakened slowly, shaking his head as he did so, for he had not realised just how strenuous the past few weeks had been for a man of his age, and had not realised just how tired he actually was.

He stood, taking a long drink from his tankard before he followed his wife to the door where she stood for a moment gazing at the scene outside the house.

Edric joined her and was stunned to see that the green and the township itself was literally packed full of people who were crowding around the trestle tables which were groaning with all kinds of food and drinks imaginable.

As soon as his people saw him, they ceased their chatter causing a deathly silence to fall upon the throng, until his brother Hal (as ever his saviour) stepped forward and raised his half full tankard aloft, and cried, 'To Lord Edric!' And every man woman and child raised their cups aloft and bellowed, 'To Lord Edric!' And a silence again descended on the crowd as they emptied their cups.

Then a deep voice bellowed loudly from somewhere at the rear of the crowd, 'To Edric the Saxon!' followed by a roar that came from perhaps a dozen or so male throats, as 'Rolf of Scania!'

Rolf the Viking and his men pushed their way across the crowded village green towards the front of the crowd.

'Well, you did say that if we came to Wentnor on the borderlands we would be made welcome,' he cried grinning from ear to ear. 'For I have never been a man to pass up on a good feast and some free ale, and this feast that you have spread here is almost as good as the ones that we used to enjoy in Scania,' he said with a smile, adding, 'besides, I owe you my life, and I know that this is not ample to the debt that I owe you but here is a little something on account,' he said with a wide grin as he threw a heavy purse full of gold at Edric.

Edric caught the heavy bag with both hands but the gold did not equal the delight in seeing his Norse friend again. He stepped forward and took the massive, dirty, sweaty hand of Rolf in his own, saying, 'You and your men are indeed welcome, come, join us in our feast. I'm sure there is enough here for you and your few skinny Norsemen.'

'Ah,' laughed Rolf as he smiled and slapped Edric on the back nearly knocking him off his feet. 'We will soon make short shift of your puny offerings here, for not a man amongst us has eaten naught but scraps for longer than I care to remember.'

But then he became more serious and stood facing Edric, placing both of his huge hands on Edric's shoulders, saying in a very serious manner. 'Laddie it should be us, and not you providing this feast, for without your help at Alnwick, me and my stout lads here would be naught but bones picked clean by the crows, and not here with you, about to enjoy this feast that you have set before us.'

The serious look left his face to be replaced with his usual wide grin and without further ado he strode forward, followed by his men, who crowded around the nearest table, stuffing food into their mouths like they had not eaten for a week (which were the very words that Rolf had uttered a few moments ago.)

There were roars of approval not only from the Vikings, but from the English and Welshmen when a dozen maidens emerged from the house, each carrying four large drinking horns brimming with best beer. The poor girls were pounced upon by the warriors who grabbed for the horns, spilling much of their contents in the process. Then the thirsty warriors emptied most of their drinking horns almost immediately, spilling even more of the precious liquid down their beards and jerkins in their haste, but laughing and shouting with joy as the girls dashed back into the house only to return a few brief moments later with yet more beer-filled drinking horns.

It was not long before the men became drunk, and the drunker they became the noisier they became as they drank and drank. They began to sing the songs of their people with the Vikings and the Englishmen roaring louder and louder, whilst the Welshmen who were just as drunk as their allies, sang melodious songs which were so unbelievably beautiful to hear, that many of the serving maidens and women of the township were so moved, that tears streamed down their cheeks. The singing slowly ceased and the men either staggered away to retch and bring back most of the food and ale that they had consumed, or slipped quietly to the ground where most of them remained until the cock crowed in the cold, damp dawn of a dull September morning.

*****

The tenth day of October came and went, much to the relief of both Edric and Godda, for although neither of the two made any mention about the day or about the dream itself, both of them were well aware of the fateful date and were happier people once the eleventh day dawned.

Amid much confusion, back-slapping and fond farewells Evan the Bwylch's and his Welsh warriors left, with nearly every man carrying a sackful of booty slung over his horse as they made their way down the slope, towards their western mountain fortress, singing quietly to themselves as they happily plodded down the muddy pathway, delighted to be on their way home.

Hywell was now the only Welshman remaining at Wentnor, and although he would sorely miss the companionship of his kinsmen, he had found love in the township, having literally stumbled over the woman when he had made one of his regular journeys down to the bottom of the hill to wash in the stream, for he much preferred the crystal clear water from the fast flowing stream to the well water that the villagers drew from the deep well that stood in the centre of the village.

On this particular occasion Hywell barged his way through the bushes in order to reach his favourite spot, having already ripped off his leather tunic as he approached the bank of the stream, singing quietly one of his favourite melodies when he literally fell over the kneeling figure of a woman who was in the process of wringing out her washing by the side of the stream.

With a loud cry he tumbled over the woman and with a loud splash, plunged face first into a deep pool, from which he emerged spluttering and spitting a jet of water out of his mouth, and cursing loudly as he did so. When he finally began to wipe his long dark hair off his face, he looked up onto the bank to see a woman who was bent double with laughter, holding her sides as if she was suffering from the colic.

Agatha was by no means a raving beauty, having a mop of bright red hair, which framed a round face mottled with freckles.

Her nose was small and bent slightly to the left, which had taken that shape as the result of a childhood fight, and her blue eyes seemed to be either too small for her large round face. Or perhaps the face was too large for her small blue eyes.

Her figure at the time of her marriage had been slim and shapely, but after her husband had been killed in a feud over the ownership of a bull, some ten years ago, the once slim waistline had now expanded to much the same size of her ample bosom, which at times attempted to free itself from both the neckline of her dresses or through the loose sleeves, which she preferred to wear. Her large size and her fiery temper had caused her to be alienated from most of the womenfolk in the village. There was only one woman who she could now call a friend. Hywell sloshed up onto the bank where he stood dripping alongside her trying, unsuccessfully, to wring the water out of his trousers, waddling around like a duck as he did so.

This caused Agatha to laugh even louder, to such an extent that as she bent double with laughter she clashed her head with Hywell who had also bent down in an attempt to wring out his long, soaking wet mop of hair, causing both of them to recoil backwards, holding their foreheads and staggering slightly as they did so,

Despite her sore head, Agatha continued to giggle, and her laughter infected Hywell who had finally seen the funny side of the situation and joined in, chuckling as he held his sore head and looked down to watch the water, which was still cascading down his breeches.

But suddenly he felt as if he had fallen into the stream for a second time as he looked at the still giggling woman, for a cold shiver trembled through his body, followed by an immediate sensation of warmth which engulfed his entire being, especially his face and his loins.

The sensation of this kind was a first for him. It felt as if it was not actually happening to him, but was happening to another person or perhaps a spirit that had taken over his body, and for some unexplained reason he reached forward and held the still shaking Agatha by her shoulders, then pulled her close to him, covering her mouth with his own in the type of passionate kiss that he had been unaware until that very moment in time, that he was capable of giving.

Agatha froze for a moment and her bright blue eyes widened as she stared into the face of this man who was kissing her with a passion that she too had never before experienced. Her freckled face reddened until it seemed to him that the freckles had merged into one single, massive freckle that covered her entire face and neck.

She relaxed a little, then returned his passion with the savage passion that the red-haired Albian people are famous for, meeting his ardour with her own even more passionate needs. Yet then she suddenly broke away, gasping for breath.

She stepped back a pace to stared at the man and for the first time recognised him as one of the Welsh warriors who had accompanied Lord Edric on his campaign in the North. A man who she had seen on more than one occasion in the company of Edric himself, and was not, she thought, merely a common warrior.

'I, I, I don't know you,' she spluttered. 'How dare you take such liberties with me?' She snorted haughtily, and yet the smile had still not left her face.

'I do beg your pardon,' said Hywell, and bowed low, as he had recently seen the Norman noblemen do. 'But in truth, I could not resist kissing a lovely woman such as you.'

Her smile widened, for no man had ever called her lovely, and for a moment she thought that the man might be in his cups. Yet then instantly rejected the idea, for in truth, the sun had only just risen, and it was far too early in the morning for a man to be drunk.

She tossed her head, as a mare does when she meets a stallion, causing her long, red tresses to fly about her head like the red beech leaves being blown about in the autumn.

The movement of her body caused her ample breasts to sway from side to side.

Then she stepped forward and did a thing that in later life would cause her cheeks to redden again with embarrassment at her own forwardness; for she threw her arms around his neck and kissed him full on his lips, thrilled at the tingling sensation that his bristly moustache gave her.

They held each other tight, kissing one another passionately as they sank to the wet grassy bank of the stream where they made long, passionate love.

Three weeks later Hywell ap-Bleddyn, King of Gwynedd, and the widow Agatha of Plowden were married in a quiet ceremony in the small chapel at Wentnor, and where, that very day and much to the disappointment of many folk, including Edric and Godda, they left the village, riding westwards towards his new domain, deep in the valleys of northern Wales.

A large proportion of the English warriors also left for their respective villages, farms, and townships, many carrying the spoils of war with them, be it a looted shirt of mail, a shield or some other weapon that had been gleaned off the dead. Or in a few cases, a silver neck or arm bangle, or in a fewer cases still, a small leather purse containing gold and silver coins that had been found on one or two of the fallen chieftains.

The men of Scania were loath to leave, and lingered in and around the village spending or gambling their spoils, whilst a few of them, including Rolf found maidens to woo.

Rolf seemed to be falling in love with a wealthy widow, for he seemed quite content to remain in Wentnor for the entire winter rather than risk the perils of travelling through Norman-held England in the hope of finding a boat that would take him to his home in Scania.

Edric was delighted with the match, for he enjoyed Rolf's company and the two men spent many a long dark evening drinking the dark ale that Godda's maidens excelled in brewing, telling yarns. Some true, whilst others were perhaps stretched just a little too far.

Twenty-seven of the thirty-one Vikings left soon after the Christmastide celebrations, bored with the dull life of the village, and eager to return to their northern homelands.

As the dark days of late January began to lengthen, giving the villagers a little more time to enjoy the longer daylight hours, Rolf moved into the widow's house, remarking to Edric, 'Well, she is a better cook than my Elfrieda in Scania, and,' he added with a wink, 'her bosom is far bigger. So I shall stay a while and enjoy a few of the home comforts that she offers so freely.'

Edric merely smiled and nodded, for he had known the widow's husband who had been slain at Hastings, saying quietly to his friend. 'I knew her husband and he was a stout warrior as well as a good friend of mine.'

Adding, 'I have given your friendship with her much thought and think that perhaps he left this world because he could see that you were coming, so I see no reason why you, my friend, and the widow should not enjoy one another's company,' trying to be serious as he struggled to keep his face straight, causing Rolf to grin from ear to ear, for he was sorely stricken by the lady, and Edric knew that Rolf bringing up the subject in the first place had been his way of seeking approval from Edric.

The end of January was bitterly cold with the snow lingering on the hilltops and in the shaded spots, where the weak winter sun never penetrated, not melting until the middle of February when the torrential winter rains washed it away along with trees and shrubs whose roots had been weakened by previous floods.

During the first week of the month of March, two of the remaining four men of Scania decided to leave, and although Edric could not believe his eyes, there were genuine tears in the icy blue eyes of his friend Rolf, as Roland the berserker and Hugh of Gotland made their way through the muddy gateway of the small fortress.

'Well,' said Rolf unashamedly wiping the tears out of his eyes with his newly spun woollen shirt, as he turned to the one remaining Viking who was standing alongside him. 'That just leaves you and me here, Ragnar my old friend,' he said to the squat, muscular figure of Ragnar, who merely shrugged his shoulders and grunted some unintelligible reply, before turning his back on Rolf and the small crowd that had gathered to wave farewell to the two men of Scania. Making his way back towards the small cottage where he had spent the past two months, living with one of the most beautiful maidens in the township, and mayhap, not merely in this small township, but without a doubt, she was one of the most beautiful maidens in the entire district.

'What the devil does she see in the dirty old sea dog?' said Rolf, as he shook his head in disbelief as the grubby figure of Ragnar disappeared under the thatch and through the maiden's doorway.

Edric nodded in agreement, for the union between the beautiful Beatrice, and the uncouth Norseman Ragnar had been the topic of many a conversation in the village since they had got together, with people shaking their heads in wonder as Beatrice, who had been the dream woman of many of the older village boys, all of whom had been scornfully rejected, had apparently fallen in love with this grubby, smelly man who was old enough to be her father.

Godda had knowingly informed Edric that the union was 'The attraction of the opposites,' whilst others said that perhaps she was looking for a father figure. Or perhaps she merely wanted a strong warrior, no matter how old or how uncouth he may be, just someone who could protect her, and mayhap father strong warrior sons. Yet in truth no one had plucked up enough courage to ask either of them, for both of them were quite formidable in their own way.

Ragnar was quite a ferocious-looking man for he was built like a bull, with arms and legs at least twice as broad as an average man, and Beatrice had always been a maiden who had been totally unapproachable, due to her haughty manner, her quick tongue, and her way of 'talking down to people.' As the three faults she had possessed since the day that she had learned to speak, they had caused her bewildered parents a lot of concern during her childhood and teenage years.

Ragnar the Viking was not the only man to find love that winter. For a few weeks before the end of the month of April, Winnifred the Healer rode into the village on a white mare, escorted by no less than three of her four brothers, and after stopping briefly at the longhall to pay her respects to Edric and Godda she left her brothers, urging her tired mount towards the large figure of Garth who was standing some ten or twelve feet away, and when she was alongside him, she gazed down at him, speaking in the sultry voice that he had all but forgotten.

'How now, my Lord Garth, think you that we have waited long enough?' she said, as if they had been parted for a few short days rather than the number of years that had passed since she had nursed him back to good health in her home in the midlands.

'Too long my love,' answered Garth in his deep voice.

He then stepped forward, reached up and literally heaved her out of her saddle, crushing her to his chest, leaving her feet some way off the ground and her lungs crushed and breathless.

'For heaven's sake put me down,' she gasped, and although he obeyed he did not release her, merely held her a foot away and gazed lovingly into her eyes.

They were married two days later, and the two middle-aged people caused much ado as they cavorted around the village like two thirteen-year-olds who were out on their first date.

CHAPTER 42

March brought the winds that swept over the hilltops, only to be funnelled along the narrow valleys and the exposed plains where they howled like banshees released from the very bowels of hell.

However, on the first day of spring the sun shone brightly, and no less than eight black-faced ewes each gave birth to twin lambs. The old people of the village muttered at such a marvel, shaking their heads in wonder, swearing that such a thing had not happened before, or at least, not in their lifetimes.

Lambs were not the only things that arrived on that sunny first day of spring, when the weak sun was at its zenith Edric, who was about to sit down to his midday meal, heard three distinctive raps on his iron-studded, oak door.

He walked to the door, which he opened to reveal two tall figures, dressed in grey capes and hoods, standing on his portal. He stepped back a pace, for he was not sure whether they were friendly or no.

Nor was he certain of the gender of the two. They were tall enough to be men but, on the other side of the blade, they were also slender and willowy.

Nonetheless, erring on the side of caution, he stepped back and his hand sped to the *seax* that he always carried in his belt.

The two figures reached up and slowly removed their hoods, revealing the faces of two very attractive – nay – two very beautiful women.

'I am Ella,' said the one to his left, in a deep sultry voice that he swore he had heard before.

'And I am Elfrieda,' said the other in an almost identical voice.

'And I am Edric,' he answered, 'lord of this holding.'

'We are sisters,' said the first.

'So I gather,' he answered, for they were too alike to be anything other than sisters.

'Nay, sire,' said the second with a slight sneer.

'We are sisters of Godda, The Queen of the Light Elves. And I am Elfrieda and she is Ella,' she repeated as if Edric had been too stupid not to have registered their names in his mind upon the first telling.

'We have come to see our sister,' said Ella.

'Ah!' gasped the still stunned Edric, as he stepped backwards and with a gesture that a Norman courtier would have been proud of, he bowed low and with a sweep of his hand, bade them enter.

He led them through the small hallway into the great hall where he said, 'Please, take a seat and I will find the Lady Godda, I think she is through here,' whereupon he disappeared through the doorway and into the kitchen where he found no less than three serving maidens preparing food whilst Godda herself was sitting on a chair at the end of the serving table, apparently directing operations.

'Your sisters are here,' he gasped, expecting her to be either shocked, or perhaps excited by the news. Yet she merely nodded and said, 'Ah, I had not expected them for at least another hour.'

'You knew they were coming?' he accused.

'Well, no. Well yes. I did know that they would be coming although I was not quite sure when they would actually arrive. It may have been this year or next year. I really didn't know.'

But before the astounded Edric could reply, she asked, 'Are there two of them?'

'Yes,' he answered. 'Two.'

'Ah,' she said again.

'And what does "Ah" mean?'

'Well, it could mean that all is not well in my kingdom, and that I am needed there.'

'God's blood,' Edric swore. 'What would it mean if three or even four of your sisters turned up?' For he had immediately felt the hostility that seemed to radiate out towards him from the two sisters, and had somehow retaliated by taking an instant dislike to both of them.

'Or even five or six,' he ranted. 'Would it mean that your kingdom has burned and gone to hell?'

Godda had seen him annoyed before. Indeed, it was not too rare an occasion for him to shout and bellow, as well as occasionally storm out of the house, slamming the doors so hard that the whole house would shake. Yet she had never seen him in such a cold rage as this, and yet she could not really see the reason for his rage, for what had happened? she asked herself.

'Naught had happened,' she answered her own question, other than two of her sisters had paid her a visit. She rose from her chair and walked slowly into the other room in order to greet her two sisters.

They met, as sisters should meet, with hugs and kisses, plus the usual kind words.

'You are looking well sister,' said Ella.

'Marriage must suit you,' clucked Elfrieda.

'And you both look well,' retorted Godda. 'How are things at home?' she queried, for she was anxious to know why they had left the comfort of their own land to visit her in a land where cold and wet weather prevailed (unlike her own kingdom which was a land that never experienced the inclement weather of England, or the hunger and deprivation that periodically blighted the land).

'Things are fine,' lied Ella, with a smile.

'Yes all is well at home,' confirmed Elfrieda. 'We just thought it would be nice to see you again, and to tell you all the news from home.' She chuckled quietly.

Godda clapped her hands twice and the serving maidens immediately appeared carrying trays full of the food and drink that they had been preparing for the past hour or in order to greet their expected guests with a spread 'Fit for a Queen.'

Edric spent the rest of the day hunting wild boar in the forest of Clunn, returning home late, tired, wet, empty-handed and in pretty well a more foul frame of mind than ever.

Godda was waiting up for him, sitting alone beside the fire with a small tray of fresh bread, cheese and smoked ham beside her. For she knew (as always) that he had been unsuccessful in his hunt, and would return angry and ravenously hungry.

He squelched across the freshly laid reeds up to the fire where he grunted as he took off his wet clothing, which he left in a heap upon the reeds, then put on the dry clothing that Godda had placed near to the fireplace so that they would be nice and warm for her husband to get into.

'Where are they then?' he grumbled as he stuffed a small chunk of cheese into his mouth.

'Gone to bed,' she answered.

'Why don't you like them?' she asked.

He didn't answer, merely stared into the flames as he crammed a piece of bread into his mouth and continued chewing until he had emptied his mouth.

'I don't really know,' he answered in all honesty. 'I just feel that they don't like me and there is just something about them that angers me.'

'Well, they are of my Elfin Folk,' she said demurely.

'But so are you, but they are different.'

'Different. How?'

'Oh, I don't know, just different.'

'Well, of course they are different. We are all different. Are we not? And anyhow,' she continued trying to smile as she added, 'I am the Queen so I am bound to be a little different, am I not?'

He grunted and continued eating until he had cleared the plate of all of its contents except for a few crumbs, and then he emptied the small silver flagon of ale that she had place on the table.

'Time for bed,' he said and rose to retire for the night.

He had expected the two sisters to stay for a couple of days or mayhap a couple of weeks at the most. Yet as spring turned to summer and the summer slowly drew to a close, his tolerance, which had never been one of his good points, grew shorter and shorter until open hostility broke out between Edric and the two sisters.

It was during one of those shortening autumn evenings as the colder weather took hold of the countryside, when the east wind roared over the hills and through the valleys wrenching the leaves from the oak, ash and other forest giants when Godda thought that she had chosen the right moment to tell her still angry husband the news that she had been dreading to break to him, saying as pleasantly as she was able:

'Edric my dearest, you know that my sisters and myself are not like your good self and can only come into and go out of your world on one day only, and that day is, as you may recall, the first day of the season of Spring, the very day that you and I met.'

'Now I do know that you and my two sisters dislike one another. But as their Queen as well as their sister, I feel it my duty to tell you that they cannot leave us until the first day of spring, so I implore you to try to be civil to them whilst they are with us.'

Edric, who had feared hearing the news that he had long expected, rose from his chair, storming out of the house again, staying away for three nights and only returning on the fourth evening, dishevelled and filthy from the hunt in which he had slain no less than three wild boar and a stag.

Godwin had also fallen out with the two sisters, so one day he felt that he was at the end of his tether and stomped heavily down the stairway carrying a large bag which contained most of his personal effects and announced that he was leaving.

'Nay son, stay a while,' said Edric, 'Where will you go?'

'I shall go and stay with Matthew. He's got a cottage up on the Clee Hill,' he said haughtily as he left the room.

Edric spent more and more time hunting in the vast forest of Clunn as well as venturing up on the long mountain for the elusive red deer and wild boar.

He hunted throughout the autumn, and into the bleak winter when his prey hid themselves in the thickest parts of the forest, secreting themselves in the most inaccessible hidden valleys where they hoped to elude their predators during the long, dark winter months.

*****

Breakfast that particular morning was a solemn affair, with none of the three sisters speaking to Edric, as he ate his bacon, eggs and sausages in silence, glancing at his wife who seemed totally unaware of the unpleasantness that appeared to seep out from her two sisters towards her husband.

Ella finally broke the silence by saying to her sister, 'My dear Elfrieda, would you be so kind as to pass me the bread?'

The bread was, as usual, kept in a small wicker basket, which was at the far end of the table, near to Edric.

Elfrieda reached across and pulled the basket towards her, whereon finding that the basket was empty, said in a haughty, snide way, 'The bread has all gone, Godda's greedy husband must have eaten it all,' as she slammed the empty basket down onto the table.

Edric looked up in amazement that this woman, who, despite being the sister of his wife, was still, after all, merely a guest in his house, and a very unwelcome guest at that, and to show him such disrespect was, in his mind totally inexcusable.

He rose to his feet, knocking his heavy oak chair to the floor as he did so, bellowing in a loud voice, 'Yes he has eaten the last of the bread, and as he is the lord of this house, it is his God-given right to do so. And if you were not such a rude and stupid woman, you would perhaps think twice before abusing my hospitality.'

He added, as he stalked out of the room, 'Hospitality that would not have been given to such as you, if you were not the sister of my own wife.'

Hunting in the remote valleys of the forest of Clunn that day, his mood became blacker and blacker. So much so that when the opportunity of a kill presented itself to him, he slew the boar and, as the dead beast was lying on its back in the long grass, he hacked and hacked at its carcass until there was hardly enough undamaged meat on the beast to afford him a good supper. In his mind he was seeing not a dead boar lying before him, but the faces of the sisters, Ella and Elfrieda.

He brooded and sulked as the winter months dragged by, waiting for the first day of spring to arrive so that he could be rid of the two abhorrent sisters.

The day dawned dull, wet and miserable, but he cheerfully made his way down the stairs and as usual sat at his usual place at the head of the table in order to commence to break his fast.

However as he began to eat, he suddenly realised that Godda and her sisters had not appeared to break their fast this morning, for they were usually sitting at their places, watching him with their usual scowls as he clumped down the dark oak stairway towards the breakfast table.

The food and drink were, as usual, on the table.

The four places were laid, as usual, for himself, his wife and her two sisters, but the womenfolk had not, as yet, descended the stairs.

However, on Godda's chair there was a single petal of May blossom.

Slightly concerned, he rose and shouted up the stairs.

'Godda? Come and break your fast with me.'

Silence.

He shouted again, but the silence prevailed.

Now he began to get a little anxious. He ran up the stairway and crashed through the bedroom door where Godda had spent most of the winter nights, only to find the room empty, with the exception of a few petals of the may blossom that had been strewn over the bed and across the polished oak floor

The bed had been slept in, but her carved ash chest, where her clothing was usually stacked in neat piles, was gaping open and, more to the point, it was totally devoid of any clothing.

Suddenly he remembered the first day that he had met Godda, and recalled her words whilst she had been still standing in that bright room, whilst the petals from the maytree were still cascading down over her head and shoulders, remembering that she had spoken.

She had said in that deep, sultry voice of hers, that she had known of his coming and had long been waiting for him, and that she would be his for as long as he wished, as long as he did not fall out with, or insult her sisters, and if he were to do so, then she would leave him and he would never find her again.

Well, he certainly had fallen out with her sisters, but in all fairness, who could blame him? For they had treated him badly, had they not?

They had abused his generosity and his kindness, had they not?

He had fed and entertained them for most of the year, and he had tried his best to be civil.

Surely it would have taken a saint not to have fallen out with them.

'For God's sake, surely even Godda could see that,' he raved. 'It was always their intention to take her from me,' he said aloud. 'That was why they came in the first place.'

He stood and banged his head against a wooden wall panel, cursing himself for not seeing it sooner.

He literally ran out of the room and into the room where the sisters, Ella and Elfrieda, had been sleeping, only to find that their room was also completely empty.

He ran down the stairs, out of the door where he met a startled boy who was in the act of feeding one of the horses in the stables.

'Have you seen the Lady Godda?' he blurted out.

'Nay, my Lord,' came the answer from the lad.

'Is her horse missing? Are any of the horses missing?' he demanded, grabbing the stable boy by his shirt and lifting the startled youngster off his feet until the boy's face was level with his own.

'Nay, my lord,' gasped the near choking boy. 'All the horses are here.'

'Ah!' gasped Edric slightly relieved as he dropped the boy who landed on his knees on the cobbled stable yard

He mounted Chieftain, leaping onto his back in one mighty bound then galloped out of the stable yard, across the green but was held up at the gates, which were closed, forcing him to wait, frustrated and barking at the top of his voice as the two guards, struggled with the locking beam in order to open the gates and let him through.

'Have the Lady Godda and her two sisters passed through this morning?' He bellowed as they heaved the beam onto the ground.

The two men shook their heads saying in unison. 'No one has passed us this morning my lord,' they said, struggling to swing the gates open wide enough for him to gallop through.

Within minutes he was across the meadows and into the vastness of Clunn forest, heading for the place where he had met Godda years before, although he did not really know where the cottage was, for he had searched for it many times in the past whilst out on his hunting trips, but despite his many searches he had never been able to locate the cottage, however, he felt sure that as today was. 'The first day of spring,' then the cottage would miraculously appear as it had appeared on the first day of spring, when he had first met Godda, many years ago.

He urged Chieftain along the trails, up and over the hills and down into the narrow valleys where he had always suspected that the cottage would be, but the valleys were empty except for foxes, badgers, squirrels and bird life which scuttled and flew out from beneath the iron-shod hooves of his stallion.

He sat on his sweat-soaked mount for a few minutes, convinced that he was in the correct valley and that the cottage or his wife would appear before him at any moment.

Alas neither the cottage, his wife or her awful sisters appeared.

Doubts clouded his mind. He spurred Chieftain up the steep slope and headed for another valley, which he began to convince himself would be the correct one.

It was not.

Nor was the next or the one after that.

He rode as he had never ridden before, sobbing with frustration until Chieftain could go no further, standing with his legs splayed and his head drooping as the saliva dribbled off his protruding tongue.

He had been unaware of it but darkness had fallen, and he virtually fell off his stallion's back and lay on the floor where he fell into the deep sleep of exhaustion.

After a few short hours of fitful sleep the dawn chorus woke him with a crescendo of birdsong as the sun rose in the east.

For a moment he felt confused as to where he was and why he was there, but then reality and sorrow flooded back into his brain as he walked wearily a few paces over to a nearby stream where he knelt in order to splash the icy cold water over his face and head to chase away the sleep that still clogged up his brain. Then he stood and walked over to his faithful stallion who stood nearby, still caked with dust and sweat from the previous days hard riding.

He searched all day long, and the following day, and the following week, returning exhausted and bedraggled, a totally miserable man on a stallion that could barely stand on its own four trembling legs.

His people greeted him with apprehension, for they could see by his face that he had not found Godda, shunning him as they turning their faces away as he passed them, afraid to meet his gaze.

The house was cold and empty, despite the roaring fires, the chattering serving maidens and the vast array of hot food that was immediately prepared for him at meal times.

He barely touched the food.

He rode out on a fresh horse as soon as dawn had lightened the sky on the following morning.

And the day after that.

And the day after that.

He searched and searched, until he finally realized, that after probing every hill and valley in the great forest, that he had lost his beloved Godda, cursing himself for not being gentler towards her sisters. Then, in the same breath, cursing them for stealing her from him.

CHAPTER 43

Sitting on a moss-covered hillock overlooking the valley, Edric surveyed the peaceful scene below, watching as one of the herdsmen ushered a small herd of milking cows down the hillside on the opposite side of the valley.

The man sang loudly as he walked behind his cows, stopping now and again as they made their way slowly down a steep pathway that led towards the valley bottom.

Now aged sixty, it had taken Edric a long time to walk up to this spot, leading his equally old stallion up the steep hillside, and although his knees ached and his left hip pained him, he was now one of the oldest men in the village and in better health than many of the village men who were twenty years younger.

His trimmed beard was white, but his hair was still brown with a goodly smattering of grey, marvelled by many who had either turned to grey by the age of forty or had lost their hair completely.

It was rumoured that strangers visited the village in the hope of obtaining a single strand of his hair which it was said held magic properties that had been bestowed upon him by Godda, the Queen of the Light Elves before she had so suddenly returned to her own kingdom.

These people would chop the stolen strands of hair into minute particles, mix them with flour and a certain mushroom that grew in the forest, then swallow the concoction one gulp.

Then, or so it was rumoured, bald men would re-grow their hair and impotent men would beget sons.

Edric, of course, merely smiled, saying nothing when he heard such stories, for he no longer had any time for such silliness.

The village had grown tenfold over the years and now consisted of eleven good-sized farms, a smithy, a potter, a wheelwright and a full-time bowyer.

The only thing that spoiled this perfect view was the fact that he was seeing it alone, and was not sharing the beauty with his lovely wife.

The beautiful Godda.

A sudden gust of wind brought a white shower of may blossom from the hawthorn tree that he sat under, falling onto his head and his shoulders, causing his thoughts to return yet again, to the love of his life.

'Godda, oh how I miss you,' he said out aloud.

The love of my life.

The so, so beautiful Godda.

The woman, who had magically entered into his life and had filled it with light and laughter,

The Queen of the Fairy Folk, who, it had seemed, had wafted into his life as if by magic, and had filled his days with joy and happiness, only to have just as mysteriously vanished.

He would never be content again

He must renew his search and find her.

He turned and began to lead Chieftain up the steep hillside.

****

For many years reports were whispered from hunters and forest men of seeing a man dressed in animal skins. A man with a long white beard but a head of thick brown, tangled hair, a man who carried himself like a warrior but when hailed by the few people who saw him, he appeared to vanish into thin air.

Many people thought that this was the famous warrior.

'Wild Edric.'

FOOTNOTE

Readers may pose the question as to whether any of *The Broken Shield* is true? and the short answer is 'Quite a lot!' For whilst much of the book is obviously historical fiction, no one really knows the words, actions and hopes of the conquered English people nearly one thousand years ago, following the defeat of their army and the consequent occupation of their country by their Norman conquerors. However, unlike the legend of Robin Hood, and King Arthur who may or may not have existed, we do know that Wild Edric did live and was an extensive landowner in what had been the old Earldom of Mercia (now the counties of Herefordshire, Shropshire and Cheshire).

Wild Edric is known to have fought against the Normans and along with his Welsh allies, the kings or princes Bleddyn and Rhiwallon, they led at least two rebellions against the conquerors, capturing many towns and villages before finally bowing to the military might of the Normans. Edric, like his counterpart, Hereward the Wake, eventually made peace with the all-powerful Normans, joining them in their war against King Malcolm of Scotland who the joint forces of Norman, English and Welsh warriors defeated and slew at the battle of Alnwick in 1093. Whilst history tells us that 'Wild Edric' did fight at 'The Battle of Alnwick', it is a moot point as to whether or not he personally fought at either 'The Battle of Stamford Bridge', or 'The Battle of Hastings.' However, as a wealthy landowner he would certainly have been called upon by King Harold Godwinson to provide warriors for the King's army, and from what we do know about the character of 'Edric,' it is highly likely that he would lead his own contingency of warriors to swell the numbers of the Kings army.

Whilst myths and legends abound regarding Godda, the queen of the Fairy Folk, the word Fairy did not come into the English language until the 14th century, some 300 years after Wild Edric and Godda existed and were first believed to be mentioned by Piers Ploughman. I have reverted back to naming Godda as Queen of the Light Elves, i.e. Aelf or Ielfe as described in Norse and Anglo Saxon chronicles.

The legend of Wild Edric is still alive and well, and it is rumoured that on dark, wild windy nights he can still be seen spurring his black stallion across the craggy hillsides as he searches even to this day for his beloved Godda.

Queen of the Fairy Folk.